ancient spirit messenger

Giant stone snake

Cherry Hill, New Jersey

Max Blue
Leah Blue
Angelo
Sonny Blue
Bingo

Albuquerque

Laguna Pueblo Reservation

Sterling
Aunt Marie

Sterling accidentally goes to Tucson

organized crime family goes west

TUCSON, ARIZONA

Home to an assortment of speculators, confidence men, embezzlers, lawyers, judges, police and other criminals, as well as addicts and pushers, since the 1880s and the Apache Wars.

◉ **TUCSON**

El Paso
● Marilyn
Angelo

I C O

ATLANTIC OCEAN

Bartolomeo

The Twin Brothers walk north with hundreds of thousands of people

The First Black Indians

CUBA

HAITI

The Police Chief
General J
Vico ●

torture video tapes,

Bartolomeo's
"Freedom School"
● Mexico City

David
Serlo
Beaufrey

SOUTH
TO CARTAGENA
AND
BUENOS AIRES
▼

THE INDIAN CONNECTION

Sixty million Native Americans died between 1500 and 1600. The defiance and resistance to things European continue unabated. The Indian Wars have never ended in the Americas. Native Americans acknowledge no borders; they seek nothing less than the return of all tribal lands.

By Leslie Marmon Silko

ALMANAC OF THE DEAD
A Novel

STORYTELLER

CEREMONY

LAGUNA WOMAN

a novel by

LESLIE MARMON SILKO

ALMANAC OF THE DEAD

SIMON & SCHUSTER

New York London Toronto Sydney Tokyo Singapore

SIMON & SCHUSTER
Simon & Schuster Building
Rockefeller Center
1230 Avenue of the Americas
New York, New York 10020

SIMON & SCHUSTER and colophon are registered
trademarks of Simon & Schuster Inc.

Designed by Laurie Jewell
Manufactured in the United States of America

1   3   5   7   9   10   8   6   4   2

Library of Congress Cataloging in Publication Data

Silko, Leslie, date.
Almanac of the dead.
p.   cm.
I. Title.
PS3569.I44A79   1991
813'.54—dc20   91–19978
                                                                CIP

ISBN: 0-671-66608-8

To Larry,
For all the love

CONTENTS

ACKNOWLEDGMENTS

THANK YOU, Robert and Caz, for your patience, love and understanding these past ten years.

Thank you, Gus, for being there.

Special thanks to J. Roderick MacArthur (1917–1984) and to the John D. and Catherine T. MacArthur Foundation for the 1981–1986 Prize Fellowship which launched this novel.

PART ONE

THE
UNITED STATES
OF
AMERICA

BOOK ONE

TUCSON

UNANSWERED QUESTIONS

THE OLD WOMAN stands at the stove stirring the simmering brown liquid with great concentration. Occasionally Zeta smiles as she stares into the big blue enamel pot. She glances up through the rising veil of steam at the young blond woman pouring pills from brown plastic prescription vials.

Another old woman in a wheelchair at the table stares at the pills Seese counts out. Lecha leans forward in the wheelchair as Seese fills the syringe. Lecha calls Seese her "nurse" if doctors or police ask questions about the injections or drugs. Zeta lifts the edge of a sleeve to test the saturation of the dye. "The color of dried blood. Old blood," Lecha says, but Zeta has never cared what Lecha or anyone else thought. Lecha is just the same.

Lecha abandoned Ferro, her son, in Zeta's kitchen when he was a week old. "The old blood, old dried-up blood," Ferro says, looking at Lecha, "the old, and the new blood."

Ferro is cleaning pistols and carbines with Paulie at the other end of the long table. Ferro hates Lecha above all others. "Shriveled up," he says, but Lecha is concentrating on finding a good vein for Seese to inject the early-evening Demerol.

Zeta stirs and nods: "Old age." The day a woman put on black clothes and never again wore colors. The old-time people had not gotten old season by season. Suddenly, after eighty-five years, they'd catch the flu later in the winter, and by spring their hair would be almost white.

The old ones did not believe the passage of years caused old age. They had not believed in the passage of time at all. It wasn't the years that aged a person but the miles and miles that had been traveled in this world.

Lecha is annoyed that Zeta is being so dramatic about their sixtieth birthday. Lecha keeps the black dye for her hair, not her nightgowns. "Who said anything about getting old?" Zeta answers without bothering to turn from the stove. "Maybe I don't want to be visible at night."

"Like a witch!" Lecha says to Seese. They are all laughing, even Zeta. Ferro laughs but watches Lecha intently as he rubs the barrel of the 9mm pistol with a soft rag. Paulie goes months without saying more than yes or no. But suddenly his pale rodent face widens with excitement. "In the joint they don't allow dark colors. No handkerchiefs or socks dark blue. Nothing black. No dark brown." Paulie pauses. "Night escape."

"If you're quiet, Paulie, no one will know you're here," Ferro says, shoving an empty rifle case at Paulie. But Paulie's face has already settled far from the reach of human voices.

Paulie came home one night with Ferro years before and had never left. He asks for nothing but to work for Ferro. What Ferro says or does to Paulie makes no difference. Zeta, not Ferro, keeps Paulie around. He is utterly reliable because they are his only people. This is the only place Paulie can remember except prison.

Seese gathers up the dirty cotton and used syringe. The pharmacy has sent a box of small clear cups. They remind Seese of shot glasses at the bar. But no whiskey for Lecha. Not as long as she can get Demerol or codeine. The kitchen table is littered with paper wrappings from sterile bottles or rubbing alcohol and boxes of disposable syringes. Tiny bottles of Demerol line the dairy compartment of the refrigerator. Lecha gets chatty right before the dope makes her dreamy. She laughs and points at all of them together in the same room. No food anywhere. Pistols, shotguns, and cartridges scattered on the kitchen counters, and needles and pills all over the table. The Devil's kitchen doesn't look this good.

Sterling, the hired man, is standing by the dishwasher studying the instruction book. Sterling is in training for a special assignment. All of them are in the kitchen because of recent developments. Sterling has been told very little; Ferro is coiled tighter than a mad snake. Everywhere he looks, Sterling sees guns.

Ferro says the needle slips in like a lover's prick and shoots the dope in white and hot. That's why Lecha wants them all to watch her get off, Ferro says, but *he* doesn't watch junky orgasms not even for his *own* mother. Zeta shakes her head, her lips tight with disgust. Ferro laughs, then jumps up from the table with the 9mm in its holster and bolts out the door to the garage. Paulie's expression remains calm. He is alert in case Ferro calls him. But the remote-controlled garage doors and security gates light up the control panel on the kitchen wall. Paulie presses the display key on the video monitor screen: Ferro is skidding the big black four-wheel-drive truck down the driveway.

Seese looks at Sterling, who shrugs his shoulders as he hangs up a dish towel. Lecha has sunk back into her wheelchair, with her bliss dreams. Zeta runs the sink full of cold water to rinse the clothes she's dyed. She has been dyeing everything she wears dark brown. No reason, Zeta claims, just a whim. But Lecha had warned Seese not to be fooled. Nothing happens by accident here. The dark brown dye stains the white grout between the Mexican tiles patterned with blue, parrot-beaked birds trailing serpent tails of yellow flowers. Lecha's mysterious notebooks have drawings of parrot-beaked snakes and jaguar-headed men. Leave it to Zeta to have the kitchen counters redone with these Mexican tiles only two weeks before Lecha returned to transcribe the notebooks.

The first time Zeta had seen Seese, Zeta had told Lecha the white girl would have to go. No strangers around the ranch. Zeta still called it "the ranch" although the city was crawling closer month by month. But Lecha had lied to Zeta, claiming that Seese already knew everything anyway.

Zeta had stared at Seese for a long time, and then she had laughed. Seese could sense the old woman knew when her twin sister was lying. Seese had known very little then except that Lecha was a well-known psychic who was returning home to Tucson after many years because she was dying of cancer. Lecha had come home to get things in order before she died.

Seese could tell by the way Zeta had searched her eyes the first week that Zeta had suspected she was Lecha's lover. It wasn't true. Lecha had hired Seese as a secretary. Lecha wants to transcribe the old notebooks and needs Seese to type them into the word processor. There are two conditions of employment: two subjects that are off-limits, although a job was not what Seese had been searching for when she came to Tucson. What Seese is searching for is one of the forbidden subjects. The other forbidden subject is that of Lecha's personal life, including that of her son, Ferro. As for her lost child, Lecha tells Seese she must wait. Seese must be careful never to ask Lecha *directly* to find her baby son.

Lecha cannot predict how long the wait might be. Well, Seese thinks, this is better than what I was doing in San Diego. Working for Lecha has got Seese off cocaine; still, she only feels secure knowing she still has the remnants of the kilo Beaufrey had given her as a "go-away" present. A suicide kit from David's faggot lover. As long as Seese knows the gallon-size freezer bags wrapped in newspaper are safely in the back of her bedroom closet, Seese feels no craving for the drug. Seese had been an addict the night she went crying and pounding on the side of Root's old house trailer, searching for Lecha. But playing nurse to a woman taking Percodan and shots of Demerol all day long had taken away her cocaine appetite. She had weaned herself down to glasses of burgundy and fat marijuana cigarettes. Seese likes to think the cocaine was part of another life. A life she no longer knows or remembers very well. She had wanted Lecha's help more than anything, more than she had wanted the drug. Lecha was her last chance, or maybe the only chance she had ever had. That is how it had begun, with Seese so desperate for Lecha's help, and so afraid to do anything that might cause Lecha to refuse to help Seese find her baby. The cocaine hidden in the back of the closet was her rainy-day account, as good as cash, legal tender in Tucson.

Lecha had brought up Seese's old connections with Tiny and the Stage Coach because Root, Lecha's biker boyfriend, had recognized Seese as one of Tiny's nude dancers four or five years before. All Lecha said was she preferred that Seese stay away from Tiny and the Stage Coach. Zeta would not like it. No other reason was given.

"Well, there are a lot of unanswered questions," Seese told Sterling the first day he was there. She had noticed him wandering outside the house with a rake although nothing was growing there but the desert itself. The old ranch house is low and long, lost in the brushy foothill paloverdes, giant saguaros, and thickets of greasewood. Seese figures this location, this house, is no accident either, but part of the old woman Zeta's secrecy about herself and everything she and Ferro and Paulie are doing.

Sterling looks too harmless to be working here. He is graying and chubby and brown. His eyes look a little lost and sad. He rakes the pebbles and smaller rocks, and she can tell he knows how to appear busy when there is nothing to do. He sees her looking at him and gets bashful, looking down at the rocks he is raking. "Hi." Sterling looks up at Seese and smiles. He says he was hired to be the gardener. He gestures with his chin at the paloverde trees, jojoba bushes, and big barrel cactus surrounding them. He is a little bewildered at this "Tucson-style garden," he says. All of it looks like rocks and sticker trees to him. They both laugh.

Seese had wanted to tell Sterling how much alike they were. That she had been hired to nurse an old woman who is not so much dying of cancer as she is addicted to Demerol. But Seese had said nothing then because Sterling was new, and part of the job here was minding your own business. Sterling had been anxious to talk that first day. The ranch was a lonely place. Hiring was based upon the employee's willingness to pass weeks at a time without going into Tucson. Sterling says he doesn't know anyone in town anyway. "Like me," Seese says, lying a little because she didn't want to talk about Tiny and the Stage Coach Bar or Cherie. Seese and Sterling like each other right away.

Seese follows as Sterling rakes small orange stones around the swimming pool. Sterling checks the surface of the water. Two small lizards float blue bellies up. "It's mostly this pool of water that takes up my time," Sterling says as he uses a long pole and net to skim the corpses off the water. Seese watches the dead lizards fly over the edge of the pool, down the embankment. Sterling says he thinks other creatures will eat them. "That way their lives aren't wasted," he says hopefully. Seese would like to tell him as far as she can see all lives are wasted, but she doesn't want to scare the old Indian guy too much. And if she made a remark like that it would bring on that choking feeling in her throat. Sterling sees something is wrong. He tells Seese how nice it is to have someone around while he is working. Because all those years on the railroad section gang had got Sterling used to working with other people. "Then when I retired—" He starts to tell her something but stops.

"Retirement *is* a big change!" Seese says, feeling sorry for the old guy. "Changes are real hard." Seese closes her eyes and shakes her head. Right then Sterling had decided he didn't care if they fired him for talking to the young blond woman. He hadn't had anyone to talk to for such a long time.

"Well, this is mostly easy work," he says, "these drowned lizards don't weigh very much." Seese laughs and is surprised to feel the laughing go deeper than she can remember feeling it for a long time. "And everyone wants to retire to southern Arizona," he continues. Seese laughs some more and Sterling can't help stealing a look at her breasts when she is laughing. He hasn't even had the heart to look for such a long time. He remembers his *Reader's Digest* magazines—"Laughter, the Best Medicine." So maybe this job wouldn't be so bad with a pretty blond nurse to joke with.

Seese asks questions then. Is he an Arizona Indian? Why did he come to Tucson? How did he ever get hired by Ferro? Sterling had been carefully following advice printed recently in a number of magazines concerning depression and the best ways of combating it. He had purposely been living in the present moment as much as he could. One article had pointed out that whatever has happened to you had already happened and can't be changed. Spilled milk. But Sterling knows he's one of those old-fashioned people who has trouble forgetting the past no matter how bad remembering might be for chronic depression. Just then the woman Lecha, twin sister of the boss lady, had called out the patio door for Seese. Sterling had seen Lecha in the wheelchair, yet the strength of her voice that day was remarkable. Later on he had learned Lecha only used the wheelchair occasionally. From the start there, Sterling had known to watch his step with the women. Because Sterling had seen older women and younger women too, in action, and the lessons had not been lost on him.

It was just as well that Seese had been called away because he had not been sure where to begin his story or even if he should disobey the magazine advice. What had happened to Sterling was in the category of things magazine articles called "irreparable" and "better forgotten." Water under the bridge.

Seese returned before long. While Sterling was pouring chlorine pellets into the pool filter system, she had pulled a wrought-iron deck chair to the edge of the pool. As Seese stared into the deep end of the pool, Sterling suddenly realized she probably would not understand about the Pueblo and the village officers and the Tribal Council. "I would like to tell you about it," he began in a voice so faint she had to say, "What?" Sterling repeated himself and then said, "But it's sort of complicated, you know."

Her blue eyes swerved away from him back to the surface of the pool churning from the filter jets. "You could tell me part of it. I might understand more than you think."

"The part I will tell you some other time is the part where I am forced to go." Seese nods. She understands that one firsthand. "I just took what I could carry. Right now I'll just tell you how I ended up working here." They both laugh together. "Some story, I bet—for both of us!" Sterling adds.

EXILE

STERLING HAD NOT intended to go to Tucson. He had bought a bus ticket only as far as Phoenix although he didn't know a soul there either. Somehow he had been sleeping when the bus stopped in Phoenix, and the driver had not bothered to count the passengers who got off. At home in his own bed, Sterling had tossed and turned, unable to sleep. Yet now he had managed to sleep through roaring bus engines and diesel exhaust fumes as well as the loudspeaker announcements of departures and arrivals. Somewhere in the past, his life had taken a wrong turn, and Sterling had awakened to find himself surrounded by small rocky hills thick with what had first appeared to be utility poles. When he had put on his glasses, he saw they were giant cactus you always saw in cartoons with Mexicans in big hats sleeping under them.

In the old cowboy movies Lash La Rue and Tom Mix had chased outlaws among the giant saguaro cactus. It had been near Tucson that Tom Mix died when his convertible missed a curve. Sterling thought of himself as modestly self-educated through the magazines he subscribed to. He had never been interested in television except to watch the old movies. Though it was very sad, Sterling thought it would be interesting to actually see the historic Tom Mix death site. It would be nice to look at a giant cactus close up. Sterling had been trying to emphasize the positive aspects of life and not dwell upon the terrible things that had happened at home between himself and the Tribal Council.

Since the trouble any thought about anything that had gone wrong or might go wrong left him exhausted. There was nothing he could do now. The bus was approaching Tucson. He might as well sleep while he could.

In the dreams Sterling is always running or chasing after them— sometimes he rides a bicycle or horse, but usually he is on foot. The Hollywood people—the producer, the director, and the cameraman— are always driving a big four-wheel-drive Chevy Blazer. The convertible top of the Blazer has been removed so they ought to be able to hear Sterling's shouts. But this is a nightmare, and the director is leaning over the seat conferring with the cameraman and the producer in the backseat. They take no notice of Sterling racing behind them, yelling as loud as he can.

The Chevy Blazer is racing toward the restricted area of the tribe's huge open-pit uranium mine. The gate guards at the mine are armed with .38-caliber police specials because the Tribal Council is fed up with journalists writing scare stories about their uranium mine. The gate guards' orders are "Shoot to kill. Ask questions later." Journalists are no better than foreign terrorists as far as the Tribal Council is concerned. Sterling is yelling, "Stop! Stop!" when the old black man in the bus seat beside him gently touches his arm. "Mister, mister, are you okay?" Sterling feels sweaty all over despite the bus air-conditioning and tinted windows. The black man goes back to his newspaper. It is a Phoenix paper with headlines about the Middle East. There is killing everywhere. Jews and Arabs. Sterling doesn't understand international killing. But he has made it his hobby to learn and keep up with the history of outlaws and famous criminals. Sterling will ask the man if he can just read the headline story. But right now the dream has left him sick to his stomach. He peels open a new roll of Tums. The big SceniCruiser is the fastest bus on the highway. Maybe it is the bus's swaying as it passes cars that makes him feel sick. He closes and opens his eyes. Up ahead there is a white Arizona Highway Patrol car parked by a skinny tree with no leaves and green skin on its branches. Sterling expects to feel the bus driver brake suddenly to slow to the legal speed limit, but the driver takes no notice, and the big SceniCruiser zooms on to Tucson. Since it had all happened, Sterling couldn't help thinking about the law, and what the law means. About people who get away with murder because of who they are, and whom they know. Then there were people like him, Sterling, people who got punished for acts they had no part in.

Sterling had been interested in the law since he was a kid in Indian boarding school. Because everything the white teachers had said and done to the Indian children had been "required by law." Reading his magazines, Sterling had made a modest study of the law on his own, the way Abraham Lincoln had. The *Police Gazette* and *True Detective* magazines gave the most detailed explanations of the law. Sterling had bought subscriptions to both magazines so he would never miss a single new development in the law.

As near as Sterling could tell, injustice had been going on for a long time. Pretty Boy Floyd had struck back at bankers who were taking small farms and leaving Floyd's people homeless during the Dust Bowl days of the Great Depression. When Pretty Boy Floyd came through small Oklahoma towns, even local sheriffs waited until he was on his way again before they phoned state authorities to report his sighting. Sterling had studied photographs of Floyd and he could tell right away that Pretty Boy Floyd had been part Oklahoma Indian. Floyd's stronghold had been in the brushy oak hill country of Indian Territory. Ma Barker had been part Creek Indian, and John Dillinger's girlfriend, Billy Frechette, had been a Canadian Indian. Of course Sterling did not go along with what Ma Barker and her boys had done. All the people from Southwestern tribes knew how mean Oklahoma Indians could be. The Bureau of Indian Affairs had used Oklahoma Indians to staff Southwestern reservation boarding schools, to keep the Pueblos and Navajos in line.

Sterling woke up in the bus outside the Tucson depot. All the other passengers had already got off. Gathering up his shopping bags and bundles at the back of the bus, Sterling tried to estimate Tucson's heat by looking out the bus's tinted windows. It was the last day of July.

In the air-conditioning of the bus, Sterling found it difficult to estimate the outside temperature. He did not think it would be too bad, but when he stepped down the bus steps into the blinding white sunlight, he collided with a wall of desert heat. An instant later, like a cold beer bottle on a hot day, Sterling felt himself covered in an icy sweat. The dampness lasted only a matter of seconds before waves of heat sucked away the sweat, and with it, Sterling's breath. What he needed right then was someplace cool to sit down to think. He pushed down the contents of both shopping bags to resettle anything that might have shifted on the bus ride. Then he took both bags, threw back his shoulders, and went into the bus depot.

Sterling looked around for the old black man he'd sat with, but the old man was gone. At least the lobby was air-conditioned. It was two o'clock and the benches were full of people who didn't look like travelers but refugees from the heat. He didn't see any depot employees behind the ticket counter. Everyone seemed to be dozing or staring off into space. The effects of the heat. He saw a couple of Indians, but they were the ones stretched out on the benches.

Sterling pushed his suitcase into the locker with his foot and squashed the shopping bags on top and slammed the door. No siestas for Sterling. He wasn't going to be like everyone else, he was going to have a "take charge" attitude. He was going to walk around and see the downtown area. There must be hotels. There must be places to buy a cold drink.

Crossing the street, Sterling could feel the asphalt sink a little under his tennis shoes. All surfaces—concrete and plate glass—radiated heat. But at the end of the first block, Sterling wasn't even sweating. Because the heat was so dry, moisture could not even form on his body. The thermometer on the bank building read 103, but Sterling decided he was feeling pretty good considering.

Downtown Tucson looked pretty much like downtown Albuquerque before they had "urban-renewed" it—and tore down the oldest buildings with merchants who had catered to Spanish-speaking and Indian people. Sterling walked up and down the streets. He liked Tucson's bright pink courthouse. He put his fingers in the fountain; its water was not as hot as he had expected. He walked past the Santa Rita Hotel and decided it looked too expensive. He rested awhile on a bench in the shade at a park across from the city library. There were a lot of flies. Sterling fanned them away with his hat. A few of the hippies dozing on the grass opened an eye when he approached. But they pulled newspapers over their heads against the flies and went back to sleep again. Hippies in Albuquerque or Barstow pestered Indians with questions about Indian ways. In Tucson hippies were more like regular white people, who ignored Indians. That was all right with Sterling. He had learned his lesson with white people who had questions about Indian ways. A Tucson police car cruised by the city park. The cop looked sleepy, but Sterling was careful to avoid the cop's eyes. Even if he was well dressed in his black-and-white-checkered slacks and blue short-sleeve shirt, Sterling knew some cops didn't need any excuse to go after Indians.

The only other sign of life Sterling found downtown was in front of the blood-plasma donor center. Two white men were loading insulated containers into an air-freight truck. The containers looked like ice chests for cold beer. Of course Sterling knew they were full of blood. That was one thing he had never done and hoped never to have to do. Sell his own blood. The donor center was probably why the little park was so full of hippies and run-down white men.

A cold beer was what he needed. He walked north again, past the music store and the wig shop. Then he saw it: the Congress Hotel. Suddenly he remembered. This was the place John Dillinger's gang had made their worst mistake.

Sterling started to feel better. Tucson was going to be an interesting place. It had history. Where else could he have a cold beer at the same place Dillinger and his gang had been drinking beer in 1934? He opened the bar door and a gust of cold air-conditioning hit his face. Going from bright sun outside into the dimly lit bar left him blind for a moment. Even if they didn't like Indians in this bar, Sterling wanted to have one drink there, for John Dillinger. When he could see again, he found the bar almost empty, except for an old woman on a stool talking to the bartender, and two old white men arguing over a video game. Sterling watched the bartender's expression, to see if Indians were unwanted. But what he saw was relief. Maybe the bartender had wanted an excuse to get away from the old woman. Of course Sterling was well dressed. Even in the heat he was wearing his bolo tie made with a big chunk of good turquoise. The bartender was even friendly. He set the mug of beer in front of Sterling and started talking. "She's trying to get me up to her room," the bartender said. He was a small, balding white man with tattoos up and down both arms. The old white woman was wearing a dark purple dress with little white dots all over it. She wore open-toed, white high heels she had hooked around the bottom of the barstool like a pro. Her white hair was carefully waved in little curls around her face. She had drawn careful circles of rouge and used just the right amount of lipstick. Forty years ago she had probably been a beauty. "Don't be fooled by the bartender," she said to Sterling. "I've had him up to my room plenty of times."

Then she went back to her drink—something pink in a tall glass. The bartender moved away from Sterling then, wiping the bar and rinsing glasses. The two old men were no longer sitting at the video game. They were pouring beer from a pitcher and arguing over pinball machines and video games. How could you trust a video game? It was all electronics, all programmed like a computer to beat you. You had no chance. But at least with the pinball game, you could see the effects of gravity— the edge of the flipper with just the right leverage to fling the steel ball up the ramp and ring the bells and buzzer.

Sterling could begin to see how the place must have looked in Dillinger's day: the seats in the booths and the stools were covered with red plastic now, but he could see they had once been done in real leather. Only the bar itself was still dark mahogany. All the bar tables had been replaced with red Formica. The floor was covered with red indoor-outdoor carpet pockmarked with cigarette burns. But at the doorway an edge of black marble tile could still be seen. It had been a classy place in its day. Sterling paid for another beer and asked the bartender if it was always that quiet. "Oh, this is about average for a Tuesday," he said. "At happy-hour time they come in." He nodded in the direction of the two old men and the old woman. Retired people living in the cheap rooms downtown. The old woman was hanging off the stool by her high heels, leaning toward the old men, who were still arguing about pinball machines and video games. Occasionally the old woman would leer at the bartender or at Sterling. "You're not an Arizona Indian," the bartender said. Sterling shook his head.

Just then two men had come into the bar. Both wore dark glasses and were nervously scanning the room, for somebody. The men wore identical white jeans and pale yellow polo shirts, and big gold wristwatches. The Mexican with the cruel face was staring at Sterling. The young white man with him stared at Sterling too. Sterling smiled at the bartender uneasily. The men were looking for old Fernando, who worked as a gardener when he wasn't getting drunk, but nobody had seen the old man for weeks. The Mexican with the cruel face stepped closer to Sterling. "You," he said. "What about you? Can you work?"

"Gardening?" Sterling suddenly felt light-headed from the beer and the heat. "Ah, yes!" Sterling said. "Yes!" Trying to come up fast with the answer the men in dark glasses wanted to hear.

"Oh, yes!" Sterling heard himself answer. "Big lawns! All kinds of lilac bushes—dark purple, lavender, pink, white, blue!" Before Sterling could go on about the pool full of giant goldfish—all of it made-up—Ferro had turned and pointed to the door. "You're hired. Let's go."

The Mexican had the young white man drive the four-wheel-drive truck. No one spoke during the entire ride. They drove north and then west from downtown Tucson. The dry heat had parched the leaves of the desert trees pale yellow. Even the cactus plants had shriveled.

Sterling had never seen dogs like these before—leaping high against the chain-link fence—snarling, barking guard dogs. They were either black or reddish with short coats and brown or black markings on their faces like masks. Sterling had noticed the dogs each wore heavy leather collars mounted with tiny black metal cylinders.

THE STONE IDOLS

"WELL," STERLING SAYS, pushing the broom back toward the shallow end of the pool. He pauses and stares at the Catalina Mountains to the east. "I hope I am going to be here awhile, because I don't have any other place to go." Sterling has to clear his throat to keep the tears back. Seese wipes the back of her hand across her face but never looks up from the water. Her sadness startles him, and Sterling is seized by memories and lets down his guard. Remorse, bitter regret.

The stone idols had got Sterling banished. How many times had the theft of these stone figures come up during the hearings and Tribal Council proceedings? So often his brain had gone numb and lost track. The stone figures had been stolen eighty years before. Yet at Laguna, people remembered the crime as though it had just been committed. But the incident involving the Hollywood movie crew and the shrine of the great stone snake was no crime; it had been the result of a simple mistake; a small misunderstanding, a total accident.

The theft of the stone figures years ago had caused great anguish. Dark gray basalt the size and shape of an ear of corn, the stone figures had been given to the people by the kachina spirits at the beginning of the Fifth World, present time. "Little Grandmother" and "Little Grand-father" lived in buckskin bundles gray and brittle with age. Although faceless and without limbs, the "little grandparents" had each worn a necklace of tiny white shell and turquoise beads. Old as the earth herself, the small stone figures had accompanied the people on their vast journey from the North.

Generation after generation the protection and care of the stone figures had passed to an elder clanswoman and one of her male relatives. She prepares cornmeal and pollen sprinkled with rainwater to feed the spirits of the stone figures, which remain in her house when they are not in the kiva. She lifts them tenderly as she once lifted her own babies, but she calls them "esteemed and beloved ancestors."

The stone figures were stolen from a kiva altar by "a person or persons unknown" according to the official report. A ring of anthropologists had been crawling around the Pueblos all winter offering to trade for or buy outright ancient objects and figures. The harvests of the two preceding years had been meager, and the anthropologists offered cornmeal. The anthropologists had learned to work with Christian converts or the village drunk.

The people always remembered the small buckskin bundles with anguish because the "little grandparents" were gone from them forever. Medicine people at all the Pueblos, and the Navajos and Apaches too, were contacted. All those with the ability to gaze into still water or flame to locate lost objects or persons, all those able to gaze into blurry opals to identify enemies sending sorcery, began a search. The gazers had all agreed the stone figures were too far away to be seen clearly. Far, far to the east.

Years passed. The First World War broke out. The elder priests had all died without ever again seeing their "little grandparents." Fewer and fewer remained who had actually seen the "little grandparents" unwrapped on the kiva altar, smooth stones in the swollen shape of female and of male.

Then a message came from the Pueblos up north. Go to Santa Fe, in a museum there. A small museum outside town. The spring had been wet and cold and only increased the suffering caused by meager harvests. The federal Indian agents didn't have enough emergency corn rations to go around, and reports came from Navajo country of people dying, starving, freezing. In Santa Fe the state legislature was two years old, and did not concern itself with Indians. Indians had no vote in state elections. Indians were Washington's problem. A muddy wagonload of Indians did not attract much attention. The Laguna delegation had traveled to Santa Fe on a number of occasions before to testify in boundary disputes with the state for land wrongfully taken from the Laguna people. The delegation's interpreter knew his way around. A county clerk had told them how to find the museum.

The snow had melted off the red dirt of the piñon-covered hills except for the northern exposures. It was early afternoon but the sun was already weak as it slipped into the gray overcast above the southwestern horizon. An icy breeze came off the high mountain snowfields above Santa Fe.

At the museum, the interpreter for the Laguna delegation left the others waiting outside in the wagon. The old cacique was shivering. They built a small piñon fire and put on a pot of coffee. Museum employees watched out windows uneasily.

"Yes, there were two lithic pieces of that description," the assistant curator told the interpreter. "A recent acquisition from a private collection in Washington, D.C." The interpreter excused himself and stepped outside to wave to the others by the wagon.

The glass case that held the stone figures was in the center of the museum's large entry hall. Glass cases lined the walls displaying pottery and baskets so ancient they could only have come from the graves of ancient ancestors. The Laguna delegation later reported seeing sacred kachina masks belonging to the Hopis and the Zunis as well as prayer sticks and sacred bundles, the poor shriveled skin and bones of some ancestor taken from her grave, and one entire painted-wood kiva shrine reported stolen from Cochiti Pueblo years before.

The delegation walked past the display cases slowly and in silence. But when they reached the glass case in the center of the vast hall, the old cacique began to weep, his whole body quivering from old age and the cold. He seemed to forget the barrier glass forms and tried to reach out to the small stone figures lying dreadfully unwrapped. The old man kept bumping his fingers against the glass case until the assistant curator became alarmed. The Laguna delegation later recounted how the white man had suddenly looked around at all of them as if he were afraid they had come to take back everything that had been stolen. In that instant white man and Indian both caught a glimpse of what was yet to come.

There was a discussion between the assistant curator and the Laguna delegation's interpreter, who relayed what the delegation had come to say: these most precious sacred figures had been stolen. The museum of the Laboratory of Anthropology had received and was in the possession of stolen property. The white man's own laws said this. Not even an innocent buyer got title of ownership to stolen property. The Lagunas could produce witnesses who would testify with a detailed description of the "little grandparents" as the people preferred to call them. For these were not merely carved stones, these were *beings* formed by the hands of the kachina spirits. The assistant curator stood his ground. The "lithic" objects had been donated to the Laboratory by a distinguished patron whose reputation was beyond reproach. As the head curator was out of the office, the Laguna delegation would have to return next week. When some of the members of the delegation raised their voices, and the interpreter had tried to explain the great distance they had already traveled, the assistant curator became abrupt. He was extremely busy that day. The Indians should contact the Indian Bureau or hire a lawyer.

The delegation led the old cacique out the door, but the war captain lingered behind, not to whisper to the stone figures as the others in the delegation had, expressing their grief, but to memorize all the other stolen objects he could see around the room.

Outside, the old cacique acted as if he had drifted into a dream. While the war captain and the tribal governor and the interpreter argued over starting another lawsuit, the old cacique was rocking himself on his heels in a blanket close to the ashes of the campfire. The governor was right. Of course they could not afford another lawsuit.

All of that had happened seventy years before, but Sterling knew that seventy years was nothing—a mere heartbeat at Laguna. And as soon as the disaster had occurred with those Hollywood movie people, it was as if the stone figures had been stolen only yesterday. Each person who had recounted the old story seventy years later had wept even harder than the old cacique himself had, and the old guy had not even lasted a month after the delegation's return from Santa Fe.

There were hundreds of years of blame that needed to be taken by somebody, blame for other similar losses. And then there was the blame for the most recent incidents. Sterling had already gone away to Barstow to work on the railroad when uranium had been discovered near Paguate Village. He had no part in the long discussions and arguments that had raged over the mining. In the end, Laguna Pueblo had no choice anyway. It had been 1949 and the United States needed uranium for the new weaponry, especially in the face of the Cold War. That was the reason given by the federal government as it overruled the concerns and objections the Laguna Pueblo people had expressed. Of course there had been a whole generation of World War II veterans then who had come home looking for jobs, for a means to have some of the comforts they had enjoyed during their years away from the reservation. The old-timers had been dead set against ripping open Mother Earth so near to the holy place of the emergence. But those old ones had been dying off and already were in the minority. So the Tribal Council had gone along with the mine because the government gave them no choice, and the mine gave them jobs. They became the first of the Pueblos to realize wealth from something terrible done to the earth.

Sterling had not quit his railroad job, as many other Lagunas had, to return to the reservation and to work in the mine. He had no close family there except for Aunt Marie. Once Sterling had got settled into his railroad job, and his life in Barstow, he did not want to go to all the trouble of moving again to work in a uranium mine. So Sterling had avoided being caught up in the raging arguments made by the old-time people who had warned all the people would pay, and pay terribly, for this desecration, this crime against all living things. The few times Sterling had come home to visit at Laguna fiesta time, he had been relieved that his railroad job saved him from being involved in the controversy. Aunt Marie and the old clan mothers in the kitchen used to predict trouble because of the mine. Sterling had listened quietly while they talked on and on. The old ones had stuck to their predictions stubbornly. Whatever was coming would not necessarily appear right away; it might not arrive for twenty or even a hundred years. Because these old ones paid no attention to white man's time. But Sterling had never dreamed that one day his own life would be changed forever because of that mine. Those old folks had been right all along. The mine had destroyed Sterling's life without Sterling's ever setting foot near the acres of ruined earth at the open pit. If there hadn't been the mine, the giant stone snake would not have appeared, and the Hollywood movie crew would never have seen it or filmed it.

The film crew had not understood what it was they were seeing and filming at the foot of mountains of grayish mine tailings. To Sterling's thinking this meant the secret of the stone snake was intact. But to the thinking of the caciques and war captains, the sacrilege had been the story of the stone figures all over again.

Sterling had tried to reason with the Tribal Council members. Nothing had actually been stolen or removed. Sterling had tried to argue a good many points. But nothing could be done. The Tribal Council had appointed Sterling to keep the Hollywood people under control. They had trusted him. They had relied on his years of experience living with white people in California, and Sterling had betrayed them.

Seese looked puzzled and shook her head. They had banished him forever, just for that one incident? Sterling had been coiling up the garden hose by the pool filter. He let out a sigh Seese could hear clear across the pool. "It was the last straw," Sterling said, looking mournfully into the water. "But the other things hadn't really been *much*—."

THE RANCH

STERLING PROMISED to tell Seese the rest of the story another time. There was too much to tell right now, and Sterling had thought about it over and over. The magazine articles all seemed to be in agreement: to cure depression one must let bygones be bygones. Sterling unfolded the magazine clipping on mental hygiene from his billfold. Seese looked, but did not seem to be listening. She was intent on the lower left corner of the page, which wasn't even the article on depression. Suddenly big tears filled her eyes. She looked at Sterling hopelessly, shaking her head, then shoved the magazine clipping back into his hands. Seese ran toward the house. Sterling felt all his strength drain away through his feet. His legs felt heavy. Maybe he would not be able to stay here after all. Some days he felt as if the atmosphere in the house was electric with tension. After years of working on the railroad section gang, Sterling knew better than to ask questions about the bosses. He fought off a wave of discouragement. He was still new to this place. Here the earth herself was almost a stranger. He could see the desert dip and roll, a jade-green sea to the horizon and jagged, blue mountain peaks like islands across the valley. When he worked in the yard with his rake, he was amazed at the lichens and mosses that sprang up on northern exposures after the least rain shower. The few times Sterling had ventured off paths that led to the corrals or water storage tank he felt he had stepped into a jungle of thorns and spines. Strange and dangerous plants thrived in these rocky hills.

For a moment the expanse of desert and sky was motionless. No hawks circled. The coyotes were silent. No sound out of the day dogs patrolling the arroyo and foothills or the night dogs in their kennels. Sterling had a great urge to stretch out on the chaise lounge by the pool.

But it would be no good for the new Indian gardener to be found asleep on the job, even if the old boss woman and her fat, strange nephew had more important business to tend to. Sterling felt safe in his room at the back of the toolshed. The small outbuilding near the corrals was easy to dismiss. But he had a space for his bed, and the other area contained a toilet with a tiny refrigerator and a two-burner stove. The shower was in the corner of the room near the tools and storage shelves. The pipe wrenches and screwdrivers had been lying untouched for a long time. Gallon cans of dried-up paint lined an entire wall of dusty shelves. Sterling was waiting to get nerve enough to ask Ferro or the old boss woman if they might want him to clean out all the no-good stuff in the shed.

His bed was comfortable, although Sterling thought the mattress was probably softer than the experts and doctors had recommended in their magazine articles. But whenever Sterling sank into the softness, he always slept without waking until morning. Yet that afternoon, by the time he had got to his room, the drowsiness he'd felt by the pool was gone. He could not stop thinking about the poor blond girl who had suddenly got so sad, who seemed even more alone than he was. She had started crying when she saw an article below the report on depression. The article was about a woman who had murdered three of her own babies. The police detective who had finally cracked the case had noticed a silky, white, stuffed toy dog sitting on a shelf in the nursery. Silky, white fibers had been found in the dead babies' nostrils and mouths, and snagged on their tiny fingernails. The woman had persuaded every-one—husband and relatives, doctors and police—that her babies were victims of crib death. Sterling could understand how such an article might have upset a young woman such as Seese. Sterling himself had not been able to read the article without imagining a poor helpless baby struggling to breathe while its own mother pressed a toy dog over its face. Sterling had never liked dogs of any kind—stuffed or alive. He got chills each time he remembered those poor babies and the ugly glass eyes of the stuffed toy dog.

Paulie was in charge of the dogs at the ranch. Sterling had only been instructed once by Paulie, but with attack dogs such as these, Sterling vowed never to forget. No one was allowed to feed the dogs but Paulie. Sterling had to wait until Paulie opened the kennels, one by one, for Sterling to sweep and hose down. If for any reason Sterling were ever to find himself in an outer perimeter where the dogs patrolled, he was to stand perfectly still when they spotted him. If a dog attacked, Sterling was to lie facedown, motionless, knees drawn up to his belly, with his hands and arms protecting his neck and head. Paulie had rattled off the instructions in a low, mechanical voice as if he couldn't care less if Sterling got torn up by dogs or not. Later on, Sterling had asked Seese what she thought about Paulie. Sterling himself thought Paulie would really like to see the dogs get somebody. Seese did not answer, but Sterling could tell by her expression she had noticed Paulie's contempt for her and Sterling. "Yeah, the dogs. Well, just think about their names," was all Seese had said. The only names Sterling could remember for the attack dogs that patrolled the property were Cy, Nitro, Mag, and Stray; and there were eight other dogs whose names were too hard to remember. Cyanide, Nitroglycerine, Magnum, and Stray Bullet were the day-shift dogs.

Sterling had asked Seese if she was afraid, but she had only shrugged her shoulders. "Those collars are electronic," Seese told him. "They have radio transmitters in them. Lecha says one of them wears a bigger, heavier collar. A TV collar."

Seese laughed. "She says they can stop the dogs by remote control. Give them little electric jolts. Give them signals and commands."

Later Sterling had watched Paulie adjust and tinker with the dogs' collars. The only time Sterling had ever seen Paulie's face relax and soften was when he was handling the dogs. Paulie had whispered to them in a low, baby-talk voice and had stroked them before he commanded them in or out of the kennel. He stroked them while he completed the transfer of a collar from a day-shift dog to a night dog.

The dogs were Dobermans with ears cropped so short their heads looked more snake than dog. Even so, the dogs came off their shifts with cactus spines in their ears, and between the pads of their paws. Paulie, who usually moved so fast, worked with infinite patience to remove the spines and dress the wounds. Paulie had caught Sterling watching him and had given him a glance so murderous Sterling had stepped in a big pile of dog turds in the kennel he was cleaning. Paulie did not want anyone to see how carefully he probed and examined each dog. As time went by, Sterling began to realize Paulie was perhaps more strange than anyone, more strange even than the two old women or the man, Ferro.

It had been around Ferro that Sterling had felt the strangeness of Paulie most clearly. Paulie's pale blue eyes avoided all faces, yet never left Ferro's face even for a moment. Ferro had a habit of abruptly turning away from Paulie's gaze. Sterling always felt a load lift off his chest when Ferro and Paulie drove away. The day dogs barked and howled at the four-wheel-drive truck as it passed through the succession of electric gates. Even the old boss woman and her sister did not make Sterling as uneasy as the two men did. The old boss woman had not cared about anything except that he was not an Arizona Indian. She would not hire somebody who would have hundreds of relatives nearby, dozens of in-laws who would make the ranch their second home.

Zeta had looked pleased when Sterling said he was alone in the world since his aunt Marie had died. Ferro had even asked what mail Sterling expected to receive. Ferro's expression was indifferent as Sterling began with his railroad pension check. He did not expect letters. Then Sterling rattled off his magazine subscriptions. Ferro turned away abruptly before Sterling had finished. There was no mention of days off or trips into Tucson. After Sterling had got settled in his new job, it might be nice to go to town once in a while. He wanted to get a library card. He was curious about the town itself because Tucson had a notorious history. Besides Tom Mix, other famous people had met their downfall in Tucson. Geronimo and John Dillinger to name two. Old Mafia godfathers and their loyal lieutenants retired to Tucson where they waited for strokes to carry them away in their sleep. Sterling would like very much just to stand on the sites of these historical events.

Sometimes the *Police Gazette* ran specials on famous crimes of yesteryear. These had been his favorites. He had been most excited the time they had the special on Geronimo. Geronimo was included with John Dillinger and Pretty Boy Floyd and Billy the Kid. Sterling had often heard Aunt Marie and her sisters talk about the old days, and Geronimo's last raids, when even a platoon of Laguna "regulars" had helped patrol New Mexico territory for Apache renegades. Somehow Sterling had never quite imagined old Geronimo in the same class with Bonnie Parker and Clyde Barrow. Geronimo had turned to crime only as a last resort, after Mexican army troops had slaughtered his wife and three children on U.S. territory in southern Arizona. Despite the border violations by the Mexican army and the murder of Apache women and children who had been under the jurisdiction of the U.S. Department of War, no U.S. action had ever been taken against the Mexican army. Geronimo had been forced to seek justice on his own.

But it had only been a matter of a few years before Geronimo's second wife and another child were killed. They had been part of a small band of women, children, and old folks who had voluntarily come in from the mountains for the safety and peace promised on the grounds of Ft. Grant. Alerted to the approach of a mob of deranged white people driving buggies and wagons from Tucson, the army officer in command had sent frantic appeals to cavalry units away on patrol. But help had arrived too late to prevent the slaughter of the defenseless Apaches.

Thanks to his magazines, Sterling was aware that many famous criminals had similar grievances with the governments or communities that had failed to deliver them either protection or justice.

Of course Sterling knew there was no excuse for crime. But for Geronimo it had been war in defense of the homelands. He liked the way the *Police Gazette* specials took an understanding view of the criminal's life. Still it was clear that the law did not accept any excuses. They had all died violently. Got the gas chamber or the electric chair. Or got shot down. Except for Geronimo. The specials always ran a whole page of inky, fuzzed photographs showing them after they'd been gunned down; halos of black blood around their heads; then later propped on snow-white marble slabs.

It was clear that crime did not pay. Geronimo had been one of the few famous American public enemies who had not died in an ambush or at the end of a noose. But Geronimo had been sentenced to live out his days a prisoner at Ft. Sill, Oklahoma—punishment worse than death. Geronimo and the great warrior Red Cloud had both been condemned to the gallows in their day as savages and murderers. But both had been masters of guerrilla warfare; one fighting the U.S. cavalry on the upper Great Plains, the other outrunning five thousand U.S. cavalrymen in the impenetrable desert mountains of northern Sonora. But some years later, elected for a second term, President Teddy Roosevelt had scandalized his political adversaries by inviting Geronimo, Red Cloud, and Quanah Parker to ride in his inaugural parade. To critics, Teddy Roosevelt said all a new president owed voters was a good show—precisely what he had delivered to them!

Sterling was pretty sure Cole Younger and some of the Jesse James gang had been part Indian by their looks in old photographs. Sterling knew the Starrs had been Oklahoma half-breeds. Sterling thought he was probably one of the few Indians interested in famous Indian outlaws. He knew tribal leaders and so-called Indian experts preferred that Indians got left out of that part of American history too, since their only other appearances had been at so-called massacres of white settlers.

What Sterling knew about the Great Depression of 1929 he had learned from his detective and crime magazines. The government boarding-school history teachers had seldom ever got them past the American Civil War. Sterling had been a boy during the Depression, but it had made little or no impression on people at Laguna. Most, especially the old-timers, had said they never even knew a depression was going on, because in those days people had no money in banks to lose. Indians had never held legal title to any Indian reservation land, so there had never been property to mortgage. But winters those years had been mild and wet for the Southwest. Harvests had been plentiful, and the game had been fat for the winter. The Laguna people had heard something about "The Crash." But they remembered "The Crash" as a year of bounty and plenty for the people.

Seese got up from her lounge chair by the pool and helped Sterling unload colored rocks from the wheelbarrow. She didn't know anything about any kind of garden, and especially not rock gardens, whatever they were. "Where did you grow up?" Sterling was on his hands and knees arranging little orange stones around the base of a jojoba bush. He was afraid to look in case Seese did not like his question. But there was the quick little laugh she gave when she was nervous, and then she said, "Oh, I grew up in a lot of places. Military family."

"No gardens," Sterling said, clearing away some weeds that had died since the last rain. "No gardens. Not much of anything to remember." Seese was smoking a cigarette and staring off in the distance toward the city. Sterling could see she had one thing she never forgot, one thing always very near. "I was telling you about my magazine articles," Sterling said. "You know, we can go see the place Dillinger's gang got caught."

Seese turned all the way around to face him. "Here?"

Sterling felt a big grin on his face. He nodded.

She laughed. "Okay. We'll go tomorrow when the rest of them are gone."

BOOK TWO

SAN DIEGO

TV TALK SHOW PSYCHIC

THERE IS CONFUSION in her dreams and memories of the child. First there is the odd dream of the snapshots of a boy, twelve or thirteen. In the dream she knows the boy is dead by the remarks others make as they look at the photographs. She is seized by the loss of him and awakens crying. She is stunned because in the dream Monte had been older, as he might look years from now. Monte would be almost two years old, wherever he was; David had kidnapped Monte when he was six months old. Seese refuses to believe he is dead. The dreams are her contact with him. She feels she has actually been with him after these dreams. She awakens crying because the odor of the baby lotion and his skin are immediate and she feels she has only just set him down in his bed. Because of these dreams she is certain he is not dead. At other times she reasons that the child probably is not alive since David spent thousands hiring detectives and paying informants. She has read about the anguish one feels as the memories of the beloved gradually recede. She knows this is to be expected. Still, she shuffles the baby pictures like a deck of cards, trying furiously to deal up just the one that will bring her back to a moment with him. She is determined to be the first not to forget. One of the few for whom the memories never dim.

As long as she is able three or four times a year to dream about him and to awaken feeling as if she has actually been with him, holding him close, she thinks the memories are holding. She had been afraid she might become too satisfied with these dreams. She had dreamed him newborn again in her arms. The ache of the loss that woke her did not recede as the day went on, but increased with every sniff of coke, with every hit off the joint, until she was tearing open cupboards looking for any kind of alcohol, any bottle of pills. She was staying in the penthouse on her lawyer's advice. The lawyer wanted Seese. His wife had injured her back in a sailing accident. That was what he told her. Seese had never trusted him. Beaufrey once said the best lawyers were the best crooks. The lawyer liked the idea of a young mistress in an elegant penthouse overlooking a stretch of private beach outside La Jolla. Of course from the kitchen breakfast bar he could point out the high rise where the senior partners were preparing appellate briefs and corporate articles. She had quit opening his bills months ago. Beaufrey had taken David and left her with the apartment and enough money and drugs to kill herself. Beaufrey had left the country in a hurry with David. Before David could change his mind. She knows she had sex with the lawyer, but can't remember a single time, nothing they did.

She tells Sterling she does not have much of a past or much to remember, but they both know she is holding out. He isn't what she thought an Indian would be like. You don't think of Pueblo Indians reading the *Police Gazette* and knowing all about John Dillinger. When Seese said this to Sterling, his wide face had been all a big smile, and she said, "That's what I mean too," pointing at his face and his mouth. "Oh," he said, "you thought Indians didn't ever smile or laugh," and they were both laughing. Suddenly she stopped to remember how long it had been since she had laughed without a weight pulling from somewhere behind. With the lawyer she had laughed but knew that the feeling wasn't true. He did not love her. Things would not work out.

Seese wonders how far back these things go. She has nightmares about diving into a pool that is too deep. Before she can manage to surface she is out of air. High above her she can see the sky and round, puffy clouds as she drowns. She remembers having the nightmare only twice before she had the baby. Both times it was the night before a math test in college. She got lost in the lines and equations; she could imagine any number of possibilities from all the signs and symbols. She read many things into them, many more than mathematicians had anticipated. Now she knows that all of it is a code anyway. The blue sky and puffy clouds seen through the deadly jade water of the nightmare pool was a message about the whole of creation. The loss of the child was another, more final message, or at least that was how it was translating—she was only just finding out that this was a translation, that the last morning she had held little Monte in her arms loving him perfectly—that had been an end too. When the drugs affected her in a certain way she was able to study the message calmly as if watching pebbles at the bottom of a stream; she could not feel the temperature of the water. She could feel nothing after that last morning. Dark green water had closed over her head.

Beaufrey and David had taken Monte or hired someone to take Monte, but then something terrible had gone wrong. This was the story she now believed because David had had her followed, had the phone tapped and had even telephoned himself, asking to hear his son cry. The lawyer had taken the call because she knew she would break down. But David had misunderstood, and next there had been the gunman; the reasoning, the lawyer later explained, was that once Seese was dead, the court would award custody of the baby to the father. But Seese did not have Monte.

In La Jolla she had been in the habit of standing for hours in front of the glass walls facing the ocean. But it could have been a blank wall. She stared and saw nothing—not the waves rising and falling on the beach or the banks of clouds on the southwest horizon. The wind had riffled the waves so they glittered like thousands of tiny mirrors—blinding reflections that left white afterimages before her eyes. The afterimages were in the shapes of teeth—incisors, canines.

After Monte had been kidnapped, Seese could not bear to look at shadows or shapes of clouds, patterns the dampness made on the beach sand, because instantly her brain gave them definite forms. She would see the toy giraffe in a cloud. She would see the print of a small hand left by the splash of a wave.

After the gunman had fired through her bedroom window, she had called the lawyer. She was not surprised he wanted her to go away, to start a new life. He was afraid of what might happen to himself and his marriage if she remained alone in the glass penthouse above the sea. He was right of course, and her doctor had suggested it too. She had seen the doctor about her eyes, and the problems she was having with the bright reflections almost blinding her. It was the cocaine mostly, he said, and as her psychiatrist he was prescribing a change. She had to leave the surroundings so familiar and once part of her life with the child. But she could not seem to leave the place although everything reasonable and sane told her she must. She could feel an animal circling inside her, pacing around and around in her stomach and chest. It was a fierce animal; it would not stop waiting or searching the place she had last seen her child.

She had not heard the shot. The gunman might have been four hundred yards away. Broken glass had streamed across the unmade bed

like water. For an instant she had confused this with the blinding afterimages on her retinas. She had been too drunk and too high to be
afraid. The lawyer came and searched but could find no bullet. For an
instant he was about to accuse her of breaking the windows herself until
she pointed out that the glass had collapsed *into* the room. A fury she
had never known swept over her at that moment, and she turned on the
lawyer. "Even as drunk as I am, I'm not that stupid," Seese said. The
lawyer had never suspected she was capable of such anger. He moved
under the blow like a boxer trained to keep moving mechanically no
matter how hard he was hit. Later Seese decided he'd come for a last
fuck, that little gesture of comfort for a hysterical woman.

"It might not be Beaufrey and David," he warned her, still recover-
ing his balance. If he could have frightened her, he might have regained
the advantage. "It could be the others," he continued.

"We are even," she said. Her voice was loud. She wanted *them* to
hear that, so if it was *them* who had kidnapped her baby, Monte, *them*
who were shooting, they would stop.

The lawyer began to say that he had it from reliable sources that
X, Y, and Z had still not been paid for Beaufrey's last big delivery from
Mexico City. Seese stared at him while he made his pronouncements.
He worked for all of the big players. She wanted to shove her .380
automatic into his mouth and pull the trigger until the clip was empty.
"You know better than that!" she had screamed at him. "I'm out of it!
I left before I had my baby!"

The lawyer was picking up slivers of glass from the pale lavender
sheets. "I'll stay with you tonight." He was sitting on the edge of the
bed still searching for bits of glass.

"No."

"Come on, Seese, you aren't being quite fair with me. I love you,
and I want to help you."

Seese knows what the Cuban maid is thinking. The Cuban maid
had worked for the lawyer's father for years. The old judge is connected
with powerful people. The maid resents being there. She knows they kill
hired help when they come to get the big cheese. The maid does not
think much of this skinny blond woman. Small cheese. She does not
think anyone will get killed except Seese. But the maid hates missing
her evening television shows.

"What's that?"

"One of those shows—they get people—people doing things—you

know—swallow pennies, hold spiders." The maid speaks English without an accent. Elena knows that if she were blond and that skinny, she would be living here. So the hatred, Seese reasons, is not of me. Elena hates all skinny, blond women. Seese rolls another joint and pours more whiskey. "What's she doing?"

"Oh, some old Mexican Indian they claim—*she* claims she can see the past and tell the future." Elena is from Cuba where they don't have any Indians. Anyone can see Elena is descended only from white ancestors.

Seese is drunk. She can see women lining up to speak into a microphone. The television studio audience. "What? What?" Seese is too high and too drunk to hear what the woman from the studio audience has said to the microphone. The face of the talk show host fills the screen.

Elena's tone is impatient. "She asked her things!"

"What things?"

Elena is not afraid to show this bitch the truth. She is spending the night with the white trash only as a favor to the boss. The boss already has another one. This one is on her way out. Elena is tired. She has no patience for this silly blond bitch who is so stupid she lost her own baby, then cries about it when she gets drunk.

"Just watch!" The maid enjoys snapping at her. She enjoys commanding: "Watch! And you'll see. *People* who have lost things—that man there had a winning lottery ticket, then he *lost* it."

"How?"

The maid grits her teeth. She hates people who want to talk while the television is on. Elena is almost yelling now. "I don't know! It blew out the window of his car! Watch! Just watch!"

The marijuana and whiskey feel like lazy updrafts of warm ocean air the gulls ride. Seese lets herself be carried far from the angry Cuban woman and from the scattered glass slivers. Seese begins watching the television screen intently. The Mexican Indian woman seems to be speaking only to her. The woman's hair is coal-black, but the skin of her face is brown and meshed with fine wrinkles. Seese giggles. The Mexican Indian woman dyes her hair.

According to the show's host, the woman finds missing persons. The TV camera comes in for a close-up of a newspaper clipping: "Mass Murder Site Located." The old woman's face fills the screen. She is smiling but her eyes are not friendly. Her eyes know many things never meant to be seen. The contents of shallow graves. The thrust of a knife.

Things not meant to be heard; the gurgling cough the victim makes choking on his own blood while a calm voice on a tape recording narrates exactly how the execution must be performed. Her eyes said, plenty of women have lost babies and small children. They die of dysentery and infections all the time. They starve, get shot, bombed, and gassed.

Seese could feel the weight rising up in her chest, but the old woman's eyes continued: In villages in Mexico and Guatemala they lay out little children and babies every day. Their little white dresses and gowns are trimmed in blue satin ribbon. Seese was crying, but like the television, she seemed to make no sound. The maid ignored her, intent on the television show.

Now the old woman's eyes were closed and her head had fallen back as if she were dozing, but Seese could see her lips were moving. Seese could not stand it. She reached for the volume knob. When Elena started to protest, Seese pointed at the door. "Get out! I'm better off alone."

Seese did not bother to watch Elena storm out the door. She was watching the old Mexican woman. The old woman was some sort of clairvoyant. She was rattling off what she was seeing: trash cans are stuffed with newborns. Garbagemen in Mexico City find four hundred fetuses and dead newborns each day, not counting the ones found floating facedown among the water lilies in fountains outside the presidential palace.

At this point Seese had lost track of what was happening on the screen. The talk show moderator was trying to calm a woman standing at the studio audience microphone. The psychic had opened her eyes and was wiping her brow with a large white handkerchief. A woman's voice from the television says, "The dead rest just fine—it's only your mind that keeps them alive and lost," but Seese can't see who is saying this—unless the talk show host has suddenly got a woman's voice. Seese gets up quickly and turns the television off. She does not like the idea of hallucinatory voices talking about the dead. She has had too much to drink. She has to get to bed. She is going to track down that old Mexican Indian woman and get her to help.

That night Seese dreams she finds Monte's corpse in a fountain at a shopping mall. He is tiny, reduced to the size of a fetus. But all his features are those of the six-month-old child he was when he disappeared. She cannot reach him and wades into the pool. Crowds of shoppers gather to stare at her. Their faces are blank although she hears angry men's voices telling her to get out. She yells back she must get her baby. Her own voice wakes her just as the sky is beginning to lighten in the east. The air pushing in the shattered glass is cold and wet and smells like kelp. She pulls the sheet and blanket closer. The psychiatrist believes she must give up hope of finding him alive, that all she needs is to know what had happened. But watching the talk show psychic the night before has made Seese realize the doctor is wrong. She refused to give up. She had to get out of there. Before more bullets came flying.

The local TV station could only give her the phone number of the cable network in Atlanta. Seese could feel her strength begin to drain away, and her feeling of purpose dissolve into need for a drink and a sniff of coke. But when she reached the Atlanta number, a woman with a soft drawl knew all about the clairvoyant Mexican woman. "Because she helped me out with a problem," was all the cable TV station woman would say, but she did tell Seese the woman's name: Lecha Cazador. The woman in Atlanta was not sure, but she thought that from Atlanta, the old woman was flying to Tucson. "That was over a week ago, you know. We do all our program tapings at least seven days in advance. This phone just won't stop ringing. On account of her." The woman in Atlanta belonged on a talk show herself, Seese kept thinking. Daytime rates, long distance. Seese kept trying to break in to thank her for the information. Finally Seese just hung up. She didn't want to hear any more about the long-distance calls that had come in about missing persons.

Seese was certain the TV psychic could help her. It was the strongest feeling about getting help she'd ever had. She didn't know if it was the heat of the sun on all the glass or the four fat lines of cocaine she had just snorted, but sweat was running down her jawbones. After all these months she was ready to move, ready to get something done. She went through all the desk drawers for birth certificates, passports, and safety-deposit keys. She packed the extra box of cartridge shells for her gun. Sweat was breaking across the bridge of her nose. She was feeling good—she was going toward something. She felt sure of it. She had not felt anything like this for a long time. The phone started ringing, but she would not touch it. No one and nothing would stop her this time.

MEMORIES AND DREAMS

MUCH LATER Seese had realized not only had David lied about having sex with Beaufrey, but Eric had been lying too. Seese had not figured that one out until after she had been crushed with Monte's loss, and she had consumed grams of cocaine, then quarts of vodka and capsules of doxepin until her vision finally blurred and her eyes felt dried up in mummy sockets. One afternoon Seese woke up in the empty sunken bathtub. She had lain shivering, dreaming she had gone skiing with her father. In the dream he wore his dress uniform, but Seese had somehow lost sight of him in the crowd at the chair lift. She had wanted to find him because he had her jacket and gloves. In her dream, she pushed her way past the skiers, who did not seem to notice that she was naked.

She got out of the tub and sat on the toilet to pee. Out the smoky glass she could see the blaze of the sun on the sand. She checked the thermostat and found at some point she—or someone—had reprogrammed the thermostat for all the rooms. "Refrigerate, sixty degrees." Seese found a half joint in the ashtray by the sink. She took a glass of orange juice out to the roof garden. The warm ocean air folded around her on the chaise lounge. She closed her eyes, but she wasn't sleepy. She had been thinking that turning down the thermostat to sixty and lying on the cold porcelain nude could kill you. She and Cherie had known a girl from Phoenix who'd died like that. Not an OD, just asleep in the cold so long her body could never get warm enough again, not even in the hospital. Sometimes coke made her feel feverish. She had been alone in the apartment, so only she could have turned down the thermostat. Maybe her unconscious had remembered the girl from Phoenix, dead from the cold tub, because something inside Seese did not want to live anymore.

Beaufrey had gone days, and sometimes *weeks,* without speaking or in any way acknowledging Seese's existence. Eric could see when she was beginning to crack, and they would make a game of her invisibility around Beaufrey. Seese would dip into the silver sugar bowl with a teaspoon, taking Beaufrey's cocaine right under his nose, they'd laugh later, and still Beaufrey had never glanced down or made eye contact with Seese. Beaufrey's only comment had been about Eric's being a coke whore. Cocaine was a matter of indifference to Beaufrey. He kept cocaine because the young boys always liked it.

The group Beaufrey worked with had stockpiles of cocaine in warehouses packed floor to ceiling, in sealed drums. Eric said Beaufrey never stopped anyone from pigging out on the cocaine in the silver sugar bowl because Beaufrey got aroused when someone overdosed on the drug. "Beaufrey would love to watch you and me both OD," Eric had said, laughing. "He gets it for nothing. An OD was a lot less expensive than a bullet." Eric had been right on that point. When Beaufrey got rid of Seese, he had paid her off with a kilo of coke, assuming she would dispose of herself automatically. And Seese might have done that except she had never forgotten how Beaufrey had talked relentlessly about suicide. Most assholes in this world would obligingly kill themselves for you. No need for hired assassins. You might have to supply a woman, drugs, or a fast car and a gun. Beaufrey was watching Eric's face as he spoke. Eric had smiled: "Oh, yes, the power of suggestion. Let's all have a cup of poison Kool-Aid. Someone push the launch button of the big bomb."

Eric had driven Seese to the doctor's office, but waited in the car where he could smoke dope and play loud music. Eric had guessed it the minute he saw her face. "Test positive. And you want to keep it." Seese felt a sinking in her chest because Eric had said "it." Her throat was tight, but she tried to sound bouncy. "Him or her—it's him or her, not *it*."

Eric threw the car into reverse, then burnt rubber leaving the parking lot. Seese had not expected Eric's reaction to be so negative or powerful. They had discussed babies and children many times. She and Eric had even discussed how they might collaborate to conceive two children— one for him and one for her. This had been their scheme to tap into all the family trusts available to Eric the minute he married and had children.

Eric had taken the long way home, driving slowly and methodically down the winding coastal highway. They were near the apartment complex when Eric reached over and held her hand in his. Traffic was light but he didn't look away from the road. Staring straight ahead, he said, "I can't believe I'm behaving this way—faggot, sissy, queer, I never imagined or dreamed—" Eric had burst out laughing, but Seese could see tears. He did not turn into the entrance to the parking garage but drove to the beach. They sat in the car and watched the tide come in.

Eric was still gripping the steering wheel, staring straight ahead at the blazing wake of light from the setting sun.

Seese slid down in the seat and hunched against the wind off the ocean. Eric was motionless, frozen to the wheel. The wind flattened his thin, fine hair tight against his skull, and for an instant Seese saw how Eric would look when he was an old man.

They did not talk until they had parked in the basement garage. "I don't even know where to begin," Eric said, pulling Seese across the seat to hug her. As his lips brushed her cheek, Seese could hear his heart pounding. His hands were wet and cold on hers. "We have always talked and talked, you and I. And now when there is so much, I can't say anything. So many things, so much all mixed up together." Eric fumbled under the front seat for his brandy flask. "I want this baby to be mine and not his." Eric passed the flask to Seese and fished around in his pocket for the vial of cocaine. Seese took a big swallow of brandy, but shook her head at the cocaine. "Here's a change already," Eric said, smiling brightly. "I've lost my comrade-in-dope." The brandy burned all the way down. Seese reached for the flask and emptied it. The burning and coughing brought tears to her eyes.

"So now we know gay men are just men after all," Eric said. "Irrational and piggish like all the rest. I thought I had already whipped *that* demon back to the underworld." Eric paused and glanced around the basement garage for security people, then spooned more coke to his nose. "What I have to tell you now is even uglier." Seese knew by his expression Eric meant Beaufrey. "He'll go crazy when he finds out you're pregnant again."

Seese looked at Eric, shaking her head slowly. "How do you know? I'm keeping this one," she said softly. "David—" Seese began, but Eric interrupted her. Suddenly he was angry. "David? David? Jesus fucking Christ! Seese! Don't you understand about David?"

Again and again Seese had thought about that night in the basement garage. She and Eric had always been able to tease one another when one or both of them got on their "high horse." But that night, neither of them had been able to call the other back down where they could talk. Eric had been gloomy and depressed for six weeks. He had even cautioned Seese not to take the really black moods too seriously. Eric had once been David's lover. David had wanted a child, a son. Eric had watched her eyes and lips and knew Seese would not believe him. Eric suddenly felt exhausted, almost too weak to push open the huge Cadillac door. He wasn't sure of anything anymore. Maybe he had the whole story wrong the way most of the rest of his life was all wrong. He was the odd man out. How could his feelings or judgment be trusted?

"I throw up," she had told him. "Morning sickness," Beaufrey said, building a case against the pregnancy. "No, *not* that. The morphine does it." Seese had stood her ground. No abortion this time. The pregnancy had put her on a different footing with Beaufrey. Pregnancy worked to her advantage. Beaufrey was uncomfortable. He kept looking at David. He was trying to determine how much David really wanted the child. But David was intent on photographing Serlo, who posed sullenly next to a large pot of orchids trailing long sprays of yellow blossoms like a peacock tail. David wanted the blue of the ocean and the sky through the glass wall. Serlo pulled some of the long yellow spikes of flowers over his shoulders like a cape. At home, Serlo either went bare chested or did not button his shirt.

Seese has other dreams that haunt her. Dreams in which she is in the hospital again, only Beaufrey himself stands near the bed holding a white porcelain basin. A surgical procedure has been completed. There is a sanitary napkin between her legs. A nurse helps her swallow more pain pills. As she drifts, Seese can feel nothing below her neck. Beaufrey had paid doctors to reach up inside her belly while she was knocked out, and they had cut the little tendril. In her nightmare, dozens of yellow rosebuds have been scattered over a hospital bed with white sheets. The rosebuds have wilted, and the edges of the petals have dried up. She dreams she is awake, but numb below the waist—"As usual," she thinks she hears one of the doctors say, but then realizes it must be the effects of the injection the nurse has given her.

The chrome-yellow hue of the light had been all that Seese could remember clearly about the abortion she had had before she conceived Monte. The light that afternoon had been creamy yellow, the color and texture of roses. She had never met Beaufrey, but Beaufrey had made all the arrangements. Seese had been so high and so happy in love with David and delighted with her friend Eric she had not wanted pregnancy to spoil it. Still, Seese had been disturbed by the urgency with which Beaufrey had got rid of her and David's embryo.

FLYING

SEESE ORDERED a double shot of rum at the San Diego airport bar. There had been two hours before the flight left for Tucson. "Anything from Haiti," she told the bartender. "This is an airport, remember?" was all the bartender said. Once they had got drunk together—her, David, and Beaufrey—on 180-proof Haitian rum. Beaufrey had been in Haiti on business. They never talked business around her. With Haitian rum Seese saw "apparitions." "You mean *hallucinations*," David said. But *apparitions* had been the term the nuns used. Apparitions were full of beauty and wonder and holiness.

On the flight to Tucson there was a guy who looked so much like Eric that she had felt a pounding in her ears. Once the plane was in the air, she made a trip to the lavatory so she could take another look, so she could make sure. As she sat on the cold lid of the commode, her hands had been shaking so hard she could not get the tiny spoon to her nostril. She had to tell herself to breathe deep and to relax. The cocaine helped. When she moved down the aisle past the man, she saw that his face was not nearly as handsome or kind as Eric's had been. When the flight attendants brought drinks, she bought two rum and Cokes although they warned the flight to Tucson would be short.

Seese could not remember seeing the hills and trees or the ocean after Eric's suicide. They had done a lot of traveling after that, but she had no memory of it. She had tried to distract herself with new landscapes when they traveled, but after Eric died, Seese had been unable to remember anything except disjointed arrivals and departures in international airports.

She had not actually seen Eric's body. Only the photographs. David's photographs, but somehow that had been worse. All she knew was that something had happened to her eyes, something had diminished her vision.

In air turbulence the jet airliner alternately bucked and shuddered. Seese thought of children's books with storm clouds illustrated as big horses—wild-eyed, tails streaming down into rain and mist. From the blue and black storm horses it was only a flicker of thought to Monte. The doctor had said it was better not to dwell on him—especially not to imagine him at times or in activities that had never happened. Of course it was all right to remember Monte as he had been. Seese let go of the idea of the children's books. She did not think she had ever seen a book that turned thunderclouds into galloping wild horses. She looked around at the other passengers and at the back of the head of the Eric look-alike. She was proud of only a few things, but one of them was that she was as fearless as her father had been about flying in jets. He had flown navy jets and had been gone on carriers for months at a time. On his visits home, he rented single-engine planes and took her with him. He had to fly every day, he said. He didn't care what kind of plane. He loved flying. What Seese remembered best was the moment the two of them had returned to the house. Her father had bragged to her mother, "Seese is a born flyer, just like her daddy." Her mother had only shaken her head. Seese's mother never liked to fly.

The thunderclouds near Tucson had caused turbulence. The other passengers were restless and some were airsick. The flight attendants were finally able to move through the cabin to take airsick bags to the lavatories. The captain was on the PA soothing the passengers. They had passed the storm. The captain used the slow, easy tones her father had used with her to announce his new assignment to the biggest, newest carrier in the Pacific fleet. That had been the good news. The bad news was the divorce. Everyone at her high school, well, *nearly* everyone, had had a divorce in the family. The school counselor said it was because their school had so many pupils from military families.

Out the window Seese saw long lines of blue landing lights outlining the runways. In the dim light she could see the grass and weeds between runways bent to the ground by strong winds. Ah, Tucson. What a nice welcome, she thought as she swallowed the last of the rum. The only places that had worse dust storms than Tucson were Albuquerque and El Paso. Her father used to tease her about going up and never coming down. Just flying and flying forever, so whatever bad weather there was down below, dust storms or even earthquakes, you wouldn't be touched.

He had been flying bombing missions over the South China Sea when she asked him about the war. He said it wasn't really a war. She asked him what it was like. They had been at a lobster restaurant in Orange County. He always came to see her when he was "back in the States," as he put it. He described what it felt like flying very high and very fast. No earthquakes or dust storms could get him. Her father had laughed then, proud to have remembered one of their little jokes together. Seese had wanted to ask him questions so he could give her answers that would help her feel better. Every evening-news show had television coverage of U.S. planes and pilots shot down over enemy territory. Even after it happened, Seese imagined he was only away on a long cruise. Seese imagined him flying and flying forever: the aviator's vision of heaven.

From the baggage claim area Seese paused a moment in front of the sliding glass doors. Traveling with David, Beaufrey, and Serlo had taught her not to appear anxious to leave with the luggage. It was also not good to rush to a rest room either. What she was carrying with her was actually a lot more cocaine than she had ever carried alone. It was the kilo of coke Beaufrey had used to "settle up" with her. Seese knew Beaufrey would have preferred to settle up with a .44-magnum slug, but Beaufrey had David to think of.

Tucson was only one of a number of Southwest hick towns that the drug enforcement people watched relentlessly. Peepholes in toilet stalls at the Tucson International Airport were one of the airport police's big pastimes. Seese and Cherie used to flip fingers at the invisible spies in the toilets. That was when they had been traveling just for fun—her and Cherie—carrying nothing on them. Tonight Seese just wanted to get to a motel room and sleep. The automatic sliding glass doors opened, and she let the weight of the two suitcases and the heavy shoulder bag propel her out into the night where a cold, dusty wind surged in dark waves.

She told the cabdriver "Miracle Mile." She'd decide which motel when they got near there. The cold wind had cleared the rum from her brain. The four years she had spent with Cherie had taught Seese about cheap motels. The cab went to the end of Miracle Mile and she still couldn't decide. She had to be sure she didn't stay at a place she and Cherie had ever stayed, even if it had been years ago. It was patterns they used when hunting for you. Your habits and routines.

Seese wasn't taking unnecessary chances. She asked for a room that would be "quiet," meaning far from Miracle Mile, behind the other units. The night clerk was reading a textbook on basic chemistry. He was marking significant passages with a pale yellow marker. Seese hated people who marked books. But the clerk had given her the key without questions or hassle, something unusual for night clerks on Miracle Mile when a woman alone checked in. So Seese did not wisecrack about students who defaced books with yellow markers or mutter that writing in books should be against the law. Rum and cocaine always loosened her tongue, but now, she would have to take it easy for a while. She needed to lie low.

STORMS

THE ROOM SMELLED faintly of stale cigarettes, but that was all. Seese counted herself lucky the room didn't reek of urine or sanitary napkins too long in the trash. She rolled a joint and propped herself up in the bed. The wind was whining along the eaves of the stucco bungalow. The gusts splattered sand against the sliding glass doors. Nights like these when she was a girl, she had pulled the covers up to her chin and had gone right to sleep. The sound of the wind had made her feel so snug and safe inside. The sound of rain did the same for other people. Eric had been the only other person who had liked the sound of the wind and sand. Because he had grown up in Lubbock, where, he said, West Texas sandstorms stripped the chrome right off the bumpers of new cars, and windshield glass was so badly sand-pitted it appeared to be fogged.

Eric had talked about the hailstorms they had out on the West Texas plains. That was what she and Eric had done when David was gone with Beaufrey: they had talked. Because they had both been in love with David, and they liked each other too much for there to be hurt feelings. Eric had had a grand way of setting up a story. He claimed he'd learned it growing up with cowboys, but it turned out his father had had a Ford dealership. The cowboys Eric had listened to were ex-cowboys hired as car salesmen when the ranchers went broke.

The hail, Eric said, was first recorded by the Spaniards with Coronado. Hailstones the size of turkey eggs had dented Spanish helmets and shields. The Spanish horses had bolted and scattered, and a few horses were never recovered. Here of course was where the Plains Indians first got horses. Seese loved to hear Eric go on and on. He knew many wonderful things. He had so much going for himself. It had always been difficult for Seese to imagine Eric with Beaufrey. A few months before it happened, Seese had asked Eric if going home for a visit might cheer him up. Eric had managed to laugh, then shook his head. West Texas was the source of his depression in the first place.

Seese's mother had worked out an arrangement years ago. She had always known how to spend the salary a lieutenant commander flying combat received. Seese had asked about that too, but her father had laughed. What he liked to do the navy paid him to do. He told Seese she should not be critical of her mother. "She can have whatever she wants. Because she married me, then didn't get a marriage. That's grounds for a lawsuit the way I figure it. I'm not the marrying kind." So her father and mother had gotten even with one another; but Seese did not feel the score had been settled between herself and either of them. Her mother had remarried immediately after the divorce was final. Another military officer, this time air force. He was gone as much as her father had been. He even looked like her father. The last year Seese spent at home, the year she had turned sixteen and they had fought, Seese had screamed at her mother, "What's the point in being married to him? He's not even as good as Daddy!" Later Seese thought her mother's remarriage might not have upset her if her father had lived.

In her grief, Seese had hated that Al was alive when her father was not. She substituted Al for her father in the downed jet fighter whenever she visualized her father's last mission. One night she and her mother had had a terrible fight over what to cook for Thanksgiving dinner. They had no near relatives. The guests would be couples from the base or friends of Al's. Seese's mother had remarked how much Seese's "late father" had disliked turkey. Now that she was married to a man who ate turkey, that's what she intended to cook.

Seese had left the house that night, with a suitcase of clothes and $80. She had hitchhiked as far as Santa Barbara the first night. Then, as she had later told Eric, she had got lucky. She ran into Cherie and some other girls. It was a hop, skip, and a jump to Tiny and all the rest. It wasn't true that she had never seen her mother again. She had stopped in San Antonio once after Al's transfer.

She had never thought she would be tracking down a psychic. Eric would have laughed if he were alive now. Eric had thought psychics were only for the ignorant or superstitious. Seese had laughed then because that's what she had thought too. But catastrophe had changed her feelings. Seese turned off the light beside the bed, but she could not sleep. When she closed her eyes, mental images out of the past kept running through her brain like a high-speed movie. She tried to keep the focus only on those scenes or images that felt happy or good, because she had suffered breakdowns in the past. Two of her breakdowns had occurred before she had ever tried cocaine. Still, coke was probably the worst drug to use if your nerves were shaky, unless you really wanted to risk your sanity with LSD.

Seese tried to visualize Monte laughing and playing with other children in a park or school playground. Seese was convinced that a child so beautiful and intelligent as Monte was being reared by people who were loving him as much as they could love any child. Seese had asked the psychiatrist if he agreed that here was the logical way to look at it: her child had been taken because he was valuable and beautiful, and it was not likely any harm would have come to him.

DECOY

SOMETIMES A VOICE inside Seese's head cried out to Eric, "Why did you kill yourself? Is that what you do to the people who love you?" But she understood exactly why you might do that to the ones you loved. So then gradually, from the grief and the anger Seese had come to feel that she was no more alive than Eric was. That in death she and Eric would always be bound together—sister and brother. There did not seem to be a vocabulary for what they had felt. Or if there had been a vocabulary, she hadn't understood it.

Eric would start talking and mention names of books. The first few times he had done this, Seese had felt a panic—a sudden need for another beer. But later on, Eric told her he admired the people—women especially—who had gone out on their own when they had just finished high school. He had not done that, exactly, but when he had turned fourteen, he had asked the Baptist minister to remove his name from the church roster of baptized Baptists in what was a small town, Lubbock. Seese had been a little stunned. She had never belonged to any church. Her mother had not bothered to have Seese baptized.

Eric had never told Seese the whole story about his years with Beaufrey. Eric said it had been because he had been so young then, and fucked up on drugs to boot. "Those were the years before I finally came out"—Eric had smiled faintly—"before I came out and told them I fell in love with guys, not women. But it was all anticlimactic. My father had identified me years before. I had the big fight with them over my art history major. He called me queer and swish and fairy. 'Faggot.' Never just 'fag.' "

David was ashamed for anyone to know. Of course, David had been seeing Seese on the sly for some months before. But David had also started spending afternoons swimming nude with Beaufrey.

Beaufrey was always delighted with the quarrels. Beaufrey was always looking for new players. Eric confessed to Seese he had cried himself to sleep the night Beaufrey and David went driving alone in the Porsche along the coast highway. Later Eric said, he had realized how provincial, how stupidly narrow, he was, despite the years away from Lubbock. Wanting David all for himself was just a stupid version of the Bible Belt bourgeois Eric rejected. Seese could rely on Eric to be her friend and ally. After all, they both loved David, didn't they?

Seese was the decoy. Because Beaufrey was as anxious as David was about his masculine image. Eric had laughed the first time he and Seese had ever met at G.'s gallery. "Oh," he had said, "I was afraid I would hate you!" Seese had been too high to say more than, "Yeah, me too." They had ended up alone at the punch bowl. David was doing the rounds with Beaufrey on his left arm and Serlo on his right.

Seese could see it in Beaufrey's eyes, the great hunger, the greed to have all of David. Beaufrey had only kept Seese and Eric around to humor David. Beaufrey had been intent on weaning David from them.

Before Beaufrey had taken him in, before the gallery picked him up, David had worked for an exclusive Malibu escort service—live-in stud, for three to six months maximum, cash in advance, all medical and dental and incidental expenses *extra*, cash on the barrel head. Rich old queers in Bel Air, their withered vines and grapes shrunken to raisins; layers and layers of grayish, crepelike skin dropping off, flat asses covered with black hairs. David never lost the gag reflex at the sight of dewlap skin on turkeys and lizards. He'd seen too much loose skin during those years. David had a long list of sights he had to avoid. Another had been the thick, yellowish-stained toenails old men had. He had awakened screaming one night in Eric's bed, wet with sweat, crying because he had been half-buried in great mounds and fields of old men's toenails.

David had bragged about the old men who had actually taught him "his art" by begging him to pose with them in front of their video and fancy 35mm cameras and lights. David had turned the tables on them. He had gone from art object to artist. He preferred to say he had been a live-in companion. What mattered was that it was clear he was the "companion," not the male nurse or chauffeur and not the butler.

TEXAS

ERIC HAD CALLED SEESE. His voice sounded choked and hesitant, as if he was so sad he might cry instead of speak. David had given him the word, Eric said. "The straight stuff. Finito. Finished. The end." "Oh, Eric," Seese had said. "Don't try to talk now. I'll come over right away."

Eric had always said only the vibration and motion of the automobile around him calmed the roaring, surging feeling in all his blood vessels. He needed to see the southern-California coast at sundown with lovers parked at every scenic-view loop. At the edge of the water an old man had been walking an arthritic Great Dane and watching intently as the dog shit a load the size of a wedding cake. "Wedding cake?" Seese had said, starting to laugh. "Yeah, a wedding cake," Eric had said, and then they had both laughed and laughed, and Seese was glad Eric had telephoned her.

They had not talked about David or about the pregnancy. Eric had been thinking about leaving. He had lived on the West Coast—San Francisco then San Diego—for twelve years. He had been thinking about Texas again. Seese was not sure what to say because even when they had been laughing and joking together, Eric had seemed restless and distant. Seese had suggested a walk along the edge of the water. They could watch the sun go down. As the sun slid through colored bands of coastal clouds into the sea, Seese glanced at Eric, but he had been intent on his own bare feet, watching the thin sheen of seawater that oozed up between his toes and around the edges of his feet.

The marijuana they'd smoked in the car was coming on full force. Seese had laughed and run to meet the waves. "We came here to see the ocean and the sunset, and by God, we will!" They broke into a run then, and raced all the way back to the car. Eric had put a hand on her thigh and pretended to roll his eyes from the thrill. "Marry me. We'll have a great time!" Seese was laughing. She shoved her head out the window to smell the low, damp ocean smell before the heat of the freeway and exhaust buried it. But when her face was turned into the rush of air, Eric had said, "I'm serious. I mean it."

Seese turned to him suddenly to see if this was another tease. She pushed away the strands of hair blowing around her eyes to get a good look. Eric wasn't joking. Waves of dread, cold, night-sweat fear had churned up from her belly to her chest and throat. Seese fumbled in the dark trying to light the joint. Eric had known both Beaufrey and David far longer than she. Eric assumed David was finished with her too.

Eric had detected trouble from her silence and pulled the old Cadillac into an empty bank parking lot.

Seese had nodded as she took a long drag on the marijuana cigarette and glanced over at Eric. He was watching her. "I wish you would come. We talked about it before." Eric's voice was calm as he added, "David's with Beaufrey now."

The mercury-vapor lights around the parking lot gave their skin a bluish-silver glow. They passed the joint back and forth without talking. Seese had seen how David glowed when he talked about the baby when they were together alone. Eric had no way to know any of this about David. Eric had seen only what a man might see. The dark surge of fear in her chest and throat began to recede a little, like the tide going out. Dry and safe again soon. Seese had patted the car's dashboard.

Eric was watching her. Seese wanted Eric to take over, to begin telling his West Texas sandstorm stories, his West Texas grandma stories, his '67 Cadillac Fleetwood stories. But when Eric kept his eyes on hers, Seese could feel herself floundering, then sinking. Eric wasn't going to let her change the subject.

"David never loved you. He made Beaufrey jealous with you. That's all."

After the outburst, Eric had seemed to shrink, to sink into the peeling blue leather seat of the Cadillac. In the dim light, Eric had suddenly looked much older. Nearly as old as Beaufrey. Seese suddenly felt the sensation of falling inside herself. She fumbled in her purse for the vial of coke. While Eric took heaping spoonfuls up to his face in the rearview mirror, Seese glanced around, from habit, to be sure no cops were passing by. Eric let his head fall back on the car seat with his eyes closed. He nodded and smiled at her. While she leaned over to shove the little spoon in each nostril, Eric started talking. "When I was in high school, I used to imagine or pretend—yeah, pretend. I liked to pretend I was an orphan. No living relatives anywhere in the world." Eric paused and sat up, flexing his shoulders, reaching for the key in the ignition. The streetlights had been on for fifteen or twenty minutes.

They had spent the rest of the night side by side on chaise lounges by the penthouse pool above Mission Bay, and the city lights. They had finished off a quart of tequila, talking about how they would go back to Lubbock as husband and wife and pick up Eric's inheritance from Granny, drawing interest these past four years until Eric "came around."

In one version they had concocted that night, they stayed in Lubbock long enough to get married, picked up the cashier's check and left town before the sun set. She and Eric had settled on that version as the one that would make everyone—from the Baptist preacher to Beaufrey— the happiest. Eric would have the money, and they would go on together as they had before, except they'd have money. Money might give them a better chance with David.

But a week later, when Seese had mentioned the trip to Lubbock, Eric had shaken his head and laughed. "Oh, I never told you the whole story, darling," Eric had said, waving a mock limp-wrist at her before he flipped the blender switch on their frozen daiquiris. Eric had seemed cheerful, and he'd been full of jokes the last week. Seese thought he was over his sadness. They had spent almost every day by the penthouse pool where they had enjoyed laughing about having a pool fifteen stories above the Pacific Ocean. Eric pointed out that a pool might be more confining, but at least the sharks couldn't get him. "Oh, yeah?" Seese said, diving under to grab at his legs. Then David and Beaufrey had returned. David came and stretched out on a lounge chair. Seese could not see if his eyes were closed behind the dark glasses. Beaufrey had stood in the doorway only a moment and then turned away. Serlo slid the glass door shut.

MIRACLE MILE

SEESE LISTENED to the toilet flush and refill in the dark. The motel was quieter than any of the cheap joints she and Cherie had ever stayed in. She was getting anxious about Cherie. As far as she knew, Cherie was still in Tucson. Cherie sent Christmas cards no matter how broke she was. Seese had tried to tease her about it once, but Cherie, who was usually easygoing, did not see any joke in Christmas cards. But Seese thought it was hilarious that Cherie, who had performed the most bizarre sex acts for paying customers and sometimes their women, that same Cherie never dreamed of neglecting to send Christmas cards. Cherie did not merely send Christmas cards. Cherie always wrote what she termed a "personal note." Now Seese was going to cash in on Cherie's Christmas cards. If Cherie herself was not living in Tucson, then Cherie was "keeping in touch" with people who did live in Tucson. Seese would be able to track her down, and then Seese would be able to collect on an old favor she had once done for Cherie.

It was only ten to midnight. Seese put on jeans and a gray sweater and tore through the suitcases for a nylon windbreaker. Mostly the suitcases were full of the "settlement goods"—cash and cocaine. It didn't matter. She just had to get from the door to the taxi. There was still time to catch Cherie at the Stage Coach. If Cherie was still dancing there. The possibility that Cherie had quit, had left town, brought a surge of the dark, hollow feeling Seese had long connected with coming down from cocaine. But it had been hours since she had had any coke, and even the marijuana she had smoked in bed had worn off. What she was feeling was the plain old jones—all nerves and her own guts reading false prophecies to her. So a little coke would readjust the world. She scattered a tiny spoonful across the peeling night table by the bed. Being around Beaufrey had got her into any number of bad habits, and wasting cocaine had been only one of them. She and Eric had always joked about the Mexican maids who cleaned the penthouse. How the maids put clean bags into their Electroluxes before they did the penthouse, and later all got high in the basement just from the sweepings off the carpet.

Seese told the cabdriver the name of the bar. He had stared at her in the rearview mirror, and she knew what he was thinking: "Cheap whores, bikers, and small-time drug deals." The wind had died down, but the air was dusty. A double shot of brandy would help. Her heart was racing with the anticipation of finding Cherie. The cocaine made her tongue numb, made her clench her jaws, and made her want to go, to move, to do something. She took a deep breath and settled back to look at the town where things would be settled for her once and for all. Miracle Mile had a heyday once. The motel bungalows, blue kidney-shaped pools, tall palm trees, and hedges of pink oleander sprang up. Winter havens for house trailers stretched for acres. But years before either Seese or Cherie had ever seen Tucson, something had changed.

The drought had left no green. In the dust-haze any lawns or grass that might have been alive was indistinguishable from the cement of buckling sidewalks.

Even the so-called desert "landscaping" was gaunt; the prickly pear and cholla cactus had shriveled into leathery, green tongues. The ribs of the giant saguaros had shrunk into themselves. The date palms and short Mexican palms were sloughing scaly, gray fronds, many of which had broken in the high winds and lay scattered in the street. One frond struck the underbelly of the taxi sharply, which broke loose a tangle of debris. Tumbleweeds, Styrofoam cups, and strands of toilet paper swirled in the rush of wind behind the taxi. Running over the palm fronds, even if they were grayish and dead, had reminded Seese of the Catholic Church and Palm Sunday. She laughed out loud and the cab-driver had looked hard into the rearview mirror. "I was just thinking," she said, avoiding the eyes.

She could endure it no longer. She had to know where Monte was—what had happened to her baby. The old psychic was somewhere in Tucson. Seese had to get help soon. In the desert life might evaporate overnight. The dead did not rot or dissolve. They shrank into rigid, impermeable leather around their own bones. Inside the cracked stucco bungalows and rusting house trailers, people got poorer as they got older. What had once been a winter getaway eventually became permanent. One year when the heat arrived in late March, they did not return to Ohio or Iowa. Instead, they retired. They sat motionless by window coolers or floor fans with the curtains and shades drawn until November. They were only passing time, waiting.

Eric would have liked Tucson. Too bad they had never quite managed to get here. He would have liked the northwest side the best because he had been fascinated with decay and death. Eric would particularly have liked the idea of the old "retiring" to await their extinction on the edge of a desert. Eric had been excited about a certain desert somewhere in Peru. That had been before Eric had realized that Beaufrey had no intention of allowing him to accompany them to Colombia. Eric had read all about the Spanish explorers because, he said, it was good to understand the history of a place. All Seese could remember was this place in the Peruvian desert where the Indians had taken their dead. The mummies were kept in an extremely arid place. Relatives and loved ones could go there to talk to those long deceased. Seese wished she could talk to Eric tonight. She understood now what was wrong with cremation. She had never understood what the Catholic Church had against cremation before. Now Eric was scattered across the West Texas plains pushed by the same winds that gusted through Tucson.

The cab ride was taking forever. Was he trying to fool her, to cheat her? She leaned forward to see where they were. The railroad tracks. She was almost there but felt something was about to overtake her— She had to know where Monte was, and what had happened to him. The old psychic lived somewhere in Tucson. Seese had to find the woman or she would be like all the others there, suspended in one endless interval between gusts of wind, and waves of dry heat.

THE STAGE COACH

THE STAGE COACH was on the frontage road to the freeway. The semis were parked north of the truck stop where the drivers showered and ate before hitting the bar for the strippers' show. Tiny didn't want the bar parking lot clogged with tractor-trailer rigs. Truckers didn't drink enough to suit him, and what Tiny wanted to sell was booze. Tiny had also sold pills to the truckers. He couldn't beat them, so he joined them, he liked to say. But the sale of a few pills didn't mean Tiny had to have giant semis a block long congesting his parking lot.

Big Harley-Davidsons, chromed and customized, were parked in perfect rows. Seese laughed. Cocaine was behind the bikers' mania for perfect rows of bikes, perfectly spaced. Biker perfection went no further than the motorcycle. Bikers themselves tended toward beer bellies and dirty T-shirts with jeans slipped down to expose their hairy cracks.

Seese did not see Cherie, but told herself don't panic—breathe deep. Even if she wasn't dancing here, chances were good Cherie would still be in town. Cherie's oldest girl was eight or nine now. Cherie wouldn't move around so much with a child in school. A tall redhead was bobbing and weaving out of a tiny fringed cowgirl skirt. Her breasts pushed open the white cowgirl vest. She had two toy pistols she aimed from the hip at the men leaning over the edge of the narrow stage. "Mamas Don't Let Your Babies Grow Up to Be Cowboys," the jukebox played. The bikers at the pool tables ignored the dancer on the platform. She had kicked the skirt out of the way, and was now doing deep knee-bends, legs apart, with the men out of their chairs at the edge of the stage whistling and yelling. The noise got one of the bikers to glance at three or four men reaching onstage to tuck dollar bills in the redhead's G-string. The other bikers had only bothered to turn their heads briefly. Seese could imagine the contempt the bikers had for the other men.

Tiny waddled out of his office when he heard the yells and whistles. He had gained a lot of weight since the last time Seese had seen him. He had to keep watch on the girls constantly. They'd show any little thing to get big tips from the audience. Being outside the city limits still didn't make it legal to spread her legs that wide. Seese laughed. Tiny had always been scolding her when she danced, complaining that she was going to get the Liquor Control boys down on him. But that had been when Tiny was hot for her, and the scolding had been his way of letting her know how sexy he thought she was. Tiny made a sudden cutting motion with his fat hand across his throat and swore at the redhead. As she closed her legs, Seese saw a sequin flash from deep within the folds of her flesh. The men at the foot of the stage booed Tiny and gave catcalls, but they didn't want the Stage Coach shut down by the Liquor Control Board either.

Tiny had turned to go back into his office, but caught sight of Seese. She took her double shot of whiskey from the bar and walked over to him. "Seese," he said as if he were seeing a ghost.

"Hi, Tiny."

"I heard you left," he said, still surprised. Tiny meant the rumor that Seese was dead meat. "Ancient history, those rumors," Tiny said, warming up, stepping closer.

Seese took a big swallow of whiskey. "Yeah, just rumors." She was scanning the barroom for Cherie. Dancers in garter belts and no bras, dancers in baton-twirling skirts, and dancers in bikinis circulated past the tables, passing the hat for tips before they danced.

Tiny had been in love with her once, but then David had come along. Seese finished the whiskey and Tiny nodded for the bartender to bring her another. Sweat was forming in the folds where his chin met his neck. Tiny was living proof that snorting cocaine didn't always cause weight loss. "I heard about your baby. I'm sorry." Tiny sounded sincere. He patted at his neck with a handkerchief and made a motion toward his office, but Seese shook her head. "I have a little something," Tiny said, meaning drugs.

"No. I'm looking for Cherie."

Tiny seemed short of breath. He wheezed. She would not have

fucked him even if David had not come along. Tiny gave up too easily. Despite everything that had happened between Tiny and Beaufrey, Seese knew Tiny would not help her because he was afraid of Beaufrey. But Cherie owed her one.

Tiny nodded his head at a table against the far wall. Cherie was hunched over the table, her head close to a man in a worn denim cowboy shirt and scuffed cowboy boots. She was trying to convince him of something. She looked startled when she saw Seese. The cowboy was suspicious. He studied Seese intently. She tried smiling but he had already sized her up. "Seese!" Cherie scuffed the chair back from the table and hugged her. She was dressed for her act. Baby-blue, see-through, shorty pajamas and blue satin high heels. "This is my husband, Teddy. Teddy, this is Seese. Remember, I told you how she helped me that time." Seese could see that Teddy didn't like to remember anything he knew about Cherie's past.

Seese didn't know where to begin. Cherie was nervous. Probably because the husband got jealous when she danced. "I guess you heard what happened—about Monte, I mean." Seese was surprised at how quiet her voice was, almost a whisper. She felt nothing when she said "Monte."

"Did David—?" Cherie stared down at the ashtray where her cigarette was burning into the filter. The husband reached over and squashed the butt. His jaw was set hard. Cherie was trying not to cry, but Seese saw big tears. Seese hardly cried anymore except when she woke up dreaming she was holding Monte in her arms. "Seese—it's just so sad—not to know—"

Seese nodded at Cherie. The husband had relaxed. He leaned back in his chair and watched a tiny flat-chested blonde bump her way out of a belly-dancer skirt. Women's tears or sad talk didn't seem to interest him.

"You been back in town long?"

Seese shook her head. She finished the whiskey. Cherie signaled the barmaid for another round. Tiny let dancers have all they wanted. It kept them loose and limber. "I waited for a long time. I thought David took Monte."

Cherie became alert. "You mean it wasn't David?"

Seese could not shake her head or reply without something breaking wide open inside herself. She took deep breaths and sipped the whiskey. "There's a woman who can help. I have to find her."

Cherie glanced at her husband watching the stage. She was rolling the hem of her shorty pajama top between her fingers. Seese could see Cherie was nervous, afraid something from the old days might slip out.

"Listen. I saw this woman on TV. She finds missing persons."

Cherie had looked puzzled. "I don't know anyone like that."

"Look," Seese said, raising her voice, "the only thing I have to go on is something about a crippled biker—a guy who works—"

At the mention of a man, Cherie's husband sat up with both elbows on the table making a barrier between the two women. Cherie shook her head.

"The old woman is with this biker—" Seese began, but Cherie had pushed back her chair.

"I'm up now!" Cherie looked at her husband, then glanced at Seese. "Ask Tiny!"

Seese nodded slowly and leaned back in her chair. The husband moved forward in his chair, gathering himself like a rodeo cowboy. His turn next. For eight minutes he had to stay in his chair while the men at the edge of the tiny stage leaned over to pry their eyes into his wife. Cherie selects her music on the jukebox. Roy Orbison. Chubby Checker. She dances staring straight ahead, her eyes miles away from this place. Neither of them were ever really dancers. But the men never cared as long as they got an eyeful. Cherie's husband looks down at his hands. He's a blond cowboy with a pretty face. Green eyes. Hands and fingernails stained with motor oil. There never has been quite enough money for Cherie to quit dancing. The husbands and boyfriends come and go on account of this.

Cherie holds the filmy blue nylon in both hands and flips it over her face to reveal her breasts. Mangoes—golden flesh served peeled—Beaufrey's morning meal in Puerto Vallarta. Metallic-blue sequins glitter on each nipple. The husband finishes his beer and motions for another. He ignores Seese. He ignores everything but the men reaching up on the platform, with both hands grabbing for her crotch or her breasts. An old man in white painter's coveralls grins so wide his false teeth slip. He's tucking five-dollar bills in the front of the shorty pajama bottom. Next to him, two men in identical work khakis huddle together, company logos and their first names embroidered on the front pockets. The black lights overhead make the scar and stretch marks on Cherie's belly glow uranium blue. Cherie has never lost a baby. Cherie can't stop getting pregnant. Still, the stretch marks only show under the black light. It doesn't seem fair. Cherie has four, can have five more, and Seese could only have one.

"Mama's got a squeeze box—Oh, my love, darling, I've hungered for your touch a long, lonely time—Daddy never sleeps at night"—off comes the blue pajama top. Cherie drops it casually, oblivious to the whistling and clapping. She stretches her arms up and can almost touch the purple tubes in the light fixture. Her breasts jut out. She turns away and shakes the cheeks of her ass, then spins back around. They want the bottoms off. They want the G-string now. The old man is standing up. He's got a twenty-dollar bill in his hand. She smiles and tosses him the pajama panty. He tucks the twenty into the blue satin G-string. For a moment the attention is on him, not her. The old man lifts the shorty pajama bottom high over his head, then brings it down to his beer glass. He stretches the crotch across the rim of his glass and downs the last of his beer. The others applaud and laugh. The cowboy is sweating. Seese smells it—hard labor. Sweat, great exertion. His hands clenching and unclenching fists. Seese wonders how Cherie manages to always find men who will eventually want to kill her, but remembers the bullet through the penthouse window and has to laugh at herself. Cherie's cowboy gives Seese a murderous look. She starts to explain that she is not laughing at anything here, that she is laughing at herself, but the cowboy has already turned his head away. It takes a certain kind of man to watch his wife or girlfriend striptease in front of a crowd of drunk, grab-happy men and not blow up and kill them all. This pretty little cowboy was the wrong kind. The right kind would have been proud, would have had contempt for all the other men who did not have a beautiful woman—the right man would have enjoyed parading his wildly sexual woman in front of the needy and deprived. Seese had seen men who gloated over how badly the leering, shouting crowd wanted what was theirs, what the crowd could look at but never touch. But Cherie's blond cowboy did not appear confident that the others were only going to look.

Seese was drunk enough not to worry whether Tiny really did have the information she needed. If she had to, she could press Cherie in front of her cowboy, and Cherie would get it. Because Seese knew that Cherie didn't want her new husband to know any more about the past than he had already guessed or suspected. The favor Cherie owed Seese actually wasn't much. It had happened a long time ago when they had been so much younger and under Tiny's thumb. Cherie had gotten set up by some undercover cops. Seese had noticed that "the college boys" always had money for their grams, and each time they had pressed Cherie to sell them more. Seese kept telling Cherie to be careful of people who didn't beg you to front them three or four grams. Narcs always had money. But Cherie hadn't worried because they had always snorted or shot up in the kitchen, right in front of her. After that the tall one who had played pro basketball always wanted to take her to bed; then he'd always leave $50 or $60. Cherie was sure undercover cops didn't do that even when they were undercover. They hadn't been anything but babies then, and Cherie never liked to tell Tiny what was going on. Tiny didn't ask as long as the cash rolled in and the girls weren't snorting too much themselves. So Cherie had set up a half-ounce sale.

The arrangement had been that once Cherie had the money, she would tell the guys to step out to the alley behind the apartment to get the goods from Seese, who would wait in the car. Cherie had wanted Seese to keep the half ounce right beside her in the car, but Seese had been wary. She had hidden the plastic bag with the cocaine inside a cardboard milk carton, which she left next to a trash can in the alley.

When Cherie's ex–pro basketball player and his buddies had pulled their guns, and then their badges, and pushed Cherie outside into weeds and old dog shit in the backyard, Seese had not panicked. It occurred to her this might be a heist, and if it was, then they might both be killed. But Seese knew if it had been shooting they planned, the gunmen would not have marched Cherie out the back door in broad daylight. It might only have been an alley, but the alleys in the neighborhood were well populated with university students. Gunmen would have shot Cherie inside, then come out to get Seese in the car. So Seese did not move, although she could see Cherie's eyes urging her to run. One cop had stuck a .44 and a badge in her face while the other slid into the front seat beside her. Seese had pretended to glance at the cop as he opened the door on the passenger's side, but what Seese had really been looking at was the old milk carton lying in the weeds and trash next to a trash can.

"What's going on?" Seese had asked Cherie just as the ex–basketball pro had opened the car door and pulled her out. "Can't these guys take a joke? Hey, it was a little joke, that's all." The cops did not like the word *joke*. The ex-pro squeezed the handcuffs around her wrists so tightly tears came to her eyes.

Tiny had got them both out of jail before the evening shift at the Stage Coach. The interior and the trunk of the car had been torn apart by the ex–basketball pro and his pals. Seese had never bothered to have the door panels or rubber floor matting replaced afterward because as long as she owned that car, she wanted to remember the April afternoon she had outmaneuvered the narcs. The cops had searched everywhere, but they didn't notice the old milk carton lying on the ground. Without the goods, Seese had only been charged with conspiracy to distribute or sell. Cherie they hit for the sale of the grams in the past, and for prostitution. But none of the charges were big enough to interest the DA's office. "Goddamn it," Cherie said, "I wish we would have gone to trial. I wanted to testify about all those grams the scummy niggers shot up and snorted. Taxpayers' money buying toot for nigger cops."

Tiny had been furious. He had slapped Cherie so hard that she fell to her knees in the parking lot outside the city jail. Seese had tried to stop him by telling him not to worry, the half was safe. But Tiny had spun around, fast for a fat man, and the murder in his eye told Seese it was about sex with the black narcs, not the half ounce of coke. Tiny had not even thought of the half ounce yet. Cherie had, though. She started crying while she was still on the ground, promising to make it all up to him, promising to borrow the money and pay it back right away. Tiny had kicked Cherie in the ribs, and only Seese, pointing out a patrol car approaching on Stone Avenue, had stopped Tiny from really hurting Cherie.

Cherie had curled up in the backseat of Tiny's big Buick and sobbed and moaned about broken ribs. All Tiny kept saying was, "Bitch! Dumb cunt bitch!" He had repeated it again and again. He told her he should kill her for it. He told her anyone else in his place would. He told her that she owed Seese, not him. She owed Seese because the half ounce was safe. If the half ounce had been lost, Tiny told Cherie he would have killed her.

Cherie comes off the platform breathing hard. She wraps a red-flowered cotton kimono around herself tightly. At the table she takes both her husband's hands in hers and squeezes them while she kisses him so that all the others can see them. The last girl has Pink Floyd on the jukebox, and they watch her adjust the crotch of her leotard as she comes onstage. The husband relaxes and pushes his glass of beer across the table to Cherie. She is still breathing fast and the hair around her face is dark with perspiration. "Pretty good for an old lady," Cherie says to Seese, and they both laugh. Tiny would have beaten Cherie bad, but probably not have killed her. Not in those days. They had all been much younger. Actually all Cherie owed Seese was for stashing the cocaine in the milk carton. Seese had started to say she didn't like to have to ask favors when Cherie finished her husband's beer and said, "Look. I think you can find them on the south side—South Park Avenue. Almost to the airport. Look for a real old house trailer with a wrecked motorcycle outside." Seese finished the whiskey. She gave Cherie a hug and smiled at the husband, who turned away rudely. The bartender had already yelled "Last call!" Seese told Cherie to take it easy, she'd be in touch, and they would have to get together for a beer sometime. But Cherie had glanced nervously in the direction of the blond cowboy, then back at Seese. They both knew they probably would not see each other again for a long time.

Tiny had watched Seese from the doorway of his office but she had pretended that she was too drunk to notice. The whole taxi ride back to the motel she was glad she hadn't had to ask Tiny for help. Tiny calculated the loss of her baby as the price she had paid for fucking with David and Beaufrey. Tiny was right of course. But Seese didn't have to give him any more satisfaction than he'd already got.

BOOK THREE

SOUTHWEST

FAMOUS CRIMINALS

FERRO HANDED the truck keys to Seese with a sullen expression. He had already lectured them about doing Lecha's errands and then coming back. He kept asking Seese why Sterling had to go, and Seese kept telling him that she'd need help with the lifting.

"Lies, lies, lies," Seese said, laughing as they zoomed down the drive, past the toolshed and corrals, past the kennels where the night dogs slept in the shade of the big paloverde tree. Sterling was concerned about getting into trouble with Ferro or Paulie or the boss woman. Seese shook her head. Lecha wants all this weird stuff—a wing back chair with peacocks on it, a typewriter table, even the typewriter!

Sterling nodded. He decided he would let Seese take over. "Relax," she told him. "We are on important business. No one is going to bother us."

Sterling thought she took the dirt road a little too fast because the rear wheels slid a little on the curves. A roadrunner had to take to the air to avoid being run over. So he made a joke hoping Seese might slow down. He said he thought she'd make a good driver for a getaway car. But instead of laughing, Seese nodded seriously and said she had actually done that once.

"In my other life," Seese said, making Sterling feel a lot better. "It wasn't a bank or 7-Eleven holdup at least. It was a rip-off. Drug deal. You know."

Sterling nodded, although he did not know. He had read a great deal in his magazines about the drug tsars and huge drug deals worth hundreds of millions. "It would make me too nervous," Sterling said as they sailed onto the paved road, and he glanced behind them at the dust cloud the truck had kicked up, a dust cloud the size of a tornado. Sterling was thinking probably Ferro was watching them in the telescope he kept in the front driveway.

"I was too young and too high to be scared," Seese said; she was driving slower now and watched for cops in the rearview mirror. She felt happy and confident taking Sterling on errands. While she and Cherie still worked for Tiny, she had always joked that she'd be lost if she had to go out in Tucson during the daylight because they slept most of the day and usually went out only at night. Then she had left with David after only six months. Still, she felt as if she knew the town enough to get them to a shopping mall.

The plan was to do the errands and eat and then drive around. Sterling was glad to have a chance to see some points of interest in Tucson. Of course they were only places that had been mentioned in the "Yesteryear" articles of the *Police Gazette*—the Congress Hotel downtown where the Dillinger gang had been staying, the bungalow not far from University Street where Dillinger himself and his girlfriend had been captured. Just in case, Sterling had brought along copies of the magazine with two of his favorite "Yesteryear" articles: the John Dillinger and Geronimo profiles. Of course, when Sterling really thought about it, he had other favorites too, but these were the articles in which Tucson played an important role.

Sterling wandered behind Seese in the department stores. They had already bought the typewriter and typing table. They were searching for the wing back chair with peacocks on it. Sterling had realized these stores were full of furniture, but it wasn't until they started looking for this certain chair that he understood just how many sofas, end tables, and armchairs there were. Seese reached deep into the big purse hanging from her shoulder and paid cash for everything. Sterling had had a little trouble getting used to all those hundred-dollar bills. But after a few hours of going up and down escalators, wandering through mazes of sofas and beds and still no lunch, Sterling had adjusted to the fistfuls of hundreds. Sterling decided it wasn't nearly the shock that Geronimo must have had when they loaded him and the rest of the Apache prisoners on the train to send them to the prison camp in Florida. At least Sterling had spent time in Barstow, California, and some weeks outside of Bakersfield repairing the track torn up by a hundred-car freight train derailment. He had also vacationed at Long Beach and had ridden the big roller coaster that swooped and swerved above the ocean.

What a shock it must have been. Geronimo would have come from riding with his warriors, sleeping on the bare ground, and eating bits of a venison jerky and parched corn. Then suddenly all the Apaches, including the women and kids, had been loaded on a train. Most of them had probably never been inside a train and never seen such things as train seats or train toilets. Sterling had been wondering how the soldiers guarding the Apaches had taught them to use train toilets when he saw the chair they had been looking for. Seese had somehow overlooked it because she was poking and pressing sofa pillows. The chair was high backed and "winged," and it was even blue. "Blue is her favorite color," Seese said while they were eating tacos. The back of the pickup was too full of purchases to leave unattended. Sterling secretly preferred drive-ins because he had not been sure of the proper clothes for indoor restaurants since the time, years ago, in Long Beach he had been turned away from a place called the Surf Cafe. He had been wearing his black-and-white-plaid sport coat and new tennis shoes. It might have been a case of racial discrimination, but Sterling was not sure. A sullen man with a stack of menus had told him he must wear a tie. Sterling had been so horrified to be turned away that minutes passed before it occurred to him that the sullen man himself wore no tie, only a sport coat and slacks.

Seese had not felt so happy or chatty for a long time. It was this funny old guy Sterling who put her in such a good mood. He always kept his eyes open for funny things and tried to make jokes. And he had found the peacock chair, which she might never have seen. Seese wanted to get every item on Lecha's list to prove she was organized and responsible. Seese knew, however, that it was the last purchase that concerned Lecha most. Lecha might have hired any number of competent people to buy what was in the boxes and bundles in the back of the truck. On the other hand, only a few people knew how to conduct the transaction planned for after lunch.

Seese announced they had an hour to kill. Sterling said that would be fine because all of the places on their tour were near downtown. He asked Seese again if she was sure she really wanted to go see these places. "They might not even be there. Or they might be sort of boring," Sterling said hesitantly, "like the Congress Hotel."

"I *told* you—I really want to. You have to tell me all about what happened at these places—all the history and stuff."

"I guess we might start at the Congress Hotel." Seese wheeled the heavily loaded pickup through downtown. Tucson's downtown had been stunned by shopping malls, so it seemed sort of deserted. It was easy to park across the street so she could look and concentrate on the old building while Sterling talked.

"You can't even tell there was a fire," Sterling commented. "It was the fire, see. It was an accident they ever caught Dillinger. Because he was a lot smarter than they were. But the weak link was the rest of the gang. See, Dillinger sent the others ahead to Tucson. He had this girl-friend. She was part Indian, part Canadian Indian. She was real pretty. They were visiting his relatives in Florida. So Clark and Makely had this woman named Opal Long with them. There might have been a couple of other guys, but they had just tagged along with Makely and Clark. Which wasn't a good idea and was part of how they got caught."

Sterling was pleased to see Seese smiling and listening so closely to his story. It was easy to imagine all the things happening when you were parked right there on the actual site.

For a moment he considered simply reading a paragraph or two out of the magazine. But Sterling had visualized it so many times in the years since he had first read the article that he thought he would tell Seese just the way he pictured the demise of the Dillinger gang:

Clark had been tall and thin with dark hair stuck close to his head. His eyes didn't seem to match. Makely was short with sandy-brown hair. Sometimes he wore a mustache, imitating his boss, John Dillinger. Sterling imagined Opal Long looked a little like Greta Garbo. It was January when they got to Tucson. They rented rooms in the Congress Hotel. And then this is where accident and luck sort of come in. One night not long after Makely and Clark and Long had moved in there, the Congress Hotel had caught fire.

Sterling paused for emphasis and to look again at the three stories of windows, imagining the Tucson fire department's arrival. "A fire," Seese said. "Accident and luck. Yeah." Her face got sad. "I know about those two." Seese had tried to make the last few words sound like a joke, but Sterling could tell that accident and luck had not dealt any better with Seese than they had with Sterling or with John Dillinger for that matter. She noticed how Sterling had left off the story because of her sudden sadness. So she reached across the pickup seat and patted Sterling on the arm so he would continue.

The firemen had saved all the gang's suitcases and things. They had had quite a number of trunks and suitcases. Of course they were full of the cash from their last robberies. And they did have a couple of sub-machine guns. So after the firemen had brought down all their things—it was quite a lot—Makely pulled out this big roll of bills and gave the firemen $50 for their trouble. The Dillinger gang locked their luggage in the car and went across the street—right here, to the Manhattan Bar—and bought drinks for other guests driven out of the Congress Hotel by the fire. Makely was smooth and a natural show-off, but Clark knew only one way to get people's attention; that had been the reason Clark had started armed robbery at age sixteen. So, as the evening went on and Makely got so much attention with the roll of bills, Clark cornered a tourist. They were all drunk. He made the tourist step outside with him. He opened the huge trunk of the '33 Packard touring car and pulled out a big suitcase. Clark had to show the tourist one of their machine guns.

"Let's see," Seese said, smiling, "I think I can guess this one—the firemen couldn't forget the face of the stranger who gave them such a big tip."

"Right!" Sterling answered. They had been reading the *Police Gazette* at the fire station. The back section featured pictures of the most wanted, and one of the firemen thought he recognized a face. "Pretty dumb to show your machine gun to a stranger," Seese said as she turned the truck from Stone Avenue to Second Street. Sterling had the exact address, but they still had to creep along to see the house numbers.

"Oooh!" Sterling said, comparing the fuzzy magazine photo with the house they'd parked in front of. Seese had looked at the photo a moment, then laughed so hard she leaned against the steering wheel and made the horn honk. The bungalow on Second Street looked almost the same, down to the peeling white paint and a battered trash can sitting on the porch by the front door. Even the position of the trash can was identical, down to a vertical dent that ran its length. "It couldn't be! No!" Seese was laughing. Right then Sterling had noticed a man across the street suspiciously eyeing them in the pickup truck loaded with boxes, bundles, and a blue wing chair. He and the blond woman were making a spectacle of themselves, which was exactly what Dillinger's gang had done, and look how they had ended up. Sterling cleared his throat. "Maybe we should go ahead and try to find Geronimo's house." If they got questioned by the police, Sterling knew that would be the end of both their jobs.

"I'm sorry," Seese said, wiping her eyes across the sleeve of her white blouse. "I couldn't help laughing! It's the trash can."

"Well, I am amazed myself," Sterling said, carefully closing the page of one *Police Gazette* before picking up the other issue that had the Geronimo article in it.

"We can't go yet. You didn't tell me what happened here."

Sterling had glanced across the street nervously but the man was gone.

"What's wrong?"

"Oh, I saw this man looking at us."

Seese had laughed again.

"You're right," Sterling said. "I must be getting edgy because we are going to Geronimo's house next!"

Sterling joked, but he got on with the Dillinger story quickly. In late January the big red bougainvillea was thick and blossoming all across the front porch and around the sides of the house too. It had been easy for the Tucson police to hide in the backyard. "What a nasty surprise to find in your bougainvillea branches!" Seese had not felt so carefree and silly for a long time. She was beginning to believe a little more in what Lecha had said: that soon many things would be resolved.

"When Geronimo came by this way, it looked very much different," Sterling had commented, staring down at a page in the *Police Gazette*.

"No kidding," Seese said, driving down University Boulevard, lined with palm trees. "Geronimo might have been the lucky one," she said, tilting her head at the yellowish-brown palm fronds the trees were shedding; the piles reminded her of dead locusts, although she could not remember where she might have seen the insects.

"Well, it was the last time Dillinger and his gang ever saw any of this. They got Dillinger and Billy Frechette, his girlfriend, at the house too. They sat in the backseat of the police car with their legs and hands in shackles. The police were reluctant to let them roll down the windows in the backseat. Dillinger made a joke about it—the end of January and he was sweating. That was the worst of it. All of the Midwestern states wanted him, and their high temperatures were in the teens. So Dillinger hired this woman lawyer, and just as they were waiving extradition to Indiana or someplace like that, this hotshot DA with plans for higher office flew in. The Tucson police let the DA take Dillinger away in the middle of the night. They drove to Douglas, Arizona, on the border. There was an airstrip there. The DA flew back to Indiana with Dillinger. It was four above zero the day they arraigned Dillinger in Terre Haute. The rest is history."

"Oh?"

"Well, you know. Dillinger escapes the Terre Haute jail. But there is the lady in red and the movie in Chicago. The FBI shot him down outside. The extradition from Arizona was illegal."

"Well, the lesser of two evils," Seese says, but she can see that Sterling is troubled by her last remark. She senses that it has to do with whatever has sent him to Tucson.

"Well," Sterling begins cautiously, watching Seese's face for a re-action, "what concerns me is that sometimes judges and courts break their own laws or they decide something completely wrong." Sterling is thinking about the tribal court judge and the Tribal Council again. He is thinking there are instances when the law has nothing to do with fairness or justice.

Seese says, "I'm sorry. I guess I've spent too many years around scum—people that when they get caught, they deserve everything the judge can give them and then some."

Sterling nods, but now he is looking at the large old house on Main Street. It appears to be empty. There is a real estate company sign in front of it.

"Geronimo's house is for sale," Seese says, smiling.

"Actually, it is just the place they took him to sign the papers declaring he and his warriors had surrendered." Sterling follows Seese up the steps to the long territorial-style porch. They press their faces against the windows. The big room is lined with glass cases made of oak. Whatever antiques were once displayed are gone except for the remains of a skull collection. Seese identifies dog and wolf skulls. Sterling sees a pronghorn-antelope skull and that of a horse. Otherwise the big room and the smaller rooms off it are empty.

"I wonder what Geronimo thought," Seese says, sitting down on the front steps staring straight ahead at the pickup loaded with all the purchases.

"He thought he and his men would be allowed to go back to the White Mountains and live in peace."

"You mean he had to take their word for what he was signing?"

"Well, look. The U.S. army had kept five thousand troops in south-ern Arizona and southern New Mexico in the 1880s and '90s trying to catch him. They never did catch him. The only way they could do it was by tricking him. They sent word General Miles just wanted to talk to him. And General Crook had promised Geronimo the Apaches could go home to live in peace. But the territorial politicians and the Indian agents didn't like Crook. General Crook was on his way out when he met with Geronimo. None of the promises were ever kept."

Seese got up suddenly. "I don't want to be anywhere near this place." She drove slowly through the "historic district's" old mansions.

"They made money off the Indian wars, did you know?"

Seese felt a sinking sensation in her chest. She shook her head. "I even went to college for a while and I don't know the things you do."

Sterling smiled modestly. "I only happened to learn it from this magazine article. There was money to be made by getting the government contracts to feed all those soldiers. Somebody had to sell them horses to ride."

"Oh," Seese said, "I get the picture."

"I don't know if this was ever proven, but there was something here called the Indian Ring," Sterling continued. "Tucson merchants who did not want to see the Apache wars end. So they paid off a whiskey peddler. They sent the whiskey peddler to get Geronimo and his men drunk. The peddler showed Geronimo newspaper headlines from Washington, D.C., and warned Geronimo if he or his men 'came in,' they'd all be hanged. The newspaper headlines were quotes from U.S. congressmen who wanted Geronimo dead. The Indian Ring in Tucson kept the Apache wars going for years that way."

"I like that!" Seese said fiercely. "I really like that! All these fancy houses, all these Tucson family fortunes made off war—the way all money is made!" Her sudden shift in mood made Sterling uneasy. Before he could reassure her that things had not ended as badly as they might have for Geronimo and his people, Seese said, "Now I know what you meant a little while ago. About judges and courts." Sometimes her anger frightened her; it was leftover anger that surfaced while Sterling was talking about the Apaches. She had to get rid of the feeling that Monte had been lost because of anything she had done. The old Tucson mansions along Main Street were the best proof that murderers of innocent Apache women and children had prospered. In only one generation government embezzlers, bootleggers, pimps, and murderers had become Tucson's "fine old families."

They parked in an alley not far from Geronimo's house and Dillinger's stucco bungalow. Lecha had arranged everything. All Seese had to do was follow the instructions at the appointed time and place. At three o'clock exactly, the tall redwood gate swung open to the alley. Seese got out of the truck holding the purse close to her body.

After she stepped inside, the gate closed again without Sterling ever seeing anyone. Somehow her reaction to the mansions and rich people in Tucson had made Sterling feel uneasy. He had misjudged Tucson. He had never learned much about Barstow, but as far as he knew, Barstow had no mansions, old or new. Winslow certainly had no mansions. So this might be the first time Sterling had ever lived anywhere near a place founded mostly by criminals.

Sterling rolled up the window partway although it was very hot. He was glad that he had spent all those years keeping up with each issue of the *Police Gazette* and the *True Detective*. He seemed to recall there had been something about the Mafia in one of the more recent issues, something about the Mafia in the Southwest. Sterling was a little ashamed he had skipped over that article. But he had never found articles on the Mafia nearly as interesting as articles about Chicago trunk murders or the white-slave trade conducted in Wyoming boomtowns. Sterling was beginning to like the fact that the old ranch house was high in the foothills. He thought the fences and gates and even the guard dogs might be a wise precaution around people who had got rich off the suffering of Geronimo and his people.

BUSINESS WITH CALABAZAS

LECHA SPOKE FONDLY of the "old man," and she had used sweet tones when she talked to him on the phone. Seese saw he wasn't that old. He might not have been as old as Lecha. Lecha had gone out of her way to explain she and "the old *viejo*" had never "been involved." Lecha had acquired all the correct expressions for sex on the regional TV talk show circuit.

Seese had smiled and politely reminded Lecha that she of all people did not have to worry about those sorts of things. Instead of smiling back, Lecha had suddenly launched into a harangue about a dying woman. "A dying woman," she lectured, "must above all put her reputation in order. Before all other business affairs, a woman's reputation must come first!" Lecha saw Seese was frightened. She had not meant anything by it, so Lecha lowered her voice. "Poor thing! You have to hear all of this from me. But if you only knew all the lies that have been told against me!" Lecha had lowered her voice more. "Even in my own family." Then she abruptly changed the subject to her "medicine." Her last warning had been "old man" Calabazas liked to have compliments on his cactus and his burros.

Calabazas was not any taller than Seese. She knew she had Geronimo on the brain because the face Seese saw resembled Geronimo's,
although Seese realized Calabazas was a Mexican Indian, not an Apache.
She felt as if Calabazas's eyes had her pinned by the shoulders. She could
not return his glance, so she looked around the yard.

The cactus garden was intricately planned. Smooth, light-orange
rock bordered a vast collection of little pincushion cactus covered with
purple-pink blossoms. Other cactus plants were bordered with small
white stones. The largest and most formidable varieties of cactus had
been planted next to the walls of the house. Snaky night-blooming
cactus plants climbed around all the windows, and it occurred to Seese
that Calabazas's cactus also created an elaborate barricade around the
house. He startled her when he said, "Yes, you would find it rough
going." Seese wanted to deny he had read her thoughts, but instead said
how beautiful the garden was. He seemed not to hear her and disappeared through a door in an adobe wall. He left her standing there a
long time. Seese could see the corrals and the burros shaded by big
cottonwoods. John Dillinger might have done better if he had rented
this place. It was too bad Sterling couldn't see this. He could have gotten
ideas for his landscaping around the ranch house. The old man returned
with a small brown paper sack with the top twisted rather than folded
shut. He handed it to her and opened the gate without saying anything.
Just then a United Parcel delivery truck pulled up behind the pickup in
the alley. Calabazas's expression did not change, but Seese sensed he
was uneasy. She knew Calabazas didn't want her or Sterling to see what
the parcel service truck had come to pick up. Seese started the pickup
engine quickly, but then pretended to have trouble getting it into gear.
As they drove down the alley, Seese watched in the side mirror; the
deliveryman was loading boxes. Calabazas's shipments. In the truck
mirror, Seese saw Calabazas's sharp eyes on hers. She figured she would
hear about it from Lecha when she got home. "What was that, I
wonder," Sterling had said when they turned onto the freeway access
road. He had the paper sack on his lap, holding it carefully so that the
twist did not come undone and cause any suspicion of tampering. Sterling
was learning quickly that Ferro and Paulie and the old boss woman
watched closely for any signs of tampering. Sterling figured the old twin
sister would do just the same.

IN THE BACKSEAT
OF A CHRYSLER

"CALABAZAS DIDN'T LIKE either one of you," Lecha said, laughing. "He got right on the phone to complain to me!" Seese and Sterling had just carried the blue peacock chair into her bedroom. Lecha was sitting up in her bed with the paper bag in her lap. Sterling hurried out of the bedroom. Bedrooms of women not related to him had always thrown him into a panic. He had always preferred motel rooms or the backseat of a big car. While he had been living in Winslow at the railroad section-gang compound, an amazing thing had happened. A white woman passing through Winslow on Route 66 had had car trouble. The only mechanic in Winslow told the woman it would cost hundreds of dollars because the car was one of those huge '59 Chrysler Imperials. Later, the mechanic told how he had advised her to sell it for scrap and to catch the Greyhound to California, which was where she had been headed. But the woman would not hear of it. The mechanic was nervous about a down payment for all the parts he'd have to order from Phoenix or Los Angeles. So she had opened up the huge trunk of the black Imperial and had started unloading suitcases. The mechanic said later he thought she might have been a little crazy or something. They all knew the mechanic because the rail-lifter machine they used for laying new track had never worked right, and one of them, usually Sterling or one of the Mexicans, had to take the mechanic a message from the foreman to come fix it. So they knew the mechanic, they knew he wasn't exaggerating or lying later on when he told them what had been inside those suitcases: mink coats, fox stoles, and leather jackets. And shoes—every color and kind of high-heel shoe—even those platform shoes with clear plastic heels so you could see the plastic goldfish swimming inside them. When she started to open the fifth or sixth suitcase, the mechanic said he had waved his hands at the pile of furs and shoes and told her that was enough down payment.

Sterling had not gone to her while she was in the room at the Painted

Desert Motel. But he had heard stories from the Mexican guys who had. They said she was expensive, but that she knew things they had never ever heard of, let alone had a chance to try. Then, right before Sterling got up enough courage to stroll by the Painted Desert Motel, Room 23, a very strange and exciting thing had happened. Right at quitting time at the big Sante Fe Railroad maintenance yard, and on payday too, the big black Imperial had come gliding up to the gate. Sterling had been a little shocked at how many of the married men who had families living with them in Winslow also seemed to know Janey. She was smiling and laughing more to herself than with them as she showed off the car. "This is my baby," she said over and over. "Now I have to get my beautiful wardrobe out of hock." She swung open the door and Sterling thought he had never seen such a huge backseat. Later he realized the car had been a special model, something less than a limousine, but "big as a bedroom," someone joked. Of course they all started making jokes, laughing and pushing one another toward the luxurious black leather seats. Then they had grabbed Sterling. All of them—Mexicans and Indians and even the white foreman—thought Sterling spent too much time reading. He told them he had a weak stomach and any more than three beers made him sick. But they had not quite forgiven him for not drinking and carousing with them anyway. They had shoved Sterling into the backseat to get even with him for all the nights he had eaten alone at the section-gang cafeteria then gone to his room to read magazines. "Give him the deluxe!" they yelled to Janey as she drove away.

Sterling could feel the grime on his hands. The odor of the motor oil on his coveralls competed with the wonderful smell of Janey's perfume. This was about the worst thing that had ever happened to Sterling. Janey had pulled onto Route 66 and they were zooming in the direction of Holbrook until she took a turn onto a dirt road. The road wound through small outcroppings of yellow sandstone and up into the juniper forest. When she stopped and turned off the engine, Sterling thought he had never heard such silence in all his life. He must have looked scared because Janey started laughing when she opened the back door.

The backseat of the black Chrysler was so big that they could do the entire "deluxe" with the doors closed. But Janey put all the electric windows down, for the gorgeous clean air, she said, and Sterling had thought the juniper and sage in the breeze did smell good. Open windows also prevented the smell of motor oil and a day's worth of sweat from spoiling things.

Janey stayed around Winslow for two more weeks performing "the deluxe" in the backseat of the Imperial. The mechanic said later she had been able to pay the repair bill the day he had finished with the car; so the extra two weeks in Winslow must have been Janey's insurance policy. All of them were a little amazed that Janey had made enough in five days to pay for eight Chrysler valves and a camshaft.

After that, when the section-gang guys wanted to go carousing, Sterling told them he would settle for nothing less than "the deluxe." So many nights he had lain awake remembering how Janey had undressed him and how she had told him to close his eyes and leave everything to her. For Sterling that would always be "the deluxe": to lie naked on soft, plush cushions with his eyes closed so he could simply feel her hands and mouth moving over his skin. He had decided years earlier that the trouble of getting ready to have sex spoiled the sex once you ever got to it. With the deluxe it all happened like a dream—feeling the sensation spreading from his balls and cock outward, and then that last sudden squeeze that brought all the sensations rushing back to the tip of his cock, leaving his fingers and toes numb.

Sterling tried the deluxe three more times after the first go. The guys badgered him to tell them about it, but he told them he had his eyes closed. That had really horrified the Mexicans and the Hopis. They were incredulous. What had been deluxe for them had been Janey's powder-blue eyes and her white-blond hair, and the way her breasts almost pointed up—some of them swore the nipples curved up. And the pink—bright pink. You didn't get any of that with the Winslow whores even as teenagers. Well, how could a Navajo or Mexican or Negro, even as a teenager, ever give you that bright shade of pink? All dark meat to begin with.

"Oh," Sterling had said. Because he had never thought about colors with sex before, but that could be blamed on going to high school at an Indian boarding school where any sort of sexual act had to be performed in the dark of the basement or a handy broom closet. They had talked so much about the part of Janey that was so pink and how much they had enjoyed pulling it all open to look, finally the foreman got mad. All morning they had only pulled and reset two rails. After the foreman left and they were yelling at each other to haul ass, a big Hopi from Third Mesa said bitterly, "Easy enough for that *bahana* to scold us. He's been sucking little pink titties all his life."

Sterling tried a couple of times to get a "deluxe" in Barstow, but the women working there weren't a whole lot different from the whores in Winslow, who not only wanted to take your money first, they wanted you to get the motel room, and worst of all, they expected you to tell them what to do. You had to tell them everything. Take off your shoes, get on the bed, take hold of this—no, not like that—it was so much trouble Sterling decided it wasn't worth it.

Living away from Laguna all the years the other men his age were marrying had saved him from his old aunts, who did question him when he visited home at fiesta time or at Christmas. He was not against marriage or women. He was devoted to his old aunts, who were always cooking and sewing for him and sending birthday cards. He got them free passes to ride the train anywhere they wanted. His main trouble with marriage was that he was not used to telling anyone else what to do. He supposed *that* might be traced back to the way Aunt Marie had raised him when his parents were both gone. Sterling didn't even feel he needed to trace it back anywhere. He was very happy going along on his own. He liked a simple life with his magazines, visits home to his old aunts, and the occasional vacation to Long Beach to ride the big roller coaster.

The years had gone along like that and there had even been young widows set up by his dear old aunts, who worried a great deal about who would care for Sterling after they were gone. But it didn't take a genius to see that the young widows and their children would expect Sterling to tell them what to do next. Finally when all his old aunts assembled at one table for a deer dinner, Sterling had given them each long-fringed silk shawls of brilliant jewel colors. And then he had told them that unless they could find a woman as able, as wise, as strong as they were, they should not bother. Each of the old sisters spoke in turn, and by the time Aunt Nora had performed the ceremonial eating of the deer eyes, and Aunt Marie and Aunt Nita had finished the brains, Sterling was relieved and happy to realize that they agreed with him.

From that time on they pampered him even more, and Sterling was left in peace to enjoy dreaming "the deluxe."

STERLING'S ROOM

SOMETIMES IN THE MIDDLE of the night the sound of Ferro's four-wheel-drive truck would awaken Sterling. They came and they went at all hours. Fortunately, Ferro and Paulie were seldom at the house for very long. The old boss woman was more difficult to figure out because only occasionally did she go with Ferro and Paulie. Yet sometimes she was gone for days. Her absence wasn't something Sterling could have proven, but when he walked down the hall past her office or outside the bedroom windows with the shades pulled, he could sense the rooms were empty. Sterling finished a second cheese sandwich and helped himself to more potato chips. He had enjoyed the errands and the drive with Seese very much. He thought if everything would continue along this way, he might be content to stay here for a long time. He carried an extra can of 7-Up down the hill to his room. The sun had almost set. The desert birds were calling and moving the way they did before darkness. The wind off the mountain peak smelled fresh, almost as if rain might be coming. The sky to the west was clear, but clouds could be smelled long before they were seen. He remembered Aunt Marie teaching him that. Around sundown Sterling sometimes felt his mood change. He would begin to think about his life. He would think about all the dear old grandaunts now gone on to Cliff House where they had planned a great many of their favorite activities for all eternity. He missed all of them around a table teasing each other, joking about old lovers and sexual escapades. The younger generations of women had not really matched the likes of Aunt Marie and Aunt Nora. But Sterling was certain that he had not matched them either, although they had loved him and spoiled him so much their own children, his cousins, had become terribly jealous of him. And in the end, the jealousy had been what had worked against Sterling when it came down to the vote of the Tribal Council over the decision of the tribal court judge. Sterling knew that sending the children away to boarding schools was the main problem. He and the other children had to learn what they could about the kachinas and the ways to pray or greet the deer, other animals, and plants during summer vacations, which were too short. Sterling might not have been sent away so young if his parents had not died. Still, that had been the policy of the federal government with Indians. Aunt Marie used to say there was no use in getting upset over something that had happened fifty years ago. Education was the wave of the future.

Well, the wave of the future had carried him clear down here, to the Sonoran desert. Sterling tried to tell himself it wasn't the end of the world. Look at Geronimo, who got tossed clear to Oklahoma.

The twilight was luminous pearl-gray. Sterling sat down on the five-gallon gas can by the corner of the toolshed. Something about ending up down here at this place was causing him to think more. Something really *had* happened to the world. It wasn't just something his funny, wonderful, old aunts had made up. It wasn't just the scarcity of eligible brides or dependable women. People now weren't the same. What had become of that world which had faded a little more each time one of his dear little aunts had passed? Sterling dabbed at the tears with his shirttail. They ran down the tip of his nose and caused an itch.

The short time he had been in Tucson, Sterling had begun to realize that people he had been used to calling "Mexicans" were really remnants of different kinds of Indians. But what had remained of what was Indian was in appearance only—the skin and the hair and the eyes. The cheekbones and nose like eagles and hawks. They had lost contact with their tribes and their ancestors' worlds.

Inside, he piled up pillows and pulled his reading lamp closer to the bed. He needed to get his mind off such thoughts—Indians flung across the world forever separated from their tribes and from their ancestral lands—that kind of thing had been happening to human beings since the beginning of time. African tribes had been sold into slavery all over the earth.

He needed to get his mind off this subject. All the magazine articles he had ever read on the subject of depression had urged this. So he rummaged under the bed for some magazines that he had found when he first moved into the room. The good thing was they were full of pictures. The not-so-good thing was the words were all Spanish. But he only needed something to look at until he fell asleep. The pictures were grainy and blurry black-and-white, and on some pages the smear of the ink on the newsprint gave them the appearance of cartoons or drawings. He could make out the date and the place; 1957, Culiacán, Sinaloa. Sterling could not make out who was who or why, but a beetle-back, gray '49 Plymouth was skidding around a corner on two wheels in pursuit of a black '51 Ford coupe sideswiping parked cars all along a narrow street. On other pages there were victims lying where they had fallen, but the blood looked more like motor oil or tar spreading under the corpses. Sterling fell asleep wondering if Mexico had produced any criminals as outstanding as John Dillinger or Pretty Boy Floyd. His knowledge of Mexican history was sketchy, but Sterling did not think they had had anyone like Geronimo since Montezuma. And then it got very confusing because it seemed as if the Mexicans were always having revolutions, and he knew that although the winning side usually executed and jailed the losers for being "criminals," both *Police Gazette* and *True Detective* magazines disqualified crimes committed during wars and revolutions.

HOLLYWOOD MOVIE CREW

IN HIS DREAM Sterling was running after the big white Chevy Blazer, yelling for them to stop. And that was when the Mexican gangster magazines toppled to the floor and Sterling woke up with light bugs all over his pillow. He shook the collection of moths and flying ants and tiny hard-shelled insects onto the floor and snapped off the reading lamp. His heart was still pounding. He felt around on the floor by the bed and found the 7-Up. He didn't care if it was lukewarm. He sat up, sipping 7-Up in the dark. He wished the Hollywood producer and his snotty cinematographer had gotten their heads blown off by the gate guards at the mine. Sterling's sheets were soaked with sweat. At least the nightmare had truth in it: the entire incident was the fault of the dumb shits from Hollywood. Stupid assholes! He had learned a number of new cuss words during the weeks he had been around them. What horrible white people! Some of the worst white people on earth was what Sterling had concluded.

It had been a setup, from the start. Even if he had managed to get old Aunt Marie to talk about the last time the tribe allowed a Hollywood movie company to film on tribal land, he would probably not have been saved. Because all the officers from all the villages had conferred with the tribal councilmen, and they had decided Sterling must do it. The whole Tribal Council had voted to appoint Sterling Laguna Pueblo film commissioner, and he could not say no. Sterling had tried in the most gracious way to decline the honor but no one on the Tribal Council seemed to want the position of tribal film commissioner. That should have been the tip-off, his warning that he had been set up.

Four hundred dollars a month. It hardly seemed worth it now because he was paid almost that much each week in Tucson. All he had to do was skim dead lizards off the surface of the swimming pool and hose dog shit off the kennel runways. For four hundred dollars a month, Sterling's job as a film commissioner had been to keep the Hollywood film crew away from sacred places and from stepping on sacred land. The first week had not been difficult because all the filming was done on sets built down by the river. But Sterling was only one man, far outnumbered by the Hollywood film crew. The second week Sterling had not been able to maintain control. Although Sterling had explained and explained which areas were "off-limits" and why, the movie crew people seemed only to understand violence and brute force. Reports came that prayer sticks left for the spirits at sacred shrines had disappeared. The third week an assistant director attempted to snap photographs inside the kiva, three actresses sunbathed at the sacred water hole, and the script supervisor squeezed a Volkswagen convertible through the northwest entrance to the main plaza—all on the same afternoon.

Sterling had seen the production manager throw the best boy into the front seat of the big Winnebago one morning when the crew was running late. His head had left a little halo of crackled-glass stars on the windshield. Everything was rented, so no one cared. As far as the movie people were concerned, the reservation was rented too. When the prayer sticks had been recovered, the nude sunbathers driven from the water hole, and the Volkswagen convertible removed from the plaza, Sterling told the producer Snell he was going to the tribal headquarters to resign. Snell had been on the phone arguing and pleading with his executive producers long distance, but when Sterling said this, Snell had put the receiver down dramatically and said, "Sterling! You can't do this to me!" "I have to live around here after you're gone" was all Sterling had said. But later, as he looked back, Sterling shook his head bitterly. Because even as he had been resigning, and trying to explain to the tribal governor the impossibility of controlling a Hollywood film crew, it was already too late. Out the windows of the governor's office they could see the exit ramp from the highway, and the dirt road to the river where the movie company had pitched their tents. A steady stream of New Mexico State Police cars, official government cars, were skidding and careening toward the film crew's headquarters with sirens and lights flashing.

But worse than the raid by state and federal drug-enforcement agencies, and the incident that had actually determined Sterling's fate, had been the attempt by the cinematographer to film the giant stone snake. The governor, the tribal officers, and the tribal judge had all criticized Sterling, although he was actually an elder to many of them. "Living as long as you did in California," one of the younger men asked, "how come you didn't catch on to all the drugs those movie people had?" That had been the moment when Sterling had come the closest to tears. Standing in front of the tribal governor and the Council and the tribal judge. "I don't know why you are blaming me," Sterling began. "You act like I should have known everything just because I lived off the reservation. But I was working for the railroad. I was living in towns like Winslow and Barstow, not Hollywood. How was I supposed to know why they all had runny noses?"

The older men who served on the Tribal Council admonished the young governor and his colleagues to go easy. Some of them had worked for the railroad and had been acquainted with Sterling then. The older men agreed no one, not even Sterling, could have been expected to know that conspirators in Hollywood had been sending vials of cocaine with the reels of "dailies."

Sterling knew the answer he had given the Tribal Council was feeble, but by that time it had been six-thirty at night, and Aunt Marie was probably worrying and angry because dinner was getting overcooked. Sterling felt defeated and weak. He said, "I didn't have any kind of experience with that sort of thing. I thought they were all just friendly with one another." One of the elder councilmen had then remarked that someone had better explain to him why Sterling was ever appointed film commissioner in the first place. A terrible silence fell over the Council Chamber. Then another old councilman saved them from that question by raising the fatal issue of the giant stone snake.

THE WATER BED

AFTER THE GIANT STONE SNAKE had been discovered, medicine people from many tribes had hurried to the site. There had been a great deal of controversy over the interpretation of the stone snake. The concern of the Council and the elected tribal officials had been focused on the theft of the stone idols eighty years before. What was to prevent such a loss of the giant stone snake now that the Hollywood people knew where to find it—now that the whites had photographed it? Sterling looked down at the feet he knew were his, but which did not feel connected to him at that moment. He didn't have an answer, and one after the other, all the old-timers recounted the story of the loss of the stone idols. The Tribal Council building, instead of emptying at dinnertime, got more crowded. The old women were beginning to show up, and one of them launched into the story of how, one night, many years ago, jealous neighbors had smashed open the beautiful lake that gave Laguna its name. The giant water snake that had always lived in the lake and that had loved and cared for the Laguna people as its children could not be found after the jealous ones had drained the lake. Mention of the lake, or stone idols or the painting of St. Joseph, always brought out a great deal of anger, and Sterling wanted to say they should not blame him or get upset with him over deeds others had done. But just then someone had started talking about the wrongful detention of the oil portrait of St. Joseph, and the angry feelings buzzed around Sterling like wasps.

Even then, Sterling had realized he might have escaped with only severe reprimands, years of community service and a heavy fine, if it had not been for Edith Kaye. She rose up from the one and a half chairs she occupied in the visitor section of the Council Chamber. Edith Kaye was a widow three times. The joke that was told in every village was how Edith Kaye had killed those husbands through overexertion as they attempted to satisfy Edith's sexual appetites. Edith Kaye had had her eye on Sterling when he first returned to Laguna to enjoy his retirement. She had had her own ideas about exactly how he should enjoy retirement.

But Sterling had made a serious error with Edith Kaye, and as Aunt Marie had warned him, again too late to do any good, Edith Kaye was one of those women you did not want to cross.

Sterling was still horrified to think what a narrow escape he had had from Edith Kaye's king-size water bed. She had gotten very ugly when Sterling tried to explain that he didn't know very much about water beds. Actually the matter was allowing her to get on top of him. But Edith Kaye had flown into a fury because he was hesitant about her riding him.

"The *water bed*," Edith Kaye had yelled at him, "the *water bed*, you stupid man! *This* water bed sinks down! It isn't like a hard mattress! It sinks down! I won't hurt you!" But the way she had been yelling and the hatred in her face had terrified Sterling. When he tried to crawl away from her and escape off the other side of the bed, he remembered reading an account of combat soldiers who described how endless ten or twelve feet were. He floundered and sank like a horse in quicksand. The water bed really did sink down, and Sterling could never quite reach bottom to brace a hand or leg to get out. In the end, all that had saved him was Edith Kaye's fury and her feverish maneuvers to reach him. Great waves began tossing Sterling until suddenly he found himself free, lying on the floor. He had carefully avoided all possible encounters with Edith Kaye since that night. In fact, one of his motives for taking the film commissioner position had been so he would have some excuse if she insisted he come over to the house for dinner again.

So Edith Kaye had ranted and raved, waving both hands, pointing out to the Council it was sacrilege to allow outsiders to make an image of the snake on film. Why, this sacrilege might even be worse than eighty years ago when the stone idols were stolen. Because once outsiders saw the great stone snake, they would want to steal it or destroy it. Sterling was consoled a little by the discomfort the others in the Council Chamber displayed as Edith Kaye raged on. He saw he was not the only one who feared saying no to her. Finally, after she had for the fourth time stated her belief that Sterling had conspired to steal the giant stone snake, Edith Kaye sat down panting.

OLD AUNT MARIE

STERLING HAD limped home in the dark. He had always developed a mysterious limp whenever he got too tired. Aunt Marie had gone to bed and turned off her light to express her displeasure with him. But the warming oven in the old wood stove was full of warm plates of food wrapped in clean cotton dish towels. He rummaged around in the drawer for a fork and spoon. Aunt Marie had called from her bed "Is that you?" and he had managed a miserable "Yes, Auntie." He had meant to sound weak and sad, although he realized she was very old now and would not last much longer. He was happy and relieved when she came slowly into the kitchen, carrying her glasses in one hand, blinking and rubbing her eyes with the other. She was in her long flannel nightgown and her long white hair was in a single loose braid down her back. As long as he lived, he would remember how much he had loved her at that moment and how much he was going to miss her when she was gone. He wanted to throw his arms around her and have her hug him close as she had when he had been a child and she had whispered "Ahh moot" over and over again softly. But he was fifty-nine years old and he could tell she was upset about something.

"Sterling!" Aunt Marie began. "Everyone is saying that you were using drugs with those Hollywood people!" Sterling had been buttering a piece of bread. He groaned. He had forgotten that the worst that would be said about him would not be said in the Tribal Council Chamber. The worst charges traveled in wildfire gossip propelled from village to village by imaginations so uncontrolled and so vivid that ordinary and innocent actions were transformed into high intrigue. Sterling himself had never cared much about television because he had grown up with village gossip for entertainment. Sterling had never seen anything on television to match Laguna gossip for scandal and graphic details. And as for speed, Sterling was one who could never understand the need for telephones in Laguna houses unless it was for long-distance calls.

"Auntie, I never *used* drugs. I never even saw any of the drugs. All I ever did was ride around and tell them where they could or could not make their film." Aunt Marie continued. She said the story was going around that he had been involved in the love triangle involving the young man who claimed he was an Indian. The story alleged Sterling had known the young man previously in California. "California! California! Why does everybody on this reservation get so worked up against California?"

If only Sterling had not mentioned the giant stone snake to Snell. Sterling hung his head. Aunt Marie poured two cups of tea and set one down in front of him. She stirred sugar in hers and said, "They say you were going to help the movie people steal the stone snake so you and the movie people could buy more drugs with the money." Sterling didn't speak. He just sat there shaking his head, tracing little patterns with his finger on the oilcloth table cover. Sterling had only mentioned the stone snake because it was relatively new to him too; it had been discovered only a few months before Sterling had retired and returned home. On the other hand, as Sterling had tried to argue earlier before the governor and Tribal Council, there had been a number of young Laguna people employed by the film company. One of them might even have told the cinematographer about the stone snake and where to find it. The answer, of course, had been that regardless of *how* they had learned of the sacred shrine to the snake, Sterling had been appointed tribal film commissioner to prevent just this sort of incident from occurring.

"Well, don't worry about it too much, dear," Aunt Marie had said as she put a stack of sugar cookies next to his teacup. She knew they were his favorites, and all the years he had been away she had sent him a two-pound coffee can full of the cinnamon-dusted cookies each month. Sterling could not bring himself to talk about the attack by Edith Kaye because Aunt Marie had warned him about accepting any sort of dinner or lunch invitations from her. Sterling knew Aunt Marie would hear all about it the next day anyway. He suddenly felt terribly weak and tired halfway through his fourth cookie.

When Sterling got to bed, he could not sleep. He could feel himself shaking. Aunt Marie was snoring in the next room. Although Sterling had been telling himself not to worry, a voice deeper inside told him there was bad trouble on the way. The voice told him mostly it was due to his long absence from the village—first, going away to boarding school so young, and then going to work for the railroad right after high school. Then, the voice continued, there was the fact that except for Aunt Marie, his close family and clanspeople had died out over the years. Who was going to plead his case for him? It was considered shabby to stand up and defend oneself. It amounted to bragging. It was far better to have friends and in-laws vouch for your good deeds and truthfulness. He lay there in the dark and regretted that he had not done more socializing in the six months he'd been back. He had taken things easy when he first retired because he had thought he'd have plenty of time to go around renewing friendships from the past. He had taken a couple of months working on the roof of Aunt Marie's little house because it was starting to leak pretty bad, especially in the corner where his bed was. He had been careful to stop hammering or brushing tar on holes whenever anyone passed by and greeted him. In fact, that had been the reason the repairs had taken two months to complete. When Sterling had finally got to sleep, the sky was beginning to turn light gray.

BANISHED

THE CONCLUSION of the Tribal Council had been reached behind closed doors while Sterling was at the clinic with Aunt Marie. The doctor had checked her out completely and announced she had the heart of a woman half her age. But her mind was made up. She had pointed to her eyes and said, "Well, a heart of a forty-year-old isn't much good when all the rest is ninety years old. I have seen too much lately. I have begun to dislike what I see, and what I hear." The doctor did not understand her reference to the Tribal Council proceedings against Sterling. The decision came out of the Council about four o'clock, and the governor sent word for Sterling to come. The messenger was an old man who did janitorial chores around the tribal office building. He announced that the decision had not been good. He said the Council had concluded that "conspirators" could not be permitted to live on the reservation because, in their opinion, all of the current ills facing the people of Laguna could be traced back to "conspirators," legions of conspirators who had passed through Laguna Pueblo since Coronado and his men first came through five hundred years ago. Sterling shook his head. This was terrible. They had probably confused "conspirator" with "conquistador."

Aunt Marie called out from her room. Sterling brought the messenger to her bedside. "Well, Auntie, I sure am sorry to have to be the one to tell you. But the Council decided they have been too easy on conspirators all along. They really didn't want it to be Sterling, but they decided they had to begin somewhere." Aunt Marie tossed herself on the pillow and moaned. The messenger looked hopefully at Sterling. "They say you've got your railroad pension. They figure you know all about living off the reservation." Aunt Marie turned her face to the wall. She said she had decided she might as well die. Sterling pleaded with her not to say that, but she kept her back to him too. He tried to reason with her, he needed her more than ever right now. "Yes," she said weakly, "I know, dear. But I am just too upset at everyone to stay around any longer. I am ready to go on to Cliff House where my sisters are. They're all waiting there for me, you know. Oh, we will do all kinds of things together again—tamales, the first thing, because tamales require many hands." Her voice had sounded so happy and strong that Sterling was reassured. He had patted her shoulder as he left for the Council Chamber, and she had turned and kissed the fingers of his hand as she had when he was a child. "Oh, Sterling," she said, "this is all wrong. You have always been the best one. Remember, no matter what happens, I always love you."

Sterling still could not believe it had all happened so fast. Only a month before he had been tribal film commissioner in charge of permissible locations for the movie people. Now the Council had voted to expel Sterling from the reservation forever. A few people had come up to him after the adjournment to ask how his auntie was feeling and to whisper that "forever" might not be for always—in five or ten years he might petition the Council to reconsider. But Sterling could feel his heart stabbed with a pain that ran straight from his throat. He had dreamed of spending the years with his poor little decrepit auntie, keeping her company until she returned to her beloved sisters and her own dear aunties at Cliff House. He decided he would try to stall as long as he could, just to be with Aunt Marie a little more. Sterling had no illusions about waiting five or ten years to attempt to return. The time he had spent away from the reservation had been a big factor against him in the first place.

Sterling would always believe that Aunt Marie had done it for him, and not for selfish reasons. He believed Aunt Marie had calculated her death to shame the Council into reversing its decision. But the shock of having killed an old woman had been so great the Tribal Council had felt compelled to point the blame elsewhere. Or as one councilman had put it, "There is more reason now than ever to get rid of this kind of man. He has no ties or responsibilities here any longer. His behavior upset our dear sister so much she is no longer with us."

WORKING FOR LECHA

THE DRIVING had worn Seese out. But it had been fun to drive around with old Sterling telling all about Geronimo and Dillinger. She had not thought about it much, but since she had found Lecha and had been "working for her," Seese had weaned herself off cocaine. She had not even been trying to cut back because she had never wanted to know how badly hooked she really was. Beaufrey had always wanted her to try heroin. She did not know what she might have done if David or Eric had offered it to her. But with Beaufrey the answer always was no. She had not thought about it before, but watching Lecha with her pills and her injections had had some effect upon her own drug use. She thought it must be animal instinct, as with horses shying from a carcass on the trail. Not anything conscious or reasoned. Of course she had a job now, and she didn't want Lecha to have any reasons for sending her away. At least not until Lecha had been able to help find Monte. Seese had to stay alert so that Lecha herself did not overdose.

And the house Lecha had brought them to was not exactly brimming over with hospitality. The afternoon Lecha and Seese had arrived by taxi had been memorable on a number of counts. Ferro had not believed Lecha when she said who she was. The cabdriver was already in a panic because two crazy women had lured him farther and farther away from pavement into the rocky and impenetrable foothills of the Tucson mountains where, as far as he could tell, only four-wheel-drive vehicles ever escaped with oil pans intact. Ferro had refused to open the main gate and had let the guard dogs out of the inner fence so they were flinging themselves at the chain-link below the intercom button, snarling and barking so loud no one could hear anything that was said. Then suddenly the six Dobermans had moved away from the fence and stopped barking. It had been then that Seese noticed they wore bulky collars that began to make crackling static sounds. Paulie's voice came over the intercom asking Lecha to step out of the taxi and stand in front of the dogs. Lecha had shouted to the cabdriver to tell them to call her sister, Zeta, but then Ferro interrupted and said he could hear. "It is not necessary to shout," he had added coldly. Lecha refused to get out of the taxi. She said she was a dying woman. Finally Zeta's voice came over the intercom. The hair on the back of Seese's neck had stood up at its sound. Their voices were identical. Zeta was calm in a way that Seese had never seen Lecha, not even after one of her injections. Zeta merely said they should have called first. She asked that the taxi driver and "the girl" please get out and stand briefly in front of the dogs. By this time the driver was very upset. Seese waved the fifty-dollar bill Lecha had just handed her in front of the dogs, who raised their hackles but never moved or made a sound. Seese heard a faint *click-click* from one of the dog collars and saw a clear plastic globe enclosing a smaller globe that followed their motions like an eye. Then Zeta's voice told them to proceed through the gates.

They gave the taxi driver another fifty on the driveway, and Paulie had waited until the cab was out of the first inner gate before he stepped out of the wrought-iron gate from the patio. He was holding a twelve-gauge riot gun casually in one hand. His pale blue eyes registered none of the ferocity that had been in his voice. He had an odd, almost military, stiffness to his walk. Paulie carried in the luggage while she and Lecha stood in the patio with Zeta and Ferro. Lecha had not mentioned that she and Zeta were identical twins. The resemblances were stunning. They must have weighed the same. The wrinkles around the eyes were identical. Both had teeth that were broad and white and too close, so that the incisors on the bottom were pushed forward. The one difference had been that Lecha dyed her hair black, while Zeta had left the wide streaks of silver untouched. Zeta's manner seemed relaxed and casual. She had glanced a time or two at Seese, but did not seem particularly disturbed or interested. It was Ferro who had pounced forward, demanding to know who Seese was. Lecha had put both arms on his shoulders as if to embrace him, but Ferro had pulled away. "Oh, is this how you are going to be?" Lecha said softly. Seese noticed immediately a trace of a sway in his walk that made the heaviness in his lips and waist appear distinctly feminine. But his jaws were clenched and his words came hissing fast. "I am a grown man. I'm thirty years old." "Oh, Ferro, I want it to be a reunion," Lecha said. But Ferro had turned away abruptly and gone to help Paulie carry in the last big trunk.

"Oh, thank you, darling," Lecha said as they passed by with the big trunk. "Be careful with it—it has so many of my dearest things!"

Ferro had stiffened; he looked over his shoulder at her, his face full of rage. But what Seese found more remarkable was the look that Paulie had given Ferro at that instant; she had seen the same expression when Beaufrey looked at David.

Lecha had insisted on going to bed immediately. But while Seese did the unpacking, Lecha lay back on the pillows with her eyes half open and talked about her sister and Ferro. Lecha was dozing in and out so there wasn't a lot of clarity in what she said. She talked about her career. At first Seese had taken that to mean the clairvoyance, but later Lecha had talked about her career as a pilot. "Oh, I was going to run my own little flying service between all the little settlements and villages. To help with the sick and injured. I planned to take Ferro along with me. He would sleep on his Indian cradleboard—through takeoff and landing! Of course I would be one of the best—I would land an airplane like an angel! But all that had only been daydreams," Lecha told Seese. "I'd get these great ideas all by myself, but I would never get around to doing any of them. Right afterwards someone else would do the same exact thing as I'd told everyone about. Zeta was right. That's all I was—talk, hot air. Zeta said, 'Bullshit walks,' and that was when I decided to go. To get out of the Southwest, to explore new territory." Lecha's voice trailed off and she started snoring. For whatever reasons, Ferro had not spent much time with his mother while he was growing up. Seese felt sad for Lecha and for her son; she went to the bedroom that was to be hers and she had smoked herself into oblivion, with marijuana.

After Seese had been at the ranch for a while, she was less afraid of Ferro and Paulie. They both behaved as if she were invisible, and she was a little horrified when she realized the invisibility was almost identical to the nonbeing that Beaufrey and Serlo had assigned to her while she had been with David.

Seese tried thinking of it as it was or as Lecha *said* it was: pain from the cancer required these injections. Seese knew too much about the street life to be fooled by the bottles of Percodan with a legitimate doctor's name on them. Seese never asked any questions about the cancer because she thought sooner or later Lecha would mention a specific location or a past surgery. But all Lecha could talk about now was the work ahead of them and how when the work was properly completed Seese would have the answers she wanted.

Seese closed the door to her bedroom and closed the door to the bathroom she shared with Lecha. It had been a long time since she had performed everyday, ordinary routines.

BOOK FOUR

SOUTH

ABORTION

BEAUFREY TALKED LOUDLY about the best doctor he knew. Neat, quick job and totally painless because if you specify, the doc always comes through—the very best of the painless—morphine. "You'd lap it up! You'd like it just fine!" Beaufrey said suddenly, his hot breath in her face. The stink of Beaufrey's breath and his words had felt like a fist in her stomach, and Seese knew she would puke. She felt cold sweat break out across the bridge of her nose and under her arms.

Beaufrey wants Seese to have another abortion. "Morphine will be sooooo goooood to you!"

"I throw up," Seese told him.

"Morning sickness," Beaufrey had said, building a case against the pregnancy.

"No. I mean *morphine* makes me puke." Seese had held her ground. Even before her belly had bulged out, Seese had been on different footing with Beaufrey. David wanted a child. Seese saw Beaufrey's pale blue eyes dilate black with anger. Beaufrey turned away from Seese and shook the ice in his scotch. "All the dope and booze will kill it anyway." Beaufrey never said "baby" or "child." Beaufrey was uncomfortable and kept looking at David, as if to calculate how important a child was for David.

After Seese had refused all mention of abortion, Beaufrey had become obsessed with the child. Because of course it was *David's* child. After Seese had seen a doctor, Beaufrey had suddenly decided to acknowledge her existence. He began to ask her questions about the pregnancy. Beaufrey talked about fetuses and fetal development. Researchers had done a great many more experiments on fetuses alive in the womb and had filmed the experiments. Beaufrey was in partnership with a rare-book seller in Buenos Aires with a complete line of dissection films and videotapes for sale.

Beaufrey said where abortion had been legalized, the films of the fetal dissections and experiments seemed to lose their peculiar fascination for "collectors." The biggest customers for footage of fetuses was the antiabortionist lobby, which paid top dollar for the footage of the tortured tiny babies. Beaufrey watched the creatures grimace and twist away from the long needle probes and curette's sharp spoon. Million-dollar footage. He liked to watch it again and again to see the faces of the lobbyists' assistants. Lush, doe-eyed things that hadn't yet had their damp, pink rims and swollen, purple petals violated by stainless-steel rods and warty pricks. Beaufrey only laughed because he could imagine himself as a fetus, and he knew what they should have done with him swimming hopelessly in the silence of the deep, warm ocean. His mother had told him she tried to abort herself. She had never let it happen again after she had him.

Beaufrey had started by hating his mother; hating the rest of them was easy. Although Beaufrey ignored women, he enjoyed conversation that upset or degraded them. He said he liked to imagine the fetus struggling hopelessly in slow motion as suddenly all the pink horizons folded in on him. Films of the late abortions were far more popular than those of early embryo stages. The forceps appeared as a giant dragon head opening and closing in search of a morsel. By the tiny light of the microcamera, the uterine interior resembled a vast ballroom that had been draped all around in glossy-red silks and velvets of burgundy and lilac. The best operators got it all in one piece by finding the skull and crushing it. Beaufrey had viewed hundreds of hours of film searching for atypical or pathological abortions because the collectors who bought films of abortions and surgeries preferred blood and mess. There was a steady, lucrative demand for films of sex-change operations, though most interest had been in males becoming females. For videotapes of sodomy rapes and strangulations, teenage "actors" from a local male-escort service had "acted" the victims' roles.

Beaufrey wondered if while they were beating their meat, the "connoisseurs" and the "collectors" ever noticed something lacking, some animal chemistry missing. Could they sense what had only been theatrical devices—from the fake blood to slices of plastic skin and flesh? The first few times they might write off this diminishment of pleasure to stress or getting over a cold. But later would they again begin to feel as if something had been short-circuited? Beaufrey liked to think so. He liked to think how the "collector" would begin to fret over his limp cock, never suspecting the movie scenes had not been the real thing. Beaufrey spent hours daydreaming about the torture of leaving enough of the man or the woman that they still had the cravings and the urges; but fix them so they can never get off again no matter what they do. Beaufrey had known a number of punks who got their balls chopped. The doctors make implants that released male hormone—more testosterone than any of them had —ever got before from their own scrawny testicles.

Beaufrey disliked films of women's sex changes; there was no pleasure in seeing how fast doctors gave a woman a cock and balls. Women needed brain transplants before they'd ever be "men," but the ignorant public saw a movie like that and believed the woman suddenly "became" a man.

Beaufrey preferred to specialize in the surgical fantasy movies, but those customers generally had other kinks, and Beaufrey was there " to please," he used to tell them, with a smile.

The real weirdos became even more obsessed with the "real thing"—they claimed they could detect fakes—an utter lie since Beaufrey had yet to sell an actual "snuff" film. Beaufrey had got a good laugh out of the "real thing" freaks who had paid him hundreds and even thousands of dollars. The queers couldn't get enough of those flicks of the steel scalpel skating down the slope of the penis tip, a scarlet trail spreading behind it. Asian faces under white surgical masks and caps glisten with sweat as the penis is peeled like a banana and is turned inside out like a surgical glove, so that the penis skin becomes the lining of the artificial vagina. A companion sequence in which a woman got implants of balls and a dildo sewn inside to folds of specifically prepared skin had been a distribution failure, which had convinced Beaufrey he knew far more about the market than his Argentine business partners. The demand for films of ritual circumcisions of six-year-old virgins had doubled itself every year. There were waiting lists of creeps who got weak at the mention of hairless twats and tight little buds. Massaged and teased into its first and also its last erection, the little girl's clitoris in close-up looked like a miniature penis. It was a great relief to see the dark, thick fingers of the operator pressing the wet, quivering organ into full extension for the blade of the razor. The offending organ was removed and the wound was washed, then packed in gauze and bandages that were changed repeatedly as they became soaked with blood.

SUICIDE

BEAUFREY HAD AWAKENED HER. Seese had slept all night outside on a chaise lounge. A wind had come up. The sky was overcast with storm clouds. The skin on her upper thighs had goose bumps. She sat up on the chaise lounge next to the pool and rubbed her legs and arms, without looking up. Seese asked where everyone was. Beaufrey had given a strange little laugh. The hairs on her thighs and the top of her head prickled; she felt icy drops of sweat down her back. Beaufrey had not bothered to warn her sheriff's deputies and the coroner were completing their reports inside. Seese started to look for another towel or robe to cover the bikini. But Beaufrey had already pushed her firmly through the sliding glass door into the living room. The deputies stared at her and for an instant Seese thought this had to be one of those dreams where everyone else is wearing clothing, but you are naked. But in her dreams she was the only one who had noticed her nudity. This was crazy: she was wearing a bathing suit by a pool but still they were staring at her. The faces of the deputies made it clear the blame had been pinned on Seese. She tried to remember everything they'd done earlier that day. All the places she and Eric had piloted the "Big Blue Bedroom" car. Seese tried to remember if there had been any accidents. "What?" She repeated the word, looking from face to face until finally she came to David, who refused to look at her or answer; he pretended to read the statement the deputies had asked him to sign.

She did not feel drunk or high, but she was shivering and sweating. She pushed past Beaufrey and went into the hall bathroom. Seese wrapped herself in a terry cloth robe she pulled out of the laundry closet. The robe smelled sour. Seese sat on the edge of the big sunken tub and stared out the window at the swimming pool. No one stopped her when she went outside again and dived in the pool.

She wasn't feeling anything. She wasn't feeling that Eric was dead. She was feeling that he had gone back to Lubbock to visit his mother. She was feeling that this was what was true. It had to feel true or it wasn't; even if another part of her consciousness told her she had heard the doorbell and then voices. Eric was dead. She knew it was a fact. But what was a fact? Eric was gone, but did that mean he was dead? Eric had gone to Texas for two weeks when his grandmother died. The other voice persisted. "Dead" meant he wasn't coming back in two weeks. Seese lay on her back and floated in the pool with her eyes closed until the police and the others had gone. She still didn't feel anything. The cocaine had dried out her mouth. Her tongue felt thick enough to choke her. She tried to catch her upper lip between her teeth, but teeth and lips seemed a long, cool distance from her throat. The first place David had ever taken her was the gallery where his photographs had just been hung. She had met Eric there. He knew everything and she knew nothing. But Eric had liked her, and in the weeks when she had gradually figured out that Eric and David had been lovers, she felt calm because she liked Eric so much. David never showed any particular affection for her or for Eric. With both of them he acted the same. He had always been offhand and aloof with her. Now she saw him do the same to Eric.

Then Eric blew his head off. Just like that. Still that might have been bearable except for what David had done. There were many things he'd done, to all of them. Seese realized that she and Eric were what David "had done" to Beaufrey. Aha! Of course!

The next day Seese could still feel the buzz from all the champagne she had drunk. David was not in the apartment. Seese went to find David at the darkroom. Seese had knocked, but the only sounds were clattering pipes in the wall—water running to the darkroom sink—print washing. David was not there, but he had not gone far because the door was not locked. She wandered through the snarl of extension cords, reflectors, scrims, and rolls of background paper. She felt like a cartoon figure with a human body, but with a camera where her head should be. For a face she had a wide, glassy lens that brought all she saw into focus so cold and clear she could not stop the shiver. None of it could be real. This had to be a drug hallucination or a long dream. The walls were all painted flat soot-black, which gave them a strange quality of undulating velvet in shades of midnight blue and black. Eric's last pull at the trigger must have felt like this: Seese hesitated then dove into the darkness, past the long, black curtain dense with odors of acid and chemicals. The darkroom was warm. The murky orange-red safelights were soothing. Seese felt hidden and safe in the darkroom. Eric used to tease David. Eric said the darkroom was clearly a womb and the best photographers never grew beyond the earliest stages of personality development.

Seese was so high her head swayed like an under-ocean flower. She watched the rushing water and let her eyes follow the colored spirals of the prints swirling in the stainless steel wash tank. The color prints moved like fish of the deep; all the colors glowed phosphorescent in the orange safelight. Seese held the edge of the sink with both hands and let her head hang back, rolling it slowly shoulder to shoulder with her eyes closed. Where was David? Eric was dead, but David had been developing film and color prints all night. Probably he had gone out for coffee. David worked in the darkroom when he was too upset to sleep.

Seese cupped a hand under the cold-water spout next to the stainless steel tank. She swallowed the water and felt the spinning and swaying subside. She stared down at the eight-by-ten color prints in the rinse tank. Among the spatters of bright reds and deeper purples, reddish browns and blacks, over a pure white, Seese caught a glimpse of the whole image. David had been playing with double exposures again. In the center of the field of peonies and poppies—cherry, ruby, deep purple, black—there was a human figure. Seese could make out feet and legs. She thought it was a great idea—the nude nearly buried in blossoms of bright reds and purples. The nude human body innocent and lovely as a field of flowers. Seese reached in and caught a print at one corner the way David had taught her.

She didn't know if it was the shock or if somehow the champagne and dope had lasted that long but she had been able to look at the color photographs of Eric's suicide without flinching. She could see how his body had fallen across the double bed with his long legs angled at the pillows. Death had not been any more peaceful for Eric than his life had. The extreme angles of Eric's limbs outlined the geometry of his despair. The clenched muscles guarded divisions and secrets locked within him until one day the gridwork of lies had exploded bright, wet red all over. Only a few weeks earlier Eric had helped David carry the roll of glossy-white backdrop paper into the studio. David had wanted the backdrop for an "all-white" series in the bedroom. "But white shows *everything*, darling," Eric had teased. David had stared back silently. "Shows all the dirt, *shows all the nasty!*" Eric had laughed until there were tears in his eyes. David had not smiled. Later Seese had realized the warning had been out in front for her to see, only she had not recognized Eric's despair.

David had probably not called the authorities for three or four hours to be sure both the color and black-and-white film had turned out. David had photographed Eric's corpse *Police Gazette* style. The black-and-white prints David had made were all high contrast: the blood thick, black tar pooled and spattered across the bright white of the chenille bedspread. Was that why she didn't feel anything, not after she'd realized David had photographed Eric's body? David had focused with clinical detachment, close up on the .44 revolver flung down to the foot of the bed, and on the position of the victim's hands on the revolver. Or did she feel no horror because she had already been filled with it, and no photographs of brains, bone, and blood would ever add up to Eric? Eric who loved her and whom she loved was not the corpse in the photographs. Eric would have been the first one to have pointed that out to both her and David. How many times did he have to tell them? The photograph was just a photograph. The photograph was only itself. No photograph could ever be him, be Eric. That was when Eric was drunk that he lectured her and David. David was a year or two older than Eric, but David had never got over Eric's graduate degree from Columbia. The worst fights Seese had seen between them had started because David thought Eric looked down on him. David had studied art and photography in a community college in Indiana, but Eric had an MFA in art history from Columbia. Eric always said art history was what you did when you weren't good enough to paint.

David had always denied that Eric had made a last-minute call to him. But how else to account for David's arriving at Eric's apartment so soon after the suicide?

White on white: the pure white background of glossy paper; white cat in a snowstorm, white Texas fag boy naked on white chenille. "Feverish with love and need" was a part of Eric's letter Seese would never forget. The cops and the coroner had even joked about the length of Eric's letter. The "three-page suicide note" had been Beaufrey's big laugh for weeks afterward.

Beaufrey was drunk, snorting gram after gram, and rambling on, so witty, so rich, but noticeably oder than his glamour photos due to all the scotch and cocaine and all the young boys in Rio de Janeiro. Beaufrey complained when Serlo forgot and bought harsh white light bulbs instead of the soft rose bulbs. Days before the show was to open, David was still clutching the proof sheets of Eric's suicide. David could hardly bear to look at the prints for his show, so G. and his gallery assistants worked closely with the color lab technicians who printed all David's work. Beaufrey had stayed drunk since Eric's suicide. He was obsessed with Eric's secret life with David and Seese. Beaufrey accused David of being there. Of watching Eric do it.

David had left the room after Beaufrey said that. Seese followed

David outside to the pool. There was a hot, wet wind off the bay, and the city lights were blurry in the mist. David pressed his fist against his chest. David had lied at first about Eric. David told Seese they had been friends since grade school. A lie. Later Eric had told Seese when and how they had become friends. After Eric was dead, Seese had found out he had lied to her too. He and David had not stopped being lovers when Seese first moved in.

Eric had lied. Under the corpse, speckled with bloodstains, the coroner's assistant had found the envelope. "All those afternoons you didn't call, I cried," the letter to David began.

ART

AFTER DISCOVERING Eric's body, David didn't just snap a few pictures. He had moved reflectors around and got the light so Eric's blood appeared as bright and glossy as enamel paint.

Later the critics dwelled on the richness and intensity of the color. One critic wrote of the "pictorial irony of a field of red shapes which might be peonies—cherry, ruby, deep purple, black—and the nude human figure nearly buried in these 'blossoms' of bright red."

The core photograph was a close-up of the face or what remained of it. By and large, the critical as well as the public reaction was one of outrage. "Photographs that belong in the Coroner's Office and the police file." "Punk comes to photography."

A steady parade of buyers had filled the gallery a week before the opening. Everyone wanted to see. Private collectors expressed concern over the lawsuit. If the negatives were later awarded to the family or destroyed, the prints would increase in value. G. was blunt. David's success was assured. Influential international critics agreed; at last David "had found a subject to fit his style of clinical detachment and relentless exposure of what lies hidden in flesh."

A critic at the opening noted the crowd stood a peculiar distance from the photographs "as if they had arrived within a few minutes of the suicide." G. knew how to sell it. He had issued a press release when Eric's family went to court for the injunction. The lawsuit had erased any doubt there had been theatrics with greasepaint or beef blood. Eric had been David's model for three years. The modeling agreement was not written, the attorney for the gallery explained delicately; nonetheless, the terms of the agreement had been well-known to friends and "intimates" of Eric's. Of course, any agreement or contract had died with Eric, but arguably, the family was obliged to honor the contract.

The tabloids on the East Coast had caught wind of it and had called it "The Last Picture Session" and "The Modeling Job From the Grave."

When the district court refused to delay the opening of David's show, Eric's family had dropped the lawsuit. Beaufrey had taken credit for the press coverage that had softened up those hick Texans.

Seese did not remember much about the weeks before or after David's show. She did not care if she was pregnant, she just wanted to die. She used cocaine and champagne every day to float herself above the chrome and glass rooms where conversation was perfectly charming but Beaufrey and Serlo looked past her as if she had never existed.

Beaufrey blamed Seese for Eric's death. He blamed her pregnancy. Their situation would have worked if *she* had not come along. Men could manage arrangements and accommodations. Seese had not been surprised by Beaufrey's accusation.

Seese should have known right then that Beaufrey was out to get her and the baby. But he had to play by special rules. David gave him no choice. Seese always understood both David and Beaufrey used others—such as Eric or her—to taunt and to tantalize. David had wanted to break Eric's heart. But she knew David had fallen in love with her after all.

Seese had thought about it again and again; she had gone over each hour, each minute, before they took Monte. Why had she stayed in the same apartment after David left? Beaufrey had no ex-employees. You were in or you were out. You were alive or you were dead. But Seese had stayed in the penthouse after David left. She had not even bothered to change the locks.

KIDNAPPED

SEESE WOULD NEVER FORGET the instant she had seen the playpen was empty. Her confusion had caused her to stumble. Stupidly she had crawled on her hands and knees, from room to room searching for him, crying out his name. He was gone. Monte was gone. Her heart had pounded loudly and she felt icy sweat all over her body. She had argued with herself: David would not take a baby still in diapers, a child Beaufrey could not tolerate.

The first few hours after she discovered her baby was missing, Seese had been so high and so scared the police detectives would find the kilo of coke that she had not told them about the other motives. Beaufrey had double-crossed Argentines as well as Colombians. The Argentines might have taken the child in retaliation.

The police had lost interest once they determined the baby's disappearance was merely a domestic incident. Child-snatching by a bitter father. Police saw it all the time.

Seese could not tell the detectives where David was. Photographic assignments; the only one she can remember is the rum ad he went to Puerto Rico to shoot. Beaufrey and Serlo had arranged to meet him later in Cartagena. But that had been weeks ago.

As long as Seese remains at the apartment, Beaufrey's lawyer "looks in" each week. Beaufrey's lawyer locates a medical doctor who is not averse to prescribing barbiturates for emotional collapse. The lawyer brings hashish with him, and two rubbers so he won't catch anything. He is anxious to comfort her. He promises they will hear very soon from David. The child is all right. Seese raises her voice until the dry membranes in the throat choke her. She feels something terrible has happened to her baby. Not just David stealing the child. But that her baby is in terrible danger. The lawyer spouts words; he assures her all mothers of lost children have the same feelings.

The lawyer was pissing in the toilet and casually asked if she had told the cops anything about the "import-export business." He got no reply. Seese was lying in the center of the bright white sheet of the king-size bed. All feelings, all sensations, had gone from her skin and the surface layers of her body. Her eyelids were open and motionless. She was floating free of gravity. The child was gone as if he had never been born. If you simply looked at the everyday surroundings—palm trees outlining the beach at Mission Bay—nothing had changed.

Seese had been numb since Monte disappeared. Seese is still numb ten nights later as the lawyer punches his cock into her. She would have killed herself the first night, but she does not want to die until she knows for certain Monte is dead. The lawyer pumps above her as if he is doing push-ups, a brief down-curve and thrust before he rises back up, and all Seese can imagine is being fucked by a strange machine. Seese remembered it had all happened as if on cue: David's phone call before the lawyer had rolled off her. David shouting. He demands to see the baby. Seese shouts back; she is in tears. If David doesn't have Monte, then he is lost. Her baby is lost.

The lawyer is already straightening his tie. He can dress rather quickly into a three-piece suit. The lawyer could tell something was up with the child because Seese was screaming, "Then where is he? Who has him?" over and over into the receiver. Seese accused David of lying, but David's voice was strangely quiet and a little halting. He almost whispered to her, "I swear I don't have him. Jesus, Seese! Don't do this!" Seese screamed back, "You took him! I know it was you, David! You took him! Where is he? Where is my baby?"

The lawyer sat on the edge of the bed, careful not to wrinkle his trousers or shirt when Seese reached out for him. He lit one cigarette after another while she cried. Finally Seese had screamed at the lawyer, "What the fuck is this? Whose side are you on? You're supposed to help me!"

Later Seese told the detectives David had called asking for Monte.

Seese could feel the detectives' contempt for her; she had got what she deserved. They weren't interested. The file on Monte was turned over to the Missing Persons Bureau. Seese knew once a file was sent there, hope was all but gone.

Afterward, Seese had drifted as if she were a sea-green ribbon of kelp caught in a current with a voice that accused her over and over. A less distinct voice said she had done the best she knew how. Her baby had not drowned in his bathwater. He had not been born addicted. But she could find no consolation for this loss.

When she tried to cry, she felt no relief, only greater pain from her anguish. She recited to herself endlessly all the ways she might easily

have protected him, how she might have saved Monte *if* she had not
been high that day; *if* she had not worked with criminals such as Beaufrey. Her breasts had been swollen and hot. The slightest contact with
the silk kimono sent stinging to her nipples. Her milk began to soak the
rose silk in wide moons. She had been too high on pot and coke to know
if the wetness came from the tears off her chin and cheeks or the flow
of milk leaking from her breasts.

Gradually Seese realizes she had been fooling herself for a long time.
David had not been able to love the baby any better than he had loved
her. It was Beaufrey, not David, who was obsessed with the baby. Beaufrey had feared David might love the child, that the child might somehow
interfere. Week after week Seese had waited for a phone call or letter.

After the bullet had shattered the bedroom window, Seese realized
David would never telephone about Monte. David would never let her
see her baby again. Seese had been seized with a compulsion to jump,
to smash through the glass and fall thirty stories into the Pacific. Shaking
and sweating, Seese filled the sunken marble tub off the master bedroom.
She rolled fat marijuana cigarettes and set them on the edge of the
bathtub. She slid under the hot water and imagined glittering-blue salt
water filling her lungs, sucking away her breath. But a voice inside her
head argued she wouldn't die yet. Because her baby might still be alive.
Her baby might need her.

Seese awakened when the bathwater was cold. Outside, a yellowish
wedge of moon hung low over the ocean horizon. She wandered from
room to room dripping water, leaving faint damp footprints on the pale-
gray carpet. She kept the door to the baby's room closed. The kidnappers
had stolen the white leather album filled with Monte's baby pictures.
They had also removed a framed photograph of Monte from the wall.
All Seese had left were snapshots she'd kept in her purse. David had
taken all the negatives with him. The police seemed to want proof that
she had really had a child in the first place. But the neighbors did not
recognize her or remember Monte in the stroller.

Seese had suddenly been aware that her own words sounded thin,
and the details of her story did not seem convincing even to her anymore.
She could imagine how she must sound to the police detectives. Seese
threw herself over the lowered side rail of the empty crib and buried
her face into Monte's blanket, to breathe the sweetness of her baby.

The day he moved out, David had argued that Monte would be
better off living with him. Seese never forgot Beaufrey standing in the
background where only Seese could see his smirk. "Smirking, sucking

mouth!" Seese had screamed at Beaufrey. Afterward David never came alone to see Monte. Usually Beaufrey came, but sometimes David brought Serlo. "Are you afraid?" Seese taunted. Beaufrey had answered for David. Their lawyers had suggested a witness be present at all times. Seese felt Beaufrey's presence far more strongly than David's. "Your fairy lawyers?" Seese had burst out laughing, spewing a mouthful of vodka on both of them. Beaufrey had tensed so rigidly Seese thought he might slap her face, but David only turned for the door. He had not even asked to see Monte. At that instant, despite the vodka and cocaine, Seese realized it was Beaufrey who was interested in her baby. "You can buy anything else, can't you? But you can't have babies. You can't do that, can you?"

Beaufrey had stopped in the doorway and stared at her as if he dared her to continue. Beaufrey had panicked after Monte was born. Later Seese remembered his clenched fists and the unblinking eyes that seemed to pierce through her and the child. Beaufrey had misread David's interest in the baby. David was only interested in the child so long as he saw his own image reflected. Seese had been too stunned with cocaine and vodka to think clearly about Beaufrey. She had assumed Beaufrey would take David to the other side of the world to keep David away from Monte, but she had been wrong.

BOOK FIVE

THE BORDER

CHILDHOOD IN MEXICO

YOEME HAD APPEARED suddenly. Lecha and Zeta had been playing with the other children on the long wooden porch. From a distance the twins had both spotted the rapidly moving figure no taller than they were, a black shawl pulled tightly around her face so only her blazing dark eyes were visible. They all felt the eyes examining them.

Instinctively the children had huddled over the sunflowers they had picked and were arranging in old tin cans. They had waited for the strange figure to pass. Out of the corner of her eye, Zeta had seen it was a very old woman, dressed in a long black dress and black shawl. She had whispered to Lecha the old woman was an Indian. At that instant the tiny figure in black had turned into their gateway and stopped. In a clear voice as strong as Auntie Popa's, the old woman had said, "*You* are Indians!" Zeta had never forgotten the chill down her backbone. Lecha had cowered closer to her. Their cousins had jumped up screaming and fled inside.

But the girls did not run because the old woman was laughing, and she was not very big, and they both were. "Don't beat me up!" She laughed some more. "Dumb girls! I'm your grandmother!" Zeta and her sister had never heard anyone talk the way Yoeme did. But they had heard their uncles and aunties discuss a certain someone. Zeta had overheard them wishing the old woman had died. The discussion had been how many years had passed since the she-coyote had run off leaving the smallest ones, Ringo and Federico, sobbing and running down the road after her.

Yoeme's name often came up with the subject of cottonwood trees. Somehow the morning she had abandoned her children, the long driveway from the big house to the mine shafts had been blocked by the huge cottonwood trees felled across the road.

Auntie Popa had ordered the others to lock all the doors and windows, despite the summer heat. Yoeme sat on the porch swing and talked to Zeta and Lecha. What she did not understand was how her own children, conceived and borne in pain, could behave so shamelessly to their flesh and blood mother. Yoeme had said "flesh and blood" so everyone inside would hear it. Popa screamed, but the sound was muffled through the window glass: "Run! Run for your lives!" The girls laughed with the old woman. They would not get rid of her, so the girls should not worry. Yoeme could not be stopped. See? Already, she had the two of them on her side. If she wanted water, it was right there. She reached for a can full of sunflowers and drank the water. Both girls had squealed, and the windows of the house were crowded with suspicious, sweating faces. Yoeme was back and there was nothing any of them could do to get rid of her. Yoeme had slept on the porch glider until the winter rains came, and then she had moved into the old cook-shed behind the big house.

Late at night Zeta had awakened to loud voices in the rooms below them. Popa and Cucha wanted the dirty Indian out of there. Yoeme liked to lie to them all the time, but very quickly the twins had realized that what was important came true. The morons would not be able to drive her away from the big house, Yoeme told the girls, don't worry.

Yoeme teased the girls, telling them she had advised their mother to get rid of one or the other of them right away. Twins were considered by some to be bad luck. If she had been around then, Yoeme said she would have taken care of the problem. She had watched both girls' faces for reactions. Zeta had asked, "Me or her?" and Lecha had said, "You kill me when I'm a baby and they'll hang you!" which had caused Yoeme to clap her hands together and laugh until their mother had come out to see what was the matter. Amalia had already been ailing awhile when Yoeme had reappeared. Like the others, Amalia seemed powerless against Yoeme. "I was just telling them how I urged you to get rid of one of them." Their mother had looked away quickly. "You'll scare them talking like that," she said, but Yoeme had paid no attention. She had even coached the girls to ask Amalia who had given birth to her. Their mother had given one of her deep, hopeless sighs. "Yes, she is my mother, although I do not remember her well." Amalia had clasped both hands to her stomach because the pains had come again. The twins had jumped back in awe of the pain. Yoeme had told them the pain was actually a jaguar that devoured a live human from the inside out. Pain left behind only the skin and bones and hair.

Amalia had leaned back in the wicker rocking chair on the big porch and managed to tell them more. There had been a terrible fight. A fight involving big cottonwood trees. "She left you and all her other children and her husband because of trees?" Zeta had wondered if her mother's pain was also confusing the facts. Amalia had not been able to do any more than shake her head at her twin daughters. And then Lecha had said, "No, it was because she is an Indian. Grandpa Guzman's family didn't like Indians."

"Who told you that?" their mother had asked them. "Yoeme, I suppose."

"No," Lecha had said, "I just know. Nobody likes Indians."

Later, when the twins were less frightened of the old woman, Zeta had asked, "Why did you leave your children?" and Yoeme had clapped her hands together and cheered the question so loudly even Lecha had blushed. They knew their mother's accusation that Yoeme was a bad influence on them was true. "Our mother told us it was trees, cotton-wood trees," Lecha said. They had been sitting on the ground in the garden next to the house pulling weeds. Yoeme stopped the weeding and tilted her head back slightly and squinted her eyes. "Yes," she said, "trees. The fucker Guzman, your grandfather, sure loved trees. They were cottonwoods got as saplings from the banks of the Rio Yaqui. Slaves carried them hundreds of miles. The heat was terrible. All water went to the mules or to the saplings. The slaves were only allowed to press their lips to the wet rags around the tree roots. After they were planted at the mines and even here by this house, there were slaves who did nothing but carry water to those trees. 'What beauties!' Guzman used to say. By then they had no more 'slaves.' They simply had Indians who worked like slaves but got even less than slaves had in the old days. The trees were huge by the time your mother was born."

"But why did you fight over trees?"

"Hold your horses, hold your horses," Yoeme had said. "They had been killing Indians right and left. It was war! It was white men coming to find more silver, to steal more Indian land. It was white men coming with their pieces of paper! To make their big ranches. Guzman and my people had made an agreement. Why do you think I was married to him? For fun? For love? Hah! To watch, to make sure he kept the agreement."

But Guzman had been only a gutless, walking corpse, not a real

man. He had been unwilling to stand up to the other white men streaming
into the country. "He was always saying he only wanted to 'get along.' "
Yoeme slid into one of her long cackling laughs. "Killing my people,
my relatives who were only traveling down here to visit me! It was time
that I left. Sooner or later those long turds would have ridden up with
their rifles, and Guzman would have played with his wee-wee while they
dragged me away."

"But your children," Zeta said.

"Oh, I could already see. Look at your mother right now. Weak
thing. It was not a good match—Guzman and me. You understand how
it is with horses and dogs—sometimes children take after the father. I
saw that." And so Yoeme told the twins. It had been a simple decision.
She could not remain with children from such a man. Guzman's people
had always hated her anyway. Because she was an Indian. "We know,"
Lecha said. "We know that. But what about the trees?"

Oh, yes, those trees! How terrible what they did with the trees.
Because the cottonwood suckles like a baby. Suckles on the mother water
running under the ground. A cottonwood will talk to the mother water
and tell her what human beings are doing. But then these white men
came and they began digging up the cottonwoods and moving them here
and there for a terrible purpose.

COTTONWOOD TREES

"I STILL SEE THIS," Yoeme said. "Very clearly, because I was
your age then. Off in the distance, as we were approaching the
river. The cottonwood trees were very lovely. In the breeze their leaves
glittered like silver. But then we got closer, and someone shouted and
pointed. I looked and looked. I saw things—dark objects. Large and
small, swaying from the low, heavy branches. And do you know what
they were—those objects hanging in the beautiful green leaves and
branches along the river?"

The two little girls had shaken their heads together, and when they
looked at each other, they realized they knew what Yoeme was going
to say.

Bullets, she explained, cost too much. "I heard people say they were our clanspeople. But I could not recognize any faces. They had all dried up like jerky." Lecha had closed her eyes tight and shaken her head. Zeta had nodded solemnly.

"So you see, when I decided to leave that fucker Guzman and his weak children, your mother was the weakest, I had one last thing I had to do." Here Yoeme clapped her hands and let out a little shout. "It was one of the best things I have ever done! Sooner or later those long turds would have ridden up with their rifles to hang me from the big cottonwood tree."

Lecha and Zeta had looked in the direction the old woman pointed in the yard near the house. Only a giant white stump remained. "What happened to the big tree?" Zeta had wanted to know.

"Well, you don't think I was going to let that tree stand next to this house as long as I was alive, do you?"

Yoeme had waited until Guzman had gone off to buy mules in Morelos, and then she had ordered the gardeners to get to work with axes. At the mine headquarters they had only cut down six of the big trees before the foreman had called a halt. Fortunately, while the foreman was rushing to the big house to question the orders, the gardeners had been smart enough to girdle the remaining trees. Yoeme had paid them to run off with her, since in the mountains their villages and her village were nearby. She had cleaned out Guzman's fat floor safe under the bed where she had conceived and delivered seven disappointing children. It was a fair exchange, she said, winking at the little girls, who could not imagine how much silver that might have been. Enough silver that the three gardeners had been paid off.

Guzman had later claimed he did not mind the loss of the silver, which a week's production could replace. But Guzman had told Amalia and the others their mother was dead to them and forever unwelcome in that house because she had butchered all the big cottonwood trees. He could never forgive that.

The twins were solemn.

"I did not let myself get discouraged. All these years I have waited to see if any of you grandchildren might have turned out human. I would come around every so often, take a look." They were on the porch now, and Dennis, their pinheaded cousin, the son of Uncle Ringo, was sitting on the step, eating his own snot. Yoeme waved her hand at Dennis. "They had all been pretty much like that one," she said, "and I was almost to give up hope. But then you two came."

"But you wanted to get rid of one of us." Lecha had let go of Yoeme's hand in order to say this.

The old woman had stopped and looked at both of them. "I wanted to have one of you for myself," she said.

"But you didn't get one of us."

"No." Yoeme had let out a big sigh. "I didn't even get *one* of you. Your poor mother was too dumb for that. And now do you see what I have?"

The twins had looked at each other to avoid the piercing eyes of old Yoeme.

Yoeme laughed loudly. "I have you both!" she said in triumph, and from the bedroom inside they could hear their mother fumble for the enamel basin to vomit blood.

THE FAILED GEOLOGIST

WHEN ZETA WAS ASKED about her childhood or her family, she replied only that it was all vague and uninteresting to her. This was the truth. But she also realized that she had come to be where she was through a strange and long series of events that were her childhood and youth.

They had arrived in Tucson in the early summer of their fourteenth year. From the train in Nogales they had taken a taxi to the bus depot. Their father had been waiting. They had talked in low voices, all the way from Hermosillo, about Uncle Federico's "big finger." They had avoided any discussion about what would happen next. Their father had not come to their mother's funeral, but then they had been separated for over ten years. He had sent a telegram immediately, by way of the mine at Canenea, announcing that the girls were his daughters, and he was now claiming his legal right to them.

Lecha had easily identified their father in the waiting room of the bus depot. He was standing apart from the rest, in starched khakis, polished half Wellingtons, reading *The Wall Street Journal*, Far East edition. Lecha had laughed. He did not disdain the poor Indians in the bus depot so much as they simply did not exist for him. He had never associated Amalia with the Indians; as far as he was concerned, she had been white. Lecha had always joked that if their mother and they had been chunks of iron feldspar, he would have been far more engaged, far more excited than he had ever been. Zeta was not so sure. Their father had been almost sixty when they were born. When he came to Potam to survey the ore formations and new shafts, he always took the girls along. That had been their visit, their time together with him. Lecha had been the one who had gone running to him with the chunk of iron feldspar in her hand. Zeta had watched from a distance.

He had taken the dark, heavy rock and had pretended or perhaps *had* examined it, but without any interest. Lecha had not let his lack of response interfere with her excitement over the glitter and sparkle in the stone. But Zeta had realized then nothing there mattered to him—not the shafts or the ore samples red-tagged for him by the mine foreman, not Lecha's excitement; though Zeta did believe he was concerned with relieving his sense of duty. After the separation, their grandpa Guzman had maintained the mining engineer had married their mother because he had been worried the partners had become dissatisfied with him and were about to hire a new geologist.

The rumors and reports had arrived in Canenea that while the mining engineer could still name the formations and the ore-bearing stones and rocks, and could recite all of the known combinations for that particular area, his calculations on the maps for known deposits and veins had been wrong; he had directed the miners to nothing. When other geologists had been called to evaluate his projections and the samples and assay results, they could find no fault with his work. They could not account for the absence of ore in the depths and areas he had designated. They had of course been reluctant to pass judgment upon a "brother"; the geologists had discussed at length the "scientific anomaly."

Yoeme said the veins of silver had dried up because their father, the mining engineer himself, had dried up. Years of dry winds and effects of the sunlight on milky-white skin had been devastating. Suddenly the man had dried up inside, and although he still walked and talked and reasoned like a man, inside he was crackled, full of the dry molts of insects. So their silent father had been ruined, and everyone had blamed Yoeme. But Lecha and Zeta had sensed the truth years earlier. They had both felt it when they walked with him and he had lifted them into his arms: somewhere within him there was, arid and shriveled, the imperfect vacuum he called himself.

Yoeme had been contemptuous of the innuendos about witchcraft. What did these stupid mestizos—half no-brain white, half worst kind of Indian—what did these last remnants of wiped-out tribes littering the earth, what did they know?

Yoeme had not wasted a bit of energy on Amalia's ex-husband. The geologist had been perfectly capable of destroying himself. His ailment had been common among those who had gone into caverns of fissures in the lava formations; the condition had also been seen in persons who had been revived from drowning in a lake or spring with an entrance to the four worlds below this world. The victim never fully recovered and exhibited symptoms identical to those of the German mining engineer. Thus, Yoeme had argued, witchcraft was not to blame. The white man had violated the Mother Earth, and he had been stricken with the sensation of a gaping emptiness between his throat and his heart.

Zeta could feel an empty space inside her rib cage, an absence that had been growing even before their mother died. She felt a peculiar sadness when she remembered their father, the detached white man who smiled and spoke and who was a dead man already.

BOARDING SCHOOL

ZETA HAD HOPED she might be with her father long enough to learn something more about the emptiness inside her. But the day she and Lecha stepped off the bus in Tucson, Zeta had seen it was too late. Their father had already purchased their train tickets to El Paso. He had greeted them formally, holding them both to his chest awkwardly, his body and arms rigid. He was pleased to see them both looking so well. He did not know how to express his condolences to them at the loss of their mother, but they must not worry. That subject finished, he had directed the porter to a taxi with their trunks and boxes. Driving to the hotel, he had told them he regretted the boarding school in El Paso was run by Catholic nuns, but there had been no other choice unless the girls went East to school. He told them he thought God was of no use. They had rooms at the Santa Rita Hotel if they did not want to spend school vacations with him at the ranch west of Tucson. He preferred the Santa Rita himself. Money had been deposited for them in a bank in El Paso. The mother superior would see that they got their school uniforms and whatever else they might need.

They had waited three days for the next train to El Paso. Their father had not left his room until late afternoon each day when he met them in the hotel lobby. He had said nothing about restrictions, but the girls had felt shy about walking alone in downtown Tucson, which was so much larger than Potam. He never smiled or spoke, merely nodding in the direction of the hotel restaurant. His forehead was continually wrinkled and his pale gray eyes intent as if he were working constantly to solve a mathematical formula even while he sat with them and soaked bread in his coffee.

Zeta had tried to guess what it was that filled their father's head so full. She began to awaken before dawn and hear small muffled sounds—the creak of a chair, the opening of a drawer—sounds of a man who no longer slept. He had not invited them to his room. Lecha wanted to see because she thought the clues might be there. She had ruled out women and love affairs immediately, but confided that strange philosophies or religions might be responsible. Zeta had felt a surge of anger in her chest at Lecha's stupidity. "It isn't anything. There's nothing. You won't find anything," she snapped as Lecha had started for his room. When he had opened the door, Zeta saw he did not recognize them immediately. Lecha was looking past him into the room and did not see this. Zeta felt her heart fall in her chest. The bed had not been slept in. The pillows and spread had not been touched since the hotel maid. The black wire hangers in the closet nook were empty. He had been sitting at the small desk. The desk top was bare, although for an instant Zeta had mistaken cigarette scars along the edges for a pattern of decoration. "Where is everything?" Lecha said, walking around and around the small room impatiently. Their father had turned as if he suffered from stiffness in the neck and shoulders. He had begun to hunch under long, unkempt white hair. They had always spoken English with him since he had never been able to learn Spanish. But Lecha had had to repeat the question twice before he could answer. "Everything?" he had said in a steady voice. "I am trying to think about it," he had answered. The farewell at the train station had been brief. Staring past them into the distance their father had announced, "You will never see me again. I am going to die. My life has never interested me much.

I think about myself and this room. The longer I think the less I understand."

Zeta had never forgotten the room. She had gone back, years later, to the desk clerk at the Santa Rita Hotel, to ask if she might look at a certain room on the third floor. She had been dressed in her business suit, hose, and heels carrying her briefcase. She could not remember the room number and had to take the elevator up to find it. The desk clerk had informed her the room was already taken.

But she had returned, and from time to time she rented Room 312. She did not care what the clerk or bellboy thought. She spent afternoons sitting at the desk. The wall behind the desk had been plastered and painted many times. She sat and stared at it and was soothed by the emptiness.

DRIED-UP CORPSE

THE NOTE HE left had said simply, "This should have been done years ago." He had done "it" in this room. The mother superior refused to give them any details. The relatives at the big house in Potam had known nothing of his death until months later when Lecha told them. Zeta had to smile at the mystery. Her father had not used a necktie or belt. Zeta had searched old county records to know. The report said he had simply sat at his chair not eating or drinking. It had been as if he had consumed himself. When he had been discovered by the hotel maid, he was not a swollen corpse, nor was there a terrible odor. He had been as dry and shriveled as a cactus blown down in a drought. Zeta had laughed: "He sounds like one of those saints that don't decay!" The report noted the condition of the corpse had been somewhat unusual. The corpse had begun to mummify, possibly, the coroner had theorized, because of the dry summer heat and the circumstances of the death. The report included autopsy results. Zeta could not make much of these technical notations, but the coroner's assistant had noted the deceased's body weight. "All that was left of him was fifty pounds," Zeta told Lecha later.

Their father had left them a ranch in the Tucson Mountains. The land was worth next to nothing. Even in the best years, many many hundreds of acres were required to keep a few cattle from starving. The mountains were all that had remained of a giant volcano that had exploded parts of itself as far east as New Mexico and as far north as Phoenix. Every square foot of the remaining foothills was covered with rock—volcanic rock, ash, and combinations of volcanic material fused with molten limestone and sandstone blown up with the molten rock. At one time, he had told them, the area had interested him immensely, because the explosion had been one of the more rare sort—alkaline rather than acidic. The day he had hired a taxi and driven them to the site, he had had the look of an exhausted man performing a chore. He had not looked at the rocky ground though he was describing highly technical rock conglomerates created by the intense heat of the explosion. When he had pointed to the south and north, where old mining claims marked ore outcroppings, he had been looking at the sky, not at the bluish-gray veins of ore-bearing rock. The girls had gathered that he meant to make a study of the area and of the relationships between the particular sort of volcanic explosion and the deposits of silver, copper and galena. But it was also very clear that he had lost whatever interest he had once had in the geology of the mountains. Now he preferred his room at the Santa Rita Hotel.

"This will be yours," their father had said as they walked back to the taxi. The driver had been under the car poking at the tail pipe and mumbling about rough road. "I did not buy it for ranching. Eighty acres isn't enough to raise anything. But, I suppose, it is something. Or maybe it isn't."

COYOTE YEARS

THE INTERVENING YEARS was a phrase Zeta liked because it described nearly her whole life. She and her twin sister had turned sixty in March. "The month the wild flowers blossom," their mother had said one day when old Yoeme was there. Yoeme said, "Yes, the same month the coyotes whelp," and burst out laughing, anxious to see what the twins would say. Lecha had answered right back, "Well, Grandma, that means you yourself are a coyote with us!" To which Yoeme had clapped her hands, but their mother had looked upset because it had already become clear that her twin daughters listened far too much to the wild old Yaqui woman.

Coyote might best describe the intervening years—Lecha constantly traveling, from lover to lover and city to city. Lecha's best stunt had been the birth of Ferro one Friday morning; by Sunday noon Lecha had been on a plane to Los Angeles, leaving Zeta with her new baby.

Lecha had sworn the trip was very important and she had promised to return no later than "Tuesday." But Lecha had never said *which* Tuesday, and Zeta did not see or hear from Lecha again until the following year.

When Zeta had asked her why she did not at least call collect or send a postcard, Lecha had said that she was sorry and she knew that she should have but she just didn't. "I thought maybe you might think about the baby," Zeta had continued, interested in her twin's excuse. "Oh, the baby!" Lecha had exclaimed as if she had completely forgotten. "Where is he? What do you call him?" By then Zeta had left town and had moved into the old ranch buildings to take advantage of the remote location for her work with Calabazas and the others. Calabazas had found an old widow from his neighborhood who wanted nothing more than to sit all day holding a baby and rocking in a chair as long as there was plenty of food and clean diapers. Later when Ferro was a fatty and suffered teasing from the other children, Lecha had blamed the old widow for always stuffing Ferro's mouth with food.

Right then Zeta had told Lecha that unless she planned on staying around or taking the baby with her, she had better keep her mouth shut. "Well, you don't have to get so mad!" Lecha had said, and from that time on they had not discussed Ferro again.

Coyote years certainly described Zeta's time with Mexico Tours and Mr. Coco. When members of tour groups had asked Zeta why they did not run tours farther south or to other Mexican states, she used to look them in the eye and answer calmly that she did not know. She had begun to make it her business not to answer questions when the answers did not truly matter anyway. What difference did it make why Mexico Tours and Mr. Coco did not venture farther south than Guaymas or Chihuahua City? Lecha could have had ten different answers for that question: that Mr. Coco was running things other than just tours or Mr. Coco had committed crimes farther south and could not safely send his clients farther or the old Greyhounds he buys and repaints parrot yellow can go no farther without major breakdowns.

Mr. Coco had been a light gray color without his clothes. He had sat in the armchair in his office watching her undress. All Zeta had been able to think about were the staples, coarse sand, and other debris on the rug beside his desk. She had known when he promoted her to tour coordinator that this moment was somewhere on the horizon. Mr. Coco had only two suits: a winter suit of black flannel and a summer suit of blue, pin-striped seersucker. He wore one until the weather changed, and by then, the sleeves of the coat would be stiff at the wrists with oily dirt. The trousers would be blotched where Mr. Coco had compulsively wiped the palms of his hands across his own thighs. One sunny morning in March at the beginning of the hot Tucson spring, Zeta saw that Mr. Coco had changed suits. He had just promoted her from the diesel fumes, the chattering tourists, and the drunken bus drivers who stared at her breasts. But after she had undressed, Mr. Coco remained in the armchair merely staring at her breasts. Between his legs in its nest of white pubic hair, the penis lay like a pale grub or caterpillar. It did not move. Although this was to be her first encounter with a man other than Uncle Federico and his fat, dirty fingers, Zeta felt nothing. No fear, no embarrassment, no horror at standing naked in the dingy sales office of Mexico Tours, at five-thirty on a Friday afternoon. The swamp cooler droned in the window behind her and emitted periodic drips into a flat pan on the floor.

The sound of the water leaking out of the cooler seemed to arouse him. They had both known all day this would happen. He opened his arms in a gesture Zeta took as an invitation to sit in his lap. The armchair was ragged and filthy, but it had deep cushions. Zeta had never been a small woman, and when she crawled into his lap, facing him, he sank so low in the chair his lips barely reached her nipples. It seemed like a lot of exertion bouncing around on his lap, having to brace herself against the chair arms with both her knees and her elbows. Mr. Coco moaned and groaned and nibbled away at her breasts. Zeta thought she should feel some revulsion, but she did not. She felt sweaty and her legs were cramped, but nothing about the scene was remarkable. She had not expected it would be any different.

Lecha claimed sex put a new odor on you. Well, it had got the bus drivers off her. The drivers knew only Mexico Tours would employ them. They assumed Zeta belonged to the boss after that. Mr. Coco himself had been subdued. Zeta pretended not to notice. He had a wife. Zeta realized somehow she had emerged from the Friday-afternoon fucking with a considerable measure of new power. It had been the power that had attracted Calabazas. He said so. He said he had been waiting to see how the twin beauties of Potam were going to do in the big city of Tucson. Himself, he had gotten out of Sonora years earlier. "Because you are much older than us," Lecha had teased. He was a clan brother who had invited himself to dinner. He was after both of them. They both looked at him as if he were crazy. Lecha said she had a date and she left. Over the years Calabazas had learned a great deal, but not about women.

Now it was only Calabazas and Zeta. "It's about time your job worked for you," he said, lighting up a Lucky Strike and blowing smoke rings as he spoke. "I know good people who want to make arrangements."

"Arrangements?" Zeta looked closely at him.

In those days Calabazas had been handsome and wild. Calabazas had been working with their clanspeople and relatives in Sonora. His pants pocket was fat with cash. When Lecha had pointed at the wad, Calabazas laughed and pretended it was his cock. "You can get this for yourselves anytime," he had joked, meaning the money as well as sex.

As soon as Zeta had become acquainted with the people Calabazas worked with in Mexico, she had saved up a bankroll to work a few deals of her own. Calabazas should have expected Zeta to pull a stunt like that, Lecha had confided later. Her sister was not to be trusted. Zeta had quit both Mexico Tours and Calabazas at the same time. She had taken two of the bus drivers with her, leaving Mr. Coco in his sour black suit, looking stunned as she told him she was bored with smuggling live green parrots and fake Rolex watches across the border in the bellies of tour buses.

AT WAR WITH
THE U.S. GOVERNMENT

YOEME HAD GUESSED immediately what Zeta was doing with her tour bus business and her partnership with Calabazas. When Yoeme had exclaimed "You will be a rich woman!" Zeta had only shrugged her shoulders. Zeta realized old Yoeme was leading her on, setting Zeta up for a tirade. Old Yoeme had made a big point of shaming those who would sell the last few objects of the people who had been destroyed and worlds that had been destroyed by the Europeans. Yoeme had looked Zeta right in the eye when she said it. Yoeme said that the work that faced Lecha had been made more difficult because from time to time, weakhearted keepers of the old almanac had sold off pages here and there for frivolous reasons.

"Remember all this when Lecha is struggling to make sense out of the notebooks." "Ask Zeta how many of the missing pages got sold off to her tourists from the United States." Of course Zeta had never seen anything like the fragments of the manuscript of glyphs. All that had ever moved through the garages of Mrs. Mares had been pottery and figurines, with a scattering of carved stone or jade axes and knives. When Zeta had informed Yoeme that they were out of the antiquities business and "working in other areas," old Yoeme had crowed, "Sold it all away! It's all gone and now you move to something else!" Zeta nodded. She had seen no point in arguing either with her grandmother or her sister.

Old Yoeme had been in the mood to talk that day:

I have kept the notebooks and the old book since it was passed on to me many years ago. A section of one of the notebooks had accidentally been lost right before they were given to me. The woman who had been keeping them explained what the lost section had said, although of course it was all in a code, so that the true meaning would not be immediately clear. She requested that, if possible, at some time in my life I should write down a replacement section.

I have thought about it all my life. The problem has been the meaning of the lost section and for me to find a way of replacing it. One naturally reflects upon one's own experiences and feelings throughout one's life. The woman warned that it should not be just any sort of words.

I am telling you this because you must understand how carefully the old manuscript and its notebooks must be kept. Nothing must be added that was not already there. Only repairs are allowed, and one might live as long as I have and not find a suitable code.

I must always return to what the white men kept hanging in all the lovely cottonwood trees along the rivers and streams throughout this land. Swaying in the light wind, rags of clothing flapping the shrunken limbs into motion. They try to walk, they try to walk—the feet keep reaching long after the neck has broken or the head has choked. In those days the Mexican soldiers were not particular about whom they killed so long as they were Indians found near the mountains. Before dawn they fired upon a camp, taking it for Indian, and the Mexican soldiers killed a young American lieutenant and an American cavalry scout. They were all hunting the Apaches running with the man they called Geronimo. That was not his name. No wonder there has been so much confusion among white people and their historians. The man encouraged the confusion. He has been called a medicine man, but that title is misleading. He was a man who was able to perform certain feats.

I have seen the photographs that are labeled "Geronimo." I have seen the photograph of the so-called surrender at Skeleton Canyon where General Miles sits in the shade of a mesquite tree flanked by his captains as he makes false promises and lies. But the Apache man identified in the photographs is not, of course, the man the U.S. army has been chasing. He is a man who always accompanied the one who performed certain feats. He is the man who agreed to play the role for the protection of the other man. The man in the photographs had been promised safe conduct by the man he protected. The man in the photographs was a brilliant and resourceful man. He may not have known that while he would find wealth and fame in the lifelong captivity, he would not again see the mountains during his life. The man who fled had further work to do, work that could not be done in captivity.

When the mountain people came down for salt or for other necessities, they came to bring the news and maybe some herb delicacy for me. This man accompanied them. He did not remain with the others talking on the porch or eating roast mutton inside. He walked down here, right to this place we are standing.

I had walked out on the second-story porch carrying one of the babies—it was Amalia, your mother. She was always crying and puking milk. I could see the man very clearly. The others had told me that he had certain work he must do, which was why they had brought him down with them. No one was to know who he was. It was a very dangerous time then. The soldiers were killing Indians left and right. I watched the man for a long time. Amalia fell asleep in my arms. He was watching the gulls ride the waves in and out. I began to remember my wonder at the rising of the waves when I first saw the sea. The sun was setting into the water. The tide was going out. The gulls were being carried farther and farther away into the bright gold light of the last sun across the water. I never moved my eyes from the man at the edge of the water. But in an instant he was gone. All I could see was a gull riding a wave, floating and stretching its wings in the lazy way the gulls have.

That is all. Take me back. I am tired.

They argued over what was easier. Lecha wanted to go back to the house and get the car, but Yoeme refused to ride in one. Zeta thought the deep sand made uphill with the old wheelchair impossible and said she could more easily carry Yoeme. But the old woman said her bones might poke through her skin if Zeta tried something stupid like that. So they took turns struggling up the sandy road from the beach, old Yoeme sleeping through the jerks and skids. They got too winded to talk. They never discussed the story Yoeme had told them on the beach, but Lecha had been careful to write it down in the notebook with the blank pages. After she had written it, old Yoeme had demanded to see it, and it was then they realized it was the first entry that had been written in English. Zeta waited for Yoeme to break into a fury. But she had rocked herself from side to side, sighing with pleasure. Yoeme claimed this was the sign the keepers of the notebooks had always prayed for.

It had been Yoeme in the first place who talked to snakes. She claimed to consult the big bull snake out behind the adobe woodshed. Zeta had learned it from her. What did the snake tell her? the two girls had wanted to know. Nothing the girls would be allowed to hear. Old Yoeme had never got along with churchgoers. She had her own picture of things. Snakes crawled under the ground. They heard the voices of the dead: actual conversations, and lone voices calling out to loved ones still living. Snakes heard the confessions of murderers and arsonists after innocent people had been accused. Why did Catholic priests always kill snakes? The twins nodded their heads solemnly at their grandmother. Snakes moved through the tall weeds, and under the edges of rocks and up through the branches of trees. They saw and heard a good deal that way: where husbands crept away, where wives embraced lovers. Snakes saw what illicit couples did, in turkey pens after dark, in the arroyo by the trash pile, all the sexual excesses the two girls had been able to imagine, but were not allowed to hear. Yoeme had the girls begging.

Lecha could not bear to face the big bull snake. She closed her eyes and tried. But she could not bear to see him thick and coiled in the shady spot by the hole in the wall where he slept. Lecha could not endure to watch his slippery, black fork tongue dart in and out, in and out. "Well, you go on back to the porch," Yoeme had told her. "Not everyone can do this. Your sister can tell you what he says."

Zeta had waited until Yoeme called her closer. The snake was not so stupid that he did not know a stranger. Although he does know you two girls because you play out here sometimes. But you can't just go rushing at them. Bad manners. You can't have a conversation right away. It is no different from with humans. Let him hear your heartbeat. Let him hear your breathing.

It was something Zeta did alone with her grandmother. In the fall, as the days were cooling off, they would find the big bull snake sunning himself on the south side of the woodshed. Yoeme had picked him up carefully, supporting his long body with one hand as she cradled him against her chest. "He likes the warmth, you see," and it had been then Zeta understood that the big snake recognized Yoeme, because he lay quietly, only his tongue moving slowly in and out at Zeta.

Zeta had never mentioned any of this to Lecha because she could not exactly explain how it had worked. Certainly the snake didn't talk. But looking at the snake as it curled in Yoeme's arms and thinking how beautifully the light brown spots were with the pale yellow under it, Zeta had for no reason thought of Grandpa Guzman not as her grandpa, but as the "old white man," which was what others, outside the family, called him. She had thought of him overturned and moaning feebly for help. And her aunt Popa was ignoring him because she figured there would be something dirty to clean up. All Zeta had ever thought was that she knew how it worked, how one talked to snakes. But it had not impressed her.

So, years later, when old Yoeme had given Lecha the notebooks to decipher, Zeta had been surprised that the old woman said, "Your skills lie elsewhere, don't they?" Lecha had glanced at Zeta to try to figure out what old Yoeme had meant. But Zeta did not change her expression, and their grandmother drifted into one of her long naps—a long nap that finally one warm afternoon four days later had not ended.

THE INDIAN WAY

ZETA HAD NOT NEEDED Calabazas after the first loan from him was repaid, but she had played along for a while because she was interested in what he might do next. He said that the two of them could have the run of the town when it came to "commodities" crossing the border. This proposal had come shortly after he had visited the old ranch in the mountains and had realized the possibilities. Zeta thought this had also come about the time Calabazas was beginning to realize that she was not going to be swept into his bed as other women generally were.

Calabazas had gotten amorous at sundown while Zeta was explaining what her father had told them about the big volcano that had once been there and about the giant explosion that had destroyed it. Zeta had been showing him different rocks containing bits of volcanic ash melted into them. She had been explaining that her father had wanted to spend his retirement studying these rocks and the ore deposits of these mountains when Calabazas had tried to gather her into his arms for a big kiss. But Zeta had seen the move coming, and she had twisted away expertly, dropping the rock she had been showing him on his foot. "You are not like your twin sister," Calabazas had said, shaking his head. "No," Zeta had replied, "I'm not." And a week later Zeta had arranged the biggest haul of gold coins yet, and Calabazas and his people knew nothing about it. She had not trusted a deal that big to anyone. She had loaded Ferro's diaper bag, car bed, and toys into the backseat of a big Hudson Hornet. The old widow and Ferro had ridden in front beside her. Zeta purposely wore a full, loose blouse over her plain, dark skirt that might suggest pregnancy. At the border crossing in El Paso, the U.S. guards had made only a quick check of the trunk. The mighty frame and springs of the Hudson Hornet had not held their load without sagging, but they seemed not to notice. Or they had passed it off to the two large Indian women, the large baby, and the load of baby gear.

The old widow-woman had not asked questions, but from time to time she had made comments too low to make out, although once or twice Zeta had heard her mumbling something about "this" not being "the Indian way." Zeta and Lecha had heard about the "Indian way" for years and years. Their aunties and dirty-fingered uncles despised what they called "Indians" until it suited them; then suddenly the "Indian way" was all-important if and when the "Indian way" worked to their advantage. Zeta did not want to hear about "the Indian way" from anyone who was her own employee. Zeta had stared at the old woman for a long time. *What* wasn't the "Indian way"?

The people had been free to go traveling north and south for a thousand years, traveling as they pleased, then suddenly white priests had announced smuggling as a mortal sin because smuggling was stealing from the government.

Zeta wondered if the priests who told the people smuggling was stealing had also told them how they were to feed themselves now that all the fertile land along the rivers had been stolen by white men. Where were the priest and his Catholic Church when the federal soldiers used Yaqui babies for target practice? Stealing from the "government"? What "government" was that? Mexico City? Zeta had laughed out loud. Washington, D.C.? How could one steal if the government itself was the worst thief?

There was not, and there never had been, a legal government by Europeans anywhere in the Americas. Not by any definition, not even by the Europeans' own definitions and laws. Because no legal government could be established on stolen land. Because stolen land never had clear title. Zeta could recite Yoeme's arguments and crazed legal theories better and better as time went by. All the laws of the illicit governments had to be blasted away. Every waking hour Zeta spent scheming and planning to break as many of their laws as she could.

War had been declared the first day the Spaniards set foot on Native American soil, and the same war had been going on ever since: the war was for the continents called the Americas.

Calabazas said the widow did not think it was the Indian way to use an old woman and a little child as her "cover" for the business of crossing the border. He had been leaning against his pickup truck with a toothpick hanging out of the corner of his mouth, staring off in the distance at the highest peak in the Tucson range.

Zeta had laughed loudly—something she only did when she was angry or surprised. "Who said anything about the 'Indian way'?" Zeta demanded.

Calabazas turned and looked at her and shook his head. "Hey, don't get mad at me, I didn't say it, *she* did."

"Tell her she's fired then," Zeta said.

YOEME'S OLD NOTEBOOKS

ZETA GAVE UP on men after Mr. Coco. He hadn't been the first, but she had decided he would be the last. She was not afraid to know the truth. She could feel what she knew. She was different from other women, just as she and Lecha had always been different from all the others. Zeta had begun to feel a wearisome repetition in the love affairs. Hot, awkward motions, foul breath, and the ticking of a clock in the room. She knew how the love would trickle away before the sweat dried on the bed sheets.

Around the same time Zeta gave up on men, she had come across the notebooks old Yoeme had left her. Zeta had begun examining the bundle of pages and scraps of paper with notes in Latin and Spanish. Lecha had all the notebooks but this one. Yoeme said it was to ensure Lecha did not try to hog the notebooks for herself; this had been Yoeme's way of teasing Lecha, but also a reminder the old woman expected the sisters to care for one another throughout their lives.

Old Yoeme had given Zeta the smallest bundle of loose notebook pages and scraps of paper with drawings of snakes. Yoeme had warned Zeta not to brag to Lecha, but the notebook of the snakes was the key to understanding all the rest of the old almanac. The drawings of the snakes were in beautiful colors of ink, but Zeta had been disappointed after she began deciphering Yoeme's scrawls in misspelled Spanish. This did not seem to be the "key" to anything except one old woman's madness.

Pages From the Snakes' Notebook

Maah' shra-True'-Ee is the giant serpent
the sacred messenger spirit
from the Fourth World below.
He came to live at the Beautiful Lake, Ka-waik,
that was once near Laguna village.
But neighbors got jealous.
They came one night and broke open the lake
so all the water was lost. The giant snake
went away after that. He has never been seen
* since.*
That was a great misfortune for us, the Ka-
* waik'meh,*
at Old Laguna.

Spirit Snake's Message

I have been talking to you people from the begin-
* ning*
I have told you the names and identities of the
* Days and Years.*
I have told you the stories on each day and year
* so you could be prepared*
and protect yourselves.
What I have told you has always been true.
What I have to tell you now is that
this world is about to end.

Those were the last words of the giant serpent. The days that were
to come had been foretold. The people scattered. Killers came from all
directions. And more killers followed, to kill them.

One day a story will arrive at your town. It will come from
far away, from the southwest or southeast—people won't
agree. The story may arrive with a stranger or perhaps with

the parrot trader. But when you hear this story, you will know it is the signal for you and the others to prepare.

Quetzalcoatl gathered the bones of the dead and sprinkled them with his own blood, and humanity was reborn.

Sacred time is always in the Present.

1. almanakh: Arabic.
2. almanac: A.D.1267 English from the Arabic.
3. almanaque: A.D.1505 Spanish from the Arabic.
4. a book of tables containing a calendar of months and days with astronomical data and calculations.
5. predicts or foretells the auspicious days, the ecclesiastical and other anniversaries.
6. short glyphic passages give the luck of the day.
7. Madrid
   Paris   Codices
   Dresden

Leave it to Lecha to show up with the remaining notebooks and the notion her transcriptions would be unique and never thought of before. Zeta had already completed the pages of the notebook Yoeme had given her. Zeta did not believe it was an accident Lecha had returned just as Zeta had finished typing the transcriptions of the pages into the computer.

Zeta feels a sudden sadness at the sound of their voices. She is not sure why. Maybe it's because Lecha and the blond woman are friendly with each other, and she feels so alone. But she does not turn back from the bedroom door, which is ajar. Zeta knocks and the blond woman startles and moves away from her, across the room to an open window. "I haven't killed and eaten anyone for some time now," Zeta says to

Seese, who blushes and returns to the chair by the bed. "It's the color of clothes you wear," Lecha says quite seriously. "After a while the dark brown color begins to shout something at all of us."

"Superstition," is all Zeta will say, dismissing the subject so that she can begin maneuvers to get the contents of Yoeme's old notebooks into her computer.

"I have been thinking about the old notebooks," Zeta begins. But Lecha is flying high this afternoon, and she grins at Seese as she says, "I'll bet you have! I know just what you have in mind." Now it is Lecha who is watching Zeta's face for clues; Zeta has never quite known, and Lecha won't tell her, exactly how much of the psychic business Lecha controls, and how much it controls her. Zeta believes Lecha mostly has the visions or "scenes" imposed on her and can't control what she sees. Otherwise, why the remark that she "had to leave" the TV talk show circuit? Zeta has gathered it was because of something Lecha had said or described, and whatever it had been, the executive producers of the regional and cable talk shows no longer wanted to risk what Lecha might "see" or say. Zeta is pleased that the blond woman is learning to leave them alone. With Seese gone, Zeta can survey the work area they've made in the corner of Lecha's bedroom. Lecha's suitcases and travel trunk have been piled outside the closet that is crammed full of her televison clothes—mostly long black silk crepes with plunging neck-lines or blue satin kimonos with slits up the sides. A big blue chair with peacocks is littered with pill bottles near the bed. But in the center of the light-oak desk sits a new electric typewriter. The pale blue carpet is littered with what appear to be notes and old letters.

"What are you going to do once you get them typed?" Zeta asks.

Lecha scoops two fat white pills off the night table and swallows them with white wine. It is difficult to know how sick Lecha really is. Zeta looks carefully at her skin color and her hair and then at Lecha's eyes. Lecha has sunk back on the pillows. Her pills are taking effect now. "Those old almanacs don't just tell you when to plant or harvest, they tell you about the days yet to come—drought or flood, plague, civil war or invasion." Lecha seemed to be drifting off to sleep. "Once the notebooks are transcribed, I will figure out how to use the old almanac. Then we will foresee the months and years to come—everything." Lecha's eyes are closed now, but as Zeta is leaving, Lecha calls after her. "I should've started this years ago—then we'd already know what's coming. But I was having too much fun—there was no time for old notebooks and scraps of paper."

BOOK SIX

THE NORTH

LOCATING THE DEAD

IT HAD DAWNED on Lecha—the way the darkness gradually bleeds away and the light gains momentum, much as water seeps into low places in the garden. The awareness pulsed through her day and night. When it had first broken through, she had tried little tricks, little exercises, attempting to cut off the channel. She had sat adding long columns of figures, and although she was able to concentrate on the numbers and do a more accurate job of adding them than she had ever done before, a part of her brain was still spinning a voice that mocked her: They are all dead. The only ones you can locate are the dead. Murder victims and suicides. You can't locate the living. If you find them, they will be dead. Those who have lost loved ones only come to you to confirm their sorrow.

Old Yoeme would have laughed at her. Would have laughed as Lecha began to go over the past twenty years and assembled the evidence. The crazed old woman would have made jokes: Lecha is a special contact for the souls that still do not rest because their remains are lost; somewhere fragments of bone burnt to ash, or long strands of hair, move in the ocean wind as it shifts the sand across the dunes. Lecha could almost hear Yoeme's voice. The crazy laugh and then, "Where do you suppose you got that ability, that gift?" Because Yoeme must have known all along that Lecha would be the one; she might have guessed it when they were still little girls.

The power Lecha had seemed to be as an intermediary, the way the snakes were messengers from the spirit beings in the other worlds below. She was just getting accustomed to this fact and her link with the dead when she had been called to San Diego.

Police in this case knew they would not find the missing boys alive because the killer had been apprehended. On the night of his arrest, with the same cunning he had used on his victims, he had managed to kill himself. In a security cell, wearing only a flimsy paper hospital gown calculated to tear if the inmate used it for a garrote, the serial killer had choked himself with a ham and cheese sandwich. He had deliberately swallowed a wad of cheese and ham that caught just over his windpipe. "No, the queer can't tell us what he did with them. His mouth's too full," a young detective said loudly when Lecha had been brought in. "No, that queer won't be doing any more sucking either. You think he did sucking? I would have said—" The older detective looked at Lecha and let the subject drop.

As her connection with the dead had begun to surface in her thoughts, Lecha had felt anxious; her nerves were raw, and her patience with grinning, backslapping police detectives in their polyester suits was running out. She had been ready to take a long vacation or maybe to go out of business for a while so that she could think about herself and her work with this power she had. It might be a dangerous power to work with. It might be the sort of power that should be locked away, ignored, no matter the wealth or fame it might bring her.

The police detectives had just been funded to set up a special team. They had been able to offer Lecha twice her normal fee. The situation they had was similar to the one Atlanta had had a few years before, except here the boys that were missing were white and had disappeared from wealthy neighborhoods in La Jolla. The department was feeling pressure from all sides. The computer and the psychologists had located the killer, but the case could not be closed until they found all his victims. Parents and family had to know for sure.

Lecha nods. This is her specialty. The detectives are anxious to talk about the work she'd done in Houston, and the case in South Dakota. But Lecha makes excuses. Flying and traveling tired her. She just wanted to get to the hotel. She had heard all she wanted from these two assholes in the car, driving from the airport. Just some hints, the younger detective had said. This weirdo really was into some kinky shit. He rented this garage apartment behind a house in the oak-hills section. We figure somewhere in the wooded areas beyond there. State fish-and-game range. But there's way too much area. Dogs are no good after a certain point, if you know what I mean. The older detective is driving and has to get his observations in too. They've had search teams comb the area. But it is so big. They could be buried anywhere. Under all those leaves. The creep was always wandering around in the forest, way back in the thick trees.

By the time they had dropped her off at the hotel, Lecha had a terrible headache. She went straight to the bathroom and prepared the syringe. The headaches had gotten worse lately, and tablets of codeine or Demerol did not touch the pain. This was going to be a rough job. These two cops had to be almost as weird as the killer, or maybe they were worse. Because the killer must have discovered his identity in much the way she was discovering her own identity as a psychic. The killer must not have known in the beginning where his fantasies and dreams would take him. The killer might not even have known the first time until after it had been done. Lecha was lying on her bed facing the sliding glass doors to the balcony. Below the balcony was the marina and beyond that the flat, blue bay, and from there to the horizon, the Pacific rising and falling to the rhythm of her own chest.

The Demerol was untying the fire knotted inside both temples. Her bones began to feel light; they floated, and then they had dissolved. She had hoped to sleep, but was accustomed to a middle ground the Demerol gave. It was a location where thought took on a more fluid quality, but unlike pure dreaming, remained more within conscious control. She kept hearing the voice of the younger detective. He reminded her of one of those tiny yappy Chinese dogs with bug eyes. "Trees! Trees!" He was certain the bodies were buried somewhere in a wooded area. She could not think about trees. The word had no meaning. She could hear the waves roll although she knew the hotel room was much too far from them. The ocean marked the motion of the moon. Up and down in the sky—higher or lower from the horizon, thin white curve of desert thorn swelled on consecutive nights to a fat white blossom. The disappearance and the returning. Over and over. The waves wash up the sand and fall back.

The dunes spread away in all directions. The white sand sinks under his boots like water. The sound is behind him. The ocean is the color of the sky. The eyes are gone. The sand fills the sockets. Now the boy has eyes the color of sand. Only the hair is lighter—the color of the sand in a wind that darkens the ocean, that darkens all.

He imagines the boys are trees that he must go tend from time to time. He uncovers them tenderly. To see how they are developing. They thrive best at the foot of the big dunes. Out in the flats they can't take root. Rain washes them out. Exposes them where they might be found.

At first there will be an odor, but it is a sign they are growing. He remembers a baby brother long ago and the dirty diapers. But babies die. Other times the odor reminds him of fertilizer, which of course "the trees" provide for themselves.

He realizes they are trees while he is touching them. He fondles the boys between their legs, and a branch sprouts and pushes out. The tips are soft leaf-bud moist with sap. He never means to squeeze too hard or to crush. But they are tender, fragile. He plants carefully and prays for tall trees. He dreams of towering oaks and spruce that lean and sway but do not break in summer storms. He realizes his dreams are of the mountains, not the sea.

Lecha never tells how she does it, how she knows. They already mistrust the ability. One week they might hire her and the next arrest her for fraud. They like to think it is done with crystal balls and what is familiar to them from movies and TV. She is accustomed to dramatic announcements at press conferences. The high Indian cheekbones and light brown skin give her an exotic quality that television news desperately needs. But her contempt for the news media is too great to allow her to appear anymore flanking police detectives or bereaved families.

In the beginning it had been different, and Lecha had enjoyed the drama. The television talk shows were still her bread and butter. But when the detectives put the police chief on the line, she had politely declined. The beach had been closed for miles in either direction. Mounted police rode patrols to keep the curious and ghoulish out of the way of the search teams digging in the dunes. She told them she had urgent business elsewhere. She asked them to send a messenger with a check. But it was the young detective from the special squad who brought the check. She was trying to pack for an afternoon flight, she explained, but saw he would not go until he got to talk.

They always wanted to know how she knew. He said, "How did you figure the beach? His apartment was miles from the beach." She held the doorknob. He had not stepped across the threshold because she would not move. "Congratulations, Detective Pearson, and please give my regards to Detective Connors. I'm glad I could help. Now I really have to catch a plane." She refused a ride to the airport. He would have wanted to describe how they had found the remains of each victim. The jet circled over the ocean on takeoff, and as it banked and turned above the ocean, Lecha looked down. The waves glittered and flashed like fragments of a broken mirror. From the air the beach sand made a narrow white stripe down the back of a giant animal, and the ocean waves glittered and flashed—eyes of mirrors as the sun dips closer to the mouth of the beast that swallows it.

She had the full answer now. She had suspected the concept of intermediary and messenger was too simple. Lecha knew exactly how grave her condition was. After she gave the instructions to the police, she had to take the Demerol again, not for any pain in her head, but for the pounding of her heart, and that voice inside shouting. She ordered scotch and milk to take the tablets. Tablets sometimes upset her stomach before they take effect. As she drifts back and forth, she thinks about old Yoeme and what she would say. But old Yoeme has got her mouth packed with sand. Lecha remembers the ragged bundles of cheap paper and the old notebooks. "Mouths" and "tongues" old Yoeme had jokingly called them. Now that she knew how the power worked, Lecha was not so sure anymore it could be called a gift. It was about time to go back home. She had made Yoeme a promise. She had to take care of the old notebooks.

LOVER'S REVENGE

LECHA TAKES PRIDE in knowing when to fold her cards. She is no gambler. She only goes for the sure things. The TV talk show circuit had been one of those sure things. But nothing lasts forever; she laughs to herself. The fascination the United States had had for the "other"—the blacks, Asians, Mexicans, and Indians ran in cycles. She had started after word got around Denver about her successes with old lovers. It had been simple. Other women came to her to ask her to take revenge on lovers who had betrayed them or who were not as ardent as they had once been. Lecha had had an apartment right over Larimer Street in the downtown. She had settled in Denver after Tucson had got "too crowded" for her. The truth of course was otherwise, but Lecha had never felt she owed anyone the truth, unless it was truth about their own lives, and then they had to pay her to tell them. People heard about it from one person, and the next thing they were knocking at Lecha's door.

Lecha traces the beginning to the work she had done for the cable-televison producer's girlfriend. The producer's girlfriend had come to Lecha for revenge. Her old boyfriend had been a cinematographer at the big CBS station in Denver. After the woman had asked the boyfriend to move out of her apartment, he had returned to douse it with kerosene and set it on fire. Lecha had tried to determine the extent of what the woman had lost in the fire, but the woman had never been able to get past the part about her cat and two dogs that had been trapped in the fire. The old boyfriend had also made anonymous phone calls to the Internal Revenue Service and to the woman's employer, a conservative businessman who did not approve of drugs or extramarital sex. Lecha had had a difficult time discussing the course of action the woman wished her to take. At first Lecha had misunderstood the woman's silences and hesitation as the weakheartedness Lecha often saw in people who came to her seeking revenge only to discover that they still loved the offender too much. Then Lecha had realized the woman's hatred was so extreme that the woman was unable to speak. Lecha realized that although the woman was at the time without a job, without a possession to her name, the woman wanted to buy from Lecha the most brutal and complete revenge for sale at any price.

Lecha had proceeded with the woman in ways that closely resembled the work of a psychoanalyst or counselor. With the tape recorder running discreetly on the bed, Lecha had asked the woman to tell her as much as she could remember about the cinematographer. Lecha did not focus upon the failed relationship itself. People could never talk coherently about ex-lovers, not for fifty years as far as Lecha was concerned. Lecha wanted to know about the man's closest family members and relatives. Where were they, what did they do for a living? In all, the work required nearly twenty sessions. Lecha had only required the woman to pay for the newspaper subscriptions to the dailies in the hometown of the cinematographer's closest relatives. Otherwise, the agreement had been that the fee would depend upon the results obtained and upon the form of payment Lecha determined to be most satisfactory.

This had been Lecha's first big case, and night after night she had rolled up big, tamale-shaped joints and sat propped up in her bed listening to the interview tapes. As Lecha laughingly said later, she had worked mostly "in the dark" on this first assignment. As she listened to the interviews, she had begun to see patterns in the lives of the cinematographer and his immediate family. Their lives were stories-in-progress, as Lecha saw them, and often in the middle of the night when she was awakened by drunks pounding on trash cans or sirens, she would realize possible deadly turns the lives of the cinematographer and his close relatives might naturally take. Lecha had merely begun to tell the stories of the ends of their lives. The producer's girlfriend had been pleased to see results after only two weeks. The cinematographer's mother had undergone emergency surgery for an intestinal blockage only to learn that snarled threads of cancer held her liver and pancreas in a tumorous web. Lecha had been a little surprised at how quickly the cancer had developed, since she had only just made up the ending to the mother's story. Beginner's luck, Lecha had confessed later, but the illness of the mother set off a chain reaction. The cinematographer's older sister accepted the marriage proposal of a man who came to her house every evening not for her, but for her thirteen- and fifteen-year-old daughters. Both girls would set out to get their future stepfather into their beds before the wedding to prove their mother's stupidity. After the wedding, their new stepfather took them and their mother to Miami Beach.

Lecha had carefully plotted their final summer together. It all hinged on whether the fifteen-year-old would become jealous of the attention her younger sister was getting. The hot tub thermostat at their rented beach bungalow had been set too high, according to reports in the newspaper. As Lecha had imagined it, the fifteen-year-old had gone into a pout one evening after the stepfather and the thirteen-year-old planned a dinner alone "to talk." Her little sister and stepfather gone, and her mother drunk, it was a simple matter to get into the bottle of vodka her father kept in the refrigerator freezer compartment. The coroner ruled the death accidental drowning and theorized the girl passed out from the combined effects of the vodka, which had raised her blood alcohol to .02, and to the hot water. The stepfather and sister had returned home from dinner to find her floating facedown in the hot tub on the terrace.

In only a matter of weeks, Lecha realized the younger girl would become pregnant by the stepfather. While this girl would not die, the complications from the abortion would hospitalize her. The mother, now separated from her new husband, and distraught over the loss of a daughter, began to mix triple gin-and-tonics to take with her on evening drives to the hospital to visit her remaining daughter. Hers had not been much different from any other freeway accident. The triple gin had slowed her reaction time.

DAYTIME TELEVISION

LECHA SAT WITH the newspapers spread around her on the floor. She was getting to the point she hated the dinky apartment. She watched the woman's face. She glanced at the producer-boyfriend's face. The woman's face was immobile, only her eyes followed the lines on the page of the newspaper. But the producer's face had lighted up. He was nodding his head and grinning. "This is wonderful!" he began. "This reads like soap opera! How do you do it?" Lecha shook her head and said nothing. The producer babbled on. "This is really something— you know, like in the movies—*Omen* or one of those!" The woman had given her boyfriend a murderous look. "Sidney," she said, "would you mind waiting down in the car?"

Sidney had left without another word, but later he had returned alone to discuss Lecha's appearance on daytime television. The producer had tried to bring up his girlfriend's revenge, but Lecha was reluctant to violate the confidentiality of their professional relationship. The producer wanted to know why, in all the dying, had they not gotten rid of the cinematographer himself? Lecha did not like visitors like this one— full of questions but with no money for her valuable time. "Business first," Lecha had said. "I want to know how much this TV show will pay me."

"Well, that depends on a number of factors," the producer explained. "I've talked it over with my boss, and we're thinking of bringing on a police officer from the missing person detail, and then someone who is actually looking for a lost loved one. A lost child would be optimum. Eighty-five percent of the viewing audience is female." Lecha shrugged her shoulders. She told him she did not know if she could sit in the TV studio and find a missing person on command. She told him she didn't work like that. But the producer grinned inanely and insisted it would be no problem, no problem. What he thought would really go over big were stories about people who consulted Lecha to exact revenge on ex-lovers and spouses or family members or business colleagues.

"I want to get out of this dump. I need to have some money for talking today and for preparations, you know, for the show." Lecha knew he would come back to the question about the cinematographer. Lecha did not tell him until after she had got the $2,000 advance, and the producer had helped her relocate all her suitcases to the Hilton Hotel. "It's simple," she began. "I didn't want to get rid of the old lover too fast. I wanted him to watch the people he loves die first. Your girlfriend's old lover is forced to watch his mother's guts split open from tumors. Straight morphine does nothing. The old lover is becoming familiar with the special packages and offers from mortuaries." Lecha watched the producer's face and decided he was too stupid to get it. "See?" Lecha concluded. "Killing off that prick would have been too good for him. This is much better. Let him bury them all."

Lecha spent mornings shopping for the appropriate clothes. She had chosen the Denver Hilton because it was connected to the fancy department stores by a glass tube, so she did not have to step into the ice and cold of the Denver winter. She was not nervous about the first taping session, although the producer had warned her this would be a live audience and the show format called for questions from the audience. Lecha's mind had been focused on the winter storms and the snow and ice, which she was not accustomed to. She had been strangely aware of the filthy banks of ice and snow pushed between the streets and sidewalks in downtown Denver. She had sat for hours, puffing a joint, gazing out the hotel window at the big mountains to the west barely visible through the brown smog over Denver. Later she remembered the mountain peaks had reminded her of the mounds of new graves covered with snow.

So the day of the videotaping before a studio audience, when the police lieutenant gave the particulars of a missing-person case, Lecha suddenly realized why she had paid so much attention to banks of mounded snow. Lecha looked right into the huge television camera lens and said, "The man is dead. He is buried in a snowbank. The snow is dirty from muddy water cars splash over it." The studio audience had audibly gasped because Lecha seemed to forget the woman sitting beside the police lieutenant on the gold velvet couch was the dead man's wife. Lecha had learned from this episode that while audiences and producers wanted a family member of the missing person present, they also wanted Lecha to break the bad news as gently as possible. It was all an act from then on—the way Lecha would lower her voice and say she regretted what she was about to say, then reveal the location of the victim; Lecha had never been sorry, not at that moment or ever. Lecha knew her abilities had been a gift from old Yoeme.

Lecha had been born for television talk shows. She had learned to read the reactions of talk show hosts and the audiences immediately. Even on that first morning, while the new widow at the end of the gold couch sobbed next to the confused police lieutenant, Lecha had silently burst into tears. Even that day the TV cameras had adored Lecha's high cheekbones, and the chill of her grisly pronouncement had been lifted.

The talk show host had jumped up from his armchair to comfort the widow on the gold couch. He immediately reminded the widow, and the studio audience, that Lecha's "vision" was only that. No body had been found, and they should not jump to conclusions. The show had been a producer's dream—a dramatic announcement, a widow's grief, and the talk show host thrown into deep water without the teleprompter and gestures he'd rehearsed to keep him afloat.

Lecha had analyzed her talk show appearance carefully. She realized the hostility of the general public toward people with abilities to "see" or "foretell" always lay near the surface. Lecha took a white linen handkerchief from the red leather purse that matched the red high heels of her televison-appearance wardrobe. It didn't take a psychic to figure out she had a bright future on the daytime television talk show circuit. She wiped the tears from her eyes and primly smoothed the skirt of the simple white linen dress. Earlier in the show, Lecha had answered a query about her age with a plain lie. She had claimed that in the tiny Sonoran seacoast village where she had been born, no records of births or deaths were kept. "I think I must be about forty-five," she had answered the woman standing at the studio-audience microphone. Lecha and her twin had a birthday approaching on March 1. As far as Lecha could remember, it would be birthday number thirty-five.

D O G S L E D   R A C E R

THE POLICE LIEUTENANT had pressed Lecha for more information—the police wanted the exact location of the snowbank concealing the corpse. Lecha tried to concentrate on the image of the snowbank, but there had been too many distractions. Try as she might, all Lecha had been able to visualize had been rural Alaskan snowbanks, memories from the year she had spent in Alaska. As far as Lecha was concerned, the only excitement had come in the spring when the big rivers, the Yukon and the Kuskokwim began to thaw and all night the earth along the riverbanks shook with the thunder of the breakup of the ice. At breakup time the newspapers from Anchorage and Fairbanks began to catalog grisly discoveries in melting snowbanks. Except for the 1,200-mile dogsled race to Nome, the body count of winter's toll had been the only interesting Alaska news. The 1,200-mile dogsled race had been the whole reason she had ended up in Alaska in the first place.

Lecha thought this must be the tundra spirits' way of taking revenge—to cook you for playing with another woman's husband. Here she was sitting under the hot television-studio lights, a widow sobbing and the mood of the audience and host beginning to curdle, and all Lecha could think about was a Yukon River Indian and his dogsled team. She had watched the handsome racer bend over the tawny lead dog to talk in low, sweet tones; at that instant Lecha had fallen in love with him. Lecha had reasoned a man who was gentle and loving with his sled dogs might be depended on to treat a woman decently. Well, yes and no, she discovered, because the racer had a wife and four kids living upriver. The racer had been conditioning his dogs for the big race, and the distance between the village where Lecha stayed and the village of his wife and kids was just the workout his dogs required—eighty miles round-trip.

By the time Lecha managed to get the dogsled racer off her mind, the talk show host had quieted the widow and settled back in his matching gold velvet armchair. The host dramatically asked Lecha again if she could give a better description of this snowbank. Lecha closed her eyes.

"Snowbank." All Lecha could think of was the spring thaw in Anchorage when the body of an Eskimo man had emerged from a snowpile at the ambulance and emergency entrance of the hospital. Eskimos and Indians had joked that the man had died waiting to be examined by U.S. Indian Health Service doctors.

The talk show host and audience were quiet, waiting on the edges of their seats to hear more about the location of the corpse. Without hesitation, Lecha told them to search snowbanks near local hospitals. The show's host had nodded at the police lieutenant and then at the director's assistant, who had just flashed him the thirty-second signal.

In the women's rest room outside the TV studio Lecha examined the huge half-moon perspiration stains on the new white linen dress. The tension had left her exhausted. No wonder old Yoeme had answered so bitterly when she was accused of being a fraud. Yoeme used to say not many would dare trade their work to perform hers.

Lecha had been relaxing in a hot bath back at the hotel when a radio news bulletin announced the body had been located outside a Boulder, Colorado, hospital. The first phone call had been from the television producer telling her they wanted to have her appear a second time for a follow-up. The second call had been from the police lieutenant to thank her, and to ask if they might list her with the other "psychics" the Denver Police Department contacted from time to time. Lecha told the producer she would have to think it over. She told the cop she would only be staying in Denver another day or two.

Lecha dozed in the hot water and bath salts thinking about the handsome dogsled racer. The best he had ever done in the big race had been fifth. Lecha's handsome racer had carried one of his dogs while his other dogs pulled the sled across the finish line. A white man who followed the handsome racer across the line also carried a dog and had a dead dog lashed to his sled. What had been clear to Lecha that afternoon in Nome was that dogsled racers lived and traveled on a modest human scale. They sewed new dog booties at night along the trail and coaxed and cried over their dogs. Lecha wasn't interested. Two days after the finish of the big dogsled race, she had gone. Lecha made it a rule to leave a place or person *before* she had any regrets. The dogsled racer had been ardent and gentle, but he had not been as important as the two Eskimo women Lecha had met there.

TUNDRA SPIRITS

THE RACER had been in a hurry to take his dog team and sled upriver where his wife was. He had complained jokingly that Lecha had worn his penis raw. The racer had been acquainted with Rose because she had gone to school "down below" in the lower forty-eight. Lecha could tell the racer had slept with Rose when he had come downriver. Rose had carried both Lecha's suitcases and had talked nonstop. Rose had said the first thing Lecha had to understand, if she was going to be a boarder in her house, was this: a terrible thing had happened nine years ago, and nothing could ever be right again. Rose warned Lecha she might notice things in the house were not as they should be. But this was unavoidable, because of the terrible incident.

At this point in the story, they had reached Rose's old log and sod house on a hill above the river. Lecha did not see or feel anything out of the ordinary when she stepped inside and put her things on the bed across from Rose's bed. She did notice the clocks—the old-fashioned kind preferred by all the old folks in Sonora—big clocks that needed keys inserted in their faces to wind them. The clocks filled Rose's little house with their ticking.

"They are set for different times," Rose explained, "because this way I know how much time they would have had if they had lived."

"Who?" Lecha saw no snapshots or graduation photographs.

"My younger sisters and brothers. There were six. Three girls and three boys."

The little children had been left alone many times before. The parents were across the river at the bootlegger's house. Sometimes the parents stayed over there for days. All money went to the bootlegger. The children got cold. The house was only plywood and tar paper covered with tin. There was no stove. Only half of a steel oil drum where they burned kerosene. The oldest child had been a girl of nine. In the dark she went outside for the red fuel can by the father's snowmobile. But the can she had picked up was full of gasoline, not fuel oil. The explosion had blown the plywood and tin shack apart. The village people saw the six children running. Through the dark in a line along the riverbank the children ran in halos of yellow flame that flared higher each time another limb or article of clothing caught fire. "These are your angels of fire. Jesus Christ of the white people!" Rose had interjected. But the children did not quite reach the river. They fell in the snow, drowning in the fluid of their seared lungs.

Rose had dreamed about the fire four consecutive nights in the girls dormitory of the school for Eskimos and Indians. This is what Rose tells Lecha the first afternoon they are together. Nothing could be done. Not even the Yupik dormitory matrons would place a radio-telephone call to the trading-post man. She had been a mother to her sisters and brothers since she was eleven but they refused to allow Rose to go home. Rose did not remember anything after the news of the fire had reached her. School officials had sent Rose south to the psychiatric hospital in Seattle.

"I finished up school down there. I was a day student. At night I slept at the hospital. I tried to talk to the children for a long time. The doctor would ask me what I wanted to say to them. I only wanted to tell them I was sorry. I would have taken care of them if I had been there. I did not want to go away. I never wanted to leave them. I used to cry at night in the dormitory. It took a long time. Finally, after the doctor quit asking about them and started asking about my father and my mother, I had a dream about them. I talked to all the children. They were standing together, smiling at me. They seemed all right and happy. Except they were all in flames, standing there on fire, but never being burned up. The old woman told me later she had seen them too—on that night, and then afterwards, right before dawn, playing together along the river. They were always in flames."

Those nights the dogsled racer stayed upriver with his wife, Lecha had gone with the others to the village meeting hall where government experiments with satellites had brought the people old movies and broad-casts from the University of Alaska. Lecha had sat with her friend Rose. Everyone huddled close to the TV screen. Rose had translated everything that was said, all the wisecracks and remarks that were made in the Yupik Eskimo language. Teenagers who had been away to boarding school stood at the back of the hall whispering and laughing in English and in Yupik. Lecha realized Rose had befriended her because Rose was considered an odd one by the others in the village. Without Rose, Lecha might have been lonely in the downriver village where the older people had nicknamed her the Racer's Workout, and the village teenagers fa-

miliar with television called it "Love, Athabascan Style." The people
had been polite to Lecha, considering the rivalry that had once existed
between the racer's people and the Yupik people downriver.

The broadcast was a home economics show from the University of
Alaska. Even the men had watched closely. Everyone enjoyed making
wisecracks and jokes about the Yupik woman who had been recruited
from a rival village to become a "TV star."

"If she had grown up in our village she'd have a better recipe for
fermented beaver tails," one woman remarked. All the women, even
old, sleepy-looking women, had clapped their hands and caused the
metal folding chairs to squeak and clang with their laughter. Lecha had
looked at Rose and frowned because she was having difficulty appre-
ciating the humor of fermented beaver tails. "Oh," Rose said. "I forgot.
You weren't here when that happened." Rose had smiled and patted
Lecha's arm. "It seems like you've always lived here." Lecha nodded,
although she had not planned to spend the winter in an Eskimo village
eighty miles from the Bering Sea. But Lecha had met the handsome
dogsled racer in the airport bar in Seattle, and he had offered just the
change of scene Lecha had needed.

"The beaver-tail recipe is kind of a sick joke," Rose said, smiling.

"She gave out the beaver-tail recipe one week. Three old women
from a village down river tried the recipe, but instead of doing things
as they had in the old days, when they used to wrap the beaver tails in
seal bladder or wax paper, the three old women used plastic. They placed
the beaver tails in a warm corner behind the stove, like you are supposed
to. They let them ferment three or four days just like the recipe directed.
But when they ate the beaver tails, they were poisoned because plastic
encourages botulism."

Now the television home economist was demonstrating a technique
for making pie crust, but no one was watching. Instead people talked.
Even the teenagers at the back of the community meeting hall were
hunched over cigarettes and giggling and talking, waiting for "Love,
American Style" to come on.

An old woman had begun to speak in a loud voice, and the other
women turned to listen. Rose interpreted for Lecha. The old woman
was saying she was not much impressed with television, except for
movies with men on horses. The old woman repeated she was interested
in horses; otherwise, television did not impress her. She had seen far
more amazing acts performed right there in that very room. It seemed
to Lecha the old woman was looking directly at her, so Lecha leaned

closer to Rose to hear the translation. Lecha was careful not to move her eyes from the old woman, who reminded her of old Yoeme; not because of any physical resemblance, but because of the old woman's command of attention. Even the men, planning hunts or discussing snow-mobile repair, stopped talking and began listening.

"When we have visitors from far away, I wonder if they know why we live here," the old woman said, and reached into a grimy canvas satchel by her feet. Out came a heavy, curved ivory tusk. The old woman held up the tusk for everyone to see. The voices and faces on the television screen could not compete. Two university professors were discussing American foreign policy in Southeast Asia. The old woman was swinging the big walrus tusk around and around her head like a lariat. Lecha glanced at the TV screen and imagined the tusk colliding with their white faces. The old woman was stronger than she looked. Then the old woman lowered the tusk, laughing.

"I know what cowboys do when they ride horses," she said, this time addressing Lecha directly. Lecha nodded; she was not sure where this might end. Suddenly the old woman shifted all her attention away from Lecha and away from all the others in the meeting hall. With all of her might, the old woman began twirling the tusk around and around in both hands. She never took her eyes off the tusk, and Lecha realized no one in that room could move his eyes away either. Lecha did not even attempt to shift her eyes away because the old woman was watching her.

As the ivory twirled, it seemed to become lighter and lighter until the old woman twirled it easily with one hand. Then the surface of the tusk had begun to glisten and sweat; the old woman's hands and the lap of her dress caught luminous drops. Then the twirling of the tusk began to make a sound. At first the sound was faint, and Lecha could still hear the drone of voices on the television. But the whirring sound became louder, and as it did, the shape of the ivory tusk began to change. It spiraled like a giant ocean shell; it spread flat into a disk and then wobbled into a fluted wedge the shape of a fan or a bird's wing. Then the tusk had burst into flames. The whirring sound became very loud then, and Lecha wanted to raise her hands to her ears to block it out, but again she realized she would not be able to lift her arms. Just then the sound began to subside, and the old woman's twirling began to slow, and the ivory tusk lay in her lap once more. Lecha looked up and was surprised to see the old woman had fallen asleep, with her chin pressing on her shoulder.

Rose stood up suddenly. The theme song of "Love, American Style" came on the television as loud as the whirring sound had been. Lecha got up. Her legs were weak. She was exhausted. They walked back to Rose's house in the twilight of the winter sun. The old woman's performance had upset Rose. All Rose could talk about was fire. "The old woman," Rose said, "should not have done that with fire."

Rose heard the voices of her little sisters and brothers.

"Rose," they cried, "come back home and take care of us." Lecha saw tears running down her cheeks.

ESKIMO TELEVISION

THE FOLLOWING DAY Lecha did not see Rose, and when she went back to the community house to watch the national news, there had been only a few people in front of the TV set. Lecha had to laugh at herself for bothering with the world news. Television took her mind off the anxious feeling she had when she was about to travel or move again. The shortwave radio at the priest's house gave daily reports on the Iditarod Race. Her dogsled racer had been running fifth, but was only four hours behind the old Yupik man who had the lead. Lecha had promised to meet the racer in Nome.

The old Yupik woman came into the community hall alone. She did not carry the canvas satchel that had contained the ivory tusk the day before. The old Yupik woman did not seem to notice Lecha. The old woman got as close as she could to the television set, by scooting a folding metal chair across the floor with a terrible sound she seemed not to notice. Someone at the back of the hall laughed at the old woman. Lecha and the old woman both turned. It was Rose. "You should not play with fire," Rose said, and Lecha did not know if Rose was talking to her or the old woman. The old woman spoke no English. Still, Rose seemed to be pointing her finger at the old woman. The few other people in the hall remained quiet. The TV screen flashed satellite weather maps one after another. Rose walked slowly toward the front of the room. She was staring at the television set. "They taught me all about this in school." Rose spoke to the old woman in Yupik, then she sat down beside Lecha and gave a deep sigh. "The old woman wants to know if you want to see more before you go." Lecha nodded. She felt as if she were under the influence of a power such as old Yoeme had possessed.

Lecha had watched the old Yupik woman do it. She stood directly in front of the television set sliding her forefinger over the glass as she spoke Yupik in a clear, low voice. With her eyes half-closed as they had been the afternoon of her performance with the ivory tusk. Rose whispered to Lecha, "Watch. Another plane will crash." Lecha thought Rose might be teasing because she had been laughing. Rose's laughter had become less and less predictable. Rose did not want Lecha to go.

The old woman had not stopped while Lecha and Rose were talking, but the wild laughter caused her to open her eyes. The old woman seemed pained and concerned. "Oh, no! I'm all right!" Rose said. "It's for the little ones, not me!" Rose had been speaking in English, but the old Yupik woman seemed to understand. She narrowed her eyes again and pored over the satellite weather map under her finger on the TV screen. What the old woman had been able to do was quite simple, really. As Rose described it, the old woman had realized the possibilities in the white man's gadgets. Rose had been adamant. "You think I am making all this up. But look at her. Look at where she is pointing on the map right now."

BURNING CHILDREN

ROSE HAD EXPLAINED it using the closest words in English to what the old woman said in Yupik. They had been walking back from the village meeting hall. The old woman had gone off to a granddaughter's house because she heard rumors of fresh seal oil there. Before she left, the old woman had insisted on shaking hands with Lecha. Lecha reached in the pockets of her heavy coat for her leather gloves lined in fox. They had cost $200 in Seattle. As Lecha offered the gloves, the old woman snatched them greedily. She had been smiling and talking to herself as she tried them on.

Rose laughed wildly and shook her head. *"Fur and hair. That's exactly* what she said." The cold, clear air seemed to calm Rose. "Natural electricity. Fields of forces." Rose had looked closely at Lecha as if she were trying to decide how much Lecha really knew about the use of natural forces.

"They rub special fur pelts. Kit fox or weasel," Rose explained. White people could fly circling objects in the sky that sent messages and images of nightmares and dreams, but the old woman knew how to turn the destruction back on its senders.

It had taken the old woman months to perfect her system. The first time the communications satellite transmitting to their village had failed, the village people were told by researchers its batteries were defective. Rose knew better, but kept quiet. The old woman had gathered great surges of energy out of the atmosphere, by summoning spirit beings through recitations of the stories that were also indictments of the greedy destroyers of the land. With the stories the old woman was able to assemble powerful forces flowing from the spirits of ancestors.

It had not been an easy matter to get to the village meeting hall and have the television set to herself. Almost always somebody had been sitting in front of the TV even if they were just staring at the test pattern. Sometimes Rose had helped the old woman by going to the meeting hall first and pretending to hear voices. Rose usually had been able to spook the two or three old men dozing in front of the television set, who did not take chances with angry ghosts. The old woman had to work quickly while she had the TV set and controls of the satellite dish to herself.

Many village people did not trust the old woman. The local Catholic priest had done a good job of slandering the old beliefs about animal, plant, and rock spirit-beings, or what the priest had called the Devil. In her childhood she had watched a medicine woman who took a small quartz crystal found at the edge of the river and used the crystal to see exactly what people living hundreds of miles upriver were doing. Medicine people had quartz crystals that performed like tiny tiny television sets, although lesser medicine people might see actions clearly but not hear what was being said. Although the old woman had tried to stop roaming about the village after midnight to prevent further accusations of sorcery, she could not resist. She had asked Rose to help her the night she perfected her plane-crashing spell.

Inside the meeting hall only the strange bluish light of the television screen lit the room. But the old woman could hear an old man snoring. He was slumped over on the metal folding chairs directly in front of the TV. All the better. Because no one could imagine she would dare perform her mischief with old man Pike sleeping right there. The test pattern was on the screen, but she had used the test pattern last time. It was good to try something a little different. Careful to turn down the volume knob, the old woman tuned in the channel with the satellite weather map and weather information in print below it. She reached into her grimy canvas satchel and pulled out the weasel pelt. Old man Pike kept snoring right along. Thirty years ago she had gone with him upriver to trap mink and beaver. Even then he could not be awakened unless snow was rubbed on his balls.

She rubbed the weasel fur rapidly over the glass of the TV screen, faster and faster; the crackling and sparks became louder and brighter until the image of the weather map on the TV screen began to swirl with masses of storm clouds moving more rapidly with each stroke of the fur. Then the old woman had closed her eyes and summoned all the energy, all the force of the spirit beings furious and vengeful. The old woman intoned the power of the story Rose had told Lecha the first day they met:

"My dear little Rose, you must not see them so often. The fire! The fire gives no warmth. What fire touches becomes brittle as ice. Touch the charred hand, it falls to ashes. Touch the faces. They peel away in your hands. You want to get warm. You are cold. Where are they? The little ones. You often dreamed and you knew. But you can not get there in time. Do they know or is it all soothing—all warmth and no fear to them. They melt. What you find flows in the ashes."

Lecha had never forgotten what had appeared on the television screen at that instant: the junction of the big river and the sea. White steam rises off the river, but gray sea fog rushes over it, rapidly filling the river bank to bank. In the distance there is a sound that wavers in the wind and disappears in the slap of the river against the big rocks. The airplane-engine sound fades in and out with the gusts of wind. The engine strains under full power, climbing. The river presses higher and higher against the banks. The pilot descends, then climbs and descends again, searching for a hole, searching for a break in the fog he entered only a minute earlier. The needle of the compass whirls and shivers in magnetic fields of false and true north. The altimeter is frozen at 2,000 and nothing can dislodge it. The copilot works frantically. They twist the knobs and desperately try to calculate the distance to the ground.

Then the screen goes white. The old woman is doubled over in the chair, arms around herself, rocking slowly, singing to herself in a tiny voice. Years later when the ill-fated Korean Air flight went off course and was shot down in the ocean, Lecha had not been surprised to learn that the magnetic compass of the autopilot had malfunctioned twelve miles north of Bethel, Alaska.

PLANE CRASHES

LECHA AND THE DOGSLED racer flew out of Nome on the same flight. The racer had been too heartbroken to take the seat beside her. Lecha had been able to hear the faint barking of his sled dogs in the baggage hold below. The dogsled racer understood Lecha was leaving because he had not won the race. Earlier he had offered to leave his wife and kids for Lecha, but she had refused. She found it difficult to explain.

"I learned something while I was living up here this winter," Lecha said. "I might never have found it without coming here." The dogsled racer's misery turned to anger. Lecha had thought about trying to reassure him. She did not want to see him sad, but there wasn't any way to avoid sadness, so she took a seat next to a well-dressed white man with a briefcase. He was an insurance adjustor celebrating his return to the home office in Seattle, and he bought her drinks all the way to Fairbanks. After she had deplaned in Anchorage, Lecha realized her Athabascan dogsled racer had already gone to make sure the baggage handlers took care with his dogs and the sled. Anchorage was where the racer caught the mail plane to the villages, and Lecha got on a plane to Seattle. The insurance adjustor had a seat on the same flight to Seattle. He was getting seat assignments for both of them. Lecha could hear the sled dogs barking and whining, but she walked into the terminal building without looking back.

The insurance adjustor punched in his favorites on the airport bar jukebox. "Spanish Eyes" was for her, he said. He was very drunk on Black Russians. She wondered if she would be able to endure him all the way to Seattle. In those days Lecha had still got sad when she left a lover. The dogsled racer had been ordinary. Lecha didn't know why leaving him made her sad. Old Yoeme would have said leaving a dull lover was cause for celebration. Look how happy Rose and the old Yupik woman had been as Lecha climbed aboard the little airplane. The old woman had shouted something, and Rose translated, "She says she won't crash *this* airplane! Don't worry!" Lecha had nodded and waved back to them. Yes. Lecha had seen what the old Yupik woman could do with only a piece of weasel fur, a satellite weather map on a TV screen and the spirit energy of a story.

After takeoff for Seattle, the insurance man started to talk about the wild and exciting life he led with his company. They were the largest single insurer of petroleum exploration companies in Alaska. Now that the big push was on, the energy exploration companies had hundreds of employees, and millions of dollars' worth of sophisticated electronic equipment flying all over the frozen wastes. "Frozen wastes"—the insurance man really believed there was no life on the tundra, nothing of value except what might be under the crust of snow and earth. "Oil, gas, uranium, and gold," Lecha said, nodding. She was beginning to think she wasn't so smart after all because she had let this yahoo get a seat beside her. But just as she was about to move to another seat, the last Black Russian took hold of the insurance adjustor. Here comes the story about his wife, Lecha thought. But instead he wrestled his briefcase out from under the seat and opened it. It was full of forms and a stack of eight-by-ten glossy photographs. Before Lecha could make out the black-and-white images, he plopped a print into her lap. At first it appeared to be blank, but then she realized it was snow-covered tundra against a high overcast sky. White on white. The only figure in the field of white was that of a V partially buried in the snow. Lecha shook her head. She couldn't make out what it was.

"The tail," he said. "The fuselage is completely buried."

"Oh."

"An airplane. What's left of a Beachcraft Bonanza. We lost the pilot, one geologist, and a quarter-million-dollar sensor unit." The insurance adjustor spread the other eight-by-tens on the fold-down trays in front of both of them. The corpses had been draped with blankets. The focal point of the photographs seemed to be the scattered, mangled electronic equipment. Against the snow, the bundles of wires torn loose from the shattered black metal boxes reminded her of intestines. Engine oil appeared like black pools of what might have been blood. "Do you have any idea of the cost of the claims to our company?" Lecha shook her head. He was fumbling with more photographs, and this time she could see the crushed propeller and nose of a plane that had broken in half on impact. In the close-ups, an arm dangled out of the front section of the wreckage. Lecha pretended to be squeamish, and the man gathered up the photographs hastily. But then he had unfolded a topographical map of northwestern Alaska and the Bering Sea. Red Xs were scattered between the Yukon and Kuskokwim rivers. Red Xs clustered around the towns of Bethel and Nome. Before he spoke, Lecha knew what he was going to tell her. There had been dozens of unexplained plane crashes.

The insurance man was shaking his head, and Lecha was aware of the odor of alcohol on his breath. "Whiteout," he said. "Blue sky and sunshine at five thousand feet and then thin clouds or mist. Suddenly a cloud bank or fog. A tiny storm front—not much more than a squall. But they can't fly out of it. The pilot goes up and it becomes more dense. The pilot drops down and it becomes more dense. The pilot banks sharply to go back to the hole where they first entered and it's gone."

Much of Lecha's life had been spent listening to people when she already knew the story they were telling, and more; more than she might ever reveal. So to break the monotony she asked about radar and altimeters and other sophisticated equipment. He was on the last Black Russian the flight attendant was going to allow him. He blinked dumbly at the map with red Xs, then slowly began trying to refold it. Then he remembered Lecha's question about radar and electronic equipment. He drew himself up as straight as he could and shook a finger at her. "Electromagnetic fields! They raise hell with everything—the compass, all the navigational equipment! Instruments and radios malfunction. Like that movie, that movie, ah—" Lecha had to help him sit back in his seat. *"The Bermuda Triangle,"* she said. "Yeah, that's it," he mumbled. Lecha thought he had passed out, but he opened his eyes once more and said, "None of that stuff is true. It can all be explained." Then he sank back in his seat.

SEVERED HEADS

LECHA HAD LIED to doctors in strange cities, telling them the pain was caused by cancer so they'd prescribe Percodan. As she rode in the taxi from the airport to the broadcast studios in downtown Miami, she realized the "gift," her power to locate the dead, was the cause of her pain. The dream she had had on the plane had been a sort of narrative in code. She had dreamed she was tied and unable to escape. She knew there was no possibility of escape, and although she could not see her captor, she knew very soon he would begin to kill her slowly, first cutting away parts of her body, sexual organs, working slowly so that she would not die until he was nearly finished. But just as she was feeling paralyzing horror, there had come an awareness so sudden and terrifying that she had jerked herself awake. She was the torturer. She was the killer.

Suddenly in a rosy, clear light of sun just risen, a voice inside her had begun speaking. She was not sure how long she had. She only knew she could not go on much longer with this business of daytime television "psychic" and special assignments to police departments. She sensed the change as if the power were turning its face, and its eyes, to look toward the world that was emerging.

The assistant producers were running back and forth with pages of dialogue for the teleprompters. The television cameras were gliding and shifting over the bare concrete floor with a dozen camera assistants dragging cables to prevent tangles. Lecha was reminded of bridal gowns, long lace and satin trains requiring many attendants to keep them from catching in doorways or around corners. Lecha curled her feet under the armchair on the talk show set. Her feet were chilled. She had learned how to dress for television—short sleeves, cool fabrics against the heat of the lights, but her feet always got cold. TV studios were all alike— underground, cold concrete floors, and snarls of black cable thicker than her arms. Television was the same everywhere she had ever appeared. No wonder daytime television viewers were interested in all the bizarre and freakish ways one might be injured or fall ill, all the terrifying, hideous ways a psychopath might torture and kill his victims, all the possible and apparently innocent actions that lead up to the disappearance and loss of a small child. The lights they used in television studios must be related somehow to napalm: the light burns the air itself, burns anything it shines on.

Weeks on the regional daytime talk show circuit had prepared Lecha for the freezing feet and sweaty forehead, but she never quite got over the talk show hosts, who did not know what to say and had to read each word on the teleprompter. She had learned a lot since the first time she had appeared on a TV talk show. One thing was to get there an hour early to make sure the producers had her check, implying that otherwise she might not go on the air. Other than that, the work was easy. The hosts always asked her the same questions. Was she Indian and what kind? How did she learn she had this psychic power? And of course, which were the most important cases she had ever worked on? Lecha had three cases she cited, although she did not think it possible to judge "importance." To the family or loved one the loss of the beloved was incalculable. Lecha used to talk about the cases that did not end in death, although these had always been rare cases, and in time, they had become even more scarce. But television audiences didn't want to hear about those cases; TV viewers were mainly interested in death. Whatever had been in the news most recently was what they wanted Lecha to talk about. Today they were going to want to know all about the corpses of the fourteen young boys Lecha had located in the beach dunes of a state park north of San Diego.

The studio audience streamed down the aisles. Lecha closed her eyes so she didn't have to see them and tried to relax before the show. She is still feeling faint aftershocks of the headache the two San Diego detectives had induced the day before. She feels a reluctance to talk about San Diego. She feels something inside her balking, and she pictures goats from her childhood in Potam, goats that spread the toes of their cloven hooves and dug into the earth refusing to be led or even dragged against their will.

The talk show host is an aging white man who wears heavy makeup. Lecha wants to close her eyes again. Ideally they would do the show with her eyes closed and tell the viewers and studio audience it was necessary in order for her psychic powers to function at their best. Talk show hosts are the television managements' idea of what women want to watch. Watch doing what? is the question, Lecha thinks. She is good at imagining sex with men. Lecha has taken the time to check out some of her hunches, and although she never talks about it, her "powers" extend into the bed. She watches closely the way the host walks, stops to talk with one of the producers, and then disappears behind banks of long drapes. The keys to this guy are the carefully tweezed and shaped eyebrows. Lecha can't get past his eyebrows to imagine herself in bed with him. So while the host with the perfect eyebrows and the rest of the crew stumble over jungle snakes of electrical cable, Lecha thinks about high voltage that causes brain tumors. She thinks about tropical lands. Giant dams in the jungles. Hydroelectric power. Guerrillas as quiet and smooth as snakes. Break open the dams and the electric motors of the machinery, machinery that belongs to the masters, stutter to a halt. She has images of these places, because she always reads her newspapers, she always has since she first took up her line of work. Tropical lands. Old tourism movies of Mexico City. The floating gardens of Xochimilco. Didn't the priest in Potam always talk on and on about the heights of Spanish culture? And didn't old Yoeme always say that priest was full of *caca*, with his lecher stories of devil-men shadowing young schoolgirls who wore even a touch of rouge?

The smiling host joins Lecha on the talk show set, and the studio audience is hushed by the teleprompters and sweating production assistants. The show rolls right along, until the host asks about San Diego and the body count still headlining news nationwide. Lecha smiles. She is wearing a conservative black dress, carrying a black kid purse that matches her high heels. She keeps her hair shoulder length. There is no gray. Lecha smiles and prepares to confound them. Her prim appearance makes her refusal to discuss the San Diego case more shocking to the host and studio audience.

"But the killer is dead. The case will be closed as soon as all the bodies are recovered," the talk show host says, still smiling, not comprehending what is about to happen. This sudden twist means his teleprompter is of no use. He stalls and then takes a quick, desperate look at the teleprompter to see if the producers can get him out of this one. He asks why she won't talk about it, and Lecha answers that she does not feel like explaining. Although she is speaking in a calm, level tone, her refusal brings scattered laughs and tittering from the studio audience. Fortunately, time is running out for this half of the show, and at last something scribbled hastily appears on the teleprompter. The host is angered now because he has been refused, and because there have been titters from the studio audience. "Well, then," the host says in oily tones that barely smooth the sarcasm, "you can't go leaving us empty-handed. We had our hearts set on—" He stops before he finishes that sentence. Lecha nods and smiles. She is familiar with ghoulish disappointment. They must have at least one thrill. At least one hair-raiser or spine-tingler.

"Well, let's have a little demonstration here. How about next week's headlines? How about you take a look into that crystal ball—" The host held up Lecha's purse in a vulgar gesture, as if he were trying to determine whether it contained a crystal ball. Lecha had been watching the faces and reactions of the studio audience; she was also aware of the sweat beginning to erode the makeup on the host's face. But while Lecha was seeing all of this, she had been aware of the voice that had recently raised itself inside her; the voice also had eyes. And while her eyes had been watching the audience and the host, these other eyes had been watching the mossy water of the canals of the floating gardens. Lecha describes the gardens of Xochimilco, with the water lilies, yellow and pink blossoms, and the reeds and cattails parting gently to the prow of the small flat-bottom boat. Then up ahead she sees a bright red and yellow woven-plastic shopping bag floating in the dark green water. There are two large objects visible through the plastic netting. But here the talk show host interrupts, afraid that the Indian woman is just killing time, setting him up with a dumb story about floating gardens and floating trash. "So far I don't see this one making next week's headlines," he says, and is gratified when the studio audience laughs at his cleverness. But Lecha does not hesitate. She repeats the sentence he interrupted and immediately there is silence, and Lecha has them on the canal as the little boat draws even with the brightly colored shopping bag. Inside the bag there are two human heads, their blue eyes open wide, staring at the sky.

The studio audience gasps and breaks into applause. It is clear the Indian woman has won them from him again. He is forced to a last, desperate shot. Summoning his most mocking tone, he asks Lecha, "Who are these heads?" smirking at his clever phrasing. But again Lecha does not hesitate. "They are the U.S. ambassador to Mexico, and his chief aide," she says, and this time there is a long silence before the host or anyone in the audience moves.

SUDDEN RETIREMENT

THE FOLLOWING MORNING while Lecha is packing in the hotel room a news break interrupts reruns of "I Love Lucy." The U.S. ambassador to Mexico and his chief aide had been caught in an ambush by Indian guerrillas outside Mexico City. The ambassador and his aide were missing.

A cold chill swept over Lecha. The FBI and CIA would send agents after her for debriefing. The hair on her scalp and neck tingled. Lecha reached into the pouch inside one of her long kimonos and pulled out a small leather case from a special inner pocket. Her old standby. Birth certificate, Social Security card, and Arizona driver's license. She does not cancel the plane reservations to New York, but she makes reservations for Tucson under another name. This had happened before, and days had been wasted with stupid questions by agents who wanted to connect Lecha with the crime she'd just helped solve. But this one, this time would be far worse, especially when they found out she was an Indian, born in Mexico.

She was out of business much sooner than she'd thought she'd be. She'd head for Tucson and get hold of Root. He managed to keep out of the way of the law. And there were always Zeta and Ferro, the two of them obsessed with security measures, dog packs, and laser alarms. Events were moving much faster than she had expected. The yield from the green water of the floating gardens was proof of that.

Lecha left messages for Root at three or four of the biker bars he liked. He traveled only by taxi now because of his disabilities, but he would always prefer the company of bikers.

Lecha has forgotten how cold the rain can be. Tucson for her has always been the dry heat in June. A hundred three degrees, six percent humidity, and the cicadas breaking into song over the good weather. The wind blows the rain against the metal panels of the house trailer Root rents. The gusts make the "green beast" shudder. Lecha had taken one look at the big old-timer and had named it that. Root was uncomfortable. Lecha wonders if he is afraid the name means she is moving in for a long time. She laughs at him. He looks at her with the blue eyes that seldom blink. He tells her he does not like to hear fun made at the expense of beasts, monsters, or anything ugly and big. They both know what he means. Lecha had hoped that as Root got older he might develop more of a sense of humor. The wind and the rain are pounding the house trailer. Lecha remembers the Midwestern storms that have such appetites for house trailers. She wonders if anyone in Tucson would have the imagination to anchor a house trailer against high winds as they do in other places. Probably not. Life has always been cheap in Tucson.

The pounding can't be the wind. Lecha opens the narrow trailer door just a crack and gets a face full of rain from the wind. Then Lecha sees a person standing at the foot of the metal trailer steps. The woman is wearing a flimsy, clear-plastic raincoat, and under it Lecha can see a T-shirt and blue jeans. The woman has been knocking on the side of the trailer instead of coming up the steps to the door. Lecha thinks this also is typical of a town such as Tucson. People here can't seem to do things in the ordinary fashion. The blonde is thin and probably young. Lecha can't see much in the dark and the storm. The expression on the face seems desperate enough to belong to an old woman. Lecha assumes this is one of Root's customers, one of those young women who swap sex for drugs.

But when the blonde sees Lecha's face, her desperate expression breaks into one of disbelief and then joy. "Oh, Jesus!" the blonde says, trying to wipe away the rain and strands of wet hair from her face, stumbling toward the trailer steps. "I never thought I'd find you! I need your help." Lecha hasn't been in Tucson for more than forty-eight hours. Only Root had known Lecha was coming. Lecha keeps her eyes on the *gringa*'s red and swollen eyes; it is as if the blonde is a newborn creature of some sort, not accustomed to light above ground. Lecha had never been tracked down before by a client. She took pride in her control over her private life. One of the chief occupational hazards of clairvoyants and palm readers was to live under siege by the desperately lonely, and those so crazed it was impossible ever to learn what had been lost.

Lecha does not like the sudden appearance of someone looking for her. It might be the authorities. She might not have got out of Miami fast enough. "Anyone who tracks me down doesn't need me. Go find it yourself!" Lecha yells this as she slams the trailer door in Seese's face. Root comes out of the bedroom rubbing his eyes. "Who was that?" "I never saw her before." Root pats the front pocket of his baggy jeans for his compact .380 automatic. He opens the trailer door slowly, only a crack, turning his face away from the blowing rain. Then he steps outside with bare feet and closes the door behind him. A minute later he comes back inside shaking the rain off his head; his white T-shirt is soaked and clings to the beer belly hanging over his sagging jeans. "I think she's all right," Root says, "one of those clients of yours looking for her kid. I told her to come back later. That you are busy." Root limps toward the kitchen area and opens the refrigerator to get a beer. When he is tired, his right foot drags more than it usually does. The steel plate in his head had set off the airport security machine's alarm. He had brought Lecha a dozen red roses. The airline employee pushing her wheelchair had thought Root was Lecha's son. Lecha is proud of the age difference. The wheelchair is a prop. Lecha didn't want to be caught walking with suitcases full of Demerol and Percodan. Root studies her. "I thought you were dying." Lecha seldom bothers to look in mirrors anymore. Occasionally she does catch a glimpse of herself in plate glass windows or chrome trim on a car. For television she leaves the face for their makeup people to worry about. She hardly recognizes the woman she sees in the mirror, although she knows it is "herself," whatever that means. Years ago Lecha realized she had never seen any person, animal, place, or thing look the same twice. Some mornings Lecha has awakened to find a haggard, wrinkled face with Korean eyes watching her from the mirror. Other mornings, just waking up with a man in the bed beside her gives her a face in the mirror like the one she saw in the mirror when she was nineteen.

"It's cancer," Lecha lies. "But I'll last awhile."

BOOK SEVEN

WEST TUCSON

ROOT'S GRANDPA GORGON

ROOT FINISHES one beer and opens another. He offers Lecha one but she says cold beer is no good in this kind of weather. "What kind of weather?" Root says right back, and Lecha has to smile at the deadpan delivery. She throws an arm around his shoulder and kisses his neck. They settle on the couch together and listen to the wind pound the rain against the trailer. Root always was moody even before the accident. She had been forty and he had been nineteen when she had first seen him with some of Calabazas's young cousins. Lecha had always preferred short men with barrel chests on the stocky side.

They had been sleeping together only a few months when Root crashed his motorcycle. Lecha had known it would happen. It didn't take a clairvoyant to see that Root with high handle bars on the low Harley chopper would not last. Before the accident, Calabazas had not paid much attention to Root. Calabazas would only grunt when Lecha brought up the subject. Calabazas had had a run-in with Root's great-grandfather, the old Mexican Gorgon, years before. Old Gorgon had kept the whorehouses and gambling halls in Tucson. That was all Tucson had been in the 1880s, Calabazas liked to say. By the time Root was born, the family had shrewdly consolidated its holdings. Root's grandmother still owned all of the low-rent property south of downtown. "You know they got rich off the Indian wars," Calabazas said. "That's where the Irishman came in. The old man hired him to go out with a wagon and some mules to bootleg whiskey, which was illegal for the Apaches as well as U.S. troops on active duty." The demand for Gorgon's whiskey forever exceeded the supply. Corn, oats, or rye were too expensive to use for the brewing mash, so Gorgon had experimented with different recipes. Gorgon's whiskey was distilled from a fermented mash of jojoba and mesquite beans with just a shovelful of cracked corn to suggest the bourbon flavor the U.S. troops, mostly scraggly Southerners, had come to expect. Once distilled, the liquor was given a last cut—two parts Santa Cruz water, one part formaldehyde—to prevent "spoilage" in wooden barrels on Kirkpatrick's wagon. Only an Irishman or a drunk would have taken that job, but Kirkpatrick was both. The job was to stay out on the desert trails, as close as possible to both the U.S. troops hunting the Apaches and the Apaches hunting the U.S. troops. Ideally, the old man told the Irishman, he should try to keep his wagonload of whiskey cut with river water and formaldehyde right in the middle of things. Stories about old Gorgon were full of clues about Root. Gorgon's daughter married Kirkpatrick. Gorgon's daughter had clearly married beneath herself, but she had also entertained high hopes that the children would distinguish the family name. Root's mother had been a Tucson debutante. Root's mother had forbidden him and his sisters and brothers to play with the children of military families sent to Tucson during the war. Root's mother had not allowed Mexican playmates; Grandfather Gorgon, Root's mother had explained, was of "*Spanish* descent," not Mexican.

ROOT'S ACCIDENT

ROOT'S MOTHER had been engrossed in forcing her simple husband to live up to the name of the family he'd married into. Root liked to say that his father had lasted long enough to sire eight of them, and then he had dropped dead. Driven to death just as old Gorgon was supposed to have driven a team of mules to death, explaining later that the mules were worn-out and used up, and he had a chance to close a big business deal in Nogales if he was willing to press the mule team harder. Root was always bitter when he talked about his father and mother. Root preferred to say that all his family had died in his accident. That the instant his skull had bounced off the car bumper, mother, grandmother, sisters, and brothers died. When he woke up months later, each one had to be introduced to him, and the night after meeting his mother and the rest, Root had cried himself to sleep in the hospital room. "Because," Root told Lecha, "I knew they weren't really my family. All they cared about was how much I was going to cost them, and whether I was going to mean extra work for anyone."

Lecha had noticed Root right away because he had looked at her defiantly as he kick-started his motorcycle and had then roared around Calabazas's big yard in mad circles until the corralful of burros and mules threatened to stampede. Then, calculating just the point before Calabazas would come out of the house yelling, Root had turned off the engine and glided his motorcycle back to its place under the big cottonwood tree.

Lecha had let Root fuck her the first few times because he had a crush on her and he was wild and young. She told him he had a lot to learn. Meaning that he couldn't get it in without its spewing all over the sheets. But after he got out of the hospital, six months after the accident, with slurred speech, a leg that dragged, Root had stayed hard no matter how long she fucked him. In those days Lecha had not thought twice about the men she was fucking. There were too many to think about. But the few times she had been in the mood, she had got his phone number from Calabazas, because Root worked full-time for him by then. Calabazas had hired him for many reasons as it turned out. One was old Gorgon had once hired Calabazas many years before. But the main reason was Root's brain damage made a perfect front for them. Root took day and night classes at the community college. He carried gram packets of cocaine in the plastic pencil bag hooked inside his loose-leaf notebook. He used the pauses and slurs to his advantage. In the college snack bar joking with classmates after class, or with the narcotics officers who tried to shake him down. Root could deliver a punch line or an insult with mock innocence, to force strangers to realize that even with only part of a brain, he was smarter and quicker than they were. He was going to school to learn to read and write all over again, Root liked to tell undercover cops, to get them off his trail. He had enrolled in speech therapy class every semester but never attended. "I didn't want," he'd say, slowly forming each word, "I didn't want to spoil a good thing like this with speech therapy." Root would laugh, and Lecha realized he meant he had finished with the world where those things mattered.

Lecha let the blue silk kimono slip open to see what he'd do. But Root was intent on pinning down her illness. She'd called him collect from a phone booth at the airport in Miami. She had not intended to mention the illness, but Root had sounded short, a little irritated by the collect call. So she said, "I've got cancer, and I'm dying." Root had only grunted, but then at the airport he met her with roses. Until then Root had never bought her anything except taxi rides. When Lecha left Tucson, she had not thought about seeing him again. She had not thought about Root at all, except when she saw cripples or people with palsy, and then she would merely wonder what he was up to and forget him again. But when she began making stopovers and short stays in Tucson, she found she could depend on Root. He had an account with Yellow Cab, and although he only rented house trailers, they were always clean and she had always had a place to sleep and more if she wanted. Root always took the mangled motorcycle with him when he moved and parked it outside the rented trailers. He said he kept it to remind him where he'd been and where he'd come back from. A Plymouth bumper two inches into his skull had not stopped him the message ran, so the punks better think twice about pushing him around.

"You can't stay here," Root says slowly, peeling at the beer label with one finger.

"Because of that woman?"

Root shakes his head. "Business," he says, reaching over to pat Lecha's bare thigh.

That was okay because Lecha had to see Zeta and Ferro sooner or later. It might as well be sooner. At the ranch she would not be hounded by hysterical blondes who had seen her on daytime television. "I wonder what she wanted."

"Who?"

"That woman."

"Someone who knows Cherie."

"Cherie?"

"Cherie is all right," Root answers. "She's a dancer at the Stage Coach."

Lecha looks down at her own tit dangling out of the blue kimono. She hefts it in one hand the way she's seen strippers display themselves. "An old potato," Lecha says. "More like an old cantaloupe," Root says, taking her breast in both hands, pretending he wants to make a meal of it. She slides down on the sofa and the kimono falls away; even the long, full sleeves slide off. When Root was in his twenties, and even into his early thirties, he had been her slave. He would have done anything she asked. But now Root had said "business," and he had meant it. Lecha had always made it a practice to avoid calendars and clocks except where business required them. Because they were not true. What was true was a moment such as this, warm sweat sliding over their bellies so smoothly that despite everything, the size of Root's beer belly or her old full-moon ass, the connection was as hot as it had ever been, the charge bolted through like lightning. Let the years dry up the cantaloupes or potatoes as long as there's still the electricity.

SHALLOW GRAVES

SEESE IS ANXIOUS to begin working with Lecha immediately to transcribe and type the old notebooks and papers. Certain answers lie within the ragged, stained pages. Answers to problems and questions Lecha must have before they begin the search for Monte. But once Lecha has settled into her big bed, she announces work on the old notebooks and papers must not interfere with work that "brings home the bacon."

Seese learns to sort the mail into two categories: new business and old. Old business consisted of the successful clients still sending Lecha money orders and cashier's checks with letters that thanked Lecha again and again. New business wasn't so easy. Reading the letters had coiled the old sadness tight in her chest, and she had been shocked how easily she had returned to vodka and cocaine in her bedroom.

Nothing prepares Seese for the phone calls she must transcribe. A woman calls long distance from Florida. Her voice starts out clear and in control, but grief pushes to the surface, and when she gets to the color of the T-shirt, she gasps as if there is no more air in her lungs: "I know I should remember which one it was, but he was always changing clothes all day, you know. He liked to put on the Snoopy T-shirt, but then after "Sesame Street" he liked the one with the little Grover puppet on it." The woman agonizes over the color of the T-shirt she can not remember, worn by the child she will never see again. The woman describes the sneakers over and over again— blue Keds—repeating details again and again as if to prove to herself she had been a good mother although her child is gone. They called. They sent cash and an article of the missing person's clothing or a stuffed toy.

Even with cocaine again, Seese can't bear transcribing the phone calls. Lecha claims she enjoys talking on the telephone. Seese grits her teeth and slashes open envelopes with Lecha's Mexican dagger.

Seese had only read a dozen or so plea letters before she read the letter that stopped her. Without a greeting, date, or return address, a big manila envelope had come registered and certified first class. "Right there you know you got something happening," Lecha alerted Seese. *Happening* meant a cashier's check had also fallen out of a wad of typewritten pages. Anything over $500 American in new business had to be carefully considered. Every fragment, scrap, and dim memory the client might have must be meticulously reported. Lecha said they had to stop the telephone calls because no check or money order fell out of the phone.

The letters and messages Lecha got had been the exact opposite of nightmares or daydreams. The letters were invariably lists of facts, re- citations of precise locations at hours and minutes of specific months and days: height, weight, eye and hair color, descriptions of birthmarks, jewelry, and clothes. From the facts Lecha's task was to find the appro- priate or accurate emblems or dreams. Lecha said the world had all it ever needed in the way of figures and facts anyway. Lecha admitted it was difficult to understand. A matter of faith or belief. Knowledge. Or maybe grace. Something like that. Lecha only had to slit open an en- velope or listen to a recording of a long-distance phone message, and suddenly she would seize the tin ammo box full of crumpled pages and notes and sift them carefully until a single word or a short phrase revealed "the clue" to her.

Seese must remember it was only a "clue." No one but the client would ever be able to understand fully the clue's meaning. On occasion Lecha had reluctantly agreed to accept yet another fee to determine for the client the message or clue. More risk was involved in reading the clue. There were all kinds of reasons for this. Seese nodded. It was all right with Seese if Lecha sent clients weird or unintelligible messages. As long as everyone understood.

Any psychic worth her salt knew even before she opened an envelope the nature of the message inside. Words inscribed by terrified, haunted people in nightmare hours after midnight were useless and often mis- leading. It didn't matter what the letters or messages said. Each story had many versions. Had Seese heard about Freudian theory? Seese nod- ded. Lecha had got herself warmed up. Freud had interpreted frag- ments—images from hallucinations, fantasies, and dreams—in terms patients could understand. The images were messages from the patient to herself or himself.

Lecha continued with her crackpot theories: Freud had sensed the approach of the Jewish holocaust in the dreams and jokes of his patients. Freud had been one of the first to appreciate the Western European appetite for the sadistic eroticism and masochism of modern war. What did Seese think Jesus Christ symbolized anyway?

Nothing had prepared Seese for the work on Lecha's notebook. Lecha insists that Seese type up each and every letter or word fragment however illegible or stained. Lecha wants her personal notebook transcribed and typed because it is necessary to understanding the old notebooks Yoeme left behind. Lecha tells Seese not to be disappointed. The old notebooks are all in broken Spanish or corrupt Latin that no one can understand without months of research in old grammars. Lecha had already done translation work, and her notebooks contained narratives in English.

Lecha's Notebook

After days of searing heat the Earth no longer cools at night. The wind carries away the heat for a few hours, and by dawn the air is motionless, and a faint warmth emanates from luminous pale ridges of limestone and tufa. The lower skirts of leaves of jojoba and brittle bushes are parched white and shriveled from drought.

What can you tell by the color of their eyes?

Dead children were eaten by survivors during times of great famine.

Late August afternoon wind stirs a blue wash of rain clouds over the edge of the southwest horizon. Humidity increases. The paloverde's thin, green bark glows with moisture off the ocean wind from Sonora.

Meaning lies in the figures and colors of the killer's tattoos. Meaning lies in the particular disarray of the victim's underclothes.

The killer's blue eyes dilate with rage so the victim sees only the empty blackness of her own grave. The killer keeps victims long enough to wash and curl their hair, and to clean and paint the victim's finger and toenails with pink polish sold at thousands of drugstores.

The computer posits models of possible routes taken by the abductor and victim.

The abductor drives the victim west and then north into the desert foothills.

According to the computer model, the child killer acts within the first fifteen minutes after the abduction.

The abductor can wait no longer. In his excitement he accidentally makes a long, shallow cut in his own upper thigh. He has always savored the chill of steel alongside the shaft of his own cock while he pulled and beat it off.

A black, late-model sedan is parked at the mouth of a dry arroyo next to a dirt road.

The purpose of the shallow grave is twofold: to hide the shameful incriminating evidence, and to prevent the loss of the beloved corpse.

The photograph appears to be of a common grave scratched out of the Sonoran Desert gravel; scraps of cloth, bleached translucent by the sun, flutter in the wind above bits of hair and bones.

The Santa Cruz River has been running at low, summer flood-level for weeks. The mother sends the little girl a short distance, no more than two city blocks, to mail a letter.

The little girl rides off on her bike—and never comes back. Later, younger neighborhood children tell how a black car bumps her off her bicycle and a man lifts her into the black car. The small pink bicycle is found lying in the weeds on Root Lane near her home.

Computers posit models of possible routes taken by the abductor. Blue-pencil grids divide the map of the area west and north of the little girl's home. Search teams are assigned blocks within the grids. Teams on horseback and all-terrain motorcycles comb the scrubby greasewood on the gray alluvial ridges that parallel the Santa Cruz River.

Plastic surveyor's ribbons in white or light yellow are tied on branches of mesquite or jojoba after each of the twenty acre squares has been searched. After each square in the blue-pencil grid has been searched, a Sherriff's Department volunteer draws a red X over the square.

On the morning of the third day of the search, family members bring the little girl's favorite doll, a long-tail monkey sewed and stuffed with brown cotton work socks, and a pair of the child's pink tennis shoes for bloodhounds brought from the state penitentiary.

Bloodhounds are not as effective in desert terrain. Damp-woods paths and lush foliage hold scents for hours, sometimes days. The dog handler estimates the dogs must be set on a trail within the first three hours or the desert's dry, hot air obliterates the scent trail. It's all scientific, the dog man explains. Heat expands scent molecules. Pushes molecules apart—scatters them. Desert gravel and sand for an hour, and the heat and the wind evaporate molecules into dust.

You don't believe they can send you all of this in one or two letters—dozens of newspaper clippings and photographs—yet week after week they do. You don't know them. Don't know who they are. Still they imagine you may have some sort of power to bring their little girl back to them.

The child's father joins the search, while her stepfather remains with her mother. They do not go to the temporary search headquarters near the bridge on the Santa Cruz River. The child's mother waits next to the telephone with the reverend from the Church of Christ, Scientist. The call the mother waits for is from California or New Mexico. She has read about it before. Kidnappers who mean no harm to the child. Perhaps they have lost a child of their own.

Seese watched them together. The two old women. Identical twins who no longer resembled one another except when they spoke. Zeta had only to pause an instant before her wide, dark face relaxed into a brief smile. "Oh . . . ," Zeta had said. "You are going to copy her book. . . ." "Well," Lecha had said, her eyes dreamy and distant, "You could say 'her book,' but of course the book will be mine."

ARMS DEALER

WHEN ZETA THOUGHT of her father, she liked to go walking down the ridge behind the ranch house where he had walked with her and Lecha that day so long ago. She had been adamant about the security systems and fences. She did not want them to interfere with the trails she took for her walks. Because the trails were far older even than the ranching and mining that had gone on in those mountains. The trails themselves extended out of another time, and Zeta had found that walking along them enabled her to reach insights and ideas that otherwise were inaccessible.

When she walked, she always carried the 9mm in the deep pocket concealed in the fullness of her dark brown skirt. She had been surprised one day to notice that the long full skirts and dark blouses and suit coats she wore were much like a religious habit. She was able to affect the appearance of an old woman, but was also able to dress as Lecha did and give the impression of a woman barely past forty-five. Lecha did it to attract men. Zeta did it to throw the others off her trail. If Zeta wore pants, they were the English riding pants for women, and she would have had the sewing lady sew a deep pocket in them too for the 9mm. Ferro had given her a two-shot .38-caliber derringer for Christmas that year and a boot holster for it, but she preferred not to wear boots during the hot season.

She did not have to walk far to escape the presence of the house and the guard dogs and other people. She wondered if her father had felt the distance that could be gained by walking there. The desert shrubs, cactus, mesquite, and paloverde grew lush from the steep sides of the hills and ridges, which were only the debris, the ruin, of the great volcano that had once presided over the entire valley.

When she came to the large flat stone the size of an anvil but four times as heavy, Zeta used to wish her father had taught her about meteorites. Late at night, when she and Ferro had waited on the ridge or had ridden horseback into the steep canyons to wait for a drop, she had watched the meteor showers. They would begin shortly after midnight and continue until two A.M. On those nights it seemed as if the sky had overtaken the earth and was closing over it, so that the volcanic rocks and soil themselves reflected light like the surface of a moon. At those moments she could not think of any other place on the earth that she would rather be. She thought about the old ones and Yoeme and how they had watched the night skies relentlessly, translating sudden bursts and trails of light into lengthy messages concerning the future and the past. Yoeme claimed it had all been written down, in another form of course, in the notebooks, which she had waved in their faces almost from the beginning.

Now Lecha had returned with the notebooks and claimed she was ready to begin the work Yoeme had entrusted to her years ago.

"We must be getting old if Lecha is coming back complaining about a little thing like cancer," Calabazas had said a few weeks before. He had been talking retirement, but Zeta knew him better than to believe it. Calabazas would never abandon what he called "the war that had never ended," the war for the land. He wanted to call every successful shipment or journey a victory in this "war." Zeta had not argued with him, but she had her own ideas about "the war."

What did they say about fairness and love and war? What did they say about strange bedfellows? The older Zeta got the less she could remember the English expressions. They had smuggled truck tires during the Second World War. They had begun to get requests for ammunition and guns of any kind; there was a growing demand for explosives—Dyalite© with blasting caps. Guns had always moved across the border, in a southerly direction, unless they were illegal weapons—Chinese automatic rifles or sawed-off shotguns. Zeta and Calabazas had finally parted company. Calabazas had wanted to stay strictly with dope. Because with guns there was politics, right off the bat. Zeta had argued with Calabazas for years. They had always been at war with the invaders. For five hundred years, the resistance had fought. Calabazas might avoid it for another five years, at most ten. But sooner or later politics would come knocking at his door; because dope was good as gold; and politics always went where the gold was.

Zeta was the only Mexican or Indian who would deal with Greenlee. Zeta had never liked to look at Greenlee's face, which was pasty white and had no chin. His pale blue eyes had always had the shine of a true believer in the white race. Arizona had been overrun by poor whites like Greenlee. So while Zeta had avoided looking at his face, she always studied the rest of him, and of course the first thing her eyes caught was the .45 automatic.

The holster he wore in the store was bulky leather and closed with a heavy police-style snap. There was nothing his .45 automatic couldn't stop, including a Mack truck, Greenlee liked to brag when he was first introduced to people, especially women. But Zeta had always known as long as the holster was snapped, Greenlee was a lot of hot air. She also knew that Greenlee paid little or no attention to a woman unless he was fucking or hoping to fuck her. Zeta had her .44 magnum in her purse. She wasn't afraid of Greenlee. Greenlee's jokes were the most dangerous thing about him because sometimes they had nearly caused Zeta to lose self-control.

Zeta tried to keep the conversation on weapons. She talked about her .44 magnum. Greenlee said he'd been looking for one. If she ever decided to sell it . . . Greenlee had waved his hand vaguely in front of himself, smiling as if he might be recalling a joke.

"What do you have when you have twelve lawyers buried to their necks in dirt? Not enough dirt." Greenlee was preparing to move into the big warehouse building he had just bought downtown. Greenlee hinted that he had become vastly rich from secret dealings. Greenlee could not resist bragging about his money to a woman, any woman. Any brains he had were hanging between his legs.

Greenlee hinted that approval for his export permits and his federal security clearance had been given priority because certain of his friends were now located in "high places" in the U.S. government.

Zeta could have spelled it out for him right then: *CIA.*

Greenlee was not a man who did much thinking. If she said she wanted carbines or pistols to sell to rich Sonoran ranchers, that was that. She had always paid cash and she had never made trouble. Greenlee did not take Zeta seriously. She was a woman, a Mexican Indian at that.

LUST

FERRO SINKS BACK in the floating cushion, fingertips only on the edge of the redwood. Jamey wants to go "diving." Jamey likes to find it floating like a sea cucumber, he says. When he gets hold, Ferro grabs both his shoulders. Jamey nibbles like a fish. Ferro reaches for the little glass vial and twists the top. He taps a hit into the glass chamber and holds one nostril while he inhales. The rush through his head then down all veins explodes in waves he imagines in shades of pale pink— the color of Bolivian flake, the color of Jamey's tight little hole; a rose, a delicate little rose. Jamey has surfaced and is drying his face and hair. He is always grinning—those perfect rich-boy teeth beg to be smashed. He puts the towel on the shelf and searches for the glass vial. Ferro makes a fist around the vial. It takes a full minute before Jamey realizes Ferro is watching him with amusement.

"Oh! *You've* got it! Man! I was scared it fell in the water." But when Jamey reaches for the fist, Ferro pulls it away, still staring at Jamey intently. "Hey! Come on, Ferro!" Jamey shifts into his pleading tone more and more all the time. Ferro holds his arm high and outside the hot tub. "Keep away!" Ferro says, remembering how much he hated the boys who took his lunch pail and threw it back and forth and around the circle while he bellowed at them and ran at them. "Pansóna! Pansóna!" they'd yell. "Miss Big Belly! Miss Big Belly!" The nun in charge of the playground would snatch the lunch pail away from the others and send them to the mother superior's office. But when they knew the old nun had turned back to the rest of the playground, the boys used to take mincing little steps, swivel their hips, or thrust their flat bellies out in front of them, mimicking Ferro.

Jamey has a perfect body. Ferro was not content with taking measurements. He bought the expensive coffee-table book of classical sculpture. Jamey is proportioned like the discus thrower. His belly is slightly concave. His buttocks are like BBs. In Tucson, Jamey stays tan year-round. The downy blond hair on his thighs and belly bleaches platinum. Jamey's eyes are deep blue, not pale, washed-out like Paulie's eyes.

In the beginning Ferro had compared the two of them because he could not quite believe he had settled for Paulie when something so much finer had been available. But now he has nearly forgotten that Paulie had been his lover.

Ferro takes another snort and then pretends to toss it over to Jamey. But his throw is purposely wide and the little glass vial sinks in the water. "Ferro!" Jamey can sound almost like a girl. Ferro had never let on where the cocaine comes from. The glass vial is Jamey's. Jamey claims the money is from his family for college expenses, though Jamey never attends class. Ferro sells him the best because Ferro knows he will be using it too. Occasionally Ferro will bring a gram or two for all-night sex, but generally he likes to see Jamey buy it from him. Jamey is shaking. His pretty face is flushed and Ferro can see tears in his eyes. "It was nearly full! That's a whole gram. Why did you do that?" Ferro raises up and the water level in the hot tub falls so low he can almost see Jamey's neat little navel. Jamey trails after him, asking, "Why?" Ferro glances at his wristwatch on the marble shelf by the sink, then gets into the shower. He has two hours to get to the hills for the drop. Before he leaves Jamey's apartment he reaches into his coat pocket and tosses a full vial of pink flake on the pale blue carpet. Jamey looks at it and then at him. But before Jamey can speak, Ferro is out the door.

MEMORIES

PAULIE IS PARKED by the exit ramp with the hood of the jeep raised. Ferro gets out of the Lincoln and pretends to be untangling battery jumper cables. Paulie lifts the hood of the Lincoln briefly, slams it shut. Ferro slams down the jeep hood and jumps in. Paulie drives. Zeta's cardinal rule is no radios or electronic linkups of any kind. The back of the jeep is full of camera equipment and a telescope. Under it all in a telescope case there is a .223 with an infrared scope. There are two .357 magnums in the glove compartment. Paulie drives around a foothill subdivisions for a while. Ferro tries to get a good look at his face whenever they pass under a mercury-vapor light at an intersection. Ferro detects a difference in Paulie now that Jamey is his lover. Paulie senses the scrutiny and turns to look Ferro straight in the eyes.

"I was just seeing you in thirty years. How your face will be. A hook—a beak nose," Ferro says. Paulie guns the jeep and turns onto the pipeline road. Ferro continues to study Paulie's profile.

The flesh sinks away and the bones rise up. That had been Ferro's experience. In the old two-story house in Sonora with whitewash smeared over clay plaster that peels away from the adobe bricks. Whitewash everywhere—covering the wood planks and pillars of the long porch. Ferro remembers playing with chunks of white clay. Rubbing it over his hands and arms to make himself lighter. Inside the argument among the women continues for days. He thinks there is a baby in the room next to the kitchen. Cries come from behind the low wooden door, and the women arguing at the kitchen table all jump up together and rush into the room. Ferro knows that the imbecile cousins must have been around then, but does not recall seeing any of them. He had not thought of that trip to Mexico for many years and could not remember much anyway. Except that Zeta had let him order a tuna fish sandwich at the dirty café along the highway. The door of the café had been set inside a giant longhorn steer skull that rose twenty feet above the roof of the little cinder-block building. When Ferro had seen the giant steer skull, he had cried that he was hungry and that he had to go to the bathroom. Zeta had already been full of fury before they left home, and Ferro had pressed himself into the farthest corner of the big backseat of the Hudson. All he could remember about the door in the steer skull was the disappointment as he walked through. It was a dirty-white screen door and nothing of the giant steer skull could be seen. The tuna fish had been bad, and all the way from Tubac to the border he had been carsick. Or maybe it had been too hot. Zeta had not believed in air-conditioning of any kind.

Zeta had seldom taken him on any of her business trips. She had told him that children did not belong on business trips. The nuns at the school did not seem to understand how a woman could have business trips, and for a long time Ferro had not trusted her. He had decided that she simply did not want him along. But when he got older and she began to put him to work, and he started to realize what the business was, he had suddenly felt bad for not trusting her. It was dangerous business. It wasn't any place for a little child. When she went away on her business trips, the nuns kept him with the other boarding students.

He would be one of the youngest, but they gave him a tiny room alone, not in the dorm with the others. The tiny room was between the rooms of the school principal and the old nun who cooked. Zeta had seldom left him with the nuns for more than a week, but it had always been terrifying. The others hated him even more when he slept in the little room. It had belonged to the old sister, the one who had died before Ferro came to school. The others reported that all the nuns were afraid to take that room because old Sister Maria Jose's ghost had not gone to heaven but was occupying that room while she served out her time in purgatory. The stories had kept him paralyzed with terror all night. He had lain there thinking about his real mother then. He had lain there hating her with all his might. He had hated her more than he had feared dying with a mortal sin on his soul. Zeta had told him she did not know where her sister was. Zeta did not apologize or try to tell him that his mother loved him but was unable to take care of him. And yet Ferro had never known why Lecha had abandoned him. He only knew that his aunt did not raise him out of maternal love but out of duty. Ferro had seen how Zeta had cast off "business associates" after one mistake. So Ferro knew that something about his mother was special and that made him special. But it had never stopped him from hating her, with all his being.

At the old house in Sonora, Ferro had been obsessed with the stairs to the second floor, and with the second-story porch where he could drop his little metal horses and soldiers to the ground. He loved the stairs and the height because none of the houses he had ever been in had had a second floor. Most of Tucson was flat. He had so many aunts he could not keep them straight. They all looked alike to him. They were arguing over the big house and over who should have what.

Zeta had told him to stay at the house. They had crowded into the big green Hudson. The instant Ferro had seen the car go over the sandy hill he crept inside. He tiptoed to the little wooden door to the room off the kitchen. He listened for a long time. He did not know much about babies, but he also knew that mothers of his schoolmates never left babies without asking someone to look in on them. Finally he had slowly and carefully turned the cutglass knob. He did not breathe as he opened the door just a crack. What he saw were two glittering black eyes watching him from a baby crib. Just as he was trying to figure out why the eyes did not seem like the eyes of other babies he had seen, the strange baby raised up and caused the crib to shake and bump the wall.

At that instant the paralysis he suffered sleeping in the ghost nun's bedroom afflicted his legs and hands. He watched in horror as two long-fingered, bony hands grabbed the top rail of the crib and the big head with the glittering black eyes hung over the top rail. The mouth had four huge, yellow teeth. The big bony head spoke in Spanish first, and when Ferro did not move, it brought out a few English words, but still Ferro did not move. The white hair had been cut short and stuck out around the skeleton face like dry weeds. Then Ferro had heard it call his name, softly at first and then gradually louder until it made his own name into a cry. He had pulled the door shut then and had started running for the beach although Zeta had forbidden him to go to the ocean alone. He ran and ran, imagining that the skeleton man was dragging himself over the edge of the crib and then along the brick floor to the porch.

When Zeta finally came for him, it was late afternoon. She drove the car only as far as the first sand dune and then began honking the horn. Ferro had been sitting with his back to the sea, watching the crest of the dunes for the appearance of the skeleton man. The tide was coming in, and as he moved to avoid getting wet, he had begun to feel a slow panic. Before long, the ocean would push him to the base of the high dune where the skeleton man could suddenly come rolling down to catch Ferro.

Ferro stood in front of the car and stared at Zeta. He was trying to see if she was going to whip him with the hairbrush in her purse. But she was in a hurry and gestured for him to hurry and get in. When he got in the backseat, Zeta put the car in reverse, then stopped and told him to get out and shake the sand from his cuffs and to empty his shoes. Something about having to untie his shoes made him want to cry. But he clapped his jaws together and did as he was told. Zeta told him to hurry, he could always put his shoes back on while they were driving.

Zeta had never talked much. She preferred to be left alone with her scheming and thinking, that was what Ferro had figured out later. As a child he had simply known that unlike his schoolmates and their mothers, he and Zeta did not say much to each other. They spoke only when it was absolutely necessary. Ferro had come to prefer silence just as she did. He had come to believe that talk was cheap. That it was common. That was what was best about Paulie. Nothing needed to be said.

DROP POINTS

THE KEY to this drop point is the Marana Air Park across the mountain from the gas line. The subdivisions inch out from the Santa Cruz River along Ina Road. But the people living in the area are used to the small-aircraft traffic that begin landing approaches here, and they don't notice takeoff accelerations and airplanes climbing as they cross the foothills. Ferro learned from Zeta, and Zeta would not say, but Ferro thought she had learned from Calabazas and the other old-timers.

At sundown they spotted a small white Cessna that appeared to be gaining altitude slowly. The steel canister had landed at the edge of the gasline road four hundred yards away. The dull gray color of the metal was almost invisible in the twilight. Ferro continued setting up the tripod, and Paulie brought out the telescope. Although they appeared to be concentrating on the telescope, they were straining to pick up sounds that might indicate people in the area—horseback riders, hikers, or kids on dirt bikes. They never repeated the pattern of any drop, although it required much more planning. It was a simple matter to avoid the radar along the border by flying the plane a hundred feet above the mesquite groves. But Ferro had made it his job to continually invent new occasions and new opportunities to move the goods across the border. Lately prices had been down and Zeta had talked about trading arms and explosives instead of cocaine.

As the twilight darkened and Venus flared brighter in the lens of the telescope, Ferro told Paulie to go ahead. Ferro rested the .223 with the infrared scope across the hood of the jeep. He followed Paulie in the scope, occasionally scanning ahead and behind him, and all around the paloverde tree where the canister had bounced and rolled.

The easiest drops were also the most dangerous. Lately there had been a new kind of pressure. Not from the drug agents, but from the new kid in town, as Ferro liked to call him. Sonny Blue wasn't new, but what he seemed to be trying was new. Content for many years to leave the drug trade with Mexico to the old families such as theirs and

Calabazas, suddenly Max Blue and his people had begun to make moves.

The canister rode in the corner of the backseat of the jeep. Paulie had already smeared motor oil on the canister. It could have passed for a five-gallon fuel can. It might have been a waterproof case for telescopic lenses. Paulie dropped Ferro at his car. When Ferro pulled onto Interstate 10, his windbreaker was zipped over his massive belly and hips. The black rubber body belt had uncoiled from the canister like a jungle snake after a heavy meal. Ferro never felt happier than when he wore the black rubber belt concealed under his clothes.

When Ferro got to the apartment, he made sure Jamey was not there. He stood for a long time in front of the mirror in the upstairs bathroom, studying the length of zippered black rubber full of Bolivian cocaine. The over-hang of his belly hid his cock, shriveled from the breeze from the open balcony door. The black rubber belt crisscrossed his chest like Pancho Villa's bandoliers. He had always wanted thick black hair on his chest. The fat made his breasts hang like a woman's. With hair the fat would have been less repulsive. Jamey said he loved him more than anyone ever before. I love you as you are, he had told Ferro then scooted across the bed so that he could give Ferro head. The immensity of the belly interfered with the usual positions Jamey tried, but he had always been quick to figure out those things. It was other things Jamey had trouble with.

Ferro coiled the rubber body belt under the guest bed and got into the shower. As he was finishing with the hair drier, he heard Jamey's Corvette pull into the parking space below the balcony doors. Before Jamey could unlock the downstairs door and reach the bedroom, Ferro was lying naked on his back, his penis swollen into a wide curve away from his belly. Jamey would call it a special treat, although they both knew that rubbing coke on the penis head slowed the ejaculations and kept Ferro going longer. Zeta had accused him once of having only his balls and dick to think with. He knew it was not true, but he also knew that before he had found Jamey, he had made mistakes that had not happened since. He imagined there was gradual buildup—secretions, fluids in his lower abdomen, and finally his crotch. The sensation had not changed since grade school when he was sent to the school chapel alone; perhaps it was to pray for aid in curbing his tongue. He did not remember the reason, only rows and rows of tiny votive candles in red glass. When he had leaned forward as he knelt, he had brushed against the pew ahead of him. He had been looking at the bare legs of the Jesus hanging from the cross. The pleasure he got from leaning closer and rubbing against the pew made him close his eyes. What he saw then was the spear the soldier stabbed into Jesus' ribs and the gush of blood that had spurted. Ferro always imagined the soldier as large and handsome and reluctant to hurt Jesus, but some mightier force had given him orders. The older boys claimed hanged men died with penises erect or spurting liquid. Ferro realized the loincloth on Jesus had only been for the sake of good taste. When he closed his eyes, he imagined Jesus' execution conducted in the nude. The last sign of life had left Jesus' body in the same spasmodic jerks that Ferro saw his own penis make as he pulled it in the warm bathwater.

Ferro left Jamey spread-eagle on the bed, facedown. Orgasm was such a relief he no longer felt the regret he had as a child who then had to kneel and confess a mortal sin. The only regret he felt was that he could not keep away from Jamey, that he had gone from seeing Jamey two nights a week, to seeing Jamey every night, and often in the late afternoon. Zeta was already complaining that the work was suffering. That Sonny Blue and his people were beginning to make inroads around town. They were selling more and they were selling it cheaper. "Mine is better," Ferro had said sullenly. Zeta laughed. "We are not talking about sex acts," she said. "We are talking about drugs. Down on the street they don't know good. They know cheap. That's all."

MOTHER

AN HOUR AFTER Lecha had returned with the skinny blond girl, Ferro had cornered Zeta in her office. He had demanded to know why Zeta had not told him. What the fuck reason had that—that—*thing* for returning after all these years? He was shouting, but Zeta remained calm. She had a pencil and a stack of blank yellow paper on the desk in front of her. She was doodling interlocking squares in a pattern that reminded Ferro of his coffee-table book full of Greek statues.

Ferro had learned when he was still very small never to let Zeta lock eyes with him. Because it was the eyes that gave the real meaning to any words she might have spoken. When Zeta had told Ferro that his mother had left him in Tucson because she could not be bothered with a tiny baby, her eyes had told him that she did not want him feeling sorry for himself. She did not believe anything teachers or psychologists might say about the ill effects of rejection upon the child. Her eyes said that what was good or necessary for white people was quite different for them.

They had had great shouting fights after he was grown. But Ferro had always known that despite what he felt or what he wanted, Zeta knew a great deal more than he did. Ferro had come to understand this gradually. At first, before he understood, Ferro had studied and read his books, waiting for the day when the argument came and it was Ferro and not Zeta who had the definitive facts. When he would be able to tell her that he had tried X or Y or Z and that he knew which was best. But after he had finished college with a business degree and had been working for Zeta, it dawned on him that he was getting no closer to what she knew and how she knew.

"How many times has your mother said she was coming back and then we don't hear from her again for three years?" Although Ferro had taken a double shot of whiskey and a couple of lines of coke, he felt as if his heart would beat a path straight into his belly, taking both lungs with it. "Your mother," as if Lecha were *his* fault or his invention. Ferro had wanted to yell back, "She's *your* sister!" but he knew without saying the words that Zeta had him beaten right there. Every word Zeta had spoken was true. She seldom lied or exaggerated, while Lecha had many times announced returns or permanent changes and then had failed to appear or call again for years. Ferro had been furious at something inside himself that had been waiting for Lecha to return.

At that moment, Ferro looked at Zeta and was stunned to see how much she looked like Lecha, although something running in the distance behind the voice inside him kept telling him it was only the whiskey and the drug. But he could see only Lecha, his mother—the one he had hated so fervently all these years. The mouth, the teeth, and the eyes—Ferro could feel the sweat sliding down the crack of his ass—but just when he thought he would not be able to hold off the shivering in his chest, he had seen the wide streaks of white in Zeta's hair. He could see her big hands, big knuckles, dark brown from working with dusty "antiquities." No long red nails, no gaudy fake emeralds like Lecha's. Ferro took a deep breath. "You did it for her. You did it for you! It wasn't for me!" Sweat had rolled down his forehead into his eyes, stinging and running tears down his cheeks. Zeta had not moved her eyes from his.

She did not dispute Ferro. She had done it for herself. In spite of her sister, Ferro had got raised, and that was all that had mattered. Ferro whirled around blindly for the door. "Fuck you! Fuck you!" he screamed, and slammed the wrought-iron gate so hard the glass rattled in the windows.

THE WEIGHT OF GHOSTS

CALABAZAS IS IN THE CORRAL with his little mule and donkeys. He talks to them in a singsong voice. He has a bushel basket of overripe broccoli he picked up at the back door of the produce warehouse down the street. But in his pockets Calabazas has green crab apples he picked in the backyard. The little donkeys pin back their ears at each other and push to get closer to him. The spotted mule stands with its head shoved against Calabazas's left shoulder. When the donkeys try to bite the spotted mule, Calabazas claps his hands and laughs.

Root smiles when he sees Calabazas in the corral with his animals. Calabazas likes the old ways, the old tricks, best. But he won't like it if Root doesn't tell him about the Salvadorians. Root isn't sure how to bring it up, but Calabazas is in one of his talking moods.

"The story I like best," Calabazas says as if he and Root have been exchanging stories all morning, "is about the old man riding his mule along the river." Calabazas gestures in the direction of the Santa Cruz River, but Root thinks "sewage treatment" not "river" when he looks in that direction. Both are true. Tucson built its largest sewage treatment plant on the northwest side of the city, next to the river.

Farther south, near the Mexican border, the Santa Cruz runs as clear as a mountain stream. The Yaqui people know the location of the sewage plant is no accident. Calabazas's goats and little donkeys and livestock from the Yaqui barrio wander on city property surrounding the sewage plant. The Yaqui livestock fatten on the tall river grass and willows as they always have since the days before there was a city of Tucson to condemn Yaqui land.

Root turns over a tin bucket and sits down to get comfortable. Because Calabazas is in one of his moods. "In those days there were witches up and down the Santa Cruz," he begins. Root wishes he could talk as fast as he can think because he'd make a wisecrack about there being plenty of witches right now—teasing Calabazas, who has, from time to time, been accused of being a witch himself.

"The sky above the riverbanks used to glow electric blue all night from the burning witches' pots. Us kids stayed close to the house on those nights. Besides witches, we always had to be careful of Yaqui ghosts. The ghosts are always traveling up and down the riverbanks searching for their loved ones. Because the Mexican soldiers slaughtered all of them. Babies, little children, old women. Yaquis who refused to acknowledge the Mexican government or to pay taxes on their land were rounded up and shot. The soldiers filled the arroyos with their bodies, and families never knew who had been murdered or who had escaped. Those ghosts can't rest. Not even now."

Root raises his eyebrows and widens his eyes at Calabazas. Root has come to depend upon facial expressions because they don't get caught then stuttered out of his mouth. "That's right," Calabazas continues, "and that's what this old man riding his mule along the riverbank found out." Calabazas stops to light up a cigarette. He always offers the pack to Root, who always shakes his head. "What do these ghosts want? They are still running away, thinking they are escaping the slaughter. They keep traveling, but at a much slower rate of speed than when they were alive. They are just now reaching Tucson as the water and the land are disappearing. Relatives already settled here had pleaded with them to flee Sonora sooner. Now the ghosts have come, and they want to know where the lake they were always hearing about has gone. The lake their brothers and cousins were bragging about. Plentiful fresh water in Tucson. Which is what the word *tucson* means in Papago." Root nods, and Calabazas takes a couple of puffs from his cigarette.

"This man had bought a little mule. One like mine. Everyone told him he didn't want a little mule. His relatives. Relatives always tell you what they want." Calabazas glances in the direction of the houses owned by his wife's family as he says this. "All of them tried to talk him out of the little mule. They wanted him to buy something bigger. Maybe even a horse. Because it would be his money that was getting spent. Not theirs. But the man liked something about this little mule. He bought it from someone up at the village in Marana. They invited him to spend the night. But he was living alone, and he had a garden that needed care. He didn't want to ask his relatives because the melons were getting ripe, and who could resist taking a few? So early in the afternoon the man got on the little mule he'd bought. This mule was the color of red dust. It had the sign of the cross down its spine, which was good luck too. So they went along, and the little red mule did very well. The old man was pleased because now the little mule would show all those relatives of his who didn't approve of small mules. But right around sundown, the little mule started slowing down. They were near the Seven Mile crossing on the riverbank. Seven Mile crossing got its name because at the time it was seven miles from town. Not anymore. The interstate runs right by there. And there's that striptease bar there."

Root nods. He wonders about Calabazas sometimes. All the different moods. Today he wants to talk about the old times. But tomorrow Calabazas might not say anything. For days at a time he might not speak to anyone—just point or gesture. If a deal had been made and a drop had been scheduled, then nothing happened. Customers got used to peculiarities dealing with Calabazas. Root and Mosca would have to carry on until Calabazas got a change in mood. As long as supplies hold out Root just keeps working the university neighborhood and Pima College, where it's mostly college kids who want to score.

"Well, this man began to think maybe what people had been saying against the small mule might be true after all. Maybe he had been cheated. It took the man all night just to get seven miles. The red mule went slower and slower. The mule started sweating. It lay down in the sand three times. The man was ready to turn around and go right back the next morning, to return the mule and get his money back. Of course he told everyone the next day. But the old-timers just laughed at him. 'Don't blame the mule. Why do you think they invited you to spend the night in Marana?' The old-timers were really getting a kick out of the whole thing because this man had not believed in spirits and ghosts and things like that. So they said to him, 'Why do you think they asked you to spend the night? Because ghosts can make a wagon heavier for the horses to pull. The ghosts pile into the wagon. They weigh twice or three times what they weighed in life. The body carries the weight of the soul all the life, but with the body gone, there's nothing to hold the weight anymore.' "

FALLING FOREVER

ROOT KNOWS HOW heavy the body is. Never mind spirits or ghosts. He knows how heavy the body is as it falls—falls so slowly the mass and weight of it pulls everything down in slow motion. He has dreams of the heaviness, of falling forever and ever. His arms slam against the mattress. He wakes in a sweat. He knows what they told him. How much of his brain came away with the crushed skull. How doctors fucked up with the steel plate. "One in ten" had been the odds they quoted his mother during the fever.

The world had pulled away and left him lying in white, puffy clouds. He could look down and look through the clouds. He might have been in a jet airliner except for the silence. He could look down through layers of clouds and see himself lying in the hospital bed connected to the machines. He lies in the bed with his eyes closed. It is difficult to recognize the visitors who come and stand at the foot of the hospital bed since he can see only the tops of heads. He can always tell which one his mother is. But he does not remember seeing the top of her head more than a few times. The therapist asks if they are cumulus clouds. Root hates the sounds he makes. He can hear the correct sound of the words inside his head, but his mouth doesn't make the sounds clearly anymore. Words are groans or choking sounds. Does the tongue actually move or is it like the feet and toes, which feel as if they are moving, but when he watches in the mirror above the bed, they are motionless, white as candle wax. Even before the accident, Root had never trusted mirrors on ceilings. The first time he saw mirrors on the ceiling had been with Lecha in the deluxe suite at the Marilyn Motel. When he saw Lecha's back, the cheeks of her wide brown ass spreading over his skinny white legs, Root had realized that mirrors do not show what really is. So he had bellowed at the physical therapist, young, blond, and enthusiastic, when she told him he could see for himself in the mirror his toes were not moving. He could not tell her mirrors on ceilings do not show the truth because he could not even say *yes* or *no*. In the ceiling mirror of the Marilyn Motel, Lecha appeared to sit on someone he had not recognized, a teenage boy much whiter and shorter than himself, flexing his feet in rhythm with Lecha's slow, smooth rocking on top. The face Root had seen over Lecha's left shoulder should have been his, but was not. Just as now the bellows and grunts should have been words, but were not.

He had awakened after five months. He had no memory of what had happened. He thought he might have some idea of a past life with a family, but he did not feel sure. The nurse who came into the room said that she had just been transferred to that ward, but she would see that someone came who could tell him what had happened. A car had turned in front of his motorcycle. Later his mother had filled in all the details. They were fresh in her mind, she said, because she had just been talking to their lawyer. The company insuring the car and driver had made a generous offer. The car had turned in front of him where Miracle Mile intersected Ft. Lowell Road. Root thought it was funny it had happened next to the graveyard. As kids they had joked about riding their bikes past the cemetery after basketball practice in late November when it was nearly dark. They had joked about what might happen to you passing a graveyard after dark, or even in broad daylight—three-thirty in the afternoon—the time his accident had occurred. Ghosts might hop into a wagon or onto a motorcycle.

Root stands up. Calabazas has been pulling thistle burrs from the burro's fetlocks. He knows Root has something to tell him, but it takes Root time to get it out. Root stares at the tall hollyhocks blooming near the sagging clothesline. He finds something to focus on so he doesn't have to watch the face of the person listening; so he doesn't have to watch their difficulty understanding his words. Root concentrates on the intensity of the colors of the blossoms—the reds that are dark as wine, garnets, even blood. Root feels sweat break out across his shoulders. It soaks his T-shirt. It runs like ants from his armpits down his ribs. He tells Calabazas about the men who've come. Not Mexicans, but foreigners who are very short and very dark and speak strange Spanish. They say they've come from El Salvador.

Calabazas is staring at the little donkeys bunched in the shady corner of the corral. He is still calculating the weight of one ghost. Somewhere near five hundred pounds. "How did they find you?"

Root shakes his head. "They say they were told to find me to reach you." Elaborate precautions had to be taken against narcs and others. Calabazas takes a last, hard suck from the cigarette and throws the butt hard against the ground. He doesn't like strangers looking for him. "Tell me more." Root shrugs his shoulders. "Brand-new leisure suits—sort of tan colored. All identical. Everything—white plastic belts, white loaf-ers. Blue shirts. Bad haircuts." Calabazas chews the end of his thumb but says nothing. Root decides Calabazas is ready for the best part. "They pulled up to my place in an old Volkswagen with Sonora plates. They each carried a blue suitcase. Brand-new powder-blue Samsonite." Calabazas draws himself up straight, and looks Root in the eyes. "What?" "Samsonite." Usually Calabazas understands his speech much better than anyone except maybe Lecha. Root frowns and tries to repeat the word very slowly, straining to control every single sound. "Sam-son-ite—it's the brand-name luggage." Calabazas doesn't always un-derstand English. It wasn't just Root's slurring of the words. There seemed to be days when Calabazas didn't understand English at all. There was no explanation.

Root sees Calabazas still doesn't understand him. Root used to cry in the hospital from the frustration of all that he wanted to say and all the sounds he could not form. The light-blue Samsonite suitcase each man carried is important. It reveals something, although Root is not sure exactly what. He knows that if Calabazas can only understand what he is saying, he will be able to interpret the meaning of the identical blue suitcases. "What do they want?" "To talk to you." Calabazas remembers what Samsonite is. "What do they carry in these suitcases?" Root shrugs his shoulders, and Calabazas grunts. The men aren't show-ing anything unless it's to Calabazas. "How many?" Calabazas acts as if he can't remember if Root has already told him or not. Root holds up four fingers. The sun is high enough to make the mule corral hot. Root feels the sweat sticking his T-shirt to his belly and his back. This talk about ghosts in wagons and strangers with blue suitcases looking for Calabazas has left Root tired and hungry. He follows Calabazas out of the corral. Calabazas walks away from him without saying any more and crosses the bare, smooth-packed adobe of the yard to the back door of the old house. Calabazas is lost in calculating all the angles, as he himself might put it, all the ways to figure these Salvadorians with new Samsonite luggage.

Root is ready for a cold beer. Maybe Carlos wants to drive out to the Stage Coach. Calabazas calls Carlos "Mosca." Carlos claims he has no idea why the boss calls him that. Root calls him Fly. Carlos says that doesn't bother him because in English *fly* can also mean the zipper, the opening, the crotch, and this suits him perfectly, Carlos likes to say. Carlos is related to Calabazas's wife. Mosca mostly does what Root does, except Mosca's customers live on the South Side. They don't talk much. Root has no curiosity about the Fly's life. Root figures Mosca's life is a lot like his own. Mosca talks a lot sometimes, depending on what drugs he's on. Other times he doesn't say anything. Root tries sometimes to figure out why he and Fly get along, but it is no use. Root knows a question like that has never crossed Fly's mind. When they go out together, it is usually to places where there is little need to talk, only to watch and to listen. They like the Stage Coach because there is always a stripper on stage and they can watch the bikers play pool.

Mosca comes out the back door of the old house blinking rapidly until he can get his dark glasses on. The deep, dark blue of the lenses is one of his trademarks. Maybe that's where Calabazas got the nickname. Mosca is short and wiry. His head and the blue lenses of the sunglasses are a little too large for his body. Root can feel the cocaine ten feet away. The cocaine acts like a fuel for a system of electric turbines located deep inside the human body. Electricity from chemical reactions crackles and sizzles through the bloodstream. Root can look over the top of his head. "The horse races," Mosca announces, patting his pockets to indicate he had some deliveries to make there. Root nods his head and realizes he is grinning. Because Mosca is so damn happy and even the buzzing of the cocaine in him is strangly in tune with the sound of the cicadas in the giant tamarisk trees in Calabazas's yard. They will buy two six-packs on the way. Mosca estimates the distance from where they stand to the big four-wheel-drive truck Mosca is so proud of. "I'll race you," Mosca says. He is the only person who acknowledges Root's disabilities. Mosca finds Root's brain damage fascinating.

Mosca challenges Root to physical contests he figures Root can't win. "Because I like to win. I like to win against you. It feels just as good. Don't ask me why." Mosca likes to say that he doesn't believe cripples should be given special favors. Mosca parks his big, black, four-wheel-drive Chevy in spaces painted with wheelchair symbols and marked with handicapped signs. Mosca laughs. "You are not handicapped if it is easy for you to get around. Special parking places make it too easy," Mosca said.

Mosca knows horses. He sneers at what he sees in the paddock where the trainers saddle for the next race. You are betting on whether the trainer has shot the horse too full of crank and it keels over dead on the backstretch. You are betting on which runt jockey fucks up the deal and bumps his nag into the number everyone is betting. "Mosca." "The Fly." At the track Root sees another way the nickname might have come. Mosca is getting the numbers. He never bothers to look at the horses. He flits through the crowd. Root waits, leaning against the fence by the finish-line rail. The horses seem to float when they run. Hooves barely touch the surface of the track. Their eyes shine hot. They are lighter than their bodies. Root had stopped growing after the accident. The part of the brain sending those chemical messages was gone. It was better that way. Less hulk to drag around. Root had learned how to walk again after three months. He might have blamed the accident for the size of his cock if he had not seen the size of his father's and his brothers'. None of them would have won any prizes.

HORSE RACES

ENTRY NUMBERS and the odds flash across the tote board in the center of the racetrack. Root is fascinated with the foam between the horses' hind legs. The lather on their necks. Mosca is beside him now, watching the board. "Look out for the ones that sweat too much. . . . No, no, that one isn't sweating at all. That's an OD. . . . No, man; these are horses, remember?" He shows Root a number so that no one standing close can see. "It's this one. You want me to put fifty dollars on it for you?" Before Root can say anything, Mosca is gone, headed for the WIN window. A man in a white linen suit steps in line behind Mosca. All he needs is the panama hat. Root sees he's carrying something in his left hand, hidden inside a *Racing Form*. He says something to Mosca as he turns away from the window with the yellow tickets. Root imagines something familiar about the face. Italian or maybe Jewish. Root asks, but Mosca keeps his eyes on the horses loading into the starting gates on the far side of the track. "He's got a couple of horses, that's all. Personal pleasure. Strictly amateur," Mosca says. Root wants to see the face again, the face of a man who has nothing better to do than watch his horses run and snort what he buys from Mosca. But the man in the white linen suit is gone. Root tries to imagine the car he drives and the women he fucks. All "white linen" quality throughout his life, Root figures, then turns in time to get hit with dirt flying off the hooves as their horse finishes first.

Mosca reappears long enough to count out the money. Odds were only five to one, but a couple of hundred is okay for standing around drinking cold beer and watching the people. Root drifts away from the fence. He likes to watch the trainers and jockeys saddle the big horses. A few of the owners are there. Root likes to try to figure out why they own racehorses. He understands how people spend money on sex, cars, and clothes; and of course, drugs. But Root wonders what it is about the horses. The owners don't ride them. Most of the owners don't even watch the horses run except for the big races at the big tracks. But what were these horses, and what was this track doing in Tucson? Then there was the man in the white linen suit with the two gorgeous fillies, horses with class. Those horses were only pasing through, to be graded for better tracks. The fillies were led from the paddock to join the other entries parading in front of the grandstand. Root looked for the owner's name on the racing program, but saw the fillies were listed as the property of a private investment group. Half of the horses on the program were listed that way. Tax shelters: strings of nags running on two-bit tracks. The more horses that got hurt or just lay down and died, the more money people made.

In the truck Mosca pulled a pint bottle of whiskey from under the seat. He handed it to Root and then began pouring neat piles of cocaine on the dashboard. Root took big swallows and passed the bottle back to Mosca, but he shook his head and nodded at the pint. Root finished the bottle, and when he had opened his eyes and wiped the sweat off his face, Mosca was offering him a segment of a red and white plastic straw. "McDonald's," Mosca said, showing big white teeth when he grinned. "Man, you sure surprised me! I heard all those stories they tell about you, you know, things like that, but—" The cocaine was already plumping up his brain cells. Root imagined a feather pillow being fluffed and smoothed into a soft, round belly of comfort and ease. He did not care what Mosca was saying.

Mosca snorted his two piles and pointed the straw at the last two piles while holding both nostrils shut with his other hand. Root glanced around the parking lot and then took the other two. As he raised up from snorting the last pile, he saw a white Mercedes pulling out from long rows of stalls. He caught only a glimpse of the driver, but Root knew it had to be the man in the white linen suit. Root glanced over to see if Mosca had any reaction to the white car, but Mosca was fumbling with a plastic bag full of marijuana and rolling papers in his lap.

"You shouldn't take those things so seriously," Mosca was saying as he roared down First Avenue doing sixty. Root didn't mind the speed, but he was thinking about Tucson cops who instantly turned speeding tickets into illegal searches. But Root was clean. Only Mosca had been "transacting." The sensation of the engine and the motion, tires whining and the exhilaration of the cocaine, settled Root back in the seat where he watched as the world was left behind.

"Eat my dust," Mosca says then, and the big Chevy veers suddenly into a convenience store lot. He leaps down from the high cab, makes two calls at the pay phone, dashes in the store for two cold six-packs, and screeches the truck into reverse. From where Root sits it is abundantly clear where Calabazas got the name Mosca; quick and busy; all over everything at once. The Fly. Mosca shoves a cold beer in Root's hand, then lights up another joint. The dingy upholstery shops, wrecking yards, and one-stall repair shops on First Avenue fall away from them faster and faster. Root has a sensation of well-being he has not felt in years as the big four-wheel-drive truck blasts ahead.

The last time Root had felt so good he had been a kid. Eighteen or nineteen. Right after he first met Lecha. They all took acid and went riding. He had just bought a beat-up Harley. He thought he had everything he wanted. The chopper, a woman. A real woman. The acid let him feel just how good it all really was. Later Root was uncertain he could trust his feelings then because he had been high. But the acid had not lied, not that time. When it was all over, after his accident, the first time Root smoked dope, that afternoon of riding motorcycles with his friends had flashed back to him. Vividly. The fresh smell of the desert, creosote, sage, and sand. The temperature of the air and the temperature of his own body so perfectly aligned that he was no longer sure where his body ended and the rest of the world began. They had turned down Silverbell Road to get away from the city traffic, and Root remembered the instant he saw the trees on both sides of the road. Masses of brilliant-yellow blossoms seemed to cascade off the paloverdes and lie in deep yellow pools beneath them. He had just been to see Lecha a few hours before, and it was as if for a brief instant he had poured out of himself into something larger, and the motorcycle was carrying him deep into it, and clouds of yellow flowers were billowing around him endlessly until he no longer knew how he was keeping the bike balanced upright, but he was, and he believed that he always could, and that he would always be in a world as infinite as this one. The beauty and joy of that afternoon had been a premonition, Root thought later. A last taste. Because the world was never the same after the accident. Vertical became horizontal.

Mosca, all the cousins, looked at the accident differently from white people. Calabazas and Mosca did not think it was strange that Root kept the twisted, broken Harley frame. Root's mother had actually called the shrink when Root refused to sell the wreckage to a junkyard. Indians and Mexicans understood, or at least the ones Root liked understood. Root had moved out to his own place after that. He did not belong; his mother and brothers were strangers.

Root looks over at Mosca, who has broken free even from the laws of gravity; Mosca's flying high with beer foam at both corners of his mouth, nose hairs caked white, and now one of the Fly's famous cocaine monologues. It is as if they have been working on the same puzzle. Root's accident. Root knows they feel the accident has significance, that it was a journey to the boundaries of the land of the dead.

FAMILY

MOSCA KEPT TRYING to make Root remember the accident. Root did not feel the same anger when Mosca asked. But the therapist had enraged him with her constant whining "Oh, come on now, try. Try to remember!" She had been trying to get him to remember his life before the accident. Remember. Remember your sisters and your brothers? Once he did start remembering, Root had screamed at the therapist that he wanted to forget again. His family were strangers; they were repelled by his condition, by the shaved head and the scars on his skull. Big zippers. Frankenstein zippers. "See, I can unzip it," Root had said to his youngest sister, meaning to tease her and play as they once had. But she had shrunk away, almost knocking their mother into the IV bottle.

Mosca wanted Root to remember, but Mosca was not interested in the past, or memories *before* the accident. Root had teased Mosca about acting like a shrink, always trying to get him to remember "Christmas with the family," and Mosca had suddenly turned serious. "Man, don't take this personal. I have no room to talk. But man, *your family!* If I were you—yeah! I'd forget *all* of them, man." Mosca could say that because he had driven Root to his mother's place a few times on holidays.

Mosca said there was nothing worse than half-Mexicans or quarter-Mexicans who were so stunned by having light skin they never noticed the odor of their own shit again. Root agreed with Mosca. The way he had it figured, his mother and grandmother had spent their time praying he would die in the coma.

For years, for as far back as Root could remember, Mosca had wanted Root to remember what the accident had been like. "What do you mean, what it was like?" Root would say.

"Well, you know, old Calabazas, he said one time people who get wiped out like that—you know, *almost* killed—well, they get visions or they take a long journey." Mosca would pause and wait for Root to take up where Mosca had left off; he wanted Root to talk about the soul journey and about visions. Root always got exasperated and said he remembered nothing. That as far as he knew, he had not even dreamed while he was in the coma. Mosca would look disappointed, and then hurt. "I thought we were friends," he would say. But Mosca is a patient man, and Root can't think of a month gone by without Mosca's mentioning Root's accident.

Mosca wheels the truck down Ft. Lowell to Oracle. Mosca has done this with Root so many times, Root thinks he may not even realize he is doing it. Mosca drives Root through the intersection where the woman in the real estate company car made the illegal left turn that had sent Root on his way; flying on his motocycle to nowhere. But after a while, Root got used to Mosca's notion the collision with the '60 Plymouth had sent him *somewhere*. Try to think and remember, cast yourself back into months of coma.

It had taken Root a few years to decide which people were worse: the ones who gawked, mouths opened so wide they slobbered on their shoes, or the ones who pretended they had seen nothing out of the ordinary when they passed him in the shopping mall, but if Root glanced back over his shoulder, he would catch them staring at him. Root soon learned the worst were those who thought his limp and dragging foot somehow gave them the right to walk up and start telling him about their daughter or son-in-law and the fall in the bathroom or the can of poison green beans that caused the paralysis.

It had not taken Root very long to figure out that the gawkers and the queasy stomachs were invariably in the shopping malls and department stores, or were well-dressed white women passing the physical-therapy wing during hospital visiting hours. Downtown, Root had instinctively felt more comfortable. Gray-haired women loaded with shopping bags waiting for buses might look, but Root watched to see how they looked at people walking ahead or behind him. It had been a great relief to see that these old Mexican women saw nothing any more remarkable about him than the others passing by: two dark, fat Papago teenagers carrying a boxy, silver tape player shoulder-high, between them, heads cocked to the speakers; the tall, balding lawyer perspiring in his dark brown suit and vest, briefcase in hand; or the leftover rich hippie in black leather jeans, his long blond hair spreading down the back of a red silk tunic. Root felt he belonged there.

Mosca had taught Root a lot, but so had Calabazas. Not intentionally, but the longer Root worked with both of them and saw the Yaqui cousins who worked on the other end, the more Root realized they did not expect what white people might call "normal" or "standard." There had never been any such thing as "normal" for them. When Root had first begun working with them, the delivery routes had been far more difficult and remote. Hours and hours of night driving off the crude roads, careening down sandy washes for miles into the heart of the Tohano O'Dom Reservation, had taught Root not to see things as "normal." Calabazas always did the driving, and the wonder was that all three of them had not been killed as Calabazas leaped the battered '54 Dodge pickup over arroyos four feet wide. If Calabazas thought Mosca and Root were trying to catch some sleep, he would light up a Kool and begin a lecture on desert trails and secret border-crossing routes. Once Root had remarked that he thought one dull gray boulder looked identical to another dull gray boulder a few hundred yards back. Calabazas took his foot off the accelerator, and Mosca had tried to save Root by adding quickly, "Maybe in the dark they look alike." But that had not prevented Calabazas from giving them one of his sarcastic lectures on blindness. Blindness caused solely by stupidity, a blindness that Root and Mosca would probably always suffer from, just as they would always suffer from the location of their brains below their belts. "I get mad when I hear the word *identical*," Calabazas had continued. "There is no such thing. Nowhere. At no time. All you have to do is stop and think. Stop and take a look." The old Dodge truck had slowed to a crawl; the engine idle sounded wheezy. They had left in plenty of time for the rendezvous with the couriers. Calabazas stopped the truck and turned off the headlights. He made them both get out. Mosca was yawning and pretended to moan and whine "uncle" at Calabazas, but it was no use. He made Root and Mosca walk ahead of him in the sandy wash. The deep, white arroyos reflected a strange luminous-silver light from the stars even without a moon. Calabazas was only worried about his merchandise, he said. Because fuckers like them were a dime a dozen, and he couldn't care less if they got themselves lost, or ran themselves out of gas or got stuck, and then died after they'd finished the five-gallon water can.

Root suspected it might have been fatigue and the fat green joints he and Mosca had smoked hours earlier. Root's ass had been dragging he was so tired; but that night Calabazas marched them up and down, up and down the same stretch of the arroyo, until Root suddenly realized what the old bastard was saying. "Look at it for what it is. That's all. This big rock is like it is. Look. Now, come on. Over here. This one is about as big, but not quite. And the rock broke out a chunk like a horse head, but see, this one over here broke out a piece that's more like a washtub." Root had rubbed his hand over the edges of the fracture lines, and although both rocks were the same dull gray basalt, he had been able to feel differences along the fractures. One had been weathered smooth on the edges. One sat slightly higher on a gravel bench shaped by the confluences of the wash. The other rock had rested at its location long enough to collect a snarl of tall rice grass and broken twigs and tumbleweeds at its base.

Survival had depended on differences. Not just the differences in the terrain that gave the desert traveler critical information about traces of water or grass for his animals, but the sheer varieties of plants and bugs and animals. Calabazas liked to talk about the years of drought, when so many rodents and small animals died, and the deer and larger game migrated north. "Buzzard was the king those years. You should have seen. They don't have to drink much water. They get it from the rotting meat they eat. It swells up with gas and then it makes greenish water. Buzzards gather around and feast. It is like their beer. They drink and drink." The old Dodge pickup was spinning and sliding around corners sometimes in the dry wash, sometimes on a faint wagon road parallel with the wash. He parked the pickup by a big mesquite tree, but Calabazas kept lecturing even after the engine stopped.

Mosca pretended to gag on Calabazas's lecture, then he laid his head on the dashboard and went to sleep. But Root sat leaning out the truck window, catching the cool, damp smell of the summer desert night. Being around Mexicans and Indians or black people, had not made him feel uncomfortable. Not as his own family had. Because if you weren't born white, you were forced to see differences; or if you weren't born what they called normal, or if you got injured, then you were left to explore the world of the different.

Root always remembered the last remark Calabazas had made that night, just as they were drawing near the basalt knob where the drop was to be made. Calabazas said, "Those who can't learn to appreciate the world's differences won't make it. They'll die."

Mosca skids to a stop for the red light. Root knows Mosca could clear the intersection while the light was still yellow, but it has been Mosca's custom to hit the red light at Oracle and Ft. Lowell so they can pause a minute or two at the site where Root's journey to the world of differences had commenced. Root tolerates Mosca's obsession because Mosca sees the accident as supernatural intrigue and the brain damage as strange power. Mosca strides into a crowded bar on a Friday night with Root, weighing 260, dragging a foot and slurring words, and Mosca is oblivious of the stares and remarks. Root is fairly certain Mosca doesn't know any better. Mosca doesn't understand why white people become uneasy when they see cripples or brain damage; their fear is irrational. They believe another person's bad luck is contagious no matter how many times they are given scientific facts.

THE HAPPY ONES

MOSCA IS OBLIVIOUS of the bars all over Tucson where blacks, Mexicans, and Indians aren't welcome. Mosca moves in so fast and gets so caught up in the sounds and faces that he never registers the hostile eyes. Quick, quick he is around the entire room, in and out of the men's room, scanning the pool tables, poking quarters into the jukebox, and counting the whores and single women. Mosca could spend the night sipping at his beer and watching a man across the room, whispering to Root from time to time, as he tried to figure out whether the guy he was watching had gotten his face fixed by the feds for testifying in the federal witness protection program. Mosca knew all about cheap face-lifts and the "new" identities. Mosca knew a bookie in Phoenix who took bets on how long the protection of a federal witness would last once the feds had finished with the witness.

At the intersection light, Mosca smiles broadly at Root and nods his head. His nose runs a little and Mosca wipes it on the back of his hand, takes a swallow of beer, and says, "I been shot twice. Once in the shoulder with a .38 and the other time a .22 in the stomach. But you know, I never passed out or anything like that. Because right away it doesn't hurt. Later it hurts. But for me, I don't know—it was like good dope right in the vein. I sort of could see myself, you know? Everything going on around me. I just lie back and watch. I saw everything even though both times the guys who were there said my eyes were closed and I looked like I was out. But I could tell them everything. That my aunt and her boyfriend came while the medics were working over me and they left to get my father. I could even tell them that one of the pigs that came right after it happened was a woman cop.

"But you don't remember anything about your accident."

"No," Root says, and then Mosca starts repeating what Root has told him, which is the little that Root's mother and the police report revealed. Mosca doesn't care if they are zooming down Oracle Road with the graveyard and intersection far behind. He repeats Root's story lovingly. Green Plymouth station wagon, a white woman driving, works for a real estate agency. This makes Root want to laugh, but the beer and the drugs make Mosca seem as distant as a face on a television screen. But Root likes to hear Mosca's different versions of his accident. Somehow it feels less personal for Root then, and more like one of the old stories Calabazas is always telling about ghosts jumping into the back of a wagon.

"Three-thirty P.M. A Thursday."

"Wednesday," Root corrects him, although the day of the week hardly matters at all, but then it will seem more like conversation than Mosca and one of his litanies of disaster.

"Oh, yeah, man, I always get it confused—"

"With the time they shot you on Thursday."

"Yeah, right: got me on a Thursday afternoon. Cinco de Mayo party along the riverbank."

"That was the .38 in the shoulder—"

"No, man—the fucking .22 in the gut. And I tell you something, that .22 was plenty bad. These guys all want to be carrying a bigger piece." Mosca pats the front pocket of his white jeans. "Twenty-two magnums will kill you just as dead as .38 specials. Aim for the head."

Root nodded. It was the speed, the muzzle velocity, and the shock. "Yeah, like the speed of this pickup." Root nods at the speedometer. Mosca glances down, then mugs a face full of mock surprise. The truck tires squeal around the corner of a side street. Mosca likes to use side streets to ditch the heat. Mosca likes to be able to pull over to the curb in the neighborhood and pour those toots of cocaine on the dashboard. Mosca is laughing now, and Root sees just how crazy this bastard is. But so happy. One of the happy ones, as Root's own mother used to say, her eyes roaming the hospital halls, or the wards where microcephalic children rocked back and forth strapped in high chairs. Root's mother thought their moans and grimaces were laughter and smiles. "Poor little things," she'd say as she pushed Root in the wheelchair, "they are the happiest ones because they don't know any better. They are happy like they are." Root had not associated the retarded children with himself. There was no comparison. Then suddenly he realized his mother believed he was retarded by the brain damage. She had screamed at him before the accident; she didn't want him with "that element." She wanted to wash her hands of him when she saw the motorcycle. To her a motorcycle and friends with motorcycles meant Hell's Angels.

Root had sat up as straight as he could in the wheelchair. He had not made any sound, but his cheeks and the front of the hospital gown had been soaked by the time she had pushed him back to his room. She had made little clucking noises when she saw the tears, and Root had hated her so much at that instant it had been all he could do to keep from trying to smash her, smash her face with anything he could get his hands on—the bedpan, the dirty breakfast dishes and tray still lying on the table. Root identified the clucking noises with the sound he knew she would be making for her grandchildren, any day now, when his sister hatched the first grandkid. Root wanted to bash in her head because she had abandoned him, left him with the other "poor things." She would always see him as one of them. She would always reassure herself that he was happy no matter how many times the doctors and therapists had assured her Root had not lost intelligence or cognitive power; what was gone was partial motor control affecting his balance and speech. The insurance company had paid. But the money had not gone to Root. His mother had arranged the trust while he was still in the coma. Eighteen or not, a man in a coma wasn't a man. Fifty thousand dollars was a lot of money. When he could finally ask her, she had brushed him off. It was all invested in real estate, she said, and he was never going to have to worry about a thing. He'd be taken care of. Root had seen how her

eyes and attention drifted away from the covey of earnest young neu-
rologists standing in front of her, out the hospital window to the roof
of the other hospital wing where pigeons were quarreling in spiral swirls
over the huge air-conditioning unit. Root's mother did not seem to hear
them when they told her the results of the latest testing they'd done.
Her son might be missing a good portion of his brain, but that he still
had an IQ only a few points below the genius level.

"No, Mom, I'm not one of the happy ones. But Mosca is." Root
carries on imaginary conversations, inside his head. Mosca almost glows
with excitement. He is pointing to a bus stop just beyond the dry-cleaning
plant and a little way from a scrap-metal yard. Mosca turns to Root
and only his hands have anything at all to do with driving, and even
then, they flap on and fly off the wheel while Mosca babbles about
witches. Mosca says he has just figured it all out. "What?" "How the
accident happened." Mosca knows how Root's head got dented by that
Plymouth fender. They are only ten or twelve blocks from Calabazas's
place, and Root is thinking this high-wheeled truck could literally run
over the top of a sports car. How about a sports car full of secretaries?
With Mosca's luck they'd all be secretaries in downtown law firms
specializing in accidents. And Mosca added there'd be no way to tell if
any of them had got brain damage in the wreck. "You don't damage
what you don't got in the first place!"

Mosca sees that Root is with him, listening, so he turns his attention
back to driving in time to whip the truck around a city bus stopped in
the curb lane. "I don't know why I didn't think of this before," Mosca
says. "You see, it all adds up. Someone in your family could have arranged it. Or it might have to do with women or the bad things your
great-grandfather did around here. You know, in the old days. You can
never tell. Myself, I'd bet on someone in the family." Mosca pauses. "I
don't know. I hate to say this, but from what I've seen"—Mosca looks
over at Root to gauge his reaction so far—"I hate to say this but—your
mother."

"My mother." Root repeats the statement. No question mark. Not
"My mother?" but "My mother." Yeah. Root knows Mosca is right
about his mother.

Mosca finishes the beer and flings the can to the floor by Root's
feet. Mosca's brain doesn't need the extra spin that cocaine gives it; now
the brain whirs faster than the poor asshole knows how to talk. "She
was always pissed off at you, right? After your dad died. She was always

on your back about your scooter, right? She always thought you were supposed to help out more." Root nods; he knows beter than to argue with a drunk crazy man.

Root can see the tops of the tall tamarisks in Calabazas's yard looming down the block, and he wants to say, "Okay, okay, go on, go on," but Root's high is too serene and too comfortable for words. Root can only nod at Mosca, who is back on the sins of Root's great-grand-father. Mosca was born and will die a Catholic, but he quotes the Bible like a fundamentalist. Mosca goes to the tent meetings on South Fourth Avenue. Mosca claims it can't hurt to know what those cracker Baptist assholes are thinking.

TUCSON WITCHES

ROOT LETS HIMSELF slide farther down into the deep bucket seat of the big Chevy four-wheel-drive truck. All the border smug-glers drive them. They are the equivalent of Lincolns or Cadillacs for pimps. Root prefers taxis. He likes Mosca's theory of witchcraft as well as any he has heard for the accident. Middle afternoon, dry and clear, on a straight stretch of Oracle Road. The woman who hit him testifies she saw nothing. Suddenly his body was just there on the hood of her station wagon. Mosca claims witches have methods of making their victims invisible momentarily so that just this sort of accident takes place. Witches can make a two-hundred-pound man dressed in a bright yellow-and-red hunting vest appear to be a turkey gobbler with a powder-blue throat under a pine tree. An instant after a hunter pulls the trigger the body of his hunting companion falls where the turkey had been. Mosca is really hot now. He is interpreting the meaning of the spell of invisi-bility. Root knows he is right. That one meeting between Mosca and Root's mother had been enough. She had not wanted Mosca to sit on the living room sofa or chairs. She was certain they both had motor oil on their clothes from riding motorcycles. But when Root carefully showed her both of them were wearing clean shirts and jeans, Root's mother ignored him. She had been ahead of them already, telling them she had cookies and coffee in the kitchen and that they'd all be more comfortable in there. Mosca knew immediately it was his dark skin that had set off Root's mother. He had heard all about this woman's grand-parents and the early days of Tucson. How many Indian slaves they had owned? Why they had refused to sell a young Yaqui girl to her own family after her father and the brothers had walked three hundred miles to bring her home!

Mosca kept talking. "Yeah, your mother probably told the witch. She probably said something like, 'I wish he would just disappear,' or something like that, you know?" They had crossed the river and were driving down Silverbell Road; Root could feel his high level off. In a minute or two, the sensation of the ground crumbling under his feet would surge through his body, and Root would need more cocaine and more whiskey. "The witch made you disappear for a second or two, just long enough for blubber ass to turn in front of you. The witch could have been right there that day. Walking on the sidewalk by the cemetery, waiting for you to come riding along. That's how they work. That's how it happens."

Mosca has pulled the truck off the road under the tall tamarisk tree in the deep shade. He is talking while he is spooning out more cocaine. "It might look like just another old potbelly man walking his scabby dog. Or just another wino hobbling along on crutches. All it takes is a split second." Root can't dispute Mosca because he doesn't remember. He can't even remember the week *before* the accident. If he could only remember. Memory returns but in slow motion; the accident must have happened in slow motion, the way all his falls were in slow motion as he learned to walk again.

Mosca is still rambling on about witches as he skids back on the road. Mosca pinches both nostrils and throws his head back violently. Root is riding his high the way he imagines desert hawks ride the updrafts over the arroyos and ravines. Root doesn't want to spoil the feeling right now. He imagines the moment as an edge polished with fine emery cloth. In the truck, Root leans out the window and opens his mouth. He remembers as a kid he tried to drink the evening air because it smelled so good.

"When was the first time you ever really saw a witch?" Root says as clearly as he can, but Mosca is lost in blasting the big pickup down the road, swerving around slower traffic, and Root has to repeat the question patiently, two more times. Mosca shoots a curious look at Root because it is the first time Root has brought up witches. Mosca smiles, shakes his head, relaxes the foot on the accelerator, and hands Root the sack with the peanut butter jar. Root rolls up his window and reaches for the tiny silver spoon.

Mosca settles back in the seat, steering now with one hand. "I ended up in jail on account of a witch."

"What witch?"

"The first witch I ever saw," Mosca says. "You know I can see them. I can just take one look and I know."

"How?"

Mosca shakes his head. His expression is serious. "I was driving down Miracle Mile. I was on my way to sentencing. My first time. I mean 'first time' as an adult. Anyway, I was driving and I was real nervous. I was going before the worst judge—Arne."

"Arne's the federal judge," Root interrupts, but Mosca only nods.

"Now he is, but *before that,* he was a state judge. . . . I was driving down Miracle Mile and I had just made that big turn by that used-car lot across from the Motor Inn where all the whores like to stand, and I looked over at the bus stop and I saw him."

"A witch?"

"Yeah, I saw this guy, and the instant I glanced at him, he looked right at me, right into my eyes. That's how I knew. It's all in the eyes. The lawyer had said whatever happens, don't be late. But I couldn't get over it, you know? I figure the witch probably sensed I have the ability to see things like him. Anyway, all the hair on my neck was chilled stiff, you know, and I could feel sweat just pouring off me. I had plenty of time. It was just twenty to ten by the bank clock, so I thought I would go around and take another pass by the bus stop. I was sort of scared but curious too. It was July and hot, but I could see this old man wore something black and long—I thought it was a long overcoat or raincoat. Then I realized he was wearing a long black skirt. The witch pointed at me and laughed."

"A long black skirt? Did you ever do acid, Mosca?"

Mosca slows the truck dramatically so he can give Root the most intense gaze possible. *"I was going before Arne to be sentenced! You think I'm crazy?"*

HOMELESS

MOSCA VEERED SUDDENLY off Silverbell Road and turned onto a narrow tire track that snaked through the mesquite forest on the vacant lot behind the Safeway store. Beyond the forest was the big arroyo. The hobos and tramps rolled off Southern Pacific freight trains night and day during the cold months. Mosca was taking the sandy road so fast that mesquite branches had nearly torn off the big side-view mirrors of the truck. Mosca was high and talking a mile a minute and pointing out campsites and trees where he'd slept. He had been annoyed when Root made a joke about Mosca's sleeping *in* a tree like a monkey and not under a tree. Mosca said all Root had to do was take a good look at the campsite under the big mesquite trees set back from Interstate 10. "Go ahead! Go ahead! Take a look!" Root couldn't see what Mosca was pointing at. The cocaine had made Mosca impatient. "See the way they made a fort out of piled-up branches they tore off trees?" Root nodded. He could see what Mosca was talking about. It was the kind of fort he had built with the other kids in the summer down along the riverbanks. Make-believe forts where they pretended to live because they knew they could walk away anytime.

The campsite Mosca had pointed out stood apart from the other lean-tos because of the similarity and orderliness of the tents and lean-tos. Root noticed a number of the tents displayed U.S. flags.

"You want to talk about crazy," Mosca began dramatically, "those war vets, those guys are *really* something! They call this their 'firebase camp.' " Mosca was leaning against the hood of his truck fumbling to light up a joint. Root could only see a few men outside the shelters; one wore a green beret. Another wore a camouflage T-shirt and combat boots; otherwise to Root they looked like any other homeless men camped along the Santa Cruz River.

"I been inside their firebase," Mosca said, exhaling the marijuana smoke as he spoke. "They have bunkers, sandbags, everything just like the movies. One of them even calls himself Rambo." Mosca kicked at empty plastic milk and bleach bottles scattered around an old campsite circle of soot-blackened river stones.

Root had listened to Mosca before on the subject of homeless white men. Women and children were different, Mosca maintained, and the war veterans were different too. But the rest of the grimy white men who lived on the streets Mosca called "hobos" and "tramps"; they had no excuses except laziness and they liked to sleep under cardboard in a city park. Mosca knew they liked to sleep in the street because he himself had lived on the streets for a couple of years even when he could have gone to cousins or to other relatives anytime he wanted.

Mosca said he used to get an incredible high off transient living. He claimed it was really a great high—street survival. "Almost as good as coke!" Root laughed out loud. He didn't care if Mosca got upset. Mosca was crazy. Mosca was leaning against the hood of the truck, fumbling to light up a joint. He was still talking about living on the street. It was the "accomplishment," Mosca said, the accomplishment of survival all on your own, without any help, that's what made Mosca high.

"Well, you don't feel it right away," Mosca says in response to Root's laughter.

Mosca stopped to spoon coke up both nostrils, then passed Root the vial. Mosca squatted by the truck, then rocked back on the heels of his cowboy boots, both eyes closed. The rush made Mosca smile. "Okay," Mosca says dreamily. "What I mean is—you learn it's not so bad. It's not the end. You learn you can do it."

When they got back into the truck, Mosca purposely made a wide turn so they could pass close to the war veterans' camp. Mosca was talking a mile a minute about the nut who called himself Rambo and the big black man who was his lieutenant. "You ever talk to any of those guys?" Mosca went on before Root could answer. "Those guys are scary. War taught those dudes all *kinds* of bad shit! I like to hear them talk. Demolitions, night attack—" They were speeding down Silverbell Road and Mosca was laughing. Mosca thought it would be really funny if they ever got hold of a little dynamite and a few rifles. Homeless war veterans attacking the country they had defended so many years before. Mosca thought it would be the funniest thing in the world.

Mosca shook his head violently and waved both hands in front of him. Root was amazed the truck did not veer off the road. The white men on the street were genetically defective. Mosca was certain of it. Take mass murderers for example. They were always white men with educations and good jobs, even families. Symptoms of trouble never came in time to stop the slaughter. There was a lot of evidence these days, Mosca said, that the mass murder of family members might be a scientifically desirable outcome in the certain cases where the entire family was hopelessly defective. The healthiest family member killed all the others. Look at the survivors of the death camps in Germany. They had carried death with them like an incurable fever. All Germans had been infected by the Nazis—even the poor Jews. Mosca blamed all the violence in the Middle East on Israel. Each time a Palestinian child was shot by Israeli soldiers, Hitler smiled.

Root shook his head. "I never get over what a fucking racist you are, Mosca." Mosca does a "Who me?" routine, but goes right back to his theory. According to Mosca's theory, the battered and murdered children are the offspring of defective parents who instinctively kill their own offspring because none in their line is genetically fit to continue.

Root had watched Mosca a thousand times: Root watched as the rage gathered, and then Mosca erupted in a fury of words—his rage and indignation blazing like automatic rifle fire. Mosca's foot would crunch the accelerator and his hands would twist the steering wheel savagely, and the big Chevy Blazer would go skidding around corners, fishtailing into the straightaways. It had been during these berserk rages that Root had seen how he and Mosca the Fly would die. Not in a rain of bullets from the DEA or local narcs; not even shot in the back by one of Calabazas's nephews. They would die maybe even this next minute because Mosca had noticed cars and pickups carrying the middle-aged couples, mostly white people but with a scattering of Hispanics and blacks. They were the low-level civil servants and clerks: the meter readers and delivery-truck drivers who had risen to managerial level by obeying the rules, written and unwritten. Mosca became outraged by the suck-ass expressions on their faces. They were the puritans who believed they were the chosen, the saved, because they were so clean, because they were always so careful to obey every rule and every law. Every yellow and red light was one of their lights, and Mosca plowed through full speed, scattering vehicles at intersections, while he raved and ranted about the churches, rotted with hypocrisy.

Root had learned the only way to stop Mosca's outrage over the faces in the cars on the street was to get Mosca's attention on something that delighted or amused him. Root pretended to be indifferent to the screeching of brakes. Root knew Mosca did not want any response from him. All that mattered to Mosca was getting it off his chest. A reply from Root or anyone might interrupt the flow of outrage. Mosca used to laugh and agree with Root that he did have enough hate and homicide in his heart to last all of them a long long time.

The dumb faces were so full of self-righteousness after church that Mosca wanted to slit their throats. What good would that do? If they had been to Holy Communion, Mosca would be sending them straight to heaven, Root pointed out. But Mosca was pounding his fists on the steering wheel and shaking his head violently from side to side. "Look at their faces!" Mosca had shouted as the big Blazer veered head-on at the car Mosca was pointing at. Root had looked and seen puffy white faces, middle-aged female and male, frozen in stupefied horror. Mosca had whipped the truck back across the center line at the last possible moment.

After Mosca left, Root opened a beer and sat for a long time in the dark thinking about the system and how it worked. Calabazas liked to talk about Root's great-grandfather and the other white men in Tucson. "You can read about it if you don't believe me. What they did. The whites came into these territories. Arizona. New Mexico. They came in, and where the Spanish-speaking people had courts and elected officials, the *americanos* came in and set up their own courts—all in English. They went around looking at all the best land and where the good water was. Then they filed quiet title suits. Only a few people bothered to find out what the papers in English were talking about. After all, the people had land grants and deeds from the king of Spain. The people believed the Treaty of Guadalupe Hidalgo protected their rights. They couldn't conceive of any way they could lose land their people had always held. They couldn't believe it. Some of them never did. Even after it was all over, and all the land and water were lost."

Root was still sitting in the dark when Lecha came in. "I hired a nurse," Lecha said. The taxi was waiting in the driveway.

Root reached over the grimy sofa arm and switched on the lamp. "Who?"

"That blonde. The one that lost her kid. I hired her. Secretary. Nurse." Lecha sat down on the sofa close to him and started rubbing up against him like a cat. Her eyes were glittering as if she was high on something. Whatever it was, it had aroused her. Still, she was quick to sense his mood. Lecha had not forgotten the months after the accident, and even after Root could again talk and walk. She had come into town and found him sitting in the same ratty armchair or lying on the same sofa where she had last seen him two weeks before.

"So what's this about? Business?" Lecha wasn't going to let him forget that he'd told her she couldn't stay there because of "business."

"I was just thinking," Root said.

Lecha raised her eyebrows the way Root often did, when he asked a question. "About how old you are getting. And how fat I'm getting," Root joked.

"Wrong," Lecha said. "You were thinking about your great-grandfather and all the money he made off the Apache Wars. You were wondering if the sins of the great-grandfather bash in the head of the great-grandson."

Root looked closely at Lecha. "What are you on? I could use some."

Lecha laughed and laughed. "Nothing!" she said in a light, young-girl's tone, lying and hoping he'd let her get away with it. Lecha gave him a big kiss and then threw open the door of the trailer. She called out to the taxi driver that she'd be right there.

Root helped her wrestle the folded-up wheelchair down the trailer steps. The taxi driver couldn't fit it in the trunk, which was already jammed full with Lecha's suitcases and other luggage. Root knew Lecha was nervous about seeing Zeta, or maybe it was seeing her son, Ferro. Lecha had waited until she was high enough and had someone to go with her before she'd return to the ranch in the mountains. Lecha leaned out the window of the taxi. "Thanks, sweetie! Take care of that business now!" Root stood in the doorway of the trailer looking down at her. He nodded his head slowly.

IMAGINARY LINES

AS THE TAXI LEFT HIM at the end of the driveway, Root thought he could see a darker form against the black silhouette of the big tamarisk tree in Calabazas's yard. Root could hear kitchen sounds and a radio playing rock and roll from the front of the L-shaped adobe, and more distantly another radio playing *norteño*—accordions, trumpets, and guitars that made a peculiar combination of Mexican Indian music and German polka. Root had never paid much attention to classes or teachers when he was in school, but he had never forgotten the color plate of Maximilian and Charlotte in their gold and jewel-crusted regalia as emperor and empress of Mexico. Blond and blue-eyed, they had been surrounded by legions of short, dark soldiers and honor guards. Maximilian collects insects. He has more and more sexual liaisons with servant girls; Charlotte becomes obsessed with ridding the castle of spiders and vermin. Maximilian sleeps on a billiard table.

Root could see the red ash on Calabazas's cigarette. Calabazas had dragged two five-gallon buckets under the tree for them to sit on. When Root got close, Calabazas had shoved a bucket to him. Maximilian and Charlotte had got as far as any Germans were going to get with Mexican Indians. Charlotte went crazy; she kept trying to get maids and servants to kill the flies and spiders crawling and flying through the royal apartments. The chastised German ladies-in-waiting had complained to Maximilian. The Indians and mestizos refused to kill insects in the palace or the garden because spirits would be offended. When Maximilian began to execute palace chambermaids for spiders and flies found in the royal bedchamber, the days of their reign had been numbered.

Calabazas gazed toward the northwest at the quarter moon descending. They sat and smoked in silence. Finally Calabazas cleared his throat, then spit between his boots. "You two, where were you?"

"Racetrack. Getting high."

"You saw—"

"Horses."

"And Mosca?"

"He moves pretty fast."

Calabazas nods and drops the burning butt between his legs, then grinds it flat with a bootheel. Root sees that Calabazas is drawing himself into his oratory posture. Calabazas calls it "Indian style" when he talks and talks before he turns at the last moment, to the point he wants Root to get. For a long time it drove Root crazy, and he wanted to yell at the old man to just tell him what it was, what was bothering him or what had gone wrong. But over the years Root had learned that there were certain messages in the route Calabazas took when he talked.

Calabazas lit up another cigarette and took a long drag before he started. He blew big smoke rings that tumbled toward Root's face before they broke. "I was born here. My great-grandmother was born here.

Her grandmother was from the mountains in Sonora. Later the other Yaquis used to hide up there from the soldiers. I have to laugh at all the talk about Hitler. Hitler got all he knew from the Spanish and Portuguese invaders. De Guzman was the first to make lamp shades out of human skin. They just weren't electric lamps, that's all. De Guzman enjoyed sitting Indian women down on sharp-pointed sticks, then piling leather sacks of silver on their laps until the sticks poked right up their guts. In no time the Europeans wiped out millions of Indians. In 1902, the federals are lining Yaqui women, their little children, on the edge of an arroyo. The soldiers fire randomly. Laugh when a child topples backwards. Shooting for laughs until they are all dead. Walk through those dry mountains. Right now. Today. I have seen it. Where the arroyo curves sharp. Caught, washed up against big boulders with broken branches and weeds. Human bones piled high. Skulls piled and stacked like melons.

"Did the Jews know? Did the Americans know? So many Yaquis had fled north to settle here in Tuscon. But did anyone care when these reports were told?" Calabazas stands up, takes a last drag on the cigarette, then tosses the butt, ash glowing, into the center of the yard. He leaves Root sitting then returns carrying a small red ice chest. He offers Root a beer and opens one for himself. When Calabazas gets like this, he will talk all night. Root wonders if he can last. Somehow this day has wrapped up about five days in itself.

Root decides he will watch the tail of Scorpio. When the fourth star of the stinger drops below the horizon, he will tell Calabazas he needs to sleep. Calabazas doesn't start talking again until he's downed half of the first can.

"We don't believe in boundaries. Borders. Nothing like that. We are here thousands of years before the first whites. We are here before maps or quit claims. We know where we belong on this earth. We have always moved freely. North-south. East-west. We pay no attention to what isn't real. Imaginary lines. Imaginary minutes and hours. Written law. We recognize none of that. And we carry a great many things back and forth. We don't see any border. We have been here and this has continued thousands of years. We don't stop. No one stops us. You have a working name. That's nothing new. I made up my name. *Calabazas*, 'Pumpkins.' That's what you did. Invent yourself a name. See, my brothers and cousins at San Rafael grew them. Big beauties. A big river down there. Plenty of water for the pumpkins. I'd load up with altar candles in little red glasses. My wife and my sisters-in-law would spend a week making big wreaths of paper flowers. Liria, my wife's youngest sister, could make colored paper talk. Could make it sing. She had a crush on me. She made big orange squash and pumpkin blossoms—they looked so real that other people stared at me and my brothers when we spread them over our parents' graves—how they admired the flowers Liria made!

"So there I'd be at the border crossing, the back of my old green Ford pickup loaded with candles and flowers and usually a goat or fat sheep for the feast. The guards on the Mexican side don't care, hundreds of Yaquis crossed for the feast of All Souls. I never had any trouble. One time a goat tied in back got loose and ate all the paper-flower wreaths, but I've always had good luck. Right at sundown we'd cover the graves with flower wreaths and candles in the red glasses blinking. My sister-in-law and nieces would set out a bowl of goat stew at the head of each grave. We'd sit up at the graveyard drinking all night, listening to Uncle Casimiro's claims that he'd talked to the souls, and they say they don't know any more now than they did when they were alive.

"I don't know. We live in a different world now. Liars and feeble-minded are everywhere, getting elected to public office or appointed federal judge. Spoken words can no longer be trusted. Put everything in writing.

"I'm not saying where or how the marijuana was grown because it grows wild and always has. My brothers kept the pumpkin harvest in an adobe shed behind the house. I'm not saying where the *mota* was. I'm not even going to say which way we cut those *calabazas,* but while we worked in the shed, my sister-in-law and little nieces were cooking pumpkin soups and puddings. Roasting all those fat, yellow seeds.

"At the border I'd wait and cross with all the other Yaquis returning from All Souls' Day. The U.S. only has a two-man station at Sasabe. They hated to see the Indians coming because they knew that meant rat-trap cars, pickups loaded down with pigs and firewood, corn and melons. The U.S. guards were on the alert for brothers and uncles hiding under firewood. They didn't think we were smart enough to bring across anything else.

"So the first time I tried it everyone was skeptical. Except my family in San Rafael. Because *they* knew me. But my wife and her family—well, I had to prove myself. So the first time when I drove into the yard back in Tucson, the back of my old truck was piled high with pumpkins, big and orange-red like full moons. Liria was watering the chrysanthemums and Liria yelled, *"Calabazas! Calabazas!"* when she saw my load. And from that time on, that's what they call me. Younger generations don't even know I have another name. The pumpkins—well, they were something special. Even in those days, what I sold that load for was a great deal of money. My wife's family had to take notice.

"I married the wrong sister, but at least I married the right family. At one time they owned fields up and down the Santa Cruz River valley. They only saved a few fields after the outsiders came. That's when our families were forced to find other ways to make a living. We have always had the advantage because this country is ours—it's our backyard. We know it in the black of night. We know it in the July heat of hell. The gringos come in and the going for us gets rough. But we just get tougher. That's how it's always been.

"So now I get the drift of certain rumors," Calabazas said, finishing a third beer. The moon was gone but the glow off the city lights and the mercury-vapor light down the driveway illuminated their faces. Root could see that Calabazas was trying to gauge how much he knew. Root wasn't family. Wasn't one of the nephews or a husband of a niece. Calabazas had hired Root because Root's great-grandfather had hired him once. Calabazas used to laugh about the turnabout. It gave Calabazas great pleasure, and now it was causing him some doubt. Root looked right back at Calabazas. Calabazas could trust him or not.

Finally Calabazas said, "I don't know what will become of an old man like me." Calabazas had settled back with his head against the tree trunk, his eyes closed. "You—the only one that's never wanted to be boss. All the rest, Mosca included, they have a dozen deals on the side so they can be making their own profits while I ride the risks." Root nodded. The tail of the scorpion was the only star remaining above the horizon. Root felt sorry for Calabazas. Forty or fifty in-laws, cousins, and nephews had depended on Calabazas for as long as Root had known him.

"It's Max Blue—with friends in high places." Calabazas was referring to a specific cocaine route, the one used by the CIA.

That was the old story. But the new story traveled inside the bright blue Samsonite suitcases.

Calabazas wanted to keep what was his—all the years he'd worked with the Guatemalan and Salvadorian connections. Except now the pressure was on. "Your country boys with their brand-new suitcases, know where they're from? Did you see what they were carrying in the suitcases?"

Root shook his head. Root had pretended he did not understand whom they were looking for or what the transaction might be.

"I told them I have to think. I have to think about it."

Root nods.

"Politics. It's never helped any of us. But then here it is."

BOOK EIGHT

INDIAN COUNTRY

RESISTANCE

CALABAZAS WATCHES ROOT disappear into the shadows of the tall trees. He gets a last glimpse when Root steps through the silver disk the streetlight spreads at the curb. Each year one was alive, things got more complicated. In the beginning it had only been the border crossings and occasionally payments to a few border officials, and they had been cousins or kin. But more and more people came. More and more outsiders. They had only been slight obstacles, nothing more to Calabazas and his enterprises than a washout on a back road or a boulder slide in the center of an arroyo. There had always been alternative trails, or other maneuvers. Calabazas had always known they would never touch him unless they got inside. From the first moment Spanish ships scraped against the shore, they had depended on the native Americans. The so-called explorers and "conquistadors" had explored and conquered nothing. The "explorers" had followed Indian guides kidnapped from coastal villages to lead them as far as they knew, and then the explorers kidnapped more guides. The so-called conquerors merely aligned themselves with forces already in power or forces already gathered to strip power from rivals. The tribes in Mexico had been drifting toward political disaster for hundreds of years before the Europeans had ever appeared.

How many years had the U.S. army garrisoned five thousand troops in Tuscon to chase one old Apache man, twenty-five or thirty teenagers, and fifty women and small children? When Geronimo had gone to Skeleton Canyon, he had gone under a white flag of truce, lured there by one of his most trusted lieutenants. Only by betrayal of the truce flag did the white men take him. Geronimo would never have been taken except with treachery.

It had taken Calabazas years to realize what the old scouts had seen fifty years before: the motives of outsiders and others were far more clear than the motives of friends and kin. They had lasted a long time together, Calabazas and Root. Sometimes Calabazas thought Root might have known more than he let on.

Calabazas had studied Root even before the accident, when Root had been smoking dope and riding motorcycles instead of going to school. White kid with Mexican and Indian second and third cousins. Root was tolerated because he had some of their blood. He was a second or third cousin but still a white boy. They never let him forget, but Root remained calm, as if those remarks only proved they had accepted him. Root liked to be the only gringo running with them. Root liked to be the only one people stared at or remembered.

Calabazas knew about Root's mother and her mother too. The daughter of old Gorgon. How white their skin was! Nursemaids and servants had kept them all wrapped and veiled. They were not allowed to play with other children. Teachers were hired for the big house on Main Street. Root's mother had rebelled when she was seventeen. The air force enlisted man she married had been the first man she dated. Calabazas had seen it happen many times. In time Root's mother had come back around with the husband her mother called "trash," much in the same way old man Gorgon had called all his daughters' husbands "trash."

The truth was that one could not trust a son or daughter. One could not trust a wife. Calabazas had decided to trust Root because he had a theory about this great-grandson of old Gorgon. Despite his blue eyes and light hair, Root was a throwback. Mosca was a different case. Calabazas had a good idea why Mosca had taken Root to the racetrack. Mosca was doing a little business of his own on the side. It might be nothing, but the racetrack was not a good sign.

The Italian families had been content to hide out, to "retire" to Tucson. Then the nephews and cousins had come West, and the racetracks and betting had come in. At first Calabazas and the old families didn't mind. They'd let the wops have the Thoroughbreds, greyhounds, and whores. Because Calabazas's people did their best work in the desert mountains, and on the vast burning miles between Tucson and Sonora. Because it was the land itself, that protected native people. White men were terrified of the desert's stark, chalk plains that seem to glitter with the ashes of planets and worlds yet to come. So these mafioso-pimp syndicates did not move beyond the city limits. The old people did not call the desert Mother for nothing; they did not cry in vain.

Once Liria had asked Calabazas what their protection was from outsiders, and he had pointed at the sun and then out at the creosote flats and rocky foothills of cactus and brush.

"We are safe for as long as we have all this," Calabazas had told her, and at the time he said it, he had believed there could never be any end to it.

Now Calabazas realized he had finally lived so long that from then on, he would be seeing more endings than beginnings. He had heard the old men and old women in the village when he was a child. In the darkness after the sun had been down an hour or so, they'd begin talking about how things had once been. They'd say "before" the whites came we remember the deer were as thick as jackrabbits and the grass in the canyon bottoms was as high as their bellies, and the people had always had plenty to eat. The streams and rivers had run deep with clean, cold water. But all of that had been "before," and Calabazas had, even as a child, grown to hate the word, the sound of that word in the mouths of the old ones, and he hated its sound in Spanish and finally in English too.

Calabazas had resented what sounded to him like whining and crying of the old folks during the long summer evenings. He did not want to know what had happened "before." Young as he was and with as little as he knew about the killing of his people, Calabazas was part of the new generation that the old-time people had scolded for its peculiar interest in "now" and tomorrow.

Now that it was safe, Yaquis were returning for visits in the twilight of their days. They brought with them these stories of what was possible in the North, in Tucson.

Calabazas had leapt at the chance to go North. He had been fourteen or fifteen. He had been restless. The old uncle and aunt he lived with kept saying a wife would be the solution. But Calabazas had thought the solution lay in getting out of the village. The mountain village had served as a sanctuary for a hundred years or so, but finally it was just a temporary refuge, and the people were anxious to get back to shallow, narrow rivers with the tall cottonwoods. The mountain village really mattered to only a generation or two who felt a great attachment and tenderness for sheer basalt ridges and thorny brush guarding the narrow trails to precipitous peaks. The contours and textures of the mountain had encircled the Yaquis in massive stone barricades that no white man's army could penetrate. Calabazas knew his old uncle and aunt did not plan to leave because they felt loyalty for the ugly, barren mountain plateau. They wanted to be buried with their loved ones—beloved sisters and grandparents who had escaped the blood-drinking Beast to live out their last days in the high, rugged peaks.

Geronimo had spent the last half of his free life hiding in the high, rugged peaks of Sonora. He had made hits against the Mexican army on his way across the border to recruit unhappy kinsmen from the new reservations at San Carlos and the White Mountains. The Yaquis had been generous with their mountain sanctuaries and strongholds. Calabazas could remember himself the strange arrivals in the middle of the night, when he had been too young not to trust all that he had seen or heard. Nights when the village dogs gave only the low growls and whispering necessary to alert, and then had come low whispering, and from his bedroll in the corner he could press an eye to the little gap in the woven wall and see silhouettes of refugees from villages far away— loaded with bundles, the women weeping silently, dabbing at the corners of their eyes with the ragged edges of their shawls.

Years later after Calabazas had heard stories about the Apaches in Arizona at the same time the Yaquis were hiding in the high mountains. Yaquis liked to argue which groups had "it" the worst—the ones who stayed down with the land in the valleys or those who had gone to the mountain strongholds to fight. "We all fought," old Mahawala liked to say after her first glass of beer. Calabazas always bought his aunt and uncle beer when he came home. And flashlight batteries.

MISTAKEN IDENTITY

"OF COURSE THE REAL MAN they called Geronimo, they never did catch. The real Geronimo got away," old Mahawala said late one night when Calabazas was half-asleep. Although the small cook fire at their feet had died down to a few coals and there was no moon, he could still see the faces of these old-timers well enough in the light of the stars and the wide luminous belt of the Milky Way. High in the mountains, the old ones claimed they were that much closer to the clouds and the winds. They claimed people of the mountain peaks got special attention from the planets and moon. Calabazas had looked at each face trying to determine in an instant if this was a joke or not. Because if it was a joke and he appeared to take it seriously, they would have him. And if it wasn't a joke, and he laughed, they would have him too. But when Calabazas realized the old ones were serious about this Geronimo story, he had given in.

Old Mahawala started out, and then the others, one by one, had contributed some detail or opinion or alternative version. The story they told did not run in a line for the horizon but circled and spiraled instead like the red-tailed hawk. "Geronimo" of course was the war cry Mexican soldiers made as they rode into battle, counting on help from St. Jerome. The U.S. soldiers had misunderstood just as they had misunderstood just about everything else they had found in this land. In time there came to be at least four Apache raiders who were called by the name Geronimo, either by the Mexican soldiers or the gringos. The tribal people here were all very aware that the whites put great store in names. But once the whites had a name for a thing, they seemed unable ever again to recognize the thing itself.

The elders used to argue that this was one of the most dangerous qualities of the Europeans: Europeans suffered a sort of blindness to the world. To them, a "rock" was just a "rock" wherever they found it, despite obvious differences in shape, density, color, or the position of the rock relative to all things around it. The Europeans, whether they spoke Spanish or English, could often be heard complaining in frightened tones that the hills and canyons looked the same to them, and they could not remember if the dark volcanic hills in the distance were the same dark hills they'd marched past hours earlier. To whites all Apache warriors looked alike, and no one realized that for a while, there had been three different Apache warriors called Geronimo who ranged across the Sonoran desert south of Tuscon.

Strategists for both the Yaquis and the Apaches quickly learned to make use of the Europeans' inability to perceive unique details in the landscape. Although the Indians hired as scouts by the white armies were not so easily fooled, still the confusion of the white officers and their arguments with the scouts time and again gave the Apache and Yaqui women and children opportunities to escape their pursuers. The trick was to lead the chase to rocky terrain cut by narrow, deep arroyos. The longer the soldiers rode up and down the steep terrain, the more exhausted and afraid they became.

So the Apache warrior called Geronimo had been three, even four different men. The warrior of prominence and also of controversy among other Apaches had been born in the high mountains above the river now called Gila. This man had not been a warrior but had been trained as a medicine man. As the wars with the *americanos* and Mexicans had intensified, and the ranks of the warriors wanted men, the medicine man had begun riding with them on the raids. His specialty had been silence and occasionally, invisibility. With his special skills, the raiders had been able to move so silently not even the Apache scouts who worked for the U.S. cavalry had been able to hear the raiders walk past their bedrolls.

The old Yaquis liked to tell stories about the days when their beloved mountain canyons used to shelter the four Geronimos. They discussed the strange phenomenon of the Geronimo photographs and of course other matters, such as how best to exploit the weakness of the whites.

First they had settled back over mutton ribs supplied by the youngest of the three "Geronimos." They each told their most strange or amusing experience with American colonels or Mexican captains who believed they had captured the notorious "Geronimo." Denials or attempts to explain the mistaken identity were always rejected angrily by the white men. *"You* are that murderer! The savage beast Geronimo!" the white men would bellow. Explanations or denials had only been further proof of guilt for the soldiers.

General Crook had been careful to engage the services of the traveling photographer stationed in Tombstone. The photographs had been for national publicity to maintain Crook's support among the territorial congressional delegations in Washington. The old people, who generally could not agree on the details of anything that had happened more than a minute or two before, had been unanimous about the photograph. Calabazas remembered he had repeated the word *photograph* to Ma-hawala, and one of the other old people mimicked his tone of dumb surprise. At the meeting of the three Geronimos, naturally there had been discussion of photographic images. All of them, even Red Clay, the final Geronimo who died in Oklahoma, had been photographed at one time or another. Sleet, the youngest of the Geronimos, had been photographed during a stay at Fort Apache when General Crook and the Indian agents had attempted to get the War Department to order the forcible removal of white squatters from mountain land that had already been promised to Sleet and his people.

The photographer who made the photograph had been at Fort Apache for a number of weeks by the time he learned from the camp mulemaster which of the Apaches was "Geronimo." The photographer had perfected his Arizona-desert backdrop and had time enough to commission Apache women to create a huge feathery warbonnet unlike any headpiece the Apaches had ever seen, let alone worn. Sleet had dressed exactly as the photographer directed, then stood slightly to one side so that the long, trailing cascade of chicken and turkey feathers could be fully appreciated in the profile view.

Big Pine had been photographed around the same time. By then the photographer's warbonnet had disappeared, and Big Pine had posed instead with a .45-70 across his lap. The rifle had no firing pin and the barrel had been jammed with an iron rod because Big Pine and his band had been arrested at their camp west of Tucson and even the small children had been locked in manacles and shackles. The locks and chains were "punishment" for "breaking away" from the Fort while Washington made a final determination of their ancestral homelands. Big Pine had tried to explain to the Indian scouts and interpreters that he was not "Geronimo," that the one they were looking for was probably Sleet, and his band of warriors, who were headed for the border. Big Pine offered as proof their tidy little camp. Anyone could see, Big Pine said patiently, this camp had taken months to build, and that the venison drying in the sun had taken weeks of patient hunting. All this proved he and his band of women and children could not have just escaped from Fort Apache and gone there. The half-breed Apache scout knew Big Pine was truthful, and Sleet's band had headed for Mexico. But the

Indian scouts had discovered that American army officers did not like complications. The Indian scouts had already determined that if they ever revealed that mistakes had been made, and that there were probably three or maybe even four Apache warriors called Geronimo, all of the Apache scouts might be court-martialed and hanged. Every hotshot young captain had come to the Arizona and New Mexico territories eager to be the man who captured and brought in Geronimo. Cash bonuses were constantly offered to the army scout or enlisted man whose efforts led to the taking of Geronimo dead or alive.

The man who had been born at the headwaters of the Gila River in New Mexico and who had spent years as a medicine man before assuming certain duties on raids had gone by different names. He had been photographed in a group picture some years before with Nana, Mangaas Coloradas, and Jute. He was known to the Yaquis in the mountains of Sonora as Wide Ledge, which the Yaquis understood to be the meaning of his Apache name. But Yaquis also understood that a person might need a number of names in order to conduct all of his or her earthly business.

The discussion of the photographic image centered upon the group photograph, which Wide Ledge had been shown by a young U.S. cavalry officer. Wide Ledge recalled that the young white man had pointed to the flat paper. Here the chorus of voices in the darkness had quickened, and Calabazas knew they were nearing what they considered to be the heart of the story of the four Geronimos. Wide Ledge, old Mahawala told Calabazas emphatically, had done a lot of thinking and looking at these flat pieces of paper called photographs. From what he had seen, Wide Ledge said, the white people had little smudges and marks like animal tracks across snow or light brown dust; these "tracks" were supposed to "represent" certain persons, places, or things. Wide Ledge explained how with a certain amount of training and time, he had been able to see the "tracks" representing a horse, a canyon, and white man. But invariably, Wide Ledge said, these traces of other beings and other places preserved on paper became confused even for the white people, who believed they understood these tracks so well. Wide Ledge had actually observed a young soldier fly into a rage at the photographer because the soldier said the image on the paper did not truly represent him. The soldier's friends had examined the photograph, but among themselves they could not agree. The photographer only wanted to be paid.

The secret, as a Yaqui or Apache might already have guessed, was that the black box contained a huge quartz crystal that had been carefully cut, polished, and mounted inside the black wooden box. Wide Ledge had had a chance to look through the flat, polished crystal; a boulder nearby had taken on a great many different forms while Wide Ledge looked through the lens. Wide Ledge said he was just beginning to have an understanding of the big polished crystal when the photographer saw him under the black cloth and began shouting at him.

Each of the so-called Geronimos had learned to demand prints of themselves as payment for posing. At meetings in the mountains they had compared photographs. The puzzle had been to account for the Apache warrior whose broad, dark face, penetrating eyes, and powerful barrel-chested body had appeared in every photograph taken of the other Geronimos. The image of this man appeared where the faces of the other Geronimos should have been. The old man called Nana by the whites studied the photographs and conferred with his acquaintances, elderly people who had ranged in the mountains even before the Apache Wars. The identity of the Apache in the photograph could not be determined, but a number of theories were advanced by both Apaches and Yaquis concerning the phenomenon; the light of the polished crystal, the light of the sun, and the light of the warrior's soul had left their distinctive mark with the Apache face white people identified as Geronimo.

Opinion had been divided over the dangers of allowing a photographic image to be made. Could the face and body that kept appearing in place of the three Geronimos be evidence that at some earlier photographic session, the soul of an unidentified Apache warrior had been captured by the white man's polished crystal in the black box and was now attempting to somehow come back? If so, why did this warrior's soul appear only in connection with the three Apaches white people called Geronimo?

Well, there were many interesting questions surrounding the strange polished crystals in the white men's black boxes, Sleet said. Why bother with speculations and arguments over whether the crystal always stole the soul or only did so when white men harbored certain intentions toward the person in front of the camera. The point was, Sleet reminded Wide Ledge and Big Pine, whites on both sides of the border were hunting the Apache called Geronimo. U.S. newspapers from Tucson to Washington, D.C., had the biggest headlines in the blackest ink Sleet had ever seen, demanding death for Geronimo. Wide Ledge was the oldest and most tired of the three Geronimos. Constant movement through rough desert country and the endless scattering of the women and children had exhausted this "Geronimo." He had been ready to "go in" until the bootlegger in the whiskey wagon from Tucson had shown him that same newspaper. The bootlegger had read the big words to him, Wide Ledge said, and that had scared all of them. If they were going to die, to have their heads chopped off and their skins tanned for chair cushions, Wide Ledge and all his people had agreed, they would not make it easy for the whites. The people would crawl back into the stony crevices and cling fiercely like scorpions.

OLD PANCAKES

BUT WHILE THE THREE Apaches had been meeting to discuss the confusion of the whites over "Geronimo," news came that Old Pancakes had surrendered to U.S. troops in Skeleton Canyon. Old Pancakes had been the best customer the Tucson bootleggers had ever had. Old Pancakes bragged that the bootleggers in Tucson protected him from the army; Old Pancakes would only "surrender" his tiny band long enough to rest, fatten up, then they would escape again. Old Pancakes bragged he was fighting his own personal war, for his right to drink when and what he wanted to drink, and as much as he wanted to.

Wide Ledge and Big Pine did not see why this news should concern them. But the young boy who had brought the news of Pancakes' surrender stood before the three Geronimos seemed to have something more to tell them. Sleet told the boy not to be afraid to tell them whatever it was. Well, Old Pancakes had really done it. Old Pancakes had claimed he was the warrior called Geronimo. The Indian scouts doubted the story, but the attaché to General Miles had heard the name Geronimo. The attaché accused the scouts of withholding critical intelligence information. It was no secret General Miles wanted to do what his rival Crook had failed to do, namely, bring in the ferocious criminal Geronimo and make the territories safe for white settlement.

Thus Old Pancakes had finally been able to use his skills as a liar and joker to seize the opportunity to save the others. Old Pancakes had released all his men and women of fighting age early in the campaigns. For years Pancakes managed somehow to guide his small band of old women and small children left in their care, to one or two campsites in the Santa Rita mountains south of Tucson.

The boy reported that Old Pancakes had not expected the Geronimo trick to work because he was such an old man and he had no warriors with him anymore, and he spent most of his time dozing under shady trees in Skeleton Canyon or one of the other canyons in the Santa Ritas. But Pancakes had not counted on army politics. Even when the scouts failed to convince the attaché and the general that Pancakes was an impostor, Pancakes had been certain once the wagon carrying him in shackles and chains reached Tucson, General Miles and his aide would be set straight by other seasoned army personnel.

But as the troops with their captive arrived in Tucson, a strange thing occurred. A stagecoach load of East Coast journalists who had arrived a few days before came running out of bars and whorehouses. The only word Old Pancakes heard was "Geronimo!" Pancakes watched the bootlegger come out of his yard where the wooden vats of fermenting liquor were poured into oak barrels. Pancakes watched the face of his old friend who had made vast fortunes off the Apache Wars. Out came the townspeople who held contracts to supply the U.S. cavalry troops with hardtack, beans, and meat. Pancakes watched the faces of the Tucson city fathers.

Pancakes' good friends, the white fathers of Tucson, realized the Army's mistake but the swarms of journalists at the telegraph station and the army greatly outnumbered them. The news of Geronimo's capture had been telegraphed to the entire U.S. By then, Pancakes had begun to be frightened by his joke. He could see he was not going to be turned loose, with all forgiven as a big misunderstanding. When the bootlegger and other Tucson dignitaries told the army they had the wrong Apache, General Miles revealed to the press there had been cooperation between some white men and the marauding Apaches. Although Miles did not say so, the implication had been the white businessmen in Tucson might have reasons for alleging Miles had captured the wrong Apache.

Within three days the president of the United States had sent a telegram to General Miles, rewarding him with another star. By then Old Pancakes had been locked up in Fort Lowell, and he realized the bootlegger and all the others could not stop what was happening. Pancakes' last hope had been the skepticism of two reporters—one from the *New York Times,* and the other from the *Washington Post.* They had studied photographs in the general's dossier on Geronimo. The general reminded them the photographs were from years before. As they could see from Pancakes' appearance, the years of relentless pursuit had taken their toll. The reporter from the *Times* had a proposal. Would the general allow the captive Geronimo to be taken out the back door of the brig to be photographed? The man from the *Times* had already engaged the photographer. Miles, who was concerned that reporters might in some way tarnish his moment in history, reluctantly agreed. Miles remarked that he'd had nightmares since they had brought Geronimo from Skeleton Canyon. In the general's dreams, Geronimo had brushed away shackles and leg irons as if they were cobwebs, and walked away, disappearing as the troops looked on, paralyzed by an invisible force. For more than fifteen years, five thousand U.S. troops, costing $20 million, had stomped through cactus and rock to capture one old Apache man more sorrowful than fierce.

"And what do you think?" old Mahawala had said, pointing her arthritic finger so it nearly touched Calabazas's forehead. "What do you think? What did Old Pancakes see when they showed him the picture of 'Geronimo's' surrender?" They had all been grinning at Calabazas, waiting for him to pick up where old Mahawala left off. Calabazas opened the last beer and began:

Old Pancakes did not go in much for photographs anyway. He held the photograph in his hands and turned it slowly around and over, sniffing it and sneezing from the strong smell of the chemicals. All the white men watching Pancakes would have laughed; the East Coast journalists would have laughed harder than the *americano* soldiers or the general, who was probably glancing nervously at the brushy slopes of the rocky foothills above the fort, watching nervously for the legions of war-painted Apaches he'd dreamed of the night before. The journalists loved the ease with which this savage desert and its savage creatures so effortlessly yielded front-page copy.

Hours later, after the plate was developed, they compared it to the wiry old man standing in front of them. Old Pancakes had never been defiant, but he had never given up anything he cared about either. He stood before them refusing to admire the piece of paper covered with brownish spots and smudges. The lieutenant and the major thought it was not a good likeness and turned to the photographer to ask for another shot. But the photographer said he wasn't being paid by them, he was being paid by the gentleman from the *New York Times*. If the gentleman from the *Times* was satisfied, that was that. Of course there was little resemblance between Old Pancakes and the image of the Apache that appeared in the photograph.

"And so the three Geronimos suddenly were safe again." Old Mahawala gave a grin as wide as a full moon.

"There," she said to Calabazas, "you have heard that one again." Calabazas had nodded. A lot of Yaqui stories about Apaches were not so good or amusing. Until the white men came, they had been enemies; sometimes they had raided one another. Of course, as they later reminded one another, the raids and the scattered deaths were not at all the same as the slaughters by U.S. or Mexican soldiers.

Calabazas had asked if any Yaqui ever claimed to know the identity of the Apache whose face kept appearing in the photographs. But old Mahawala and the others had only shaken their heads and begun to gather up the empty beer bottles to wash and reuse for home remedies. Then an old uncle had hobbled over to Calabazas. The face in all the photographs had belonged to an ancestor, the soul of one long dead who knew the plight of the "Geronimos." The Apaches were nervous about the dead and the activities of their souls, but the Yaquis were not. The Yaquis had extensive experiences with just such occurrences. The spirit of the ancestor had cast its light, its power, in front of the faces of the three "Geronimos." Calabazas had been fascinated, and he asked the old man if the spirit had entered those warriors. "Oh, no!" the old uncle had said, waving his arms and shaking his head. *"That* is something else again! Very different! Not so good!" The spirit could move in and out easily through a crystal rock, that was all, the old man assured Calabazas. So a camera could not steal the soul as some people fear. A camera could not steal your soul unless you were already letting it go in the first place. But Calabazas had never forgotten the last thing his old uncle had said that night: "Of course in the hands of a sorcerer, who can say what might happen. Don't take any chances. Look where poor Old Pancakes ended up."

WILD ONES

CALABAZAS SAT ON HIS narrow bed with his back against the wall and smoked one of the "special blends" he preferred at bedtime: fifty-fifty Prince Albert and marijuana. Calabazas laughed at the young guys who wanted the *sin semilla,* something that might have had more kick, but that had none of the sweet calm of a female plant that had completed her full cycle. He must be getting old himself if he was thinking about a night almost forty years ago when he had made one of the last journeys back to the Chalky Place camp where the last of the wild ones stubbornly lived out their last days, refusing to come down to the villages along the riverbank where the melons and pumpkins grew juicy and big, where their grandchildren now had toddlers playing in the white river sand.

The old wild ones would not leave the mountain camp until the claws of the winter winds raked their necks and legs with icy chills. But gradually, fewer and fewer of the wild ones reassembled each February for the return trip to the mountain stronghold. Calabazas had heard time and again that these last wild people at their moment of death always spoke of the mountains. Some spoke as if they were talking to the others, sometimes in a time of siege and grave danger, but more often, they were welcoming visitors or they themselves were returning to the stronghold. The last thing old Mahawala had told everyone was that human life spans weren't much, and they should all remember that the soldiers had come once, and they would come again. The day would come when once more the people would have to flee to the mountains. Old Mahawala had even warned them they were becoming forgetful and arrogant because of all the white man's toys, radios and televisions and automobiles, which were causing them to forget a great many important things. "You think it won't happen again, that the time won't come around again. Well, you just go ahead and think that way. I will be the sudden gust of wind that overturns your lantern."

None of those old ones had ever forgotten the final year of the Yaqui struggle when Mexican federal troops slaughtered four hundred unarmed men and women at Rooster Hill. Even then, when the heart of every Yaqui was crying out, no Yaqui ever said "surrender." It was the same war they had been fighting for more than four hundred years, ever since pig-anus De Guzman had come hunting for Yaquis to enslave for his silver mines. Thinking about De Guzman reminded Calabazas about Max Blue. The newspapers had said he had been an important man in the Mafia, but he had had serious injuries that forced retirement in Tucson. Calabazas and the others kept watch, and for a long time Max Blue had performed only out-of-town work—nothing south of Salt Lake City or Denver. But Calabazas and the others had watched the two sons grow up, while the mother bought real estate. Max Blue always had the perfect alibi when a gangland execution took place in Atlantic City or Trenton or in a garden restaurant in Manhattan's Little Italy. Maybe because Max wasn't getting any younger himself, but all along Calabazas had been worried about the two sons. Not because the sons themselves were anything special, but because of the mother. The woman. The wife of Max Blue. Calabazas had never felt easy about her. Because she was doing something all the time with land and with money. And while her husband was reputed to spend all his days on the golf course north of the city, Leah was seen all over, everywhere, and she flew to Los Angeles twice a month sometimes.

Calabazas took a last hit off the cigarette and headed outside for a last look at the night. More and more he was thinking about "retirement" too, except he meant real retirement, not like Max Blue, who arranged executions from the golf course. Calabazas was thinking maybe of Sonora, of getting closer to where he wanted to rest at last. Whatever retirement was, it couldn't be any worse than the years Old Pancakes spent as "Geronimo."

The women and children with Old Pancakes had been loaded on the train in Tucson. Sometime after the Apaches arrived at the island fortress off the Florida coast, white men from a school for Indians in Pennsylvania had come to take away their children. The Indian school in Pennsylvania was in damp country, and many of the Apache children fell ill and died. The Apache scouts, those betrayers of their people, got loaded on that train too. Those scouts who had enabled the U.S. soldiers to evade ambushes and traps, those scouts willing to sell the locations of the Apache camps, those scouts had gone to prison with the Apaches they had once pursued.

Calabazas had begun to notice that he did not sleep as much as he once had, and he identified that characteristic with old age. As the human soul approached death, it got more and more restless and more and more energy for wandering, a preparation for all eternity where the old people believed no one would rest or sleep but would range over the earth and between the moon and stars, traveling on winds and clouds, in constant motion with ocean tides, migrations of birds and animals, pulsing within all life and all beings ever created. Calabazas had not thought very often about warriors because they had died out when he was still a small boy. But he could not forget Old Pancakes. The last years Old Pancakes had been proof of the surprises and the sheer wonder still left in this world. Shrewd Pancakes had made the best of the situation. And if the whites wanted to pay him to ride spotted ponies in Wild West shows and wave an unloaded rifle over his head as the character the white journalists called Geronimo, then that was okay with the old man. Because he had seen a lot of changes throughout those years of struggle. As a boy he had ridden with the great man the whites called Cochise. But he had also heard what the great man had said before his death. Guns and knives would not resolve the struggle. He had reminded the people of the prophecies different tribes had. In each version one fact was clear: the world that the whites brought with them would not last. It would be swept away in a giant gust of wind. All they had to do was to wait. It would be only a matter of time.

Calabazas woke in the middle of the night from a dream in which the old ones long dead had gathered for a celebration.

"Drink up!" they all told Calabazas. "We are drinking to celebrate your wedding! Congratulations! What a lovely bride!" But in the dream Calabazas tried to tell them he was already married. He tried to find Sarita, but she was not in the room. Then through a half-open door, Calabazas saw the bride in her dress; the bride turned, but she was not Sarita, the woman he had married. She had Sarita's body, with the big ass and small breasts, and the small, lovely hands. But the face was Liria's, her sister's.

TWO SISTERS

CALABAZAS GOT UP and made coffee. Another sign of old age. Brewing coffee long before sunrise. The dream that he was married to Liria and not her sister, his wife, Sarita, was the longest-running dream Calabazas had. Calabazas shaved while the coffee boiled. He had never dreamed the actual wedding before, probably because *that* had been the decisive moment, when both he and Liria should have spoken up. Because long before the wedding Calabazas had been in love with Liria. Liria had loved him too, but she had also been confused and frightened by her betrayal of her sister. Sarita was the eldest, the one the other children looked up to and had to obey. Liria had been just a girl, and falling in love with her brother-in-law-to-be had terrified her.

Calabazas folded the chrome legs of the shaving mirror and cleaned up the razor before he poured himself some coffee. It had been going on so long between Liria and him that even if he called Sarita by Liria's name, Sarita answered and no longer even bothered to get angry or hurt. Because Calabazas had lived up to his side of the bargain; he had accepted responsibility for Sarita, as his wife, but also for the others, Liria included. The bargain had been made by representatives of both family groups, representatives who sometimes traveled to Sonora to be certain that Calabazas's elder brothers and sisters were satisfied with the terms. There had initially been friction because the Sonora Yaquis felt the Tucson clan had adopted a somewhat haughty attitude. But already Calabazas had proven himself to be a brilliant businessman, expanding his import-export business year after year. He had taken the whole family, cousins and stray in-laws, and looked after them. Despite the thefts from both private citizens and the city of Tucson, the Brito family had managed to keep a sizable parcel of land along the Santa Cruz River.

Old man Brito, as he got older and his mind became less clear, imagined thieves were stealing his property. But when Calabazas or one of the others questioned the old man, he could not tell them what items were missing or stolen. Sarita's theory was simple. Her father's family had lost a great deal to the first whites who had settled in Tucson. The terms of the Treaty of Guadalupe Hidalgo had guaranteed protection for all land titles granted prior to the arrival of the U.S., but the treaty had been violated again and again by whites greedy for the best land. Sarita and Liria never spoke of what the family had lost without great bitterness. Any talk about the lost land caused Sarita to become furious with him, Calabazas. At first Calabazas had tried to reason with Sarita, gently reminding her the anger she was feeling was for criminal acts committed years and years before. How could Sarita be angry at him?

At first Liria had refused to discuss her sister at all with Calabazas. Liria had been so upset about committing adultery with her brother-in-law that she would hardly speak to him at all even when they made love. It had taken almost a year before Calabazas had managed to get Liria to succumb. From the beginning something powerful had pulsed between them whenever they had looked at one another or whenever one spoke to the other. The strength of this feeling had caused them both embarrassment and apprehension. Liria used to glance nervously over her shoulder. Calabazas thought Liria had acted foolishly. Years later he realized her instincts had been correct, and they should have let the truth be seen. Sarita would have recovered and would have married again. Toward the end, old Brito had confused Liria with Sarita anyway, and for weeks at a time, old man Brito had embarrassed them because he thought Calabazas and Liria were husband and wife, and Sarita was still engaged to the neighbor boy who had died.

Day and night Calabazas had schemed, locating faint trails through dark volcanic rock and thick spiny bushes and cactus that figured in all his dreams. He preferred to do all the border crossing himself, but in time, as his clanspeople in San Rafael grew larger crops, it became clear Calabazas would have to hire help. The family and clan in San Rafael were getting ambitious too. They wanted to guide "travelers" north across the border for a small fee. The business of guiding strangers through the deserts of the south had been going on for longer than anyone could remember. The so-called "explorers" Cabeza de Vaca, Estevan, and Coronado could not have lasted more than a few days without the assistance of Indian guides. Without a guide, the traveler might die of heat and dehydration within sight of a cluster of rocks and mesquite where wild desert pigs and coyotes had managed to scratch water holes.

Calabazas told his relatives to do whatever they wished. Himself— he avoided human cargoes. Too many things could go wrong during a crossing. Ten or twelve gunnysacks full of marijuana could be hidden in the limbs of mesquites or behind big boulders. Gunnysacks or boxes could be abandoned, left for weeks. But human beings—there they were. What did you do with them? Calabazas had always had the philosophy it was better to put in-laws to work for you, even if they were always borrowing against their wages. Working for you, they were automatically tied up with what happened to you. It made the prospect of betrayal less likely. They might not like Calabazas. They might say behind his back that he was nothing but a parasite, and an opportunist, taking advantage of all the land the Brito family had along the river. They might complain that Calabazas thought he was better than they were, when here he was the one born in Mexico and not a legal citizen. They might have any number of slights, injuries to pride or reputation, blamed on Calabazas. But unless one wanted to betray and destroy the entire clan, nobody was going to sell information. No one was going to talk.

Calabazas realized they could stay with the marijuana and do reasonably well. In the beginning marijuana had been all they could afford because smuggling goods demanded up-front money. During the Second World War, Calabazas had concentrated on truck tires, and spools of copper wire, he brought across the border. The truck tires were worth many times the amount Calabazas had paid in Mexico.

Calabazas had always seen his marriage to Sarita as an arrangement with the family, as well as an arrangement with Sarita. Calabazas had exceeded all the wildest dreams of Sarita's clanspeople. Husbands, brothers, cousins, and their in-laws only needed to ask and somehow Calabazas found them jobs.

Years later Calabazas could look back on that day with Sarita and laugh at himself. Because in those days he had been such a cocky bastard. He had thought back then he could "read" what was going on inside a person. How wrong he had been about Sarita!

Calabazas refilled his cup and stepped outside to watch the sun come up. Around at the front gate he thought he could hear the car doors opening. Liria had started going to six-o'clock Mass with Sarita. Did they pray for him? Did they pray for continued success for the family business? Very likely they prayed for that. But sometimes Calabazas wondered what they said to one another, now that they were getting older. Did they ever talk about what went on years before?

Calabazas had been so cocksure of himself he had never suspected Sarita. Out of the blue sky the bolt struck him. Sarita went to Mass every day at the downtown cathedral. Sarita had spent Saturday afternoons helping the women of the altar society wash the altar cloths and priests' vestments. Calabazas suddenly remembered that as Liria was telling him about Sarita's unusual devotion to the Church and to the altar society, he had sensed something strange. According to Liria, Sarita had been a goody-goody who had no time for high school dances. After school Sarita had walked downtown to assist the priests' housekeeper with the evening meal or to finish washing up noon dishes. There had been six priests as well as the monsignor.

How stupid! How blind! How arrogant! A more humble man would have seen it. Sarita had been in love with the monsignor when she had married Calabazas in the cathedral. Her lover had given the Mass and his blessing to their marriage. All of this Calabazas had not seen because he had been in love with Liria.

Calabazas had started laughing then. He could remember the strange reaction of his beloved uncle and aunt to the wedding.

GAMBLING DEBT

THE BRITOS HAD SENT an invitation to Calabazas the day after he had arrived at his granduncle's house in Tucson. Old Brito was notorious for his gambling debts. In fact, Calabazas seemed to remember that at Chalky Place camp they had laughed over Brito stories that had come filtering back from Tucson. Of course when Calabazas had arrived, he had found his poor granduncle needing someone to chop wood for him and someone to fill and carry the big milk cans of drinking water.

Old Mahawala had warned him to "watch out for Brito," but at the time, Calabazas had not been able to imagine what she meant. "Cards and dice, cockfights, dogfights, that old Brito was always there, taking on everyone. Making wild claims." Old Brito had been dark, wiry, with his top front teeth missing, and he kept an ancient revolver, almost as tall as he was, shoved down the front of his baggy trousers. That old Brito! What a troublemaker he got to be! No wonder they ran him out of San Rafael. But old Brito had saved his best trick—the big horse race—for last. Everyone was there. People had come up from Sonora because two of the horses running were from Mexico. Hands were full of fifties. They all made bets. The women sat on lawn chairs under bright-colored umbrellas although the sun was beginning to get low in the west. Old Brito was everywhere making bets. His sore hip never seemed to bother him when he was gambling. There had been four horses. The horse from Hermosillo was a big black one, and outclassed the others. But old man Brito had been taking bets all afternoon on a shaggy-looking gray horse owned by four Tucson men. The gray horse won the first race by a head, and old Brito had jumped up and down until the gun in his pants almost dropped on the ground. But for the second race, Brito bet on the black horse. Brito got a lot of money that way, betting on the black horse when everyone thought the gray would win again. By this time, the sun had just about disappeared, and a breeze was coming up from the river. The racetrack was near the riverbank, where the sandy soil was raked and packed just right.

The men at the starting line dropped their arms and the horses leaped down the straightaway. Oh, how the women in those days loved to shop for the *paraguas,* the parasols. Umbrella crazy they all were. The women went to the races to show off their umbrellas and to keep an ear cocked in the direction of the clusters of husbands and sons laying down their money. Calabazas had never forgot the festive scene at the races. The women and their gorgeous parasols might have been a dream garden of giant flowers, blossoming with turquoise roses and pink pais-leys and parrot-green vines of leaves and buds covered with brilliant reds, yellows, and lavenders.

It had been a good start, but then a gust of wind off the river caught a bright-orange umbrella and tore it from the hands of a horrified woman. It had been as if all time had slowed down so that one could look at the racehorses exploding down the straightaway, head to head, and at the same time one could see the glorious orange umbrella above the heads of spectators. The umbrella paused, as if waiting for the racehorses to catch up with it before it began its descent. The orange umbrella floated down onto the center of the racetrack just in front of the finish line, where it caused a terrible pileup. Although three of the jockeys were thrown, none of the riders or horses were injured.

Brito had leaped onto the track an instant after the horses had collided at the finish line. He had whipped out the huge old revolver, which was so heavy he had to hold it in both hands. It had been one of his blind furies, which he claimed later he did not remember. As the riders brought the panting, foaming racehorses back down the track, Brito took aim and fired. He hit the jockey on the black horse in the thigh. The black horse half-reared, and the wounded rider slid off into the arms of the horse's owner. Brito fired at the jockey again but managed to hit the owner in the arm. By then everyone had scattered, running hunched close to the ground, heads down. The sun had set and the night coolness with the damp smell of the river began to settle over them. All the umbrellas had disappeared from the spectators area, and the woman who had lost the orange umbrella had fled by way of the old riverbank path.

Brito had got himself deep in trouble because the owner of the black horse from Hermosillo had not come up to Tucson alone and had many relatives in Tucson. Before it got dark that day, word had gone out that friends of the wounded were in the mood to squash the little worm Brito. So Calabazas had paid off the irate Sonorans. Old Brito had worked a deal: Calabazas would marry Brito's eldest daughter, Sarita.

Had old Brito and his wife already suspected Sarita and the monsignor?

MARRIAGE

SARITA WAS ALWAYS SERIOUS and quiet, as if her attention were focused far away. Later of course, Calabazas realized that had been precisely the case. Sarita had fallen in love with the monsignor, who must have begun fondling and petting her the first time she had volunteered to help the women of the altar society clean the cathedral.

Now Calabazas could look back and laugh. But at the time, the discovery of Sarita and the monsignor had been a terrible shock. It had been on the afternoon old man Brito died. Calabazas had returned early from one of his "business" trips. It had been a Wednesday afternoon. Sarita would be at altar society until six. Liria and Calabazas had time to go off to the back wing of the house if they wanted. Calabazas had been relieved to see that Sarita had gone to wash the priests' dishes. He had had a lingering urge all morning to take Liria to the back room and push up her skirts.

The advantage of the massive L-shaped adobe house was that the back wing was separated by three-foot adobe walls from the front of the house. The back wing had two entrances, and if someone knocked at one of the doors, anyone inside the back wing could leave by the door on the other side of the building unseen by the person knocking. Liria kept a jungle of hollyhocks around the brick terrace of the back wing. A number of times Liria had had to hurry out one door and into the tall stands of hollyhocks and cosmos while Calabazas calmly pulled on his pants and picked up his woodworking tools to open the door to Sarita or Old Brito's nurse. It was understood that Calabazas had possession of the back wing to prepare wooden crates with false bottoms or to clean the rifles and pistols.

But on this afternoon Calabazas had only just pushed himself into Liria, between her thick, smooth thighs, when there was a frantic pounding on the door to the terrace. Calabazas could tell by the light pounding it was the day nurse. He gave Liria two quick parting thrusts before he slid off her and picked up his pants. But Liria leaped up too because the nurse said the old man had fallen. Calabazas followed the nurse to the sitting room where old Brito lay gasping in the middle of the floor. The old man's eyes were closed, but his mouth was open and his lips were making sucking, smacking sounds as if the old man were no longer a creature of air but a strange fish pulled up from the depths. Liria knelt over old Brito.

Her eyes were full of tears, but she was calm when she asked Calabazas to go after Sarita. Liria held her father's hand and watched his mouth, which frantically sucked at the air while his lungs wheezed and rattled in the bony, heavy chest. The skin on the hand was as soft and smooth as a newborn baby's, although the dark-brown pigment of the skin had faded in freckles and splotches. The day they had stood at each elbow with the old man at the grave for their mother, Liria and Sarita had known that it would not be long before they lowered their father's coffin into the ground.

Liria had cried not because the rattles and gasps from the old man's mouth were becoming less frequent, but because the old man had dictated that Sarita, as the elder, must marry first, and must marry Calabazas. Sarita had not wanted to marry Calabazas. She had not wanted to marry anyone, she told Liria. Liria cried because now the old man was leaving them, but their lives would never be their own. Calabazas had been the old man's tool, someone to carry out his orders, to guard the land holdings, to keep the keys to the locks. The old man had had that kind of power over the lives of all of them. Something was ruined now the old man was gone. Liria could feel it. The old man had been the only reason Sarita, and not Liria, had Calabazas for her husband.

Old Brito's entire body jerked once, then went rigid for a moment, then lay still. Liria lay his hand on his chest. A circle of dampness darkened the front of his trousers and spread wider between his legs.

THE MONSIGNOR

CALABAZAS WAS OUT OF BREATH and his voice sounded too fast and too loud. The women had been working in the pantry off the kitchen area of the priests' quarters when he had pushed open the door. They were starching and ironing white cassocks and white linen altar cloths. Calabazas recognized them only as the older women, most of them widows, who knelt at the front of the cathedral and took Communion at every Mass. They looked startled, as if caught in an illicit act. Calabazas had to ask twice where Sarita was. The women had looked at each other, and by the expressions on their faces Calabazas felt they required some explanation. He told them that old Brito was dying. One of the women pointed in the direction of the monsignor's apartment across the big courtyard, hidden behind a row of oleanders thick with white and pink blossoms. Later Calabazas would recall that the ladies of the altar society seemed to turn and hurry away abruptly, but at the time Calabazas had thought it was because they did not want to miss the drama of old Brito's death.

Calabazas strode across the bricked patio and past the small fountain with white water lilies half closed and clusters of tiny golden carp. Calabazas did not think the monsignor would remain in his apartment during cleaning and dusting. The massive oak carved door was not locked, and Calabazas did not knock or wait, but called out once for Sarita as he pushed open the door. Sarita's purse and shoes were on the floor next to a long wine leather couch in the room that served as the monsignor's library and parlor. Bookshelves from the floor to the high, whitewashed ceiling were lined with black-leather-bound volumes. The monsignor's desk was cluttered with envelopes and letters, and a gold-trimmed, black fountain pen with the cap carelessly left off. The polished wood floors were covered with Persian rugs in deep blues and dark reds, and the luxury of the room reminded Calabazas that parishioners and priests in the diocese had complained about the monsignor, who was, after all, a Jesuit.

The monsignor stepped out of the bedroom while Calabazas was facing the writing desk, and when Calabazas turned, he had expected Sarita, not the monsignor. The surprise left Calabazas speechless. The monsignor had closed the bedroom door behind him. Calabazas realized the long, dark-red robe the monsignor was wearing was not a cleric's robe but a bathrobe, and the monsignor's hair needed combing. Calabazas apologized for entering without knocking and explained there was an emergency at home and Sarita was needed at once. But the monsignor seemed preoccupied with something other than Calabazas's words. The monsignor watched intently as if he were examining each word as it came out of Calabazas's mouth. Calabazas could see the small kitchen through the doorway behind the monsignor. The sink and round glass-top table were spotless. The monsignor had still not spoken. Calabazas did not think he looked angry for the intrusion, but Calabazas mumbled an apology and turned to leave because he was not familiar with the ways of priests. But before Calabazas reached the door, he heard the bedroom door behind him open. Even after he saw the expression on Sarita's face, Calabazas still had difficulty understanding what had happened. It was as if a part of his brain was tossing bits and pieces of information at him but he could not hold them together. They kept scattering—skittering away before Calabazas could form any coherent idea. The monsignor's messed hair. The monsignor's bathrobe. The monsignor's silence. Sarita's stricken expression. Sarita's emerging from the bedroom. Then suddenly it was all there. At that moment Calabazas had not laughed. He had barely been able to swallow. But years later, when he thought of himself as the cocky young stud, so certain he knew the score on everything and on everyone, Calabazas had to laugh. He could imagine himself standing in the monsignor's study, Persian rugs on the polished wood floor, the white-headed monsignor in his bathrobe with Sarita at his side. Calabazas liked to laugh now when he remembered his absurd pride, his absolute belief in himself and in his little world. Later Calabazas thought he and the monsignor might have stood paralyzed, staring at each other indefinitely, if Sarita had not pushed past both of them and run out the door. Calabazas followed her. The monsignor did not move.

The monsignor sang a High Requiem Mass for old man Brito. The vaulted ceiling high above the altar enveloped all of them in the monsignor's baritone, and Calabazas realized how Sarita as a Catholic schoolgirl had been attracted to him. They had never talked about that day. Sarita continued with all her ladies' altar society activities. Calabazas had never gone to Mass or confession anyway. Calabazas would get occasional glimpses of the monsignor driving one of the new Cadillacs donated each year to the diocese by wealthy car dealers. The last time Calabazas had seen the monsignor, walking near the cathedral, the purple-edged cassock had been hanging loosely and Calabazas realized Sarita's old lover was sick. When the monsignor died, the newspaper gave his age as sixty-four. Sarita had moved on to radical young priests smuggling political refugees across the border, so the death of the monsignor did not sadden her.

JOURNEY OF
THE ANCIENT ALMANAC

LECHA REACHED UNDER the pile of pillows beside her and found the wooden ammunition box with the notebooks and fragments of the old manuscript. Her medication left her feeling as thin as an air current a hawk might ride. She sank back on her pillows with her eyes closed and thought how easily she could imagine the gliding and soaring of the red-tailed hawks that often flew near the ranch house. What she needed was her late-afternoon injection so she could be up and around and doing something. She called for Seese although she was perfectly able to get herself moving. It felt nicer when someone else did it. Seese had made friends with the New Mexico Indian Ferro had hired. The gardener. The handyman. The hired man. She called for Seese again and tried to see the face of the little travel clock on the bureau, but its face was turned away from her. No matter.

The injection got everything under way. She was up and out of the pale blue satin nightgown and into her white garden caftan. Shoes were not important. She seized the wooden ammunition box full of notebooks and the loose squares of the old manuscript; the strange parchment got drier and more curled each season until someday the old almanac would reveal nothing more to an interpreter. She headed for the chaise lounge on the patio. Lecha had never been able to get old Yoeme to say much about the old notebooks, except all of the material transcribed into the notebooks had been on thin sheets of membrane, perhaps primitive parchment the Europeans taught the native Americans to make. Yoeme had told them the skins had been stretched and pressed out of horse stomachs, and the little half-moon marks were places the stomach worms had chewed.

"A number of the pages were lost, you know," Yoeme had intoned, with her eyes half-closed so she could recall the details clearly. "On the long journey from the South. The fugitives who carried the manuscript suffered great hardships. They were the last of their kind. They knew that after them there would no longer be human beings who had seen what they saw. A dispute erupted among those few survivors of the Butcher."

They argued whether they should send the strongest to make a run for it, or whether they should give up and all simply die together. Because they were the very last of their tribe, strong cases were made for their dying together and allowing the almanac to die with them. After all, the almanac was what told them who they were and where they had come from in the stories. Since their kind would no longer be, they argued the manuscript should rightly die with them. Finally, the stubborn voices prevailed, and three young girls and a small boy were chosen to carry the almanac North. The pages were divided four ways. This way, if only one of the children reached safety far in the North, at least one part of the book would be safe. The people knew if even part of their almanac survived, they as a people would return someday.

Flight to the North had begun after the occupation by the invaders. The people in the South had heard about the tribes far, far to the North from the traders who spent their lives walking north and south along trade routes. Traders carried parrots and orchids north and returned with turquoise and white buckskins. That had been the final argument: somewhere in the North there might be a few survivors of their tribe who had been given refuge by the strange people of the high, arid mountains.

According to the story, the four children left at night with pages of the almanac sewn into their ragged garments. The eldest girl carried a flint knife. The young boy was given a torn blanket. They were told their only hope was to avoid the slave catchers on horseback with dogs. They must find people in the villages who were not afraid to associate with fugitives. They were carefully instructed before they set out. They were told the "book" they carried was the "book" of all the days of their people. These days and years were all alive, and all these days would return again. The "book" had to be preserved at all costs.

"The story of their journey had somehow been included in these notebooks," Yoeme said, thumping the notebooks with her bony forefinger. "They set out at night and traveled a great distance before daybreak. They slept until sundown and set out once more. They were only young children. The eldest girl was twelve. Perhaps that is why the people in the places they passed were merciful and did not alert the local authorities. The story is all here in the notebooks."

Many weeks into their journey, as they began to enter the edge of this stern motherland, they were weak with hunger. All along they had managed to find water and to ration what they each carried in the canteen gourds. Finally, early one morning as they prepared to sleep until dark, one of the younger girls burst into tears. She was so hungry, her stomach hurting and hurting worse than the "spike." But the eldest girl was suspicious of these tears because only the day before they had each got a handful of gourd seeds from a man tending his garden.

They had entered a dry, barren terrain of sharp stones and steep hills cut by gullies. Few people were to be found anywhere along the trail they followed now. When they had met people, they saw there was little food to be had. They were told the aliens had stolen their modest harvests year after year until the people could hardly keep enough to seed the gardens the following season. The children saw few birds or rodents and no large animals because the aliens had slaughtered all these creatures to feed themselves and their soldiers and their slaves. It had been many weeks since the four children had seen meat of any sort. So the eldest girl became suspicious and asked the younger girl to lift the sacklike cotton garment she wore. But the younger girl refused. The eldest knew then what had happened, and she jerked up the ragged dress. The other children were horrified to see the younger girl had torn an opening in the hidden pocket, exposing the edges of the almanac pages.

While the other three had slept, the younger girl had lain next to the others secretly chewing and sucking the edges of the brittle horse-gut pages. The eldest led the others, and they began slapping and kicking the younger girl until she collapsed on the ground in tears. But they were weak from hunger, and soon they stopped and sat on the ground beside her and cried too.

Of course nothing had been lost because the little girl had eaten only the edges of the pages. But as the children continued on, they began to find entire villages that had been abandoned, where the people had not even bothered to carry grinding stones or cooking pots with them. Finally they reached the point on the river where the village known as "the Mouth" is now located, but at that time, all that marked the place was the big grove of cottonwood trees there. The children found the houses empty, but fortunately they found water in a seep dug by coyotes under the cottonwood trees. The children thought they were alone in the village and had just settled themselves in a huddle to sleep when they heard the sound of a woman singing. The voice sounded happy and the children hardly knew what to make of it. She was a hunchbacked woman left behind by the others when they fled the invaders and their soldiers. The woman moved along the ground like a spider to get around in the village and could even reach the water. But of course she could not have fled to the mountains with the others.

The woman began to smile and talk rapidly to them in a language they had never heard. When they did not respond, she smiled again and gestured for them to come closer to her, and to the cook fire she had kindled in front of her house. She pointed into the big soot-layered cooking pot that was beginning to simmer. Bulbs and roots the woman had dug along the dry riverbed floated in the water like the severed arms and heads the children had seen in a lake near their home in the South. Ferny green leaves floated among the bulbs and roots, and the woman brought out a flat, small basket with crystals of rock salt.

The little boy fell asleep in the shady doorway while the girls sat staring at the hunchbacked woman whose face seemed as big as her body. They had been traveling for months and they had met people who were afraid of them—afraid of who might be tracking the children and of the disaster that contact with fugitives might bring. The girls studied the crippled woman for a while and whispered to themselves. They concluded the woman had been abandoned, left for dead. She seemed so happy to have them. She must have been alone a long time. Here was a place they might stay awhile. To rest up and prepare for the mountains. The children had concluded the bright blue mountain range below the higher and bluer ranges were the mountains they had been instructed to find. They discussed it and decided that since they were almost to their destination, they could afford to rest awhile with the crippled woman.

The woman dropped tiny pinches of the rock salt into the stew and adjusted the level of the fire carefully. She was listening to the girls whisper, but did not speak until they had scooted themselves into the shade with their backs against woven-river-reed wall. The eldest girl could understand nothing the woman was saying, but decided the woman had asked about their destination. So the eldest girl stood up and stepped into the sun, shading her eyes with one hand and pointing with the other. The woman dragged herself past the little boy without waking him and moved around the fire until she could see exactly where the girl was pointing. The woman had then pointed at all the empty houses and had nodded her head, then had pointed back at the blue mountains that filled the entire horizon from the west to the east and as far north as it was possible to see. As the sun went higher and the heat of day descended, the mountains became less distinct and their color a hazy blue.

While the others slept and the woman watched the stew, the eldest girl had slipped away as if she were going to the bushes to urinate. But once hidden, she had carefully unknotted the threads closing the hidden pocket. Although she could no more read the writing than she could understand the language of the hunchbacked woman, she looked carefully at each stiff, curled page. When she returned to the little cook fire, she glanced over in the shade to be sure the other three were sleeping, and then she dropped a page of the manuscript into the simmering vegetable stew. The girl had done it so quickly the hunchbacked woman had no chance to protest. The woman watched the stew for a long time. The girl watched beside her. The thin, brittle page gradually began to change. Brownish ink rose in clouds. Outlines of the letters smeared and then they floated up and away like flocks of small birds. The surface of the page began to glisten, and brittle, curled edges swelled flat and spread until the top of the stew pot was nearly covered with a section of horse stomach. Well, it was a wonderful stew. They lived on it for days and days, digging up little round bulbs in the soft, white river sand, and gathering ant eggs and other things the crippled woman directed them to get. Food was difficult to find, but with the four of them they managed very well, and gradually they realized if they had not come along, the crippled woman would have starved as soon as she had gathered all the roots and bulbs she could reach.

They all began to gain strength from just one potful of stew. Only the younger girl who had chewed and sucked the edges of the pages she carried knew the source of the wonderful flavor in the stew. Then, in a quarrel, the little girl who knew the secret of the stew had told the others. The little boy began to cry. He said he would not eat another mouthful because he might be eating the part of the book in which the alien invaders are wiped out forever. He might be eating the passage of the story that describes the return of the spirits of the days who love the people. The eldest girl had shared the shock of her companions at her thoughtlessness. It must have been the hunger—hunger affected the brain. They had all seen what hunger did during the last months the Butcher had starved and slaughtered their people. But then the eldest stopped crying and said, "I remember what was on the page we ate. I know that part of the almanac—I have heard the stories of those days told many times. Now I am going to tell you three. So if something happens to me, the three of you will know how that part of the story goes."

The little boy did not agree. He did not think tampering with the pages of the almanac was allowed. But the girls were brutal. They told him they didn't care if he ate or not. Every time a page had been memorized, they could eat it. Of course they hoped to reach some of their own people in the mountains of the North. They agreed they should try not to eat any more pages. They would have to be cautious. The crippled woman only watched. The children noticed she was less cheerful, and they did not hear her singing as they had when they'd first come. The eldest said it was because the woman was afraid soon they would leave her, and then she might die. The youngest girl thought the woman was sad because the others in her village had left her behind. The little boy feared the woman had already suffered the effect of having eaten a page from the almanac.

Sometime in the late afternoon, the eldest girl studied the northern horizon, calculating the last leg of the journey. She had learned the paler the blue of the mountains, the drier and more barren the land where they lay. She must not have her willpower fade at the thought of leaving the comfort of the shady cottonwood trees and the water at the little house of river reeds.

The hunchbacked woman was again boiling a potful of roots and bulbs. The woman gestured at the pot, and the eldest girl knew the woman wanted another page from the almanac. But this time the girl was well rested and not starving. She knew what must be done with these pages. They had not yet reached the mountains the color of the sky. Her instructions had been very clear. The girl pretended not to understand what the crippled woman was asking, but the girl also realized by the expression in the woman's eyes, the woman was not fooled. The children had not traveled all that distance without encountering "hosts" who had wanted favors in return. Even the little boy was not safe from such propositions. But their elders had warned them they must be prepared for "such hosts" because the epoch that was dawning was known by different names from tribe to tribe, but their people called the epoch Death-Eye Dog. During the epoch of Death-Eye Dog human beings, especially the alien invaders, would become obsessed with hungers and impulses commonly seen in wild dogs. The children had been warned. The children had been reminded. A human being was born into the days she or he must live with until eventually the days themselves would travel on. All anyone could do was recognize the traits, the spirits of the days, and take precautions. The epoch of Death-Eye Dog was male and therefore tended to be somewhat weak and very cruel.

The girl was careful to take each of the children aside one by one. She told them they must travel on and that she felt the crippled woman might try to stop them. So when they went to dig roots and gather larvae in the coolness after sundown, they were careful to fill all of their gourd canteens. The little boy carried the torn blanket. The hunchbacked woman watched helplessly and kept gesturing at the pot full of roots stewing over the coals. The girl who had first chewed the edges of pages she carried hesitated. She had also had her first menstruation because of the food and the rest, and she wanted to show the others, especially the eldest, she was not a child.

"Go on," she told the others, "I will be following right behind."

The eldest girl tried to warn her. "Don't do this! We must stay together." But the girl would not listen. "At least take off your dress so the pages will be safe." But the girl refused that too because she was confident of herself. The last they ever saw of her was in front of the house of woven river reeds, accepting a bowl of stew from the crippled woman, who was smiling broadly and nodding her head enthusiastically.

The eldest girl went sneaking back the next day while the others slept. She had gone back for the pages, not for their companion. The crippled woman was asleep in the shade of the cottonwoods. The eldest could find no trace of the other girl. For a while she thought perhaps the girl had somehow been lost attempting to catch up with them, although they had been walking in the river sand, following the dry riverbed. But as the girl quietly checked inside each of the abandoned houses, she finally came to a structure that had been used by the men for ceremonial purposes. Part of the structure was set below the ground's surface; even as she stood at the entrance she could feel cool air currents pouring out. The girl had stopped at the entrance although she knew she must hurry. She had not hesitated at any of the other houses, but the air currents she felt caused the sweat to chill on her skin; a shudder swept over her. She did not want to go inside. She did not even want to stand in the threshold and look in.

So there, in the hottest part of the day, after the sun had centered in the sky, a restless breeze kicked up the dust and rustled the cottonwood leaves. The girl was standing in front of the ceremonial house; she did not want to look inside, and yet she was certain she must. The clatter of the cottonwood leaves in the wind, and the waves of heat swelling off the packed earth of the abandoned village plaza, seemed to lull her into drowsiness and sleep. The girl realized if she did not move that instant, she would become paralyzed, and her fear startled her and caused her to lunge forward into the coolness of the dim ceremonial chamber. The heat swelling out of the parched earth had been the woman's ally; while the woman was sleeping, her ally had been instructed to guard the abandoned village.

People did not return to the abandoned village for a long time, and even now, people from the village called the Mouth suffer for reasons that can only be traced to what the eldest girl saw inside the ceremonial house. The epoch of Death-Eye Dog is, of course, notorious for just this sort of thing. Death-Eye Dog has been seated on the throne for five hundred years. His influence has been established across this entire world.

So the girl did not hesitate at what she saw hanging from the cross-beams of the roof. What she had returned for was the ragged garment the younger girl had worn. The eldest girl could only hope the crippled woman had not begun cooking the pages, but had instead feasted upon the liver or heart, known to be the preferred delicacies. The hunchbacked woman had not yet removed the pages from the dress, so the eldest slipped the garment over her head and wore it over her own dress. The children had been told the pages held many forces within them, countless physical and spiritual properties to guide the people and make them strong.

Old Yoeme had paused and looked them both in the eye before she had continued. "You see, it had been the almanac that had saved them.

The first night, if the eldest had not sacrificed a page from the book, that crippled woman would have murdered them all right then, while the children were weak from hunger and the longer journey.

"As long as all our days belong to Death-Eye Dog, we will continue to see such things. That woman had been left behind by the others. The reign of Death-Eye Dog is marked by people like her. She did not start out that way. In the days that belong to Death-Eye Dog, the possibility of becoming like her trails each one of us."

PART TWO

MEXICO

BOOK ONE

REIGN OF
DEATH-EYE DOG

MESTIZO

THE OLD MAN was that way. You could play him cards or dice, and if you beat him, he would just laugh and say you were too young to have such a bad memory. He'd claim he had won with three kings or with five threes on the dice. He would pour you more of the rotten-smelling beer he brewed out of any kind of weed or plant or cactus he could find. The old man was slow, lazy, and dangerous. He would get enough of his smelly home brew in him and then he would start bragging about his ancestors and how they had been the most illustrious and powerful. Full of beer he used to get very serious, and when I was a young child, I felt frightened. It was then he bragged the ancestors had seen "it" all coming, and one time I interrupted to ask what "it" was, and he waved his hands all around the shady spot where we were sitting and he said, "The time called Death-Eye Dog." There was no one in the area who could talk the way the old man did.

Once the old man got rolling he would talk as if others were present and they were arguing with him, debating some point or another. So whenever he addressed the present time we live in as "Death-Eye Dog," it seemed those invisible ones knew the time by other names, and the old man would quickly correct himself. Some knew it as "The Reign of Fire-Eye Macaw," which was the same as saying "Death-Eye Dog" because the sun had begun to burn with a deadly light, and the heat of this burning eye looking down on all the wretched humans and plants and animals had caused the earth to speed up too—the way the heat makes turtles shiver in a last frenzy of futile effort to reach shade. The only true gods were all the days in the Long Count, and no single epoch or time of a world was vast enough or deep enough to call itself God alone. All the ancestors had understood nothing stayed fixed in the universe. Originally the sun and the stars had come from a deep blue darkness, spinning and whirling and scattering themselves in arcs above us, called the Big River or the Milky Way.

That old man had been interested in what the Europeans thought and the names they had for the planets and stars. He thought their stories accounting for the sun and the planets were interesting only because their stories of explosions and flying fragments were consistent with everything else he had seen: from their flimsy attachments to one another and their children to their abandonment of the land where they had been born. He thought about what the ancestors had called Europeans: their God had created them but soon was furious with them, throwing them out of their birthplace, driving them away. The ancestors had called Europeans "the orphan people" and had noted that as with orphans taken in by selfish or coldhearted clanspeople, few Europeans had remained whole. They failed to recognize the earth was their mother. Europeans were like their first parents, Adam and Eve, wandering aimlessly because the insane God who had sired them had abandoned them.

Menardo had loved the stories his grandfather told him about the old man who drank stinking beer and talked about and sometimes talked *with* the ancestors. Menardo had loved the stories right up until the sixth grade when one of the teaching Brothers had given them a long lecture about pagan people and pagan stories. At that time the boys had started looking at the girls who did not go to school, but who were required to spend mornings working around the church, either in the kitchen or in the convent area where they washed and cleaned or in season put up the fruit and vegetables. The girls with quick hands learned sewing and embroidered heavy satin vestments for the monsignors and the bishop.

Menardo had been fat all his life. But in those days the others had picked on him and made fun of him. Pansón was the name they called him, and he did not mind it because one of the older boys had found a far worse name. For the rest of his life Menardo could hardly think of it, let alone whisper it. When he looked in the mirror to shave, it always came back to him. Flat Nose. A slang name the Indians were called. "Flat noses that dogs don't even have." The boy who made up the name was dark skinned himself, but he was also tall and had legs and arms of a man. When he beat up the younger boys, he always picked them up and threw them up in the air, so they were injured in the fall and not by blows from the fists or feet.

Around the time the others had called him Flat Nose and Big Belly, Menardo had made a horrible discovery. His grandfather's nose had been much shorter and wider than his was; the people the old man called "our ancestors," "our family," were in fact Indians. All along Menardo had been listening to the one who was responsible for the taunts of the others. Without the family nose, Menardo might have passed for one of *sangre limpia*. Immediately Menardo found excuses for not going down the street where the old man lived in a small *ramada* in a garden. Menardo was afraid the other boys might come by and hoist themselves up on the back wall of the garden and see Menardo sitting with the old man.

Menardo's cousin had finally come to the house one evening to tell them the old man was begging to have Menardo visit him as before. Menardo had rehearsed his lies for his mother and was able to repeat them to his cousin in flawless form: he was studying now to become an altar boy and had to spend all his free time at the rectory. Menardo almost felt sorry because the old man was the only one of all the adults who did not require anything in return, except that Menardo listen. The old man talked about other times and other worlds that existed before this present one. The old man recognized evil, whatever name you called it.

Not long after his cousin had come asking why Menardo did not visit grandpa, the old man had died in his sleep. Menardo had been relieved once they got him buried because he had studied the shapes and sizes of the noses of all his uncles and aunts and cousins; the only one with a suspicious nose was Menardo, and once the evidence the flat nose was inherited had been buried, Menardo knew exactly what to do.

He had gotten the idea out of a magazine that one of the older boys had smuggled into chapel. They had wanted the magazine because it had ads in it for women's lipstick and perfume, and one of the ads showed a woman whirling around in a dress that showed the tops of her thighs. It was an exciting picture and the boys had nearly ruined it with their sweaty hands, smudging all the black ink on the page. But later on, when the picture was ruined and the magazine was stuffed behind the cupboard of the priest's kitchen, Menardo had taken the magazine to the outhouse, in case he might still be able to make out the image of the woman whirling in her short dress. But the wonderful page had been torn out. What he found was a picture article on boxing and the new flyweight champion of Chiapas. The new champion was talking about his success and his hopes of meeting the flyweight champion of all Mexico, who was second in the world only to the Filipino champion. The champion had hazel eyes, just like Menardo, and his hair was light brown. But more important, his nose had a wide, flat look that the champion called his only regret. "An older, heavier opponent smashed my nose into my face," the champion said. "But the women still like me, don't they, Evita?" the champion said to the gorgeous, shapely blonde at his side during the interview.

UNIVERSAL INSURANCE

THE BOXING ARTICLE had given Menardo the answer he needed. He would bring it up casually. As he had later when he was courting Iliana. Menardo imagined her father was staring at his nose. Menardo had to swallow hard to keep from blurting it right out like a maniac: "It got broken in a boxing match!" Such an outburst would have finished the whole courtship right there. Iliana's family was among the oldest in Tuxtla Gutiérrez—her great-grandfather on her mother's side had in fact been part of the original Gutiérrez family that had settled the area. Menardo had risen quickly in the insurance business because he knew exactly what people wanted to hear.

Menardo sold "insurance of all kinds" to the whole region around Chiapas. As a salesman, Menardo got better and better; he moved up in the world, establishing his own company: Universal Insurance. He made appointments only with police chiefs, mayors, and owners of grocery stores. Of course there were many businesses and lives that could not be insured, not by any company, and not even by God himself, Menardo liked to joke over a cocktail during a follow-up visit with a new client. The concept of life insurance and insurance for buildings, livestock, and crops was new to the people outside the Federal District. Part of Menardo's work was to explain tactfully the new world that they were living in, the new age. What was necessary so a man might sleep soundly at night was insurance against all the unknowns stalking the human race out there. Fire, Menardo likened to a feral cat, stalking at night around warehouses full of hemp or freshly ginned cotton. The glow of the cat's eyes was seen too late to save a lifetime's struggle and labor.

They liked it when he talked to them about hurricane winds that stampeded across the bay, to trample flat warehouses full of coffee beans or tobacco drying on racks. But there were always the older business-men—elderly merchants who had seen their life's savings roll away in wagons driven by thieves calling themselves "revolutionaries" and "the wave of the future." These elder businessmen did not approve of the notion of interfering with the will of God by insuring losses. They did not like Menardo, and it took many visits and a great deal of humiliation before Menardo could get them to listen to him. He was there, he told them, because the "new world" could belong to them just as the old one had. Insurance was the new tool of the trade. What Menardo offered were special policies that insured against all losses, no matter the cause, including acts of God, mutinies, war, and revolution. The policies were extremely expensive, but guaranteed 100-percent coverage. How could they lose? How could they refuse this kind of protection?

The older businessmen inquired into the assets of Menardo's com-pany and found them sufficient. Still they thought he was a fool to insure against losses during revolution since anyone could see the years and the police crackdowns had not cooled off the rabble-rousers and the Bolsheviks. Menardo knew a few of them had developed a perversity due to their advancing age and to the losses they had sustained years ago. Menardo knew that a few of these bitter, strange old ladino busi-nessmen were hoping to see Universal Insurance destroyed and Menardo wiped out. Chiapas had the misfortune of being too close to the border, which leaked rabble-rousers and thieves like a sewage pipe. Menardo's had been the first insurance company to employ a private security force to protect clients from political unrest.

TIDAL WAVE

ILIANA'S FAMILY HAD ANNOUNCED their engagement after one of Menardo's greatest triumphs as an insurer. A frantic telephone call had come from the owner of a shipping enterprise up the coast. An earthquake in the Pacific had sent a tidal wave in the direction of the docks and warehouses. The freighters could be taken out to sea to ride out the high water, but one warehouse was packed full with new appliances just shipped from the United States.

Menardo had had no more than two hours. He chartered a crop-dusting plane belonging to a coffee plantation he insured. He telephoned ahead for trucks, wagons, wheelbarrows—anything with wheels. He offered phenomenal wages for an hour's work. He guaranteed anyone injured or possibly lost if the tidal wave should arrive ahead of schedule would have their family and orphans forever cared for by Seguridad Universal. When the chartered plane landed on the dirt strip behind the hospital, a doctor and a priest came running out to complain they could get no one to help with the evacuation of the hospital because everyone in the town had heard about the amazing wages being offered by Menardo. It was true. The men and big boys stood waiting anxiously glancing over their shoulders from time to time to check the ocean waves. A dump truck, a tractor pulling a flat hay trailer, a milk truck, and a number of smaller pickup trucks, taxis, and horse teams and wagons were ready and waiting. On the hill above the town, the women and children stood together, not watching the ocean but the activity at the airstrip. Menardo took command. He politely asked the doctor and the priest to step aside. Everything would be taken care of, he reassured them. While Menardo gave the orders for the crates of refrigerators and stoves to be loaded and moved to high ground, he questioned the doctor and the priest about the number of patients who were ambulatory and those who would require stretchers. Menardo could feel the power swell inside himself. He assured the doctor and the priest he would return with help.

The warehouse emptied so rapidly Menardo imagined the rising wind was pushing the crates of washing machines and deep freezers out of the building like leaves. On the grassy, green hilltop near the shrine to Our Lady of Perpetual Hope, the women and children and their hastily gathered bundles were surrounded with crates of new appliances. Finally, as time began to run out, a lookout was appointed to fire a pistol from the hilltop so the crews emptying the warehouse would have time to escape. Once it was clear the contents of the warehouse would be saved, Menardo had sent ten workers, three pickups, and a dump truck to evacuate the hospital. Patients strapped on stretchers were transported to the hilltop where they, along with all the others, watched as the great wave approached with the roar of a freight train. A fierce wind rode the giant wave, tearing off hats and flapping hospital gowns. Menardo had glanced away for only a moment, to remove a speck of dust in his left eye, and when he looked again, the huge wave had toppled over itself like the stone seawalls the wave pushed ahead of itself. The crowd let out its breath in a sigh—an *aahh* so loud it almost sounded like a cheer. When Menardo looked again, the warehouses lay folded like squares of cloth at the foot of the hill.

The next day Menardo is famous all over Chiapas State and in the most remote villages and towns of southern Mexico. Newspapers proclaim that Universal Insurance makes good on its promises to protect clients from dangers of all kinds. Not a single new appliance has been lost, and the patients have been safely evacuated although the hospital is destroyed. The publicity from the tidal wave brings hundreds of letters and calls from prospective clients. Menardo can not allow the security of his great new enterprise to depend on the teenage boys and village farmers. Menardo sees then the necessity of a crack team of troubleshooters. Also, a delicate matter has recently developed in a town farther south. A client reports that "agitators" have been talking to his field hands; in the night, vandals have come to destroy the coffee trees. The client, a white-haired gentleman, is a believer in the old order, and in the old ways. He pays Menardo in gold, not currency. "I am solid," the old man says. "I wish to remain that way."

ARMS AND MUNITIONS

MENARDO CARRIES GOLD sewn inside his underwear and socks, which he covers with another plain layer, in case of searches at the international border. In Tucson, he scans the yellow pages. He walks past gun shops, lingers near their doors, hoping to find someone he might approach about a special business deal. He wants his security men to have only the best. He wants an elite security force, one that the wealthy and the powerful will rent for special occasions—elections or funerals and even weddings—when the possibilities for violence proliferate. He prices the guns inside and settles for 9mm Lugers because many of his wealthy clients are Mexicans of German descent. He is a novice. The owners of the gun shops are all white men who wear guns and holsters in their shops. They unconsciously touch their holsters when Menardo walks in their doors. He knows they will call the police if he raises the subject. U.S. laws are strict regarding the sale of firearms to foreigners or citizens of other states. Menardo is once again self-conscious about his flat, thick nose; his skin looks darker in Tucson too.

Menardo sits back in the taxi and ignores the English words of the driver. The taxi stops at the army surplus store near the railroad tracks. Before he goes inside, Menardo checks his reflection in the plate glass. He fears his suit coat is wrinkling and spoiling his image. Menardo sees a man staring at him from the other side of the window. The man is short and slight and has a huge bundle of yellow nylon billowing in his arms. The man does not take his eyes off Menardo as he walks in the door. Menardo refuses to be stared down, but once inside, Menardo realizes he is staring at a man whose face is more than half covered with a reddish-purple birthmark. Menardo drops his eyes, and at the same time the strange little white man drops the parachute and steps over to the glass-front counter. Although the day is hot, the man is wearing tight black leather driving gloves. Menardo admires the parachute in halting English. He might find uses for those in his company. The man pulls nervously at the driving gloves and asks what the company sells. "Insurance and security," Menardo answers, not sure he has used the correct English word for insurance. The man has a pistol strapped on his hip. He smooths the leather of his gloves compulsively; first, with the right hand, then the left. Greenlee sees Menardo staring at the pistol and smiles for the first time. The smile goes on and off like a light switch, as if the man does it only to relax his jaws. The man motions at the back of the warehouse crammed full with racks of surplus army jackets, used parachutes, and empty ammunition boxes. Menardo tries to see everything as he follows Greenlee, but every shelf and corner, every square foot of the floor, is piled with canteens, helmets, glass radio tubes, and spools of copper wire.

Menardo can hear someone hammering on hollow metal. Menardo can't see. He removes his tinted eyeglasses, but it's of little use. The back room of the warehouse is hot and smells like railroad ties and train diesel and crankcase oil. In the dimness he makes out the hood of a jeep. Leaning in a far corner, almost touching the fifteen-foot ceiling, are what appear to be some sort of antitank missiles. Menardo is new to all this, but he has every confidence a businessman of his brilliance and skill can arrange the purchases and delivery of certain high-quality American firearms. But just then Menardo turns to find Greenlee kneeling, pressing on a floorboard. It comes up with a *pop!* and Greenlee lets himself down into the hole in the floor. Menardo later wonders why he followed crazy Greenlee into the basement. Later, when Greenlee has renovated the warehouse basement, they both still laugh about that day. Menardo had followed Greenlee without hesitation. He stepped off the bottom rung of the ladder, and Greenlee flipped on the lights dramatically. For as far as Menardo could see, in the vast basement of the old warehouse, there were stacked boxes of rifles and ammunition. Later Menardo asked Greenlee why he had trusted Menardo, and Greenlee had laughed nervously, smoothed the leather of his gloves, and said he trusted no one. But with Menardo, Greenlee knew anyone stupid enough to just walk in like that and follow him into a hole in the floor could not have been any government's agent.

Menardo had returned from Tucson with a full, satisfied feeling, not only from the big meal Greenlee had bought him at the airport before he left, but with the vision in his head of all those crates of rifles. The rifles with ammunition and delivery charges cost once again the amount of the gold coins Menardo had carried. But Greenlee had been happy to open Menardo a charge account. "This is only the beginning, my friend," Greenlee had said, patting Menardo on the shoulder as Menardo stepped into line with other passengers bound for Mexico City and points south. It had been just the beginning because Greenlee refused to deal with the others—the hotshot colonels who bought "supplies" once or twice. There were other arms suppliers, of course; but Greenlee got the best even when "the best" was unavailable anywhere else. Even then, Menardo used to have fantasies about Iliana dying, and himself falling in love with a lovely young girl who would immediately give him the son he wanted, the son who would inherit the yearly percentages and all the rest. "All the rest" was what occupied Menardo. Selling insurance and security had been a good beginning. But it had not taken Menardo long to realize, as Greenlee hinted, the real future lay in insurance and security of a different sort.

ALEGRÍA

MENARDO HAD MADE AN APPOINTMENT with the most prestigious architectural firm in Mexico City. There, on three floors of a skyscraper, rows and rows of young engineers and architects toiled away, "designing the face of Mexico's future," as one of the senior partners of the firm told Menardo as they toured the premises. But when they reached the upper floor, where the offices of the senior partners and associates were located, the senior partner had led Menardo into a suite where a beautiful young woman sat working at a drafting table, her knees together and the high heels of her shoes hooked daintily on the rung of a high stool. When she turned and looked up at them, Menardo saw the lovely blue silk dress she wore was protected by a starched, white smock that gave her appearance a certain authority. She was, the senior partner told Menardo, their most prized young associate. Menardo did not remember crossing the pearl-gray carpet with the senior partner. All Menardo knew was that he was breathing the odor of many gardenias and carnations blooming together as Señorita Alegría Martinez-Soto took his thick, damp paw in her delicate, dry hand. Menardo glanced down to look at his hand in hers and saw that despite her work with pencils, rulers, and compasses, Señorita Martinez-Soto kept her fingernails long and perfectly enameled. Later Menardo had felt like a bumpkin because after the senior partner had left them alone together,

Menardo had been so flustered he had accidentally stumbled over the wastebasket next to Alegría's desk. But instead of appearing disdainful or stiff, she had laughed at the wadded balls of paper scattered over the carpet. "Little paper rabbits," Alegría had said, pointing and then smiling broadly at Menardo. He had fallen quickly to his knees to retrieve the crumpled paper, but again she laughed and waved a hand with the long, dazzling fingernails and told him the janitors were accustomed to finding far worse. She explained when she really got an idea in earnest and began to make headway with a design, she would lose all track of time; then pencils and pencil leads and wads of torn paper would fly all over her office. "Fortunately," Alegría said, looking deep into Menardo's eyes, "they aren't paying me for being neat and clean or to keep this office orderly." Just as Menardo thought he sensed a certain boldness on the part of the young woman, she indicated the chair across the desk from hers and invited him to sit down.

The first order of business, she told him, was to get a general idea of the client's immediate needs. Menardo had been greatly relieved that Señorita Martinez-Soto was proceeding slowly and from the very beginning. For although Menardo had boldly ventured into many business arenas in previous years and had become a self-made "millionaire," he was quite aware that many of the intricate customs and rituals of the upper classes were still unknown to him. He had never engaged an architect before. He had simply understood this was the practice when one wished to build the castle of one's dreams. Menardo was aware of a feeling far stronger and more urgent than simple gratitude toward this young beauty who had spared him embarrassment or discomfort. She must be one of these "modern liberated women" who did not need to resort to bitchery to get what she wanted. While she talked on and on about the "options" and "alternatives," Menardo's eyes darted furtively over her body, ready to dart back to her eyes whenever she looked away from the big window where she stared as she spoke. She had a fast, breathy way of talking about her ideas and goals—the interplay of structure as sculptural form with light.

"Light?" Menardo had echoed. He had narrowly escaped her eyes catching his on her breasts. Light had been the lead-in topic to their fateful discussion, enthusiastic planning, splendid rolls of blueprints, and finally, the opulent marble staircase to the second level. Menardo had learned that day to speak of "levels" rather than "floors." Before he knew it, the time was up, and Señorita Martinez-Soto was showing him to the door. Menardo saw that all of the other offices were dark, and all but a few of the cadres of draftsmen and typists had left for the day. It was seven P.M. and Menardo had been so entranced he had forgotten his promise to call Iliana at six P.M. Now all that seemed too far in the past to matter. The lights of the capital were blinking and blazing, and without weighing the considerations, Menardo asked Señorita Martinez-Soto if she would not like to accompany him to the tearoom of his hotel for refreshment. Menardo was very self-conscious. He thought "dinner" would have been too forward, and "cocktails" or "a drink" sounded too vulgar. He had only heard gossip or read about liberated women in popular magazines. He was not sure what he should do or what he should expect. But Señorita Martinez-Soto became very cool. She explained socializing was specifically forbidden by company policy unless both husband and wife could be present. Apparently something unfortunate had happened between a client and a junior partner, but it had been long before her arrival at the firm and she did not know the details. Certainly he understood, did he not? Menardo broke into a cold sweat of embarrassment. It was the sort of mistake he tried always to avoid because he knew what separated the social classes were these intricate and confusing rules of etiquette. As she showed him out of the suite to the elevators, she had smiled and told him he should discuss with his wife the points she had raised, and she would have the firm's receptionist telephone the following week to schedule her visit to Tuxtla Gutiérrez. It would be impossible, she reminded him, to design any structure without first surveying the building site.

Menardo could not get her out of his mind. He speculated on her background. She could not have been of high birth or from great wealth. Menardo knew the daughters of those families would never have been allowed to take up a profession. Menardo was relieved she was not too far out of his class. He was not sure, but he thought in another year or two, as the bigger arms sales were made, the millions might raise him to her level and he and she might possibly be considered social equals.

ILIANA

BACK HOME, MENARDO FELT a little ashamed at the way the spell of the big city had overcome him. Iliana was happy and excited about the plans and the design of the new house. It was her chance to get even with sisters and brothers and in-laws who had been skeptical about the marriage. But Menardo had money, and her family had lost much of its wealth over the years. Still Iliana had been reminded, every day since she was three years old, that her great-great-grandfather on her mother's side had descended from the conquistador De Oñate.

Menardo had been cautious about mentioning Señorita Martinez-Soto. He had even let Iliana go on calling the architect "he" until it was time to dress for the party at the Governor's Palace. Then he had said:

"Oh, by the way, it is interesting, and I know you will like her—the architect who is doing the drawings is a woman." Iliana had been intent on discovering whether Tacho, the sullen Indian chauffeur, had remembered to pick up the dry cleaning. She knew Menardo did not like to wear the brown suit to the Governor's Palace where the governor and the general and the ambassador would all be in military regalia. Naturally Iliana understood the importance of these details. In the months of their engagement she had done all she could to give helpful hints to Menardo so her parents and relatives would find him more acceptable. The consequence of these months of exchanging brown shoes or tan shoes for the dignity of black had made Menardo prone to fits of temper just before leaving the house for society "functions" as he called them. But Tacho never forgot anything, and almost as if he knew what the Señora was thinking, he sent the cook from the kitchen to remind the Señora the dry cleaning was hanging in the hall closet. Tacho favored the Señora because she had permitted him to keep his pet macaws in a tree behind the old garage.

Iliana brought Menardo the black suit and ruffled white shirt. She asked Menardo if the senior partner was sure this woman had the necessary capabilities. Menardo could feel himself move within, away from excitement and anticipation he could not pin down, to irritation, then fury, with Iliana and her dumb questions. Iliana had spoiled the new feeling he had been enjoying as he bathed. She was always raising worries where none should be. Iliana was insisting on an expensive automobile, a bulletproof Mercedes, because she felt they had reached "that level," the highest of society. Iliana had only attended the nun's school through the seventh level because her parents believed further education only confused young women. Iliana had never been confused, but she had always been uneasy. She had been born into a family set on the brink of ruin by dirty, stupid Indians who had no understanding of how much they needed their *patróns* to keep the world running productively. Even after Menardo had loaned large sums of money to her father and three brothers, thus establishing himself, Iliana still was gnawed by the fear that disaster was stalking all of them. Sometimes the fear surged up in her stomach causing her to have to excuse herself from her parents' dinner table, or to have to leave the ballroom for the ladies' lounge. Iliana had thought for a long time that a house that was slightly larger than the old family home would *prove* her husband to the rest of the family. Iliana did not want the design spoiled. She felt a little angry the architecture firm had put their dream house in the hands of a woman.

Iliana did not exactly argue. From their house to the Governor's Palace she had listened as Menardo reeled off Miss Martinez-Soto's academic honors and professional prizes. But when Menardo would look to see if that had satisfied her, Iliana would say, "I don't know," which prompted Menardo to launch into another description of the size of her office and its proximity to the offices of the junior associates and senior partners. The last time Iliana said "Well, I'm not so sure," Menardo had taken his head in both hands as if to shake his brains around. All he could think of were the years they had been engaged in this ritual to prove he was worthy enough despite all the money her family had received from Menardo. Iliana shut up when she saw the violence with which he seized his own head. Menardo had never laid a hand on her, but he had often shouted at her and told her how stupid or how greedy she was.

Dinners at the Governor's Palace were business affairs, Menardo reminded Iliana. However gay or social they might seem to her, she should be careful not to interrupt or join in conversations with him and the men, although the former ambassador's wife often did. The governor's wife used to remain so the former ambassador's wife, an American woman, would not be alone with the men. The American woman did not speak or understand Spanish well, and the other women had devoted part of the evening to a discussion of the lack of refinement in certain women who slipped into places and occasions where they had no business. Iliana leaped upon the subject tonight with a special appetite because the woman architect had begun to worry her. Iliana was anxious to have the other women agree with her because Menardo seemed so determined to leave their dream house in the hands of Miss Martinez-Soto.

The judge's wife said that she had recently read a magazine article that concluded that work outside the home caused infertility and sterility in women. The police chief's wife cleared her throat, and the judge's wife appeared flustered for a moment. The women had an understanding: they avoided topics and names, and even words that might in any way connect one of themselves with an upsetting incident or circumstance. Iliana had been trying for years to carry a child to term. How many times had each of them carried bouquets of gardenias and miniature roses to the hospital bed where Iliana sat clutching the bed sheet to her belly, tears streaming out of her eyes, without a sound. But Iliana took no notice of the reference to barrenness, perhaps because Menardo had stopped sleeping with her. It had been kind of the judge's wife, really, to mention the effects of careers on women such as Miss Martinez-Soto. Iliana felt better. That other woman was no threat.

Menardo could hardly concentrate on the conversation after dinner because he was rehearsing imaginary conversations between himself and Miss Martinez-Soto. This was very unlike Menardo, who had learned it pays to listen closely to the conversations of men such as the judge and the police chief. In this district, the judge and the police chief had certain powers that rivaled those of the governor and even the former ambassador. The ambassador had retired from his post in Washington, D.C., to manage business affairs for a wealthy American with vast holdings in Guatemala and Colombia. The women informed their husbands the former ambassador's wife had complained he traveled far more now than he ever had. The wives did not expect to know what importance, if any, might be attached to all this travel. They reported the information so their husbands would praise them. The former ambassador's wife complained in public and sometimes even argued with him. The wives were encouraged to report gossip and incidents out of the ordinary so they would be useful to their husbands not simply as wives and the mothers of their sons, but as patriots.

VIDEO SURVEILLANCE

POWER CENTERED IN THE INVESTIGATIONS the chief of police might authorize independent of any other agency or bureau. The southern border was particularly vulnerable to secret agents and rabble-rousers, sewage that had seeped out of Guatemala to pollute "the pure springs of Mexican democracy." The chief of police had often requested secret meetings with the governor and the judge and former ambassador to brief them on the current investigations or to ask for emergency funds, since over half of the manpower and physical resources of the State Police were committed to the "protection" of state security. The difficulty, the governor had often complained in bitter tones, was that the Federal District did not appreciate what a poor state Chiapas was, and how little money the state had. "None of them understand that we are the ones responsible for protecting our border. They don't know the dangers we face daily." The police chief did not like to hear the governor use the word *we* when clearly the governor did nothing all day but doze in his red leather desk chair and scribble his signature on the piles of papers his secretary brought him. The secretary had been a runner-up in an International Teenage Miss competition only a few years earlier, and the police chief took advantage of the governor's conspicuous absences at their golf games to complain to the judge and to the former ambassador.

"She is as thin and flat as a young boy. She is a mere child. How can that old pig mount her without tearing her open, without ruining her insides?" The police chief was careful to wait until they had finished nine holes and had retired to the shade of their big white umbrella before he mentioned Miss Teenage Chiapas. The manager of the country club had set up a white wrought-iron table and umbrella especially for them on the far side of the ninth hole. The steep slope of the back side of the ninth hole made a perfect backstop for bullets, and it had become their habit to play nine holes, refresh themselves with a few pitchers of margaritas, and then fire a few rounds with their handguns. The police chief had ruined golf games before by allowing himself to become upset over the shocking sexual appetite of the governor. Each had an idea about what the police chief was feeling during those moments when the tequila was whispering in his ears, and he would yell and reach for his service revolver if anyone disturbed him. Menardo thought the police chief must be imagining the governor and the girl together, in the small conference room off the governor's main office, the long, thin legs spread open and skirts pushed up high.

The judge knew the police chief had called the governor's young secretary into his office after midnight for a confidential security check. The judge thought the police chief must be remembering how easily the white silk panties had slid down her long, thin legs as he began what he termed "a body search," which was perhaps a bit uncomfortable, but all a part of official procedure in the line of security duty. The judge thought the chief must be remembering how the girl and governor appeared on the secret video cameras that had recently been installed in the governor's office while he was away at a national conference in the Federal District.

The chief of police could not remember the girl's face, much less her dark buds of breasts or her small, thin buttocks, which he had seen on the video screen. What he could not forget, what remained in his thoughts, had been something far more horrible, something that he had not expected to see but that the video camera had revealed. It was the long, thick erect organ of the governor; in low light it might be mistaken for a loaf of bread. He had of course been with the governor many times in the locker room of the country club after a shower or in the sauna room. But even standing beside the governor at the marble urinal in the Governor's Palace in the capital had not prepared the chief for when the governor first took down his trousers and boxer shorts.

On the videotape, as the governor ran his fingertips over the girl's breasts and belly, his organ would increase its girth but the length remained the same, and most strangely of all, the organ did not twitch or jerk or move as the governor pushed his finger in and out of the dark bush area between the girl's legs. Even at the instant the governor knelt astraddle the former junior miss, the organ hung down with its own weight and had to be lifted and then guided to the threshold with both the governor's hands, a maneuver that reminded the police chief of a mortar crewman loading a shell.

Even if the girl knew how to type and was past sixteen, the legal age for such carnality, the police chief could not help but think that such conduct left their administration, and the entire government party, wide open to charges of scandal the filthy communists relished. At a time when the unrest and turmoil to the south were in a ferment, the police chief felt the governor should not take these weekly golf games lightly. They needed the solidarity and brotherhood more than ever. It was not fitting for this serious business of men to play second fiddle to the flower-pink cunt that already suffered bruised petals, if security's new color-video camera was telling the truth.

As their car pulls out of the governor's private driveway, the former ambassador's wife tells him that Iliana could do nothing but talk and brag about the huge new mansion she and Menardo were having built. "Oh, where?" the former ambassador asks, pretending he is interested when he had hoped for a nap on the ride home. She is a clever bitch and immediately takes offense at his languid response.

"Don't you think *that* is interesting?" she demands. "Don't you wonder how all the money goes to that monkey-face who passes himself off as a white man?" Here the former ambassador is struck by the difficulty in balancing one interest with another. Her information comes in handy now that he is working for the American company. But it is not necessary for her to know anything, and yet the former ambassador hears in her badgering tone signs she is attempting to construct possible links and plots. The former ambassador clamps a hand to his forehead and apologizes, saying he feels one of his terrible headaches coming on. That quiets her immediately because the severity of his headaches necessitates days of bed rest in total darkness with high dosages of morphine. What the former ambassador does not tell his wife is he knows exactly where Menardo is getting the money to build the big new house.

Menardo rises before daylight and nervously showers twice, once upon rising, but then again before it is time to leave for the airport because he feels oily from the humidity and his own sweat. Iliana insists on coming along to the building site with Miss Martinez-Soto. Menardo has always known Iliana would have to participate in the planning and the design. But since the senior partner had put their project in the young architect's hands, Menardo's previous expectations and plans have also changed. Had a senior architect done the designs and blueprints, Menardo might have felt at ease about leaving Iliana to work alone with her. Old man Portillo was a proven master architect and he would know how to sidestep graciously any of Iliana's stupid ideas. But this young woman, though she had been a prize winner and top graduate from Madrid, might lack the experience needed to deal with the likes of Iliana,

who could talk of nothing but greenhouses and conservatories and or-
chid-raising as her new hobby.

Everything about Iliana irritated him this morning. He wanted to
bash in her rouged cheeks and eyes ringed in turquoise. She kept asking
why he wanted to leave for the airport an hour earlier than necessary,
when everyone knew the plane from the Federal District always ran two
hours late. He ignored the questions the first two times she asked, but
the third time he had slammed down his briefcase so hard that the
downstairs maid and the cook scurried out the back door. Iliana stood
with the expression she assumed when her feelings were hurt. She went
back upstairs, and a few minutes later, when Menardo yelled for her to
come, that Tacho had brought the car around, she appeared at the head
of the stairs in her pink satin kimono and said she did not feel well
enough to go. Menardo felt small and helpless clinging to the briefcase,
which felt heavier and heavier in his hand as he stood looking up at
Iliana. He did not want Iliana along on the day he hoped to spend
exclusively with Miss Martinez-Soto.

Iliana was the kind who picked up the telephone and spoke with
the husband or father of any woman she had suspected with Menardo.
This had caused Menardo a great deal of embarrassment. Menardo
believed it went back to the status of his family versus the status of hers.
Had he been from origins equal or higher than hers, like other husbands
he knew, Iliana would not dare make her poisonous telephone calls and
send hate-filled, unsigned letters. Menardo had given her as much money
than any husband of the upper class ever could have. Iliana's own family
would never have afforded an expenditure the size of which the new
house was going to require. Menardo was proud his wife had large sums
of cash to spend. Iliana's own sisters and brothers remarked how much
money she spent. Everyone knew how expensive Iliana's collections
were. She had begun collecting antique perfume bottles after the first
miscarriage; Iliana's deep sorrow over the loss had necessitated some
diversion. Menardo had tried to dissuade Iliana, citing the costliness of
these perfume bottles, but he had not fought very hard. After the antique
perfume flasks had come enameled pillboxes, odd demitasse spoons,
rosary beads of precious stones, pearls, and gold.

Menardo left Iliana, arranging to drive by later after the visit to the
building site so Miss Martinez-Soto could meet Iliana. They would discuss color charts and features Iliana wanted in the mansion. Menardo
had calculated this move to calm any worries Iliana might have had
about his intentions toward Miss Martinez-Soto.

ADULTERY

TACHO ROLLED PEBBLES of different colors on the ground near the airstrip and small terminal building. Menardo sat in the front seat straining his eyes, almost blinding himself even with the dark glasses as he peered into the bright sunlight searching for signs of the flight from Mexico City. Tacho was tossing the pebbles in the old Indian game that Menardo remembered seeing his grandfather play, when Menardo was a small child and his grandfather still had enough eyesight to see the little stones. Menardo had known it was a gambler's game, but today Tacho told him it was a fortune-telling device too. Menardo had been pretending to read the newspaper between glances at the blinding sky, but he stopped long enough to make a guttural sound expressing his impatience with Indian superstition.

"The pebbles can't tell you any more than I already know," Menardo said crossly. "The plane is two hours late from Mexico City, and my guest will be exhausted and half-sick by the time she arrives. She will regret she ever heard the name of Tuxtla Gutiérrez." Tacho was kneeling beside the driver's door, rolling the pebbles while Menardo made his dismissive remarks. "Oh, I wouldn't worry boss," Tacho said without raising his head. "I asked the pebbles. They say she will like it here, sir." Menardo said nothing to this. He hated the way Indians tried to please you, telling you whatever they thought you wanted to hear so you would be tricked and believe their stupid superstitions or at least be manipulated to give them a bonus on payday. Still, Menardo had heard the cook and the downstairs maid quarreling over hot tips they had purchased from Tacho, hot tips on numbers for the lottery. Tacho had not asked them to pay in cash, which Tacho never lacked. He had required them to accompany him to the garage where he kept a hammock handy for naps and such transactions as these. The women had been fighting over the numbers he had given them. The cook had the little maid in tears. The cook maintained Tacho preferred older, bigger women and therefore had not given the maid as many winning numbers as he'd given the cook. Sometime later Menardo learned the cook had been right. Tacho had given the skinny girl only one winning number while the cook with the big fanny had won with five numbers.

Miss Martinez-Soto was escorted off the aircraft by a fair-skinned man in a captain's hat and uniform coat. The captain was apologizing profusely, and Menardo realized Miss Martinez-Soto was wearing an airline galley smock. The captain tipped his hat to Menardo and apologized for the delay and moreover for the "terrible inconvenience" Miss Martinez-Soto had suffered and for which the airline would pay. Menardo took Miss Martinez-Soto's hand and got a faint whiff of vomit. She seemed so much younger and far less formal outside the big city. She laughed and ran her hands down the sides of the smock.

"A man in the seat behind me stood up to go to the lavatory. Just then he got airsick. I am lucky he missed my hair. But he got my dress." Menardo was enchanted. She was talking to him as if they had always known one another.

Alegría did not like the sullen Indian chauffeur. Negroes made better drivers. She did not like the way the Indian looked at her. He seemed to know already. She decided the Indian chauffeur must be Menardo's way of keeping in touch with his humble origins. That ass, the senior partner Mr. Portillo, had insisted on taking her for a long lunch to discuss Menardo, their prospective client. This man was "self-made," as Mr. Portillo put it delicately, which meant here was a man of darker skin and lower class who had managed to amass a large fortune. Alegría hated the way Portillo bit into the olives skewed to the martinis he kept slinging back. Portillo was the only one of the partners who had not tried to seduce her. Portillo drooped in his chair, suddenly giving way to the weight of the martinis.

The courses of the meal seemed to wash in and out relentlessly; Alegría played with her spoon and imagined the plates and bowls were garbage washing onto a beach. When he saw Alegría did not care for the soup, he cut short his lecture on the holy man Bartolomé de Las Casas. He turned to Menardo and the mansion Alegría would be designing. It would be her first solo commission, and he naturally wanted to give her the benefit of all the knowledge his years in the profession had accumulated. Alegría did not tell him so, but Portillo would have nothing to worry about with this commission. The Señor was head over heels for her after one look. No, there would be no offenses, no ruffled feathers. If the wife wanted Gothic vaulted ceilings in the closets, Alegría was prepared to give them to her, and to concern herself only with structural stability.

That night, Alegría had had a bitter argument with Bartolomeo. She told him she had to fly to Tuxtla Gutiérrez the following week. Bartolomeo had been angry at the length of the lunch she had had with Mr. Portillo. Bartolomeo was furious at the time her firm spent with the rich, "petting their swollen little egos!" Bartolomeo had shouted at Alegría, "And then you! You they keep there to pet the swelling trousers of the rich!" Alegría did it instinctively. When Bartolomeo got upset, she groomed her fingernails. The steady motion of the nail file was soothing. Stroking on the bright-colored nail enamel somehow distanced his words. Once when she teased him about *New World* being the terminology of the exploiter, Bartolomeo had slapped her across the face. Staggering back from the blow, tears blinding her, Alegría's hand had brushed the electric coffeemaker. But instead of recoiling from the burn she had seized the handle and slammed the coffeepot into Bartolomeo's chest, scalding him. Alegría had found that a manicure prevented such incidents.

Alegría thought the Indian chauffeur exemplified the worst characteristics possessed by the Indian. He had listened to every word Menardo or Alegría said, from the airport to the dress shop, to the moment he opened the door of the Mercedes for them in front of the Royal Hotel. He not only made eye contact with his social superiors, this Indian alternately had mocking, then knowing, eyes. Alegría hated what he had said with his eyes as she was escorted off the wretched plane by the captain. Tacho had looked right at her as if to say, "The captain wants to reach right into your panties." As he held the car door outside the hotel, Alegría had glanced up and to her horror saw the Indian was smiling as if he knew she was going to seduce his boss later that afternoon.

MARBLE STAIRWAY

ALEGRÍA HAD BEEN IN Mexico City, quarreling with Bartolomeo over the affair she had been having with Menardo, when the shocking message had arrived. Iliana was dead. The accident could be traced back to the first afternoon Menardo ever spent with Alegría, and their visit to the building site on the edge of suburban Tuxtla where a last hilltop of jungle trees and vegetation had persisted. The light that shone down on the site had been magical. It was the most luminous and soothing sunlight Alegría had ever seen. When she commented on it, Menardo had been quick to point out the southern climes had much to offer a person who had spent most of her life farther north. It was true. She had hated the winters in Madrid. Sometimes she thought she might die before the overcast and the wet winds passed. Sometimes she had borrowed money from another student and simply fled on the train to the sun and the ocean in the South. Alegría had nodded, still looking with wonder at the wide, flat jungle leaves and the fretwork of the innumerable vines and delicate mosses, which transformed the blinding tropical light into a light which was soft but which illuminated all crevices with a glow of pearls. The quality of the light instantly became Alegría's focus. Whatever Iliana and Menardo said they wanted—entryways, carports, closets, whirlpool baths—Alegría scrutinized to determine how these details or items might be built without interfering with the quality of the light. It had been for this special light that the fatal marble stairway had been designed. The high wall of glass in the conservatory would supply the cascades of glowing white light.

Iliana and Alegría got along surprisingly well. They had agreed on nearly every detail—from built-in appliances in the kitchen to the size of the storage closets on the second floor. Alegría won over Iliana completely when she presented the drawings for the wall of glass display cases for Iliana's collections. Alegría made the journey from Mexico City twice each month during construction. Menardo could not reveal to Iliana and certainly not to Alegría that the cost overruns were beyond his wildest fears. It was during this time that Menardo began to notice burning sensations in his stomach, no matter what he ate for lunch. The doctor gave Menardo big bottles of liquid chalk to drink when he felt the burning. Dr. Gris asked if Menardo was under any unusual stress. Was anything going haywire at home or with the business? Dr. Gris had protruding eyes magnified many times behind thick glasses. When he asked these questions, he leaned close to Menardo's face, smiling all the while, as if he knew everything. Menardo could smell the doctor's sour breath, and the face seemed more frog than human. The froggy sounds their skin and bodies made in the sweat still embarrassed Menardo. Alegría was part of a different generation; the *slap slap* and *suck suck* sounds paralyzed him with embarrassment, but excited her to new heights. Menardo did not tell Dr. Gris about any of this, but the huge, bugging eyes seemed to miss no detail. At one time Menardo had been much closer to Dr. Gris. They had often golfed together with the former ambassador and the police chief. But after Menardo's young secretary had needed the sudden confidential attention of Dr. Gris, they no longer saw each other socially. Menardo had felt betrayed. He had always given Dr. Gris a wholesale price on the night security patrol that kept the doctor's estate secure from trespassers. The doctor's bill had been item-ized. Besides the initial test and consultation, and the "surgery," Dr. Gris had added nearly ten thousand more for "confidentiality"—an item Menardo had assumed was part of the deal, after all the golf they'd played together. When Menardo had expressed shock at the bill, Dr. Gris had only smiled. His eyes protruded in proportion to the width of his smile. Gris told Menardo saving face in a town the size of Tuxtla Gutiérrez was expensive indeed. A little later, after Menardo had thought about it, he sent a statement to Dr. Gris indicating the price of security against burglars and trespassers had risen due to the revaluation of the peso. Dr. Gris had paid without question, and although Iliana still saw Dr. Gris, and Menardo had brought his nervous stomach to him, their golf games were no more.

Alegría and Iliana had ganged up on Menardo. Alegría saw the jungle as a distinctive feature the house should not deny. At first Iliana had wanted high walls to shut out the jungle. She had not even wanted windows facing east where the clearing gave way to thick vines trailing down from the limbs of giant jungle trees. But Alegría had worked patiently, explaining the glass and steel of the conservatory walls would be as secure as any wall, which of course was not true, but was the kind of reassurance that Iliana needed before she could move on. Alegría argued that in order for the marble stairs to create the effect of a cascade of light, a waterfall of jungle light down the polished marble, the entire east wall would have to be glass. The marble staircase branched from the midway landing up to the second-floor level where one could stand and gaze down into the masses of orchids and bromelaids Iliana collected for her conservatory. One could then turn to survey the great *sala*, which held four long dining tables for winter dinners and had electrical hookups in one corner for dance-band amplifiers. But as Alegría told them both in her breathless enthusiasm, no visitor would ever enter this house without immediately turning to the staircase and to the wall of glass and the lush green jungle vegetation outside the conservatory. Iliana had wanted something grand for her mansion, and the cascade of white marble stairs had been exactly what Iliana wanted. Guests would be forced to notice the conservatory, filled with her latest collecting interest, rare jungle orchids.

All the women Iliana lunched with at the club buzzed with excitement and envy. The judge's wife wrinkled her brow slightly and said that the whole house plan and even the size of the swimming pool seemed "so very modern." To which Iliana had smoothed the bodice of her linen dress and laughed. Of course the judge's wife would not appreciate such a staircase. She weighed close to three hundred pounds and it would have been an ordeal for her. Certainly the judge's wife had no use for the swimming pool—no bathing suit would fit her.

Iliana had been taught by her mother to pretend ignorance of those things that cannot be changed. She had picked up the telephone before and had made trouble for married women sleeping with Menardo. But she had "not recognized" those women and those situations over which she had no control. If Iliana had suspected anything initially, when Menardo kept flying to the Federal District to review drawings and floor plans, once she began working with Alegría, she chose to ignore her suspicions and mistrust. Alegría often took her side against Menardo. Both women were of the opinion that as long as they were going to the trouble of building a house, it should be exactly the way Iliana wanted it. When Mr. Portillo had discussed the commission with Alegría, he had reminded her such opportunities to design a private home of these dimensions came seldom to young architects. Fewer and fewer could afford such luxury.

Iliana had wanted a house the size of Maximilian and Charlotte's palace. But with patience Alegría convinced Iliana that to have a house which was so "out of scale" would be a crime against good taste. The discussions of "scale" had not meant much to Menardo except it might save him millions of pesos. He was a little surprised at how quickly the two women had warmed up to one another after he and Alegría had sex together. Menardo had expected the love affair might affect Alegría in a negative way. Menardo certainly had no desire for Iliana, but he had recovered his old fondness for her in the heat of his passion for Alegría. It pleased Menardo to see the two of them together intently studying blueprints and to understand the various terms used by architects and builders.

Iliana began to miss the club luncheons, and when she did attend, the other wives noticed she no longer complained about the female architect. Instead, Iliana had begun to talk about scale and proportion and clever ways to conceal storage space behind wall panels. Finally, the judge's wife, as the senior woman in the luncheon group, took Iliana aside and warned her she had been absent far too often. Actually the others were angry because Iliana was talking about things they did not understand. Iliana had not been surprised the envy of the other members of the luncheon club had manifested itself in this manner. She had rather expected it and had maybe even hoped for some little confrontation that would set her apart from them. Of course she knew that one did not let such things get too far out of hand.

Menardo spent afternoons with Alegría in her hotel room. Alegría had made it known to all that under no circumstance was she to be disturbed. The afternoons were her time to rework the design plans.

When he came to Alegría's room, he carried a cardboard tube of blueprints. Menardo had long ago learned never to be caught without an explanation or excuse for himself.

LOVE TRYST

ALEGRÍA HAD NEVER AGAIN received him as she had the first time, the afternoon of her harrowing plane flight from Mexico City. Menardo had insisted she buy the most expensive dress that fit her, noting proudly the dress shop had few dresses in her size. The wealthy women of Tuxtla Gutiérrez were too fond of their luncheons and rich snacks at their canasta games. Actually, Alegría chose a white pantsuit of raw silk. She pretended to be shy about spending her client's money. She was aware Iliana shopped there also and did not want to give the saleswomen of the store any extra details for their inevitable gossip. She had come only for the day, to survey the building site. Of course, she had not brought a change of clothes. The disgusting old man on the plane had vomited all over her white linen skirt and matching blazer. This was what Menardo had argued to Iliana after Alegría had returned to Mexico City, and word had reached her that Menardo had bought clothes and a hotel room for their female architect.

Menardo had given her two hours to rid herself of the filth from the plane ride. When he rang up to her room, she had recovered herself and took a businesslike tone. When she stepped out of the elevator, leather folio in hand, she looked as cool as the icy white silk. She had slipped on her big sunglasses before she stepped outside. Tacho was holding the car door. She stepped around the chauffeur, leaning as far away from him as she could. All the way to the building site she sat with a shoulder slightly turned to him, only nodding when Menardo pointed out the court building, the police station, the entrance to the country club, and the Governor's Palace. Menardo had offered her a hand as she stepped out of the car, but she had not taken it. She walked ahead of him to survey the clearing. Menardo had lost all hope then and was about to join Tacho, who was leaning against the hood of the car, when Alegría suddenly turned and called out. Menardo had jumped, fearing a poisonous snake or a drunken Indian. But Tacho did not move, and Menardo was embarrassed to see Alegría laughing. "I didn't mean to frighten you," she said. "I was only calling you over to see this." Menardo hurried to the place she was standing.

"Look," she said, but when Menardo looked he saw only the ragged edge of the jungle where the bulldozers had stopped.

"What do you think?" Alegría had been pointing up into the fringe of wide, waxy leaves. Menardo looked vainly for a bird or a green tree frog or a lizard or snake. All he saw were branches, leaves, and vines in a tangle and dappled by a few shafts of sunlight. "If it's a flower of some kind," Menardo said, laughing nervously, "don't expect me to see it! I leave that to the florists."

"The light," Alegría said with a lovely tone to her voice, as if she were in love with the light. "See?"

"Oh!" Menardo said quickly. "Yes, yes, I do!"

"There is nothing more lovely than the veiled sunlight the jungle gives. We will let this light be the theme of the entire house."

"Yes," Menardo said, squinting up at the tops of the jungle trees, wondering how Iliana would ever agree to have her dream home built so close to the jungle.

Alegría had grown more and more excited about the light and the ways in which the special qualities of the softly filtered sun could be enhanced by the design of the building and the placement of windows. She had talked nonstop all the way to the hotel. Menardo could only watch her breathlessly, because when Alegría was talking about her vision of what the new house could be, her face and her hands—her whole body—were vibrant. Suddenly Menardo felt sweat rolling down his sides, sliding over his ribs and soaking the top of his shorts and trousers.

In the hotel room Menardo stood in a daze as Alegría unrolled rolls of buff tracing paper and made broad sweeps with her felt pen, quickly sketching walls of glass, a central stairway in front of the glass, and a wall that partially enclosed the jungle rather than shutting it out. When she stood back and looked at him for some words, some response, Menardo felt his desire choking him. He tried to speak but the effort made his eyes water. All he could do was move his head rapidly, and the sight of him, short, stocky, eyes wide, and head nodding, was almost more than Alegría could bear.

Later Menardo would see it again and again. Alegría had turned away from him, and when she turned back, suddenly the white silk blouse had been unbuttoned so he could see her pink brassiere and her navel. He regretted he was not a polished, finished man because he knew she must be used to that sort. The two steps he took toward her he remembered were uneven. The last step he might have stumbled. He blamed Alegría's sudden move. Just as he reached her and put his hands on her shoulders (she was as tall as he), she had stepped back, deliberately falling backward onto the hotel bed. Menardo had never experienced a seduction of this kind before. The whores had never wasted a single motion. Their moves were methodical. They left nothing to surprise. A few of the small-town girls had hoped to catch him for a husband and had made lavish displays of themselves, spreading their legs wide, hitching skirts and dresses high, slipping panties to their ankles for him. But Menardo had not been surprised; that had been the sort of behavior he had come to expect as a rising star, a man bound for wealth.

Menardo squeezed his hand down to unzip his trousers, and Alegría had moaned and pushed against him as the back of his hand pressed against the mound between her legs. She was holding him by the shoulders, pulling him down so it was difficult to get the trouser's zipper all the way open. He felt her raise her hips high and felt her peel off her panties beneath him. At that instant, a warm, perfumed scent enveloped them, the zipper opened, but Menardo knew he would never be able to get the trousers off. He settled for an open zipper. He was barely able to push his cock inside her before he had the sensation of a runaway horse leaping from under him, leaving him, falling far far behind, then spiraling up to the explosions of light, and at last deep, soft darkness.

Alegría listened to herself. When she was of two minds about anything, she created an internal debate. She was surprised she had even considered an affair with this provincial businessman. If word ever got back to Portillo and the rest of the old men at the firm, her future in the profession would be ruined. She would immediately be fired, and she would never work again unless she went far from Mexico City. Alegría could imagine Portillo saying, "There is a fine line, a fine balance between keeping the client happy and satisfied, and absolute surrender of good taste and moral values." Portillo had of course been referring to the problem of clients' demands for Roman columns and Gothic vaulted ceilings. Alegría could feel the sticky wetness leaking out between her thighs and running under her buttocks soaking the bed. With each breath Menardo's weight on her chest was suffocating her. When she tried to shift the weight, Menardo rolled off her quickly, apologizing, asking her if she was all right. Alegría wanted to laugh at Menardo's awkwardness and his fear that he might have caused her discomfort. Instead she rolled over with her back to him and looked at the sky out the window. It was nearing sundown. The light was a rich chrome-yellow on the white walls of the hotel. Even as she was watching, a pink tint was beginning to wash into the yellow-gold. Alegría felt her chest and throat thicken, and tears began rolling down her cheeks. She was remembering what one of the Basque students had said to her in the smoky coffeehouse near the campus in Madrid. The Basque had been the only one who had really tried to persuade her. The other communists had never taken her seriously, especially not the women. But the little Basque had shaken his head at her and warned that class defined sex for your family and you. She had laughed gaily and he had said, "Some-day you'll know. You'll feel it. How men use you. Treat you like a thing. The rich man. The powerful men. You feel how they fuck."

HIGH RISK

THE LITTLE BASQUE had died in the riots. She had been taking final examinations in the school of architecture, so Alegría had not cried. She could not afford to be upset during examinations. The Basques had been all they had talked about at the coffeehouse. Dying for the cause. It was what he wanted, Alegría would say when the others brought it up. But now ten years later she was lying on a hotel bed in the capital city of one of the poorest states in Mexico, crying for the Basque who

had been so short none of them had ever known his real name. "Shorty."
Was she crying for the Basque? The proletarian women would have said
she was crying for herself, who else? Because they said she would always
be looking out just for herself. Alegría wished she could tell the Basque:
   "You are right. Menardo here thinks I am out of his class, and so
he fumbles and apologizes." Alegría had not had sex before with a man
so anxious to please her. She had not had sex with a man who sensed
so quickly her moods. She had been blunt with Menardo. She had told
him she was risking not just her position at the firm but her entire career
as an architect for him.
   Menardo had listened to her discuss the dangers. But he did not
share the anxiety or fear Alegría felt because he was so certain he could
take care of her in the event anything happened. He had just concluded
negotiations with an arms dealer in Tucson. If plans were successful,
Menardo knew he would in a few more years be one of the wealthiest
men in the south of Mexico. Menardo wanted to take her hand and
lean close so he could get the full effect of her lovely hazel eyes. But
Alegría had insisted they go downstairs quickly afterward. They had
both carried rolls of blueprints when they entered the hotel dining room.
Alegría was still discussing the ruin of her career and her life in low,
calm tones lest any of the busboys or waiters sense urgency and eaves-
drop. "You have nothing to worry about," Menardo said expansively.
"Believe me. Arrangements would be made." Alegría had looked at the
brown moon face and flat nose and the shining dark eyes and thought
how little he knew or understood, despite the wealth he had begun to
accumulate.
   "I would hate doing nothing," Alegría had warned him. "I would
go crazy." Menardo began to outline what he would do for Alegría in
the unlikely event of dismissal, but she had cut him short. She had refused
to discuss it further. It was upsetting her. There was no need to talk
because nothing was going to happen.
   For a long time, as Alegría and Iliana worked together closely on
the interior designs for the house, Menardo was convinced their arrangement was safe. Of course he longed to have Alegría come down
from Mexico City more often than twice a month, but the policies of
her firm did not allow that even during the construction phase. Menardo
obeyed Alegría's dictates. If she felt that a visit to her hotel room was
not wise, then Menardo was a gentleman and met her only in the hotel
bar. Sometimes Alegría restricted him to visits only when Iliana was
present. Iliana liked to dine at the country club when Alegría was in

town, because then Iliana could show off in front of the women from her club. Iliana would carry a roll of blueprints to dinner with her although they never discussed the plans there. The factor of Iliana and her friends at the women's club had fooled both Alegría and Menardo. They had been so careful to watch out for Iliana and to include her in every phase, they had forgotten the trouble might come from Iliana's so-called friends.

The other women could tell by the way Iliana talked about the female architect that she suspected nothing between that woman and her husband. None of them thought twice about the casual encounters their husbands might have. There was no worry because, if anything, casual activity kept their husbands in line at home. What they all feared was a woman who would settle for a house, maid, and money for herself and the bastards she would bear. It became a matter of sheer economics. None of them wanted their husbands' money spent anywhere except in their households.

Like the other wives, Iliana seldom interfered with Menardo's affairs of the heart unless it appeared a great deal of money was pouring into the other woman. In a town the size of Tuxtla Gutiérrez, a phone call or two and the woman in question would be warned that her job, if she had one, and her family members, if they lived nearby, were all in jeopardy. There was an understanding among all the women in the club that there was no need to discuss such matters except perhaps in a discreet conversation between two or three club members. Certainly it was considered bad taste to bring up the subject of a husband's escapades unless the wife herself raised the issue. All the rules were thrown to the side this time. The women in the club could not maintain the silence. Iliana's behavior—her talk about the blueprints, color schemes, and then all those color photographs—had been more than the others could tolerate. They would have been forced to tolerate Iliana's airs had she been invulnerable. But Iliana had been so caught up in her pretensions of reading blueprints that she had missed a fundamental fact: her husband was fucking the architect. The judge's wife spent three days making discreet midmorning calls on all the members of the club, speaking in whispers about the duty and obligation they had to inform Iliana of the seriousness of her position. Iliana had her reputation to think of. After all, Menardo wasn't simply fucking the company receptionist or the teenage mail clerk. Iliana had mentioned Alegría's name more often than Menardo's.

"The foolishness of it. The irony," as the former ambassador's wife had put it. The other women were not as irritated with "Mrs. Former Ambassador" as they usually were. The former ambassador's wife did not say so, but she also happened to know Menardo was very busy then with a business deal that, if it went as planned, would give Iliana so much money the club women would never ever be able to cut her down to size. The former ambassador's wife knew they had to move fast. It was this: if Iliana had not talked so much about Alegría. If Iliana had not acted as if Alegría were her best friend, the other women would not have done what they did.

Alegría had guessed what had happened the instant she saw the Indian chauffeur's face. Workmen were finishing the interior—the plastering and painting, and final cleaning of the white marble staircase.

EXPOSED

ALEGRÍA HAD COME for the last inspection. She could not see Tacho's eyes behind the mirror lenses of his sunglasses, but she could see his thin lips pulled up in a smile. She thought she would not be able to speak or even to breathe. Menardo asked what was wrong. He was gripping her hand and smiling and talking happily as he always did when she arrived.

"She knows," Alegría said in a weak voice.

"What?" Menardo let her hand loose. "No! How could she? What makes you say so!"

Alegría sank her head back on the seat with her eyes closed. "Ask him," she said, barely lifting a hand to point at Tacho. Tacho was watching them in the rearview mirror. Tacho nodded his head. Menardo felt his world had split into halves, one half flying behind him in the airliner with Alegría, the other looming ahead of him as Iliana's old aunt stormed from the airport lobby, towing Iliana behind her as she rushed toward them. Menardo had fended off Iliana's old aunt while Alegría rushed to catch a flight back to Mexico City.

Iliana's aunt had already called the Portillo firm to speak with the senior partner. After the old aunt and Iliana had confronted Menardo, the old woman's driver had taken her directly to a telephone to relay a message to the Portillo firm: "Whore arrives P.M. flight." Old man Portillo himself had met Alegría at the airport, with the firm's lawyer at his side. Except for the surroundings and the noise, both of which had been chosen by Portillo deliberately, the whole affair had been surprisingly civilized and quick. She had agreed to resign her position immediately, and the firm had in turn presented her with a generous severance check. Portillo and the lawyer had concluded the business before the luggage off the arriving flight had been unloaded. Old man Portillo had been pleasant because she had proven all his arguments against hiring women at any level in their firm.

Just like that, Alegría had thrown away six years of university classes and her professional career, at least in Mexico. There had been "the tight white knot," as the student radicals called the Eurotrash oligarchy. They themselves were all grandchildren of the worst oligarchs, which gave them, they argued, a special privilege to attack those who had spawned them. How the radicals would have laughed if they could have seen her paid off and dismissed in public with people staring at the tears running down her face after Portillo and the lawyer walked away. Just like that her career as an architect was gone. Obliterated. All for Menardo, and she had not even been aroused much by his chubby hands and the short, fat prick. She could have handled Menardo as she had handled dozens of others—clients, colleagues, and senior partners. Portillo himself had "accidentally" brushed her arm and breast a time or two himself; she could have bought a little "job security" from Portillo, but she had been too proud. She didn't know why, but the pride was gone now. Had it been because Menardo had made promises right from the start? Was it because he had kept insisting he would take care of her? She had loved her work. She did not need a man to give her money. Something inside herself had listened each time Menardo had whispered in her ear. Had she believed Menardo's promises about a business of her own? In the same town where his wife lived? Alegría had completely lost her good sense.

Somewhere in the equation, Bartolomeo's name appeared. Alegría had dreamed about him and awoke crying because in a dream he had boarded an airliner to leave her forever. Bartolomeo would only make jokes about the loss of her job. Bartolomeo argued Alegría's services rightfully belonged to the poor who needed shelter, and not to the sweat hogs of capitalism. Alegría's designs—whitewashed walls and stone breezeways above sapphire-blue water—were pure decadence, capitalist pigstys.

Her job was lost, and her career in Mexico, maybe everywhere, was ruined. Bartolomeo would die laughing. All her schooling, all her bourgeois delusions cut down to size. And now maybe she would come to be with the rest of them, the people about to deliver Mexico a great revolution.

Mexico had never seen a great revolution, only rehearsals for the greatest uprising. Here was Alegría's big moment. Her choice. She had only to say yes to Bartolomeo and she could be part of "it." Whatever "it" was.

HIGH COMMAND OF THE PEOPLE'S ARMY

ANGELITA LA ESCAPÍA had been at the airport for nearly twenty-four hours. She had watched the comings and goings of cars and bodyguards and overheard heated phone calls by the old maiden aunt. Menardo was memorable that day. La Escapía had noticed him the first time when he greeted the young white woman who had arrived on a flight from Mexico City. Hours after Iliana and her old aunt have been driven home, La Escapía sees the pudgy half-breed monkey return, this time wearing stiff new jungle-camouflage fatigues and black combat boots. What was the deal? Red Monkey had passed La Escapía both times, the second time so close she could smell the alcohol fumes around his face. The monkey drank tequila. Red Monkey was the code name for Menardo when they discussed him and the trading and services he had increasingly been performing for General J. The long delay at the airport was a windfall for their people. Red Monkey was about to fall into the soup.

La Escapía watched the three small planes land one after the other as delicate and quick as moths. They taxied to the hangar area where she watched Menardo greet each pilot in turn, shaking hands and nodding vigorously all the while. Marx had been right about a great many things. The history of the Americas made revolution against the European domination inevitable. But Marx had also been a European, and he and those following after him had understood the possibilities of communal consciousness only imperfectly. European communism had been spoiled, dirtied with the blood of millions. The people of the Americas had no use for European communism. That was why she and the others had voted to break with the Cubans. La Escapía strolled outside to the area shaded by hangar buildings. General J.'s jeep was parked next to the black Mercedes. The general and Red Monkey were standing in front of the three airplanes, gesturing wildly at one another and smiling. La Escapía and the others had expected the private air force for some time; after all, Menardo maintained his private security police as a service to the customers of Universal Insurance. La Escapía had been furious with intelligence reports because nothing had been found out about the link between the arms dealer in Tucson and General J.'s friends at the U.S. CIA. Yet they had collected volumes of detailed surveillance of Menardo's sexual liaisons with the little lady architect from Mexico City. El Feo had only shrugged his shoulders at the intelligence officer. La Escapía had really been angry then. Why didn't they admit it? They enjoyed watching the architect because she slept with comrade Bartolomeo, their Cuban friend.

La Escapía disliked the waste of valuable energy spying on their own members. Yes, she knew Bartolomeo was not strictly one of them. Bartolomeo was the liaison with Cubans and other friends of indigenous people. Bartolomeo was the funnel for financial aid wheedled away from comrades all around the world. She did not like Bartolomeo either. When the issue was the indigenous people, communists from the cities were no more enlightened than whites throughout the region. Still, Bartolomeo was weak enough for her and El Feo to manage as they wished. Accounting and receipts would be no problems. Bartolomeo was too lazy to be bothered to keep accounts.

"Yes, sir!" El Feo was saying triumphantly. "Things *were* what they appeared to be! Comrade Bart was fucking the architect at the same time she was fucking the enemy, Menardo."

La Escapía kept hold of her temper. "So what?" she wanted to know. Were they implying Bartolomeo was a double agent? Did they know if the architect was also an agent? What was their proof? Only lunatics believed in guilt by association. El Feo had not disagreed or argued with La Escapía. He only smiled and nodded; La Escapía knew he was agreeing with himself and not with anything she might say, the stubborn, smelly he-goat. La Escapía could tell the direction El Feo's thoughts were running, and she had to agree with El Feo this time. There was no revolution and there would be no revolution as long as "outsiders" like Bartolomeo were telling the people how to run their revolution.

AIR FORCE

MENARDO THANKED GOD a thousand times for the three airplanes that had been delivered that afternoon. The airport, which earlier had been the scene of such terrible humiliation, before the sunset, had become the site of another of Menardo's milestones, his greatest triumph since he had saved ten thousand new appliances from the tidal wave. Universal Insurance now boasted its own private air force. Menardo and General J. had kept themselves spellbound for hours talking about their partnership in the insurance business. Wherever revolution, mutiny, uprising, or guerrilla war might strike, Universal Insurance *would be there* to offer complete protection to clients. No need to depend on poorly equipped government forces. Besides, "government forces" could not be trusted. Military officers hatched mutinies left and right, and disgruntled police might develop "blue flu" and call in sick if the price wasn't right. Universal Insurance would provide the answer for every security need. Legislative assemblies had fallen into the hands of radicals and madmen. Urgent needs to bolster the national defense were ridiculed by communists, terrorists, and anarchists of every sort. Chief executives of the future could buy policies with Universal Insurance to indemnify themselves against violent uprising or revolution.

"With the services of Seguridad Universal, all the client does is signal us with a Code Blue. Even if we have only the sketchiest details, we go to our computerized files where we locate the client's instructions. Code Blue from a head of state guarantees said chief of state instant and complete mobilization of Universal's Special Security Forces."

The three light planes would become "gunships" equipped with .50-caliber guns.

Whenever Menardo recalled the terrible scene with the weeping woman in the airport lobby, he felt as if his intestines had dropped into his underpants. But Menardo had only to catch a glimpse of the three small planes to feel reborn. The beauties were in his possession if only for a few hours, until General J.'s pilots flew them to Guatemala. Menardo almost broke into a run to reach the small, sleek planes. Greenlee had delivered one of the Piper Cherokees himself. He was standing with the other two pilots who had flown the planes from Tucson. Greenlee stopped talking and smoothed the imaginary wrinkles of his black driving gloves before he crossed the concrete apron to shake hands with Menardo.

Menardo ran his hands over the metal as if the planes were racehorses. Was Menardo pleased? Greenlee was only there to please one person: that person was the customer, Menardo. For purposes of confidentiality, Menardo had not introduced Greenlee to General J. The general's own position was rather complicated, and he had cautioned Menardo to reveal their partnership to no one, certainly not the wives. The general reminded Menardo "women are blabbermouths." The general had not mentioned Iliana by name, but Menardo's heart began pounding again. He felt the familiar surge of adrenaline rush through his limbs. Menardo was afraid the general knew about the affair between himself and the woman architect. Everywhere the walls had eyes and ears. Only the other afternoon they had been discussing internal security over drinks at the ninth-hole shooting club. General J. had been drunk and loud as he had said, "No one can be trusted. A great storm is gathering on the southern horizon." Menardo did not want anything to go wrong; he did not want a woman, not even a woman such as Alegría, to upset his partnership with the general. They would have the perfect arrangement: the general would not only perform his official military duties along Mexico's southern border, he would oversee security operations for Universal Insurance Corporation. The general liked to say he had suffered the inadequacies and impotence of the army too long. It had been a lonely job for the general. He himself had seen Marxists in the highest levels of the Mexican government, Marxists who routinely castrated the budget requests from military commanders such as himself. Marxist conspirators in government refused the general the manpower and the modern equipment necessary to protect the southern border while Cuba was supplying Indian bandits and criminals sniper rifles with infrared scopes. All the general had for his troops were assorted carbines, some left over from the Second World War. The same subversive elements in the government sent him raw recruits—not soldiers—scrawny Indians who wore their army-issue boots dangling by laces around their necks. "Savages," General J. was fond of calling them. They had calluses on their feet thicker than the soles of any boots. Well, now the general had his own air force at his disposal. Soon Universal Insurance would have an entire security force on continuous standby call: a private army all their own.

DISGRACE AND RUIN

HE HAD BEEN CAUGHT by Iliana before, and Menardo already knew her preferred tactic was to inflict great damage on the "other woman." At first Menardo thought a young professional such as Alegría was beyond the reach of a sour matron in a provincial town such as Tuxtla Gutiérrez. But then he remembered Iliana's uncle was acquainted with Mr. Portillo, and fear for Alegría swept over him. Surely the quality of her work and her high standing in her graduating class would insulate Alegría from Iliana's hysterical allegations.

Menardo had hoped to lure the general home with him, knowing that Iliana and her old maid aunt dare not attack him in front of General J. But the general was wound up like a mechanical toy, and one of the pilots had promised to explain the intricacies of jet fighters.

Menardo thought Tacho might know something about Iliana's terrible discovery. As they drove from the airport through the downtown district toward home, Menardo cleared his throat a number of times. Tacho glanced into the rearview mirror each time, to see if the boss had got up the nerve to ask. But each time Menardo backed down. It was unseemly to let servants know anything was amiss. Anyway, Iliana always told Menardo how she found out.

"That is the worst thing!" Iliana sobbed. "The whole club knew! They were all delighted! I trusted that woman! Filthy pig dripping your slime while she talked oh so nicely to me! Well, they have gotten back at me now for all the jealousies they've had! I can never hold my head up again!" But this time Iliana's crying did not affect him. He did not feel guilty or sad or remorseful. He was numb. Iliana had greeted him at the door with the news that Miss Martinez-Soto was no longer with the Portillo firm. The club would love Iliana all the more now that they had cut her down to size. No, this time Menardo felt nothing except perhaps the urge to drive a fist smack into the middle of Iliana's puffy, damp face. The old maid aunt was upstairs napping or he might have. He was a man of his word. Alegría had become his responsibility. Fortunately, his Universal Insurance Corporation had a limitless future ahead of it.

Alegría had been thinking about the mansion with its glass wall toward the jungle and the white marble staircase. She had taken a camera with her on the day of the confrontation, planning to photograph the complete construction so she might add the house to her portfolio and résumé. Now she was ruined. Bartolomeo would be delighted. He would make her work for the "people" now. Menardo had sent a cashier's check and a spray of pale yellow orchids from the most expensive shop in Mexico City. The money was enough to cover her expenses. She thought she should take a vacation. But when she returned to the apartment, she could not bring herself to lift the phone book to the bed. She would follow the doctor's orders. Call the travel agent to arrange a week in San Diego. She needed to go far away. She needed time to think. She lay down, but instead of sleeping her mind raced over the events again and again. Mexico did not need many architects, Bartolomeo was fond of saying, since the ruling class was so small and all the others were too poor to build "designer houses." Her stomach clutched around the thought she had ruined herself. She had lost an inside position on the track to the top. She remembered as a child the horse races in Montevideo. A horse running far in the lead had inexplicably pulled up, allowing all the horses to run past. She had remembered it because it was one of the few times she had ever seen her father lose his poise. Her father had bet a large sum on the horse. He was no longer joking and talking.

Alegría's father always bragged she would go far. Alegría decided she would not tell her parents until she had definite plans. But she also could not delay too long, since either one of her parents might telephone the firm. Her father might forgive the accusations, but he would hate to get the news from strangers. She had to call her parents, but she could not raise herself from the unmade bed and reach down for the telephone. She thought a short nap might help.

Iliana refused to speak to Menardo except to clarify logistical details concerning purchases and deliveries to the new house. Since the incident she had thrown herself into interior decoration. Menardo was relieved. It had occurred to him Iliana might insist the house be sold immediately. But Iliana had her own concerns. She had gone to great lengths to make sure that Miss Martinez-Soto would not find new employment in any of the prestigious architectural firms. This had been accomplished rather simply via the grand old family connections in Mexico City, and with the aid of the women at the club. Alegría after all, was Venezuelan, not a Mexican citizen. Iliana let the club members make strategic phone calls. If Miss Martinez-Soto attempted any legal action, Iliana and her allies made sure no law firm in Mexico City would take her case. Iliana had been afraid to stop or in any way relax her vengeance for fear she might slide into one of her depressions as she had after miscarriages. It was not possible to know for certain if Miss Martinez-Soto was ruined in Mexico, but Iliana had made every effort.

The betrayal by Menardo and Alegría did not shake Iliana's fascination with the structure she herself had designed. The design had been Iliana's idea. Alegría had only drawn what Iliana had told her to draw. The grand entry hall had been Iliana's idea. The new house excited much jealousy. To settle old scores, Iliana knew it would be necessary to furnish this house more lavishly than she had planned originally. Iliana sent Tacho to the big newsstand downtown for all the French and Italian magazines on interior design. The contractor had completed the pool and the landscaping. Iliana took out the buff tracing paper without flinching. She unrolled it on the big mahogany table in the dining room. Her reply to all of them was to appear at the weekly luncheon carrying the familiar cardboard tube. The wife of the former ambassador shook her head when she reported to her husband that night. "We thought she went on while that woman was designing the house. But today we had to listen for two hours about water lilies for the swimming pool! Finally I had to say, 'Iliana, darling, we believe you. You are spending a fortune!' " The former ambassador only nodded. He knew all about Menardo's business, especially now that Seguridad Universal was available throughout the entire region.

THE FALL

THEY HAD BEEN LIVING in the house for less than five weeks. The accident took everyone by surprise. The wives of the police chief and the judge had of course known about it immediately since their husbands' offices were involved directly. There might not have been so much excitement had Iliana not been from a founding family. And of course there was the fact the new house was in the suburbs too close to the jungle where anything or anyone might emerge. Therefore, a full inquiry and a special investigation were ordered. The maids and the cook had been unpacking dishes in the downstairs pantry. The three women said they never heard Iliana cry out, although one of the maids said she thought she remembered hearing a faint sound. Of course outside, the crew finishing the pool area had been using a cement mixer with a loud gasoline engine. By the time Menardo reached his house, the driveway was full of police vehicles. The white Pontiac ambulance from the local mortuary was parked with its tailgate down. As he rushed through the front entrance, the drama of the grand entry hall immediately struck him. The wall of glass at the far end glowed with a luminous light filtered through the jungle leaves. The light was strange. Reflected off the high polish of the brilliant-white marble stairs, the light seemed more pervasive than the summer-afternoon sun at one o'clock. Menardo had been given no details. He only knew a terrible tragedy had occurred at his home. Now under the high vaulted ceiling, a crowd of plainclothes detectives, medics, and Dr. Gris were gathered at the foot of the marble staircase. Menardo saw they had covered Iliana with a blanket off her own bed, an expensive white cashmere shawl Iliana had preferred on winter evenings. The cook and two housemaids were huddled by the kitchen entrance. The cook was crying and wringing her hands, and the maids were trying to comfort her. Menardo took one look and knew the cook was not crying over Iliana. The cook was merely afraid. Because the cook had worked for them eight years, and police investigators knew the passage of time had a way of creating certain conflicts between the wealthy and their Indian servants.

The police chief was conferring with his detectives, but sensed Menardo's arrival by the sudden shift of the huddle near the corpse. The chief hurried across the wide hall. His big Luger in its black leather holster slapped against his fat hip. Menardo had seldom seen the police chief in uniform. He preferred civilian clothes, he said, for security reasons. Today he was in his full regalia. The black was set off by generous amounts of silver braid and silver medallions dangling from their pins on his thick chest. Iliana would have liked that, and she would have liked the effect of the big hall filled with police detectives speaking in low voices. The chief had worked himself into a good deal of emotion crossing the big hall. Like any husband, he had often daydreamed about somehow losing his wife so he could enjoy his middle years as a playboy and lover. But the sight of Iliana's body sprawled at the bottom of the dazzling white staircase had caused the hair on the chief's neck to stand up. For the moment, the woman architect seemed to have slipped the chief's mind. Menardo had to look closely to see if the chief was serious or only pretending. But when Menardo realized the chief was sincere, the loss of Iliana struck him. Menardo could not think why exactly, because Iliana's fury over his affair with Alegría had not abated as quickly as with past affairs. Menardo could not think what the loss was, but he knew it was connected with the shock the chief seemed to feel. Menardo felt as if he were onstage, and the audience was waiting for him to perform. But he could think of nothing. Fortunately, the chief and the detective took the cue. The chief strode over to the foot of the stairs. He walked up the stairs, and then as he turned dramatically, to face the group below, the chief lost his footing and slipped back flat on his ass. One of the uniformed men, a quick, thin man with dark skin and eyes, leaped forward to aid him, but the chief pushed his hand away. "She might have been pushed. Due to the location of the house, and the increase of, shall we say, 'subversivism.' " Hearing this, the cook broke into sobs. "Everyone will be questioned." The chief nodded in the direction of Tacho, who was staring at the body. Tacho stiffened and looked at Menardo. "My driver was with me at the time," Menardo said.

"You must understand everyone—those workmen—everyone will have to be questioned," the chief said, trying to straighten a pin on the back of one of his medals. A detective took the chief aside. "Sir," he said, "the marble steps—something is not right. The angle is rather acute. The steps were made too close together even for a woman's step. The foot catches the edge of the step." The other detectives nodded silently, behind their spokesman. "Unsafe design." They might have said anything—that they thought he had killed his wife, that terrorists crawled out of the jungle and pushed her—anything. But for them to dare criticize the design of the cascading white marble staircase was more than Menardo could tolerate.

"It could not have been the stairs! They are perfection! Look at them!" Menardo shouted.

But the questioning of the cook, maids, Tacho, and all the men plastering the swimming pool revealed nothing. Menardo was interrogated by his friend the chief himself. The questions centered on Menardo's business dealings and business connections. The chief wanted to know more about General J. and his consultant work with the Guatemalan government. Why exactly were the two of them buying airplanes from the United States? The chief had it from reliable sources two planes would be located, at least some of the time, in Guatemala. Naturally there were concerns about national security. "After all," the chief said, "invasions by one nation upon another are not unknown. Such a move on the part of Guatemala is not unthinkable or impossible." Menardo found the chief's questions alarming. He realized that his recent business expansion had excited a good deal of jealousy and suspicion. "I have had so very many troubles come down on me now," Menardo said in a weak voice. He was worried because Alegría did not answer his long-distance calls or letters. The chief's fleshy lips broke into a wide smile. He put his arm around Menardo in a ritual of brotherhood. "My poor friend," the chief said.

Menardo had not been able to contact Alegría until the night after Iliana's funeral. Alegría seemed not to understand anything he said to her on the phone. Alegría sounded drunk. She had just returned from Cancun and was exhausted from the traveling. Her flight had been late. Alegría could only echo Menardo's words: "Accident," "found dead," "broken neck," "buried today." The shock of the news of Iliana's death did not touch her, but instead thudded against the layer of numbness Alegría wore like a strange skin. At Cancun she had not been able to break free of the crushing waves of exhaustion and sleep. The sun flashed off the white sand and water as if the molten metals of the planet had never cooled, but had only coalesced into polished surfaces, mirrors upon mirrors. She had ordered meals in her bungalow, but found despite how ripe the fruits might appear or how fragrant the watercress or parsley, they had little flavor, as if they had been picked too soon, still green, and had been forced to ripen. She knew the waiters and help at the resort were gossiping about her. She had registered under her parents' home address in Caracas. She knew the resort staff expected a man to arrive shortly and join her. When no man had appeared and the young woman slept away the days, the resort staff had deduced the end of a love affair.

Alegría had intended to call her parents after she had rested and thought things out. But the prospect of planning her next move caused her eyelids to feel heavy and evaporated all her strength. She had tried to fight this lethargy first with strong coffee and then with tiny white pills, but the effort had only left her nauseous. Alegría had felt time leaking away with the tides. Her father would telephone the firm asking for her. He might already know. She did not think she had the strength to hold the phone receiver. She was forced to let it all go, just like that.

The funeral had been unpleasant. Iliana's parents were old-fashioned and were horrified Menardo had sent the body to the mortuary, which they considered barbaric and a sin. They followed Church dogmas so old most of the priests had not heard of them. Her parents had always known Iliana's marriage to Menardo would bring her to a bad end. Only an inferior creature would have chosen to build a new house in a jungle area exposed to so many dangers. Iliana's parents didn't care that the local inquiry and special investigative officers had ruled the death accidental. The coroner's officer noted that while the marble staircase was by far one of the most stunning focal points of this most modern and beautiful mansion, still the stairs themselves had been made with a peculiar design. From discussions with the workmen, investigators determined the stairs had been cut and polished in an unusual manner. The officer did not know what the desired visual effect might have been, but the practical result was the close spacing of the stairs took no account of a person's natural stride. The police investigator noted he had spent the morning at the death scene and had even asked a maid and a gardener to walk up and down the stairs. He himself had repeated the procedure over ten times. All of them, the report noted, had experienced some difficulty, and the maid had nearly fallen, because of the slippery surface; however an adult might negotiate the steps, the foot seemed to land on the edge of an adjacent step.

It is the husband's right to dictate all funeral arrangements. Menardo found himself relishing this last act as son-in-law and husband. Menardo had wanted to use the mortuary for many reasons. What he had argued with his inlaws was that after autopsy, only morticians had the skills to make the body once again presentable. But he also wanted to avoid the "old customs"—the open coffin in the main hall, a steady stream of visitors, mostly members of her clan, the very people who had opposed him and a few who had continued to snub him at weddings and baptisms. Iliana's mother had fainted, but Menardo thought Iliana looked as good as could be expected after the fall. Bruises from the fall were covered under layers of powder. The only fault Menardo found had been with the eyebrows, which Iliana had always penciled with a thin line of reddish color. The mortuary had given Iliana fat, black eyebrows.

It was difficult for Menardo to remember he was a widower and officially in mourning. Of course he was sorry Iliana was dead; she had not been sick or old. She might have enjoyed many more years. But then, on the other hand, everyone had to die sometime. There were no children, and Iliana had never cared for her nieces or nephews. Her parents were elderly and in failing health, but they had all the others to fret at and complain to. She had gone suddenly and, the coroner had said, "painlessly." Menardo wondered a little bit about that, but of course the first blow to the head or snapping of the neck or spinal column caused loss of all sensation. Menardo knew he was expected to make some show of grief for the benefit of Iliana's family. But now that she was gone, he kept feeling a spitefulness that he was almost ashamed of. Iliana was gone and it mattered little whether he kept the in-laws anymore. As for his own family, none of them came. Menardo's ties with them had nearly dissolved.

Menardo took a last look at Iliana, and he did not see anyone he'd ever known. He tried to remember tender moments, those days in the courtship when he had actually anticipated the evening all the day before. Menardo had the feeling he kept changing; he had become different people until little of the original person remained. Menardo could feel he was headed toward the headlines and history. The dawn of the new age Menardo had so often cited to the provincial businessmen had suddenly burst forth into the heat of the day. The high noon was approaching.

Menardo realized he had paused by the coffin somewhat longer than usual. Menardo pulled himself up straight and made a little bow to Iliana, patting her crossed hands. He had not touched the dead before and was surprised at the nothingness he felt. Not woodenness or wax-iness or cold—just nothingness. Death had made her hands a mere surface; already her body was becoming an illusion. Death had flattened her out. She had no more substance than a photograph. He almost wished they did not have to bury her. He almost wanted to watch, day by day, and to check from time to time on the progress of decay.

BOOK TWO

REIGN OF
FIRE-EYE MACAW

TERRORIST BOMBS

PERHAPS IT WAS NOT the normal thing so soon after a wife's death, but Menardo was succeeding brilliantly with the new business deal General J. had set up, and Alegría had finally agreed to marry him. Still, change was everywhere from that time on. Sometimes Menardo told himself these changes were his fate, and it was only with Iliana gone that his eyes had cleared enough to see. Iliana had always kept him so tightly tangled in the world of club luncheons and dinner dances Menardo had not noticed the shiftings or the rise of the river. Now there were more "incidents." Tuxtla had always had its share of petty crime and murder among the Indians. But not a week after Iliana was buried, Menardo found himself back at the funeral home, this time for rosary of the eldest daughter of the bank president. The girl had been walking on the main street in downtown Tuxtla. A bomb had exploded in an alleyway across the street. The girl had been killed by a piece of roof tile knocked loose by the explosion. At the funeral-home chapel, Menardo tried to get a good look at the dead girl. While all the others prayed aloud softly, Menardo leaned hard against the polished wood of the front pew, clicking his rosary loudly so none would suspect he was studying the corpse, not praying. She had not been a pretty girl. She had a beak nose and black moles on her neck and cheeks. Death had changed her skin color very little. All the banker's daughters had cultivated skin white as milk. Menardo could not determine much by looking at the dead girl. He knew he would have to touch her as he had touched Iliana. Even after the rosary was finished he stayed on his knees with head bowed, waiting for the others to leave. All he wanted was to touch the dead girl's hand, but he did not want anyone to see. Because they would not understand it was something he needed to do in order to clarify his thinking. Menardo had even spoken to Tacho about the matter.

Tacho's expression never changed as he listened to the boss. The black, piercing eyes in the rearview mirror studied Menardo and made him self-conscious. Menardo had inquired what the Indians did when there was a death. "The usual things like the white people do. And then . . ." Tacho let his voice trail off, as if the boss would not want to hear more than that. The eyes in the rearview mirror kept watch.

"No," Menardo said, "tell me more. What I wonder about is . . ." But Menardo could not say it. Not even to this Indian who had no idea of propriety, of which questions might be asked and which could not. Tacho said no more, and Menardo had decided it was not worth the trouble to ask him again. Tacho was waiting outside the funeral home for him. Menardo looked around quickly to see if there were any windows Tacho might be able to peek through. Menardo checked to be sure no funeral-home employees were nearby.

Menardo's throat was dry with excitement. He could feel a tingling down both legs, which he blamed on the hour he'd been kneeling. As he walked toward the coffin, he dropped the rosary beads into the pocket of his suit coat. He could justify what he was about to do only because it was necessary. Once he had done it, he would be free of it and would never have to concern himself again with these thoughts. This was all a result of Iliana's death. It was not his fault. Menardo held his hand above hers, working himself up to touch the dead girl's hand. He extended his right forefinger slowly, as if approaching a reptile which might startle. Menardo could smell his own sweat. It had the odor of fright he recognized from that morning he had rushed through the doors of the new house to find medics, police, and servants milling at the foot of the stairs.

He was not sure he was actually touching her hand, but when he pushed, the corpse's left arm had shifted, leaving the right hand alone on her chest with a pink rosary threaded through the fingers. The movement of the left arm horrified Menardo. Everything was supposed to be in its place and remain there. It had frightened him so badly he could not remember *what* he had felt with his forefinger. He had not been able to distinguish her flesh from his own. What embarrassment! He would have to try to fix the left arm before any mortuary employees appeared. Menardo took a deep breath. The odor of candle wax and gardenias made him light-headed. He took the left arm by the wrist, but this time there was no mistaking it. He could see he was touching the dead girl, but the arm felt as if it were an extension of himself, a strange growth on the ends of his thumb and his fingers. He let the arm drop again, took his own right hand into his left, and squeezed each finger. There was nothing wrong with his fingers. He looked at the dead girl again. He had to hurry. His hand was shaking so badly now he could barely rearrange the rosary in the hands. He lifted the arm by the white chiffon and guided it back to its place on top of the right hand and the rosary.

Menardo could see the red glow of Tacho's cigarette. Tacho was leaning against the side of the car staring up at the sky. It was a moonless night and clouds were scattered over the stars. Menardo was relieved Tacho would not be able to see his face clearly. He was sure his face must be the color of ashes. Menardo rolled down both windows in the backseat so he would not have to smell his own sweat. But Tacho had already picked up his scent. Tacho's eyes stayed in the rearview mirror watching him all the way to the house. Suddenly Menardo felt an anger almost bursting his chest. Menardo was angry the bomb had killed the young girl. He was angry at the stupid fall Iliana had taken, a fall that she could as well have taken two months sooner, before she had made her poisonous phone calls to Mexico City. Menardo was angry at Alegría, paralyzed in her apartment in Mexico City, refusing to allow him to see her. Alegría insisted they observe some rules of decorum before their marriage, since Iliana had died in a freak accident. Luckily, Iliana had done the design of the steps herself. It had been Iliana who had insisted the marble be highly polished. Alegría had argued for a more subtle effect.

Menardo had to see Alegría. The operator rang and rang, but Alegría was not answering her phone. She had told Menardo she was keeping the phone unplugged because she did not wish to receive calls from her parents, who had learned of her disgrace and who called to question her more closely about her dismissal from the firm. What she had not told Menardo was that she could not bear to be in the apartment alone. The pale blue rooms were a prison. Everywhere she turned there was a reminder of the career she had dreamed of.

COMMUNISTS

ALEGRÍA KNEW BETTER than to tell Bartolomeo or any of the rest of the group about Menardo's marriage proposal. They would have sneered. Still, it was comforting to hunch in a corner and listen to them drone on and on about revolution. Mexico was being robbed blind. Mexico had been robbed blind. "Yes," Alegría wanted to say, scanning the faces quickly, "and only one or two of you were not weaned on the stolen fruits of Indian land and Indian labor."

She had been exhausted by the time the taxi dropped her at Bartolomeo's apartment. His comrades did not seem to be at home, although anyone might have been sleeping in the piles of newspapers and dirty clothing. Alegría had quit asking who or how many because Bartolomeo delighted in the "open door" policy their group had. As many as twelve "comrades" sometimes slept in the tiny room. So there had been little privacy. The room served Bartolomeo well. The politics of the room kept intimacy at bay and had forced his family to disown him.

Alegría wished she had a shot of brandy. The comrades and roommates often came marching into the little room right in the middle of the night. Bartolomeo kept her pinned on the tangle of old blankets until she convinced him she had had an orgasm. When the roommates walked in, she always shut her eyes tight. She was grateful then not to have electricity. The candles they kept lit in the red and blue glass jars cast long shadows, and Alegría imagined the comrades saw hardly more than vague figures. This night she lay listening for the *trump trump trump* of the comrades' boots while Bartolomeo labored on top of her. He could not pierce the shell of her concentration on sound. She could hear a baby crying on the floor above. She could hear a slow, metallic ticking of a cheap alarm clock down the hall, a radio, and a musician playing an Indian flute. She could hear the voice of a woman pray, "Hail, Holy Queen Mother of Mercy, our life, our sweetness, and our hope"; she could hear the sound of retching and vomiting and the scrabble of rodents' feet, a dull thud, a door slamming, a groan.

When Alegría awoke, she was lying alone on the pile of blankets. Their voices were low, but they were not arguing Lenin or what is to be done with the writings of Mao. Alegría detected an atmosphere of alertness, and a certain suspense. From the floor she could make out the legs of men at the table, though later she heard a woman's voice. One voice kept saying, "Slowly, slowly now—be careful!" Then she knew. She was wide-awake in an instant. The comrades were making bombs ten feet away from her. She moved very slowly, as one might move to avoid startling a wild animal. She did not bother with bra or panties and crushed them into her purse. She was glad she was wearing a simple dress with no buttons or zippers. She listened for a lull, for one of the people crowded around the table to move, and then she got up and said, "Bartolomeo?" In the strange candlelight at the table all the faces seemed elongated. A voice said, "Who's that?" and another said, "Just the one Bartolomeo fucks." "He's not here. He went to get something." Suddenly Alegría felt how much she had hated all of them. To them Alegría would always be just another woman Bartolomeo fucked. Nothing she could do or say would ever make them trust her. Bartolomeo needed her to stir up their anger, to remind them who and what it was they hated and opposed. They would not care if Alegría agreed the system that starved and destroyed human beings for the profit of a few was a system that must fall from the sheer weight of the bodies of the dead. "Stay with your own kind!" one of the women drunk on the cheap beer had shouted at her late one night, and Alegría had shouted back, "I know my own kind! The bourgeois! You are one and the same as me!" The drunk woman had tried to fight her, but Bartolomeo had pulled Alegría away by her arm. She didn't like the sound of what they were now doing at the table. The voice that kept urging, "Easy! Easy!" didn't seem able to answer back when another voice demanded, "You know so much then— you do it!" Alegría wanted to laugh out loud. She had to get out of there. She had listened to their discussions enough to know that their grasp of dialectics was weak; she feared their grasp of wiring blasting caps to explosives might be even weaker. She preferred to take her chances on the street at three-thirty in the morning. Overhead the smoke, dust, and clouds had formed a luminous canopy that glowed a poisonous orange. As her eyes became accustomed to the dark, she saw the glow was bright enough to throw faint shadows on the decaying walls. The early November frost had come down from the mountain peaks. Alegría turned up the collar of her coat to cover her mouth and nose.

She returned to her blue rooms just as the sun was blazing up behind the layers of orange and pale brown. The phone was ringing as she came in, and it continued ringing until finally she lifted the receiver.

Menardo had to see her. The situation was urgent. His voice sounded desperate. "What is it?" she said. "Oh," he said, "everything is breaking loose! Subversives are everywhere!" Menardo had to swallow hard before he said, "They bombed this week, killed a young girl." He thought he might sob when he said, "The bank president's daughter." Alegría managed to calm him. They must not see each other until their engagement was announced. Wedding plans must wait until at least eight months had passed since Iliana's death. "You know that," Alegría reminded him. "Yes," he said reluctantly, he knew.

Alegría had tried to make a clean break with Bartolomeo in Madrid. She had. They had. Bartolomeo had gone to Mexico City. But later her best job offer had come from Mexico City. She had been careful not to go near the university because she knew where he'd be. In the end, he had come looking for her.

Menardo met her at the Tuxtla airport with his arms full of red roses. He put them into Alegría's arms and hugged her close. The paperwork at the civil registry had taken no time. A magistrate had read the vows, and two of his clerks had been witnesses. Menardo's dream had been an intimate little chapel wedding, but under the circumstance, he had agreed with Alegría that a quiet civil ceremony was called for. All Menardo wanted was for her to be his wife this night of all nights when she would truly be his and he would truly be hers. Driving to the hotel afterward, Menardo had taken Alegría's hand and had gently pressed it to the crotch of his trousers so she might feel the strength of his ardor. The organ flexed and pulsed before she had moved her hand away. Alegría felt nausea sweep over her; she had no choice. Alegría pressed against Menardo and leaned over so he could reach into her bodice to take the nipple of her left breast between his fingers. As they reached the hotel, Menardo straightened his tie and rearranged his hair. Did she want to dine? In the light of the big lobby she could see him so vividly, the large black mole right above his lip, the perspiration of his sexual excitement soaking under the arms of his white polyester sport coat. Alegría would not have been surprised to see a spot of moisture near his fly, but fortunately his sport coat had been buttoned.

No, she did not want to eat. The idea of food left her nauseous. She needed to rest. But Menardo interpreted the words "to rest" to mean she wanted sex with him. She wanted to try to explain, but saw that his ardor had already returned, and words would do no good.

Menardo had ordered the honeymoon suite filled with dozens of white roses. The champagne was iced, and he insisted she drink a glass. The champagne did settle her stomach, and she had two more glasses before Menardo could wait no longer. His penis was as short and fat as he was, and it was lost in the overhang of his belly. He insisted on kissing her all over, then licked and sucked the parts he'd kissed. The champagne and the fatigue had left her drowsy, and the kissing had irritated her more than it had aroused her. Alegría wanted to tell him just to stick it in and get it over with. But now she had to pretend she was his bride; from that night on, she would have to be his wife. She had to endure his lips on her shoulders and her arms. When he kissed her thighs and inched toward her pubis, Alegría imagined he was a giant mollusk trailing slime over her as he prepared to nose into her vagina. The urge to jerk herself away, to draw her legs to her belly and then to kick him violently was almost uncontrollable. So she had groped desperately for his penis. But the crouching position he had assumed for the licking and kissing had put the organ out of reach. Fortunately, Menardo interpreted her gesture as a great demonstration of desire, and he had lost all control and embarrassed them both with his ejaculation across the sheets.

COMRADE LA ESCAPÍA
AND THE CUBAN

"COMRADE LA ESCAPÍA," people in the villages called her, teasing, and not teasing. She didn't care. All her life she had heard them whisper behind their hands and gossip behind her back. Call her comrade, call her anything you wanted, but she had worked her way up to the rank of colonel in the Army of Justice and Redistribution. Delegates sent by all the villages had warned that everyone would be quarreling and fighting if military rankings and military discipline were used. No one was supposed to set herself or himself above anyone else, not in the family, not in the clan, and they sure better not in the village. No, the village delegates had recommended military rank not be used except in their dealings with the outside world.

The village delegates had not recommended anyone be called comrade either. People had seen enough TV and movies to know what *comrade* meant. They had been taught by the missionaries to hate communism. Things had begun to shake, and La Escapía knew the uprising would be in full blossom soon enough to silence all her enemies and critics. Big things were going to start happening so fast. She and the other leaders of the People's Army had been able to amass one of the largest and most sophisticated arsenals in the region. The Indians had managed to obtain the weaponry and supplies from at least a half dozen different groups representing more than a dozen foreign governments as well as underground groups. The Indians had even got two big checks from a famous U.S. actor. La Escapía laughed at critics. Of course the tribes took money from anyone they could get it from. They agreed only on one point: they must retake their land despite the costs. From the missionaries, La Escapía (known to the nuns as Angelita) had gone to the Cuban Marxists. She was a silent but ruthless critic of the months of "political instruction" she and the others had received at the Marxist school the Cubans ran in Mexico City. La Escapía's favorite instructor had been a blond Cuban who had taught her how to fuck. He used to take her to his rich woman's apartment, "his fiancée," he called her, then Bartolomeo had dripped his juice all over the blue velvet bedcover. When La Escapía had tried to wipe off the bedcover, Bartolomeo had stopped her. He said the woman needed to be brought down a notch or two. Bartolomeo had tried to get rough with her. Not physically, because she was certain she weighed more than he did. Bartolomeo had tried to bully her. He had threatened to report La Escapía and the others for harboring nationalistic, even tribal, tendencies. But Angelita only laughed. Her laugh meant the end of the afternoon sex instructions with Bartolomeo. Let him fuck his rich-bitch architect girlfriend. La Escapía and the others would deny they had secret intentions. Whatever the rich outsiders wanted to believe was all right with the tribal people. They just wanted the means to take back their lands. That was their secret and the only "truth" tribes could agree upon. Angelita had never hesitated to admit she had fucked Bartolomeo because she had learned a great deal from him about obtaining aid from others besides Cuba. She had graduated at the top of her class at the Marxist school. Later when enemies in the villages, people related to her by clan or marriage, accused La Escapía of being a "communist," she let them have it. Didn't they know where Karl Marx got his notions of egalitarian communism? "From here," La Escapía had said, "Marx stole his ideas from us, the Native Americans."

The school classes had been conducted in the basement of a down-town building. Lectures on Marx had been all that kept the Cuban school open. Constantly the Cubans reminded La Escapía and the other Indians about the expense and trouble involved in trying to educate them. La Escapía had expected to hate everything the Cubans taught. She and the others from the villages had only agreed to attend the school because the Cuban made such classes a condition for the delivery of arms and other supplies. In the early weeks of class La Escapía had dozed off and actually snored during the classes. Then in the fourth week, the lazy Cubans had begun to read directly from *Das Kapital*. La Escapía had felt it. A flash! A sudden boom! This old white-man philosopher had something to say about the greed and cruelty. For La Escapía it had been the first time a white man ever made sense. For hundreds of years white men had been telling the people of the Americas to forget the past; but now the white man Marx came along and he was telling people to remember. The old-time people had believed the same thing: they must reckon with the past because within it lay seeds of the present and future. They must reckon with the past because within it lay this present moment and also the future moment.

After the lecture, La Escapía had gone to Bartolomeo's office. She had questions about Marx. What Marx said about history and about the change that comes and that can not be stopped. Bartolomeo had stared blankly at her breasts while she talked. He was not interested in what the old Indians thought about the passage of time or about history. He was not even interested in what Marx had to say about time or history. Pushing the door shut with one foot, Bartolomeo said all he was thinking about was sucking her left nipple in his mouth. La Escapía had not bothered Bartolomeo about Marx again.

VAMPIRE CAPITALISTS

MARX WAS THE FIRST white man La Escapía had ever heard call his own people vampires and monsters. But Marx had not stopped with accusations. Marx had caught the capitalists of the British empire with bloody hands. Marx backed every assertion with evidence; coroner's reports with gruesome stories about giant spinning machines that consumed the limbs and the lives of the small children in factories. On and on Marx went, describing the tiny corpses of children who had been worked to death—their deformed bodies shaped to fit inside factory machinery and other cramped spaces. While the others dozed, La Escapía sat up in her seat wide-awake. She could not get over the brutality and all the details Marx had included. She could never have imagined tiny children wedged inside the machinery just to make a rich man richer.

El Feo was sent by La Escapía's elder sisters to take stock of her political views. El Feo wanted to know how she knew this man Marx wasn't a liar like the rest of the white men. La Escapía shrugged her shoulders. She wasn't trying to convert anyone. Tribal people had had all the experience they would ever need to judge whether Marx's stories told the truth. The Indians had seen generations of themselves ground into bloody pulp under the steel wheels of ore cars in crumbling tunnels of gold mines. The Indians had seen for themselves the cruelty of the Europeans toward children and women. That was how La Escapía had satisfied herself Marx was reliable; his accounts had been consistent with what the people already knew.

From that point on, the words of Marx had only gotten better. The stories Marx related, the great force of his words, the bitterness and fury—they had caught hold of La Escapía's imagination then.

La Escapía used to walk for hours around and around downtown Mexico City, in a daze at what she was seeing—at the immensity of wealth behind the towers of steel and concrete and glass, built on this empire for European princes.

In the filthy, smog-choked streets with deafening reverberations of traffic jammed solid around her, La Escapía had laughed out loud. This was the end of what the white man had to offer the Americas: poison smog in the winter and the choking clouds that swirled off sewage treatment leaching fields and filled the sky with fecal dust in early spring. Here was the place Marx had in mind as "a place of human sacrifice, a shrine where thousands passed yearly through the fire as offerings to the Moloch of avarice." La Escapía really liked the way Marx talked about Europeans.

El Feo kept quiet but nodded vigorously at the right places. La Escapía was going to make him pay through the ears for acting as go-between for the elder sisters. The elders just wanted the land back; they didn't want to hear about "revolution." While he was listening to La Escapía talk about Marx and the cities of werewolves and England's dead children, El Feo had already been formulating his report to the elder sisters. He would advise them to listen: La Escapía was on to something important.

El Feo didn't worry about the world the way La Escapía did. The thought of retaking all tribal land made him happy; El Feo daydreamed about the days of the past—sensuous daydreams of Mother Earth who loved all her children, all living beings. Those past times were not lost. The days, months, and years were living beings who roamed the starry universe until they came around again. In the Americas the white man never referred to the past but only to the future. The white man didn't seem to understand he had no future here because he had no past, no spirits of ancestors here.

CRIMES AGAINST HISTORY

EL FEO HAD SPENT HOURS talking with the elder sisters and the special committee. They were concerned that Angelita might already have become a communist. No, her thoughts were from her heart, aimed at helping them. She was their soldier. She was no communist. La Escapía had merely carried out her assignment at the Cuban school to the fullest extent possible. He could not possibly tell the story the way La Escapía had. Perhaps the elders should consider listening themselves. Words could not be blamed simply because stupid or evil persons slandered the words or corrupted their meaning. *Commune* and *communal* were words that described the lives of many tribes and their own people as well. The mountain villages shared the land, water, and wild game. What was grown, what was caught or raised or discovered, was divided equally and shared all around.

No, El Feo was relieved to report, La Escapía had not been brainwashed by the Cubans. In fact, she was contemptuous of their ignorance of Marx, and she had clashed with the Cubans over which version, whose version, of history they would use.

La Escapía had originally made notes because she had to locate so many of the words in a dictionary. Gradually she had learned the words, but La Escapía had kept writing in the notebook anyway because people were always liable to ask you to prove what you were saying wasn't just a lie. The notebook had tiny marks and numbers only she could decipher, for page numbers and titles and authors of books. La Escapía had kept the notebook to back her up when Cubans wanted to argue or the "elder sisters" tried to give her trouble. She had written "Friends of the Indians" across the front cover of the notebook as a joke. Friends of the Indians! What a laugh! The clergy and the communists took credit for any good, however small, that had been done for the Indians since the arrival of Europeans. The world was full of "friends of the Indians." The Dominican priest Father de Las Casas had been a great friend of the Indians. La Escapía had searched through their canyons of books, but she had found it: all in printed words just as Marx had said. The Dominican priest Bartolomé de Las Casas had been a rich slave-holder with an inheritance of a plantation and Indian slaves to work it on La Isla de Hispaniola. Las Casas had gone to Cuba slave-hunting with other businessmen, although Las Casas was not present when the rebel Indian leader Hateuy was burned alive. Why hadn't the stupid Cubans running the communist school in Mexico City talked about this part of Cuban history? Later La Escapía had pointed to this as one example of how little the Cubans knew about Cuban history. La Escapía called it further proof Cubans didn't want indigenous people to know their history. When they denied indigenous history, they betrayed the true meaning of Marx. Not even Marx had fully understood the meaning of the spiritual and tribal communes of the Americas.

El Feo and the others had been reluctant to execute Comrade Bartolomeo without "due process" in a trial of some sort. "Kangaroo court?" someone joked at the back of the meeting hall. Because nobody had cared what they did with the Cuban white man who was no good to anyone anymore.

Bartolomeo had somehow managed to exceed all the others in his disdain for history before the Cuban revolution. Before Fidel, history did not exist for Bartolomeo. That was his crime; that's why he died.

La Escapía had pronounced the death sentence because Bartolomeo had had no respect for the true history of Cuba or any of the Americans except for the singsong "Fidel Fidel Fidel Fidel!" Bartolomeo had died because he had betrayed the truth with half-baked ramblings he alleged were the words of Karl Marx. La Escapía was indignant. The Cuban school in Mexico City drove people away; it did not gather new comrades for the great struggle to regain all the lands of the Native American people. Angelita had read the words of Marx for herself. Marx had never forgotten the indigenous people of the Americas, or of Africa. Marx had recited the crimes of slaughter and slavery committed by the European colonials who had been sent by their capitalist slave-masters to secure the raw materials of capitalism—human flesh and blood. With the wealth of the New World, the European slave-masters and monarchs had been able to buy weapons and armies to keep down the uprisings of the landless people all across Europe.

La Escapía was not acquainted with Cubans of African or Native American descent; but the European Cubans were a race of hairdressers. Bartolomeo had kept quiet about the great Indian rebel leaders because Fidel had not been around back then. The Europeans had destroyed the great libraries of the Americans to obliterate all that had existed before the white man.

Bartolomeo had died for other crimes too, but La Escapía, El Feo, and the others had always felt proud as they remembered that mainly Bartolomeo the Cuban had lost his life because he had neglected to mention the great Cuban Indian rebel leader Hateuy.

Five hundred years of Europeans and nothing had changed. The Cubans had lied and distorted the words of Marx; worse, they had attempted to suppress the powerful warning Hateuy had sent to the people of the Americas. Hateuy had refused baptism before Europeans burned him alive because he said he did not want to go to heaven if Europeans might also be there. Cheers and shouts had come from the back of the crowd when Angelita La Escapía had finished.

The stories of the people or their "history" had always been sacred, the source of their entire existence. If the people had not retold the stories, or if the stories had somehow been lost, then the people were lost; the ancestors' spirits were summoned by the stories. This man Marx had understood that the stories or "histories" are sacred; that within "history" reside relentless forces, powerful spirits, vengeful, relentlessly seeking justice.

No matter what you or anyone else did, Marx said, history would catch up with you; it was inevitable, it was relentless. The turning, the changing, were inevitable.

The old people had stories that said much the same, that it was only a matter of time and things European would gradually fade from the American continents. History would catch up with the white man whether the Indians did anything or not. History was the sacred text. The most complete history was the most powerful force.

Angelita La Escapía imagined Marx as a storyteller who worked feverishly to gather together a magical assembly of stories to cure the suffering and evils of the world by the retelling of the stories. Stories of depravity and cruelty were the driving force of the revolution, not the other way around, but just because the white man Marx had been a genius about some things, he and his associates had been wrong about so many other things because they were Europeans to start with, and anything, certainly any philosophy, would have been too feeble to curb the greed and sadism of centuries.

Marxism had a bleak future on American shores. Irreparable harm had been done by the immense crimes of his followers, Stalin and Mao. To the indigenous people of the Americas, no crime was worse than to allow some human beings to starve while others ate, especially not one's own sisters and brothers. With the deaths of millions by starvation, Stalin and Mao had each committed the sin that was unforgivable.

Only *locos* such as the Shining Path mentioned Mao anymore. The Shining Path refused to hear about any mass starvation except what they themselves had suffered; to them, all history outside the Americas was irrelevant. The earth could be flat as far as the Sendero knew or cared. If communists had starved *some* millions, the bankers and Christians of the capitalist industrial world had starved *many many* millions more. Look all around and in every direction. Death was on the horizon. Talk to the Sendero about Stalin's or Mao's famines and they will simply shoot you to shut you up. Marx and Engels could not be blamed for Mao or Stalin or Sendero any more than Jesus and Muhammad could be blamed for Hitler.

El Feo had worked out the wrinkles and snags between Angelita and the elder sisters. The time was drawing near for the "beginning," and they did not want misunderstandings or hard feelings among their people or allies. Many of the older people had been reluctant to hear about Marx because theirs had been a generation that had seen the high water of the flood of Christian missionaries, who had recited the names Marx and Engels, right after the names of Satan, Lucifer, and Beelzebub.

So Comrade Angelita did not hesitate to talk about anything the people wanted to ask. There was nothing to be nervous about. There was nothing they couldn't talk about.

Was Comrade Angelita trying to get the village to join up with the Cubans?

How much were the Cubans paying her?

Wasn't communism godless? Then how could history so full of spirits exist without gods?

What about her and that white man, Bartolomeo? To questions about her sexual conduct, Angelita was quick to laugh and make jokes. Sex with the Cuban was no big thing.

BULLETPROOF VEST

"JUST A LITTLE SOMETHING for you, Menardo, a little gift."
"Ah, Sonny, what is it? Size extra large? What are these? Falsies? You don't think I've got a big enough chest and belly?" Menardo laughs as he holds up the bulletproof vest his friends in Tucson have sent him.

Menardo sits with the sun at his back by the pool. The gardeners are swimming on the bottom, cleaning bits of soil and stray rootlets from the water lilies. Twice daily this is done to keep the big pool crystal-clear as glass. The vest's gift wrapping slides from his lap, but the maid catches it before it hits the blue tile decking. Sonny Blue finishes the piña colada, and another maid, older, with a face like an Olmec mummy, brings him a fresh drink. Sonny pokes a finger at the gardenia floating in the drink. He watches Menardo stand up and try on the vest.

"These pads—"
"They are called inserts."

"These will stop a .357 magnum."

"But they are heavy, hot to wear."

"Yes," Menardo said. "Still, I don't mind. Hot and alive are better than cold and dead."

Menardo fumbles with the bulletproof vest, then slips his white silk shirt over it. *"Pues! Qué guapo!"* Menardo struts up and down the length of the pool to get the effect of the vest. He glances at the big yellow and pale pink blossoms floating on the water. A gardener surfaces at his feet, but he is looking at Sonny Blue.

Sonny Blue was beginning to feel tired from the flight that had left Tucson so early. He traveled for their "friend," Mr. B. Mr. B. rented warehouses in Tucson from Leah Blue. Mr. B. sent Sonny to Mexico to become familiar with a key supplier, Menardo. The U.S. government supports covert forces and supplies them with weapons got by trading cocaine through Tucson. Mr. B. has explained it before. Max Blue had worked for the U.S. on secret projects a time or two. Sonny found the secret war exciting.

"No, no worry my friend," Menardo says in English. "We are shooting them to hell. We are making them a bloody pile."

There is a woman laughing. The sound pours through the French doors of the balcony. Both men look up. "Alegría," Menardo says, and smiles again at Sonny. "She loves beautiful, expensive things." Sonny suddenly hates Menardo's tone of certainty about his wife. He longs to tell Menardo what Alegría really loves, what she wants to take and take all night long. Instead Sonny Blue stands up suddenly and extends his hand. Menardo points at the piña colada Sonny has not finished. "Alegría will be furious if she misses you," Menardo says. Sonny Blue knows he should go. Menardo works with all the factions. His number may be coming up—bulletproof vest or no vest. Sonny shakes his head.

"Next trip I'll come for dinner."

"Your word of honor!"

Sonny Blue lets Menardo embrace him and kiss both cheeks. "My word of honor," Sonny says softly.

The older maid escorts him out. Her face is a mask, but in the eyes Sonny sees danger. He looks around the vast mansion, the pale marble staircase and the white and black checkerboard of marble in the entry hall. Beneath the glass dome of the conservatory, gardeners' assistants hang like monkeys from ladders, tending orchids with cascading spikes of yellow blossoms flecked with bright red. The sky above the dome is the blue of gemstones, not sky. The glass dome is Alegría's dome. It is her design. Sonny is impressed. Alegría had graduated from architecture school in Madrid. Menardo wasted no time in replacing the dead wife with one as young as his daughter. Sonny knows there are rumors Alegría killed the old wife.

All the thick hairs on Menardo's stomach and chest have turned white. He will be fifty in the spring. He wants to wear the bulletproof vest to the ambassador's party. But he can not decide if an undershirt should be worn to prevent chafing.

"I don't want to be in the middle of dinner and have it pinch my ribs."

"There's no chance of that happening unless you mean pinching the layer of fat hiding your ribs." Alegría is angry because Menardo scolded her for the new shoes and purse to match.

"Reptile, aren't they." He frowns. "You know how I dislike snakes."

She laughs and he turns suddenly from the silver box containing his cuff links. She realizes then he is serious. He has never been so angry with her before. She stands motionless and stares at him like the little doe blinded in the headlights of their Mercedes the night before. She is selfish and thoughtless but she knows it. All the shoes and dresses with his money are intentional. Why else is she married to him?

Menardo turns back to the mirror and fumbles with the thin metal inserts that slip into pocket panels sewn in the front and back of the vest. The insert that belongs in the pocket over his heart does not lie flat. He had read the instructions that came in the box. The vest is the finest body armor made. The vest is sold only to the U.S. military and U.S. police forces. The instructions must be followed or the maximum protection will not be obtained.

"Is everything all right?" The sight of the vest makes Alegría uneasy. Lately there is an unidentified dread that shadows her.

"Of course. Don't be silly." Menardo says, taking a silk shirt from the closet. "We are going to be late." Alegría feels the tears. She had not thought of tears, but there they are in her eyes.

The scene is a replay of her afternoon with Bartolomeo, who complains he can't even tease her anymore.

"You will look good as a widow," Bartolomeo had told Alegría as she was dressing. She was wearing a black silk slip.

"What do you mean?"

"Just that you look ravishing in black."

"You know something else—tell me!" But Bartolomeo rolls over on his side and laughs. He tells her paranoia comes from guilt, but she had been frightened. Had spies seen her with Bartolomeo? Bartolomeo teases her after they make love; he calls her "the double agent."

"On whose side?" Alegría says, though she knows it is dangerous either way.

Tears get nowhere with Bartolomeo, but fortunately Menardo is different. Menardo refuses nothing to her tears. She removes the black lizard shoes and carefully wraps them in the white tissue paper. She wipes the back of her arm across her face like a child. He is right. They are all right. About her. She's selfish. She lives for herself. She knows this but can not stop. There is no other use for her. She knew this even while she was in school. The others at the university sneered at her drawings full of delicate lines.

"Whom are those buildings for? What meaning do they have for any of us?"

She laughed nervously and pretended to erase a smudge. "When you take power, you will want big buildings too," she teases, but the hostility from them is always there even though she uses her key to get into the architecture building late at night to mimeograph leaflets for them. She loved making the drawings—floor plans of vast rooms, interiors flooded with light from high windows and domes, the pearly-yellow light framed on white walls. She wanted the gardens to penetrate the rooms. The only criticism of the drawings for her final project had been that they contained no human figures. The professor of the design class finds the figures of little dogs, parrots, and monkeys too whimsical. She does not tell him the human figures she draws spoil everything. They always look like police or men in dark suits, and they are always too large. She cleverly drew little dogs on the stairway. A monkey played in the orchids of the hanging garden, and she drew a scarlet macaw on a perch.

In the backseat of the Mercedes, Menardo pats Alegría's hands absentmindedly; ahead of them are two bodyguards in a truck, and two more guards follow in a white jeep. The vest causes Menardo to hold himself straight. He moves stiffly when he turns to take a second look at an armored personnel carrier parked outside the Governor's Palace. Mexico is almost bankrupt and the country is about to explode, that is what her mother and father write to her each week. "Come home to Caracas," they plead.

"You are upset about something," Alegría says to Menardo, who has a sour look on his face. He tugs at the corners of his small, neatly trimmed mustache. "It's nothing you need to worry about, darling."

"But it is," Alegría answers.

At the party he watches her dance with each of the host's four handsome sons. Alegría is the only woman dressed in black. She is the most beautiful. He had not meant to scold her about the shoes. But somehow black reptile skin is part of the nightmare he has from time to time. He struggles to remember the dream, but knows only somewhere in the dream there is scaly, black, reptilian skin. He had been startled that Alegría had found shoes and a purse identical to the reptile skin in the nightmare. She could not have known about the reptile skin because he told no one his dreams except Tacho, his driver, who came from a village near a Mayan temple ruin. In Tacho's village they were all trained to decipher dreams. Menardo paid Tacho twice the going rate to ensure strict confidentiality. Enemies could use your dreams to destroy you, that's what Tacho had told Menardo in the beginning. Right then Menardo knew he must double the Indian's salary or tell Tacho nothing about his dreams.

Menardo talks to Tacho about other delicate matters. He asks Tacho who these Indians are who join up with the guerrillas in the hills. Tacho turns and flashes a big smile into the backseat of the Mercedes.

"They are the brothers of the soldiers who guard the Palace," Tacho says, and pretends he is serious. Menardo likes a servant with a sense of humor. Sullenness upsets him. He had been relieved when Alegría had changed out of the black lizard shoes without pouting. Gardeners, servants, and the Indians had become more sullen since guerrilla forces had made regular strikes across the border. Guatemala had too many educated Indians. It was the fault of the Church. From the very beginning priests treated them like human beings.

"Nowadays you educate an Indian and he becomes a Marxist," the former ambassador says. The governor signals for the expensive champagne. Although they have been discussing the guerrillas, and before that the upcoming elections, Menardo's attention wanders. It is probably due to lost sleep from the nightmare. He watches Alegría dance with an investment broker from São Paulo. She smiles up into the man's face. It occurs to Menardo he could ask Tacho if Alegría had ever been unfaithful. Indians could detect such things. The governor jokes this is the last of his French champagne, now that the socialists had spoiled everything in France. Someone jokes about the Americans with money frozen in Mexican bank accounts. It isn't a mistake any wealthy Mexican would have made. Menardo allows the dark-skinned servant to refill his glass again. He is getting drunk, but he wants to. Alegría is dancing with the host's youngest son. They stop. The boy gestures with both hands.

"It's not just the Indians, really." Someone behind him is talking about guerrillas. "A few come from the best of families." Menardo takes a big swallow of champagne. He wants to dance with his wife. The boy sees him and bows away graciously. Alegría looks surprised. "Are you all right?" she asks.

"Can't a man dance with his wife?" Menardo answers, laughing from the governor's good champagne.

Alegría can feel the vest under his tuxedo. It is unyielding. He draws her closer to him, and with her eyes closed his steel-padded chest might belong to someone else. Alegría's breasts are small, but they press the edge of the bulletproof panel into his chest. The pressure of the padded steel against his ribs is reassuring. He waltzes with his eyes closed. With champagne on the inside and the vest on the outside and his beautiful wife in his arms, Menardo forgets about the terrorist bombs and reports of new unrest. How nice it is to forget. But Alegría twists away from Menardo before the waltz has ended.

"That vest of yours is crushing me!"

"Ssh! It's no good if you tell everyone!"

She laughs and replies, "So serious!" But she glides away to the ladies' room downstairs. Menardo watches her until she disappears. Perhaps he was taking a risk to marry a woman so young, so full of modern attitudes. He smooths his shirt under the tuxedo jacket, feeling the padding and the steel of the vest. Iliana would never have complained about the vest. How often she had urged him to buy the bulletproof Mercedes. Before that, Iliana had worried about traffic accidents and insisted on big cars. It was good Iliana had not lived to see the world now where terrorists routinely attached bombs to cars. In his nightmare Menardo is riding in the Plymouth from years ago. He can not see who is driving. It appears to be early afternoon because the streets are empty. Here Menardo is puzzled because the empty streets of the dream frighten him. This is not a dream in which brown tarantulas swarm over his bed or blood-drinking bats attack him. Such dreams had awakened him but had not left him soaked in sweat. In the nightmare, he knows somehow the month is August. The empty streets of the nightmare are hot and bright from the sun. There are no spiders or monsters, only the empty street where Menardo is driven in the Plymouth.

Somehow the dream awakens him stiff with terror, and with the bed sheets soaked in sweat. Menardo always awakens before the car passes the Governor's Palace. Tacho can not explain why this dream leaves him shaking and dreams about spiders, bats, or big jungle cats do not. Tacho claims this dream can not be read until the car proceeds around the plaza past the Palace. Tacho urges him to stay in the dream long enough to reach the Palace.

Alegría returns with her fur stole and beaded purse. "These shoes hurt my feet," she says, and Menardo regrets scolding about the black lizard shoes. Other guests follow them. Outside, a three-quarter moon is dropping over the edge of the horizon. The breeze is surprisingly cool for late July. On the drive home, Alegría dozes with her hand in his hand. He leans over carefully and pulls a bottle of brandy from the backseat compartment. He suffers more often from a nervous stomach. Old age, Dr. Gris tells him, and laughs. But Menardo knows the nausea arrived that night with the nightmare.

READER OF DREAMS

TACHO SUSPECTS HE IS FORGETTING important details from this dream. Tonight Menardo understands this. Though he can not say why, the dream takes place in early August. It is just this sort of detail Tacho claims he needs in order to interpret the dream. Menardo remembered the black serpent skin. He is irritated that Tacho can't interpret its meaning without knowing more. It is not a snake or lizard itself in the dream. Maybe it is around the corner, once you pass the Governor's Palace. Tacho, like all the Indians, finds it easy to make jokes about the problems of others. They could care less about their own situations. No wonder they were such a poor and ignorant lot, although Tacho could at least interpret dreams—or could until the same dream came night after night. Before, when Menardo still had ordinary dreams, Tacho had told Menardo what numbers were associated with which dreams. For a share, Tacho offered to instruct the boss how to use dreams for the lottery. Tacho's boldness in asking for 10 percent had been a little shocking. Still, for an Indian, Tacho knew a lot about percentages and odds. They had won each day he had placed a bet. Tacho was firm about the amount of money that could be placed on a number. Tacho claimed that if one got greedy and bet more than the prescribed amount, then the number would not pay. Working together they had won over 20 million pesos. Not bad, not bad. The work with the dreams had brought him closer to a servant than he had been since his childhood. His own father had always advised against it.

Tacho is slouched in the front seat. In the darkness the red ash of his cigarette stares like the eye of a ghost. Tacho has the car door open for them before Alegría reaches the driveway. Brandy on top of the champagne makes Menardo talkative. He doesn't care if Alegría hears him ask Tacho about his dream. But tonight Tacho only grunts. Nothing more. The silence of Indians is maddening. Menardo understands why his ancestors found it necessary to kill a few. But then Tacho turns to the backseat and whispers, "Tonight stay until your car has passed the Palace."

Alegría has gone to her own bedroom. The cigarette smoke has given her a headache, she says. Menardo postpones turning out the light. He makes a list of important phone calls for tomorrow. He wants to reassure Mr. B. that he knew nothing of General J.'s plan to resell the merchandise to an air force colonel in Honduras.

He gets up abruptly and goes over to the massive black-walnut chest where the bulletproof vest is lying. He removes the inserts and lays it tenderly into the box. The guarantee and other printed materials are scattered on the bed. Menardo plans to read himself to sleep. But just to be sure, he pours another brandy. The advertising brochure is printed on expensive, slick paper. The pages are filled with color photographs of police officers—a few in uniform—but most bare-chested. They pointed at marks left by the impact of the bullet against the vest. The bruises ranged from purplish black to scarlet and fading yellowish brown. With each photograph there was a brief description of the encounter and the weapons used. The clock by the bed shows three-thirty. Menardo has read each of the accounts in the magazine carefully. He is pleased the vest repels knife attacks as well as bullets. Menardo feels happier than he has felt in many months. Perhaps the danger was becoming a strain. But the stakes were even higher now with General J. and their new air force. Now there was Sonny Blue, who worked for Mr. B. Menardo felt drowsy from the brandy, but after the light was out, thoughts continued to dart and flit through like nighthawks. The magazine had many details concerning ballistics. The metal inserts for his vest have STOPS .357 AND 9MM printed on them in large black letters. Of course a .38 slug was no problem. Menardo was curious about the blade of a knife. According to the brochure, cheap switchblades or butcher knives would break off in the vest. Menardo imagined an attack on him by masked assailants. The first attacker would fire a .38-caliber revolver at Menardo's chest while the second would lunge with a big knife for his belly, but the knife would skid off the steel insert. Stunned by their failure, they would stand helplessly as Menardo pulled out his 9mm automatic, and the faithful Tacho opened fire with the Uzi he kept beside him on the car seat. The scenario was exhilarating. The bodies of the two guerrillas lay crumpled on the steps behind Menardo as he strode into the club for his afternoon meal. The scene soothed him to sleep.

When he woke, Menardo heard a bird singing in the wisteria outside the window. He felt more refreshed than he had in many weeks. The vest had kept away the nightmare. Despite the brandy and the governor's French champagne, his head was clear. He felt alert. He whistled while he bathed. He smiled at the maid who brought in his white silk suit. However, he waited until the maid left the room before he took the bulletproof vest from its box. He examined it carefully, running his finger over each seam, each nylon stitch. The knock at the bedroom door annoyed him. He pushed the vest back into the white tissue paper on top of the two inserts. But it was only Alegría.

"Still fondling your vest," she teased. She had only come to go through her special closet where she kept her most expensive dresses. She paused to choose between a pale yellow suit of raw silk and a white linen dress. Although she was in a bubbly mood and seemed to have forgotten the incident the evening before with the lizard-skin shoes, Menardo felt a distance between them. He was glad when Alegría gave a little wave and darted out the door again. He wanted to be alone with the vest to read all of the technical information in the new owner's manual. The vest must not be allowed to become oily or soiled and was less effective when wet. The nylon covers on the steel inserts could be washed gently by hand in a mild detergent without the steel inserts. The vest itself was guaranteed effective against knives and .22 and .38 calibers. Steel inserts were necessary for protection from larger calibers. Of course the inserts were less comfortable than the vest alone, but except for dancing with his wife, Menardo had not found the inserts to be annoying. The unyielding panels felt reassuring. He decided he would always wear the steel inserts. That way he could be certain.

Tacho had been relaxing behind the steering wheel as if he were ready to hear about the nightmare. But Menardo had slept without dreams that night as he preferred. A man of his stature and financial success should not be confiding his dreams to a servant. Without intending to raise the subject, Menardo told Tacho the problem of the dream had been solved. He told Tacho no more than that. Nothing about the vest, although the vest had done the job. No one must know he wore a bulletproof vest.

Night after night Alegría refuses sex with Menardo. Her quarrels with Bartolomeo leave her too angry for sex with her husband. "Fat red monkey" is the name the Indian guerrillas in the hills call Menardo, Bartolomeo delightedly reports. Finally Alegría agrees to sex with Menardo to avoid suspicion. She lies to Menardo and says she must go to her private bathroom for birth control. Away from him, Alegría sits on the closed lid of the toilet and stares out the window. The sky is full of stars. Alegría wonders what will become of herself six months from now. She tries to remember the names of some of the constellations. Where would she be tonight if she were not here? With whom would she be having sex right now? Sonny Blue in Tucson? Bartolomeo claimed the uprisings and strikes all over Mexico were only the beginning. In six months the war would spread from the South. The Indians talked to sacred macaws. Bartolomeo gave up. The Indians were hopeless. Bartolomeo was returning to Mexico City. He asked Alegría to accompany him. Menardo wouldn't last long once the Indians got started. All this time the Indians had been misleading Bartolomeo and the others. The Indians couldn't care less about international Marxism; all they wanted was to retake their land from the white man.

After a while, Menardo comes searching for her. But by that time she has decided to leave Menardo. It is perfectly clear to her that something will soon happen: "great changes" as the gypsy fortune-teller used to say, using the bundle of divining sticks to brush away black ants from the cushion he sat on. Well, Alegría understood great changes all right. She could feel them surge warmly through her veins with the blood. Sometimes she thought about the big dumb animals with their identical instincts. She had had no idea of why she was getting ready to leave Menardo. It was all in her blood, the tingle of apprehension but also anticipation. Bartolomeo says they are out of control—these mountain tribes who hate Europeans, and who believe they know communism better than Lenin or Marx. Bartolomeo predicts only trouble from these Indians; he is about to advise his supervisors to suspend all shipments of aid.

Menardo sweet-talks her through the bedroom door. He wants her very much. He tells her he will even remove the vest, an attempt on Menardo's part to humor Alegría with a little joke. Alegría feels as if she owes sex to Menardo at least twice a month. Alegría unlocks the door, then bends over the side of the bathtub, displaying her ass, and then calls for him to come in. She has learned to prefer this position because she need not be near his face. When she thinks about leaving Menardo, she thinks about escape from this. She is just as bored with Bartolomeo. Alegría can feel herself falling in love with Sonny Blue.

GENERAL J.

"GOBBLE, GOBBLE, GOBBLE!" the general says. His little grandson is playing with a woven-straw turkey with a red head and red feet. The general catches the toy just before the child drops it into the toilet. It is a cheap toy the Indians sell at the market. The maids spoil Nico, then run off and leave the general baby-sitting. None of the Indians could be trusted. The old woman who raised him had volunteered to rig an explosive to the general's mattress. What is the world coming to when the oldest servants can not be trusted? General J.'s newly divorced daughter consoles herself with luncheon dates with her ex-husband's friends. She is three ax-handles wide, the general teases. She hates him for the teasing.

"Gobble, gobble, gobble!" the general says, and runs the turkey across Nico's head. He laughs at the child's shock when he tucks the toy into the pocket of his dress uniform. The general's daughter blames him for the disappearance of her husband, who was fat and soft and had a hind end floppier than hers.

"He ran off with another man," the general tells her, but they both know her husband had enemies. The general had never seen a eunuch, but he had read many descriptions. The son-in-law had had the eunuch's swinging hips and mincing steps. His fat fingers had been covered with gold rings. Still, the general could be philosophical; reading the great literature of the world had prepared him for anything that might happen. So when his only child had married a faggot, General J. had simply reread *King Lear*. When deserters bolted off to the mountains to lead battalions of other stinking mestizos and Indians, the general had reread *Paradise Lost*. One had to take the philosophical view: the sky rained down dirty-brown angels over the rugged coastal mountains. Indians were the work of the devil. The general is late for his meeting. He slips the straw turkey out of his pocket while the driver and the bodyguard talk soccer in the front seat. Each minute that ticks away reiterates his rank over the rank of the others. A true leader must consistently show those under him he is the boss. He is the man who can afford to arrive late.

"Gobble, gobble, gobble!" he says, waving the little turkey at them. They are already on the third pitcher of margaritas. He props the little turkey against an empty glass pitcher. The purpose of the meeting is to assess their position in these days of upheaval. Menardo arrives late at the country club. The others have already taken golf carts to their private pistol range. At first the golfers had complained, but rank was rank. The golfers had little to fear at the ninth hole. The pistol range merely used the back of the mound to muffle the sound. The shooters aimed past the ninth green and fairways toward the tropical forest. "If anyone gets hit, it will be us. None of these yokels in Tuxtla knows anything about swinging a golf club," the governor jokes to the police chief. Menardo has played golf with the former ambassador, and it is true golf balls pose far more danger than stray bullets from their pistol range. Menardo pats his chest. He has had to ask Alegría to buy him shirts a half size larger. The bulk from the vest makes his old shirts too tight under the arms and across his shoulders. In the old shirts he can't breathe right. He feels as if he is being suffocated.

He can hear them shooting. All the grass and forest trees muffle the shots. *Bump! Bump!* The flat, loud pop that means the chief is there. He is fanatical about his .44 magnum. He'll match it against all the others anytime.

Someone has brought unopened gallon cans of vegetables and fruit to use for target practice. A can flies into the air awkwardly like a heavy seabird. Only full, unopened tins simulate the sounds of bullets hitting flesh and bone. Another bullet spins the can around on the ground. The police chief is always satisfied with his .44 magnum. He holds the cans away from himself so he will not soil his uniform. One drips a golden liquid. The other leaks runny red juice. Menardo can't identify what the contents are until the chief motions for all of them to come closer to compare the sizes of the bullet holes. Menardo smells peaches and red peppers. What excites the police chief is the size of the hole the bullet leaves as it exits. The .44 leaves a hole as big as a child's head. That morning the police chief kept turning his finger around the exit hole made by his .44. He pretended not to notice the little cuts on his fingers and the specks of blood. The purpose of the pistol range was to pass Friday afternoons and to give country club VIPs an opportunity to practice marksmanship.

Menardo understands why the golfers hate the arrangement. It sounds as if the ninth green has been ambushed. Ten, even five, years ago it would not have mattered so much. But now terrorists had invaded everywhere—even golf courses. Everything reflected the change. This vest, the .44s and .38s, the pistol range. Security matters were a change for all Europeans. They only vaguely remembered stories about the uprisings of the Indians against their ancestors in the great castle wars.

They are all wearing earplugs and are watching the police chief fire a short-barrel automatic rifle. The police chief turns from the target and sees Menardo first. "How do you like this baby!" He waves the automatic rifle above his shoulders to demonstrate its light weight. The governor is sitting on a white plastic lawn chair. They all take white lawn chairs and surround the table shaded with the white umbrella.

"The umbrella is to keep off stray golf balls," the former ambassador jokes. They repeat the same jokes to show their solidarity. The police chief gives their stock reply: "You are here with us, so there's no danger!" Menardo reaches to pour the big glass pitcher of margaritas. The police chief's little joke has caused an uneasy surge in his blood. Politics had no place in their common cause, which was survival, whatever their minor political differences. Earlier that same morning more severed human heads had been found floating among the flowers of Xochimilco.

EL GRUPO GUN CLUB

THE POLICE CHIEF wants action. The general is biding his time with the guerrillas, but some of the guerrilla leaders had once been the general's officers. The general gets emotional when he talks about the defectors. General J. rapidly confuses the rest of them with his talk about theology and Lucifer. The defectors had been trusted aides.

Things were veering out of control in their region, and the entire meeting of the shooting club would be devoted to a discussion of recent developments that might aid their "joint interests," as General J. so delicately describes their business deals with one another.

The general suddenly finds himself in a reflective mood. He takes a deep breath and looks away from the table to the western horizon where jagged mountains lie majestically in the blue mists. He gestures to the waiters, who bow respectfully and bring iced pitchers of margaritas. Theirs is a business of the most serious nature: they govern the many; all the more reason they had to fortify, even indulge, themselves in every way.

They drained a fifth and sixth pitcher of margaritas. The governor is tipped back in his chair, snoring. The general notes that lately the old lecher can't keep awake. The general signals his driver to bring the new chromeplated .44; he is ready for target practice. The general motions for the others to keep still, so the governor will not awaken and spoil the joke. Theirs has always been a group that appreciated practical jokes and laughter. The general wants to startle the old governor with the gunfire. Menardo keeps thinking about strokes and heart attacks as the chief pulls the trigger. Flames blaze out the end of the .44's barrel. The explosion is deafening, and the governor leaps up from his chair and overturns the table, spilling empty pitchers and glasses. The governor clings to the former ambassador, shaking with terror. He clings to him even after the police chief has collapsed on the shooting bench in tears from the laughter. Menardo is laughing, but is not enjoying it. They had been discussing the infiltrations and the saboteurs. Of course the assassins must be everywhere. Fortunately, they have designed everything around them for maximum security. Fortunately, they did not have to worry within El Grupo, as they called their afternoon shooting club. Menardo was not sure, but he thought the police chief had looked at him a bit strangely just now as he said this. Menardo had never quite felt secure with the police chief because there was rivalry between the chief and General J. Menardo motions to Tacho for his holster and gun. He can shoot as well as the others. The police chief doesn't shoot that well.

Menardo fired his 9mm again and again and watched a party of golfers scurry away from the ninth hole of the golf course. The rest of El Grupo had started on the fresh pitcher of margaritas and seemed not to notice how widely the bullets had missed the targets. Menardo had trouble concentrating on the target. He kept thinking about the worst that could happen if they were to begin to suspect him someday, for some reason. Of course he had nothing to hide; Menardo was completely innocent, but he knew his remarriage had angered El Grupo. Rumors about Alegría's political activities years ago in Spain still circulated in Tuxtla. Greenlee had told Menardo not to worry, that Mr. B. and the others at the "Company" were looking out for all of them. But Menardo was not sure the gringos understood the rift between the police and the military.

When Menardo returned to his chair at the glass-top table, the police chief was still laughing. His big belly had jerked his shirt loose from the trousers. He was quite drunk now, and his eyes were bloodshot. "That is the trouble," the chief was saying, "none of you want to stand and fight. None of you are prepared." Menardo touched the edge of the bulletproof vest. He wanted to tell them he was ready, he was not running away.

Menardo listens to the governor and the former ambassador as they fire at human silhouettes of black cardboard. They talk about bank accounts and real estate in Arizona and southern California. Their strategy is to invest across the border. The Mexican economy is a sinking ship. The governor is drunk on margaritas. He will embrace Mexico and love her, but his money goes to a safe place.

The police chief spins the cylinder of his .44 magnum and winks at Menardo. Each time he fires, yellow flame blazes from the barrel. Let bankers and politicians talk all they want. Let them wave their pieces of paper. The chief won't buy that horseshit about economic conquest or economic domination. The judge shuffles a deck of cards and gestures at the others to see if they want to play.

The chief keeps talking while Menardo takes his turn at the firing line. He is too drunk to notice he missed all six shots. The governor keeps pushing wads of cash and stacks of silver to the center of the table. He makes stupid jokes about banks and foreign debt soon being eclipsed by the accumulated interest and late penalties. The police chief makes a sloppy shuffle that barely mixes the cards. The police chief leans farther in his chair so he can watch the former ambassador's hand of cards.

The police chief draws one card, holding his first four. The greatest threat Mexico faces is rape and bondage by foreign bankers. The former ambassador does not blink. The air under the *ramada* sinks under the weight of the relentless afternoon heat. Menardo wipes his hand across his upper lip. Menardo has never felt such tension in a poker game before.

The police chief gulps a double shot of tequila and deliberately stalls the game. "Where would we be without bankers?" he says to no one in particular, and draws two cards. The governor snaps his cards together and drops them on the cash in the middle of the table.

"Sounds like Marxist talk to me," the governor says, laughing, then goes to take a piss at the edge of the fairway. Menardo watches the police chief's eyes. The eyes study the former ambassador, then the judge. Menardo is startled when the chief looks at him, and Menardo drops his eyes to the cards he's holding. They have all dealt with foreigners. Besides, Greenlee was no banker, only Mr. B.

When the cards are no good, they throw them down in the center of the table and take another turn on the firing range. Shooting, cards, and drinking are required activities. All cardplayers had to shoot and to get drunk; all shooters had to get drunk and play cards. Tequila makes everyone jabber.

They all knew stories about local uprisings. Priests had complained fewer Indians attended Mass. Everywhere there were rumors of religious pilgrims slowly marching north. The judge and Dr. Gris argued the pilgrims were unarmed and harmless. How could anyone take seriously thousands of landless Indians who obeyed the orders of sacred macaws? In a neighboring district they had outlawed Indians from keeping the birds for purposes of fortune-telling. Menardo suddenly felt they were all looking at him. His heart was pounding. Of course they probably all knew Menardo had allowed Tacho to keep some birds in a big tree by the garage. Suddenly Menardo knew he should go. He tried to think of excuses. He settled on a promise he had made weeks ago, to take

Alegría to lunch at the Royal Hotel; this month was the "anniversary" of their first love-making. He felt ashamed to use their anniversary to escape El Grupo. But he did not feel comfortable today, with all the talk of strange native religious cults and Mexico City "Reds."

But Menardo also knew the police chief didn't like anyone to leave during his stories. When the chief was drunk, he easily became enraged. Menardo gritted his teeth to keep the appearance of relaxation. The afternoon heat was beginning to bear down, and too many tumblers of margaritas rested uneasily in his stomach. Suddenly Menardo felt as if a drug had been injected into his veins, and he could move his head and neck only with the greatest difficulty. His legs felt like sandbags and his arms were too heavy to move. Menardo felt panic. He was sure it was a sudden medical crisis brought on by the heat and the alcohol and the loud voice of the police chief. He was certain it was something like a heart attack or a stroke, because it had come over him so suddenly. When Menardo tried to speak, he found his tongue entirely filled his mouth. None of the others seemed to notice, but by then they were all drunk. The former ambassador sat swaying back and forth in his lounge chair. Even the bulletproof vest seemed suddenly to tighten around his chest and press his ribs too close to his lungs. Menardo could not move his hand to his face to wipe away the sweat. He could not even move his eyes to the left to catch Tacho's attention. The governor got up and started firing his .38 special.

The sound of the governor's shots broke the paralysis, and Menardo was able to wobble to his feet. He had to go, he said. Just then he saw the manager of the country club frantically speeding across the golf course to stop El Grupo from shooting up the ninth hole. Three or four times a year it had been a custom of theirs after the sixth pitcher of margaritas, and what could the manager do? All but two of the group served on the country club's board of directors. They had hired him. Still, when the manager came, usually that was a signal for the party to break up.

Time to go home for siestas before dinner. The governor had a date with his new sweetie. Just thinking about her made his manhood stiffen.

STRIKES, UNREST, AND UPRISING

MENARDO LET TACHO HELP HIM into the backseat. Tacho could tell that he was not feeling well, but said nothing. That was one good thing about these Indians. They didn't say much. But then Tacho did a strange thing. Tacho drove him past the mortuary, and suddenly Menardo recognized the sensation of paralysis he had felt earlier; he realized it was the sensation of a body being embalmed. He had felt the embalming fluid course through his veins. He could feel the sweat under his arms and down his back. He could feel sweat on his balls.

Menardo was surprised and frightened at how long it took to pass the mortuary. He realized it was partially his fault because he had told Tacho to drive slowly to conserve gasoline that every day became more expensive. The mortuary is visible for a long distance because it is a two-story building in the style of a Castilian mansion. At first the red-tile roof was all Menardo could see. Then he could see the purple blossoms of vines that climbed the outer walls. The plump flowers were grotesque. They seemed to have been approaching the mortuary for the past twenty minutes, and still they were not quite even with the mortuary's entrance gate. He tried but could not think of what the purple flowers of the vines resembled except human intestines. Menardo regretted he had gone to see the victims of the ambush. Corpses were not yet a common thing, as in lands to the south. The bodies had barely begun to swell, and there was only a faint odor when the wind stirred. Although they had each been shot at the base of the skull, all the stomachs had been slashed open. Menardo could only think of the travel brochures for the Hawaiian Islands where Alegría wanted to go. Human intestines resembled Hawaiian necklaces of flowers. The car seemed not to quite reach the mortuary, even as it moved along the road. Menardo had felt the same sensation in a dream in which he was always just approaching but never quite reaching the treasure. Sounding as indifferent as he could,

Menardo asked Tacho to speed up a bit because the Señora would be waiting. This was a lie, because Alegría always played tennis on Friday afternoons. He felt the Mercedes surge forward, and the added speed broke the strange spell so at last they were past the mortuary.

Menardo had taken to sleeping in the bulletproof vest after university professors had been awakened by masked men and marched to the big fountain in front of the university library. The assassins shot the night watchman too, but he had lived long enough to describe the execution. With pistols buried in their victims' stomachs, the assassins shouted, "Test this!" Of course the professors had all been communists, and the assassins were likely men working for the Police Chief's special unit. Still, in times such as these one could not be too careful. So Menardo had slipped his silk pajamas over the vest. The vest no longer chafed or caused heat rash over his stomach. Without the vest, Menardo felt strangely exposed and somehow incomplete.

Alegría had made fun of Menardo in his vest. They no longer shared the same bed, and he was careful to remove the vest before he slipped into the velvet robe he always wore to her bedroom. She had joked about Menardo without his bulletproof vest.

"Aren't you afraid the communists will shoot you right here?" Alegría said, laughing. Alegría had a cruel side, which his first wife, Iliana, had never had. "They have a small size for women you know." Menardo wanted to please her. Sex required such effort now that Alegría had moved to her own bedroom. It was her design showcase, she said, but the next thing, she wanted to sleep there alone. Her excuse had been fear of pregnancy, but Menardo knew the vest he wore to bed was responsible. Still Menardo had no choice; without the vest, his sleep was lacerated with nightmares.

Iliana had been dead little more than a year and already the world had changed a great deal so she might not recognize newspaper headlines these days. The rebels rely almost entirely on dynamite. They hit key railroad and highway bridges. Last week terrorists had wired the staff car of a general called Fuentes with ten pounds of dynamite. The blast had blown away both legs and both balls and only left a flap of skin for a piss tube where his dick once was. Let that story get around. Later the rebels had scattered flyers with cruel cartoons of General Fuentes in a wheelchair with a comical dildo strapped on attempting to fuck a cunt labeled "Capitalism." Menardo had been shaken by the bombings. He had met Fuentes on four occasions briefly. Strangely, they had once stood side by side at the Governor's Palace urinal; Menardo had not been able to resist the compulsion to glance quickly to his left to see the size and the shape of Fuentes's cock. To think General Fuentes had been unmanned by exploding steel fragments—the very organ Menardo had so recently seen in the men's room—had left Menardo nauseous.

BLOOD MADNESS

MENARDO HAD ASKED TACHO what he thought about men cutting off the sex organs of other men and women. Menardo had conversations with Tacho he would never have dared with a white man. Tacho had watched Menardo in the rearview mirror as he answered. The blood fed life. Before anything you had the blood. The blood came first. At birth there was blood.

Blood was powerful, and therefore dangerous. Some said human beings should not see or smell fresh blood too often or they might be overtaken by frightening appetites. Usually Tacho said little, but on gruesome subjects, Tacho was like all the other Indians, even Menardo's own grandfather, who relished stories about accidents and death. Menardo wanted to take advantage of Tacho's mood to ask certain questions. Were there human sacrifices anymore? Not by the Indians, Tacho said, but the human sacrificers had not just been the Mexican tribes. The Europeans who came had been human sacrificers too. Human sacrificers were part of the worldwide network of Destroyers who fed off energy released by destruction. Menardo laughed out loud at Tacho. Tacho believed all that tribal mumbo jumbo Menardo's grandfather had always talked about. Tacho looked at Menardo in the rearview mirror as if the laughter had insulted him, but Tacho continued.

Blood and its power had been misused by sorcerers. Long before Europeans ever appeared, the people had already disagreed over the blood and the killing. Those who went North refused to feed the spirits blood anymore. Those tribes and people who had migrated North fled the Destroyers who delighted in blood. Spirits were not satisfied with just any blood. The blood of peasants and the poor was too weak to nourish the spirits. The spirits must be fed with the blood of the rich and the royal. God the Father himself had accepted only Jesus as a worthy sacrifice.

Menardo thought Tacho had finished on the subject, but then Tacho had blamed all the storms with landslides and floods, all the earthquakes and erupting volcanoes, on the angry spirits of the earth fed up with the blood of the poor.

Menardo did not raise the subject again with Tacho. The talk of blood and spirits thirsting for blood made Menardo feel nauseous. Then later in the day the disgusting subject had been raised again by General J., who wanted to talk about castration over lunch. The general fancied himself a bit of a scholar.

Menardo was disturbed that both General J. and Tacho had been so anxious to talk about sex and blood; he expected it of Tacho, but not of the general, who was highly educated. Yet the longer the general had talked to Menardo, the more animated the general had become, and a flush had spread up his throat to his cheeks, and Menardo had thought he saw a suspicious bulge in the general's trousers. The general had continued with a theory some French doctors had had: he speculated that the sight and smell of blood naturally excited human sex organs. Because bloodshed dominated the natural world, those inhibited by blood would in time have been greatly outnumbered by those who were excited by the blood. Blood was everywhere, all around humans all day long. There was always their own blood pumping constantly.

Here Menardo had interrupted the general to ask, surely the general was referring to savage tribes—Indians and Africans—and not to civilized Europeans? But the general had laughed and shaken his head, draining his glass and wiping his mustache on the back of his hand. "No, these are the ancestors of the French we are talking about. The cave people of France." Menardo did not recall the nuns and the priests or even the high school teachers ever mentioning that the early ancestors of the French had lived in caves eating raw meat. But the general was an intellectual, and Menardo knew the Catholic Church was old-fashioned about modern science. The French doctors had further speculated that the sight and smell of blood of the castration caused the body to release chemical signals to the genitals so that in primitive times, the conquerors who had castrated their prisoners would immediately impregnate the geldings' women. The general had asked Menardo to forgive him for going on so unabashedly as he had about the unpleasant subject. But the general was about to complete a scholarly treatise on the use of physical measures such as castration to subdue rebel, subversive, and other political deviants. General J.'s main thesis was that only the body remembered. The mind would blank out. Tortured nerves and veins had a memory; what the torturers did to prisoners was to make human time bombs. General J. believed the best examples of the Nazi torture work were Jews who proclaimed themselves survivors. Because their bodies had carried cruel memories for years and years, and when the Jews thought they were home free, and safe, then the time bomb went off and they committed suicide.

The general's other theory was that man had learned the use of rape through the observation of the sexual behavior of stallions in wild herds. The soldiers of the invading armies had simply made certain all pregnant captives had been repeatedly and violently raped until bleeding commenced. Like stallions, they replaced the aborted with seed of their own.

The talk about blood had left Menardo shaken. He tensed his muscles to feel the firm outline of the vest on his belly and chest. Oddly he had never feared wounds in his back. All he had ever been was a serious businessman, a pioneer in the world of casualty insurance. Menardo had never lifted a hand against anyone except those who had in some way threatened damage to one of Universal Insurance's clients. Even then, Menardo himself had never touched a hair on anyone; he had always left those decisions in the hands of General J., who commanded their security services. As the president of Universal Insurance, Menardo enjoyed state-of-the-art protection around the clock. Expense was of little concern. It would look bad for business if anything happened. Menardo had been thinking about a dealership for bulletproof vests. He liked the name Body Armor and knew it would sell strongly with his regular insurance clients. "We cover you for everything" was the slogan he would use.

Menardo began to make plans. It would be such a simple matter. He and Tacho would conduct a test. A simple but dramatic test of the bulletproof vest. By none other than himself. Menardo had studied the body armor brochures closely. Bullets had only left dark-purple bruises. Testimonials that accompanied the photographs again and again described the moment that vest users saw the end of the gun barrel and got ready to die. The velocity of the bullets had slammed them to the ground, but a miracle of high technology had given them a second chance. Menardo wanted to feel it, to experience it and to know the thrill, to see the moment of death and not have to pay.

SPIRIT MACAWS

TACHO HAD OBSERVED WHITE PEOPLE all his life. He had learned to follow Menardo's moods and ignore whatever Menardo might say because Menardo was a yellow monkey who imitated real white men.

Tacho knew Iliana had warned Menardo many times about telling his dreams to an Indian. Tacho had been overjoyed the day Iliana took her fall. The marble stairs were imitations of the temple staircases the Indians had built. Tacho laughed all the more when the boss had married Alegría. Tacho had smelled Alegría, and he had correctly guessed the day Menardo's new wife had gone back to fucking the Cuban, Barto-lomeo. Tacho knows about the Cuban from his people living in the mountains.

Only Tacho and a few others knew about the macaw spirit beings that followed him, always roosting in nearby trees until they located Tacho again. The big blue-and-yellow birds had cruel beaks and claws. They followed Tacho wherever he went, and for a long time the big parrots refused to talk to him. Tacho stole cake from Menardo's kitchen, and one of the blue-and-yellow birds had spoken to Tacho. The bird addressed Tacho as Wacah. Tacho was reluctant to hear any more and left the birds in the tree outside. Birds and animals that were too friendly toward humans might be sorcerer's animals, not real animals. The blue-and-yellow macaws shrieked Tacho's new name over and over from dawn to dusk:

"Wacah! Wacah! Wacah! Wacah! Big changes are coming!" For a long time after that, Tacho had hurried past the tree into the garage to avoid the two spirit macaws. But they had stayed high at the top of the tree and ignored Tacho, or Wacah. They refused to leave. The macaws kept reading off lists of orders, things that Tacho-Wacah must do. Tacho bribed the birds with candy, and then for two or three nights Tacho had beautiful dreams.

All Menardo's dreams had contained the terror of a doomed man, and always the dreams were of ambush on the highway, dreams in which the cars and guards usually accompanying the Mercedes were suddenly gone. No matter how deadly the omens in the dreams, Tacho told Menardo there was nothing to fear; Tacho lied to Menardo every chance he got. Tacho watches the gradual changes in the yellow monkey. The change that the vest brought to the master and mistress's bedroom is quite extensive and funny. They no longer fuck because Señor prefers to cower in his vest.

For weeks the vest keeps Menardo's dreams simple and blissful. Then one night Menardo dreams of an asphalt highway in the moonlight where the white lines give way to a giant silver rattlesnake warming itself on the pavement. Menardo screams at Tacho, but he can't brake. The car tires explode as they tear into the huge snake, hurling bloody chunks of reptile skin and flesh against the car windshield. Tacho says no need to worry, the giant snake is from the Bible, and it is good luck for Christians to kill serpents. But after the dream, Menardo can no longer eat red meat. He is haunted by a smear of reptilian tissue across glass. The sight of reptile scales makes Menardo's skin crawl. Menardo proceeds with plans to experiment with the vest. If Tacho is going to assist in the test, Menardo wants him to understand a little. Menardo opens the brochure and points at a series of pictures of white men without shirts.

"Look! See?" Menardo's fat brown forefinger slides over the white man's left nipple. "The big dark spot! Right there!"

Tacho looked, then nodded slowly.

"A criminal shot him with a .38 special, but the vest saved him!" Menardo pats his own chest over his pajamas.

Tacho is cautious. "This very same vest?"

Menardo is suddenly impatient. "No, not *this* one, but one just like it. So today," he says with a flourish, "today, my friend, we are going to perform a scientific test!" Today they are *compadres*. This will be their secret. Their secret alone.

Tacho is careful to take side streets to avoid the route of Menardo's fatal dream. Although Menardo had talked excitedly about the tests and actual cases reported in the illustrated brochure, Tacho is not sure he understands.

POLICE INTERROGATORS

THE VIDEO CAMERAS and equipment had been gifts of the United States government. Their U.S. friends were concerned about the growing political unrest in Mexico. Their U.S. friends only asked to receive duplicate tapes of the interrogations. Menardo had always envied the police chief's extensive knowledge of electronic technology. The chief had made a point of inviting them all into the conference room to review police interrogations on video. The chief said he needed their suggestions. While the others stared at the hundreds of tiny switches and lights on the panel, the chief had waved a thick instruction manual at them, saying it was so simple and easy, even an Indian could do it. Then the chief had laughed, and they had all laughed because none of them acknowledged any Indian ancestors.

The police chief needed the suggestions of El Grupo. They could not continue these interrogations with such stupid questions for the suspects. For example, *Question:* Do you know why you are here? *Answer:* No. *Question:* You are lying! This was to be an anti-subversive campaign. On the video monitor the young whore's hard, upturned breasts filled the screen in freeze-frame. He watched the ten minutes of videotape over and over, listening to the questions the junior officers had asked. Of course they were asking her how many other girls were working as she was, and whom the girls were working for. Halfhearted questions. Girls such as her did not last long on the streets. Personally, the chief thought it was better for the girls when they got taken over by a pimp.

Communism was responsible for all the young girls, and yes, young boys, lining the streets downtown, and the parking lots outside tourist hotels. The chief had always felt his work was indispensable. They lived such a great distance from the Federal District. If the police chief was not constantly vigilant, the agitators from the South would stir up trouble. The police chief began writing furiously, hitting the pause switch on the videotape deck, rolling close-ups of females' organs across the TV screen. The chief had sent his aide away before he had noticed the colors on the screen were all wrong—all yellows, greens, oranges, and browns and blues where they should have been rose-pink or bloodred. Still, the chief had been inspired by the whipping the junior officers gave the whore with the belts of their uniforms.

The police chief complained to Vico, his wife's brother: the Argentine interfered and often interrupted interrogations. The Argentine had persuaded them to use lipstick and makeup on the genitals so they might show up better on the video screen. All the Argentine talked about was "visual impact" or "erotic value." Making a little on the side selling the tapes—that was one thing, so long as police work was not hindered. The chief was delighted to make money from the filthy perversions of thousands hopelessly addicted to the films of torture and dismemberment. But a short time later the police chief had an idea. The videos Vico sold to the Argentine pornographic film company were only copies. With the originals, the chief's idea was to educate the people about the consequences of political extremism. He wanted the people to see the punishment that awaited all agitators and communists. Stern messages could be interwoven in the interrogator's questions, something perhaps like this: *Interrogator:* Why are you performing traitorous acts against God Almighty and the sovereign nation of Mexico? *Whack!* with the rubber hose across the soles of the feet.

But the Argentine cameraman did not want to be delayed while new questions were drafted for the interrogators to use. Vico was no better than the Argentine. They both only cared about a "quality product." Vico was blunt. They didn't use the sound track except for the prisoner's cries or the torturer's grunts and the sound of breaking bone. The chief canceled all interrogations and videotaping by the police until the official list of interrogation questions had been completed.

The chief purposely stayed away until his interrogation questions were completed. He prided himself on the perfection he demanded in all he undertook. But in the ten days the chief was absent, the Argentine had completely taken over. It probably was the first time the Argentine had been surrounded with such yokels. The chief despised the junior officers and their kowtowing to the Argentine. So during the ten days he had been away, they had become grinning idiots in officers' uniforms. Whatever the Argentine told them, they did without question.

The chief looked at the report by Dr. Guzman. The Argentine had made a mess of everything. The prisoners were covered with welts, bruises, and burns. "The videos sell for more money that way," the subordinate answered when the police chief had questioned him about the medical report.

It all gave the chief a dizzy, unbalanced feeling. Suddenly everything about the way the chief had understood his assignment, even his own life—all of it seemed to go up in steam, evaporate. None of them understood what the bruises and burns might prove to the outside agitators or international commissions.

The light-headedness came again when the first images blinked on the video monitor screen. It was far worse than anything the chief could have dreamed. The Argentine had turned the basement of police headquarters into a movie studio. They were out of uniform. Dressed in civilian clothing. The chief tried to keep his composure. By whose order had the junior officers performed interrogations out of uniform? But even before he could speak, Vico and the Argentine were at his side. A junior officer stopped the videotape. Vico whispered in the chief's ear. Vico urged the chief to remain calm. The money involved here was considerable.

"Look at the laws of supply and demand," Vico continued, and the chief was wondering if his brother-in-law was on some kind of dope because his talk just seemed to be getting faster and faster. For years there had been no shortage of "raw material" in Argentina. But recently there had been a drastic interruption. A change in government, so to speak. The chief nodded. Vico put his hand on the chief's arm. They were supplying half the world. Think of it! Vico raved on and on. But somehow in stepping back from the idiot Vico, the chief had inadvertently nodded his head in the direction of the officers by the video machine. The idiots had assumed the gesture was their signal to start the video again. On the video monitor he could again see his men. He could not believe it. Things had been changed. The interrogation room had been decorated with colored paper and paper flowers as if for a party, but in the center of the room on a tinfoil "throne" sat the prisoner. The prisoner's eyes had been taped with the silver tape the Argentine used to bundle cords on video equipment. But the chief had not been prepared for masks on their faces. The interrogators wore carnival masks—the wolf, the rat, the vampire, and the pig. In this video they wanted no trace of the police. This they had done for a special video called *Carnival of Torment*. How quickly they had lost sight of their true purpose. Of course, they wanted to make money, but what had been most important to the chief was the message, the warning that must be sent. The chief kept a notebook beside his bed. Every night he woke at least twice for his bladder, and while he was up, sudden ideas came to him. The videos could carry warnings to more than leftwingers and subversives. Thieves and criminals of all types, molesters of children and small animals, traitors, spies of enemy nations—all would receive warnings. This is waiting for you, the warnings would say. This is what's waiting for anyone out there who dares violate the law.

But not this! This circus was a crime! A beast feast! This was perversion that had involved his own junior officers. The video was still rolling; now the images on the screen were silhouettes and the prisoner's nipples and vulva were spotlighted. On the screen they thrust a cattle prod inside the vagina. The junior officers were laughing.

The chief did not feel well, but blamed the odor of his coat. The odor of cleaning solvent made the chief ill. His wife had become less attentive in recent years. She no longer looked after the household and the hired help after the children were grown. She spent all her time with the women's club. Playing canasta and drinking gin with the governor's wife and the others. The chief would make a note as soon as he reached his office: "warnings to loose women" would be the theme of their next interrogation session.

The Argentine cameraman talks too much after three beers. He brags about the movies he made while he was in the Argentine army. The chief did not care for the Argentine's loud mouth always bragging. The Argentine didn't know a hole in the dirt from the hole in his butt. The chief does not like the cameraman's smart-ass attitude. Argentines are all like that. The bastard talks as if it is a sex movie. But first and foremost the videotape is an official record. The chief does not allow Vico or the swine Argentine to change his standard procedures for interrogations. Vico doesn't argue, but from his next trip to Buenos Aires he returns with a suitcase full of video cassettes the buyer-distributor has sent to give them more ideas. Watching the Brazilian and Taiwanese sex shows after practice at the pistol range began around that time. The chief brought the cassettes Vico had borrowed.

He let the Argentine think they were going to let him call the shots. The chief even made a point of telling Vico how well the Argentine was working out. The chief wanted the Argentine to get sloppy and maybe become insubordinate with him or one of the staff officers once or twice—something like that. Because the arrogance of the Argentine was almost more than the chief could swallow. The Argentine was Mr. Know-it-all! The chief really enjoyed setting him up. They start out the interrogation with a beating. The prisoner is handcuffed with hands pulled behind him. The Argentine said he had more than enough footage of the lolling tongue and swelling, blackened face. They had already poked and jabbed with broomsticks. Such limited imaginations these Mexicans had! The Argentine did not attempt to mask his contempt for them.

Finally the Argentine had turned to the chief and said, "Do they understand words or do they just grunt?"

The Argentine had been lured to Tuxtla by Vico, who had promised him the latest in high technology and equipment. Otherwise the Argentine would have taken a job in Mexico City. The job in Mexico City had paid less, but all the actors, including the girls, were professionals. Tuxtla was the pits. Police interrogators made even torture dull and repetitive. The chief had been embarrassed when the Argentine pointed out the inadequacies of their interrogation methods. All of the big fish were taken away from them and sent to Mexico City. The little ones would tell you anything about anyone even before the sergeant and his men got past the preliminaries—stripping off prison trousers and the insertion of the copper wires up the prisoner's ass. The copper wires were connected to a tractor battery. Prisoners would shit all over themselves trying to expel the little wires.

The Argentine cameraman was always on the police chief's mind. He should never have gone into business with his brother-in-law, Vico. The Argentine had been Vico's idea. Despite the business at hand, the police chief found he often lost his concentration, and he would find himself thinking about the smirk on the Argentine's face. The chief had always been able to control personal impulses and urges because he'd seen strong men, intelligent men, ruined by their lack of self-control. Many times the chief has had to fight back the impulse to slug incompetent subordinates in their faces, but with the Argentine, the chief can no longer ignore the arrogance.

The day they get the Argentine the timing is perfect. They seize the Argentine as he walks through the door of the interrogation room. The man behind the camera wears a pig mask. The chief wears the hangman's mask of black cloth. The Argentine pales when he hears the electric doors clang shut up and down the basement corridor. The Argentine does not struggle as they tie his arms and legs spread apart on the chair. The chief wonders if the Argentine has guessed who the movie star will be. Imagine the surprise of Vico and the others in Buenos Aires when they see this video. There was no need for the expense of a surgeon's table or any of the other props. The chief had never needed more than the heavy, high-backed oak chair. If it was the genitals the chief wanted to get at, the chair worked best. The victim's sitting position pushed all the guts and tallow down on the sex organs, forcing them out. The best way to geld a horse was to hobble it with its head snubbed tight against a tree or post. One slit and the testicle was visible inside the slippery, marbled-blue membrane. Men were not much different.

PART THREE

AFRICA

BOOK ONE

NEW JERSEY

AMBUSH

THE DAY THEY HAD BEEN AMBUSHED outside the dry cleaners in Newark, Uncle Mike Blue had been lecturing Max about
security precautions. Max got bored with turnpikes and big thorough-
fares. Max favored narrow roads through the backwoods. He liked the
orchards and fields full of dairy cows. But Mike Blue had been vehement:
back roads placed Max where any cheap punk could gun him down.

Suddenly Max had found himself in the batter's box where he could
actually see the blurred shadows of the .38 slugs dropping away from
the gun barrel straight at him. But the concentration necessary to see
the slugs had slowed his body. The dive Max had made for the open
car door had been from his baseball days too, but the slugs he had seen
shattered the radio. The ones you don't see are the ones that get you,
Max had been thinking the instant a slug tore across his back and
exploded in his left shoulder.

Leah's eyes were bloodshot from crying. The newspapers were calling it a major gang war. Uncle Mike was dead on arrival, and the doctors
did not expect Max to live. Leah had not been naive. She had known
since she was a young girl that theirs was a family special and apart
from all other families. But nothing had prepared Leah for the violence.
Leah's father and two brothers had always administered vast real estate
holdings in Florida and southern California. All Max Blue had ever done
since Leah had met him was court death, although she knew she could
not blame Max for the military plane crash. Each time she saw him lying
with a bottle of blood dripping into a vein, bandages soaking up the
blood as it leaked out, Leah wanted to end it, if that was how the
marriage was going to be.

Max had wanted to talk. He had seen the anger in Leah's eyes. Later Leah had blamed her mother's death for her anger at the hospital. What Max wanted to tell Leah was how Uncle Mike had been talking about carelessness not five minutes earlier. About the precaution of the well-traveled street where assassins hesitated because of the exposure and numbers of witnesses. What Max wanted to tell Leah was about the argument they had had over lapsing into a pattern—regular route and daily routine enemies could read like a book—the morning stop at the bakery where the driver waited with the limousine idling in a tow-away zone while Uncle Mike bought strawberry pastries and a thermos of espresso. Then the drugstore where the driver left the white Cadillac double-parked to buy the morning papers. Uncle Mike Blue stopped by the cleaners once a week on Friday to pick up his shirts and suit. Max had wanted to laugh and tell Leah how they were on schedule for death. Both Max and Uncle Mike Blue. But Max had had a tube down his throat, and Leah had needed to talk, to pour out her fear and her anger. Max had tried to keep his eyes open and struggled to focus on her mouth until he saw her words in thick, bloodred waves. Behind his eyelids he kept seeing the last words from Uncle Mike's mouth take the shape of shirts floating off the hangers as the old man sank beneath the suit and shirts he carried. In an instant Max had seen the words, the shirts, flutter into angels.

Moving to Arizona had not been what Leah had wanted at all. Then she had realized how much Max had been changed by the shooting, although the change in Max had actually begun after the plane crash. Much later, Max Blue had told her: he could not remember what it felt like to be Max Blue, to be who he had once been before the plane crash. It had been as if Max Blue had died that day in the sand and tumbleweeds next to the runway at Fort Bliss. After the plane crash, Max had still pretended to enjoy Leah's thighs spread open on the bed. But the .38 slugs had blasted away the Max Blue who could pretend. The Max Blue who had survived no longer bothered to conceal what he felt. When he came home from the hospital after the shooting, Max preferred to sleep alone. He told Leah there was only one thing he wanted, and that was to move to Tucson, Arizona. He liked the looks of the skies around Tucson. He did not tell Leah, but after the shooting, the New Jersey skies had reminded Max too much of the gray fabric inside a coffin lid. He could not explain the importance of the high, open dome of bright blue sky except to connect the sky with the army plane crash outside El Paso.

Max had lain in the dry tumbleweeds and sand dunes overnight. He had hurt so bad in the night he had passed out and thought he had died. But in the morning he had lain on his back, unable to move his legs or arms, and he had watched the sky emerge from the darkness of the night, and he had seen the inky stain smear into thick gray terraces of clouds he realized later were no clouds but merely the fuzziness of his vision from loss of blood. But then Max had awakened into the deep, bright-blue depths of sky all around as if he were flying high above the desert, above the earth so he could easily see how it curved into the Pacific Ocean just beyond Yuma. Only Max and the plane navigator had survived the crash. Max had never forgot the instant he had seen the bright blue of the sky with full El Paso sun; he had awakened on a sand dune as the army jeeps approached. The old Max had died in the crash. A different Max had somehow pulled himself back into this world, but not completely. He could not rid himself of the sickening fear he felt each time he began to feel drowsy and drop off to sleep. "Dropping off" was so much like dying.

WHEELIE

THE OLD WING of the El Paso Veterans Hospital had housed First World War veterans and veterans of the Spanish and Mexican wars who had contracted tropical fevers and lung diseases. Supposedly they responded to El Paso's dry climate. Most of the old wing had been taken up with the oxygen tanks and compressors, the hiss and hum of respirators for lungs seared with mustard gas in the First World War. Leah had pushed Max in a wheelchair down the dim, high-ceilinged halls of the old wing during visitors' hours. But few of the old men had visitors. They had been sent far from their homes for the dry, warm climate, and gradually they had lost touch with their families and their lives before the war. Although they sat upright in bed, green plastic tubing from nostril to oxygen tanks, their eyes were motionless and blank. Max saw these men had been dead for years—worse than dead to their families, who got no insurance money for a vegetable hooked to a machine.

The new wing was full of Second World War and Korean War veterans, although new policy had placed patients in hospitals as close as possible to their homes. Max had noted that most visitors came for the "temporary admissions" like Max—people who could walk out the front door again. Families soon recognized when a man was as good as dead. Max had found no fault with his mother and sister or Leah. They had not left him for dead. All of them wanted to move to El Paso until Max had yelled at all of them—he was getting out. He wasn't permanent like the other poor bastards in wheelchairs.

Max observed the permanent "wheelies": they tended to marry bulldozer-sized social workers in their forties; wheelies married loud-mouths who abused them. "Wheelie's" huge social-worker wife threw him out of his chair when they had fights. While he was in a wheelchair himself, Max could not avoid these monologues from the wheelies. Max swallowed a pill and settled back with his eyes closed. Here is an army colonel's son who talks a blue streak. He had broken his neck in a swimming-pool accident when he was fifteen and drunk. He tells Max he feels out of place there.

"Wheelie" must return to the veterans' hospital from time to time for the bedsores he gets on his legs and butt, despite the sheepskins his huge wife buys for his wheelchair and bed. Wheelie has lifetime benefits from the veterans' hospital because his neck broke at National Guard summer training camp. Max opens his eyes from time to time or nods and says "yeah" and "ah-huh," but Max is not listening to Wheelie so much as he is drifting along in his own thoughts when Wheelie whispers that his prick gets hard and the women can't get enough of it.

BLUE SKIES

✻ THE MORNING THEY HAD KILLED Mike Blue and hit Max, the world had changed for Max. He had seen everything—every person—differently from before. Then gradually the truth had emerged for Max: he had already begun the change after the plane crash. The hit on him and Uncle Mike had been far worse than the plane crash. Max was beginning to wonder, how many chances did Death get in five years? What kind of lottery was it anyway? How soon before Max's number did come up?

When Max had awakened, he did not recognize any of the people around the bed in his hospital room. Some were obviously hospital staff, but Max knew the others assembled there must be his family members. He looked at the women and tried to guess which might be his wife. Max had lost all sense of connection with the world the instant the .38 slugs hit his chest. Max had told Leah exactly how he felt; emotional bonds between everyone and himself had been severed.

Max kept other thoughts to himself because he knew how people were, especially his family, and the thoughts were thoughts better left in silence. The thoughts were always about death. One death or many deaths: how many times, how many ways, did a man die? Max knew there was nothing after death. Nothingness and silence. The silence and the emptiness were darkness. Max had recovered consciousness after the plane crash, but he had never forgotten the darkness and the silence that flowed endlessly. There were no devils or Jesus. Death was the dark, deep earth that blotted out the light of a vast blue sky Max called life.

In his delirium after the shooting Max had confused memories of the shooting with earlier memories of the plane crash Max never knew he had. The shooting and the plane crash had become a single nightmare, darkness flooding light until Max awoke sweating with terror.

The priest who had visited Max at the hospital after the shooting urged Max to meditate and pray for the precious gift of faith he had lost. Max did not tell the priest he had spent days and weeks drifting on painkillers meditating on death; all forms of death. All death was natural; murder and war were natural; rape and incest were also natural acts. Serial murderers who chewed their signatures on victims' breasts and buttocks and even the baby-fuckers—they were all consequences of human evolution.

Now years later, Max thinks of himself as an executive producer of one-night-only performances, dramas played out in the warm California night breezes, in a phone booth in downtown Long Beach. All Max had done was dial a phone number and listen while the pigeon repeats, "Hello? Hello? Hello? Hello?" until .22-pistol shots snap *pop! pop!* and Max hangs up.

Max believed in death because death contained certainty. The changes in once-living tissue, the decay, were absolute. The dead were truly destroyed and gone. Max was fascinated by the thought that death terminated all being; death changed a man to a pile of rotting waste.

Max believed killing a man was doing him a favor; life insurance policies were good once the widow and family were cleared by police and private investigations. The men and women Max had got contracts for all deserved it. "Don't play if you can't pay." Max had had little cards printed up for the hits. Cops ate up weird messages on calling cards left at the crime scene. Cops were criminals at heart. Leave the calling card and the cops would think they had a serial killer on their hands. Cops liked to believe the victims had it coming, so the printed cards were the finishing touch. "What goes around comes around," was printed on another batch of cards. The cards had functioned as codes to alert contract-holders the job had been performed by Max. Max never lifted a finger, or if he did, he was hundreds, even thousands, of miles away lifting only a telephone receiver.

Max had spent considerable time thinking about the best modes of assassination. Max preferred the word *assassination* because each death had been "political." Max had made a set of guidelines he followed. A death that disgraced or discredited the victim was, of course, the form of death most in demand in the international business world. The value of this guideline could easily be seen in the Philippines, where Marcos had made the mistake of assassinating Aquino at the airport, instead of the whorehouse. The result had been instant sainthood for Aquino and political jet-power for his widow.

Max favors .22 caliber pumped four times into the nape of the neck, point-blank, followed by a liberal dousing of white gas. Sign the .22-caliber bullet "Anonymous." Under microscopes in the crime lab, even the best ballistics men could not distinguish which .22 had fired the bullet.

Arson after the hit was almost a necessity nowadays, due to the increasing sensitivity of lab tests for hair, blood, skin, and fibers. Fire took care of everything. Max had followed the fishing-boat murders in Alaska because the State had been able to produce so little physical evidence at the murder trial. The secrets of success had been a cheap .22 rifle and five gallons of white gas. The intense heat from the fire had melted dental fillings and the teeth of the corpses had shattered so that no identification on one corpse was ever made. Max liked to think of himself as somewhat a scholar, an expert in a very narrow field. He had favorites that regrettably no one would ever know about.

Max believed the ordinary details and normal circumstances of accidental death had been the components of his success. The one-car accident at night, the hit and run while the subject jogs a residential street, the garden hose to the car exhaust and the victim at the wheel with the engine running; irrefutable accidents. People slipped and died of blows to the head in tubs and showers all the time. People suffered strokes and heart failure in hot tubs; people died all the time while swimming laps.

Max had favorites. A lawyer had been found facedown in the swimming pool in his shorts with a wedge-shaped gash in the back of his skull. Tucson police were as stupid as they were corrupt. Tucson police saw accidents where Max had only tried for unsolved homicides. The lawyer had gone to a small apartment complex he owned to collect rents early one Sunday afternoon. Tucson police had ruled the death a swimming accident, and the head wound a result of "colliding with the edge of the diving board." The guy who had whacked the lawyer had panicked and thrown the golf putter into a big tree near the swimming pool. Only by accident had a gardener found the golf club in the tree. Weeks had passed and the dead lawyer was just another unsolved murder.

Max had always delivered top-quality work because he had been careful to observe and to refine his methods. The key to success was to give the cops ample simple explanations for the death. Any appearance of even a remote possibility of accident or suicide was explanation enough to satisfy police and relieve them of further investigative work.

Max called the categories "big time" and "small time," although they were all murder or *assassination,* the word Max increasingly preferred. In the "small" category Max had one or two he liked: the swimming-pool accident and the motorcycle accident. Max the choreographer and designer had been home asleep while "subcontractors" had followed his blueprints all night. They had done the neck-breaking and had then loaded the corpse, with his motorcycle, and driven them to a little grove of paloverde trees growing by the Speedway Exit ramp off I-10. Max had rather liked that it was March and the paloverdes had been thick with bright yellow blossoms when they had hung the "motorcyclist" upside down in a paloverde and left the bike appropriately skidded and smashed lying at the bottom of the exit ramp. Max had liked the newspaper report that a woman on her way to work had sighted "strange fruit" in the flowering desert tree at six o'clock in the morning.

GOLF GAME

MAX RUNS HIS BUSINESS from the men's locker room of a municipal golf course. He uses the pay telephone in the lobby or outside the Jacuzzi. As far as local people know, Max is a retired businessman who plays golf every day for his health. But Max goes to the golf course every day for the light, and for the blue vastness of the sky. He played golf to savor the single instant of perfection when the ball and the head of the club met in absolute alignment, and the ball arched gracefully above the pale ribbon of grass. Max loved the purity of natural physics and geometry. When he watched the arch of the ball against the sun, Max thought of the great cathedrals he had seen in Europe where light was celebrated as the presence of God. After the shooting Max could remain indoors only a few hours before he felt claustrophobic. He returns to the house only for messages. Weather permitting, Max takes a nap on a chaise lounge on the patio. At night Max no longer sleeps more than a few hours.

Many nights Max stays on the driving range with two shifts of bodyguards until two A.M. The secret of Max's security plan is the helicopter and .44 magnums with infrared scopes for all his guards. Max hires and trains the bodyguards himself. The most important parts of the process are the testing and the personal interview. Max hires the shy loners with the dreamy eyes who answer no when Max inquires about wives, children, parents, or close friends in the area. Max watches the men. He rotates the guards so he can watch them at the golf course. Max watches a few weeks and then he can tell which of the new men can be trusted for special assignments. Max has found the optimum number of men is twelve. Max provides the car, the housing, and pays for a telephone. The guards don't seem to care that Max is able to keep an eye on them with this system. Max never pays armed guards anything less than top dollar because, after all, they do have guns. The quiet ones who worked out constantly and swam in icy rivers alone seemed relieved to have Max take a special interest in their personal lives. Max knew loyalty was always bought. A man had to eat. Humans bought the loyalty of the dog and the horse with food. The worst betrayals came from one's own blood. Brothers sold out sisters, and sisters betrayed one another; mothers informed on their own children. Max had always avoided hiring family members or "friends" of friends. Preference was given to out-of-town applicants who had recently lived abroad in the Middle East or Asia.

Max sketches out the entire operation step by step, act by act, so all the gunman has to do is pull the trigger. Because Max had learned the hard way about assassins: if they did not have each step mapped out for them, the least decision became overwhelming for them. Assassins easily pulled triggers, but they might be paralyzed for hours deciding what model or color of car to rent. Max favors .22 calibers with cheap silencers he buys wholesale from a Church of God minister in Tucson. Max still can not get used to working with the white trash of Tucson. But he has little choice; the Mexicans and Indians all stick together in this town. The preacher who makes silencers fights income tax laws; the silencers are just a sideline to pay legal fees. White men had never been able to control Tucson or the Mexican border. In Tucson white men got the leftovers, as Sonny Blue had bitterly called them—cigarette machines, pinball games, and racetracks—dogs and ponies—kid stuff. Or garbage and toxic waste.

Naturally Max was pleased at the prospect of working with Mr. B. Mr. B., of course, was ex-military, still called "the major" by Greenlee. Max knows Mr. B. has important friends because the senator gives Max a call.

On the golf course Max finds out a great deal about a man; if he is deliberate and slow at the tee or if he rushes a hole or panics in a sand trap. Mr. B. has a nervous, tight swing that pulls the ball into the cactus and mesquite so many times Max quits keeping score. Max marches him through eighteen holes; Mr. B. talks about national security, and the need for good men.

Max likes to watch his guests flail at golf balls while attempting to carry on business discussions. Golf-course meetings give Max every advantage. Max is aware of a growing sense of satisfaction and well-being as he finishes off the last hole.

Max watches the major clench his jaws as he swings. Mr. B. jokes that he is more at home at a poker table as his ball disappears into the big arroyo curving near the eighteenth hole. As Max drove him back to the clubhouse, Mr. B. leaned out the golf cart to get a better look.

"What's the real estate market like around here?" Mr. B. had asked.

Max smiled. "Ask my wife. The real estate developer."

"Commercial property?"

"Absolutely!" Max said, proud that Leah had taken Tucson real estate by the throat. "Industrial parks—warehouses, showrooms, business suites."

Mr. B. smiled. "These friends of mine," he began, looking directly at Max, "are looking for warehouse and office space."

Later Max had phoned Leah from the clubhouse. While Mr. B. was in the shower. Could she possibly join them for drinks at the Arizona Inn in an hour?

LEAH BLUE

MAX WAS NEVER HOME anymore with Leah and the boys. Max knew she would not say it, but he did not make love to her anymore either. Max had looked at Leah as she made the accusations. He said nothing. He did not feel angry or irritated. Leah was not a stupid woman. She knew what she needed and what her two sons needed. Leah was much like her brothers and her father, who operated real estate ventures in California and Florida. From time to time her brothers and father had found the "liquidation of certain assets or deficits" was necessary. Rival developers or difficult contractors had suddenly disappeared. Max had been attracted to that killer's quality about Leah. But the attraction—the feeling—had been lost, left behind that morning he had slipped on the sidewalk in his own blood. Max had not forgot the murderous expression that had seized Leah's face when he had told her about the move to Arizona. He had promised her the real estate business then. The money would be hers and she could run it any way she wanted. He didn't care. Max had tried to sound lighthearted and tried to make a joke: "Almost a widow twice." Leah would have the real estate to support herself and the boys if Max ran out of luck.

As the only daughter and with her mother dead, Leah had been a daddy's girl. Her brothers had always taken her with them to parties and the beach. Her father had explained business deals to her and the brothers at the table after supper. Leah was one of them, and they had taught her to be bossy and had let the killer shine in Leah's eyes. So Max had bought Leah off. Otherwise, no Tucson unless Max went alone.

Max left Leah alone and Leah left Max alone. The real estate market in Tucson and southern Arizona was wide open, ripe for development. Leah only had to visit her father and brothers to see the possibilities. Her father had driven down to San Diego by way of Palm Springs. Her father would only nod his head as they passed huge tracts of desert that had been bulldozed into gridworks scraped clean of cactus and lined with palm trees. Leah didn't say anything. She just nodded. She got the idea, she got the idea.

"Max wants Leah to go into Tucson real estate."

"Real estate what? Industrial, commercial, apartments, condos—what?"

"That's what we were just trying to figure out."

But Leah had laughed at all three of them. "This is Tucson, Arizona, we're talking about—a dusty one-horse town," she reminded them.

"You'll knock them dead, sweetheart," Daddy had told her at the airport, and given her a big kiss. Her brothers both stared out the windows at the airplane. It wasn't any secret who was number one with Daddy.

Leah wore whatever she wanted when she went to look at acreage or city lots. If the housekeepers looked busy or if the kids wanted to go, she took them. They were good for about forty-five minutes playing with the knobs and buttons on the dashboard of the big Chrysler. The lights would flash and the wipers would go. The windows went up and down. But then Sonny would lose interest and tease Bingo. Finally Bingo would slump against the wheel in tears. The first time it had happened, the agent representing the seller turned pale. He paused, expecting Leah to rush across the vacant lot to get the kid off the horn. And Leah might have done that except she saw the agent's discomfort. Cars on the street were slowing, and it was Leah, in her bright green mumu and matching heels standing in the center of the vacant lot, people were staring at. Leah had sensed the agent was about to give in on the interest rate; the sound of the car horn had worked like a vise. Leah never even glanced in the direction of the car. The agent broke. Leah opened her bright blue straw handbag and fished out a ballpoint pen. A light breeze shivered past carrying a springtime odor of blossoms—desert trees, she didn't know which ones. The agent unfolded the real estate sale contract. At that moment she had felt something she had never felt before. The horn had stopped and she could hear the voices of the boys approaching behind her. But nothing could interfere or change what she had just experienced. She had outwitted the agent. The sensation was the closest to anything sexual she'd felt since Max got shot. Sometimes when she was driving back from the county recorder's office or her lawyer's office downtown, she would think about what she was doing. Max had told her to put the land titles in her name or the names of the boys. Max was busy with more important things. Anyway, she had already started financing her own deals. She didn't have to wait for money from Max. If something really big came up, she'd call her brothers.

There was nothing to talk about. Max was working on something. That was all he would say. Max slept on a big leather couch in his office and took phone calls in the middle of the night.

DESERT REAL ESTATE

THERE DIDN'T SEEM to be any way to explain to Leah what had happened. A great deal of what had been his life before had vanished. When Max took a piss, he'd look down at his dick in his hand. He'd watch the urine spread in yellow clouds in the water of the toilet bowl. He'd watch the yellow stream flow away in urinals. In the shower he'd lather his balls with soap, then work the suds in the tip of his dick. But that was all. It might have been his foot he was touching.

Some nights Leah would lie with her eyes closed and imagine that the city limits of Tucson and surrounding Pima County were a gridwork of colored squares for Chinese checkers. They had been in Tucson for a year and a half, and Max had not had sex with her or even slept in the same bed with her. Going over offers and counteroffers and joint-partnership deals was Leah's way of getting back to sleep. Otherwise Leah would be engulfed by loneliness and she would cry. All Max could tell her was the shooting had changed him. He lived and sometimes even slept at the golf course.

Buying real estate was a real rush, Leah was fond of saying. Max had hardly noticed the changes in Leah's schedule or the full-time house-keeper. Max did not ask questions if Leah did not ask questions. In the beginning Leah had had to work late nights and all weekends to catch on to the real estate investment business. She called her father and her brothers and asked their advice. She canvased neighborhoods on the edges of the city, leaving her business cards in case large parcels of desert became available. Within the family and the organization, Leah's real estate business was looked upon as evidence of how bad off Max really was. None of them, not even those who were suspicious of Max and his strange "retirement" to Tucson, bothered to look closely at his wife's investments. Most assumed that her half dozen duplexes and bungalows next to the air force base constituted a modest real estate business the family had arranged to support Max. The ones who were suspicious kept close watch. Those who did not play golf had to learn. Max did not meet with anyone except on the golf course. Always outside, always in the open air. Max played foursomes three times a day every day. Max's preference was to play in hot months; he had teed off by six A.M.

Leah had said nothing to anyone. Max wanted the confusion. Max could not leave Tucson, that was the rumor. It was supposed to have something to do with the hot, dry climate and how the doctors had sewed him back together. Something about the cold made his bones and joints ache.

For a long time Leah had not much enjoyed sex with the men she got. If they were not too terrified to fuck her, then they were either crazy or stupid.

Leah had been intrigued with the reactions men had when they learned they'd just fucked Max Blue's wife. Some sent dozens of roses or pots of orchids in bloom addressed to Mr. and Mrs. Max Blue. Leah knew she would never get those suckers in bed again. But those who did not send flowers but telephoned with inside information on classy municipal bonds, followed by a call for lunch later in the week—well, *those* babes were few and far between. Leah sensed their sexual excitement was aroused by danger. They might race motorcycles or sky-dive, or they might be aroused by the danger of having the wife of Mr. Murder himself. Leah tries to imagine their fantasies—the race to pump a load into her before the gunmen break through the door, and everything explodes right then, every pore wrenched by prolonged throbs.

Later Max tells Leah she is a hundred percent wrong about men's fantasies; those are *her* fantasies—the excitement of the orgasm before the bullets. Max knows what the men are thinking as they ram it home to Leah:

" 'His wife, his wife, I bury it in his wife! Over his dead body.' They imagine you spread over my dead body." Leah knows Max is right.

Only a woman fantasizes bullets striking a man's back at orgasm; a man's fantasy at orgasm was firing bullets into the wife's husband. Leah wonders if Max gets excited when they talk about sex.

FAMILY BUSINESS

ANGELO SANK BACK in the seat of the big Mercedes and let Sonny talk. He only half-listened because he was noticing that his Aunt Leah's realty corporations owned every other commercial parcel in northwest Tucson. Sonny was talking as fast as he was driving, cutting in and out of traffic, doing sixty up Oracle Road. Before Angelo had come West, one rumor he'd heard was Uncle Max played golf only on *one* golf course. The course with the desert landscaping. He had pictured the holes with their colored flags and numbers on the pin surrounded by a green of solid rock or adobe clay. The first visit to Max on the golf course had disappointed Angelo. The greens had finely manicured green grass, and the fairways connecting the holes, while a little sparse and yellow on the edges, were still grassy. The hazards were desert hazards, and Angelo had found them quite wonderful. Not only did the unwary golfer risk sending a ball into a sand trap, the spiny desert trees— paloverde and mesquite—growing along the edges of the fairways created an impenetrable jungle. The best hazard was formed not with deep sand or boulders and big rocks or even with the desert trees. The best hazard was a wide strip of cholla cactus branching up as tall as six feet, their spines so thick they resembled yellowish fur. Max had all kinds of funny stories about vacationers, winter visitors, playing golf there for the first time and attempting a save from the center of the cactus hazard. Teddy bear or jumping cactus, Max called the chollas, and he claimed he'd seen golfers with segments of the spiny branches sticking to their heads, their asses, and even stuck to an ear.

What Sonny is talking about is the task facing their organization. He is talking about percentages of nets and grosses. Sonny is talking expansions and resistance and what the competition is hoping to expand into. Angelo always feels a vague uneasiness when he hears Sonny or

Bingo talk like that. Angelo likes what he does with the horses: checking up on the racetracks the organization controls.

In the parking lot at the golf course Sonny wraps up his monologue with, "That's where you come in," and Angelo grins and laughs so his cousin won't catch his inattention. At the pro shop the man behind the counter says, "Fourteenth hole," and points, the minute he sees Sonny Blue. Sonny points, at one of the canopied golf carts. Everyone on the East Coast has theories about old Max Blue and the golf course. Most of them agree he is stupid or crazy. But Angelo sees how quickly the four bodyguards with his uncle sight the golf cart as he and Sonny approach. Angelo feels a wave of sweat break over him as Max Blue's four bodyguards pull out their Uzis. The three golf carts and armed men in front of them barricade Max, who tees off calmly. Max hooks the shot and the ball disappears into the mesquite grove below the sixteenth hole. Angelo wishes he'd eaten more for breakfast. He knows what his uncle is going to ask him. Angelo prefers to leave things just as they are. He will tell his uncle that if he has to. He will remind his uncle they won't find another man who knows horses as Angelo does. Unless you know horses, you can't tell how much funny stuff is going on at a racetrack—throwing races, needles, and hopped-up ponies—all the monkey business Uncle Bill had taught Angelo to watch out for at the track. Uncle Bill had taught Max for a while. Max will listen when Angelo says Bill's name. Angelo has had the fillies on the Southwest pari-mutuel circuit for two years now, and the best part is he had only seen a gun once and that was over a dope deal. The Southwest tracks are cleaner and quieter than any on the coast. Angelo wants to stay with the horses. Someone had to do the job, and Angelo and the racing fillies were assets.

Max can see Angelo is uneasy with the bodyguards. Max jokes that the best bodyguards trust nobody, not even your grandmother. Max is smiling and nods his head in the direction the lost ball flew.

"You can't practice enough," Max says, and glances at the gold watch on his wrist and then at the clubhouse. He is expecting a threesome at eleven, Max says.

Angelo is always surprised at how much Max and Bill look alike. Angelo is always embarrassed at how his heartbeat quickens when he first sees his uncle Max's face. But the eyes are different. None of them had eyes like Bill's. Uncle Bill had been the only one who had wanted to give Angelo a chance. Because, Bill liked to brag, he and the boy were alike in their love for the horses—"the ponies," Uncle Bill liked to call them. Bill had wanted the rest of the family to know Angelo belonged working with the horses.

Angelo didn't want to get involved with the expansion. The expansion involved the Mexican border and shipments from friends of Mr. B.'s. Angelo spots two golf carts speeding toward them in the distance. Angelo knows this is the threesome for the game at eleven.

"Election year is coming up," Angelo says when they get back to the car, but Sonny Blue doesn't acknowledge the remark. Angelo as a horse owner has worked out well, Sonny Blue tells him. Angelo hates the condescending tone his cousin uses.

"Bring your fillies to Tucson. Run them here this winter," Sonny Blue had said. But all that time they had been maneuvering Angelo into position.

MARILYN

ANGELO HAD BEEN a little surprised at Marilyn. It was the difference, Marilyn said, between the East Coast and the Southwest. Angelo asked her where in the East she'd been, and she had hesitated for only a split second before she said, well, she hadn't ever been anyplace outside New Mexico except for Texas, and then only to El Paso, which wasn't really like Texas. But she'd heard. She'd heard about how people in New York City and New Jersey and places back there were not friendly. Marilyn had winked at Angelo. People had been lining up behind him at the quinella window, and some of them were beginning to get nasty and mutter at her out loud. But there again Marilyn had surprised him. She had told all of them, even the meek-looking old men with only one twenty-dollar bill in their hands, they could damn well stand there and wait, they could hold their horses (she had laughed at her own joke), that the gentleman ahead of them was placing a rather large wager. Angelo did pull out the roll of fifty-dollar bills then just because Marilyn had said that. Later on, after she got off work and Angelo met her at the ticket windows, he had teased her. Angelo told her that he had been at every window at just about every track on the East Coast since he was a kid standing beside his uncle. Angelo told her that he had never heard anyone, woman or man, anywhere on the East Coast talk like *that* to irate customers. She was, Angelo teased, a whole lot more like the East Coast than she was an Albuquerque girl. But she laughed that off and said that if you didn't get tough, you got trampled, and she took off walking a little ahead of him, fast, determined, rooting around in her big tooled-leather cowgirl purse for a cigarette. Angelo had to hurry a little to catch up with her, and when he said hold your horses, hold your horses, what's the rush, Marilyn laughed and then looked him right in the eye and said:

"I am dying for a cold beer and a joint, and then I want to hit the hay with you." Just like that.

Marilyn picked the bar she said all the track employees went to. She said the good thing about it was the jukebox because it had all the old Bob Wills and the Texas Playboys albums on it. As soon as they'd stepped in the door, she had asked him for quarters. Give me all your quarters, she had said, winking again. And then even before they'd got their beer, she had gone to study the jukebox, sliding quarters and pushing buttons. The people on the barstools looked like track employees all right. Angelo saw a couple of the assistant starters, and two of the exercise boys, rubbing their hands around the coolness of the beer mugs. They all stared at him because of the white linen suit. At first that had bothered Angelo a little. Because in the East, sharp dressers were everywhere. What you wore mattered a great deal so far as how clerks or cabdrivers treated you. But in El Paso or Albuquerque around the race-tracks where all that remained of the cowboys could be found, snappy suits, and fancy shoes or hats, brought out the worst in people. The remains of what were once cowboys were the most nasty. The few blacks and all the Mexicans and Indians behaved a lot better, mostly to spite the broken-down white men in faded, torn jeans hanging so low the tops of their ass cracks showed. All that got better as soon as they found out that Angelo had no intention of giving orders or looking down his nose.

Or as Marilyn used to like to remind him, even when they were in bed together, "Out here we don't like people bossing us." And the first time she had said it, something about the way she was raised up on one arm, her tiny breast dangling, made him burst out laughing. He had said, well, what do you think—that people in the East *like* to be bossed? And she had thought about it a moment before she had let herself slide down, hand and arm buried under the pillow, facedown on the bed. She had looked up at him slyly and said:

"I boss you a lot and you don't even know it!"

Now, Marilyn glanced up and gave him a big smile as she took her beer. And then she hastily pushed two more buttons before she took Angelo by the hand and pulled him in the direction of a booth near the pool tables.

"I noticed you the times you bought fifty-dollar WINS and quinellas and daily doubles," she said. "I tried to imagine what you would be like."

"And were you right?"

Marilyn was taking a long swallow of beer, so she just nodded. "I'm mostly right," she said. "Mostly." And then Angelo had seen an instant when the glitter in her blue eyes had gone. But she had bounced right back. The way her long blond hair bounced in the loose ponytail she wore. Long, lovely strands pulling loose along both temples and behind her ears so she was most like a racing filly, all motion and speed and spirit. Angelo wondered if this was another of those differences between East and Southwest: the suddenness that things happened here. Angelo wasn't more than half through a bottle of beer and he was in love as he had never been before.

Marilyn talked and told him everything, but then Angelo would see the glitter in her blue eyes flicker, and she would spring questions at him. Why did he grow up with aunts and uncles and grannys and no mother or father? How did he get away with not going to school? What was he doing wearing those white linen suits, strolling around the track every weekend? Had he watched too many movies? Too much TV? How come he was always alone? Didn't he have girlfriends? A family? Marilyn had fired all the questions like a shotgun, but then she had backed off, letting him know he could answer one or some or none. And so he had pointed down at her scuffed cowboy boots and the bell-bottom blue jeans carefully faded and then embroidered with flowers and butterflies and rainbows.

"So now you're a cowgirl? Not a hippie?" Angelo was smiling as he said it, but something had disturbed Marilyn. She looked down and picked at the label on the beer bottle. Just as quickly, she brightened up again because one of her favorites was playing on the jukebox, "The Milk Cow Blues." The bartender brought over two more bottles of beer and indicated that one of the exercise boys had bought them a round. Angelo looked in their direction and nodded. Marilyn glanced over her shoulder.

"You know why I like this song? I like it because it's about two things at once, you know? If you only want to hear the part about the milk cow, you can." Marilyn winked as she added, "Or you hear the *other* side too." Angelo nodded. He left a couple of dollars on the table and they walked out hand in hand.

Angelo was staying at the Hilton. Was that okay? Marilyn clapped her hands together. The Hilton! That was better than any motel!

She couldn't keep from walking ahead of him, to pinch the plastic leaves of the fake fig trees decorating the halls. Angelo enjoyed her excitement at the small details. He liked the cowgirl belt with MARILYN tooled in white letters wreathed in red rosebuds and green ivy. She had pulled off her boots and rubbed her toes along the carpet. The socks she wore were men's socks, mismatched, one black, one dark blue. Then she had spread-eagled herself facedown to sniff the nubby, white bedspread. Marilyn had only seen king-size beds, she told Angelo. She had never actually tried one. Angelo had undressed while Marilyn explored the bathroom and the closet. She laughed at how carefully Angelo hung up the linen sport coat and trousers. Her faded bell-bottoms were in a heap with torn white panties and the men's socks. She left the red, pearl-button cowboy shirt for Angelo to take off.

Marilyn was the expert. Afterward she told Angelo that all the guys wanted a good blow job, and so she had practiced and practice makes perfect, doesn't it, and it had been all Angelo could do to smile and nod his head. She had said she was too nervous and excited about being in the Hilton to want sex very much. But Angelo had not been able to get enough of her. By morning Angelo had realized Marilyn preferred oral sex. Although Angelo held his weight off her, Marilyn seemed panicked when he was on top of her. She clawed at his shoulders, panting, fighting to escape suffocation. Later she admitted the feeling of suffocation was just something crazy, and her girlfriends told her that if that was true, then why didn't she gag or feel as if she were choking when she sucked cock. Marilyn said she didn't know. Even being on top of Angelo frightened her, although not as much. Marilyn had described the sensation nervously, defensively. All she could think of was one of those barbecue skewers piercing all the way through her. After breakfast as Angelo was driving Marilyn to her house, she had been silent, then suddenly she had informed him that blow jobs were what the professionals did. No diseases that way, no pregnancies. She didn't like to be pinned down, not since her big brothers had teased her and wrestled her when she was a little girl.

Marilyn did not explain her reason for leaving Angelo any better than she had explained her sensation of being suffocated. Angelo had thought she was as happy and as much in love as he was. The racing season in Albuquerque had ended when the state fair was over, and Marilyn wanted to water-ski at Elephant Butte Lake. "We were wild," Marilyn said, and then she talked about Tim and the others. "Those were really bitchin' days," she said right before she fell asleep. When they stopped for gas in Truth or Consequences, Marilyn had asked for money for a long-distance call. Marilyn did not say whom she had called, and Angelo didn't ask. She continued with the water-skiing story about taking acid at Elephant Butte Lake and the guy who had skied right over a rattlesnake.

"I didn't know rattlesnakes could swim," Angelo said.

"They climb trees too," she added, lighting up another joint. Angelo could feel a strain even while they both laughed at the prospect of water-skiing legs spread wide open and suddenly straight ahead, swimming for the cattails on the lake edge, the big diamond-back rattler coming at you straight on. Marilyn was trying too hard to keep the mood funny and a little crazy. She kept passing Angelo the joint.

Marilyn was staring out the window now. She had let go of the funny, silly mood. Angelo could almost feel her gathering up the words. He thought he could almost see the words rising up in her chest and then up into her throat. When she turned her head from the window, Angelo saw big tears in her eyes. Marilyn would not let him park the car or wait with her at the El Paso Airport. She said it was better that way. Somehow Angelo had known how it would be, after the first time they had made love and Marilyn mentioned Tim. She and Tim went back a long time together. Marilyn had told Angelo. She had warned him.

CHANGE OF HEART

ANGELO SAT IN HIS CAR for a long time in the El Paso Airport parking lot. Marilyn had been getting ready to return to Tim for a long time. Angelo had just been playing a long shot. He had known it all along, but it had not stopped him from loving her. Angelo sat and felt the street shake under the car as the big jets landed and took off. Marilyn had never told Angelo what had caused her to leave Tim. Or even if she had been the one to go. Once she had described her "crowd" as the last survivors. Survivors of what? Angelo had wanted to know. "Oh, you know, we were the first hippies and now we are the last. Just us. Just our crowd. The people that hung out together." Angelo felt Marilyn wanted the crowd again. Wanted that group that was hers, where what she did was what they all did. Angelo thought he had some idea of how to entice a woman away from another man. But with Marilyn, every expensive dinner, every shopping spree, had been followed with a strange remorse. She would tell Angelo how they had gone for weeks shoplifting what they needed in grocery stores. Cigarettes, beer, even steaks. Once she had got caught with two rib-eye steaks stuffed down the front of her jeans.

An airport cop finally came over to the car and asked if he was okay. Angelo nodded. He drove slowly until he got outside the airport, and then he purposely took the narrow, twisting road over Mt. Franklin. Bingo had a black Trans Am and was always bragging about how fast he could get to the El Paso Airport from his house. Angelo made himself game rules that afternoon: he could shift down and use the accelerator, but he could not touch the brake. If he made it to Bingo's without touching the brake and under forty-five minutes, then he would get Marilyn back. When Angelo skidded into the long, sandy driveway, he had not used the brake once. He did not have to glance down at his wristwatch to know he had come in well under forty-five minutes.

The Hacienda of the Wall was what Sonny called the house Bingo had custom-built on sixty acres of yucca and white sand dunes northwest of El Paso. Sonny had made jokes about the design, asking if the architect also designed jails and prisons. Bingo argued he needed his home to be his castle; "like a fortress," Angelo had suggested, and Bingo had leaped on that phrase, nodding his head enthusiastically.

The terrace above the pool was where Bingo spent most of his time. He had arranged all the furniture an executive suite might have—a big L-shaped desk of chrome and glass, two plump champagne sofas, with matching armchair. Although the terrace had a high redwood canopy, it was open on all sides, and whenever thunderstorms threatened, Bingo's entire house staff—three Mexican women and the Vietnamese gardener—had to drag Bingo's executive suite indoors.

Angelo did not get out of the car but sat looking at the high, massive walls of Bingo's "hacienda." A minute later he heard the voice of Bingo's bodyguard, and Angelo followed him to the terrace. Bingo was in his swimming trunks; his hairy beer-belly sat like a stuffed toy in his lap. He had been looking at a *Penthouse* magazine. Bingo tossed the magazine down and reached for his short terry-cloth robe.

"Hey, Angelo, what's wrong, man?" Bingo said, gesturing for the maid to bring Angelo the same as she was bringing for him. The maid brought them both double or triple margaritas in long-stemmed glasses that looked as wide and deep as fish bowls.

"Wow," Angelo managed to say, "whatever's wrong with you, this size will fix it!" And for a long time they sat in silence, both staring off at the southwest, where the sun was rapidly disappearing behind the dunes along the horizon. Halfway through the margarita Angelo thought he could feel a great pressure under his lungs and heart, pressure that seemed to press his ribs and the bones of his chest outward like limbs bending in the wind. The pressure was only there if he thought about it. If he remembered that Marilyn wasn't back in Albuquerque in the little apartment she rented near the fairgrounds. If he remembered that she had arrived at a decision. If he remembered that she was gone. Angelo drained the glass, but before he could reach over to the glass-top coffee table in front of the armchair, the Mexican maid had taken the empty glass and disappeared inside. Bingo was used to the service so he just nodded and smiled, still gazing over the dunes edged in sage and last year's tumbleweeds bleached white. Angelo could tell by the way Bingo puffed away at the marijuana cigarette and gazed out at the expanses of desert, Bingo liked to listen to the sounds around them, to the calls of nighthawks and crickets.

"I could just sit here like this forever," Bingo said, but a moment later the phone beside him rang and Bingo disappeared inside. "Sonny," was all Bingo said.

The maid set another margarita in front of him, but Angelo didn't move. He sat facing the south with the bloodred sunset in the corner of his right eye. Bingo's property was actually in New Mexico rather than Texas, where, as Bingo put it, state government is less flexible. New Mexico was one of those states with "a lot of flex," Bingo liked to wisecrack. To the south in Mexico, Angelo could see the pale blue ranges of mountains, like layers of paint growing progressively paler. The distance and the space did not seem to end. Not ever. The colors changed rapidly after the sun set. The sky ran in streams of ruby and burgundy, and the puffy clouds clotted the colors darker, into the red of dry roses, into the red of dried blood. The dunes of the horizon were soaked in the colors of the sky too; then the light faded and the breeze slashed at the ricegrass and yuccas. The cooling brought with it deep blues and deep purple bruising the flanks of the low, sandy hills. By the time Bingo reappeared, the sudden dark blue of the night sky had descended. Angelo looked south and could see nothing but infinite night. He took a deep breath. He knew he was drunk, but the awful pressure inside his chest had rolled back momentarily. Women were always leaving but then came back. Everything would be all right. Things would work out. He would get Marilyn back.

The wrecking yard—all the equipment, the car crusher—all of it Uncle Bill had paid for himself. That was the source of the trouble. Bill had been so careful not to give them any reason to collect. No favors to collect on, no loans, nothing fixed up by old men. Nothing. Still they had come, and Uncle Bill had moved like a man tied in steel wire; the tension grew tighter by the day. Angelo had only known that something was wrong, something was brewing up day by day, and he could tell the men in the yard knew; it would enter through the wide chain-link gates in back. The waiting went on and on, and Angelo wondered if they were like him, hoping that whatever it was would happen late at night when they were all far away, safe at home.

Angelo watched the light become darkness. He had always thought before that the darkness was separate, that the darkness was a heavier liquid that displaced the shimmering, diaphanous glow—the darkness fell across it, overcame it. Tonight, with the peppery warmth of the tequila in both nostrils, Angelo realized that the light in the sky had receded, but not disappeared; instead it had undergone a change in the minutes that passed. The light had grown thick; it had grown heavy. The light had ripened into the darkness that now filled the sky from horizon to horizon. So the family had waited a long time for Uncle Bill. They had waited for years and years. And then when the time was ripe, they had come. They had come to Angelo now. First Sonny Blue in Tucson, and now Bingo outside El Paso. He was their man, they said. "Our man in Albuquerque." Our liaison on all the Southwest tracks. You've done so well, man, you make us look great." And now they were giving him a promotion. "It will be good for you, kiddo, believe me. Just what you need to forget that girl."

Bingo came out, and even in the dim light Angelo could see the cocaine ringing his nostrils. His hair was messed as if Bingo had just finished sticking his head between a woman's legs. Bingo was too high to notice Angelo had been crying. Bingo was talking too fast now to make much sense, rambling on about Sonny and his father in Tucson. Bingo tried to show off when his brother and father were not around because the minute one or the other of them appeared, Bingo became the dumb one. The one they had to tell to shut up. So with Angelo, Bingo had to launch into what he kept calling the "technical aspect" of the "operation." Bingo needs to feel important.

At that instant Angelo thought how good it would feel to kill Bingo. To shut him up. To get the white-nostril clown face and cocaine breath away from his own face. To smash up Bingo's face so he would never again have to be reminded of Bingo, flunky brownnose, and asshole-sucker. It was about killing all right. It was about Uncle Max, the "semi-invalid." Uncle Max who made the front page of the *Times* when he "retired," for "reasons due to health," to the sunshine and year-round golf of the American Southwest. A little cow-town called Tucson. What had the movie been called *Dial Max for Murder?* No one had ever bothered to explain what Max did, but Angelo was convinced it had been Max Blue who had sent the men to crush new Lincolns and Cadillacs at Uncle Bill's yard.

After Max Blue had been shot and had come so close to dying, the family had sent him to palm trees, perpetual sunshine, and enough golf courses that Max would never have to play the same one in the same week. Angelo had learned here and there, from his cousins and from others, that Max Blue had the perfect layout: as far away from the action as possible. All day out on the golf course for sunshine and fresh air, always following the orders of his doctors, and getting checkups every year at the Mayo Clinic. Max Blue had come West to unknown territories of vast, untapped riches. This was the modern age. Max Blue could take care of everything by phone. By private couriers. As the dust cleared, the smoke blew over, and the corpse got stiff, thousands of miles away Max Blue would be teeing off, looking off in the distance at the arid, blue mountain commenting to a congressman or federal judge that the mountains were as blue as lapis lazuli.

Marilyn used to laugh and say she did not mind helping Angelo play the part. She got to drive the Porsche. She liked living in hotel suites because she never liked being tied down to one place. She had started to keep a diary of the hotel suites they'd had as they moved between Sunland and Turf Paradise in the cold months, and Santa Anita and Ruidoso in the warm months. Marilyn rated the hotel suites according to the stale odors lingering and to mysterious stains on ceilings. Angelo thought she should not bother with cheap-wad polyester pillows and sour drains clogged with hair. But Marilyn even rated the free envelopes and postcards in bureau drawers, and soundproofing in the ceilings and walls. When dope was legalized, she liked to say, she'd include an index for each of the racetrack towns. "Where to Find Cocaine in Ruidoso, New Mexico," and where to score decent smoke in L.A.

There was not enough for her to do. Marilyn had mentioned that twice or maybe three times on that afternoon they drove south to Truth or Consequences. The Porsche was right on ninety as the El Paso Airport came closer and closer, and the moment Marilyn would leave him loomed like heavy black lines across the horizon. She wanted them to be *doing* something together. Something more than fillies? She had nodded and stared down at her hands, because she had not been able to say exactly what was wrong. Not him. Nothing he had done. Yes, she had everything. She could do what she wanted. She came and went without having to explain anything. All the money she wanted. All the drugs. Well? She didn't know. It was all too set. You know? Suddenly Angelo had seen Marilyn's face light up. She had found an explanation. It wasn't the best one; he could tell by the way she kept hesitating, then repeating the same phrases. "I just need to think. I just need time."

Angelo would not let her go so easily. Why was she going back to Tim? She could have time. She could think without going back to Tim. Marilyn had grasped the armrest on the car door with both hands. She had clenched it until the knuckles of her hands went white. Angelo had kept one eye on the road and one on her feet. Angelo was afraid to press her. He loved her. He wanted to let her have anything she wanted. They had lain in bed after making love and talked about it. If either of them had ever asked, the other had sworn to give it freely. "My freedom," Marilyn had said, looking into his eyes intently. "It is the most important thing I have. I will die before I give it up."

So Angelo had let Marilyn go that day. He had stopped the car on the departure level of the airport where Marilyn had pointed because she did not want him to come in. She said she'd already cried enough. She didn't like to find herself crying when it was her decision.

VENICE, ARIZONA

MAX SAVORED THE TEE-OFF for every hole. Every time was the first time, a fresh start, the moment before the best possible shot off a driver ever possible and the soaring of the heart with your eye following the arc of the ball into the center of the fairway before the green. Max preferred to have the strange Sonoran desert enclose the fairways and greens. He and Leah had argued for hours about building lakes and fountains in the desert. Max wanted Leah to build a desert golf course in her city of the twenty-first century, Venice, Arizona. But Leah had only laughed. No deserts in Venice, Arizona, not for an instant, and certainly not for eighteen holes of golf. Tucson had enough desert. It was ridiculous for longtime residents to try to pretend Tucson wasn't any different from Phoenix or Orange County. People wanted to have water around them in the desert. People felt more confident and carefree when they could see water spewing out around them. Max had frowned. "I didn't say human beings were rational," Leah said. "Tell me they are using up all the water and I say: Don't worry. Because science will solve the water problem of the West. New technology. They'll *have* to."

Max had lost all respect for science after he had been shot. Leah threw around the words *science* and *technology* like everyone else. Max had been hooked up to their science and technology—stitched up, then reopened for bleeding half a dozen times.

Leah had made it despite obstacles she had faced because she was a woman. Show her an obstacle and she would work harder, that had been Leah's standard line at Chamber of Commerce banquets. The scarcity of water in Arizona and other Western states was an obstacle to the land developer. But Leah was accustomed to seeing obstacles removed—rolled or blasted out of her way. The market for new homes in the Tucson area had always been extremely competitive. Leah had to use every ounce of her will just to keep up with giant home-building corporations also pushing luxury communities. The water gimmick had really worked in Scottsdale and Tempe. A scattering of pisspot fountains and cesspool lakes evoked memories of Missouri or New York or wherever the dumb shits had come from. Leah wanted Venice to live up to its name. She had planned each detail carefully. No synthetic marble in the fountains. Market research had repeatedly found new arrivals in the desert were reassured by the splash of water. They are in the real estate business to make profits, not to save wildlife or save the desert. It was too late for the desert around Tucson anyway. Look at it. Pollution was already killing foothill paloverde trees all across the valley. Max catches himself looking at Leah. She had not talked about the effects of pollution on the desert until she met the owl-shit expert.

Leah had never cared whether Max knew about her lovers. In the beginning she had hoped he would find out and be moved, by hurt or anger or simple jealousy. What a joke. The spies Max used had been discreet. The spies were to prevent infiltration by an undercover agent in the guise of Leah's lover. Max had always been especially careful about the household and grounds staff.

Max is surprised Leah is flirting with the owl-shit ecologist, but remembers "opposites attract," and Leah does have an angle. She needs to head off protests by environmentalists against her plans for Venice, Arizona. Real estate development makes strange bedfellows. But Max is not interested in what happens in the bedroom. Instead, Max instructs the spies to learn what Leah talks about when she is alone with the owl-shit expert. Leah talks about water rights, the spies report. Max has to smile. Leah never misses an opportunity to save time; she fucks an expert witness on owl shit and water conservation. Max complimented Leah on this one. Had he been chosen by design or had the ecologist merely been a happy coincidence?

With the ecologist Leah has been doing two kinds of undercover work: her dream-city plans revolve around water, lake after lake, and each of the custom-built neighborhoods linked by quaint waterways— no motorized watercraft please! The amount of water needed for such a grand scheme was astonishing. Leah could not deny that. She was hoping her owl expert could help her and her lawyers make a case for Venice, Arizona, city of the twenty-first century. The water had to come from *someplace,* and Leah wasn't about to settle for reclaimed sewage or Colorado River water. Leah's "someplace" for obtaining all the cheap water she wanted would be from the deep wells she was going to drill. She had got a lease on a deep-well rig cheap because some Texans had been hiding oil-field equipment from creditors in Tucson. Leah had also bought three gigantic bulldozers from the Texans to scrape out the canals and lakes.

Max does not bother to catch all the details, but Leah wants him to play golf with Judge Arne. The case in question had already been heard by Arne in Federal District Court in Phoenix. Arne had the case "under advisement." Leah could not have hoped for a better opportunity. No link would ever be made between the outcome of an obscure water-rights suit brought by some Nevada Indians against a subdivider in Bullhead City, and Blue Water Land Development's applications for deep-water wells in Tucson. All Judge Arne had to do for Leah was dismiss a cross-suit by the Indians in the Bullhead City case, and the State of Arizona would have to grant Leah Blue her deep-well drilling permits. Indian tribes or ecologists might try to sue to stop her deep wells later, but by then the deep wells would be flowing in Venice, Arizona.

Judge Arne had made a good drive right down the center of the fairway. He was a better golfer than most who came to play Max. Of course, the others were usually coming to ask big favors—to have people shot or factories burned to the ground. Max was the one who needed the favor. Judge Arne, on the other hand, was simply "moonlighting." Three "moonlight" jobs equaled Arne's salary for a year.

Max had a good feeling for his irons that day while the judge seemed to have problems, overshooting the green on a couple of holes so that Max had finished strong, four shots up. Arne was a shrewd one though. Max could not detect any temper in Arne over the loss, but after all Arne had been in a somewhat official capacity that day, and Max had been the host. Max did not usually leave the course until sundown, but he and his bodyguards had walked the judge to the locker rooms. The judge had been in a generous mood. He told Max he felt he could influence the holdings in this water case at every level, all the way up to the Supreme Court. Arne believed in states' rights, absolutely. Indians could file lawsuits until hell and their reservation froze over, and Arne wasn't going to issue any restraining orders against Leah's deep wells either. Max could depend on that. The judge had lurched the big Volvo sedan out of the parking lot, swerved, and disappeared down Tortolita Road.

Max had made no secret of his security measures for Leah's "friends" or "associates." He had called Leah to listen to an audiotape of the last "nature lovers" board meeting. As Leah listened with Max, she was relieved her owl-shit expert hadn't been at the meeting. Leah was not sure if her "eco-defender" would have defended her or not. Still, the "nature lovers" had learned long ago to court the rich and their corporations with promises of tax breaks for large donations of money or land. But the tape Max played had not contained any talk about endangered waterfowl habitats or even how to get a million dollars out of Blue Water Land Development Unlimited. The "nature lovers" had discussed the owl expert Keemo, and Leah, and whether Keemo was fully aware of *who that woman was.* The Nature-Lovers Committee was composed of seven board members; six were women, and five had fucked Keemo in the desert at least once. Keemo himself had told Leah this. He was not bragging about himself, he said, but rather he was trying to communicate a mystical power he felt whenever he walked into the desert. Leah had made a mental note then never to walk in the desert alone with Keemo. She did not want to leave imprints in the sand with her bare ass the way the other women had.

Golf was pure geometry and physics; angle, trajectory, and wind speed; the wood and steel, the rubber and cork grasped in a human hand, and all in perfect alignment with the grass fairway clear of the sandy wash lined with green mesquite. Golf was ancient and ritualistic. A replacement for the Catholic Church. The little ball, Max imagined, had at one time been an enemy skull. Max did not complicate golf with any connection with business or personal life. He watched players better than he was with pleasure, though not many played better than Max when they came to the course for a "business game" to ask Max Blue a favor. Even the celebrity golfers the senator had brought around had been too tense and nervous to play well. The desert was too close for most of the Californians and New Yorkers. Texans could not swing their irons for fear of rattlers they imagined coiled on the fairway. Those not disturbed by the desert setting of the golf course got nervous because Max Blue made most people nervous. People had difficulty understanding why Max lived most of his life outside on the golf course. With the money Max had and with the favors owed to Max by those in the highest levels of government, Max could have enjoyed the life of a Persian prince.

Max and Leah had made no secret about their terms of marriage. Max's friends and even some of his closest advisors had fantasies about the ripe young women in a secret room in the clubhouse. Max only laughed. Let the would-be assassins stumble around the clubhouse locker rooms looking for nonexistent love nests. Max could have any person or any thing in the world if he wanted it badly enough to make the series of telephone calls to his lawyers or his bankers. Even the worst trouble could be handled this way.

For a long time Max had brooded over the changes. Max had sent for sucking and fucking movies and had in expensive call girls, and then the more expensive and more ugly licensed sexual therapist. Max still lay awake for hours trying to feel even a spark, a last shiver of desire, some remains of an urge or a fantasy that brought even a tingle of excitement. Max could remember the daydreams and fantasies, but nothing about them excited him anymore. The bullets had torn Max loose from his own body. Now Max got pleasure only from precision planning, from perfect timing and execution. Max funnels money from his "contracting" business to Leah's Blue Horizons and Blue Water corporations. Max is relieved by Leah's happiness buying and selling real estate. For a long time Max had not seen any point in going on; he had felt the hopeless monotony of sleeping, eating, and shitting. Then one day he wandered into Leah's office with its map scattered with blue, green, and yellow pins. Max had felt a flicker of interest stir. Max had leaned close to the display tables of the architect's scale models of the canals and lakes and golf courses for Leah's Venice, Arizona, development. Max had not been interested at first, but as Venice began to take shape with maps and models, Max had begun to feel faint anticipation stir. Leah saw Mediterranean villas and canals where only cactus and scraggly greasewood grew from gray volcanic gravel.

STEAK-IN-THE-BASKET

CALL IT A JOKE, a twist of fate, that after Max had endured hours of "Wheelie's" rambling wet-dream scenarios in the Veterans Hospital, Leah should, years later, have an affair with Trigg, the Realtor in a wheelchair. Steak-in-the-Basket was what Max called Trigg. Leah had made it her practice to alert Max to her love affairs, and to give Max the names and descriptions of all business associates she was planning to see during the week. Max did not ask, but Leah had done this as a courtesy to Max. It was also a precaution. Leah did not want the security men to shoot a business client or new lover.

Max did not ask Leah about her lovers because he had no interest or curiosity about the men or anything these men did in bed with his wife. Max could imagine innumerable sexual postures and practices without feeling the least hint of arousal. Max had tried imagining himself anywhere with anyone doing anything, but nothing worked. It was as if folds of wet, pink flesh were as ordinary as the sky or the sidewalk, though Max could remember when he had got hard-ons every time he saw a pair of big tits. But Max had been more curious about Leah and Trigg because Trigg was a loudmouth in a wheelchair. Trigg considered himself a "legitimate businessman," but in Tucson that only meant no firearms were used. Trigg had a specialty with zoning laws and property that was worthless unless the zoning changed. Trigg bragged once he got started, it was too late, no one could stop him. Leah pointed to red pencil dots on blocks of downtown real estate. The grid of blocks and lots on the Tucson city map was a chessboard. Trigg was buying downtown block by shabby block. Trigg had started out with ratty bungalows near the university, and Trigg had got one of the houses rezoned to allow Blood Plasma International to lease the building from Trigg. Naturally Trigg was Blood Plasma International. Trigg bragged to Leah that blood-plasma donor centers busted neighborhoods and drove property prices down without moving in blacks or Mexicans. With property prices down, Trigg came and cleaned up, buying most property at forty cents on the dollar. Max didn't blame Leah for her interest in Trigg; in fact, Max himself was interested in Trigg. Max wanted to know the deals and schemes in Trigg's mind.

"Wheelies" had something to prove. Short men needed to prove themselves, but for men sitting in wheelchairs, the need was absolute. Leah confided to Max that she had taken full advantage of the manhood Mr. Trigg had managed to resurrect between his legs. Trigg had managed to squeeze the blood flow to his groin with both hands until Leah had got what Trigg called his "rod" to ride. Leah had ridden herself raw the first afternoon. Trigg could not ejaculate, but claimed he felt orgasms inside his head. Leah had not intended to bring up sex, but there had been something in the way Max loathed Trigg for being paralyzed that had infuriated Leah. She hated how little sex mattered to Max. Leah had no intention of drying up just because Max had. Leah had gone after sex with the same confidence she had when she made her first real estate deal. Leah had thrived on afternoons in Phoenix with male clients who later invited her for drinks or dinner.

The first words Trigg had ever whispered into Leah's ear had been a little breathless. "My cock gets real hard," he said, the scotch smelling bitter on his breath.

Trigg had been in a wheelchair since his freshman year in college. He had spent eighteen months in hospitals and intensive physical rehab. He had read all the books in the hospital library and had asked his father to use his connections at the country club to get Trigg access to the doctors' medical library at the university hospital. Trigg was adamant about the eventual miracle of medical science and high technology for spinal-cord injuries and nerve tissue transplants. It was only a matter of time and Trigg would be out of the chair.

Leah thought sex with Trigg might be interesting. She had not been disappointed. Trigg's desire had a sharp edge, as if he still hungered for all he had lost. After Max Blue, Leah found she had enjoyed the fervency of Trigg's desire almost as much as she had enjoyed the durability of his erections. Max had not been able to resist a bad joke. How lousy a lover was Max Blue? So lousy his wife replaces Max with a paraplegic lover. Leah had preferred sex at the Arizona Inn because it was elegant and neutral ground. But after six or seven weeks Leah had yielded to Trigg's insistence that she come to his "condominium." Trigg never used simple words such as *home* or *house* as long as words such as *condominium* or *town house* were available. Trigg didn't just want sex with Leah, he wanted Leah to get to know the "*real* him," "the man inside." Although picking up men on the university campus was potentially dangerous to amateurs, sex with strangers did have a few advantages; at least you did not have to be bored with self-revelations.

Trigg's condominium had been even worse than Leah had imagined. The development itself was no worse than other pseudo–Santa Fe stuccos, but Trigg had decorated the penthouse himself. Trigg had dragons everywhere. The front door knocker was a brass dragon's-head knocker. The hat rack in the foyer was a black lacquer dragon with hat poles for spines. The dark red rugs had black and green dragons running their length. The draperies were fake oriental tapestries of intertwined gold and green and black dragons. Trigg kept the draperies closed carefully so the dragons could be clearly seen. The table lamps were writhing red and black dragons of plaster. The only decent object seemed to be a small jade incense bowl with a dragon's head and tail for handles. Even the shower curtains had been custom-made to match the dragon pattern on guest bath towels.

All doorways were wider to accommodate the wheelchair. In the kitchen, the refrigerator and the shelves and counters were all at wheelchair height. Trigg wasn't dependent on anyone for anything except "one thing," and Leah had been too shocked to respond when Trigg had slipped his hand lightly over her crotch. When Leah had warned him never to touch her like that again, Trigg had been puzzled at her anger.

Leah hated handicap-designed toilets because they were so high off the floor to give easy access to the wheelchair. She sat on the toilet and only her toes touched the floor. Leah wondered if Trigg had thought about a custom development strictly for the physically handicapped. Was there "soft money" available from the government specifically for the disabled?

Trigg had already got out of his chair and undressed. From the bathroom door, the huge four-poster bed looked like a Viking ship, and the red dragon lacquered on the headboard was the mainsail. Leah slid into the bed beside Trigg pretending to squeal because the sheets were cold. She did not mention the idea she'd just had in the bathroom. She did not know how much further she and Mr. Trigg were actually going to travel together, and she wanted to get first crack at any preferential loans for housing the handicapped. The Viking ship tossed and rolled, and Trigg bragged later about all the ideas he had for future developments. The sky was the limit. Leah had enjoyed Trigg after they had fucked and smoked a cigarette because he had a childlike enthusiasm for all the schemes and plots he had. The word *conglomerate* had the same gravity as *condominium* for Trigg. He wanted to create his own conglomerate in southern Arizona. Cover all the squares. Touch all the bases. Own a hospital, an ambulance service, and a mortuary as well.

"Diversification," Leah had said when Trigg had stopped talking. He had covered all her squares and touched all her bases, and Leah was in a tolerant mood. She let Trigg keep talking. Trigg claimed most of his ideas were outgrowths of his months in the hospital, and the medical texts he'd read. Trigg was convinced he was a genius. All his ideas and the connections with the accident, the months in the hospital and the wheelchair—*all of it was in his diaries.*

Trigg had reached into the drawer of the bedside table and pulled out a thick three-ring binder. Trigg had pointed at a closet door. He had all the other notebooks stored there—notebooks all the way back to the accident. As he talked to Leah about himself, his diaries, and his accident, Trigg's eyes sought Leah's eyes urgently, as if he feared Leah did not understand the extreme importance of the diaries. He wanted Leah to know the person he was deep inside. All Leah could do was to nod when Trigg said this. The notebooks in the closet were stacked three feet high. Leah resigned herself to sitting in bed naked surrounded by dragons, reading the story of Trigg's life on lined, loose-leaf paper. She was mixing business with pleasure, and Trigg's diaries were homework. She was fascinated with Trigg and his "orgasms in his head." Orgasms had to be in his head. The scars across his lower back looked as if Trigg had been chopped in half and sewed back together.

But when Leah had reached for a notebook to settle back with and read in bed, Trigg had had other ideas. She could take the diaries home with her to read. Right now, though, Trigg said he wanted to talk about "diversification." The health-care industry is a sleeping giant, Trigg said. His plasma donor centers had got Trigg thinking about alcohol and drug treatment centers. There were millions and millions to be made from treatments for people addicted to alcohol and other drugs. That had been what Trigg wanted to talk about.

"Talk?" Leah had said in a teasing voice. "Who said anything about talk? This was all I came here for." Leah laughed. She had not felt so good in months. Trigg had fucked her one way, and in typical Tucson fashion he was ready to try to fuck her with a slick real estate deal too. Trigg wanted Leah's Blue Water group to finance and build his detox and addiction treatment hospital. In return, Leah's Blue Water Investment Corporation would receive stock in the blood plasma business as well as stock in the detox hospital. Leah said she'd have to think about it. She did not want to see Trigg's tacky dragon logo within ten miles of her dream city. But if Leah herself took over planning and design, then the addiction treatment center might be one "jewel" in a triple crown of high-tech medical care facilities, within the first luxury community designed for the handicapped and the addicted. When Leah had finally got loose from Trigg, the trunk of her car was full of loose-leaf notebooks, pages filled front and back with Trigg's urgent scrawls in pencil and ink.

DIARIES

MAX HAD NOT BEEN ABLE to resist Trigg's diaries. Leah had not seemed interested. "Go ahead, save me the trouble—let me know if there's anything juicy," she said, and then laughed at the memory of Trigg, his face wet from his own saliva, grinning at her crotch.

Trigg's diary entries appeared to begin in a rehabilitation center. The diaries were obviously kept for mental hygiene or group therapy. Max had experience with therapeutic diaries himself. Therapists were Peeping Toms. Your dreams and fears were their windows. Therapists were merely satisfying themselves though they claimed they were helping you.

Trigg had only ever had one thing on his mind, and that was the meat dangling between his legs. The accident had only served to intensify Trigg's attention to his cock. The diaries were page after page of notes on attempts to get pretty girls from his college classes to go to bed with him despite the wheelchair.

Max shuffled through the stack of notebooks; the older they were, the more filthy they were. Max had started in the middle and flipped through the pages to the beginning, then fanned back through to the end of each notebook.

From Trigg's Diaries

The black and Hispanic orderlies hate their jobs. Women's work. They wipe shit off butts and mop up puke. They always smile for no reason when they lift me out of the bath.

My mother smiles that smile too. I catch her staring into mirrors behind my back to see the width and length of the scar.

Cut you down to size, I hear the orderlies say when I wheel by the nurses' station late at night. I can't sleep because I have the same dream every night.

Helpless baby. I don't dream anything but the words themselves written in white on black. The whole dream consists simply of those words. Nightshift orderlies close the nursing station door and smoke reefer. I am the only patient with enough of a brain to know. The others are snoring.

The orderlies (blacks) hate white people. I can tell by the way the short one smiles when I complain about cold bathwater.

You will find out who your friends are. The guys from school. At first they call a lot. Then it's only one or two. Rick and Brett still come over and play chess. Sally and her friend Elaine will bring over a new album. They always ask for dope to smoke. Say I am the reefer man. My parents' friends are not the worst ones. They always try to show they are confronting my "handicap" head-on. They go out of their way to watch me to prove their minds are as broad as their fat asses.

Elaine came over with her friend Patsy. My folks were gone for the weekend. First vacation alone since the accident. A year and a half. Mother calls it "essential." Elaine's friend is a big girl but friendly. Pours Dad's Black Label scotch too easily. I won't bother with reefer if Elaine's friend isn't going to get friendlier. I want to reach down her white peasant blouse and pinch her nipples.

Max finds the diaries extremely satisfying. For one thing, they have enabled Max to begin to piece together details of the crash that had put Trigg in the chair. Trigg had been drunk when another drunk turned left in front of Trigg's sports car. Both his parents had been corporate lawyers and alcoholics.

Susan is gorgeous. She has long blond hair and big tits. She smiles when she sees me, not like the others who smile but don't want to look me in the eyes. I see Susan before class, then drop my notebook and feel really stupid because the chair almost tips when I reach down for the notebook. The dumb jock with F on all his quizzes sits and stares at the notebook. After class Susan talks about her fiancé. Two weeks to go to the third anniversary of my accident. In the hospital I had dreams about walking and running. The chair is not me. The chair is not part of me.

Diane, a girl from my language class, walked with me to my van. I wanted to ask her if she wanted to sit in the back of the van with me. But I could see her get nervous. She had to meet her aunt. Something for a birthday.

I don't know what women really think of me. Even when they start out friendly and interested, I do something wrong. I scare them.

I want women to accept me for who I am and not what I have or do not have. They look down on me in my chair, so why not overlook my feelings too?

I can't stand people who think they are better, who act superior. Bad day. I miss my swim because the city pool is closed for cleaning this week. I feel the difference in my bowels. Rocky roads as the chair bounces across campus to see if I can swim between collegiate workouts. But after I climb the chair over the curbs and fight the elevator up to the fourth level, the secretary cunt bitch tells me there are no exceptions to the athletic department's rulings.

Mother won't have time to see me in Key West over Christmas. The fourth "anniversary" in two more weeks.

My MBA classes look okay. All my friends are in law school. I tell them what I need from life only money can buy. I want to make as much money as fast as I can. Lisa is upset that I am not going to Baltimore for Easter. I can't tell her I feel like I'm drifting—that I want to date other women again. I want a woman up to my level.

Lisa wants to get married in the summer. I try to explain my dream goal: to walk down the aisle with my bride, not roll in this fucking chair.

Tried to call Diana again today. She quit coming to language lab. I suspect it is because of me, no answer. I embarrassed her at the pool. After class I asked her to come watch me swim. I spat on an asshole crowding into my lane. Diana said she didn't understand my hostility. I had to laugh.

Lisa calls while I have Diana half-undressed. While I'm on the phone, Diana gets dressed and leaves. Later I find her at the sorority house. She doesn't want to let me put my arms around her. Goddamn Lisa. Diana says it won't work out. I ask, can't we go someplace more private? Diana told me she is dating another guy, but she did not tell me he is black. How does it feel? she wants to know. How does he feel? I ask her back. What do you mean? Aren't cripples lower than niggers? I say, and I already see tears in her eyes, the kind that used to get my dick hard. I tell her about the orderlies in the hospital. I tell her she doesn't know anything about them or the hospital.

Dad says Arizona does not have the best MBA program. But the weather is easier here in the winter. In the ice and snow it is easy to fall in the chair. I hate lying there waiting for someone to come over to help me. Time seems frozen while people look at me. I feel all my clothes getting soaked. Finally one of the morons comes over and asks me if I need anything.

All the women in MBA classes are ugly—no—"double uglies" like Rick and Brett and I always called the sows.

The review class is going to be terrible. Boring. Brokerage license, rules and regulations. But I will get rich off this.

Lisa called off our engagement. I try to sound upset. The telephone connection echoed and I couldn't hear her. I estimate the money I make will more than finance all the costs of the breakthrough technology.

Max skips to the last notebook Trigg had lent Leah.

Breakthroughs in electrochemistry of the human brain. The rewiring of human nerves severed or badly crushed. Money buys anything.

Ike calls from West Germany. Says he's got a deal over there. They will buy all the blood and bioproducts we can deliver. Blood plasma centers are only the beginning.

I see myself as being superior to the others. I am better than all of them.

Tucson, city of thieves. Third-generation burglars and pimps turned politicians. These alleged human beings, the filth and scum who pass through the plasma donor center, get paid good money for lying with a needle in their arms—an activity they pursue the rest of the day anyway. I could do the world a favor each week and connect a few of the stinking ones up in the back room and drain them dry. They will not be missed.

BOOK TWO

ARIZONA

BIO-MATERIALS, INC.

AS TRIGG BOUGHT MORE AND MORE real estate, he had become paranoid about Mexicans and blacks. He could be rid of his own plasma donor centers anytime he had a hot prospect from the East Coast looking for condominium property in Tucson. But Mexicans and blacks could drift up from the bottom of the cesspool—and it only took a few of those brown floaters to stink up and ruin an entire neighborhood Trigg was "rehabilitating."

Trigg said he knew right away not to bother bullshitting Leah. Look who her old man was anyway. Rumors went around that Max Blue had never retired.

Trigg wanted to talk about the blood and organ donor business because he had contacts who were developing a whole new market beyond plasma and whole blood. Trigg wanted to use the plasma donor centers to obtain donor organs and other valuable human tissue. Trigg had never known a woman like Leah. He had never found a woman who could listen to descriptions and price quotations for whole blood, human corneas, and human kidneys without turning green. Trigg had seen plenty of big guys faint over an ice-packed carton of cadaver skin for grafts. Trigg liked the way Leah was always thinking. He got ideas off her ideas. Leah was on track about a medical hospital. They could build the facility near the detox-rehab hospital. They would need a regular hospital from time to time for their detox patients. Leah had got the idea for a kidney dialysis machine that would serve the sector of town houses and condominiums that would presumably be bought by kidney patients and their families or by health insurers to house their Arizona dialysis patients.

Trigg had to stop and look in the mirror sometimes to believe his life now, and the new three-piece suit he had just bought. The problem with most of them in wheelchairs was they did not care about their personal appearance. They were ragbags. Many of them smelled ripe. Trigg had always known that to be a success you had to look a success. Money was the measure, and all Trigg had needed was a couple of lucky breaks in a row—a string of winners. Leah was the queen in his ace-high royal flush.

Trigg did not trust employees. Trigg handled all the bookkeeping and banking himself to ensure privacy. Trigg shipped out fresh-frozen plasma and whole blood and took pride in delivering the shipments himself. The Bio-Materials company van had a rear lift system that allowed Trigg to remain in the wheelchair while he was driving. A new Mercedes would not be so convenient. Trigg would have to pull himself in and out of the wheelchair into the driver's seat and still stow the wheelchair. But the extra trouble would be worth it because the Mercedes he had bought was a beauty—a custom convertible for Tucson's lovely weather. Trigg imagined speeding along the beaches heading for mother's place in Palm Beach. He would buy a white three-piece suit for the occasion. All it would take was enough money and his mother would be telephoning to invite him for tea.

Trigg took pride in the strength of his shoulders and arms. He was always pleased when women asked him if he worked out. A stupid question when he was wheeling his body weight and that of the chair around campus eight hours every day before the wheelchair ramps became the law. The worst had been the dumb broad who had said, "Oooh! You really do have a great *upper* body!" Trigg hated the sorority-house piggies, pink and sweating in their bikinis. If they encountered him around the university pool, they invariably shrank back from him as if he were the Boston Strangler.

But when Trigg had finished his laps, if the mood struck, he could always buy himself a quickie with a piggie. All he had to do was offer a coed a joint in the back of the van, and then he'd tell them about his land development corporation and the Mercedes, and the little piggies would shed their tops and bottoms in a flash. Trigg was happy that Leah was a married woman. She could keep her gangster husband and Trigg could keep his panhellenic piggies.

Trigg made it his policy to check the daily ledgers and receipts as well as the contents of the freezer units at each of the plasma donor centers. Luckily Tucson employees were ignorant of the value of blood and other "bioproducts." Nurses and medical technicians would steal any drug they could get their hands on. Except for pints of blood or frozen cadaver skin, there wasn't much to pilfer from a plasma donor center except needles and syringes and the usual thefts of toilet paper and garbage bags by employees.

Trigg had had an idea buzzing in the back of his head for weeks, maybe months; he had not been able to forget the price quotes for fresh whole blood, human corneas, and cadaver skin. Trigg was becoming acquainted with human organ transplant research teams at the university hospital. Someday Trigg would walk again with the aid of their electronic-impulse hookups to his legs and skull. He wanted to help research teams obtain the fresh biomaterials they needed.

GREEN BERET

TRIGG DIDN'T LIKE THE RECEIPTS for the week from the two new locations. Volume was the name of the game, and no way were the two northwest plasma donor centers pulling in enough donors. The northwest locations had been intended to exploit areas where copper strikers were unemployed. Trigg had placed help-wanted signs in the donor centers because he wanted to find "one of them" to hit the streets and start recruiting plasma donors for him. Trigg could not implement his plan without substantially increasing the number of "resident" donors and donors who could be counted on to return month after month.

Trigg interviewed the job applicants himself. Trigg had noticed the big guy before. The staff members said street people called him Rambo. Trigg had looked him over without looking him in the eyes. The combat boots and the camouflage T-shirt made the guy "Rambo." Trigg had to laugh to himself at the moron standing in front of him. But when Trigg finally looked into Rambo's eyes, he saw something that had chilled him; after that, Trigg believed Rambo *had* been to Vietnam. Trigg had enjoyed Rambo's military posture and the way Rambo would almost salute before he left the room.

Trigg had never regretted the money he had paid Rambo—fifty cents a head for a donor who returned at least twice. Rambo didn't get paid until the donor had returned the second time. Trigg couldn't lose. Rambo had showed up riding a really nice ten-speed bicycle one day, and after that Rambo had pulled in plasma donors he found in the unemployment-office parking lots and in the food stamp lines and at the government free-cheese lines. At first Rambo had not enjoyed riding the bicycle because he had been afraid of the cars. He had not been afraid the cars were going to hit or kill him; he had been afraid of the people inside the cars and what they might be thinking about him. He had vowed to always wear some article of clothing—combat boots or jacket and of course the green beret—to remind all of them of Vietnam and where he and a million others had been. He had to laugh. Americans got paralyzed with fear every time they saw a Vietnam veteran still wearing combat clothes; Rambo enjoyed the advantage this gave him. Army surplus stores had resupplied him when his last pair of combat boots wore out. On the road or living on the street, Rambo had found the green beret and combat boots did the trick; even cops and railyard bulls had been strangely transfixed by the green beret. They could not stop staring at the Silver Star and Purple Hearts pinned on the beret. But Rambo refused to discuss his medals or what he had done in the war. If people still pressed, Rambo simply told them the past was history and no longer mattered, and even the strangers had always walked away more relaxed. Rambo did not spend money on much, but he was careful to always have the beret dry-cleaned, and not at one of those dinky one-hour places either.

Rambo had tried going without wearing the green beret; the wool in the green beret did not make the top of his head any hotter in Tucson than it had in Thailand. A little sweat, a little discomfort, was necessary to give men the fighting edge. That had been one of the primary lessons at the Special Forces training school in Florida. The wool acted as an insulator against the heat as well as the cold. He had been sent home before the others in the Special Forces unit. When Rambo had awakened in the hospital, he had thought he was wearing his beret; he could feel the beret on his head, though somehow in his sleep the pillow had pulled the beret far down over his ears. But when Rambo had tried to reach up, he had not been able to get his arms loose from the mass of bandages that were somehow tangled with the bed sheet. He had bellowed and grunted a long time before one of the other patients in the ward had repeatedly hit the nurse-station button. Rambo had asked them what day it was, and where he was. Wednesday, and somehow he had ended up in Manila. He had demanded to know where the rest of his unit was, and they had told him that all the rest of his unit had gone home. They had already gone? They had left him? When was this? The nurse had been apologetic. He would have to wait until the following day and ask the doctor. The nurse said she was new; she had been rotated up from Australia and was headed back home herself.

"Don't worry. You'll get home too. If you want something, you can have a pill to help you sleep." He had asked her about his beret. She had repeated the word, dumbstruck. "Beret?"

"Beret! Beret! Green beret! You know, you fucking cunt! My god-damn green beret!"

The following day the doctors had come. Rambo noticed immediately they were afraid of him because they had all approached his bed in a tight group, pretending they were merely crowding around to look at his medical chart. Rambo could see immediately the young doctors in their starched and pressed khakis were not real military because they did not wear their caps with the scrambled eggs—the gold braid army doctors got with rank. The war was over so they thought the men would not detect civilians in uniforms. He did not see why the military had tried to deceive wounded veterans.

Roy was a special name because it meant "king" in French. His mother had always loved the romantic sound of French, and she had never let him forget his name was special. After Vietnam, they had not got along. She had not liked the "vulgarity" of Roy's vocabulary and the repetition of four-letter words; she had objected to the loud *klomp!* of his combat boots on her hardwood floors.

The young doctor had explained slowly and carefully that what Roy felt around his head were bandages, not a hat.

"Beret!" Roy bellowed. "My green beret!"

"Yes, of course," the young doctor had said, smiling apologetically. It was not a hat on his head that he felt. The doctors had even showed him, pointing in a shaving mirror. That was him with a cone of bandages on his head. Of course then he had been called Roy, not the nickname Rambo. He had not even liked the movie because none of it was real or true. But the nickname Rambo had stuck with the younger men in the homeless camp. They had seen all the Vietnam War movies.

For a long time the doctors had not understood where Roy's injury had been. He had not minded the bandages around his head, but he certainly had no wound on his head. That had been the most absurd notion the doctors had; Roy had screamed at them.

"*Head!* My head? You stupid cocksuckers! I never got hit in the head!'' He got control of himself again after that outburst because he wanted the doctors to think he respected their military rank, when, in fact, he had guessed their charade. One of the other doctors had tried to trick him by saying that it was shrapnel, not a bullet. Of course he knew it was shrapnel! he screamed at them. But why did they have his head wrapped up? The army was always making mistakes. Here was another one. His head and arms all wrapped up and both legs bare. Roy had told him he did not understand it. They could see the scars on the leg where the wound had already healed. Why had they flown him to the Philippines with bandages around his head?

Roy had been happy when he had got the nickname Rambo because that meant the homeless men along the river had decided to let him in. Because at first they had all been certain Roy was an undercover cop in jungle fatigues and green beret. They had lost his green beret in the hospital in Manila. Because Rambo knew the pictures his parents had taken of him walking off the transport plane by himself showed him *without* his green beret. He had been wearing the bandages on his head, which they had finally forced him to admit were necessary. Bandages on his head were necessary. That was all he allowed to be said about the bandages. He had no head wounds. The beret had been stolen by custodians who scrubbed the floors of the wards. At the time Rambo had felt a great deal of hatred in his heart for the filthy gook who stole his green beret. The green beret had protected him from harm. Roy had never let on to the others, but he thought the Rambo movies were full of shit because Sylvester Stallone would have been blown to bits eight million times in his first week in combat in Vietnam.

Roy had worked the longest with the doctor who wanted to find out more about the killing of Sylvester Stallone. Finally Roy had had to tell the doctor it was no use. If the shrink did not know why Stallone had to die, then the doctor ought to give up psychiatry. Right after that, Roy had been wandering near the train station in Albuquerque and had seen the green berets in the front window of the army surplus store. The new combat boots had cost a lot too, so Roy had to cash in the remainder of his bus ticket. Wearing the green beret again all the time greatly changed the sort of thoughts Roy had. If he had still been talking to that shrink, he would have been happy to inform the doctor that he never gave Sylvester Stallone a second thought these days. He would have said, "Doc, unbelievable, but I never even think of him when the guys call me Rambo. Stallone the actor, who is he anyway? In a way I am more Rambo than Stallone is because I have a Silver Star and three

Purple Hearts, and where was Stallone in the war years? Prancing naked in porno movies."

No, Roy knew who he was. With the beret on his head, Roy's thoughts had been crystal clear; it had been as if steam or condensation had been wiped off a window inside his head, behind his eyes. Too many of them had made money off the Vietnam War. Not just the actors, the Holly-weirdos, but all the giant corporations—Dow and Du Pont, Remington and Colt, General Motors and General Dynamics—the fat cats glutted with blood. Someday his army would arrive at their doorsteps; Rambo would lead his ragged army against the government. When he wore the green beret, all of the future became clear to him.

Rambo ate only peanut butter and the macaroni and cheese the homeless shelters fed the men year-round in Tucson. He had not been able to eat meat or fish or anything that had once wiggled or had blood. Someday he would show the fat cats blood, but the blood would be theirs. The fat cats had helped Roy's thinking clear. He now thought of himself as Roy who was also known as Rambo. Communism had killed itself. Now the United States faced a far greater threat—the danger from within—government and police owned by the fat cats. Roy had seen for himself women and children hungry, and sleeping on the streets. This was not democracy. Police beating homeless old men was not the United States of America. Something had to be done, and Rambo and his army would do it.

The green beret made anyone—a man or a woman—look strong and clean. Roy's beret had kept him alive on the helicopter ride to the hospital.

PLASMA DONORS

ROY SAID IT WAS HIS LUCK; he had spent two blistering years in Thailand crossing borders back and forth fighting the secret war. Television news had never mentioned it. Roy thought it was funny; his parents had not believed their own son when he told them he had been fighting in Thailand. His parents had believed what they had been told by television. What do you think of that? Your *own* folks don't even believe you. They believe the TV."

Trigg smiled and nodded. This Rambo guy would be perfect for the job; another certifiable nut case on the payroll. There might even be some kind of government money or a tax break for hiring a veteran. If the guy went nuts later, whose fault was it? "Independent contractor" like the rest of them, that was what Trigg had always had his attorney tell the police and the prosecutors. Unfortunate occurrences, tragic misunderstandings, and fatal injuries abounded in the world; when your time comes your time comes. Trigg had actually enjoyed listening to his attorney sweet-talk and seduce a jury. Trigg liked the lawyer's philosophy: juries consisted of the leftovers who never watched the news or read newspapers because the world had left them behind years ago. Juries came from the bottom of the barrel; juries secretly resented their lowly position but also secretly believed they deserved the bottom. The lawyer believed it was important to talk directly to the jury about chance, fate, and luck.

Roy and Trigg get along fine. Roy's job is to hand out leaflets to homeless people. He gets fifty cents for every new plasma donor he brings in. Avoid the ones with scabby arms and legs from needles, and don't bother with the ones with runny noses or runny eyes. After a week or two, Roy had learned his job. Trigg hired him as a night watchman at the main cold-storage unit.

His secret was, Rambo knew how much the bastards wanted to be like him. He had listened for years, and he had got so he knew which ones had really been to war and which ones only talked. Rambo was most interested in the guys who'd actually gone. Sleeping in dry washes or rolled up in cardboard under mesquite trees above the river, they would be ready when he called. It was simple arithmetic. The punks would have been in diapers the first time Rambo had gone to 'Nam. The younger generations were weird. What they wanted most of all was to have been somewhere so they'd have a place to start from. Let them take whatever they needed, because the only legacy the U.S. had given them was as worthless as the string of dingy foster homes they had endured. Only a great and terrible war could explain how so many could find themselves sleeping in the street. They had lost fathers and brothers they could not remember to that war. That had been how Rambo explained their attraction to him. A few had had the stories down right.

So a few of the young drifters had heard stories about the real thing from Vietnam vets along the way. The past could never be pinned down. Each person remembered a moment differently. Rambo had seen photographers and journalists in the combat zone. If that was how history got written, then the punks' lies made no difference either.

"This is the issue," Rambo had told the first few men. "Look where we are." Rambo had paused so the men could look around. They were in a dry arroyo that ran parallel to the Southern Pacific tracks. Rambo had calculated all the distances: they were 850 yards east-southeast of the Tucson Police Department headquarters downtown and 840 yards due north from the university branch of the blood plasma donor center. Some of the men had seemed dazed by raising their heads high enough to see beyond the bank of the dry arroyo.

"Look where we are. We fought and shed blood for this nation and look where we are. I'm looking for a few good men," Rambo said, and smiled at the tall, skinny guy nearest him. But the skinny man plucked at his beard nervously and never looked up from the ground. Some of the older guys, one black, had done tours in Southeast Asia, but they had stood clear of the others who were liars. For an instant Rambo had felt something in him sink, the feeling he got when no one believed him. But Rambo quickly caught himself.

"This is America! The land we laid down our lives for!" What Rambo had liked was that he didn't have to do much talking. They all knew what it was about. They had fought and suffered for the U.S., but the U.S. had no place for them. Rambo saw them nodding their heads, all eyes on him; except the older ones who were drifting away, walking west down the arroyo. At a certain age you wore out. That was all there was to it. Rambo had seen it in veterans all the time. So young ones who did all the lying about Vietnam worked out better actually. What had to be done now required young men. Because after a certain age, a man learned to fear the sound of bullets as they split bones.

ARMY OF THE HOMELESS

"THE DAY WILL COME when I'll need volunteers to head units," Rambo had said carefully, because he didn't want to scare them off like some nut case. He stood and watched their faces and waited to see who would step forward. He had begun to use silence. All eyes were on him. Rambo could tell a number of them thought he was crazy. As if they could judge! All of them were thin with scraggly hair and patchy beards. Most of them were white, but a few were brown and black. They all slept on cardboard in the bottom of the arroyo. They had been waiting for someone like Roy. They knew him when they saw him, and no name or nickname mattered. A leader for them was what was important to the men.

Roy didn't want to confuse their minds with talk about the future. They would be ready when the moment was right. Roy didn't want anything premature. The nickname Rambo had been a little premature.

Roy walked a distance west along Twenty-second Street to vacant land that was still desert bushes and cactus. He liked to sit in the desert alone, away from lights so he could see the stars more clearly. The sight of the millions and millions of stars had always got Roy's thoughts channeled in the direction of man and God. How puny and vicious men were. Was God to blame or was man ruined?

All questions and no answers had been Roy's life up until that night. But when Roy had returned from his walk in the desert, he knew what he would do. Everything was beginning to fit together; all these years Roy's life had been scattered, and now suddenly he had seen how all the parts were going to fit together. Trigg has a sign-up program too. Now Roy carries a manila folder full of patient information-release forms. Donors in the monthly program were examined by a doctor periodically. The idea was to get a healthy and dependable source of blood products. Once Roy had asked Trigg if he had had to dump any plasma or blood because of AIDS. Trigg had laughed and rolled his wheelchair in a slow circle. "It's a whole new ball game now," he had said. In the beginning the feds and of course, the public, had been slow to catch on. Whole-blood and plasma products were too valuable to dump simply because of unverified reports and rumors. By the time the government had sent out bulletins with precautionary guidelines, Trigg had emptied his freezers. A short time afterward, fire had swept through Tucson Blood Products, and Trigg had left the old company's name in the ashes. Trigg wanted no AIDS victims' lawsuits.

New laws, new rules, new regulations, new tests, new procedures— all of it cost money. Recruitment and screening were critical. Trigg paid Roy to go out and find donors. Roy started with the city parks in the morning when the homeless men were at the water fountains washing up; by noon Roy would have worked his way south to the church kitchen and the sandwiches on Fifteenth Street. Roy used the soft sell. He didn't know any other way to get men to sell blood or plasma every week. He told them up front he was getting fifty cents a head for their names if they showed up at the plasma donor center.

Roy wore the beret and the combat boots because he had to walk the arroyos and big washes to find the campsites and lean-tos. Even when he did not wear his camouflage pants, the green beret and the combat boots had been enough. Right away they wanted to talk about the war.

Roy had known a number of assholes and crazies who had been to Vietnam or the Gulf. They had not been "talkers" for one thing; that separated them from the liars. But he had watched them listen and stiffen with rage while skinny, pimply boys lied and bragged. Crazies let their silence simmer, sometimes for years; then all at once their silence exploded in the faces of all the liars.

What difference did it make years later whether a man had actually served in Vietnam and was now wandering the streets, or only repeated stories he'd heard from older guys who had been in combat? Roy was not going to pass judgment on what were lies and what were truths. The U.S. had used false figures; the enemy body count had been inflated.

No, Roy would never humiliate the skinny, young "Vietnam vets" who had signed up with him for twice-weekly visits at the plasma center. In America a man needed some kind of story to explain himself, to explain why he was here and how he had got here. The only good they would realize from that war were the stories.

Roy had read the mimeographed newsletters piled on a card table inside the Methodist soup kitchen where social justice and social activism were the name of the game. It had been simple dollars and cents. America's wealth had bled away during Vietnam; now the U.S. was buried in debt. So Roy could not bring himself to expose the skinny, young impostors in filthy camouflage pants and field jackets. Because they had all been casualties of that war, all Americans no matter how young, even the unborn.

Roy could sense Trigg's growing attachment to him as a "captive audience" for Trigg's endless monologues about how much he was worth, meaning "assets" and how much he had bought at pennies on the dollar from government liquidations of real estate once owned by little savings banks established only to go belly-up. The best way to rob a bank was to own one. Roy had nodded his head and had pretended to be impressed because a plan was beginning to take shape, and Roy wanted to learn as much as he could about Mr. Trigg. Trigg blabbered on and on about profit-loss, percentages, and world markets, but Roy was thinking about the man in the wheelchair. Roy wanted nothing Trigg owned, not the Mercedes, not the big house with the special therapy pool, not the cashmere socks or the rich bitch who sat on Trigg's face.

The world market was definitely changing. Real estate was going to take a dive.

Trigg congratulated himself on his wisdom and foresight in getting into the biomaterials industry. "Biomaterials," not new antibiotics or drugs, were going to be the bonanza of the twenty-first century.

"Biomaterials?" Roy asked questions because he liked to watch Trigg preen and condescend to answer him.

"Biomaterials! Not just plasma, not just blood!" Trigg could not contain his excitement. The vodka had taken over, and Trigg listed to the left in his wheelchair as he attempted to be buddy-buddy with Roy and leaned toward him as he whispered loudly:

"Biomaterials!" Biomaterials—the industry's "preferred" term for fetal-brain material, human kidneys, hearts and lungs, corneas for eye transplants, and human skin for burn victims.

Roy had heard rumors about Tucson before he ever hopped the freight train in Baton Rouge. Hoboes said Tucson had communist priests and terrorist nuns and even the Methodist churches in Tucson were communist. Then Roy heard the opposite too, that just outside Tucson the U.S. military had begun to create a "bastion of strength" to run the length of the U.S. southern border. In Baton Rouge stories circulated about the mysterious recruiters in white shirts, dark blue suits, and dark glasses who were looking for "good soldiers" willing to relocate to Tucson.

The afternoon Roy had hopped off the freight train in downtown Tucson, a group of homeless activists had been taking showers on the steps of City Hall. His first night in Tucson, Roy had watched himself shave and shower on the local TV news at the men's shelter where he had gone with the other "shower protesters." Roy had not stayed at the men's shelter long. As the weather had cooled and the autumn rain storms came in November, Roy could see there were old men and sick men who needed the shelter. As he listened to Trigg run on about growth and opportunity, Roy had recalled the other reason he could not live at the men's shelter. The homeless activists had wanted Roy to "become" involved in the struggle.

Roy had not answered them. He had packed his razor and toothbrush in the pockets of his field jacket and moved into a cardboard piano crate in the arroyo off Eighteenth Street. Roy had got Trigg to buy him a bicycle for his recruitment work, and as winter brought more and more drifters and homeless from the snow in the north, Roy had begun to carry two notebooks with him as he signed up "clients" for the biweekly bonus program. He carried Trigg's notebook and he carried the homeless army's notebook. He was not afraid to write the words *Homeless Army* across the notebook cover; he felt the excitement rise up into his chest and throat, and he felt his heart beat faster at the word *army*.

The skinny, starving Mexicans who managed to reach Tucson had to find people willing to let them sleep in a shed or chicken coop, otherwise the Border Patrol got them. The cardboard boxes and tin shelters under the mesquites along the Santa Cruz were filled with white men, though occasionally a Yaqui Indian with land on the Santa Cruz River rented camp space to blacks and Indians. Roy wrote down all the names and did not bother to note which were "phony" and which were "real" Vietnam veterans. What was past did not matter. What was important was how the men felt right then. Roy was looking for men who were incensed, who were outraged, at the government. He was not interested in the "shower activists" with their protests and polite lawsuits to acquire shelter for the homeless.

Trigg used to ask Roy what he did with his money. Trigg was repulsed by Roy's cardboard and plastic held together with corrugated tin. Roy always smiled, shook his head, and told Trigg nothing. Trigg never pressed because Trigg had to do all the talking anyway. Trigg claimed he was only making money because he wanted to save enough to design and build a computerized walking machine; this had been

Trigg's dream since the day he had learned his spinal cord was severed. This dream of Trigg's had also led him to buy the small private hospital in Verde Canyon. Trigg bragged about his plans to diversify; Trigg wasn't going to make the same mistake other real estate investors had made. "You don't know anything about Verde Canyon, do you?" Roy shook his head. Actually he had been reading through Trigg's files methodically and knew exactly *what* Verde Canyon was all about. Money. Verde Canyon was a rehabilitation hospital for alcoholics and drug users.

Roy had read the hospital's prospectus to shareholders. Trigg had shrewdly chosen a New Age theme for the brochure enclosed with the financial report. The brochure reverently described the cleansing, healing powers of the Sonoran desert. The Verde Canyon Hospital would depend chiefly on contracts from federal and state court systems to provide court-ordered "treatment" in lieu of jail. The advantages of sentencing a person to "treatment" rather than jail had a more hopeful outlook, although "treatment" was far more expensive than simple incarceration. Trigg had been rather careless with the keys to filing cabinets; Roy had learned a great deal about Trigg and was still learning. The night-watchman job meant a dry, warm place to sleep during Tucson's winter rains. But Roy had also begun to spend more time around the plasma donor headquarters because the cold weather had sent hundreds more homeless men south, more men who wanted to look up to Roy, men who wanted Roy to lead them against injustice. They all knew him by the other name. He refused even to utter it. His men might call him any number of names; if one nickname was Rambo, Roy didn't let it mean anything.

VACANT HOUSES

THE GROWING BAND OF HOMELESS "Vietnam vets" in the lean-tos along the arroyos and the Santa Cruz River had left Roy tense and self-conscious. Tension was inevitable because the men knew and Roy knew that he had something important to say to them, that he had something that would explain what it was they must fight for.

To shake off the tension, Roy had begun to ride his bicycle north of Silverbell Road and then west on a dirt road into the desert. Santa

Fe or California-style houses were scattered on the tops of foothills and ridges, isolated from the desert as well as from one another. All winter Roy had bicycled up and down the dirt roads past the winter homes of the wealthy, who had begun to arrive in rented Jaguars and Mercedes in mid-November, and who left for Aspen on New Year's Day.

Roy had learned to spot evidence of vacancy: the cables or chains with padlocks that had gone back across driveways. At first Roy had only explored outside the vacation houses because he did not know much about the new, high-tech security systems. Then Roy had realized the wealthy left little of value in their Tucson winter homes, and the alarms and security systems had been for their personal protection and were shut off once they had departed. The wealthy were so carefree; Roy discovered curtains and drapes carelessly left open to reveal rooms strangely bare except for a sofa or bed or chest of drawers. Carpeting was always wall-to-wall in shades of ivory-beige or light silver that reminded Roy, somehow, of coffins. He noticed blank spaces in the middle of walls, and empty corners where objects had been.

Roy tells no one what he does with his time. Trigg only cares about the steady flow of blood plasma donors. Trigg has too many other hot propositions and fancy deals. Roy had begun to make a map that pinpointed the vacant winter homes, and he jotted down information about security patrols, gardeners, or operative security systems. Roy no longer worried about what would happen next. All tension had dissolved the night Roy began to make the map. Because at the top of the map Roy had written *Locations of Resources: Army of the Homeless.* When Roy had finished snooping in Trigg's files, he would quit. Trigg had been getting on Roy's nerves lately on account of the mortuary and ambulance schemes.

Trigg had flashed money at Roy before, but this time Roy was thinking ahead. Number one, they would need money. Number two, what did Trigg need done so badly that he waved hundred-dollar bills in both hands? Trigg had said all he needed was the "right" ambulance driver, and then he had winked at Roy. Sure Roy would drive the ambulance or hearse, whatever meat wagon Trigg wanted. Trigg had winced at the mention of *meat wagon.*

Roy had begun to meet with the men in the arroyo two or three times a week to share a bottle with them. He did not try to pretend he was broke, but he did not let them borrow from him either. Roy didn't care if he brought the bottle or the paper bag full of greasy tacos to the guys sleeping in the park. Roy met with four different "units," as the men called themselves. Roy was content to keep the units low-key; he did not bother to inform the men he'd chosen as unit officers. No democracy in the army, not even this army. They would know soon enough what he had planned. For now he had to keep the secret; otherwise some of the braggarts or liars might snitch to the police. Food, drink, and companionship were exactly what the men needed in this phase of the plan.

Roy could feel the change taking place in his blood. Alert, but calm, if such a condition was possible. There was no hurry, no rush. It was coming, it was inevitable; nothing he did either way could or would affect what was coming. But Roy also knew that with planning, some casualties might be avoided. Roy had been going through Trigg's files late at night, but he had not decided what use to make of Mr. Trigg's files. Roy had no plans for snitching or for blackmail either. Roy no longer had any use for the Bible or people who called themselves Christians. Roy trusted the feelings he had in his chest and throat; that was how God led a man, not by TV evangelists or puffed-up shitbag reverends and cardinals. Roy hated all churches and organized religion because they had sold out Jesus Christ for sure, and probably Muhammad and Buddha.

Most of Trigg's corporations existed only in manila folders. Beyond naming and registering the corporations, Trigg had done nothing with them. He had conducted no business through Alpha-Bio Products, Alpha-Hemo-Science Limited, Biomat, Bio Mart, or Biological Industries. But for Alpha Healing, Amalgamated Hospices, and New Century Corporation, Roy had already made real estate purchases.

Part of his job was to listen to Trigg shoot off his mouth. Roy had known guys in wheelchairs who liked to talk a lot; Trigg's was that same nervous chatter sending out secret signals—I'm-not-a-freak-I'm-not-a-cripple-I-am-all-right. Trigg had shifted into his "benevolent asshole" pose and touched Roy's sleeve to prove his sincerity. Trigg thought his wheelchair made him a goddamn hero. Trigg had big plans. Big big plans. The cornerstones of his empire were real estate and the plasma donor centers. But the cornerstones had got boring. So now Trigg wanted to branch out, and he would have great opportunities and benefits for his employees.

Roy had merely nodded. He knew all about Trigg's plasma center employees. They were all women, and from what Roy had seen, they all took pills or drank vodka out of lab beakers. Trigg had no favorites. He was careful never to call the same one into his private office twice in a row. He was against favoritism. Trigg spooned out little lines of "employee incentive" on the glass desk-top. At least Roy didn't have to sit on Trigg's face to get a shot of vodka from him.

Roy had got to know the women at all three centers. They called for Roy if they had trouble with crazy, stinking bums who wouldn't take no for an answer: "No, we don't want your blood." Roy was always gentle with the crazies; he talked to them as he escorted them out to the street and told them they didn't want to sell their blood anyway; they needed to keep their blood. Their blood made them strong. Their blood was what kept everything moving inside them—everything—their eyes, their lungs, their brains; blood even moved their cocks.

Roy had only meant to soothe the crazies when he told them to keep their blood for themselves; but as he had talked to the urine-stinking, wild-eyed drifters, Roy had realized that he was telling them the truth, or at least what he himself believed to be true. Later at one of the unit meetings Roy had warned the men about the habit of selling their plasma or whole blood. He promised very soon there would be alternatives that would provide shelter and food without the sale of blood.

Roy did not waste his time on the women at the plasma centers because they talked about money and marrying men with money. But after a few months Roy had got to know Peaches. Peaches had worked for Trigg the longest; the others said she had lasted because she was in charge of cold-storage inventory and never had to see that chairload of shit-for-brains they called the boss. Peaches had a purple birthmark around her left eye, but Roy thought she was beautiful. The others had warned Roy not to feel bad if Peaches ignored him. Except for Trigg, they did not think Peaches had ever said more than a dozen words to any of them in the seven years she had worked in the freezers.

The doors to the refrigeration units were always kept locked, and the alarms were always set. "No entry. Strict orders," Peaches had said. She was not rude, but she stood firm. "Are plasma and whole blood *that* delicate, *that* perishable?" Roy had wanted to know. Peaches seemed to understand that Roy found her attractive. She had laughed so Roy could watch her round tits bounce in their prim bra cups; these were how she had got the name Peaches.

Roy sensed her suspicion of him. Peaches was not like the others. She was right. Curiosity was stupid. He was wasting his time in the basement. Roy had been about to turn and go back to the freight elevator when Peaches had rapidly punched in codes on the freezer-unit door. "See—there's nothing; all the units are enclosed."

"All this for plasma—"

But Peaches shook her head. Her mouth had slowly spread into a smirk. "No, all this *isn't just* for plasma. Huh uh."

The first time Roy and Peaches fuck, Roy gets her so good she tells him about the arrangement between Bio-Materials and the human organ transplant industry across the U.S. The Japanese had developed a saline gel that kept human organs fresh-frozen and viable for transplants for months, not hours. Peaches did not explain where or how Trigg had obtained the human hearts and lungs carefully packed and clearly labeled: *Type A Positive—Adult Male.*

Frozen human organs, less reliable, sold for a fraction of freshly harvested hearts and kidneys. Of course, fetal-brain tissue and cadaver skin were not affected by freezing. Peaches said Trigg bought a great deal in Mexico where recent unrest and civil strife had killed hundreds a week. Mexican hearts were lean and strong, but Trigg had found no market for dark cadaver skin.

FIRST BLACK INDIAN

CLINTON WAS THE BLACK VETERAN with one foot, but he wore the best, the top of the line, the best kind of prosthetic foot you could buy. Clinton had to wear his full Green Beret uniform every day. Otherwise there would just be trouble for him because Clinton didn't bow and scrape for no Arizona honkie-trash crackers. Clinton had grown up outside Houston where the cops and Texas Rangers really hated African-American folks. Clinton lives alone in a Sears garden shed he bought for himself. Roy hears rumors Clinton has relatives in Tucson, but Roy doesn't ask questions because that sets something off in Clinton's head. Some days Clinton says he's okay. Other days he warns you ahead of time you better steer clear. Roy is not afraid of Clint's bad days; on Clint's bad days, Roy is free to talk wild-talk right back at that crazy black fucker. They don't talk to one another; they talk *at* each other, and neither of them bothers to listen to the other. What is important is Clinton's outrage—Clinton's pure, pure contempt for any authority but his own.

Clinton reads books when he goes to wash up at the downtown branch of the public library. What he can't get off his mind is what man does to man over and over again. A slave was the first thing any man thought of; someone to do the dirty work. Clinton thought women were correct about being enslaved by men; otherwise, Clinton had no use for bitches because what at one time had been so good in them had been ruined by their enslavement. Clinton's paranoia knows no boundaries. He has cousins and stepbrothers in the army, and the word gets around among the brothers and the sisters. The army has to have lab technicians; there are security guards; there must be cleaning crews. The word leaks out.

Clinton always prefaces his remarks. He says no black American would ever betray his country. But a black man's country was different from the white man's country, no matter they both called it the same thing: United States of America. Clinton says the AIDS virus was developed in a biowarfare laboratory by the U.S. government and was stolen by military personnel sympathetic to white supremacists in South Africa. Naturally they had been careful to set AIDS loose in the African-controlled states; whites in South Africa would never have risked setting loose the virus on their valuable labor force. Still, the growth of populations in all-African states had to be stopped. Somewhere the men who had paid for the stolen virus sat around a conference table brainstorming.

"Mad scientists?" Roy tried to interject, but Clinton had waved away Roy's remarks; white man's words were always being shoved in the black man's mouth.

"Mad scientists, mad generals, mad Church of God preachers—all of them want to see black folks disappear, but sort of gradually, you know." Clinton says J. Edgar Hoover ordered the assassination of Martin Luther King. Right there Hoover's wings got clipped. The old faggot was crazy. Assassination wasn't "gradual," and assassination had a way of creating folk myths and heroes. A secret bipartisan congressional panel had hastily concluded only a cover-up could save U.S. cities from burning and the outbreak of a race war. Clinton said J. Edgar had first practiced assassination on John F. Kennedy because Hoover hated the Kennedys. Kennedy supported civil rights, but John Kennedy hadn't been the big fish. "Hell, no," Clinton said, "all you whites can think about is 'white.' John Kennedy couldn't lead no one; he couldn't even lead the U.S. Congress." Clinton had warmed up good on this topic. Later Clinton told Roy he was the first white man ever to listen through the whole rap to every last word Clinton said. Roy could see why Clinton pissed people off, even some black people. Because Clinton said Kennedy had only been used for target practice; J. Edgar's dress rehearsal. Martin Luther King had been dangerous because he was a leader. He could lead all different kinds of people—more and more, white people had listened to and followed King. That was what had driven J. Edgar, the old butt-fucker, over the edge.

Clinton understood the cover-up; the whitewash. Clinton said young blacks would have burned down the United States that summer if the truth had come out. Clinton understood the need to be practical. He will be the only black unit leader, but he won't have an all-black unit. Roy wants integrated units in this new army. They have more whites than blacks anyway. What Roy does not say is for now it is better to have whites outnumber blacks in integrated units. Otherwise whites feel uneasy. Roy and Clinton get along because neither man tries to argue good or bad, right or wrong, only what is necessary. Clinton likes to test Roy's reactions.

"What if I get me an all-black unit?"

Roy shrugs. None of them are fortune-tellers, are they? For all they know, they may end on opposite sides, battling one another. Neither man rules out a race war, but both tend to agree, battle lines will be drawn according to color: green, the color of money, the only color that had ever mattered. The richest, whatever their color, had always escaped. Clinton has read about the wealth and greed of slave-dealing African tribes. The richest Jews had escaped Hitler's ovens. Only poor Jews had died. Roy said he didn't know if Clinton was right about that.

Clinton nodded his head. "The rich got the news; then the rich had the money to get away."

Clinton had been curious about the tribes that had sold slaves on the African coast. But Clinton had not been fooled by the white man's lies about African slave-holding tribes. To read the white man's version, Africans were responsible for the plantation slavery in the New World. But African slaves only replaced the Native American slaves, who died by the thousands. Before the European slave-buyers had arrived, African coastal tribes had practiced only local war-hostage slavery. Prisoners of war worked until their ransoms were paid. Children born to war hostages were adopted and enjoyed all privileges. Where a tribe might capture fifty slaves in ten years, the demand for slave labor in Spanish and Portuguese colonies of the New World greatly increased tribal warfare for the procurement of slaves. Hundreds and finally thousands of slaves were needed in the gold mines and plantations that were worthless without slave labor.

Clinton had gone to Vietnam. It had been easy to see it was a white man's war; the colored man was sent to do the dangerous, dirty work white men were too weak to perform.

On the GI Bill at the University of New Mexico, he had met a black woman, Reneé, who was reading about black history and black culture. Black studies had been a radical new subject for Clinton; the more he learned, the more angry he got as he realized how whites had had to scheme and manipulate day and night to keep blacks from realizing the power and beauty they had always possessed.

Clinton seldom talked about the two or three years he hung out at UNM in Albuquerque holding black power meetings in the basement of the student union building after midnight. They had had FBI influence in their group in those days, but the undercover FBI Toms all had to go home before midnight because they were flunking English. Clinton wasn't sure now if the door whites offered America's "colored" people was an opening or merely another trap. Vietnam had been a trap for people of color. White man expected the colored man to "lift himself" by killing little yellow people. Clinton had sat through all his classes the first semester, but his mind had always been on organizing the brothers and sisters on campus. Clinton didn't expect to get grades when his real work on campus had been to try to warn his people, honest black folks who still believed all the lies fed to them about the United States of America. Clinton had seen how many dark American faces had been in the Asian war. Clinton had seen the white toads, Lyndon Johnson, and his generals smacking their lips at all the splattered brains and guts of black and brown men. Forces sent to destroy indigenous populations were themselves composed of "expendables."

Roy generally had no problem following Clinton's line of reasoning through the first bottle of wine. But halfway into the second wine bottle, Clinton tires of cursing the white man and begins to curse the black man and the brown man who sold their brothers down the river for the white man. Who was the blubber-bellied god of treachery, that god of snitchery and lies? Why did the brother betray the brother? Why did the mother call the police on her son?

Roy likes to get well into the second bottle of wine with Clinton before they start talking about rich people. Then Clinton starts sounding like a communist, something Roy has to caution Clinton about. According to Clinton, the entire war in Southeast Asia had been fabricated as a location and occasion for the slaughter of the strongest and most promising young men of black and brown and poor-white communities. Clinton swears he is no Marxist. African and other tribal people had shared food and wealth in common for thousands of years before the white man Marx came along and stole their ideas for his "communes" and collective farms.

"White man didn't even invent communism on his own," Clinton said, wiping his mouth on the sleeve of his shirt.

Black people called men like Clinton "crazy niggers" and blamed Vietnam for them. Everyone had the same thought: black people all knew deep down the Vietnam War had been aimed at them to stop black riots in U.S. cities. The war had destroyed some of their best young men. The war had destroyed two generations of hopefulness and cultural pride. A dangerous generation had emerged from the Korean War. Black warriors and warrior women who sat down at the lunch counters and refused to ride at the back of the bus had changed the face of America. Efficiently, the white man had sent sons and daughters to burn down Vietnam instead of Detroit, Miami, or Watts. Vietnam had been designed to stop the black man in America.

Roy nodded. The FBI probably had assassinated Martin Luther King. He did not agree with Clinton about the war in Southeast Asia. Roy thought it had been a war for the usual reasons. But Clinton's conspiracy theories were his own business, and Roy didn't worry about them; some of the other unit leaders whined about Clinton's "racist theories." All Roy would say was Clinton had a constitutional right to his views, the same as they had a right to their views. Southern whites nearly always agreed with Clinton. The FBI got rid of King, and Vietnam had been a war to eradicate gooks and niggers.

Clinton had "found" a good little mountain bike on the University of Arizona campus. Clinton and Roy rode together on the dirt roads between the vacant winter homes in the desert foothills. Clinton casually opened mailboxes.

"Rich folks really are different from the rest of us assholes," Clinton said, "because they don't care what happens to their mail.

"Everything we need is here," Clinton had said, sipping some of the homeowner's scotch as he reclined on a white leather couch. The rich were different all right. The Tucson vacation homes came complete with Tucson cars and Tucson bank accounts. Beside Clinton, on the pink-marble-top coffee table, were piles of letters he had opened. Everything they needed was there. Clinton had located a gold mine: gasoline credit cards, Tucson bank-machine cards, bank statements. In one instance, he had even found an Arizona chauffeur's license among the piles of catalogues and junk mail flyers.

Roy helped Clinton finish the bottle of scotch. They had the giant-screen TV on with the volume down so they could talk. The setup with the vacant houses had great potential, but their timing would have to be right. "Timing is everything, timing will be everything," Clinton said, happy and drunk. Until the appointed time, locations of the vacant houses, and the contents of the mailboxes, all were to be top secret, known only to Roy and Clinton.

Roy could not explain to himself why he confided in Clinton and not one of the other Green Berets. Roy thought it must have to do with Clinton's color, but he didn't know how. Maybe because Clinton was black, Roy could trust the man to know how to wait, how to lie low and wait. Roy had put himself in charge of recruiting. He beat the bushes in the city parks and in the mesquites along the interstate where homeless men slept. He was determined to find all the homeless Vietnam vets in Tucson, and Roy had started hitchhiking to Phoenix twice a month looking for guys around the free-cheese giveaway warehouse.

Late at night Clinton sometimes dropped by. Roy's night-watchman's job with Trigg came complete with an office. Clinton lit up the reefer and took a big hit before passing it to Roy. The basement "watchman's office" was nothing but a janitor's closet, with a mop sink at one end. But Roy had fixed up the closet with a light bulb so they felt cozy. While Roy sucked the joint, Clinton exhaled slowly and began to laugh softly, shaking his head. "You got keys to this place?" Roy was still holding the smoke in his lungs, so he only nodded.

"You know how much all this stuff is worth?" Clinton said, and gestured at the dark expanse of basement filled with refrigeration units, electronic cables, and consoles of switches, lights, and gauges that, in turn, were connected to computer terminals and a red telephone. Roy shook his head and slowly exhaled the smoke.

"But I know someone who does know." It was too soon for Roy to know whether Peaches would tell him all she knew. To judge by the backup generator system for power failures, the contents of the freezer compartments were worth a great deal. They passed the joint in silence, and they both scrutinized freezer locker units that filled the basement. Clinton pulled another fat joint from his shirt pocket. What Roy likes best about Clinton is his sense of timing. They are almost alike in that respect; Roy thinks how funny it is to find out the man most like you in temperament is black. No one will ever know this because Roy will never tell, and he doubts whether Clinton feels the same way. Clinton would probably swear and laugh at the notion. So Roy carries these thoughts around with all his other thoughts. He imagines his ideas are popcorn kernels popping inside his brain. Into the third reefer, they are back to strategies and planning. They will wait out this year just to lay down the groundwork. Timing was crucial. They would prepare and wait until the riots across the United States kicked up again, and Arizona's meager National Guard forces were deployed to aid California police and National Guard. Roy and Clinton know that all across the U.S. there are others who are also waiting for the right moment. When Arizona and southern California had consumed the last drop of groundwater, entire cities such as Tucson would be abandoned to the poor and the homeless anyway.

After Clinton became "relief" watchman, the basement closet becomes "headquarters." Clinton drags in a filthy, torn crib mattress and a busted-up tape player held together with silver tape. Nights when Clinton is watchman alone, he presses the buttons and shakes the tape player twice to get it going. Then Clinton begins to dictate messages they will need later on, once their Army of the Homeless has begun to seize radio stations. The people of the United States, ordinary citizens, had set out to reclaim democracy from corruption at all levels. U.S. citizens by the thousands had been put out on the streets while elected officials gave away government money to their cronies. Taxation without representation!

Clinton's messages would be a call to war. Homeless U.S. citizens would occupy vacant dwellings and government land.

SPIRIT POWER

CLINTON'S FIRST BROADCAST in the reborn United States was going to be dedicated to the children born to escaped African slaves who married Carib Indian survivors. The first broadcast would be dedicated to them—the first African–Native Americans. Clinton talked about the tapes he was making for radio stations, but he never let Roy hear any of them. Clinton said he could describe all the tapes, and Roy would have a better idea if he just let Clinton talk.

Roy had seen the box full of newspaper clippings. The one on the top was about an African woman who was leading an army of rebels somewhere in Africa. The headline had called the woman a "voodoo priestess." Clinton said the African woman was only twenty-seven, but her troops loved her like children and called her Mama Marie. Mama Marie and her troops had raised hell with government troops. The ordinary people, the citizens in Africa, had the same problems with government politicians as the people had in the United States. The people worked day and night to pay taxes, but still found themselves hungry and homeless.

The voodoo priestess and her soldiers believed that with her power, sticks and stones would explode like grenades and bees would become bullets. Mama Marie had rubbed the chests of her young soldiers with special oils to stop bullets. Now here was the kind of army to have, the kind the voodoo woman had had in Africa, because Clinton had seen years ago in Vietnam that the little jungle people weren't just good fighters. They used all kinds of poisons and spells and prayers to spirits to attack the GIs in Vietnam.

"You should know," Clinton said to Roy. "You musta seen that stuff, little monkey gods on altars—things like that." That was Clinton's latest theory: the U.S. military had lost the Vietnam War because the Viet Cong had used magic and spirits. How else had the U.S. lost? They had had superior firepower, they had bombed every square foot of the entire country, and still the U.S. had lost. Clinton wasn't saying the spirits had done it all or spirits had even done half of it; but the spirits had tipped the scale in the Vietnamese's favor.

Roy did not bother to argue with Clinton about ghosts winning the Vietnam War. Clinton might be right. Roy had felt like a ghost himself since the war. When he saw Roy wasn't going to argue, Clinton admitted he didn't totally believe in that kind of superstitious stuff. He wasn't convinced magic oil could stop bullets. Clinton still believed in the M16, don't worry. He had seen saturation bombing by B-52s. He'd seen how napalm burned like a laser through flesh and bone. "I just mean that kind of spirit stuff helps," Clinton said.

"Like God is on our side? That kind of stuff?" Roy said. He smiled so Clinton wouldn't accuse him of being an asshole. Clinton believed it was important for the people to understand that all around them lay human slavery, although most recently it had been called by other names.

Everyone was or had been a slave to some other person or to something that was controlled by another. Most people were not free, Clinton knew from experience, yet man was born to be free. The first slaves Europeans kept had been white. Slave keepers didn't care about color so long as the slaves were strong and stayed alive. The European kings had slaves called royal "subjects" who worked obediently and paid their taxes to the kings. One kind of slavery had often been traded for another slavery as bad or worse. Slaves of past centuries had shelter and food. Yet today in the United States, so-called "free" men, women, and children slept under cardboard on the street.

White people wouldn't like being called "slaves" by a black man, but Roy didn't think most radio listeners would know what color Clinton was except red, commie red. Roy had found out the hard way Clinton couldn't be teased about communism. Clinton had been all over him so fast Roy hadn't ever seen where the razor had come from.

"Don't ever call me that again! Don't ever say my name *Clinton* and *communism* in the same breath!" Communism was dead. Communism was a failure, and that was *not* what Clinton was talking about. Maybe Rambo-Roy himself was the communist, Clinton said. Rambo was the one who had gone to all the rich people's houses to steal in the name of the homeless and poor.

Roy had laughed out loud then, at Clinton and his razor; he laughed at himself. No wonder human beings never improved themselves over hundreds of years. He and Clinton would just as soon fight and kill each other as go to the trouble to confront a crooked politician.

Clinton had explained why his camp was separate from the others this way: he had been kicked out of rooms and then out of shelters or halfway houses because of his religion.

Roy studied Clinton's face. "Religion?"

Clinton nodded, his face full again with indignation: "Because of my shrine. You think in the United States of America—" But then he broke off, shaking his head. Roy nodded. No one could argue: the U.S. was a Christ-biased nation. So Clinton kept his camp separate from the others because of his shrine. He set up the shrine in the center of his storage shed. At night he slept behind the shrine, keeping it for protection between himself and the door. Clinton had done that in his hooch in Vietnam at the firebase camp where the enemy had crept in at night to slit men's throats while they were dreaming.

Clinton's shrine held the knife, or the blade of a knife and what remained of a handle, a skeletal piece of metal. Clinton had kept the blade razor-sharp; he had carried the knife in combat because it had never failed him in the dangerous alleys and streets at home. Clinton's people—women and men alike—all carried knives. Clinton had been hit by flying shrapnel that killed three men nearby. The handle of the knife had been shattered by shrapnel, but miraculously, Clinton had escaped with minor injuries. Clinton woke up and learned the medic had sent the knife along because anyone could see, the knife had saved Clinton's life. The knife had power all its own. Clinton felt this power long before he studied African religions in black studies and realized his family's regard for knives was a remnant of old African religion. Clinton had carried the blade wrapped in a piece of red velvet he had cut from the draperies in a whore's room in Manila.

When he was not wearing the knife sheathed on his combat belt, Clinton kept the knife on its shrine. He had bought the local incense to burn for the shrine, which of course worked to cover the odor of opium or reefer. He bought tiny Japanese porcelain dishes he put in front of the red velvet bundle surrounded by small candles burning in glasses. Clinton put pinches of food on the tiny dishes and sprinkled rum on the blade each time he unwrapped the red velvet.

Roy pointed out that people might not want someone burning candles and spilling rum because it might cause a fire. Typical white-man thinking! Clinton had learned to expect that even the best of them, such as Roy, sometimes just didn't see. Candles, rum, and incense didn't necessarily mean a fire. The white man would stop everything before it started; the white man would pretend to know all the answers ahead of time, but of course, really, the white man didn't have a clue. The white man had made some monumental errors in the five hundred years Europeans had disrupted Africa, China, and the Americas. The Chinese and Africans had broken free; now it was only a matter of time before all captive people on the earth would rise up.

Clinton talked to the blade when he poured the rum over it. The cutting metal edge of the knife was Ogou's favorite dwelling. In Africa, metalworkers were Ogou's priests, Clinton's people all revered the knife. Clinton offered this prayer:

> Ogou, Warrior and Metal-maker,
> Ogou wages war every day.
> Ogou, we suffer a great deal in this battle with
>   our oppressors.

Ogou protects those who serve him.
Ogou is watchful.
Ogou has boundless energy.
Ogou is powered by anger.
Ogou-Feray you magnet power!
Pull iron fragments together
gather the lost to your chest!
Ogou, your father-love heals them—
all the scattered fragments—
ancestor spirits gathered!
Ogou-Feray you lead them to war
for the sake of us, their descendants.
Ogou-Feray, Commander of the Army-of-the-Lost-
    Is-Found,
Ogou fires the cannon to announce the uprising.
Rage blind rage destroys all in reach,
mad dog warrior, Ogou!

The shrine had made people, even other blacks, afraid of Clinton because Americans had swallowed all that Hollywood bullshit about voodoo and the Devil. Some guys even objected to the apples Clinton left out for the spirits. Clinton did not blame people for their ignorance, but at some point a man had to teach himself or learn something. He explained the apples had to be left to rot so the ancestor spirits could "eat" them.

OGOU, THE KNIFE

THE ONLY SUBJECT Clinton had ever cared about in college had been black studies. In black studies classes they had read about the great cultures of Africa and about slavery and black history in America. But Clinton had not agreed with Garvey and the others who wanted to go back to Africa. Clinton disagreed because blacks had been Americans for centuries now, and Clinton could feel the connection the people had, a connection so deep it ran in his blood. Clinton had been told by the old women talking when he was still a kid; they had been discussing all the branches of the family. The original subject had been marriages with whites, but one whole branch in Tennessee had been married to Indians, "American Indians." "Native Americans." And not just any kind of Indian either. Clinton had not got over the shock and wonder of it. He and the rest of his family had been direct descendants of wealthy, slave-owning Cherokee Indians. That had been before Georgia white trash and President Andrew Jackson had defied the U.S. Supreme Court to round up all the Indians and herd them west. Clinton had liked to imagine these Cherokee ancestors of his, puffed up with their wealth of mansions, expensive educations, and white and black slaves. Oh, how "good" they thought they were! No ignorant, grimy cracker-men dare touch them! So pride had gone before their fall. That was why a people had to know their history, even the embarrassments when bad judgment had got them slaughtered by the millions. Lampshades made out of Native Americans by the conquistadors; lampshades made out of Jews. Watch out African-Americans! The next lampshades could be you! Clinton did not trust the so-called "defenders of Planet Earth." Something about their choice of words had made Clinton uneasy. Clinton was suspicious whenever he heard the word *pollution*. Human beings had been exterminated strictly for "health" purposes by Europeans too often. Lately Clinton had seen ads purchased by so-called "deep ecologists." The ads blamed earth's pollution not on industrial wastes—hydrocarbons and radiation—but on overpopulation. It was no coincidence the Green Party originated in Germany. "Too many people" meant "too many *brown-skinned* people." Clinton could read between the lines. "Deep ecologists" invariably ended their magazine ads with "Stop immigration!" and "Close the borders!" Clinton had to chuckle. The Europeans had managed to dirty up the good land and good water around the world in less than five hundred years. Now the despoilers wanted the last bits of living earth for themselves alone.

Military solutions were no solutions at all; Clinton had seen what a "military solution" was in Vietnam: destruction on all sides; everywhere burned earth, and the souls of the people tortured. Clinton believed education was the answer although he had had his education cut short. Still, while others off the street used the downtown public library to wash and shave, Clinton always went from the rest room to the reading room. Clinton had plans. He kept pages and pages of notes from the books he read at the public library. Then Clinton had moved up to the university library where little blond sorority sisters roamed in fours looking for black athletes; no other black men would do but jocks.

Clinton took careful notes of inspirational passages and sudden ideas that came to him while he was reading. He was saving all his notes for use on the broadcasts he planned to tape for the radio. Clinton didn't waste time worrying where or how he'd get hold of a radio station for his broadcast. That was something the white man did—worry ahead of time. The white man had had the radio waves all to himself; but funny thing was, white man didn't have nothing alive left to say. Clinton wanted black people to know all their history; he wanted them to know all that had gone on before in Africa; how great and powerful gods had traveled from Africa with the people. He wanted black Americans to know how deeply African blood had watered the soil of the Americas for five hundred years. But there had been an older and deeper connection between Africa and the Americas, in the realm of the spirits. Yet for a while, it must have seemed to the Africans who had survived ocean crossings that their gods had indeed forsaken them. The Spanish plantations and mines of Hispaniola had been a fate worse than death for the Caribbean tribes, who had deliberately died rather than live as slaves. African slaves had been shipped in as replacements for the Indian slaves, who had proved to be nearly worthless.

From the beginning, Africans had escaped and hid in the mountains where they met up with survivors of indigenous tribes hiding in remote strongholds. In the mountains the Africans had discovered a wonderful thing: certain of the African gods had located themselves in the Americas as well as Africa: the Giant Serpent, the Twin Brothers, the Maize Mother, to name a few. Right then the magic had happened: great American and great African tribal cultures had come together to create a powerful consciousness within all people. All were welcome—everyone had been included. That had been and still was the great strength of Damballah, the Gentle. Damballah excluded no one and nothing.

Clinton wanted his radio broadcasts to emphasize the African people's earliest history in the Americas because slave masters had tried to strip the Africans of everything—their languages and histories. The slave masters thought Africans would be isolated from their African gods in the Americas because the slave masters themselves had left behind their God, Jesus, in Europe. The Europeans had been without a god since their arrival in the Americas. Of course the Europeans were terrified, but did not admit the truth. They had gone through the motions with their priests, holy water, and churches built with Indian slave labor. But their God had not accompanied them. The white man had sprinkled holy water and had prayed for almost five hundred years in the Americas, and still the Christian God was absent. Now Clinton understood why European philosophers had told their people God was dead: the white man's God had died about the time the Europeans had started sailing around the world. Clinton found himself smiling.

Clinton did not think of the knife blade itself as Ogou. He did not think the tribal people had confused the gentle, huge snakes at the shrines for the Great Damballah or his wife. The spirit of God had only been manifested in the blade and in the giant snakes. God might be found in all worldly places or things. Clinton was careful not to use any names that had been poisoned by Hollywood's lies. Clinton simply called the religion "ancestor spirits." Clinton wasn't trying to scare anyone with his radio broadcasts; scared fuckers would kill you faster than any cocky son of a bitch. Clinton simply wanted people to know the truth. Clinton's only regret was not listening more to the old granny women talking. The "spirits" had emerged as the most dangerous and potent forces against the European colonials after only two hundred years. Then once the spirits of Africa and the Caribbean Islands had made their marriage, the white man had heard rumors about the union of African and Indian spirits. The "spirits" had been outlawed by the French in Haiti, but too late. The French plantation men of Haiti went gunning for the traveling herb man the other slaves called Don Petro. Planters put a big price on the old man's head. Creole slaves could only laugh privately at the white men's mistake. Because old Don Petro, he was one of the "ancients" the white man could never catch. And each year this Don Petro had stirred up more and more trouble for the plantation and mine owners. Don Petro was the head of a new family of spirits, high in the Caribbean mountains.

The people found in the Americas that the spirits did not quite behave in the same manner as they had in Africa. In Africa the spirits had been predictable and generous. Ogoun, the Ironmaker, had been a gentleman-warrior and doctor back in Africa. The slave-hunting and the death on the ocean's crossing had changed everything. The Africans had been changed by the journey just as Ogoun, Eurzulie, and Damballah themselves had been transformed by the slaughter in the Americas. Ogoun was no gentleman-warrior here; Ogoun was the guerrilla warrior of hit-and-run scorched earth and no prisoners.

Clinton wanted to make his point about the spirits. Not because he was some kind of missionary twisting people's arms and reaching into their pockets. Clinton didn't care about the religion part. Clinton just wanted black people to know the spirits of their ancestors were still with them right there in the United States.

Clinton remembered those old granny women sitting with their pipes or chew, talking in low, steady voices about in-laws and all the branches of the family. The branch of the family that was Indian always bragged they were the *first* black Indians. The old women had chuckled over this claim; they had only meant they were first black Indians in Tennessee, someone had joked; that made more sense. In the old days Tennessee had been nothing but trees and Indians anyway. The black Indians of the family went so far as to paint a black Indian in a warbonnet on the front wall of their house. The black Indians of the family had stories about the very first black Indians.

The first black Indians had lived in high mountain strongholds where they launched raids on the plantations and settlements below. Some said the first black Indian medicine man had been a Jamaican who wandered Haiti, calling himself Boukman; this Boukman of course was working for Don Petro's spirit family. On an August night, Boukman, the black Indian, had performed a ceremony. A terrible hurricane came up during the ceremony, and then suddenly, an old woman appeared who danced wildly then killed a black pig. Everyone there drank the blood of the pig and swore to follow Boukman, whose name meant "spirit priest." Ouidambala, Great Ocean serpent, was consulted about undertaking war. The storm winds and floods had struck a terrible blow to the Europeans and gave the slaves advantages they sorely needed to launch their revolution.

Right then the difference between the spirits' behavior in Africa and the spirits' behavior in the Americas had been clear: Don Petro's mean old wife, Martinette, had come dancing up a storm, and she did not care if the winds blew away everyone's things. Don Petro's family was like that, harsh even with family members, harsh even with one another. In Africa the spirits behaved much more gently and peacefully.

On American soil these spirits had been nurtured on bitterness and blood spilled since the Europeans had arrived. To judge from the ferocity of Don Petro's family, the spirits had tasted blood even before the white man came. Some nights when Clinton had felt the most desperate in his own mind or in his heart, he had squatted in a corner of the homeless-shelter shower room and read himself notes he had taken on African religion. Sometimes Clinton had nightmares about Africans and American Indians chasing him. The first nightmares had come after Clinton had been evicted from his room because of the rotting food on his shrine to Ogou.

Clinton was able to interpret his own dreams the way doctors did. Anyone would have had dreams of terror if they had slept on the street. The same dream night after night had become less frightening. Finally Clinton had dreamed the feathered tribal warriors were not chasing him to do harm, but only to bring him a message. The spirits were talking to dreamers all over the world. Awake, people did not even realize the spirits had been instructing them. It was perfect. People would not know why their feet were marching them north; people would not understand the joy they felt walking together side by side. Clinton knew what work was cut out for him and for Rambo-Roy and the others.

The old grannies had been sisters or sisters' cousins, and they had constantly argued about the branches of the family. French colonials, terrified of poisonings and slave uprisings, but more terrified of the spirits, had asked the black Indians to lead the great opening Mardi Gras parade to acknowledge the people who had been in that place the longest. The white man needed the black Indians to quiet the anger of the spirits. The old grannies used to laugh. White man didn't do enough for the spirits because the next thing they know there's the Civil War and the old spirits drink up rivers of white man's blood while the slaves run free.

CREOLE WILD WEST INDIANS

EVEN BLACK STUDIES CLASS got boring sometimes, especially once European conquerors showed up in Africa. The early history in Africa was great because the African kings had built great empires and African metallurgists had created great works in iron. In the North, African mathematicians created the zero, key to higher mathematics, while African astronomers charted the planets and stars.

But Clinton had always got a sick feeling in his stomach as the days in class passed and the terrible, fateful day approached; the day was when the first European slave-traders had appeared at African slave markets and not at the slave markets in France and England. The semester assignment had been to collect old folks' talk about their memories of the past. Black studies had been a good class for Clinton in that respect: he had gone to talk with one of the last of the old grannies right before he got sent to Vietnam. She had talked about the spirits watching over Clinton. She saw them. Later in Vietnam when he woke up alive with the knife and its shattered handle, Clinton had known for sure the spirits were watching over him.

Clinton remembered the old grannies arguing among themselves to pass time. The older they got, the more they had talked about the past; and they had sung songs in languages Clinton didn't recognize, and when he had asked the grannies, they said they didn't understand the language either, because it was spirits' language that only the dead or servants of the spirits could understand.

Clinton had only taken notes on particular details that had interested him. A lot of the African-American studies classes had been bullshit honkie sociology or psychology. Having a black professor didn't make it the gospel. Clinton only took notes on the subjects that excited him, such as the black Indians or the spirits and African people.

From Clinton's Notebook
Black Indians at Mardi Gras

Black Indian guards and scouts walk ahead of the Mardi Gras parade. The tribal queen is very black, but her face is painted intricately and she wears the feathers of the Kushada Indians. The medicine man strides beside her. Black Indian marchers in tribal costume and feathers are everywhere. "Wild creatures" are dressed in animal skins, and grass aprons with headdresses of horns and antlers. They wear huge cattle rings in their noses. "Wild creatures" dance by jumping up and down, and screeching and spitting. "Wild creatures" have been enraged since time immemorial, over human behavior, but now especially, they reserve special fury for white people along the parade route. They sing:

The Indians are coming   *The queen is coming*
The Indians are coming   *The queen is coming*
The cacique is coming   *Golden Blades are coming*
The cacique is coming   *Golden Blades are coming*

The black Indian tribes call themselves Little Red, Little Blue, and Little Yellow Eagles. The Golden Blades do battle to see who's chief each year. Wild Squatoulas and the Creole Wild Wests (cowboys from Opelousas) sing:

> Get out the dishes,
> get out the pans!
> Here comes all the Indian mans!

Black Indians dance with wild abandon. The dances are tribal.

No outsider knows where Africa ends or America begins.

A huge snake of pearls writhes on the black Indian queen's gold-lamé cape. An immense spider of silver beads crawls over the flame-red satin of the queen's dress. The cacique priest has chosen the pure white of crystal beads, snowy-egret feathers, white velvet, white satin trimmed in miniature roses of white rhinestone and crystal sequins.

The black Indians march, tribe by tribe, leading the Mardi Gras parade. Tribes sing their songs of arrogance:

> Oh, the Little Reds, Whites, Blues,
> and Little Yellow Eagles,
> Bravest in the land.
> They are on the march today
> If you should get in their way
> Be prepared to die!

In 1933, a policeman was injured by a war spear thrown by some rival tribes in battle. After that, the tribes agreed to act friendly in the Mardi Gras parade. They sang this song:

> Shootin' don't make it no no mo no!
> Shootin' don't make it no no mo no!
> Shootin' don't make it no no mo no!
> If you see you a man sitting in a bush
> Knock him in the head and give him a push.
> 'Cause shooting don't make it no no mo no—
> Shooting don't make it no no mo no!

Along the parade route young girls and boys act as spies for rival tribes waiting down the street, reporting the boasts and challenges that have just been made to give rival tribes and individuals enough time to make up songs in reply.

To a challenge from another black Indian woman, the black Indian queen answers:

> *Shoot! She don't look so hot to me!*
> *She don't have no life in her!*
> *Man! She's got to have it like I have it!*
> *Use it like I do! Do it like I do it!*
> *Like a tribal queen! Like a tribal queen!*

Here the queen darts her tongue out like a snake's, and her hips and stomach writhe like a snake's because black Indians still keep in touch with the serpent spirits Damballah and Simbi.

Chief Brother Tillman, leader of the Creole Wild West Indians, is dressed in simple buckskin with black fringe and black feathers. Late as 1947, white people of New Orleans feared the black Indians from the Wild West and tried to avoid them. Still the braves leaped on the trucks of white maskers and yelled, "Mardi Gras! Mardi Gras! Chew the straw! Run away and tell a lie!"

The notes Clinton had made on the black Indians never failed to make Clinton feel somehow hopeful and proud. Clinton especially enjoyed how rowdy and frightening the black Indians had been to whites. Clinton loved to imagine the exhilaration, the feeling of power, the Wild West Indians must have felt. But after 1947, black Indians had no longer appeared in the Mardi Gras parades. The black Indians were outlawed from the parade because changes were already in the wind in 1947. Blacks who had defended the U.S. overseas had come home to demand civil rights.

The black Indians had been part of the white Mardi Gras parades since the days wealthy Indians had owned slaves like the whites. The black Indians had been allowed in the parade because they were American Indians. Clinton felt proud the black Indians had shown the white people whose side they were on even if all the black Indians did get kicked out of the parade. The Negro Mardi Gras was held on March

19 in New Orleans, and he wondered if the Negro Mardi Gras parade had invited the outlawed black Indians to march in their parade. That would have been the right gesture for black people to make to their Indian brothers, but Clinton knew black people and Indians had not always been free to make the appropriate "gestures." Clinton was no fool. He could remember how his old aunties and grannies had loved to sit smoking their pipes, teasing about one another's lineage. Indians were Indians, even if they looked black. The black Indians didn't get invited to any more parades, certainly not to the Negro Mardi Gras parade. Because the black Indians were troublemakers, and trouble had been the last thing the Negro middle class of New Orleans needed.

The old grannies and aunties used to say the people who had first come from Africa had been shocked by what they had found in the Americas. Even the African gods they had found in America had been toughened-up by their experience on this continent. Except of course for the pure-hearted Damballah, gentle but distant, who did not concern himself with worldly things; Damballah had not been affected. But right away it was clear that in America, the African gods were short-tempered. What the African slaves had met face-to-face in this land was Death. Death roamed freely night and day in America; in Africa, Death only went about late at night.

ARMY OF JUSTICE

SPIRITS DIDN'T FRIGHTEN CLINTON. He knew how to talk to them silently; he had ordinary conversations with them unless they had come to Clinton with a message. Clinton had not always believed. Then he got hit in Vietnam, and the knife changed everything. Vietnam had been full of Vietnamese spirits. Vietnamese people spent the better part of their time, and money, on incense, candy, liquor, and flowers for the spirits. The example the Vietnamese set had been inspiration for Clinton, and luckily, he had begun to "feed" his knife a little rum every morning, and every night. A month later, the knife had saved his life.

Back in the United States, the spirits seemed to be angry and whirling around and around themselves and the people to cause anger and fear. Clinton had seen madness and meanness everywhere in the United States, among whites and blacks too. Because people everywhere had forgotten the spirits, the spirits of all their ancestors who had preceded them on these vast continents. Yes, the Americas were full of furious, bitter spirits; five hundred years of slaughter had left the continents swarming with millions of spirits that never rested and would never stop until justice had been done. Clinton didn't like to waste energy quarreling over little things. If Rambo-Roy wanted to call their army the Army of the Homeless or Army of the Poor and Homeless, that was okay by Clinton. But Clinton would have called it the Army of Justice.

First came the great serpent spirit, the pure and gentle Damballah. Damballah was so shy and apart from the world that he did not involve himself in the trials of humans except as a messenger. All the other spirits were more than eager "to work" for people who fed them generously.

The "Americanized" spirits used the name Ge Rouge after their African names. That was a warning: red for "danger." Clinton had not been able to remember all the names and disguises the spirits took, but he knew Ogou Ge Rouge was a great warrior; it had been Ogou Ge Rouge who had saved his life. Native Americans had been talking to ancestral spirits who lived in clay jars when the African slaves had appeared. The Native Americans had died off deliberately to spite the Europeans. In death their spirits had been set free to roam at will and to help other powerful ancestor spirits already set loose on the slave masters.

Now it was simply a matter of time, that was all. Clinton knew his life, body and soul, belonged to the world of the spirits. When Clinton had looked around, he saw that people were all terrified, all fearful of death. Poor people were just as scared as rich people. Clinton had noticed that each time he had traveled. Clinton had read somewhere that the number of baptized Christians had been steadily falling in America since the Second World War. Clinton wondered if this had been the effect of the atomic bomb—to drive people away from churches; people blamed God so they did not have to listen to him anymore. Clinton had done the same; he had let go of one God when another had protected him in battle.

The time had come when people were beginning to sense impending disaster and to see signs all around them—great upheavals of the earth that cracked open mountains and crushed man-made walls. Great winds would flatten houses, and floods driven by great winds would drown thousands. All of man's computers and "high technology" could do nothing in the face of the earth's power.

All at once people who were waiting and watching would realize the presence of all the spirits—the great mountain and river spirits, the great sky spirits, all the spirits of beloved ancestors, warriors, and old friends—the spirits would assemble and then the people of these continents would rise up. People would rise up as they had for old Boukman and old Koromantin, the Gold Coast man who had raised the people in 1760.

The spirits worked in many ways. European overseers fell victim to terrible vices urged on by the spirits. Overseers no longer concerned themselves with business; instead, overseers lost themselves for hours in savage sexual pleasures, which commonly began after a midmorning corn-liquor toddy. White overseers had amused themselves with their slaves for hours on end, pausing only for more liquor or occasional naps. The spirits had been behind the excesses of the mine owners and plantation bosses who began to forget their purpose was to make money; the excesses they had committeed on their slaves had required time that had once been spent on keeping accounts, and inspecting the slaves' work. Gradually the output from the mines, the harvests from the plantations, would begin to decline. The white men would be seen less and less except by a few of the house slaves. Second- or third-born sons without land, the Europeans overseas had been alone, without families to call them back to their senses.

Valuable slave women and children had been mutilated and slaughtered, had been driven mad by the depravity of the colonial masters. Smelter walls had cracked when the fires were allowed to die out, and still the spirits had ruled the overseers' appetites. Each day the colonials had retired more and more into their private world, a world that shut out their terror because each instant had celebrated their personal power with the flesh of their slaves. European lords had had slaves; so had the Arabs and the Chinese; even some tribal cultures had kept slaves. But nowhere except in the Americas had the colonial slave masters suddenly been without their own people and culture to help control the terrible compulsions and hungers aroused by owning human slaves. Nowhere had so many slaves been consumed so lavishly or so quickly. Child rape and murder had been perfected in the New World by European slave owners, who had later returned to Europe infected with bloody compulsions they had indulged in the colonies, hidden away from the eyes of their peers and their God as they smeared the fresh blood of slaves on their thighs and genitals.

LIBERATION RADIO BROADCASTS

CLINTON NO LONGER FELT HIMSELF choking on anguish— on the rage and pain he had felt every day of his life, even in the army. What had made the difference were the spirits, and the army he and Rambo were putting together. Clinton was happy Rambo was in no hurry; Clinton had wanted to travel around a little to see which way the wind was blowing in such places as L.A., Houston, and Miami where recent rioting had been worst. Clinton wanted to do a little scouting work, that was all.

He reminded himself to be realistic. He wasn't going to find many poor blacks in L.A. or Miami who would waste time listening to him. The poor were tired and sick. They would rather watch TV. A few were making big money from the others who bought a few minutes of forgetfulness from a pipe or a needle. Illness, dope, and hunger were the white man's allies; only dope stopped young black men from burning white America to the ground. Clinton felt an obligation to try to locate recruits because numbers were not as important as loyalty or determination. Small groups had been changing the history of the world from the beginning. Clinton had seen the bloodshed in the black and brown neighborhoods—all the ammunition and guns, all the energy young people used up every night in L.A., San Jose, Oakland—never mind Washington, D.C. and New York City. For now, Clinton would settle for recruiting a few of the best men, and women too, who wanted to fight a real war, instead of selling crack to keep white men rich *and* safe. If he couldn't find young recruits, then Clinton would go after old ones like himself, Vietnam vets. There might be one or two like himself still alive.

Clinton did not expect success overnight. He knew they would call him a crazy old man. But he would just keep hammering away at the young ones—he knew someday they would find out money alone wasn't enough, because money didn't buy respect. Sure, they could make money off one another; they could bleed on the street while white men got richer and richer selling them dope, and future warriors were killed by booze or dope. They were free to continue with all that. Clinton did not want his radio broadcasts to sound like Hitler's, but people had to be warned: alcohol and drugs were intended to keep them weak, to keep them from rising up—to demand justice. Black slaves had labored to make the United States rich and powerful. The United States still owed African-Americans just as the U.S. owed Native Americans.

Clinton's Slavery Broadcast

Opening music (Bob Marley, Jimmy Cliff, Aretha Franklin)

Voice reads: Now is the time to keep the promise you make.

Curse him as I curse him!
Spoil him as I spoil him!
May he have no peace in bed
   no peace at his food
   nor can he hide!
Waste him and wear him!
Rot him as these rot!

Voice-over continues:

1. Slavery is any continuing relationship between people and systems that results in human degradation and human suffering.
2. Women and children are the most frequently enslaved because slavery relies on violence and systematic terrorism to maintain control.
3. Terrorism takes many forms, but most often the violence is sexual, to convince victims suffering is part of their very identity, as unchangeable as their sex or skin color.
4. The slave is the polestar of the Master's life. The slave will always receive the Master. The slave becomes part of the Master, and perfection becomes possible.
5. The slave has no identity but through the Master; slave identity is not a fully human identity.

6. Slaves may serve as laborers, but slaves exist primarily to satisfy sexual and ego needs of the Master.

7. The Master craves the pulse of cruelty and pleasure the slave arouses in him again and again.

8. Strike the Master's son but never the Master's slave; the son is a separate being, but the slave and Master are one and the same.

9. Slavery is highly productive and yields fabulous profits. Slavery makes cruelty valuable and useful.

10. Europe got fabulously wealthy off slave power in the Americas. Where does the greed of the European originate? Greed arises out of terror of death. People of snow and ice are haunted by freezing and starving. The wood on the fire never lasts for long.

11. Wealth from slavery buys storehouses of food and armies and the finest physicians. Wealth obtains more slaves and more property to barricade the Master in the world of the living.

12. The slave is offered to Death in place of the Master; thus the slave "becomes" the Master if only for an instant as the slave dies.

13. The slave accumulates power in the realm of the Master's dreams. Gradually, the slave inhabits the Master's idle thoughts during his waking hours. The Master's obsession enslaves him. (End of broadcast.)

Clinton's Radio Broadcast #2
First Successful Slave Revolution in the Americas

Slavery joined forever the histories of the tribal people of the Americas with the histories of the tribal people of Africa. On La Isla de Hispaniola escaped African slaves called maroons fled to the remote mountains where the remaining bands of Arawak Indians took them in.

In 1791 the slaves' war for independence began with a ceremony to the spirits. Boukman, Biasson, and Jean François led the people into battle. Guerrilla army units of maroons and black Indians came down from mountain strongholds at night to leave various charms and "poisons," and to burn barns and the mansions of the rich. In 1801, the Revolutionary Army of Slaves at Santo Domingo defeated 25,000 of Napoleon's soldiers, commanded by Bonaparte's brother-in-law. The French are defeated with the help of the spirits.

The spirits of Africa and the Americas are joined together in history, and on both continents by the sacred gourd rattle. Erzulie joins the Mother Earth. Damballah, great serpent of the sky and keeper of all spiritual knowledge, joins the giant plumed serpent, Quetzalcoatl. When someone dies, the spirit goes to the Dead Country. Legba-Gede, Lord of the Crossroads of Life and Death, directs the traffic of the human souls.

Spirits inhabit the "thunderstones" or flint blades the Arawaks and Caribs once carved. The spirit inside one "thunderstone" caused the stone to sweat profusely; another famous stone named Papa Gede urinated. The spirits are the most powerful beings. That is how the outnumbered and ill-equipped people's army had held off the French navy and army.

First Legba-Gede takes on his favorite incarnation, Lord of the Cemeteries, who gave his secret followers special power against European soldiers occupying Haiti. The Lord of the Cemeteries had given his secret followers the power to hypnotize then overpower victims along the road. The soldiers of the Lord of the Cemeteries carried nooses of dried human gut to strangle new victims after midnight. Europeans are terrified.

Gede Ge Rouge has always been a cannibal. *Ge Rouge* is synonymous with the Americas. The power of Gede and spirits of the dead is original to the Americas. Gede was not worshiped in Africa. Ogoun had traveled with the other spirits to the Americas, but Gede, Master of the Dead, protector of small children, tricksters, and sexual athletes, Gede, who connects the living people with distant ancestors and forward in time to descendants yet unborn, Gede belongs to the Americas.

The signatures of the spirits are outlined in ashes and cornmeal on the ground. For Legba-Gede they paint the cardinal points, the crossroads of the universe. Sometimes the old man, Legba-Gatekeeper shows up, crippled, covered with sores and maggots. He is both male and female; he is both fire and sun. Old Gede prances like a horse in his old black overcoat, jabbering away and sipping champagne. His rites are performed during the new moon. Old crippled Gede sometimes has only one foot; then they call him Congo Zandor because a snake has only one foot, which is his belly that he crawls on, and he mashes his victims between giant stones.

Sitting across from old man Legba is Petro-Mait-Carre-four, young and strong, spirit of all points in-between, spirit of the moon, spirit who regulates all demons. Gede-Brav is Lord of the Smoking Mirror, wearing dark glasses; his words and gestures are full of constant sexual innuendo. Gede-Brav, Keeper of the Gate, is the cosmic phallus, muttering to himself and rubbing against objects.

> *Gede-Brav can swallow the hottest drink.*
> *Gede-Brav has a ravenous appetite.*
> *Gede-Brav always shows up at the wrong moment.*
> *Gede-Brav shows up where he is not welcome.*
> *Gede-Brav cross-dresses.*

Old bent man, Cinq-Jour Malheureux, is Gede-the-dying-sun-soon-to-be-reborn; Cinq-Jour Malheureux represents un-named, empty, and unlucky days at the end of the Native American calendar.

In Africa, Ogoun, spirit of the warrior, statesman, and metallurgist, reigned over the villages and towns of Dahomey and Guinea; but in the Americas, Legba-Gede, Lord of the Dead Spirits, Keeper of the Crossroads of Life and Death, became more powerful because the Europeans had killed so many people in the New World, dead souls far outnumbered the living. In Africa, Ogoun did not have to share his power; in Africa, Ogoun had great armies with the best weaponry. But in the Americas, Ogoun Ge Rouge must share his power with Legba-Gede, and right here you know this military spirit hates this "political maneuver," this "compromise" in which he must share power with the Lord of the Dead.

The rage of Ogoun is terrible. Even in Africa, Ogoun's anger had accidentally killed his people, and in despair he had thrown himself on his sword. But in the New World, where Ogoun faces far greater outrages, his fury has no limit. Thus it is that Ogoun Ge Rouge and his followers have many times outnumbered and double-crossed Legba-Gede and the people after they've won their independence. Ogoun Ge Rouge Jaco is the fast-talking, crooked politician who appears from the smoke and ruin after the revolution. Jaco tells lies and spreads rumors. Jaco works to create misunderstanding and suspicion among the people. Jaco and his cronies work fast; before the people realize, Jaco and the others are long gone with all the people's money in the national treasury.

Ogoun Ge Rouge Feraille is the spirit of a great national hero who outlasts and finally defeats the spirit and followers of Jaco. Trouble is, politicians all call themselves "followers of Ogoun Feraille" and only later reveal themselves as followers of the crooked politician Ogoun Jaco. So far, Ogoun Jaco and his followers had been busy all over the world, not just in Haiti. Others had seen their revolutions eroded and betrayed, otherwise a Chinese poet could not have written: "Before the revolution we were slaves, now we are the slaves of former slaves."

Clinton didn't care if his radio broadcasts sounded like lectures from a black studies class. After the riots and Vietnam War, there had been no more university funding for black studies classes. That was no accident. The powers who controlled the United States didn't want the people to know their history. If the people knew their history, they would realize they must rise up.

BOOK THREE

EL PASO

SONNY'S SECRET SIDELINE

SONNY HAD BEEN EXPECTING a phone call from the Mexican, Menardo. Sonny hadn't told Max anything about his contacts in Mexico. Sonny told Max he liked Mexican "beaches," but "bitches" was more like it; Menardo's wife, Alegría, was sensational in bed. She had been all over Sonny again and again.

Sonny was looking forward to doing business with the Mexican because Menardo's prices were much better than what Mr. B. had offered. Sonny didn't care if Max had worked with Mr. B. or the government; what Max did was up to Max. Sonny didn't like B. He'd work for B. because Leah rented warehouses to him and because the job was so simple.

Sonny Blue had always thought Angelo was pathetic. Raised like an orphan by the fat uncle in a junkyard, Angelo had surprised Sonny Blue. Angelo had managed his racehorses and done his "accounting" for the family interests at both the horse and the dog tracks. Angelo had not been fooled by sob stories or excuses from the peons. Sonny liked to call white men in Tucson "peons." Sonny used only *white* peons; he never used Mexicans when white men were plentiful and cheap.

Sonny Blue had been impressed when Angelo's racehorses had won a race here and there. All the Tucson horses ran on California tracks. Angelo did not seem the type to work in the family business. Sonny Blue figured him for the type who would work for a while and then quit when he had the money he needed for legitimate business. The fat uncle who had raised Angelo had refused to take part in family business activities. Sonny Blue had heard the story of "Fatty," and how he had never touched a penny of the family "dividends" and how he wanted to keep his fat hands clean. For what? Angelo had had to live in a small trailer crowded together with the fat uncle. Sonny Blue thanked his lucky stars he had been born who he was.

Sonny Blue saw many similarities between Angelo and his brother, Bingo. Bingo had been slow and had struggled through school. Bingo was taking care of the El Paso operations for now, but already Sonny had been thinking about sending Angelo over to assist Bingo. They needed a border toehold, and they needed someone in El Paso who would be ready to act when their "new friends" began making deliveries to them. Sonny Blue could not trust Bingo. Bingo stuffed too much coke up his snout. But the family politics were sticky; Sonny could not let Max or Leah find out how much cocaine they both used because heads would roll then. Max was old-fashioned. Cocaine was a drug the white man sold to niggers.

Max had given Sonny the vending machines and pinball games: the family organization had exclusive distributorships in Tucson and El Paso. Bingo was a poor manager, and the family organization was losing money in El Paso. Sonny Blue and Bingo had strict warnings: stay away from dope. Dope was the territory of the Mexicans. Max Blue had reminded them about the law of diminishing returns: they could start a war with the Mexican and Indian smugglers, but when the dust cleared, what would they have gained? The family had had some good lessons taught them over the years by Mexican and Indian smugglers.

Max Blue had gone on and on, preaching to Bingo and Sonny about their vending and game machine distributorships—*exclusive* distributorships. Distributorships such as these did not grow on trees. What more did they want? Sonny Blue had always known to be careful what he said to Max. Sonny had always felt a little uneasy, and secretly, he was afraid of his father. But it had been difficult for Sonny to hold his temper when Max had asked "what *more*" Sonny wanted. "Money!" Sonny wanted to scream. He wanted his share. He wanted a chance to show he was *somebody* besides Max Blue's son. What did the vending and pinball machines bring in a year—$275,000 or $300,000? Exclusive distributorship? Well, Sonny had to watch constantly for "squatters" and independents who tried to go around Sonny with video games and hot-sandwich machines. The games division's profits were shrinking because of all the home videos; but the instant-food dispensers were offsetting the games' losses.

Sonny hated even to think about it. The stale smell of greasy lunch meats and rotting lettuce permeated Sonny's office at the main warehouse. Sonny was sick of the pig slop. He was sick of the way things had been going for him and Bingo. He did not understand why his old man had rolled over so easy for the Mexicans, who thought they ran the town.

Sonny Blue had lived in Tucson all his adult life. In Tucson, the big thieves hanged the little thieves. It was that simple. In Tucson money talked louder than bullets. In Tucson a man might dare you to shoot him; but no man in Tucson ever refused a hundred-dollar bill. For five hundred dollars "trash" in Tucson would shoot their own brothers.

"Legitimate business"? That was the joke of the century in Tucson. Even the new Federal Building sagged dangerously because so much steel and concrete had been "diverted" by subcontractors during construction. Tucson had families of thieves going back three generations; they had been stealing from the U.S. government since the Apache Wars, so what were a few hundred thousand yards of concrete or a few dozen steel beams?

Sonny didn't know which ones he hated worse: the white-trash "gringos," the pigtailed biker gangs, or the filthy Mexicans. Human sewage all of them. What a relief there were only a few blacks; Sonny had counted this as Tucson's *one* selling point. Sonny had not wanted El Paso. Tucson was bad, but El Paso was only more of the same two-bit players. Bingo had hated Tucson too. Bingo had been the smart one to jump on the El Paso deal. What difference did it make where the stinking food-vending machines were leased? Sonny had stayed in Tucson deliberately. Sonny wanted to prove a point.

Sonny Blue did not trust Mr. B. because he was a retired major. "Military" meant "police" as far as Sonny was concerned. Telephone call from the senator or no, Sonny Blue was not impressed by Leah's half-million-dollar lease. The entire economy was shaky; the military would face huge budget cuts. Sonny Blue laughed at the expression on Leah's face. "Snip! Snip! Off go their fat budgets!" But Leah Blue had had the last laugh. She wasn't a bit worried about the money. The major had paid cash up front: out of his blue Samsonite suitcase. Leah pretended to fan herself with a bundle of hundreds. The warehouses that the major had rented had been vacant since their completion. Leah had used cheap government loans and development grants to finance the construction. Friends of the family had been generous in approving interest-free loans from certain banks the senator controlled in Phoenix.

Sonny Blue did not call her "Mother." Sometimes he could more easily imagine Max was his father than he could imagine Leah as his mother. Sonny had been watching Leah with her men from the beginning when she had taken Sonny and Bingo in the car with her to show real estate. Sonny had sensed right away something was going on when she had bought them candy and pop and left them in the big Chrysler with the engine running and the air-conditioning on. Sonny had wanted to sneak into the house and spy on them. Bingo had been afraid of getting caught. Bingo had started to cry and would not shut up until Sonny had kicked and punched him.

"You can be with me or you can be with them," Sonny had said to his brother, and even as he spoke, he could see fear in Bingo's eyes. Without Sonny, Bingo had no one but the housekeepers or gardeners, who did not last more than a year or two. Sonny had taught Bingo to call her Leah and not Mama or Mother. Whiney babies called for their mommies.

Sonny Blue could not wait to see the expression of shock, the stunned look, of Max when he found out Sonny had got his own business rolling with the Mexicans. Sonny didn't need any major as a go-between. Sonny wasn't worried; his "business partner," Menardo, owned something called Universal Insurance. As Menardo had explained it, the company was far more than a mere insurance company. For your money, you not only got insurance from tidal waves, fires, earthquakes, and hurricanes; Menardo had waved a thick contract in front of Sonny's face. At Universal Insurance, for only a few thousand dollars or a few million pesos more, a businessman such as Sonny Blue could be protected against uprisings, riots, unrest, and even mutiny by government forces. Universal Insurance maintained its own highly trained, well-armed security forces for land, sea, and air. As governments went bankrupt and no longer paid police or armies, the services of private police and private army units became more important.

Menardo had talked at length about the federal troops and the police, who were in the pay of everyone (including Universal Insurance). Menardo did not think bribes alone were reliable any longer. In the end Sonny agreed to purchase the "foreign businessman's protection package"; the package had been expensive, but had included everything. "Everything" included the use of Universal Insurance's "air force," and in the event of emergencies, one of General J.'s Learjets. Sonny Blue had savored the feeling of power and satisfaction that had spread over him like good wine; he gunned the Porsche and pulled away from the traffic on I-10. He would show Max.

Max had not been the same since the shooting. How many times had Sonny heard his uncles and aunts whisper about his father, about the changes in Max Blue that caused them to shake their heads. Sonny did not exactly blame Max; it wasn't his fault he got shot. Max must be unlucky because he had got hurt in a plane crash in the army. Sonny couldn't blame his old man for bad luck. What irritated Sonny was Max Blue's assumption that Sonny and Bingo would be satisfied with some chicken-shit pinball games and sandwich machines in Tucson and El Paso while everyone else was getting rich running dope or guns across the border. Something was wrong with Max since the shooting. Max wasn't interested anymore in women or money; Max might as well be dead. All Max did was play golf; all day, weather permitting, seven days a week, for fifty-two weeks.

Sonny had only heard rumors. He had not been able to bring himself to ask. Max would have told Sonny if Max had wanted Sonny to know. Killing was cheap, and getting cheaper every day. Sonny could make more on one big truckload of cocaine than Max Blue could make whacking a dozen bastards. Max must have done it for kicks. Sonny didn't blame his old man. If sex didn't work any longer, there had to be substitutes. Sonny could remember that when he was in grade school, Max had worked in his office all night even on Sunday and at Christmas.

Sonny knew his father did not like to be touched or to touch others. Sonny tried to imagine what the thrill was. Max didn't even get the satisfaction of squeezing the trigger. He must have been excited by the planning and the step-by-step preparations for an execution. Sonny had not seen his father excited or happy when the family was together. Sunday dinners had been for the benefit of the grandparents, even if they only came to Tucson in the winter. Otherwise, they themselves seemed to know it wasn't a real family, that the boys were separate parts of the lives of Max and Leah; *small* parts, pushed aside by bigger plans and greater schemes.

Sonny's way was to be one of the cool ones—the kind girls went after. Sonny had made a study. A guy did not have to be much in the looks department as long as he had great-looking clothes and a great-looking car; women were looking for status, not good looks; good looks didn't buy them champagne and strings of pearls. Sonny kept all his fraternity-alumnus dues and fees current so he could drop by the "house" whenever he wanted to pick up some nice fresh coed. Sonny had got used to dating college women, and after he had graduated, Sonny discovered he was attracted only to the coeds. Working women were a turnoff; they were always calculating what a man's salary added to their salary might buy for them. The coeds lived on their family trusts or their papas' monthly checks. Coeds had flexible schedules, so Sonny could screw them all afternoon if he felt like it.

Sonny had dated a few women who had good bankrolls or were hotshot businesswomen. But he had not felt comfortable talking with them about hydraulic lifts on trucks delivering video arcade games. Sonny took the precaution of announcing he did not wish to discuss business on a date, and the women had quickly agreed.

Sonny had never been serious about any of the coeds he had dated; he had no desire to see the same ass and same tits over and over 365 days a year. Sonny had never dated the same woman two nights in a row; that had been one of his frat-house trademarks. Fresh pussy every night. Of course he had dated a couple of the "better" girls more than once. Sonny had also dated not two but three coeds who had gone on to become Miss Arizonas; but they had been no different. Once Sonny got them in bed, he could begin to see things close up; sometimes he switched off the lights so he would not see the freckles or moles; Sonny did not watch them walk naked across the hotel room because he knew he would notice something—one tit larger than the other, dimpled cellulite on the thighs or the ass—even on the skinny ones.

Sonny had a secret that always worked. Once he got the girl in his Porsche, he poured out fat lines of coke on the dashboard and handed her a gold straw. Liquor might work quicker than candy, but nothing beat good cocaine for getting the panties off sorority girls. Sonny could take coke or leave it; he had watched Bingo stumble around half-blind from the drug, still searching for more.

Sonny and Bingo had started dealing a little while they were at the university. Everyone knew hometown boys had access to any drug you wanted—name it and Tucson had it, and at the lowest price. Now that Sonny had hooked up with Menardo, he and Bingo would have cocaine by the kilos. Mr. B. had only vague plans for Leah's warehouses. Sonny had pegged the retired major right away as an arms dealer. Mr. B. wore a khaki safari jacket and matching pants and fussed a great deal with the chin strap of his broad-brim canvas safari hat.

Sonny had talked to Bingo about the possibility of expanding their enterprise in three or four years to include guns, but Bingo had not sounded interested in anything but the kilos of coke coming out of Mexico. Bingo had wanted to know what market there was for guns in

Mexico. "Guns and dynamite," Sonny had added, to see the expression on Bingo's face. But Sonny could tell that Bingo's mind was on the kilo packages.

BROTHER'S KEEPER

BINGO HAD ALWAYS WAITED for Sonny to tell him what he should do. Bingo didn't care if the idea was not his own; Bingo never had any good ideas of his own anyway. There were leaders and there were followers, and Bingo knew what he was. He had always looked for Sonny during lunch or study hall when they were in school. Bingo had pledged the same fraternity; he had even graduated with the same 2.0 grade average.

Bingo had been known as the quiet one, who was shy with girls. But Bingo had changed all that when he had got his big house in the sand dunes outside El Paso. Sonny had given him pep talks; let the big Lincoln and the Olympic-size pool work their magic. "Linen suits and cashmere overcoats speak louder than words," Sonny said.

Bingo had always had violent nightmares that woke him crying and sweating with terror. Sonny had been the one who had turned on the light and gone to the far end of the house to the master bedroom for Leah. Max Blue had just returned home from the hospital, and Leah did not let the boys in their bed. Bingo had cried and begged his mother to force Sonny to let him sleep in Sonny's bed. Sonny demanded payment, although Bingo seldom wet the bed anymore. Bingo had to do whatever Sonny told him. Whatever Sonny said, Bingo was his slave; otherwise, some night when Bingo's nightmare of the exploding gas furnace had woken him screaming, Sonny might refuse to let Bingo get into bed with him. Sonny had demanded to know what was so scary about the exploding furnace. Did Bingo see himself blowing up or burning? Bingo had not seen any of that; Bingo had only dreamed the furnace and then its explosion as if he had been blown to bits but was still able to describe the fiery clouds of debris and butane gas.

Bingo awoke sobbing because the explosion had been the end of all of them—Mother and Father as well as Sonny and himself. The effects of the dream, the grief, did not end once Bingo had awakened. Bingo could not stop himself from grieving for hours after he woke from the nightmare. Sonny had pointed out that once you were dead, love didn't matter. Bingo had loved Sonny so much, but that day, Bingo had detected Sonny's pleasure at seeing him cry. When Sonny wanted Bingo to shut up, he would threaten to push Bingo out of his bed. Lying next to Sonny was all that soothed the terrible feelings of grief and loss in the nightmare.

Bingo had always loved Sonny more than anyone. Sonny had whispered they were not wanted by their mother and father; Bingo started to cry when Sonny teased him. Or Sonny had been "wanted," but Bingo had been an "accident" and had spoiled everything. Bingo had been a crybaby who had driven Max out of the house the morning he got shot. Sonny had told Bingo a number of lies, claiming they were true stories. Their parents weren't like other kids' parents. Bingo believed Sonny because Sonny talked to him, for hours and hours in the dark. Other kids' parents didn't get shot. Other kids' parents came to their bedrooms if they got scared at night. Later Sonny told Bingo that he had lied; Sonny said he had been afraid to go all the way through the house in the dark to the master bedroom. So Sonny had only pretended to go tell their mother Bingo was calling for her. Sonny used to lie and say Leah was coming; then Bingo had waited hours and hours until he knew his mother would not come. "She never did come," Bingo used to complain to Sonny. Sonny used to shrug his shoulders as if it were none of his concern.

"You know I would come running in a minute if I knew you were crying and wanted me!" Leah had said years later when they talked, but Bingo had not quite believed her; or he had believed Sonny more.

Sonny had been the only one Bingo had ever been able to talk to, but even in high school, there had been certain things Bingo had not been able to tell Sonny. The things Bingo wasn't able to tell Sonny were things so weird Bingo didn't dare tell them at confession. They were just dreams or strange ideas that had come to Bingo suddenly. He had imagined his homeroom teacher and the entire class sitting at their desks naked. When Bingo had told Sonny, Sonny had asked if Bingo was seeing Sister Thomas Mary naked at her desk; what about the *guys* in homeroom, was Bingo seeing them nude also? When Bingo had nodded, Sonny had become very animated; Sonny had begun laughing and dancing around the room.

"You're a queer, Bingo-Boy! That's what it means! Queers like to see old nuns and young guys naked!" Bingo had imagined far worse, far stranger scenes, but he could never tell Sonny.

Bingo often found himself daydreaming that Max and Leah and Sonny had all been killed in a plane crash or a car wreck. The daydreams left Bingo very sad; he felt as if he had really lost them. The move to El Paso had not helped, except in the beginning when the big house and the car and the expense account had all been new. Whatever money Bingo had, he always spent, and now that he was closer to the border, he could get all the good tequila and scotch he wanted and all the good pills and pharmaceutical cocaine. The Mexican maids had been the frosting on the cake. Bingo had been warned not to let the maids see him use cocaine; but Bingo had developed a taste for cocaine on damp flesh, and he found he enjoyed two women at a time more than one woman who expected all his attention.

The first mess Sonny had had to save Bingo from was the two coke-hungry Mexican maids. Sonny had driven the new Porsche from Tucson to El Paso to check on Bingo. Reports from the office in El Paso had been that Bingo was seldom seen except to sign paychecks on Thursday afternoons and to write himself $3,500 checks to cash for the weekend. Bingo had been glad to see Sonny climb out of the black Porsche; the two women had been fighting all night. Bingo had admired how Sonny knew exactly what to do: one call to Immigration and the women would disappear into the vast deportation process. Employers in El Paso and Tucson preferred illegal aliens because they worked so cheaply and they were afraid to make trouble. The cocaine and wild sex with Bingo had caused the maids to forget their manners. Sonny teased Bingo about sex. Bingo had learned his lesson with the maids; from now on, he would simply go back to telephone escort services. What had worked for Bingo in Tucson would have to work for him again in El Paso.

That was the chief disadvantage of Bingo's big hacienda that was so far from downtown; escorts had cost more, and the better services did not allow their employees to leave the El Paso city limits. Bingo had not wanted to mention to Sonny that he was lonely at his house, and the Mexican maids were the only ones he had for company. Escorts were only good for part of the night; Bingo needed more. "Maybe you should get married," Sonny had said as he was starting up the Porsche for the trip back to Tucson. Sonny had felt full of mischief that morning because Bingo looked so lost and sad to see Sonny go.

"Hire a live-in companion," Sonny said as he wiped off his blue-mirror sunglasses. "I don't care. Only next time don't fall in love with two Mexican lesbians."

Bingo had been uneasy when Sonny had showed up a few months later with Angelo. Bingo had let the general manager run the day-to-day business; how much intelligence did it take to refill candy machines? Bingo wasn't going to waste his time pretending to be busy. Bingo was not as anxious as Sonny was to expand the business. Bingo did not like the fact the retired major knew so much about Angelo's old girlfriend, Marilyn. Bingo did not believe this was mere coincidence. Bingo did not trust the phone calls from the senator. Bingo was the stupid one, but still he had been able to figure out the connection between the retired major and the pilots smuggling cocaine.

Bingo was reluctant to get involved; he shrugged his shoulders. "How about Angelo?"

"What about him?"

"I was only wondering." Bingo had avoided Sonny's eyes.

"Christ, Bingo! Just tell me! *What? What* is it this time?"

"Fuck you, Sonny! Never mind. Forget it! Do what you want! I don't care! But I'm not fucking around with your fucking Mr. B.!"

Bingo did not care if Angelo took over everything in El Paso. Bingo did not want to be bothered with anyone, and he sure didn't want to get involved with the government. Max Blue hinted he and others had performed special "services" for the U.S. government at home and abroad. Bingo didn't give a shit about "rendering service" to his country. He didn't trust the government, especially not if that government had got favors from Max Blue in the past. Because Bingo knew exactly what open on Bingo's saw his father's The article con- nhattan. A grue- gripping a cigar been on his way n of cocaine, but the room sipping agazine article. from prominent ie meaning of the explanations, the was Max had only *pretended* to be badly wounded, and Max had only *pretended* to retire to the golf course in Tucson. The most macabre speculation had been that Max had indeed almost died from gunshot wounds, but that close call with death had also changed Max Blue. Max Blue and death had made a deal, according to the magazine reporter.

Bingo had never forgot that night. He had never snorted so much cocaine by himself before; he had never been so high or drunk so much tequila. Something about the cocaine had made Bingo read the article again and again; he thought it was quite funny to learn about his own father from the Crime section of *Time* magazine. All night Bingo had sat at his desk, snorting coke and sipping tequila with Pink Floyd tapes in the background while he brooded about himself and his family. Sonny had always tried to tell Bingo their parents didn't want kids; but Bingo was not so sure. Everything had ended the morning Max had got shot and Uncle Mike had died.

The roommate had been away for the weekend. When he returned, Bingo had not mentioned the magazine. The roommate had already arranged for a new room the following term. Bingo could trace his all-night affairs with booze and blow to that night he had spent reading family history in *Time* magazine. Bingo had seen no reason to change anything now that he was settled in El Paso. In a family of go-getters, Bingo was the flop. Bingo wanted nothing more than to stay high in his hacienda in the sand dunes.

ORGAN DONORS

ROY HAD MADE IT a practice always to refuse the cocaine Trigg offered him. Roy was aware Trigg was watching him walk. If Trigg had not watched Roy, the cocaine might have been nice. Trigg had made a point of bragging about its origin and quality. Always a rock as big as a fist; always pink flake.

Trigg had not acted edgy before. Roy glanced at the glass desk top for signs of cocaine, but the glass was clean. Trigg had laughed nervously. "No, it isn't *that*," meaning cocaine. "I have something I want to talk to you about." Trigg kept his eyes on Roy's eyes. Roy wondered what meaning a blink might have had then. Would Trigg back down?

Roy could see Trigg was uneasy about something but at the same time anxious to talk to Roy. A sixth sense Roy had developed in 'Nam told him when a woman or a man wanted to talk about sex. Roy had not pegged Trigg for a faggot, just a pervert in a wheelchair. Roy expected a double date with a couple of whores to the hot tubs or maybe dirty videos of Peaches going down on Trigg in his chair. Later when Roy had been rethinking everything, he had to laugh at himself for being so slow. Born yesterday.

Roy had always known Trigg felt inferior. At first Roy had assumed it was the wheelchair, but Trigg had felt inferior long before he had collided with the car. Trigg liked to get drunk with the help, that had been one of Trigg's negative points according to Peaches, who took her work for Bio-Materials seriously. Peaches had caught Roy staring at her titties. Still she had happily talked for hours with Roy about "negatives and positives." Peaches didn't consider discussing negatives and positives about coworkers as gossiping or snitching. Impulsively Roy had asked Peaches to tell him his own negatives and positives, but she had refused, saying she did not know him enough to say anything. Roy had looked down quickly before she could see his face. He had been surprised at the pain her words had pushed into his chest. He wondered how it felt to have a heart attack.

Peaches knew but did not care about Trigg's "illegal" sales to certain West German biomedical consortiums. Peaches said once you were dead, it mattered little what became of your body. Peaches had seen something, but later when Roy had tried to get Peaches to talk, she had refused. Trigg had to be very drunk and use a lot of cocaine before he would start talking about "it." That had been all that Peaches would say.

Trigg did not consider the subject sexual, but rather a story about the blood plasma and biomaterials market worldwide. Trigg disliked psychiatry and psychology, which could be twisted to explain anything. Trigg had never denied that picking up hitchhikers had excited him. He had thought of it as a roll of the dice or a hand of five-card draw. The winners and the discards. Discards were "locals" or those with too many kin. Trigg had found that his wheelchair automatically took the suspicion away from the hitchhikers who might have been uneasy about a drive with him. Trigg would always wave his hand at the backseat and his wheelchair. Trigg had not minded the killing.

They are both getting drunk and they have snorted a gram of cocaine between them.

"Nobody ever notices they are gone. The ones I get," Trigg had said, looking Roy in the eye. Trigg had been too drunk to remember that Roy was himself "homeless." Trigg talked obsessively about the absence of struggle as the "plasma donors" were slowly bled to death pint by pint. A few who had attempted to get away had lost too much blood to put up much fight even against a man in a wheelchair. Of course the man in the wheelchair had a .45 automatic in his hand.

Trigg had paid extra if the victim agreed. Trigg gave him a blow job while his blood filled pint bags; the victim relaxed in the chair with his eyes closed, unaware he was being murdered. What Trigg does with the swollen cock in his mouth never varies: he catches an edge or fold of foreskin between his teeth. The cock might shrivel temporarily, but then it would encourage greatly from the nibble. All this Trigg performs from the wheelchair. Trigg blames the homeless men. Trigg blames them for being easy prey. He holds their jizz in his mouth until he gags. They got a favor from him. To go out taking head from him. He doubted any of them could hope for a better death. They were human debris. Human refuse. Only a few had organs of sufficient quality for transplant use.

"Trigg the Pig," Peaches had said bitterly, "he blabs his big mouth too much." Peaches had been upset about Trigg's drunken ramblings. Her face had reddened. "Did he tell you about 'the harvests'?" Roy nodded his head, but Peaches had refused to talk any more except to say everything was done legally. She had seen court papers signed by a judge authorizing everything. Peaches recovered her composure. "Transients die all the time. They don't go to doctors and they don't eat right," Peaches said. She had looked Roy squarely in the eye to let him know that was how she would testify under oath.

Clinton said there had been some grumbling among the men because their leader was not eating with them and sleeping in the tin-and-cardboard hooch the men called Command Headquarters. Roy told Clinton to tell them to assemble that night and he'd give them a full report. Rambo had no secrets from his men. Rambo had been working on secret sources of money for their group.

Clinton had got a group of blacks and a few Hispanics together for his own brigade. All of them were older men, and one look in the eyes and you could see they'd been there all right. Clinton's men said they'd take women in their brigade too, although this was a signal for joking and laughing about the "orders" they'd give these women.

In private Roy had warned Clinton about accepting women into his unit. An integrated unit was one thing; all the men had fought together before in Vietnam. Most homeless women had a bunch of kids; they would be a mess. Women would be more trouble than they were worth.

Roy would not tell Clinton his suspicions about Trigg's biomaterials business until the right moment. Unless they found a better "incident," Rambo planned to mobilize and rally his army of homeless to accuse the blood and biomaterials industry of mass murder.

KILL THE RICH

THE DAYS WERE GETTING COOL by evening, and when Rambo came to "brief" the men in the evenings, they would be standing around bonfires, passing bottles, smoking and talking. Each week more tents and lean-tos appeared along the gray clay banks of the Santa Cruz River. The mesquite groves along the riverbanks were checkered with plastic-tarp shelters, and blankets and sleeping bags drying on mesquite branches. Rambo and Clinton marched their men in Homeless Day rallies, but they were careful not to have any member of their unit arrested in the protests. Rambo and Clinton got high just retelling the events over and over again, how the "activists" were keeping the poor and homeless stirred up and assembled, which was all Rambo and Clinton wanted or needed. The activists had urged the people to occupy vacant government buildings, but Rambo and Clinton were no longer interested in the scraps thrown to them.

Rambo let Clinton evaluate the volunteers. Clinton had a good eye for white men. Clinton's blacks were always doing comparative studies among themselves, and they'd compare notes on white-man behavior. All Rambo said was he was glad it was they who had to observe white men's behavior and not him. Observing the behavior of "white" people, his "own kind," had been what had cut Roy loose from the world. He had no regrets. He was where he belonged. Corporations and big business had seized control of America during the Vietnam War, and only a poor man's army of patriots could hope to restore the people's democracy to the United States.

Clinton and Roy inventory the empty vacation houses twice weekly as the winter visitors begin to arrive in Tucson for the winter holidays. Clinton keeps the records and sorts through the mailboxes at each of the vacant houses. Some were so rich they forgot they had Tucson bank accounts. In the piles of letters at one house they had found blank checks and an all-time teller card; in a separate bank envelope they had found the personal code number.

Roy and Clinton regret they can't tell the others about the vacant houses, but they don't want to move too soon. Their operation requires a great deal of planning and thought. But when the cold rains come in November, Clinton is angered by the men who are shivering, and they begin to outfit their men with used field jackets from the surplus store. The bankcard works every time at the automatic teller machine. Clinton keeps careful records. Clinton organizes reconnaissance marches into the desert on the edge of the northwest side of the city where the men scavenge firewood for the camps. The trouble with these men is they are all wrecks—smashed by cheap wine and car wrecks, ruined by police and nightsticks. Clinton takes all the men who volunteer to go. He uses his wood-hauling patrols to weed out the drunks and the crazies from the "dependables." Clinton organizes patrols when he feels the jumpiness begin to spread from his hands into his stomach. Moving the feet always helps, he says.

Clinton claims he can tell if owners of the vacation houses are keeping close watch or not by the mail that keeps coming to the home. Clinton is careful to avoid creating suspicion. The thrill was to open the mail, read it, and reseal it. Clinton had known guys who worked for the censors in Vietnam. The only tricky part, Clinton thought, would be to empty the automatic teller machine at the rate of $400 a day. "Did you ever stop to think how long it will take us to get that much money out of the teller machine?" According to bank statements, the account with the automatic teller card has thirty thousand dollars in it.

Late at night Roy and Clinton had talked about money—what they would buy with it, what they would do to get it. Neither of them wanted the usual stuff such as fancy cars, women, investments, or silk shirts.

Roy had decided he would buy his own island to live on. Clinton said he didn't know what he would do. Maybe he would travel to Africa and to Haiti to learn about the old religion. But after Roy had bought the island, and after Clinton had learned voodoo, they could not think what else to do with their imaginary money. Roy could not think of anything he needed beyond his jacket and sleeping bag. Clinton had done a lot of background work on "their" money-machine bankcard. The card would work at bank machines in fourteen western states.

"Meaning what?" Roy said.

"Meaning I could go and keep on going." Clinton was smiling, watching Roy's face.

"I already thought about all of it. Before we ever started this. Before I ever saw you. I decided to let things fall where they will."

"You mean you figured me for a thief?" Clinton said, still smiling.

"No, not that. I just mean that whatever turns out, all of this has happened before, somewhere in the world. Some will go and some will stay."

Clinton had touched Roy lightly on the shoulder. "Don't worry, man. Me and this bankcard, we'll be back."

Roy touched Clinton's sleeve. "You don't have to say anything. You probably should just take it all and go. You, me, probably we'd be better off."

Roy didn't like the idea of trying the bankcard out of state, but Clinton assured him they had nothing to worry about. Clearly the owner of the vacation house used his Tucson bankcard as infrequently as he used his winter vacation house. Roy trusted Clinton to come back with the bankcard because they had talked about that.

Roy said, "We have endless wealth."

Clinton's face got tense. "That's stupid. No one has endless money—"

"Except the U.S. government, who just prints more."

Roy had tried to lighten Clinton's mood, but Clinton sometimes got set off.

"Rich don't want to give away any, but poor will come and take it all."

The others in both units were afraid of Clinton's storms of anger. Roy had overheard the men discussing him. The men had been drinking and were talking freely. A young white kid about eighteen said he was scared Clinton wanted to kill all whites. But the Mexican called Barney shook his head.

"Clinton, he's after the rich. Clinton, he'd even go after Oprah Winfrey because the bitch is rich!"

"Kill the rich?" the skinny white kid said. "But someday I might get a lot of money." All of them had started laughing then, even the guys who hated niggers and expected race wars, because the skinny kid was *really* stupid if he thought he'd ever have any money, let alone get rich.

The bank statement for the automated-teller card arrives at the house each month. Clinton says he is counting on there being only one bank statement sent out, the statement sent to the vacant house. They both agree they will have to clean out the bank account before cold weather to play it safe. They do not want to chance losing that kind of money. Because with that kind of money, they could equip their little guerrilla army. Speed was more important than size in guerrilla armies. The money was going to buy them everything they needed, the money was going to get them launched.

Clinton drops off to sleep every night thinking about the others. Far far away there are others like himself, men, right here in the United States, with nothing to lose. In the morning while the coffee is still heating in the campfire, Clinton tells Roy he wants to do some traveling.

Clinton's argument had been a good one: they had some money to cover traveling expenses; the thing was to take advantage of the cold weather, which drove all the homeless and able-bodied to travel far to the south. Clinton could get one of those $99 bus passes and go right across the country. But Roy did not like the idea of Clinton moving around like that, from homeless camp to homeless camp. A black man in army camouflage pants was sure to get the wrong kind of attention.

Clinton had laughed bitterly. "Oh, I see. I travel like a bum and sleep in the ditch." Roy realized his mistake then. Clinton was going to talk to people on the street, but he wasn't going to sleep there. They wouldn't find Clinton haranguing crowds outside soup kitchens. Not yet. Roy had only sighed loudly and walked away. He stopped himself from explaining. Explanations meant nothing. Clinton might figure it out for himself later; Roy had assumed Clinton would travel the way Roy traveled. Roy got a rush out of hopping freight trains. Roy liked to imagine he was a bullfighter with only split seconds and inches standing between himself and the charging freight train.

Clinton was quiet the night before he caught his bus. He was going to San Diego and L.A. first. The California riots had stopped when the weather cooled off.

Roy had told the men Clinton had to go to his grandmother's funeral in Los Angeles. Roy tried to avoid the appearance of secrecy. Week by week the homeless men arrived, and always a few drifted to the 'Nam Veterans' Camp, especially if they had run afoul of regulations in church soup kitchens or city shelters. The men who came to the 'Nam Camp were usually the crazies—the ones who "believed" they had fought at Khesanh or Mylai. Roy did not turn anyone away, but he had to watch each new arrival carefully because sooner or later the government would send undercover men posing as drifters as they had earlier in October, to report on any political activities by the homeless.

Roy had made it his business to listen closely to the men when they talked and drank; Roy visited Clinton's unit each evening after he had checked with the men in his own unit. The fatigue jackets had helped pull the two units together. Just as uniforms were supposed to.

Roy was not as worried about police spies and informers as he was about the questions that came from local advocates for the homeless—Tucson church people and "liberals." "Why don't more veterans join in class-action lawsuits? Why don't more veterans join in the marches and demonstrations?"

"*More?* You want *more* of us? You've already had enough!"

The men in camp had cheered Roy, and the "advocates" had hurried away. Later in the week, Roy read a newspaper article on the "apathy" of homeless Vietnam veterans. For Roy the article couldn't have been better.

Apathy. Let them believe what they want to believe.

.44 MAGNUM HAS PUPPIES

STERLING HAD SEEN BULLETS and guns everywhere for days, but he had tried to avoid looking directly at the weaponry. He had tried not to be within earshot of Zeta, Ferro, or Lecha, who seemed to be constantly crowded into Zeta's office door just as the computer printer began to chatter. Paulie had been strangely inactive during this time, and Ferro had complained about Paulie's lethargy when they were loading or unloading gear. Sterling had also noticed the change in Paulie because one of the Dobermans had had puppies. Paulie had spent hours watching the dog before the pups were born.

Sterling could tell Ferro and Paulie had been fighting because more and more Ferro called Sterling to help him lift tarps into the back of the pickup while Paulie repacked the hot-air balloon or refilled water cans and plastic bottles. Paulie moved more slowly when Ferro was not speaking to him. Sterling had learned to stay out of Ferro's way whenever Paulie's eyes were swollen.

Sterling had found out a little from Seese about homosexual men. She said they were no different from other lovers, or other couples. Sterling could not explain his curiosity without sounding prejudiced. Paulie would have been strange even if he had not been gay. That was Sterling's point. Sterling had watched Paulie become more and more worried about the pregnant dog. Mag had been a favorite of Paulie's because she had crouched and growled at him even when he brought her dish full of food. "Mag" was short for her full name, .44 Magnum.

Sterling hosed down the kennels, raked dog turds into piles, and shoveled them into the wheelbarrow. The daily schedule was always the same. Paulie had been adamant about consistency. No consistency and these high-octane dogs would explode all over the place, and someone, probably Sterling, would get killed. At eight A.M. Paulie brought in the night dogs and set loose the day dogs in the twenty-acre outer perimeter. Paulie had trained the dogs to accept only the food either he or Ferro fed them. Under no circumstances were others even to attempt to feed the dogs. When Ferro and Paulie were away on business, the dogs ate from automatic feeders full of dry dog food.

Sterling was used to being ignored by Paulie. Sterling had ignored Paulie so they were even. Weeks had passed without either of them speaking to the other. Sterling had found Paulie in the kennel stroking the bitch and examining her belly. Sterling had stopped in his tracks with a wheelbarrow full of dog shit because he had never seen Paulie's face so strangely expressive; Paulie's eyes were filled with tears. Paulie's voice sounded thick with his concern for the dog. He didn't want the red bitch to die. Sterling asked if the dog was sick or having trouble because he had been cleaning kennels all morning and had not seen the red bitch lying down or vomiting. Paulie had seemed to misunderstand the question because he had started talking about there being "too many puppies." "Too many" would kill the dog. Paulie's voice had quickly dropped almost to a whisper, as if his throat were tight. "Too many."

Sterling could see emotion had choked off Paulie's words, so he nodded and pretended not to notice the tears.

"Too many puppies will kill her. Too many and she'll die."

Paulie had not left the kennel until Ferro had telephoned twice; on the second call Paulie heard something bad because Sterling had watched Paulie's muscles tighten the longer he talked on the phone.

Sterling had been startled to find Paulie still smoking cigarettes and talking to the dog at eight A.M. when Sterling came on duty. Paulie had spoken to Sterling without looking away from the dog. "I counted them," Paulie had continued in a soft, even voice. "I counted them with my hands—feeling them through her belly like this." Sterling watched the rough, bony hands, fingernails chewed to the quick, gently press the dog's abdomen.

Sterling had begun to get a strange, almost light-headed feeling as he listened to Paulie talk about a dog. Not this dog, .44 Magnum, but another dog long ago. Had the other dog been *Paulie's* dog? No, it had belonged to a man. A man who came to the house but who did not like Paulie. Sterling had been relieved when Paulie had clarified which dog he was talking about. "This other dog" had been Paulie's dog, but the dog had died from having too many puppies.

"You mean too many all at one time? You mean too many *inside her?*" Sterling had floundered for the words to say it without making it sound too gruesome. Paulie did not respond after that. Sterling decided he had asked Paulie too many questions instead of just shutting up and listening.

For all his reading about the art of becoming a good listener, Sterling had forgotten all the cardinal rules with Paulie. Paulie had something inside him that frightened Sterling a great deal, so much that Sterling had forgot the art of good listening.

Sterling had been wakened almost every night for the past two weeks by the headlights on Ferro's returning truck. Just before dawn when Sterling awoke to nature's call and groped his way to the toilet, Sterling had looked out the window and saw the silhouette of only one person, the driver. Ferro had stayed out all night and left Paulie at the ranch alone.

Sterling kept an eye on .44 Magnum throughout the week, but she had eaten all her food and had gotten more fierce and lively as her stomach had grown. Paulie had increased the dog's daily rations. Sterling had no choice but to obey orders. Day by day Sterling could feel the tension grow.

MEN IN LOVE

STERLING HAD WAITED around the swimming pool hoping to find Seese on a break from the nonstop typing she was doing on the old manuscript. Seese had difficulty looking at computer screens for long without developing a headache. Seese had come outside to smoke a joint. Sterling always said no to marijuana because it made him too hungry and too horny.

Seese had taken a big drag on the hand-rolled cigarette and closed her eyes for a long time before she spoke. Sterling could see something was bothering Seese because she seemed exhausted and distant on the lounge chair, intent on sucking and inhaling the pot as deeply as possible. Sterling had begun skimming leaves and dead moths off the surface of the pool. He thought it might make talking easier for Seese.

Seese said she was feeling strangely exhausted by typing Lecha's old book or manuscript or whatever it was. Sterling thought Seese looked close to tears. Sterling had done a great deal of thinking about Seese: her pain did not recede because she was a mother whose child was lost. But Sterling had hoped maybe typing all the mess of old notepaper scraps and shreds of cards might help Seese, by occupying her mind with the stories or old reports or whatever Lecha wanted Seese to type.

"I dream all night about pages I typed the day before, except they aren't the pages I've typed, they are pages I *dream,* but when I awake, the dreams feel they are real even though I know they are only dreams." Seese was staring into the water at the deep end of the pool. "When I sit back down at the keyboard, the real manuscript page reads completely differently than in my dreams."

"You are working too hard with the old papers," Sterling said gently. He did not want to add to Seese's trouble by giving bossy advice. He wanted her to know he cared with no strings attached. If and when Seese wanted him to know about the dreams, she would tell Sterling; it was that simple. Sterling was grateful he was no longer suffering from bad dreams. Now when Sterling slept, he remembered no dreams at all the next morning.

"I wonder what is bothering Paulie." Sterling had decided that maybe focusing on someone else's problems might help Seese get her mind off the sadness.

"Men in love," Seese said, and Sterling thought she sounded bitter. "I never figured them out at all. I mean, the thing with David and Eric and Beaufrey."

Paulie watched Mag almost constantly as milk began to fill her teats. Paulie was no longer Ferro's shadow, available in an instant for Ferro's orders. Ferro telephoned the kennels, and with a throat tight with fury, Ferro demanded to speak to Paulie. Paulie never said more than "yes" or "no" over the phone.

Thirteen puppies had been born a little before dawn. By the time Sterling had arrived at eight o'clock, Paulie was already pacing nervously outside Mag's kennel, stopping frequently to look inside the doghouse. Sterling had seen no headlights at three A.M. as he had previous nights. Ferro had not come home.

Paulie had actually touched Sterling's elbow briefly, but Paulie's voice was still sullen. He ordered Sterling to take a good look. What did Sterling see? "Puppies." Sterling started to feel nervous because Paulie had never looked at Sterling so directly before. The pale blue eyes were bloodshot and distant. He ordered Sterling to count the pups, but Sterling pointed out, the red dog growled each time she heard Sterling speak and was growling then as Sterling spoke. No way could Sterling count Mag's puppies.

Paulie had already counted them three times himself; he just wanted to be sure the total was correct. The number had upset him a great deal: thirteen. Thirteen puppies were far too many. They had almost burst open her belly; now they were about to devour her, to eat her breast by breast. Sterling was horrified at Paulie's description of the pups eating their mother; but when he checked, all he had seen were layers of little tails and little legs, and pup heads bobbing and weaving. Sterling didn't know much about dogs, but he told Paulie the dog and her puppies looked okay to him.

"You don't know anything about dogs," Paulie said matter-of-factly. Paulie had spoken with such vehemence, Sterling had whole-heartedly agreed with him. Never argue with a crazy man, old Aunt Marie used to say.

Sterling had been pushing the wheelbarrow past the corrals when Ferro had come blasting up the long driveway ahead of a cloud of dust. Ferro had skidded the Blazer to a stop at the kennels and leaned on the horn until all the dogs were barking and howling, even the red bitch. But Paulie had not come out of the kennels, so Ferro spun the wheels and kicked gravel all the way up the hill to the house.

JAMEY LOVE

FERRO DID NOT LIKE the way he was feeling even when he was high on coke. He knew he had to do something about Paulie. Ferro knew he was obsessed with Jamey, but he wanted to work it out before Jamey realized what power his smooth, blond thighs had over balding, fat men the wrong side of thirty. Ferro had never felt the lust so strongly or the jealousy so quick in his blood. Jamey had appeared one fall day as Ferro was cruising the university for the tanned, blond jocks in their skimpy satin gym shorts. What else was the University of Arizona famous for?

Ferro had never had one as gorgeous as Jamey. Ferro had no trouble finding boyfriends while he was in his teens and twenties. He had never been good-looking, but when he was younger there had been a smooth-ness to his skin, and a roundness to his face that, coupled with expensive Italian shirts and leather trench coats, had won him almost any boy he had wanted in Tucson. Ferro had had a Porsche since eleventh grade and "income from the family ranch" as he delicately put it to the hand-some country-club boys. But the big meals, all the imported beer, and weekends with his lovers at the best hotels had made Ferro fat. By thirty, Ferro was thick around the belly and the face. Ferro took no chances. He made sure the young, handsome men rode in the Porsche and con-sumed grams of coke so he already "owned" them before he ever brought them to his bed. Afterward Ferro took extra precautions to dump the boy before the boy dumped him. Paulie of course didn't count as one of the "boys." The "boys" were clean and elegant and from the white upper-middle class. Paulie was hardly more than a gardener or a chauf-feur in hire to the household. Paulie was a convenience; similar to a valet or bodyguard.

Jamey did not mind if Paulie stayed on as the bodyguard and chauffeur for Ferro. Jamey had always held out for certain of his "old dear friends," and now Ferro was exercising his right to keep "a dear old friend." Jamey thought Ferro was too possessive and had encouraged Ferro to keep Paulie, although Paulie hated Jamey. Ferro took care the paths of the two men never crossed. Ferro had rented the town house so Paulie would never see Jamey. Zeta and Jamey had been indifferent about meeting one another so Ferro had let it drop.

COP CAKES
OR NUDE COP PINUPS

FERRO HAD ALWAYS been a sullen, distant child, but Zeta had seldom ever had to correct him or speak to him about anything he had done. Jamey or Paulie made no difference to her. Zeta told Ferro it was his own business whom he slept with. Ferro worked hard. He sat up all night on mountain ridges, in the wind, or in the rain, because drops in bad weather were risky enough that the law did not expect them then. Ferro had ridden horseback when it was 108°, gathering the skinny cattle to drive across the border at the bitter-water windmill. Later he and the two Papago cowboys had wrestled the skittish Mexican steers, to retrieve plastic packets of cocaine taped under their bellies. Zeta never argued. Ferro earned his leisure time. It was his money.

Ferro had savored Jamey's silky, smooth skin, imagining he, Ferro, was a captive. A victim of homosexual rape by lovely, cruel Jamey, who had immediately abandoned him. At first Ferro had waited for the kiss-off: Ferro would telephone and get a busy signal, the unreturned calls and unanswered messages. But Jamey had seemed oblivious to all the wobbling jelly-fat Ferro so much despised and abhorred about himself. Gay men especially hated fat, but not Jamey. Jamey loved to be "crushed" and "smothered" under Ferro's body, and Ferro had felt Jamey lovingly poking his big cock into Ferro's creases and folds of fat.

Ferro had never wanted anything, any high, any drug, the way he wanted Jamey. He had begun to think about Jamey at all times of the night and day.

Even when Jamey did not bother to go to his classes, Ferro had not been able to get over the awful feeling that Jamey would find a new lover on campus; someone who was blond and slender, and blue eyed as Jamey was. Jamey did not need money, but he was always ready to buy coke at a discount for himself and friends. Ferro could not stop making comparisons between Jamey and a runt like Paulie. Paulie had a grimy white face and the close-set eyes of a rodent. Paulie had wandered in like a stray dog that got fed and had stayed. Ferro had never wanted Paulie. Paulie had only been there to work for them—Ferro and the old woman, Zeta.

Jamey was Ferro's opposite, yet somehow they were equals. Jamey was as blond and willowy as Ferro was swarthy and fat. Jamey's diet consisted of raw fruits and vegetables chased down with expensive champagne and Ferro's top-line cocaine. The foods Ferro ate and drank disgusted Jamey. Pure cocaine in moderation was not as bad as rich food or heavy whipping cream, Jamey said. Ferro had been open-eyed from the start. He knew he got the young pretty men because he spread around the cocaine. That was no mystery.

Jamey was Ferro's opposite in temper; not a nervous bone in Jamey's smooth, white body. Roll over, lie back grinning, take another snort. Jamey wanted nothing more in life than that: to snort and fuck all morning and all afternoon. Ferro had been through hundreds of boys, and he had immediately seen Jamey was too good to be true. The catch with Jamey was his taste in friends. Because of these "friends," Jamey could not be trusted. A few of Jamey's friends were actual Tucson cops, but most of them were like Jamey and only liked to dress up like cops; uniforms, even nurse's uniforms, aroused them. Ferro found uniforms of all kinds disgusting. Jamey dressed like a cop for poster photographs and for videotapes and movies. Jamey's friends called their calendar-publishing company Cop Cakes. Cop Cakes advertised all the calendar pinups were actual law enforcement officers. Ferro laughed and tossed the old Cop Cakes calendars on the floor. They could put out better pinup calendars themselves. Ferro wanted to finance his own pinup calendar. No cop or nurse uniforms either. Ferro did not trust Jamey's friends, especially not the faggots who got hot when they wore a pig's uniform.

A calendar would only be the beginning. The family business was about to consolidate. Now Zeta's computers had completed projections designed by Awa Gee. Zeta's computers were telling them to sell out because the wholesale price of cocaine worldwide was about to take another "nosedive." Ferro hated Awa Gee and his stupid puns, but the gook son of a bitch was a master at invading or destroying enemy computers.

Calendars and publishing would be just the beginning. Ferro had been bored with the routine for years; he had begun to hate the endless driving all night on back roads, alert and tense for any sound, waiting and watching, for low-flying aircraft blinking tiny Christmas-tree lights to signal without detection. How many hours had Ferro and Paulie waited for donkey pack trains or teams of backpackers to emerge from the desert, uncertain whether the border patrol who took the bribes remembered which night the crossing was to take place. As long as the wholesale price of cocaine had stayed up, smuggling had been worth the danger and boredom; but not anymore.

Ferro would not forget the balloon trips they'd made with cocaine shipments. They had had a close call on one of their last balloon flights. Their balloon had been caught in a whirlwind as it was descending, and Ferro had seen how fragile the balloon was, how any strong wind might rip the nylon so the balloon collapsed into itself.

With their "guest ranch" business, hot-air balloon cruises along the border had been the perfect cover for moving large parcels. But after their near-miss with the whirlwind, Ferro had seen color photographs of a balloon crash in Albuquerque. The balloon and basket were on fire; tiny human bodies dangled from ropes as one body fell high above the Rio Grande. Later Ferro had lied about the reason he no longer used the hot-air balloon. But Ferro had kept dreaming over and over, he was dangling at the end of a long rope; all above him there were sparks and cinders and smoke from the fire engulfing the balloon.

Ferro was relieved he was about to retire. He did not want to risk losing Jamey; all the nights Ferro had to spend alone with Paulie waiting for drops or shipments might jeopardize their love. Jamey had been edgy about Paulie. Jamey did not like "rough trade" and Paulie was the roughest. Jamey was afraid Paulie might hurt him. Ferro had to laugh. Paulie did what Ferro told him. Paulie never questioned Ferro's orders.

The reappearance of worthless Lecha, his mother, was another sign it was time for him to retire with Jamey and enjoy life far from smugglers' paths and jeep trails. Ferro would leave the stink of old women behind in the old ranch house. He would finance Jamey's calendars, and later they might branch out and publish a magazine or books. The subject of the books wouldn't matter so long as they were not about women. As book publishers they would travel the world together.

The return of Lecha plus Jamey's "cop cakes" pals were reason enough to leave town. Ferro did not trust the so-called artists Jamey snorted coke with. Jamey never stopped to think, did he? Where did these "artists" get money for coke? Bullshit artists were what they were. Undercover cops had plenty of money. Jamey had laughed at Ferro's wild imagination. Tucson was full of "trust fund" artists, didn't Ferro know?

Ferro wanted to savor each moment and all the pleasure he could get with Jamey. Ferro and Jamey. He can think of nothing else. Ferro wants to stop all of Jamey's nights on the town without him. Suddenly that seems like the answer. There were important details he could not work out when his mind was always whispering, "Jamey, Jamey." It seemed funny how Jamey had eclipsed all else—the return of the old women, the rise of Max Blue, or the rumors out of Mexico. Just the sound, the thought, of Jamey's name gave Ferro a chill along his spine until something flashed bright in his brain. Ferro is consumed with pleasure as long as Jamey is close by. But if Jamey happened to be out, then the first burst of pleasure at his memory was immediately followed by the most terrible feelings of doubt and fear that somehow Jamey and his love would be lost. Jamey carries the beeper Ferro gave him, but it isn't always on, and Jamey isn't always near a telephone. Ferro tries to avoid confrontation over the beeper. Jamey laughs and says his friends think he's a drug dealer because of the beeper. That showed what his pals were thinking about, Ferro said, although they had agreed not to quarrel over Jamey's "friends" anymore. Jamey wanted to tell his friends, but Ferro had forbidden it. Jamey had wanted to announce to everyone he was Ferro's love slave and that's why he wore the beeper.

Jamey finds a great deal of amusement in Ferro's suspicions and fears. Jamey is able to manage with his friends quite safely. One of the Cop Cakes calendar group was the undercover man called Perry. Jamey laughed and laughed because Perry the undercover cop loved to snort coke. Perry sells twenty-four-hour notice of police or drug strike-force raids in Pima County. Perry always takes his pay in ounces of cocaine. Jamey says the coke is for personal use, but Ferro suspects Perry the Pig sells half grams to other Tucson cops. Jamey finds straight men, especially straight men in uniforms, very exciting. Ferro sneers. Perry the Pig isn't straight. Straight men did not pose nude in the positions Perry had taken with the other men for the Cop Cakes calendar.

"Touchy, touchy," Jamey says, and laughs at Ferro's hatred of Perry.

Jamey did not worry himself the way Ferro did with suspicions and questions. Jamey called it second-guessing or paranoia.

"Ferro, you can't start thinking like that. Sure Perry might be a decoy. But he's not. Perry is a cop who sells information because he wants the money. It's that simple."

Ferro does not argue, but he does not think bad cops or spies are that simple. Blond, dumb Jamey. Ferro doesn't bother to point out that Perry sells information at below the current market value. Let smart-ass Jamey Boy learn the hard way. The Perrys of the world claimed to sell the secrets for the money; but the sums they accepted betrayed their true motive, which was not greed but revenge. Traitors were driven by the strongest human impulse, the deepest human instinct—not for sex or for money but to get even. Secret crimes or hidden injuries required secret and hidden acts of vengeance. Ferro was no stranger to the plea-surable sensations revenge excited—the exquisite pulse-surges behind both eyes and the tingling in the groin while the scalp prickles and sends a chill down the spine at the instant vengeance is performed. Ferro was willing to bet the undercover cop got a hard-on every time he "leaked tips" about planned raids and stakeouts. As "cop cakes" went, Perry's pinup photo had been forgettable; his ass was flat and he had a pencil prick. Perry had begun as "Officer January," bare assed in department-issued SWAT gear, brandishing a riot stick. In riot helmet and gas mask, Officer January appeared anonymous and cruel. The joke had been on the Tucson Police Department. All the cop beefcake shots on last year's calendar had included badge numbers and squad-car numbers for blow jobs. Internal memos had been sent to all precinct chiefs from department of internal affairs investigators requesting photographs of all uniformed officers under their command. The latest edition of the Cop Cakes cal-endar had been comedy shots—tricks of photography in which the Tuc-son police chief's head appeared on the nude body of a sexually aroused male with a nightstick up his hairy ass. The comedy calendar had been a best-seller in adult bookstores in Salt Lake City and Phoenix and had made the national television news. According to Arizona's senators, the comedy calendar was an outrage and an attack on police and law enforcement in the United States.

The Tucson chief of police had been forced to hold a news conference televised on the national evening news to deny that the nude men on the Cop Cakes calendars were presently or had ever been law enforcement officers for the Tucson Police Department. The chief said pornographers' actors and models had posed for the calendar, and all rumors about rampant homosexuality among police officers were untrue. The chief said he had been especially disturbed by rumors that neatly trimmed mustaches signaled gay cops. The chief had declined to discuss the photograph with the nightstick. The department was not taking the calendar lightly; when police were under attack in Arizona, then the whole American way was endangered. Law and order was threatened by these subversives—homosexual artists who printed their filth on calendars to incite disrespect for the law and contempt for the police and court system.

OWLS CLUB

JUDGE ARNE FOUND A BIG SCARE inside his copy of the Cop Cakes comedy calendar. Somehow, someone had got hold of a color negative from a roll of the judge's "sensitive snapshots." The color-film processing plant was fully automated—the judge took care to know important facts. The judge had paid the film-lab receptionists fat tips each time he had picked up one of his rolls of "fun film." The judge would have to have a word with the lab manager—unless there was a security problem at the Owls Club. Fortunately, the yokels at the Tucson Police Department had been so stunned by their own "pinups" they had not noticed that Judge Arne's "pinup" for the month of August was no trick-photography shot. Printed from a single negative, the color print clearly showed the federal judge merrily penetrating his own basset hound. For September, the Cop Cakes comedy pinup had been the Pima

County sheriff superimposed over the figure of a man with his fly open and half-hard cock poking out, holding a stuffed owl in both hands. The judge did not like the use of the stuffed owl. The owl might be coincidence, but the judge did not think so. Whoever had found the color print of him with the dog had found it at the Owls Club. Because only members and honored guests knew that stuffed owls were one of the dominant motifs in the club's decor.

The judge had to smile at himself and his maturity. Twenty or even ten years ago he would have been in a cold sweat, paralyzed with fear of detection; instead he had been secretly quite pleased with the bold, exotic figure he had made on the calendar. He could easily imagine hundreds of young men locked in bedrooms nude and gazing at the calendar on the wall hypnotized or weak with pleasure. Trick photography indeed! But the "weak link" in the chain had to be located. The judge would have to go to the Owls Club on a regular basis again and familiarize himself with the regulars and the pretty homeboys off the street. He would be careful not to partake, but merely to sip cognac downstairs in front of the oversize color TV. Since he had been appointed to the federal bench, the judge had had to stay at home with his photography and basset-hound stud. The judge liked to say delicately to old friends he was now retired from all that—as if the wave of his hand swept away all the rose-bud rumps of all the brown street boys. Still the judge had regulars who were more worldly-wise than the light-fingered street boys. The blond University of Arizona boys were Midwestern hustlers who could swing both ways for a few bucks extra. The brown ones knew their place, the white ones didn't. But wasn't that what increased police spending was for? Alleys and vacant lots across Florida and the Southwest were littered with human refuse from the Midwest and Northeast—cast-off white men, former wage earners from mills and factories. Remnant labor-union ideas made older workers dangerous in times of national unrest. Now there was the chaos spreading across Mexico. The refugees were thick as flies in barbed-wire camps all along the U.S. border.

The judge was scheduled for golf on important matters. The senator would be part of the foursome as would the chief of police. The senator had flown in from Washington with a top-secret briefing concerning internal American security as well as security along the international border with Mexico. Of course the judge had been privy to classified documents because of his military friends in high places at Ft. Huachuca. The Cop Cakes comedy pinup might not be such a light matter at the judge's security-clearance renewal. But secretly the judge did not think

they would bother to pursue such a trivial matter as trick photographs
that libeled the police and courts. Over the years the judge had learned
a great deal about lie-detector tests and the evaluators of the testing.
The judge knew that the worst offenders remained serene, absolutely
innocent in their own minds because the victims had always started the
trouble. The judge thought the Tucson Police Department had botched
the whole affair because they had been too quick to issue absolute denials
that the calendar of nude cops had ever existed. Too many people in
Tucson were like the judge and secretly subscribed to "art books and
art calendars" for the discriminating male. The judge had breezed
through all inquiries by the press concerning the comedy calendar. The
judge had brushed aside the whole matter; trick photography could show
anything—the public should not be misled.

The judge was not being premature when he put the finger on one
of the "regulars" at the Owls Club. He was used to inhabiting a world
in which one lived in dread of the plain envelope with no return address
or the series of awkward phone calls. The Cop Cakes calendar had been
a subversive act, not a simple act of blackmail. A storm of lawlessness
was surging at the edges of respectable life in the United States. The
judge thought the golf game might be a good opportunity to raise the
subject of a large donation from the senator's foundation to help south-
ern-Arizona law enforcement. The volatile political situation in Mexico
made donations imperative, especially since Arizona State government
was nearly bankrupt.

The senator's staff had printed briefings, which were stupid and
useless on the golf course. Max had only glanced at his copy, then had
stuffed it in his golf bag. Max hated the pretensions of sleazy politicians
such as the senator. Max particularly enjoyed how conducting business
on the golf course disrupted all the smoothly oiled routines; Max had
exposed more rough edges and hidden dangers during a golf game than
the best spies and informers could gather in weeks. The golf game interrupted conversations—the senator would just get puffed up to begin
one of his "order and control at home, order and control abroad"
speeches and *whack!* Max Blue had teed off, sending a lovely arcing ball
hundreds of yards down the fairway to the edge of the green. The golf
ball soared like a bright white bird, though occasionally the arc of the
ball had reminded Max of the spring rain arching down from the clouds.
The sight of the ball's perfect flight, the ball's absolute accuracy, silenced
even the biggest assholes, such as the senator. Max could not imagine
why the senator was alive at all. The senator was stupefied with greed.

He had stared blankly as Max explained the near-hypnotic quality of golf's graceful marriage between physics and geometry. The senator's aides had telephoned all week, begging for a golf game with Max.

Max had begun seriously to question what value *this* U.S. senator or any other U.S. senator had any longer. The U.S. Congress made laws and more laws. But laws meant nothing without enforcement. In today's world, judges were a better buy; they gave more for the money than other politicians or the police. More and more often the senator had come for help and to ask small favors.

PART FOUR

THE
AMERICAS

BOOK ONE

MOUNTAINS

ANGELITA, AKA LA ESCAPÍA, THE MEAT HOOK

EL FEO HAD NEVER TOLD ANYONE how he had felt the first time he had walked into the downtown hotel where the negotiations were being held. The strobe flashes and videocam lights were blinding as he entered the lobby. The other Indian leaders were more well-known and had aides along to carry their briefcases. El Feo had been lucky to borrow a pair of new shoes from the village mayor; no one in their village, not even the mayor, owned a briefcase. Later El Feo and the other Indian leaders had been driven in buses to the university campus to meet with student leaders. In those days, La Escapía had gone by her Christian name, Angelita. She had been baiting university students the first time El Feo ever saw her. Angelita had been drunk on politics; a raving orator who might someday gather together hundreds and hundreds of fighters for El Feo's army. Then suddenly Angelita's attention had turned to El Feo; he could feel her eyes on him. Angelita had started laughing at him—squinting in the bright lights and pointing a finger at El Feo. El Feo disliked her instantly; she knew nothing about him. He had purposely not brought a briefcase or notebook. He wanted to make it clear he was not interested in white men's pieces of paper; El Feo had simply come for his people's ancestral lands.

El Feo had heard stories about Angelita. She was dangerous. She laughed and made fun of everything. She got the people laughing when the meeting or topics were serious—Angelita even made jokes about uprisings. She was dangerous. Nothing tiny or angel like about this woman, El Feo had decided, not unless you were thinking of an angel from hell. El Feo felt his throat get dry and his feet and hands tingle.

He could feel beads of sweat on his scalp. Great dark angel from the thirteen nights of the old gods—here was the angel El Feo had been searching for all his life.

Until El Feo had met Angelita, he had felt passion only for retaking stolen tribal land; big brown women with big breasts and big bellies interested him for only fifteen or twenty minutes at a time. Market days in the mountain villages found the women gossiping, whispering, and giggling behind their shawls about one so handsome his mother had to call him El Feo to protect him. His mother got him at birth from a coastal village. At one time the people had all lived closer together; at one time life had been a great deal different down in the low valleys that ran to the turquoise sea. He had come from a village close to the turquoise sea. He had been sent as an infant to the mountains so the coastal clans and the mountain clans did not forget they were one family; and because he had had a twin brother. Later as El Feo and his mother had traveled to the coastal village where he had met his other mother and father, and his twin brother, Tacho, nicknamed Wacah because he tamed big *wacahs* or macaws. The people on the coast had all the fish they could eat; otherwise they were poor. Tribal land the people had cleared for farming had later been claimed by the federal government; then the land had been resold to German coffee planters.

Angelita had questioned El Feo about certain rumors going around; they said El Feo was already married—married to the earth. They claimed El Feo had sexual intercourse four times a day with holes dug in damp river clay. El Feo had laughed and shook his head. He said he did not discuss his religion with anyone, not even with warrior angels. Later the village gossips claimed El Feo had been seduced by Angelita La Escapía, the crazy woman from the coast.

El Feo used to watch her face and watch the faces of people in market crowds who listened to her.

"A great 'change' is approaching; soon the signs of the change will appear on the horizon." Angelita's words filled El Feo with rapture. The earth, the earth, together they would serve Earth and her sister spirits.

El Feo had been content to watch from a distance. Men probably watched to see her big breasts heave and jiggle. But the women listened because they had never heard a woman like her before.

TWIN BOYS

EL FEO AND HIS TWIN had been separated because twins often attracted dangers from envious sorcerers; later there might be accusations of sorcery made against the twins together. El Feo had been initiated by the elder men in the ancient fashion, while Tacho had only the small ceremony the coastal village people still practiced. They both had been confirmed in the Church by the same traveling bishop on the same day. The elders had remarked that the twins had been reared in different villages to prevent just such coincidences as that.

Then one day Tacho had appeared in the mountain village. Tacho had worn his driving uniform, although he had hired an old taxi to drive him. The taxi had been full of gifts for all of them. Tacho had spent all his wages for the first month on the taxi ride, goat, and black piglets. Tacho had butchered the goat himself, but had left the task of dividing the meat to El Feo's "mother." Tacho's parents had sent the goat; but Tacho himself had chosen the black pigs for his brothers. Clanspeople broke out the home brew, and the village celebrated the visit from their dear brother Tacho.

Long into the night Tacho and El Feo drank with the other men around the glowing coals. They had talked about the black pigs and the wild-boar spirit the coastal people fed parched corn. Before dawn El Feo had looked at the piglets and at Tacho; El Feo had looked around at the figures squatting in their blankets, many of them dozing.

"The black pigs will feed an army," El Feo said softly.

"Four of them?" Tacho had his eyes closed, but he was listening.

"Of course four of them. Four is a good number. One boar, three sows. They will combine themselves over and over."

In the mountains the rich farmers hired armed patrols to watch for Indian squatters in the coffee plantations, and to shoot the wild pigs. Pigs rooted out the coffee seedlings and stripped off bark from mature trees.

"On the coast, people say the black boar and his kind have helped the people's uprisings more than once. The black boar and his troops stampede through thick undergrowth and trees. The stupid army chases the pigs deeper and deeper where the paths sink into moss. The black boar leads them into the swamp where hundreds of soldiers can easily be picked off by a few snipers," Tacho said.

El Feo took the pigs to his campsite in the hills above the village because pork was a great temptation even for El Feo. When the pigs were large enough to fight off wild dogs, El Feo would let the black pigs run wild. El Feo had explained to Tacho only one thing mattered: the stolen land; someday wild black pigs would help feed the people's army as the people took back their land.

MORE FRIENDS OF
THE INDIANS

TACHO WAS CAREFUL not to raise suspicion with El Feo's visits. Tacho made a point of having El Feo help him wash and wax the black Mercedes. The boss and the new wife had been quite nervous lately; rich white people needed reassurance because of the political unrest. White people can see the tribes in Africa have retaken all their ancestral lands, blood-soaked though they were.

Tacho entertained El Feo with stories about the "old wife" and the young mistress from Mexico City. El Feo had especially liked the old wife's tumble down the marble stairs, but that had been everyone's favorite story, from the housemaids to the rich society matrons. The boss would not mind if El Feo spent the night in Tacho's space at the front of the garage. El Feo had wanted to sleep one night in the backseat of the Mercedes, but Tacho had refused. "The boss doesn't sleep so good at night. He might surprise you."

El Feo liked the woman on top so he could look over her shoulder at the faint glow of tiny human souls awaiting conception in the ceiling rafters overhead. Souls of children who died before their second year remained nearby, hovering in cracks of the ceiling; homes of sorcerers were barren. Sorcerers captured only the souls of adults or children over two. El Feo and Angelita don't talk. They have food and sex together twice a day, that's all. She does the talking. El Feo had given up on talk years ago. He had thought he was through with fucking too, but sometimes El Feo was wrong in his predictions. This woman had chosen him. He had not done the choosing. All his life El Feo had been the one chosen.

The one chosen would be asked to do special favors for the whole group; late at night, at the end of the party, the ones who had been chosen would be asked to carry back gifts for others or to take special messages.

El Feo left the fund-raising and the gifts from all "the friends of the Indians" to Angelita, who did not mind the politics or politicians. Tribal leaders as far away as Nicaragua had heard of that woman who knew how to get the goods for the Indians. All sources of "direct" and "humanitarian" aid were known to Angelita; one week she would be gone, and the next week she would return, with little Korean vans to transport the village "baseball teams." Her secret had been simple: the world over—from foreign governments to multinational corporations—they all wanted to be called "friends of the Indians." They had just witnessed the bloody end of European control in South Africa. They had watched the tribes of Africa retake the land from Europeans; in the Americas they might have another fifty years or even one hundred, but time was running out. The Indians had risen up in Peru with the Shining Path. Everyone wanted to be "friends of the Indians"—the Japanese and Koreans as well as the Germans and Dutch. There were "friends of the Indians" all around the Persian Gulf.

Angelita had sent El Feo down into Tuxtla to get reports from Tacho. Tacho was ears and eyes for them. They kept track of General J. and the "security forces," as well as the police chief and the others in El Grupo.

WACAH THE SPIRIT MACAW
INTERPRETS DREAMS

TACHO HAD WORKED A LONG TIME to gain the boss man's trust; he had spent months pretending to be interested in Menardo's endless dreams; Tacho had not told Menardo the truth about the dreams and had instead substituted lucky numbers. Tacho had himself dreamed on the same night. Menardo's dreams had been full of numbers, but all of them had added up to less than zero. Tacho did not care if he had given away lucky numbers he might have sold or bet himself. Guaca-maya, the Blue Macaw, who had taught humans to talk, had taught Tacho the use of luck with numbers. Oh, gamblers might rush out and bet lucky numbers from dreams, but they paid a price; there was always a trade-off. Gamblers who got lucky numbers lived short lives. Tacho had been taught by the macaw spirits to look for numbers that kept bullets from their mark or numbers that kept disease or sorcery from one's bed.

The boss's dreams had been the worst dreams; even the slow-witted boss had understood that his days were numbered. Tacho traced Men-ardo's decline to the visit by the *norteamericano* who had given the boss the bulletproof vest. Tacho had watched the boss's wife as she studied the *norteamericano* talking with her husband beside the pool. Tacho had seen her look at the boss with the same attention the last year the "old Señora" was alive; now that Alegría had the boss, she was already looking for another man. Tacho had to be careful because the boss's new wife was quick to detect spies; Alegría was far more clever than the first Señora had been.

Tacho had guessed from the start the house the boss had been building was for this Alegría, not for the barren wife. Now Menardo had his mansion of white marble and his pool of water lily blossoms; on the ironed linens of his king-size bed, Menardo, the mestizo, savored the luscious fruit of a skinny white woman. Menardo had General J.

for a business partner and the former ambassador and the governor for country club pals. But Menardo's dreams were the dreams of a man soon to die; in Menardo's nightmare, the white lines of the highway suddenly became a giant snake that exploded into bloody flesh beneath the wheels of the speeding car. Menardo had awakened from the dream screaming, soaked in cold sweat. He had changed his pajamas, but the lining of the bulletproof vest had remained damp.

Menardo had discovered then, he could not fall asleep unless he wore the bulletproof vest. Even the strongest sleeping pills failed Menardo after a few hours, leaving him groggy and sick with anxiety until he put on the vest.

Tacho had been amused by Menardo's pathetic attempts to interpret the nightmare as a "good luck" sign from the Blessed Virgin, sometimes shown crushing the head of Satan, the serpent. Menardo worries the dream may be the Blessed Virgin's warning about assassins throwing bombs under the wheels of the car. For an instant Menardo catches Tacho's eye in the rearview mirror and Tacho sees Menardo's fear: "I still feel its flesh under the car—the tires sinking into slime." Menardo opened the tiny liquor cabinet in the backseat, poured himself a glass of brandy, and said nothing more.

Dream of the cuckolded husband; dream of the *double-cuckolded* husband; besides Bartolomeo, the communist, Tacho knew the *norteamericano* had fucked the boss's new wife too. Tacho had lied and made up winning numbers for Menardo at the horse races. He never gave any client the numbers to win all the races; word got out and they started to follow you, or worse, other gamblers tried to kill you. Tacho gave Menardo some winning numbers to fool him; Tacho wanted Menardo to keep dreaming nightmares and to keep telling Tacho his dreams.

Next Menardo had dreamed of sea turtles torn loose from their broken shells, bloody and dying; later the same night, Menardo had dreamed of two men who stood on a bridge and dropped a pistol into the brownish water. Tacho had been delighted with the information he obtained from Menardo's dreams; Menardo had been talking to the *norteamericano* without General J.'s permission; Menardo feared the general would have him murdered. Menardo had seen the general's notorious videotapes of intelligence interrogations; the turtle shells peeled bloody from live flesh were a reference to the torturers who removed fingernails and toenails.

SWARMS OF SQUATTERS

EL FEO AND ANGELITA had organized their village defense units along the same order as the village baseball teams. Priests and other missionaries had been fooled by the devotion and enthusiasm the Indians showed for baseball; what the outsiders did not realize was each baseball team was composed of males of the same clans. Thus the priests and government authorities had failed to realize that baseball practices and baseball games were opportunities for more than mere sport and amusement. Tacho had listened to his brother and the woman relate the long, complicated stories, the alibis and excuses necessary to persuade foreign governments to send Indian villages direct aid of baseball uniforms and cases of dynamite. The dynamite, they lied, was for clearing land for new baseball diamonds. Tacho had told El Feo and the wild woman Angelita what he thought: if even the lowest police louse got wind that baseball teams were secret guerrilla units, then all of them were going to be ground into bloody pulp by the federal police and the military.

Tacho had gathered the information they had requested because he liked the tingle in his balls when he lifted the telephone receivers to hear the boss talk to the police chief or the general. He could hear them discuss the "solutions." Universal Insurance's clients were urged to telephone the boss at the first sign of worker unrest. With Tacho's information, El Feo and Angelita had been able to deduce weak links and spies within the villages. Tacho had listened as the boss ordered Universal Insurance Company's security forces to coffee plantations to sweep the surrounding hills of Indian squatters, their shanties, and their gardens. Over and over it happened; the squatters dragged together debris for shacks and scratched out small garden plots. Then armed "security guards" trampled the gardens and burned the shacks. The strategy of the squatters was simple: make a thing unprofitable and watch the white man leave. Over and over; again and again the squatters had reappeared in other locations. The land was theirs and they knew it. Tacho had listened as businessmen whined to Menardo about expenses, and costs. The Indians were worse than insects; it cost the squatters nothing to breed and to swarm over the land, while a unit of five security specialists with weapons and one vehicle cost hundreds per day. For swarms of squatters, Indians thicker than weeds, Menardo had developed more economical methods: Universal Insurance sent a crop-dusting plane to dump insecticide and herbicide on the squatters. Luckily crop-dusting planes flew low and were easy for snipers to shoot down. Tacho wasn't interested in being squashed like a flea with the others; Tacho was happy to leave the teams and units and chains of command to El Feo and Angelita. Himself, Tacho was at work on the boss man's dreams. Tacho's strategy was to let the dogs turn on one another. Tacho was learning patience; the macaws did not always speak clearly to him. The macaws said the battle would be won or lost in the realms of dreams, not with airplanes or weapons.

In the old days the Twin Brothers had answered the people's cry for help when terrible forces or great monsters threatened the people. The people had always feared the Destroyers, humans who were attracted to and excited by death and the sight of blood and suffering. The Destroyers secretly prayed and waited for disaster or destruction. Secretly they were thrilled by the spectacle of death. The European invaders had brought their Jesus hanging bloody and dead from the cross; later they ate his flesh and blood again and again at the "miraculous eternal supper" or Mass. Typical of sorcerers or Destroyers, the Christians had denied they were cannibals and sacrificers. Tacho had watched enough television and movies to realize those who secretly loved destruction and death ranged all over the earth.

The old parrot priests used to tell stories about a time of turmoil hundreds of years before the Europeans came, a time when communities had split into factions over sacrifices and the sight and smell of fresh blood. The people who went away had fled north, and behind them dynasties of sorcerer-sacrificers had gradually taken over the towns and cities of the South. In fact, it had been these sorcerer-sacrificers who had "called down" the alien invaders, sorcerer-cannibals from Europe, magically sent to hurry the destruction and slaughter already begun by the Destroyers' secret clan.

Tacho himself had tried to avoid the spirits. He had heard others complain the spirits demanded too much, cost too much, because nowadays people did not bother to look after the departed souls of their own family and relatives. Younger people refused, saying they didn't want to take money or the time away from their jobs in the fields. But one day two big blue macaws had appeared in the tree by his door, and it was too late; the macaw spirits had chosen Tacho as their servant. What did the spirits expect? What did they want from people who were working all day and part of the night and still they were starving? The duties of the macaw servant were innumerable; all requests, warnings, and orders from the macaws had to be obeyed, no matter what was asked. Tacho had to guard the macaws from parrot traders and common thieves, who might shoot them for their feathers. Fortunately, the birds had a big tree by the garage where no parrot traders or thieves could get near thanks to the latest in security forces and technology.

When the spirits called, Tacho had to go to them; their name for him was Wacah. Tacho had to sit for hours on end under the big tree, or sometimes he parked the Mercedes there while he polished it so he could listen to the birds. The macaws had come with a message for humans, but it would take a while for Tacho to understand. The macaws had been sent because this was a time of great change and danger. The macaw spirits had a great many grievances with humans, but said humans were already being punished and would be punished much more for their stupid human behavior. He no longer thought about anyone— not his parents or his twin, El Feo. He had not thought about the village. Tacho had cleared his mind and his heart of all others so he could understand what was going to happen next.

VILLAGE OF SORCERERS AND CANNIBALS

TACHO HAD BEGUN to see changes all around Tuxtla. The government was uneasy about the relentless stream of refugees from the wars in El Salvador and Guatemala. Maybe the white men had counted themselves, then counted the Indians. What Tacho saw as the refugees increased was white men would soon be outnumbered by Indians throughout Mexico. Police patrols had been increased, sweeps were made twice a day through the market for refugees to drag away for "interrogation," and if they survived, to refugee camps miles away from the border. Tacho had watched the patrols arrest three Peruvians who were not refugees, but merchants accustomed to travel who carried all the necessary papers. But papers made no difference to police since infiltrators and spies always carried the "correct" papers. The police patrol had seized the bundles of dried plant stalks and leaves, the odd roots and envelopes of seeds and dried leaves the Peruvians had displayed on their blankets. After the police had left with the Peruvians, Tacho had joined the others on the spot where the Peruvians had spread their blankets. No one said anything. The children poked around in the dirt looking for coins that might have been lost in the confusion. In the weeds and debris where the police van had been parked, Tacho looked down and saw a bundle wrapped in newspaper. Tacho moved away from the bundle casually and waited until the crowd had scattered.

Tacho had tried to slow his heart's pounding by staring up at the sun in the sky; somehow he had known the packet would be lying there. Tacho stood a distance away. The bundle was waiting for him to pick it up; Tacho could feel this more strongly than he had ever felt anything before. Tacho felt an urgency as if a beloved or person of great importance were waiting for him, *expecting* a welcome, expecting hospitality.

"Sorcerers work in cities," people say; maybe the Peruvians had been "witches." But he wasn't afraid; he did not feel his guts churn or cold sweat on his feet as sorcery victims usually reported.

A life might be short or a life might be long; duration mattered little. What did matter was how one lived until one died. Tacho examined his conscience carefully; he must not go to the bundle if his motives were selfish; he must not pick up the bundle if he wanted riches or a long life or an easy life. For riches and a long life Tacho knew all he had to do was continue to serve Menardo; the boss was more superstitious than ever; he had even split the winnings 80–20 the last time Tacho had correctly "read the numbers."

Tacho placed the bundle inside the cigar box where he kept his other valuables. He did not open the bundle until El Feo was with him. Luckily the wild woman had not come with El Feo. Tacho was not sure if Angelita should see the bundle. She believed in diesel generators, minivans, and dynamite; she had gone to Mexico City with the Cuban, Bartolomeo, to ask for more "direct aid" from their "foreign friends." Angelita said this was because an Indian *woman* on television made white men feel less afraid than if they saw a handsome devil such as El

Feo. If that was what white men thought, then whites were fools; because a woman such as Angelita was more deadly and fierce in battle than many men.

El Feo did not speak for a long time after Tacho told him about the bundle. With El Feo present, Tacho had been aware of the bundle again as a presence; with El Feo there, the bundle wanted to be opened.

"Well, well," El Feo said as he carefully unwrapped the bundle. Inside was an opal the size of a macaw egg. The stone had been "dressed," wrapped in red wool string and downy, white feathers. Twelve big coca leaves and a pinch of cornmeal had been packed with the opal to feed it. El Feo touched the opal cautiously. "You don't know anymore with these Peruvians and Bolivians all crawling out of the hills to sell 'Inca long-life capsules.'" The twelve perfect coca leaves were religious objects too.

Tacho shook his head. He thought 95 percent of supposed witch-craft and sorcery was superstition and puffed-up talk. But 5 percent . . . "Only five percent?" El Feo had laughed loudly and shook his head at Tacho. For twins, they did not look much alike. When they were arguing, Tacho got stiff and did not say much, while El Feo thought everything was funny. Someplaces there were entire villages populated by sorcerers, all living together by mutual pledge to prey only on out-siders. Their pledges were frequently broken, and they turned upon one another in the most bloodthirsty manner; brother killed brother, sister devoured sister. This destruction, this sorcery, this witchcraft, occured among all human beings. The killing and devouring occurred behind bedroom doors, inflicted by parents and relatives, and the village of sorcerers continues generation after generation without interruption.

El Feo had had actual experience himself with a village of witches. El Feo's baseball team had attended national playoffs one year in Ve-racruz and had had to play the baseball team sent to represent a village of witches. The village of witches was wealthy because they had tapped into the great inter-American market for "Inca secrets" and "Aztec magic". European descendants on American soil anxiously purchased indigenous cures for their dark nights of the soul on the continents where Christianity had repeatedly violated its own canons, and only the Indians could still see the Blessed Virgin among the December roses, her skin color and clothing Native American, not European.

The village of sorcerers had got rich making up and selling various odd sorts of alleged "tribal healing magics" and assorted elixirs, teas, balms, waters, crystals, and capsules to the city people, mostly whites.

But more and more mestizos too had secretly begun to consult the Indians. They all wanted to keep the consultations secret to avoid embarrassment or possible excommunication from the Church. The sorcerers listened to the ailments and complaints of the city patients to gain knowledge of the patients' lives; the cures the sorcerers had then sold their "patients" had cost hundreds, but consisted mostly of floor sweepings containing rodent dung and cotton lint. A piece of paper had been packed with each talisman, amulet, charm, or medicine the village salesmen sold. It was called a simple remedy for all illness and evil; it had been written in crude Spanish and copies had been made with faded-purple mimeograph ink.

Ritual of the Four World Quarters

> Jesus, Mary, St. Joseph! Holy Trinity!
> All the saints, and all the souls of the living and the
>   dead!
> The Heart of Heaven who is called Huracan is the long flash
>   of lightnings
> The green flash of lightning
> And the deafening crash of lightning.
> Grandmother of the Dawn
> Grandmother of the Day!
> They looked like humans
> They talked like humans
> They populated the earth
> They existed and multiplied
> They had daughters and they had sons.
> These wooden figures had no minds or souls.
> They did not remember their Creator.
> They walked on all fours aimlessly.
> They no longer remembered the Heart of Heaven and so
> They fell from grace.
> They were merely the first attempt at human beings.
> At first they spoke but their faces were blank.
> Their hands and feet had no strength
> They had no blood, no substance
>   no moisture, no flesh.
> Their cheeks were dry, their hands and feet dry
>   and their skin was yellow.
> Burning pine-pitch rains from the sky.

Death Macaw gouges their eyes
Death Jaguar devours their flesh
Death Crocodile breaks and mangles their nerves and bones
     and crumbles them to dust.

THE OPAL

THE OPAL DID NOT appear to be a fake, wrapped up to fool rich society women. They both knew the danger of looking at the opal unless they were prepared; the eye of the opal might show them anything; the "eye" might take them anywhere. El Feo had glanced down for only an instant, but he had seen the Cuban, Bartolomeo, his hairy bare bottom bouncing on top of Angelita in Mexico City. That hadn't been news to El Feo, but all the same, the opal might show anything, even the most trivial or embarrassing. El Feo said that was another reason Tacho should keep the bundle; the opal might show too much; a man might see the struggle and suffering to come and lose heart. Angelita with the Cuban wasn't pretty, but it was necessary: to get back the land was everything.

After El Feo had gone back to the mountains, Tacho had not been able to resist; the bundle was inviting him to take a look. All he had to do was to ask, and the eye would show him everything everywhere— all that had been, all that would be. All El Feo had done was glance down and he had seen more than he had bargained for; Tacho took the stone in the palm of his hand, and with his eyes closed he had exhaled to feed the opal's spirit his own breath. When Tacho had opened his eyes, the unpolished surface of the opal appeared as thick layers of clouds high over the earth. Tacho peered down through the clouds and could see glittering sapphire blues and emerald greens of the Pacific Ocean, and the long coastline, longer than Tacho had ever imagined, the coast- line of the Pacific all the way from Chile to Alaska. Then the clouds seemed to darken and thicken and there was fire; Tacho watched great cities burn; torches of ruby and garnet mushroomed hundreds of feet into the sky. Tacho had strained to see landmarks more clearly, but one city was larger than any Tacho had ever seen. Then he knew: he was watching Mexico City burn again, but this time the sacred macaws had watched as cages full of human cannibal-sorcerers went up in smoke.

Before Tacho returned the bundle to its box, he tried to ask the opal to show him his own life, but all Tacho had been able to see was the unpolished gray surface of the stone. Carefully he rewrapped the opal and returned it to its box. The eye had closed for now.

RIOTS WORLDWIDE

MENARDO HAD WATCHED satellite television until dawn. Menardo sipped hot brandy and chocolate to soothe his nerves. At dawn a strange fatigue and sleepiness would overcome him; then Menardo would be able to sleep without dreams for a few hours. Recently though, Menardo had found the satellite television news irritating, even upsetting; images of the hordes of dirty rabble—the mobs shrieking and stampeding in front of police armored cars or military tanks did not calm his ragged nerves. All over the world, everywhere, the TV cameras showed civil wars. The video images brought back the university riots many years before in Mexico City. Menardo had had heavily insured businessmen in the Federal District, and he watched himself age ten years in one week as the rioting began to spread to involve other sectors of Mexico City. If the riots had not been stopped, Menardo's losses might have run to billions of pesos, and Universal Insurance would have been ruined.

For years Menardo had not had to worry about the "civil strife, strike, or insurrection" clause of his insurance policies. The long-haired, filthy communists had disappeared from television screens, and Menardo believed the days of mobs and riots had truly passed. Then suddenly one night Menardo had awakened to a loud buzzing sound. The screen of his television had been filled with what appeared to be larvae or insects swarming. When Menardo had raised the volume and looked closely, he saw the swarms were mobs of angry brown people swarming like bees from horizon to horizon. At first Menardo had thought he was seeing a rerun of videotapes taken at the Mexico City riots years before; then, looking more closely, he had seen the city was Miami, and the

mobs, American. All over the world money was the glue that held societies together. Without money or jobs even the U.S. was suffering
crippling strikes as well as riots and looting. Cities such as Philadelphia
that were bankrupt had to appeal for the National Guard, but riots in
Detroit, Washington, and New York City had also required federal
troops. Menardo shook his head. He didn't like the look of things in
the United States. What a shame such a power as the U.S. had gone the
same direction as England and Russia. Almost overnight, the people had
discovered all their national treasuries were empty, and now everywhere
there were riots.

Menardo dozed off, only to suffer a bad dream. In the dream,
Menardo had been running to find his security units in armored trucks;
but when he reached the village square, the trucks were there, but his
men were not. With the crowd advancing toward him, Menardo had
frantically tried to fire upon the mob from a truck, but the mechanism
in the machine gun had malfunctioned, and instead of exploding shells,
all Menardo had heard was *click-click, click-click.* Then the armored
truck with Menardo inside had been engulfed by the mob, who rolled
the vehicle down the street ahead of them. The mob pushed the vehicle
into the sea. As the dark, cold water had closed around Menardo to
suffocate and crush him, he awoke sweating and panting with the bed
sheet twisted partially around his neck. All the other bedding had been
kicked on the floor.

Menardo asked Tacho what the meaning of such a dream might
be. Menardo had lied and said the dream was not his, but belonged "to
a friend." Tacho had asked if the "friend" was a white man or an Indian,
but Menardo refused to say. Why should the meaning change for an
Indian? Menardo had demanded to know. Tacho had only smiled faintly
and did not answer.

"If your friend is a white man, the dream is about his fear of being
born. But if your friend is an Indian, the dream is about a sacrifice for
close family members." Tacho had watched Menardo's expression in
the rearview mirror. "Oh, oh, I see." Menardo began nodding his head;
he didn't really "see" at all, but he was hoping the Indian would let it
go at that because he had drunk too much brandy getting back to sleep
after the nightmare.

Menardo blamed television. Monkey see, monkey do. There was
nothing wrong with television for entertainment, but the broadcasting
of mobs and riots was precisely what the terrorists had wanted. All

anyone had to do was look around. At the market, rival food vendors had rigged tiny Korean televisions with wires to car batteries to lure customers, who ate friend dough or tripe while their eyes never left the TV screen. Television showed everything—it showed too much. Menardo had to shudder whenever he recalled the videotapes the police chief had showed him and the others in their shooting club. Still the use of video to control criminals and terrorists was entirely a different matter.

Menardo blamed television commercials designed to seduce and bewitch viewers who would never get any closer to the objects of desire than the television screen, or store windows, which looters smashed with bricks. That was the trouble! Television spoiled secrecy. What common people did not see, they did not covet. If you had a little money set aside, you had to hide it or your relatives and in-laws would borrow and steal you blind. How could storekeepers fill their shop windows with televisions and not expect the ignorant rabble to steal them? The ignorant rabble did not understand the struggles of the small businessman; even Menardo, as successful as he had been, had to face competition from giant insurance companies with multinational holdings to cushion their losses. Looters saw window displays of tape and CD players, and to them, the merchant who owned the store appeared to be a millionaire. What did ignorant Indians know about conducting a successful business? All they wanted to do was waste money and time on village feast days, special "remembrances" for beloved relatives, and ailing clanspeople. Menardo could have been like the others—like his cousins who stayed up all night listening to old men talk about devils and ghosts. Menardo could have taken the easy way out like the others and lain back in a dirt-wall house playing with the babies and the children while his Indian wife supported them from sales of eggs and poultry at the market. In cities, the Indians behaved no differently. The men did nothing. Menardo hated to see them smoking and talking in twos and threes on street corners. Not only did the Indians not make anything of themselves, they had tried to *unmake* any of their own people who tried to succeed. Menardo had seen Tacho's brother and the other village louts slinking in and out of Tacho's quarters, no doubt to beg money or to sleep. Ordinarily, Menardo would have forbidden the visits, but Tacho was different from other Indians Menardo had employed; Tacho had special abilities to interpret dreams.

SONNY BLUE AND ALEGRÍA

JUST AS HIS FRIEND Sonny Blue had said, the world wasn't such a pretty place these days. That had been the reason for the special gift of the vest. Menardo had examined the vest again and again, running his fingers along the reinforced nylon stitching that secured the "wonder fiber" panels in the vest. A modern miracle of high technology, the wonder fiber was neither bulky nor heavy but possessed a unique density that stopped knives and bullets, including .357-magnum slugs, the brochure said. The brochure also included color diagrams, and a number of actual photographs of test models who had been shot and stabbed in laboratory tests. The miracle fiber made the vest comfortable and inconspicuous.

Menardo had adopted a policy of strict secrecy about the vest. He warned Alegría not to mention a word, nothing about body armor, without secrecy what good were the precautions? He had even asked Alegría to wash the vest by hand in the bathroom sink because Menardo did not trust the maids. No one but the two of them, and of course Sonny Blue, must know about the vest. Menardo had not told General J. or the police chief, though he had been tempted because he knew they would be envious. But since the flood of refugees from the South and the strikes and demonstrations in the northern cities of Guadalajara and Juárez, Menardo had noticed a change in his two friends.

The chief usually laughed and talked when others were firing; but last week he had appeared startled when the governor took his turn on the firing range. The former ambassador, the doctor, and the others had joined in making a big joke out of the jumpy police chief. "An angry wife, a neglected mistress, a scolding father-in-law?" the former ambassador quipped. But Menardo had seen General J. was not laughing. The general had been traveling a great deal lately, and although Menardo believed in secrecy, he felt a seed of concern taking root in his lower intestines. After all, he and General J. were partners; in the years they had done business together, they had become *more* than partners, and yet the general had told Menardo nothing about these trips. Now the police chief's edgy behavior had added to the tension.

EMPEROR MAXIMILIAN
AND CHARLOTTE

ALEGRÍA HAD NOT had sex with Menardo since Sonny Blue brought the bulletproof vest, but the ugly surprise of Bartolomeo had made her worry about the spy, Tacho. She knew how much Menardo relied upon Tacho's "dream-reading"; it would not be easy to get rid of the Indian. She might have to settle for Tacho's "promotion," perhaps to caretaker at the beach house. Sex with Menardo used to get Alegría almost anything, but she could hardly remember it seemed so long ago that Menardo had been her lover in the Rose Suite of the Royal Hotel. To endure sex with Menardo, Alegría had imagined she was making love with Sonny Blue in the honeymoon suite of a faraway hotel, perhaps in Singapore. One glimpse of Menardo cinched with the white webbing of the vest had been enough to fill her with loathing. The bulletproof vest felt unyielding, but this had aroused Alegría as long as she imagined Sonny Blue wore the vest, and not Menardo. Menardo had snorted and huffed away on top of Alegría, who had orgasm after orgasm, one wave following another in a great warm ocean. Once Bartolomeo had accused Alegría of engaging in mutual masturbation because she had admitted to him that fantasies were necessary to her pleasure. Menardo had labored a long time before he had finally come, and Alegría could feel what feeble, dry ejaculations they were. His University of Arizona fraternity brothers had taught Sonny Blue to be proud of the quantity of his ejaculation; he had even cautioned Alegría about the mess on the sheets. Whispering his confession seemed to excite Sonny even more.

Sonny had asked Alegría why she stayed with Menardo, but she had refused to discuss her marriage. Sonny had heard rumors about the "other wife" and her strange accident on the marble stairs.

"You don't love him," Sonny had said, trying to push her. "Why him?" But Alegría had just shaken her head. She did not want to talk or think about Menardo; she wanted to think about Sonny Blue and to imagine herself as the love of his life, pampered and protected. Sonny Blue had asked more questions about Menardo than he had asked about her; the whole time Sonny had been talking he had been stroking her breasts and flicking her nipples.

Alegría had to talk fast before Menardo rolled over and fell asleep with his arms wrapped around himself and his vest. "I'm worried about the beach house, Menardo. The federal police are worse thieves than the Indians."

"Don't worry now! Don't worry at a time like this!" Menardo laughed wickedly, as if his sexual performance had been so astounding it had left Alegría panting for more.

"We could send Tacho down to watch the house."

"I need Tacho here. The others can't drive like he does. I'll send security patrolmen." Menardo's breathing was slowing, and Alegría could feel his fingers gradually loosen from her breast as he drifted to sleep.

"I don't trust Tacho," Alegría said, raising her voice slightly. "You worry," she said, tugging at the edge of the bulletproof vest that pressed into Menardo's soft flesh at the belly button. "You worry about assassin squads—"

"*I worry* about sleep. Tacho isn't one of them. Go to sleep."

Alegría had never liked the Indian chauffeur, but from the start Menardo had been stubborn about getting rid of Tacho. Alegría knew Tacho had got a hold over Menardo with all the baloney about dreams and numbers. "Menardo, listen to me. I lived in Mexico City. I know."

"Know what?" Menardo had almost dropped off to sleep.

Alegría said nothing. She waited until Menardo began to snore, then she got out of bed and walked to the French doors that opened to the balcony.

There was no moon and the jungle foliage seemed to absorb all light from the stars and even reflected light from the town. Alegría stared at the garage where the chauffeur slept; sometimes she was not able to sleep and had walked downstairs in the night only to see lights on in the garage, and sometimes a figure or figures moving past the small window. Alegría left Menardo's room, but did not feel sleepy. She could feel the adrenaline pulse in her veins, left over from Bartolomeo's visit. Something did not add up: Bartolomeo had been able to find her and her store too easily. Bartolomeo had been talking to his Indians—his puppets, his toys; he had got the information from them. Tacho was the link. Alegría had walked slowly down the polished marble stairs, aware of the gridwork of grooves that had been chiseled the length of each stair after Iliana's tragic fall. Alegría seldom thought about Iliana, but she thought a great deal about the house. Alegría went to the lights and the switches of the alarm system to flick them off so she could walk outside to the pool.

After the house air-conditioning, the night air felt steamy; the night cries of birds and small animals in the jungle were interrupted by the barking of dogs, big Alsatian shepherds that guarded a coffee-grower's estate nearby. Universal Insurance had, of course, provided the coffee-grower's security system. How would it look if the president of Universal Insurance and Security or his next-door neighbors were attacked by thieves or terrorists?

The house, the gardens, and the pool had all been designed by Alegría, yet she felt indifferent about them the way she had felt indifferent about her apartment in Mexico City. Alegría blamed her father's diplomatic corps assignments because they had always kept moving—Lisbon, Madrid, Mexico City, and finally, Caracas. Her father had transferred them deliberately so she might become a citizen of the world, not just Mexico. Sometimes her indifference frightened her, and she willed herself to feel something, even hatred. She had been attracted to Bartolomeo and other leftists because she could feel the hatred they had. She was fascinated by the intensity of their hatred; otherwise politics bored her.

Her father claimed his family had descended from royalty—Emperor Maximilian's cousins. On her fifteenth birthday, her father had presented her with "a history of the family," a book about Emperor Maximilian and the empress, Charlotte. Her mother had disapproved of the book for a young girl; this opposition had made the book irresistible. In the evenings Alegría's father had called her into his study and closed the door; but before her father quizzed her about the pages she had read, he would launch into his speech about diplomacy. The art of diplomacy. The Empress Charlotte had been lacking in the art.

Her father had endlessly meditated on Maximilian's fall; but for the fall, their family might have reigned as monarchs in Mexico; territories in the North would never have been lost to the gringos. Patiently her father had explained that when noble individuals fell from high positions, the correct term, the only word adequate, was *tragedy*. When he talked about what might have been, Alegría saw tears in his eyes. The sight of his tears had been strangely exhilarating. Alegría never forgot the story. Her father had researched and read obsessively about Maximilian's fall. Heartless and craven, the European nations had turned their backs on one of their "own" while the wolves closed in on the palace.

The European powers had sent young Maximilian and his wife, Charlotte, to reign as emperor and empress of Mexico. Maximilian became impotent on the voyage to Mexico. Maximilian regained his potency only in the dark flesh of Indian women. Charlotte wrote to her mother of her disappointment; she was twenty-five years old and her time for love and lovemaking were over. Charlotte traveled to Yucatan, and at the ancient ruins of Uxmal she had paused before a carved stone, undecipherable and erect. Although it was late December, the empress was suddenly overcome by the tropical heat. Charlotte returned from Yucatan anxious and depressed, although she did not understand why. Rumors in the palace named the toloache, a toxic plant, possibly sacred datura, which in small doses is known to disturb the mind.

Charlotte became hysterical as new clutches of spiders' eggs were discovered on the red damask sofa. She gave strict orders the entire castle at Chapultepec be fumigated. She accused Maximilian of carelessly allowing his live specimens to escape from their jars and crawl downstairs from the attic laboratory. Charlotte's nightmares were of insects and vermin in the Montezuma Castle. The emperor began to sleep on the billiard table.

Maximilian had been stunned by the expense of fielding troops to fight the Indian Juárez and his partisan army. The Imperial Treasury of Mexico was dangerously overdrawn. Maximilian's scheme for raising money called for the colonization of Mexico by Confederate refugees from the American Civil War. A commander from Texas named McGruder administered the Land Office for Confederate Colonies across northeastern Mexico. Juárez and his army of partisans were joined by Indians dispossessed by the Confederate settlers.

Charlotte was no longer able to sleep at night and roamed in her carriage to revisit sites of past banquets and balls. The European powers did not respond to Maximilian's pleas for money; Charlotte traveled to Paris to beg help from her sister, Eugénie, wife of Emperor Napoleon.

At Acalcingo, Juáristas stole the six white mules that pulled Maximilian's carriage. Meanwhile, at St.-Nazaire, nothing had been prepared for Charlotte's reception. Prussia had invaded Bohemia, and the European powers had forgotten about the empire in Mexico. The Empress

Eugénie assured her sister privately, but the European powers had written off Mexico as lost.

Charlotte's mental confusion increased during her private audience with Pope Pius IX, and she insisted she must drink the Pope's hot chocolate because all her food was poisoned.

Maximilian's secret messengers were betrayed, one after the other. Their corpses were hung from poles in Liberal trenches with signs from their necks that read "Imperial Courier."

Charlotte's madness in no way diminished her physical health. She was more beautiful than before, shut away with her servants in a wing of the palace at Tervueren.

Maximilian died before a firing squad. Juáristas refused to deliver his corpse to sympathizers. The embalmers failed at their first attempt and there was a threat of international protest. Maximilian's corpse had to be rewashed in arsenic solution and wrapped in bandages followed by a coat of varnish. The corpse was then suspended by ropes from the hospital ceiling to allow the varnish to dry. Juárez and his personal physician visited the hospital secretly in the middle of the night. All others were barred until the varnish dried. Juárez remarked the smell was not so bad after all.

Alegría knew the story by heart; it had been Bartolomeo's favorite story. He was dead now. How he had enjoyed tormenting Alegría about her butchered faux royal ancestors.

Alegría had been thinking about the future, her future. She had to get out of Mexico. Bartolomeo might not get to first base with his accusations against her, but his sudden appearance was an ominous sign about local politics and the mood of the Indians in the mountains. The least connection with Bartolomeo would be enough for General J. and the police chief to make a stink to Menardo. All over Mexico, local skirmishes between rival political parties had convinced both General J. and the police chief that communist agents were everywhere spreading their cancer of communism among ignorant, lazy Indians and half-breeds who would like nothing better than to see communism feed them while they idled away the day.

Bartolomeo spelled *blackmail*. Next he would be asking Alegría for little favors, not just sex. Next Bartolomeo would ask Alegría to hide caches of ammunition or even weapons in her store warehouse. Back upstairs in her own bedroom, Alegría took stock of her jewelry and the cash in the closet floor vault. Bartolomeo might not be able to convince

General J. or the police chief about Alegría's leftist "flirtations," but their wives and others in Tuxtla society would persuade them. Alegría had already provided Tuxtla society with sensational gossip, which had climaxed with the death of Iliana, whom they had all secretly hated. Yet they expected Alegría to give them more sensational gossip, and Bartolomeo was liable to deliver what they had been waiting for.

Alegría remained calm. She was thinking about Sonny Blue in Tucson. She wasn't worried. She had a plan, and if it failed, then she would find Sonny Blue. She had been thinking about the bomb accident in Mexico City; funny thing how Bartolomeo always escaped while the others died. There was always the spy, Tacho. Maybe Tacho could be of some use to her; maybe he would obligingly carry back certain misinformation about Comrade Bartolomeo.

As for Menardo, he had become a virtual basket case, obsessed with assassins since he had got the bulletproof vest. Menardo had begun to spend hours driving around Tuxtla making notes on intersections and possible ambush sites for terrorist kidnappers. Menardo had insisted that Alegría be accompanied at all times by her own bodyguard, though so far Alegría had refused. She said she did not want to call attention to herself, but Alegría had a great deal she wished to conceal.

How would it look to the world if the wife of the president of Universal Insurance and Security had been kidnapped by terrorist kidnappers? Alegría had only shrugged her shoulders at Menardo. Did he really care about her or was she merely a prized possession? Menardo apologized desperately: Alegría could have anything she wanted and she would have nothing she did not desire; that included bodyguards. She no longer had to ride with Tacho if she felt taxis were safer.

UNEASE AND SUSPICION

MENARDO HAD TRIED months before to stop Alegría from going to her interior-decorator shop every day. He feared she would make an easy target for leftists at her shop. He wanted her to remain safely occupied with the other wives, who shopped together, then played canasta until seven at the country club. Why didn't Alegría make things easier for him? Menardo had been disappointed to wake up alone in his bed. Alegría hated the vest and had returned to her own bed sometime after he was asleep. Iliana had been barren, and Menardo wanted children; but Alegría did not stay in bed long enough for him even to start a baby. Only the year before, they had been newlyweds, and Alegría had wrapped her naked body around his and begged for more, more, more!

Menardo had not seen it coming, whatever it was that overshadowed him now. He could feel a presence that had gradually occupied his consciousness, an intuition that very soon this world would become fragmented and scatter apart. His partnership with General J. and the "silent partners" had begun to suck Menardo into the dark undertow of politics. Bombings by terrorists had been stepped up in Guadalajara and Mexico City; huge power-transmission-line towers had been dynamited outside both cities. In the darkness, looting started; then police and soldiers arrived and opened fire. The looters became rioters, and soldiers and rioters had been killed.

Like satellite TV, everywhere available to everyone, dynamite in Mexico was also everywhere available, sold too cheaply and in great volume to foreign mining companies who wanted to blow up all of Mexico looking for gold or uranium. Meanwhile the dynamite was being stolen by the ton, and leftists were trying to outblast the mining companies. Menardo hated bombs; only bullets were precise and just. Bombs too easily killed innocent people. After the bombing in Tuxtla, Menardo had given Tacho strict orders. Three times a day like clockwork Tacho had removed his chauffeur's coat and slipped clean overalls over his uniform trousers and shirt. Then Tacho had groomed the undercarriage, frame, and motor of the Mercedes, combing it from front to rear as he lay on his back, scooting along on a piece of cardboard on the lookout for bombs.

The others at the shooting range had not seemed to notice, but Menardo began to wonder if they had only been pretending. Others less acute might not have noticed, but the general had no longer looked directly at Menardo. If Menardo tried to lower his eyes or in any way catch the general's eye, the general had avoided his gaze. The general had been so casual the others had not noticed, and when Menardo had asked if something was wrong, the general had smiled broadly and laughed, saying, of course not, how ridiculous, as he gazed at the wall behind Menardo's head.

Menardo began to regret he had brought Sonny Blue to Tuxtla

when they could as easily have met in Mexico city. He regretted the secrecy, which had really been unnecessary, and might now have undermined the general's trust in Menardo. Menardo blamed the political upheaval in the South. He had begun to receive emergency calls from clients in Guatemala, San Salvador, and Honduras—day and night— with claims for warehouses and property gutted by fires set by Indian guerrilla units. Menardo had stepped up security patrols for all industrial and commercial clients, marking their locations on a wall map with colored plastic pins. Red pins were units of five men; blue pins were units of ten men. The black pins marked the scenes of labor-union disputes, riots, or demonstrations, which were strictly the domain of General J. because federal troops were sent out in those cases, at no charge to Universal. Because what was good for businessmen and industrialists was good for Mexico.

The refugee situation had suddenly filled the town with foreigners and suspicious-looking Mexican tourists from the capital, who were undercover agents for internal security. The police chief had pointed out the secret agents to Menardo and the other members of their private shooting club. Later Menardo had noticed the police chief sneaking glances at him, and one evening at dinner at the country club Menardo had noticed General J. staring at him from across the club's main dining room. But when Menardo had crossed the room to greet General J., he pretended he had not noticed Menardo.

Menardo knew the general had been flying to Honduras and Costa Rica for a series of meetings with certain Americans. The general had called the meetings "strictly military"—but Menardo could feel tension in their phone conversations. The general had been uncharacteristically gracious and reassuring about the gringos. It was not a question of losing something but of both Menardo and their company gaining a great deal.

The general reminded Menardo about the video cameras the Americans had given the police chief; these were good examples of the usefulness of gifts from the United States government. Security had been too strict to allow Menardo to meet the Americans until later. Menardo felt uneasy, but security was the domain of the general, just as the accounts, policies, and premium payments were the domain of Menardo. General J. seldom had questions about auditor's reports, so he did not expect questions from Menardo about security matters.

Menardo did not feel better after General J. went on to explain the U.S. government had new military field equipment they needed to test under actual combat conditions. Test equipment given away by gringos was equipment the police and the army did not have to buy from Menardo. In the years they had done business together, they had become more than partners. They had been like brothers who looked out for one another. The general had also been fortunate to marry into a prominent family from Tuxtla. They used to get drunk together regularly in the early years to talk business and to make future plans. They had both faced the opposition from the families of their wives, but what sweet satisfaction, what revenge, Menardo and the general had had! What mattered nowadays was money, and even though the "high society" of Tuxtla might groan or grit their teeth, their sisters and daughters had gone to the highest bidders as they always had. The difference now was men such as Menardo and the general had more wealth than the "blue bloods," who had squandered billions since the Second World War. The general had always gone further to insult the manhood of the upper classes, saying there were no virile blue bloods, and that the aristocratic class owed its continuance to the secret liaisons between their women and real men such as himself and Menardo.

Menardo had tried to telephone his friend the general twice earlier in the week, but each time the secretary had said the general was out of the office. After his last round of secret meetings with the U.S. military, General J. had promised a full report to Menardo. Fortunately there was always Friday afternoon at the shooting range. Menardo could take his partner aside and they could arrange to have dinner later. Menardo had not felt such uneasiness since his childhood, when the others had made jokes and kept secrets from him.

Even Alegría had noticed Menardo's nervousness on Wednesday. At first Menardo had tried to deny anything was bothering him, but Alegría had been strangely insistent; she wanted to know what was wrong. Alegría had even guessed it was something to do with the general. She got quite excited and demanded to know what was wrong between him and the general. "Wrong? What could be wrong?" Menardo had raised his voice indignantly; he did not see how Alegría could jump to the conclusion something was wrong. Women did not understand the friendship men shared, otherwise Alegría would have known that everything was fine, everything was going great and was about to get even better. Let the general do the talking. These United States "businessmen" wanted to remain behind the scenes; they needed reliable local "partners." Wednesday evening at dinner Alegría had mentioned the women's club was only meeting twice a month now. Alegría said she did not care since she had wanted to take some business trips to the United States later anyway.

Changes were all around. The phrase repeated over and over inside Menardo's brain. The old man had always put the phrase at the beginning of the story about Prince Seven Macaws, who had been undone by two sorcerer brothers. Menardo had no control over his thoughts lately because of the worry. Somehow the worry had mobilized Menardo's earliest memories, and he remembered the voice of the old man, his grandfather, acting out stories and changing his voice for different characters.

Changes were everywhere. Aircraft and helicopters supplied by the United States government were on patrol for groups of illegal refugees, who anyone could see were leftist strike units disguised as Salvadorean or Guatemalan refugees. Menardo had agreed with the police chief and the general: only blood spoke loudly enough; "shoot to kill" was the only answer, but the politicians and diplomats weren't buying. Satellite television was to blame. Blood spoke too loudly for television. International outcry followed. That had been the reason the police chief had "secret units," and the military had always had "counterintelligence units."

ILLEGAL REFUGEES

AT THE CLUB on Friday, Menardo intended to talk with the police chief, and then to the general, each separately. Menardo sensed a growing conflict between the military and the police. The police chief supported the capture and incarceration of illegal refugees by the State Police, who had always attended to matters of internal state security. But the general argued the military must be called in. The police chief did not deny the refugees might be secret enemy agents—saboteurs and provocateurs sent north to wreak havoc on Mexico City. The chief favored refugee prison camps where the refugees could do field work at nearby plantations during the day. The plan called for hiring hundreds of new police officers and would cost millions. General J. opposed any more refugee prison camps. He advocated harsher measures.

Menardo agreed with General J. that the bands of illegal refugees trying to make a run for it should be gunned down from the air like coyotes or wolves. A little blood here and there was better than big pools of blood flashed across the globe by satellite TV. Mass the refugees in camps and sooner or later, as their numbers grew, so would their unrest and boldness until a bloodbath occurred.

Menardo agreed with the general the best policy was to kill them as you found them. Otherwise, you ran into all the logistical problems the Germans had encountered with disposing of the Jews. General J. thought Hitler had underestimated the German people. The Jews could have been killed by mobs and death squads without the cumbersome and incriminating death factories. Fifty here, a hundred there—the numbers added up over weeks and months at a steady rate; this was why "disappearances" and death squads were superior to Hitler's death factories.

General J. prided himself on his knowledge of military history. If Hitler had not been crazy, he might have realized it was not necessary to kill all the Jews. The general himself would have killed only key figures, and the remaining Jews would have been demoralized and docile the way the remaining Indians were. But the Jews would have made far superior slaves than Indians ever had; Hitler had wasted great potential. German factories might have hummed night and day powered with Jews, and the Germans might have been the first nation to enjoy complete leisure and wealth in the industrial age.

Indians however were the worst workers—slow, sloppy, and destructive of tools and machinery. Indians were a waste of time and money. No refugee camps for them—the best policy was quick annihilation on the spot, far, far from satellite TV cameras. The general and Menardo had agreed on that. Menardo and his friend had agreed on nearly all things.

Thursday evening Menardo had quarreled with Alegría at the dinner table, and she had left the room in tears. She had been asking question after question about the general, about the governor, about the chief of police. She kept coming back to the police chief until finally Menardo had lost his temper. Alegría was not just another wife—he knew that. Other women did not bother about their husbands' colleagues.

Later Menardo had knocked softly on Alegría's bedroom door and had held his breath so he could hear if she replied. Menardo wanted to explain himself. He wanted to explain the entire situation; he had never told her about "the concerns" his partner and others in his club had expressed when he had announced his marriage with her. Menardo thought Alegría should be alerted about some of the people she had associated with at the university. Subversives and radicals were thick— communists were everywhere, so Menardo could hardly blame Alegría. She had told him about the classes she had taught at the university, and of course it wasn't her fault if communists had enrolled.

Alegría did not answer his knocks, so Menardo had poured himself a big brandy to carry to bed. With the brandy he could gradually put distance between himself and the worries that lined themselves in rows like soldiers. Riots and looting had resulted in heavy casualty losses, millions and millions in claims that Universal Insurance had to pay. Menardo felt the brandy begin to ease the tension he felt in his stomach. He sat in bed watching satellite television with the sound off—an international beauty pageant on a beach somewhere. Innocent enough, but sometimes lately, a word or even a phrase was enough to set off a tight, panicky feeling in his chest. The hot vapors of the brandy rolled down his throat and pushed aside all effects of the words. Words, only words. *Rifle, revolver, return.*

Menardo had dozed off for only an instant because when he awoke, again the bathing suit contest was still on the TV screen. But in the instant Menardo had fallen asleep, he had begun to dream. He was a tiny child in the village again, carried in the old man's arms; Indians from nearby villages had joined the others in long lines to greet Menardo in his grandpa's arms. The faces Menardo saw in the dream he recognized as all the old people who had passed on; they called him storekeeper and asked him to sell them food on credit. Although only an infant in the dream, Menardo had been able to talk, but only Spanish, which none of the old ones seemed to understand. He felt the greatest anxiety trying to make himself understood by the Indians, who could be seen in the distance joining the line of people already waiting to speak to Menardo. *Return. We return.* He was trying to explain to them he did not have enough to feed everyone, not enough to go around, but they understood no Spanish, only Indian, which Menardo had refused to learn.

The dream did not frighten him, but he was puzzled because he had not dreamed about the village or the old people there since his youth. Then suddenly they had all been lined up—probably because the TV beauty-pageant contestants had all been lined up. Menardo poured himself more brandy. The liquor created an invisible, warm wing that lifted him up, out of the reach of the words, where he floated more powerful than any of them—the general, the governor, or the police chief. He finished the brandy and closed his eyes to enjoy the sensation. He rubbed his fingers lightly over the left front panel of the vest inside his pajama top. The triumph of modern science—man-made fiber, rayon, nylon, and now the deceptively thin and soft fibers of "wonder fabric" that stopped all bullets and knife blades.

The beauty pageant was no longer as soothing to watch because the young, ripe beauties who had just been eliminated were huddled together bewildered, while ten smiling finalists stood front stage in the spotlight. Menardo frowned. He did not like to see weeping women, not even when they were beauties in bikinis. What did they expect? They could not *all* be chosen. Menardo had never been chosen for school teams—soccer or baseball—because he had been too fat. Menardo snapped off the television and reached for the information booklet about the vest. He was familiar with the diagrams and the cross-section drawings illustrating how bullets became enmeshed in the wonder fibers that saved your life. He did not like to admit this to himself, but he had begun to enjoy the nightly ritual of the brandy, then looking at himself in the mirror wearing the vest and pajama bottoms. The vest was bright white against his skin. He appreciated the low cut in the front and back, which protected his genitals and lower spine. It was perfect. Lightweight and whisper soft; only your wife knew you were wearing body armor. Secrecy was essential; otherwise assassins aimed for the head. The brochure on the vest always made good bedtime reading because the technical details gradually put one to sleep. The photographs of actual tests filled Menardo with confidence. All of it was a matter of trust—trust of the high technology that had woven the vest fibers, and trust in those most intimate with you. *Trust.* Menardo had repeated the word over and over until he was asleep.

THE TEST

MENARDO HAD AWAKENED Friday morning feeling well rested and happier than he had felt in months. He had not awakened sweating and moaning in one of his nightmares. The day was sunny, and a mild breeze smelled of Alegría's roses and mock orange blossoms in the garden. Menardo felt happy and confident about his meeting later that day with his friend the general. Alone together, just the two of them, they could iron out any misunderstandings that might have sprung up if the general had learned about Sonny Blue's visit. Conducting business with the U.S. government or its citizens had always aroused some nervousness and wariness even between friends and partners. Menardo expected General J. would have a good deal to report to him too, although he understood some of it was top secret between the U.S. and the Mexican military commanders.

Menardo had not felt so happy at breakfast with Alegría since the wedding. He had skipped his newspapers and looked across the table at her while he drank his coffee. He had felt love shining in his eyes, but Alegría apparently had not because she had demanded to know what was wrong, why was he staring at her? Was he trying to drive her crazy? Menardo did not get angry, but got up from his chair to hug her and soothe her. Couldn't she tell? His worries had gone, they had disappeared suddenly during the night. All his little insecurities about his friend the general—all the little fears that his partner would throw him over for a deal with the U.S. military.

By the end of breakfast, Alegría had seemed more relaxed. She was talking about a business trip to Phoenix and L.A. Alegría said she wanted to see what interior designers in the United States were doing; too much of the French or even the Italians was boring; Alegría wanted what was fresh and exciting. "I feel fresh and exciting," Menardo had said to Alegría as he rang Tacho to bring the car. But Alegría had been too intent on her travel plans to notice his wit. He kissed her on the cheek when he heard the car pull up. Before he stepped out the door, Menardo straightened his tie and collar, then patted down his suit coat, smoothing the fabric to better conceal the outline of his vest. He wanted the vest correctly in place when he stepped outside.

Tacho did not speak unless spoken to. Menardo waited until they were out of the driveway before he began telling Tacho his dreams. These were good-luck dreams—Menardo was certain because suddenly everything had seemed hopeful: his wife was happily planning business trips; Universal Insurance was about to close a deal with the U.S. government and his friend the general would fill him in on details in a matter of hours. Menardo gazed back over his shoulder at the shining white palace that was his home: how silly his lapses of confidence had been! All was safely protected, securely guarded, and shielded; each detail, each element, each person, in his life was secure. No one and nothing could touch him!

His dream the night before was proof of that. No one could lay a hand on him. Menardo had dreamed he was in a village of stone walls. Inside an abandoned room, a skeleton had been unearthed. "You dug this up?" Tacho asked.

"No!" Menardo answered quickly, shaking his head. "Not me! The skeleton had already been disturbed by someone else. Not me!"

Tacho glanced into the rearview mirror where he caught Menardo's eyes for an instant. Menardo nodded. "The skeleton wore a necklace of green stone beads. But it wasn't like a nightmare. I wasn't afraid of it!"

"Because it had no feet or hands?" Tacho said.

Menardo had felt a chill excitement. "How did you know?"

Tacho had smiled broadly and tilted his head back so Menardo could see him in the rearview mirror. Menardo had forgotten how arrogant Indians could be. "Some say don't leave the dead feet or hands to chase you and grab you." Tacho seldom volunteered so much information. Stupid superstitions. Whenever Menardo had observed Tacho or other ignorant Indians from his home village, Menardo found it difficult to believe his own family had ever been connected with such ignorance and superstition. Menardo's ancestors had adopted European dress—brocades and silks as befit royalty. They had worn the old feather capes on ceremonial occasions, and to satisfy the rabble when they paid their taxes once a year.

Menardo did not see what difference hands or feet made if you were dreaming about a skeleton. In dreams, anything could happen anyway—feet or no feet. He was tired of Tacho's superstition. "I was not afraid because I was wearing body armor."

"Armor? In your dream?" Tacho's eyes were shining in the rearview mirror; Tacho had started laughing as if Menardo had made a joke. Menardo could not endure Tacho's ignorance. Indians such as Tacho stayed poor because they feared progress and modern technology.

Menardo had not intended to reveal the secret to Tacho, but suddenly it had happened: Menardo realized what he had wanted to do from the beginning, after Sonny Blue had first given him the vest. Menardo had wanted to see a live bullet hit the vest. He wanted to witness the superiority of man-made fibers that stopped bullets and steel and cheated death.

The armed escort cars remained at the main gate to bolster country club security. They feared car bombs crashing through. Universal Security provided armed patrols outside and inside the country club. Leftist rabble were all terrorists, and terrorists might try anything. Last Friday the police chief had killed a stray dog that had wandered too close; they had feared terrorists had strapped explosives to the dog for use with a remote-control security device. They had found nothing on the dead dog except fleas.

The waiters had been putting up the blue-and-white-striped awnings that completed the tent where their shooting club relaxed in the shade with cuba libres and margaritas while bets were made and members took turns firing. Menardo glanced at his wristwatch. There was enough time before the other shooting-club members would arrive. Menardo directed Tacho to park the Mercedes behind the tent for privacy. Without speaking, Menardo had first removed his coat and tie, laying them carefully on the backseat so they did not wrinkle. Tacho had watched intently in the rearview mirror. Menardo thought he even saw a ripple of amazement cross the Indian's big face as he had unbuttoned his shirt to reveal the bulletproof vest. Tacho had been embarrassed and reluctant as Menardo removed the vest and handed it to him. "See that? Feel it!" Menardo could hardly contain his excitement. He did not need their brochure of pictures; he would prove it to himself. Tacho was still examining the nylon straps of the vest when Menardo thrust the information brochure into Tacho's lap. Menardo took the vest and slipped it back on. He leaned over the driver's seat and looked over Tacho's shoulder at the color photographs of police and others whose lives had been saved by the vest. Menardo was not sure Tacho could read, so he had read aloud the caption of each of the photographs. Menardo savored Tacho's amazement that soft, man-made fibers with no steel or metal at all could stop a bullet. Menardo had not felt so happy in years—not since he had first made love with Alegría. They could not lay a hand on him, that was the meaning of his dream. He did not need an Indian such as Tacho to tell him that. What a lovely spring day it was! The breeze was dry and cool, and Menardo felt as if suddenly a great weight had been lifted off his shoulders. The general might have secret meetings in Honduras or Costa Rica, and the police chief might get video cameras from mysterious U.S. agents, but Menardo has his connections too: with Sonny Blue, who represented certain U.S. businessmen with trade proposals.

All his nightmares, his premonitions, about assassins' ambushes— gunmen on motorcycles and exploding bombs—had meant nothing more than too much rich food before bed. Menardo felt lighthearted. The general would never deceive or betray him. They were closer than brothers—he and the general. The general did not know how to talk to those rural merchants. Certain rivalries between rural families and clans had made security policies easy for Menardo to sell. Menardo sighed with satisfaction. Changes all around only made the insurance and security business better. The sky was the limit, even the general knew that. Menardo opened his pistol case on the backseat and laid out the Ruger, Colt, and Smith & Wesson—all of them bought from Greenlee in Tucson. "You want to see how the body armor works?" Menardo had to repeat himself twice because Tacho did not seem to understand Menardo's plan. Tacho was still staring down at the color brochure of huge purple bruises on hairy white chests where wonder fiber had stopped the bullets before penetration.

Menardo felt the breeze cool his arms and shoulders as he got out of the car. He knew he looked ridiculous wearing only the vest and trousers and shoes, but he saw no reason to spoil a shirt and sport coat. The color brochure had not done any good with Tacho, who seemed stupefied and unable to understand Menardo's most simple commands. "I will stand here. You will stand over there. . . . Yes, there. Right on that spot. Whatever you do, don't step over that line. . . . No." Tacho's smile wasn't so arrogant now. He had Tacho scared. "I want you to see this, Tacho, so you understand." Menardo had brought the 9mm Smith & Wesson to Tacho, who seemed rooted to the ground where Menardo had ordered him to stand.

Menardo's heart was pounding with excitement. He could hardly believe what fun he was having with the bulletproof vest. Later, after the others had arrived, Menardo would ask one of the waiters for a carving knife, and they would witness still another amazing escape from death. He glanced down at his watch and realized he was impatient for the others to arrive. Because he wanted to stun and dazzle them. He imagined how dramatic it would be for the others—the governor, former ambassador, the judge and the doctor. Because the general and the police chief would surely guess the vest's secret, but to the others it would appear as if Menardo faced certain death.

WORK OF THE SPIRITS

TACHO HAD KNOWN all along about the vest. What Tacho did not see or overhear was reported to him by the maid and the cook's helper. The household staff felt betrayed by the loss of their prestigious lady, Iliana. She alone had been respectable. Tacho had mentioned the vest to El Feo and the woman called Angelita La Escapía. The wild woman had known immediately about this "body armor," a miracle fiber that stopped bullets. Angelita talked too much, but she knew interesting facts. Politicians and the rich. Police, politicians, and the very rich wore body armor under their clothes whenever they went out in public. Bulletproof wigs for men and women were available to prime ministers and presidents, who wore bulletproof glasses with the wigs for optimum protection. "Nothing is foolproof," Angelita said. "Professionals aim for the mouth or the ear."

The fetish suffered night sweats, and one morning Tacho had found a puddle of urine at the foot of the bedroll. Tacho had been afraid to disturb the bundle since then. He was not sure if the opal or the coca leaves had been responsible for the night sweat and urine. Tacho worried the police had killed the bundle's Peruvian caretakers and the bundle had been angered and desired revenge. The twelve coca leaves belonged to a powerful spirit.

In the South, there were thousands who worshiped Mama Coca, because she had loved and cared for the people for thousands of years. Mama Coca had taken away the pain, she had numbed the hunger, and she had given tired travelers a last push over the mountain. Mama Coca had sustained them all along, and now Mama Coca was going to help them take back the lands that were theirs. That was why the white men feared the coca bushes and poisoned and firebombed them. Coca leaves gave the Indians too much power, dangerous power; not just the power money buys, but spiritual power to destroy all but the strong. All things weak, all things European, would shrivel, then blow away. Nothing would stop their passing; all their apprentices and toadies whatever their ancestry, would disappear too.

Tacho tried to pretend he did not understand what Menardo wanted done with the pistol. The upstairs maid had told Tacho about Menardo's wearing the vest to bed; she often found the color brochure about the vest in the bedcovers, evidence Menardo fell asleep reading about the vest. But Menardo was crazier than Tacho had thought. Menardo was babbling about playing a joke on the others. He would make fools of them!

Still, nothing had prepared Tacho for Menardo's request to shoot him in the chest with the 9mm Smith & Wesson. Tacho's hesitation had only excited Menardo more. At the end of the country club driveway limousines and escort cars could be seen passing the main-gate guard-house as if traveling in a convoy.

Menardo wanted perfect timing—he wanted Tacho to wait until the cars had pulled up, then he would greet his fellow shooting-club members, then Tacho must shoot. Snap! Snap! Snap! One two three! Before the others could even open their mouths! What an exhibition they would see! Here was a man to be reckoned with—a man invincible with the magic of high technology.

As the convoy of Mercedeses and escorting Blazers slowed to a halt, Menardo had gestured extravagantly with both arms like a windmill above his head; then he had pointed at both front panels of the vest, then at Tacho, who was holding the pistol at his side. The heads inside the cars stared dumbly at Menardo until he yelled at Tacho to point the gun; as soon as Tacho had raised the automatic, all eyes had been on Tacho. Menardo shouted at his fellow club members, "Watch this! Watch this!" Tacho looked at the stupefied faces of the general and the police chief; he wanted to be sure they did not order their bodyguards to shoot. They seemed to realize Menardo was giving the orders. "Go on! Now! Do it! Fire!" Menardo's voice had been shrill with frenzy as he slapped the left panel of the vest; right over his heart. "Here! Here!" he urged Tacho. Before General J. or the police chief or any of the others could leap from their cars, Tacho had fired the 9mm automatic once, striking Menardo in the chest.

The fall surprised Menardo, and somehow he had no air in his lungs to speak to the general and the others who knelt over him. Tacho had stood looking down at him, still holding the 9mm in his hand. The police chief and General J. fumbled with the nylon webbing and zipper of the vest, and Menardo could feel himself sinking into their arms. What was the general saying? Had Tacho fired the pistol? Why had he fallen? Menardo could not remember. He felt a warm puddle under himself. Why had the waiters poured soup over him? What were they looking at? They could examine the vest later for damage, but right now he needed help to stand up. He was getting too wet and cold lying there.

THE HEAT IS ON

ALEGRÍA HAD BEGUN to feel uneasy when Bartolomeo showed up in Tuxtla. She did not like how easily Bartolomeo had located her at the shop. He claimed he was working with Indians in the mountains; some "internal committee" in Havana wanted him to investigate the Indians. They could not be certain any longer which groups of Indians were true Marxists, and which tribes were puppets for the U.S. military, or worse, tribes which were corrupted by nationalism and tribal superstition.

"They know all about your husband in Mexico City," Bartolomeo had continued with his familiar smile. Alegría knew his tricks. She laughed. She would tell Bartolomeo herself.

"He wears a bulletproof vest to bed. The Mercedes is armored. Two cars—bodyguards—one goes before, one goes behind."

"Oh, not *that!*" Bartolomeo said with a wave of his hand. "We are talking about a *business relationship*—the general—"

"You Cubans! You're crazy! *Of course,* there's a business relationship! That's public knowledge!" Alegría had sent the sales clerks home early when she saw Bartolomeo walk through the door; her excuse had been the inventory report.

Alegría and Bartolomeo wandered through the brass lamps, leather armchairs, massive sofas, and rolls of expensive wool carpeting imported from all over the world. As Bartolomeo gazed at her interior-decorator's shop, she could see his upper lip slowly begin to curl into a sneer. "*Haute* bourgeois!" Bartolomeo said, pronouncing the last word slowly as he looked her in the eye.

"What do you want?" Alegría said in a hard, low voice; she was beginning to hate this man.

"What do you have?" Bartolomeo was always smiling, always cock-sure.

"I'm locking up now. I'm expected at home."

" 'Expected at home.' How nice. How respectable."

Alegría could feel her heart pounding. She had never felt hatred so purely before. If she had had a gun close by, she would have killed him on the spot. Her anger had always aroused Bartolomeo. She could see his face change, his eyes glisten as he moved toward her. "Too bad you didn't explode with the others—it's funny how they died but you didn't! I hope they kill you here!" she hissed. But Bartolomeo was unconcerned with insults or accusations. He was the first to admit he had saved his own hide and the others were expendable. Bartolomeo merely shrugged his shoulders and smiled. "To have you, my plum, *this instant,* I would gladly die later!" Alegría saw he was scheming to get her near one of the beds. "Go stick it in an Indian!" Alegría hissed through her teeth. She was thinking too bad she couldn't alert the police chief and the general about Bartolomeo's presence because she could imagine how much they would enjoy interrogating this communist. Too bad, but she was not well liked in Tuxtla; the authorities would likely take the Cuban's word over hers; too bad, but Bartolomeo could link her to the Mexico City group.

After Bartolomeo left the store, Alegría had been too shaky to dial the phone for a cab. She poured herself straight shots of rum from a bottle she kept at the store for her nerves. Menardo got on her nerves. The Indian chauffeur, Tacho, got on her nerves. Menardo was obsessed with the bulletproof vest. He wore it to bed; for all she knew, he wore it in the bath and shower. Alegría had heard the general's wife whisper to the police chief's wife about Menardo. The whole town had begun to suspect one another. Menardo had had visitors from the United States. The former ambassador had also had visitors from the United States. The police chief not only had had visitors, he had got himself video cameras and equipment with promises of more to follow.

This town got on her nerves. Alegría found she had been thinking more and more about Sonny Blue in Tucson. Menardo kept safety deposit boxes full of gold and U.S. cash in Tucson. She did not like the

way Tacho watched her and everything that went on. Alegría was sure
he was a spy.

Alegría more and more appreciated how much better the rum made
her feel. Alcohol was important medicine for her. Tacho suspected her
and Sonny Blue. Tacho might "interpret" one of Menardo's dreams in
such a way that Menardo would catch wind of the affair. Or Tacho
might try blackmail.

Alegría no longer slept in Menardo's bed. All night Menardo tossed
and turned, jumping out of bed or sitting up in bed, muttering in his
sleep. His nightmares were always about bombs exploding under the
Mercedes, or masked assassins stepping through the bedroom door.

Security no longer permitted dinner and dancing parties at private
homes. Social functions and entertaining were conducted at the country
club, surrounded by walls and electric fences and helicopter surveillance.
Alegría continued to play cards with the other wives three times a week
at the club. Some weeks there had not been enough players for five tables
because the husbands of some of the women no longer felt their wives
were safe driving to the country club. Years before, of course, the women
had only met one another in their homes. Iliana's had been the first
generation of women to realize the advantages of luncheon and cards
at the country club where the women could drink cocktails, smoke
cigarettes, and gossip about in-laws uninhibitedly.

Alegría did not have any illusions. A number of Tuxtla's best ad-
dressees were off-limits for Alegría; and while the wives of the governor
and former ambassador might play bridge or canasta with Alegría at
the country club, this did not mean she would ever be invited to their
homes. At the club, rumors provided the only entertainment. If Alegría
missed a Tuesday or a Thursday, she was aware of the former ambassador's wife and the governor's wife whispering behind their hands as
they watched her. All the talk is about the gringos: U.S. dollars and U.S.
equipment are up for grabs. Menardo, the general, and the police chief—
they had all had visitors from the United States recently. The former
ambassador's U.S.-born wife watches their three wives suspiciously.

Rumors say United States troops will soon occupy Mexico to help
protect U.S.-owned factories in Northern Mexico as well as the rich
Mexico City politicians on the CIA payroll since prep school. There are
shortages of cornmeal and rioting spreads. Rumors say the richest families have already opened bank accounts and purchased homes "in the
North," which is understood to be San Antonio, San Diego, Tucson, or
Los Angeles. Rumors say the refugees fleeing from the South have greatly

increased in number as civil wars ignite in Costa Rica and Honduras. Alegría imagined a map of the world suspended in darkness until suddenly a tiny flame blazed up, followed by others, to form a burning necklace of revolution across two American continents. That was another reason Alegría preferred taxis. Alegría expected the riots eventually to reach Tuxtla, and she preferred to meet rioters in a taxi, and not a Mercedes.

MIRACLE OF HIGH TECHNOLOGY

ALEGRÍA HAD BEEN PACKING her bags for a vacation at their beach house at Playa Azul. Menardo had planned to drive her himself to make a second honeymoon before he returned to Tuxtla. Perhaps she might start her painting again if she spent time alone in their lovely beach house above the shimmering Pacific. It would be a paradise where Alegría could take a serious look at herself and her life to assess the threat Bartolomeo may have posed. She daydreamed and ached for the hard thrusts of Sonny Blue; but she knew Sonny would not have built the beach house as she had designed it, the way Menardo had. No costs were too great; Menardo had sent out rush orders to Mexico City for the steel and glass to build her dream hideaway at Playa Azul.

Alegría had wanted to meet Sonny Blue at the beach house, but he had refused despite Alegría's assurance that Menardo would not suddenly appear and surprise them. The elaborate electronic security alarms would not have permitted such a surprise. Still, Sonny Blue had not wanted to jeopardize business with Menardo or to end up shot dead by the jealous husband either. Alegría realized no man would ever love her or spend his money as freely on her as Menardo had. No matter how lifeless or sexless the marriage was, Alegría knew she was well-off; look at the silks and linens. She felt a great deal of tenderness for Menardo as she packed her new bathing suits and beach caftans with leather sandals to match.

The sound of tires on gravel in the driveway was unfamiliar—too loud, too sudden—as if the car were speeding to a stop. Alegría heard a second car pull up. Her heart began pounding; she glanced at the clock: three-fifteen, Friday afternoon, and something terrible had happened. Alegría felt a strange numbness and tingling in the tips of her fingers and toes; when the downstairs maid knocked and called out at her door, Alegría knew they had killed Menardo.

The general and the police chief had come for her immediately; they had not yet removed the body from the scene, but they had brought the vest, heavy, and still wet with Menardo's blood. Alegría saw how much they hated her—the general, police chief, and the others. They probably knew about her affair with Sonny Blue. They blamed her for Iliana's death, and now for Menardo's. They wanted to rub her face in the blood; she could feel the police chief struggle to control himself. Alegría had burst into tears when she saw the ridiculous vest; it looked too small now for a man such as Menardo. They called it an accident; they had witnessed everything.

Alegría had moved toward the front door, tears running down her cheeks; she fumbled with her purse to find a handkerchief. Her hands were shaking. She wanted to take a gun and kill the Indian before more damage was done. She was furious at Menardo. How many times had she warned him about Tacho? She had never liked Tacho's Indian friends who came at all hours of the night carrying strange packs and bundles. Bartolomeo had dropped hints about "your husband's Indian" as he called Tacho; Tacho had a twin brother in the mountains who led Indian guerrilla units. Alegría usually did not trust anything Bartolomeo said, but in the case of Tacho, she had already suspected the truth. Alegría had seen the hatred in Tacho's eyes; he hated Europeans, pure and simple.

Alegría asked to be driven to the scene to stall for time, and to give the appearance of the grieving widow, though she knew she would fool no one. Tacho was sitting in the Mercedes as if nothing had happened; eyewitnesses, including the general and the police chief, had heard Menardo give Tacho the command to fire. Menardo was lying on his back covered now with his own shirt and suit coat. Alegría approached slowly. Poor silly man! From the moment Menardo had seen the vest, he had been enraptured. But instead of crying, Alegría wanted to laugh. She had sunk to her knees on the ground next to his body and buried her face in both hands, and she had laughed until tears ran down her face; and then she had cried because she knew this was it, this was the end.

The general and the police chief would make a complete investigation. She wept for herself, not the fool Menardo. Menardo had been worth much more to her alive than dead; she did not trust the general or the police chief. The general would want to take control of the company and cheat her out of everything.

Alone in her bedroom, Alegría had called the mortuary, where she was told all arrangements had been made by "friends of the family." One by one they had come—the former ambassador and the governor, the judge and the doctor, the police chief and the general—the men from the club had paid their respects, but the wives had made excuses, citing security, because they knew it was all over for Alegría in Tuxtla. One by one, the men had clasped her hands between their sweaty palms, and staring into her eyes, each had whispered they were "there for her"— anything she might need. A freak accident! How tragic! Microscopic imperfections in the fabric's quilting; a bare millimeter's difference and the bullet would safely have been stopped. The judge and the former ambassador had both suggested filing lawsuits against the vest's U.S. manufacturer; naturally they wanted to assist her. The police chief had asked what she knew about Tacho. The general had asked if she had trusted Tacho. Alegría lied and told them Tacho was utterly loyal and trustworthy. She needed time, and she did not want the general or the police chief to suspect Tacho and begin a new investigation; she no longer had Menardo to intercept and censor or destroy damaging reports about her past political affiliations. Bless him, Menardo had believed her when she called politics her "ignorant youth"; but the others would never believe her.

HOW CAPITALISTS DIE

BUT IN THE END it had been Bartolomeo who had hated Alegría most—more than the country club wives and Menardo's business associates. Alegría's heart had skipped a beat when she saw the driveway littered with handbills. Bartolomeo had lost no time. The handbills had been copied from the front page of the newspaper with the photograph of Menardo's body inside a dark circle of his own blood. *This Is How Capitalists Die,* the handbill read.

Alegría felt a strange tingling all over her body; she thought she might faint; her mouth had gone dry and her palms were cold and wet. That bastard Bartolomeo had betrayed all of them; he wanted to destroy her and the Indians in the mountains as well. Alegría had not felt hatred so violently, with such purity, before. Maybe the despised Cuban worked for the CIA after all. Alegría wanted to kill him slowly, to feel him dying under her hands, his flesh quivering and clammy; she would breathe deeply, breathe exultantly, the stench of his blood and shit, the sweet aroma of his terror. That was how liars such as Bartolomeo died.

The handbills had been scattered all over Tuxtla; the police chief and General J. had returned and began asking Alegría questions. They searched the garage where Tacho had slept but found nothing. The Indian had removed all his things and swept the floor clean. Alegría searched the high limbs of the big tree, but saw no scarlet macaws. The Indian and his blue and yellow *wacahs* were gone.

Tacho had been stunned by Menardo's death; he felt embarrassed too. Because Tacho realized he had actually believed in the bulletproof vest too, maybe not as much as Menardo had, but still this made Tacho a fool with the rest of them. Tacho had not wanted to take the pistol from Menardo's hand, vest or no vest; he had been afraid he might not hit the vest, but miss and shoot the boss in the face or in the knee. That had been the reason Tacho had stepped closer, over the line Menardo had marked in the dirt with the heel of his shoe. Tacho had been concerned about accuracy even if Menardo had been too dumb to see the dangers. As Menardo had eagerly watched the approach of his fellow shooting-club members, Tacho had moved closer. The cars and escort vehicles had formed a small procession. They were afraid and believed strength lay in numbers.

Tacho had not wanted to fire because he knew white men did not like to see an Indian shoot a mestizo unless *they* had given the order; otherwise Indians might get ideas and move from mestizos to shoot at whites. Tacho had sat patiently behind the wheel in the Mercedes while ambulance attendants and more police and curious golfers crowded around Menardo's body. Tacho felt relaxed and calm; how odd when he had just killed his longtime employer. Menardo had requested that Tacho shoot him; that was the testimony Tacho had given the police. All eyewitnesses agreed; Menardo had commanded the chauffeur more than once to fire.

Later, after the police had completed their investigation, Tacho took the long route home in the Mercedes, just as he and the boss had planned earlier that morning; now the boss was dead; they had planned safe routes downtown for the last time. For the last time, the boss had kissed his treacherous wife good-bye and pulled the front door shut on his mansion. One last time Menardo had looked up at the sky, just as he died.

For the last time, Tacho drove the Mercedes slowly past the obscure alleys and downtown street corners Menardo had seen in his nightmares, which had alternated jeep loads of assassins sent by the general with truckloads of assassins sent by the police chief or leftist terrorists. Tacho had to laugh. Menardo had not been able to trust any of them, and he should never have trusted his new wife. Tacho thought it really was funny: he, Tacho, had been in his way the most loyal, and yet, look what had happened. Nothing could have saved Menardo.

Tacho recalled the arguments people in villages had had over the eventual disappearance of the white man. Old prophets were adamant; the disappearance would not be caused by military action, necessarily, or by military action alone. The white man would someday disappear all by himself. The disappearance had already begun at the spiritual level.

The forces were harsh. A great many people would suffer and die. All ideas and beliefs of the Europeans would gradually wither and drop away. A great many fools like Menardo would die pretending they were white men; only the strongest would survive. The rest would die by the thousands along with the others; the disappearance would take place over hundreds of years and would include massive human migrations from continent to continent.

Tacho had parked the Mercedes in the driveway and left the keys with the cook; he told her he was leaving. He did not bother to warn her about talking to the police because they would torture her if she refused. Tacho packed his clothes. As he prepared the canvas for the bedroll on the floor, he knelt in something wet and cool on the floor. Blood was oozing from the center of his bedroll where he kept the spirit bundle. Tacho felt he might lose consciousness, but outside the door hanging in the tree upside down, the big macaws were shrieking. The he-macaw told Tacho certain wild forces controlled all the Americas, and the saints and spirits and the gods of the Europeans were powerless on American soil.

Tacho had been chosen by the macaws' and the opal's spirits; for better or for worse, he had to take the spirits with him, like wives. Tacho had soaked up some of the blood with a handkerchief to show his brother. In the mountains, El Feo or some of the others initiated by the old priests might know more about a bundle such as this. All the spirits ate blood that was offered to them. But where had the blood that leaked from the bundle come from?

The unborn baby drank the mother's blood; unborn chicks grew from delicate halos of blood inside the egg. The spirits of the mountains had to have their share; if people did not sacrifice to the mountains willingly, then the mountains trembled and shook with hurt and anger. The dead bodies strewn across winding mountain roads after head-on collisions provided blood to calm angry mountain spirits. Particular curves on the mountain roads not only had shrines and altars, but special feast days to pacify the spirits who inhabited the curves or crossroads.

Blood: even the bulletproof vest wanted a little blood. Knives, guns, even automobiles, possessed "energies" that craved blood from time to time. Tacho had heard dozens of stories that good Christians were not supposed to believe. Stories about people beaten, sometimes even killed, by their own brooms or pots and pans. Wise homemakers "fed" goat or pig blood to knives, scissors, and other sharp or dangerous household objects. Even fire had to be fed the first bit of dough or fat; otherwise, sooner or later, the fire would burn the cook or flare up and catch the kitchen on fire. Airplanes, jets, and rockets were already malfunctioning, crashing and exploding. Electricity no longer obeyed the white man. The macaw spirits said the great serpent was in charge of electricity. The macaws were in charge of fire.

THIS CUBAN SHOULD RETURN TO CUBA

EL FEO AND ANGELITA had moved permanently from the village to El Feo's camp high in the mountains, out of the reach of federal police and army patrols for illegal refugees from El Salvador and Guatemala and points south. The Mexican president had declared a state of emergency as thousands and thousands of war refugees from the South were spilling over Mexico's southern boundaries. The United States demanded that Mexico stop the refugees. Rumors circulated about desert-camouflaged U.S. tanks deployed along the entire U.S. border; other rumors accused the Mexican president and his cabinet of being U.S. CIA agents since kindergarten. The fair-haired sons of Mexico's elite had been given Ivy League educations in the U.S. to prepare the puppets for their jobs. The rumors spread unrest like wind spread wildfire. The U.S. president would offer the Mexican president military aid when rioters shot police protecting U.S.-owned factories in Juárez and Tijuana. The Mexican president would not accept U.S. military aid until the rebels had dynamited high-voltage lines, blacking out all of Guadalajara, and much of the Federal District.

El Feo laughed whenever he saw newspapers or satellite television because the government thought the saboteurs, rioters, and looters were part of a single group or organization. The government wanted groups because they hoped for leaders to crush or to buy off. But this time the story was going to be different because the people no longer believed in leaders. People had begun to gather spontaneously and moved as a mob or swarm follows instinct, then suddenly disperses. The masses of people in Asia and in Africa, and the Americas too, no longer believed in so-called "elected" leaders; they were listening to strange voices inside themselves. Although few would admit this, the voices they heard were voices out of the past, voices of their earliest memories, voices of nightmares and voices of sweet dreams, voices of the ancestors.

All across earth there were those listening and waiting, isolated and lonely, despised outcasts of the earth. First the lights would go out— dynamite or earthquake, it did not matter. All sources of electrical power generation would be destroyed. Darkness was the ally of the poor. One uprising would spark another and another. El Feo did not believe in political parties, ideology, or rules. El Feo believed in the land. With the return of Indian land would come the return of justice, followed by peace. El Feo left the politics to Angelita, who enjoyed the intrigues and rivalries between their so-called friends. All that mattered was obtaining the weapons and supplies the people needed to retake the land; so Angelita had lied to all of them—the U.S., Cuba, Germany, and Japan. But to their African friends they were truthful. They didn't lie because Africans were tribal people who had taken back a continent from the Europeans. Always they were poor, struggling Indians fighting for their way of life. If Angelita was talking to the Germans or Hollywood activists, she said the Indians were fighting multinational corporations who killed rain forests; if she was talking to the Japanese or U.S. military, then the Indians were fighting communism. Whatever their "friends" needed to hear, that was their motto. The Indians' worst enemies were missionaries, who sent Bibles instead of guns and who preached blessed are the meek. Missionaries were stooges and spies for the government. Missionaries warned the village people against the evils of revolution and communism. They warned the people not to talk or to listen to spirit beings.

Bartolomeo had complained about the absence of study groups and evening classes for adult instruction. Bartolomeo had a number of complaints that he termed "serious." Beside their failure to organize Marxist instruction and study sessions, there were more disturbing issues. Bartolomeo had been doing his own investigating throughout the entire region. He had talked to some *good Indians* for a change, not to *treacherous tribalists*. Angelita pretended not to notice his choice of words. Bartolomeo had been snooping through their files and logbooks since his arrival earlier in the week. He had insisted on following El Feo on his rounds in the remote villages. When Bartolomeo and El Feo had returned from the trips, Angelita sensed trouble from El Feo's stiff posture. El Feo refused even to look at Bartolomeo. El Feo was furious. Whatever had happened, Bartolomeo was involved.

Bartolomeo considered himself a policy expert now. One more big ideological victory here, and Bartolomeo was certain the central committee in Havana would reward him with promotions and a post in Mexico City. Bartolomeo was tired of the remote Indian camps; he was even more sick of bourgeois Tuxtla, of the phony rich bitches who sat on their bony butts—such as Alegría, that great whore! Bartolomeo knew he was destined for higher positions; Bartolomeo was nearly ready for his triumphant return to the capital.

Bartolomeo bossed everyone who came within range of his loud, Cuban mouth. Orders! Orders! But these village people had gathered because they were finished with big bosses and orders. Bartolomeo had never understood Indians. A squad of village women had told Commander Bartolomeo to shove his orders up his ass. Bartolomeo had then called in the disciplinary committee to punish the offenders.

Punish these warrior women? Angelita laughed. This Cuban should return to Cuba; from there, Europeans should return to the lands of their ancestors.

"This army belongs to the people, remember?" she said to Bartolomeo; she enjoyed watching Bartolomeo's temper heat up. Bartolomeo motioned for her and El Feo to follow him inside the tent that served as their office. Inside, El Feo handed Angelita a pink handbill he had pulled from inside his T-shirt.

"These were scattered all over Tuxtla last night." The handbill was a dark, smeared copy of the newspaper photograph of Menardo's corpse.

"You know what this does to Tacho," Angelita said in a low, angry whisper.

Bartolomeo waved his hand as if to brush aside her words. They had already ruled Menardo's death accidental. "Tacho needed to get out anyway. He was about to lose his cover."

"How do you know? Who told you?" El Feo was furious. Bartolomeo did not bother to look up; he had been leafing through a stack of blank squad reports that squad leaders El Feo and Angelita had refused to complete.

Bartolomeo droned on and on. The committee in Mexico City had sent warnings before. Blah, blah, blah! Unless Angelita and El Feo and the others completed reports on their activities, Bartolomeo would have no choice but to report them again. Other tribes obeyed committee directives concerning reports. Another negative report would cause an automatic cutoff of valuable Cuban aid; worse yet, the word would get around to all the other "friends of Indians" and they'd halt support. "I have suspected something all along," Bartolomeo continued. Angelita thought to herself, "This is it. Adiós, Bartolomeo, you are one dead Cuban," and while he blabbered on, Angelita made plans. Bartolomeo would be tried before a people's assembly for crimes against the revolution, specifically for crimes against Native American history; the crimes were the denial and attempted annihilation of tribal histories. Bartolomeo continued with his recitation of suspicions and accusations. The Cubans had received unconfirmed reports that these mountain villages were hotbeds of tribalism and native religion. Marxism did *not* tolerate these primitive bugaboos!

"*Us? Not us!* Their spies are *liars! We* are internationalists! *We* are not just tribal!" Angelita argued vehemently. She was thinking about all the "friends of the Indians" who had sent them aid from all over the world. Millions had come from a crackpot German industrialist who wanted to see the tribal people of the Americas retake their land. Millions came each year from Japanese businessmen who wanted to avenge Hiroshima and Nagasaki any way possible. They were internationalists all right! Tribal internationalists! They wanted to keep the Cubans in the dark about their true objectives for as long as possible. They wanted to keep aid flowing to the people's army. "Arrest this man!" Angelita had called out in tribal dialect so Bartolomeo would not try to escape. He had still been frowning over the stack of uncompleted forms and reports when the warriors seized him by both arms.

Representatives and people from the mountain villages had been invited for Chinese orange soda and parched corn compliments of the People's Revolution in Cuba. Meetings of the villages had traditionally cleared the air during local disputes and prevented bloody feuds. The meeting had been called to update the people on the most recent developments. Luckily some days would pass before police authorities would react to the pink handbills and reopen investigations into Menardo's accident.

Bartolomeo begged for his life; the handbills were trivial, he said, the handbills claimed no responsibility for Menardo's death, which authorities had ruled accidental. Bartolomeo denied he was a double agent. Bartolomeo denied he was CIA. The handbills could not be traced to the villages. The handbills had merely been part of the people's "reeducation." El Feo shook his head and left the tent to call the meeting to order. "There is a more serious charge," Angelita said. "You are guilty of crimes against history, specifically, crimes against certain tribal histories."

"You can't do this! You're crazy! The committee—!"

"The committee? Why do you think they sent you here?" Angelita smiled. The charges against Bartolomeo made her feel nostalgic. She remembered the first time she had seen Bartolomeo, so handsome with his brown eyes and light brown hair; in the bedroom his body had looked just as good. What a pity! Comrade Bartolomeo had outlived his usefulness. There wouldn't be any more free Chinese soda pop or Russian anti-tank missiles from Cuba; but foreign aid from the Marxists had been drying up anyway. Angelita looked out at the people who had come to the meeting for free popcorn and soda pop; what would they think? Most of the village meetings had included discussions about obtaining more "gifts" from "friends of the Indians." El Feo and the others were still plugging the speakers into truck batteries, while latecomers got in line for soda or wandered through the market where business was brisk.

ANGELITA LA ESCAPÍA
EXPLAINS ENGELS AND MARX

COMRADE ANGELITA stepped up to the microphone and announced she was not afraid to talk about anything the people wanted to know. She had no secrets and nothing to hide, so there was nothing to be nervous about; there was nothing they couldn't talk about. Was Comrade Angelita trying to get the villages to join up with the Cubans? How much were the Cubans paying her? Had they promised her Japanese motorcycles? What about chain saws? Wasn't communism godless? Then how could history, so alive with spirits, exist without gods? What about her and that white man, Bartolomeo? To questions about her private life Angelita was quick to snap back, "What about it?" with her jaw set so hard, the questioner was afraid to open his or her mouth again. Comrade Bartolomeo, she explained, was under arrest, about to be court-martialed for betraying the revolution with capital crimes against history.

"More about the traitor Bartolomeo afterwards, but first .... " Angelita launched into a lecture.

"Questions have been asked about who this Marx is. Questions have been asked about the meaning of words like *communism* and *history*. Today I am going to tell you what use this white man Marx is to us here in our mountain villages!"

But right from the beginning, Angelita explained, she wanted no misunderstanding; nothing mattered but taking back tribal land. Angelita paused to sip orange soda and scanned the crowd for her "elder sisters." The "elder sisters" had complained that Angelita was hardly different from a missionary herself, always talking on and on about white man's political mumbo jumbo but never bothering to explain.

"Are we supposed to take what you say on faith?" the elder sisters had teased Angelita.

"Is this Marx another Jesus?" Jokes had circulated about Angelita's love affair—not with Bartolomeo or El Feo but with Marx, a billy-goat-bearded, old white man. The elder sisters laughed; here was the danger of staring at a photograph. A glint of the man's soul had been captured there, in the eyes of Marx's image on the page. The elder sisters said Angelita should have been more careful. Everyone had heard stories about victims bewitched by photographs of strangers long dead, long gone from the world except for a trace of the spirit's light that remained in the photograph.

It was time to clear the air, especially now that Bartolomeo was about to be court-martialed by the people. Angelita set down the empty soda bottle near her feet and pulled the microphone stand closer. She glanced at the elder sisters standing at the back of the crowd; they nodded at her, and Angelita took a deep breath and began:

"I know there is gossip, talking and speculation about me. I have nothing to say except every breath, my every heartbeat, is for the return of the land." The teenage troops yell and whistle, girls and boys alike; the dogs bark and the crowd applauds.

If they could agree on nothing else, they could all agree the land was theirs. Tribal rivalries and even intervillage boundary disputes often focused on land lost to the European invaders. When they had taken back all the lands of the indigenous people of the Americas, there would be plenty of space, plenty of pasture and farmland and water for everyone who promised to respect all beings and do no harm. "We are the army to retake tribal land. Our army is only one of many all over the earth quietly preparing. The ancestors' spirits speak in dreams. We wait. We simply wait for the earth's natural forces already set loose, the exploding, fierce energy of all the dead slaves and dead ancestors haunting the Americas. We prepare, and we wait for the tidal wave of history to sweep us along. People have been asking questions about ideology. Are we *this* or are we *that*? Do we follow Marx? The answer is no! *No* white man politics! *No* white man Marx! No white man religion, no nothing *until we retake this land!* We must protect Mother Earth from destruction." The teenage army cheered and even the older people had been clapping their hands.

"Now I want to tell you something about myself because so many rumors are circulating. Rumors about myself and Marxism. Rumors about myself and the ghost of Karl Marx!" There had been laughter and applause, but Angelita did not pause. "I will tell you what I know about Marx. His followers and all the rest I don't know about. This is personal, but people want to know what I think; they want to know if I'm Marxist." Angelita shook her head.

"Marxists don't want to give Indian land back. We say *to hell* with all Marxists who oppose the return of tribal land!" Market transactions had slowed as Angelita warmed up; and the people listened more attentively. Angelita could see El Feo and the others working their way through the crowd, recruiting people's volunteers to feed or hide their people's army regulars. "To hell with the Marxists! To hell with the capitalists! To hell with the white man! We want our mother the land!"

Cursing the white man along with free soda pop put the people in a festive mood; they were accustomed to listening to village political discussions that continued for days on end. "Marxism is one thing! Marx *the man* is another," Angelita had said as she began her defense of Marx. So-called disciples of Marx had often disgraced his name, the way Jesus was disgraced by crimes of his alleged "followers," the popes of the Catholic Church.

Angelita announced she would begin with her early years at the mission school on the coast where she had first heard the name. The old Castilian nuns at the mission school had called Marx the Devil. The nuns had trotted out the bogeyman Marx to scare the students if the older students refused after-school work assignments, free labor for the Catholic Church. Avowed enemy of the priests and nuns, of the Baptists and Latter-day Saints—enemy of all missionaries, this Marx *had to be* Angelita's ally! She had understood instinctively, the way she knew the old nuns had got the story of benevolent, gentle Quetzalcoatl all wrong too. The nuns had taught the children that the Morning Star, Quetzalcoatl, was really Lucifer, the Devil God had thrown out of heaven. The nuns had terrified the children with the story of the snake in the Garden of Eden to end devotion to Quetzalcoatl.

Angelita paused to scan the crowd for reactions. Spies for the federal police or the army would use up the batteries of their little hidden voice recorders before she was finished. The people's army units could have vacated the village within a few minutes anyway. Screw the Christians! Screw the police and army! Angelita didn't care. They would not take her alive. Before she died, she must explain to the village people about Marx, who was unlike any white man since Jesus. For now—screw Cuban Marxists and their European totalitarianism!

Marx had been inspired by reading about certain Native American communal societies, though naturally as a European he had misunderstood a great deal. Marx had learned about societies in which everyone ate or everyone starved together, and no one being stood above another—all stood side by side—rock, insect, human being, river, or flower. Each depended upon the other; the destruction of one harmed all others.

Marx understood what tribal people had always known: the maker of a thing pressed part of herself or himself into each object made. Some spark of life or energy went from the maker into even the most ordinary objects. Marx had understood the value of anything came from the hands of the maker. Marx of the Jews, tribal people of the desert, Marx the tribal man understood that nothing personal or individual mattered because no individual survived without others. Generation after generation, individuals were born, then after eighty years, disappeared into dust, but in the stories, the people lived on in the imaginations and hearts of their descendants. Wherever their stories were told, the spirits of the ancestors were present and their power was alive.

Marx, tribal man and storyteller; Marx with his primitive devotion to the workers' stories. No wonder the Europeans hated him! Marx had gathered official government reports of the suffering of English factory workers the way a tribal shaman might have, feverishly working to bring together a powerful, even magical, assembly of stories. In the repetition of the workers' stories lay great power; workers must never forget the stories of other workers. The people did not struggle alone. Marx, more tribal Jew than European, instinctively knew the stories, or "history," accumulated momentum and power. No factory inspector's "official report" could whitewash the tears, blood, and sweat that glistened from the simple words of the narratives.

Marx had understood stories are alive with the energy words generate. Word by word, the stories of suffering, injury, and death had transformed the present moment, seizing listeners' or readers' imaginations so that for an instant, they were present and felt the suffering of sisters and brothers long past. The words of the stories filled rooms with an immense energy that aroused the living with fierce passion and determination for justice. Marx wrote about babies dosed with opium while mothers labored sixteen hours in silk factories; Marx wrote with the secret anguish of a father unable to provide enough food or medicine. When Marx wrote about the little children working under huge spinning machines that regularly mangled and killed them, Marx had already seen Death prowling outside his door, hungry for his own three children. In his feverish work with the stories of shrunken, yellowed infants, and the mangled limbs of children, Marx had been working desperately to seize the story of each child-victim and to turn the story away from the brutal endings the coroners and factory inspectors used to write for the children of the poor. His own children were slowly dying from cold, lack of food, and medicine; yet day after day, Marx had returned to official reports in the British Museum. Wage-earning might have saved Marx's children, but tribal man and storyteller, Marx had sacrificed the lives of his own beloved children to gather the stories of all the children starved and mangled. He had sensed the great power these stories had—power to move millions of people. Poor Marx did not understand the power of the stories belonged to the spirits of the dead.

The crowd had listened patiently because there was plenty of orange soda, and because rumor had it that Cuban "advisors" such as Bartolomeo were soon to become part of history too. But certainly the most exciting topic for the people had been the handbills showing Menardo Flat-Nose Pansón shot dead with his own pistol. People had questions about the handbills. What was truth? The man lying shown on the handbills had been killed accidentally; Menardo had been shot at his own request. Angelita waved a stack of the handbills in front of her; she tore them to pieces dramatically and threw them high over her head like confetti. The handbills were the work of an enemy who had slandered the good name of all tribal people in the mountains.

El Feo left the politics to Angelita, who got intoxicated on the subject of Marx even as she denied being a missionary for Marx. El Feo had confronted Angelita with his suspicions: somehow Angelita had been bewitched by the photographs and writings of Engels and Marx. El Feo had listened to Angelita go on and on about Marx and Engels. Angelita told El Feo about Engels's hearty sexual appetite.

They had already made love a number of times when El Feo had teased Angelita about her two other lovers, Engels and Marx. At first El Feo feared he had gone too far because Angelita's jaws had clenched and she had frowned. But El Feo had grinned and chuckled to keep the mood light, and Angelita had calmed down. She was no Marxist; she had her own ideas about political systems, and they had nothing to do with white men in Europe. But after Angelita had defended herself, she had showed El Feo photographs of Marx and Engels in books. She had remained quiet for a long time staring at the photographs. El Feo had settled back in the hammock to smoke a cigarette and watch the wild woman. Finally after a long time, Angelita had told El Feo the truth; the first time she had opened a volume of *Das Kapital,* she had been amazed at the blazing darkness of Marx's eyes. The photograph had been made when Marx was a young man. She confessed to El Feo she had never entirely believed what the old-time people said about photography until she had seen the photograph of Marx. A flicker of energy belonging to Marx and Marx alone still resided within the blazing eyes of the image; emanations of this energy had reached out to Angelita from the page. But it was only after she had heard his stories that she had fallen in love with Karl Marx. Both El Feo and Angelita had laughed and shaken their heads. Angelita warned El Feo never to repeat their conversation; enough rumors went through the villages about Angelita's lovers. They didn't need speculation about ghosts or spirits. They didn't need, and their army didn't need, any rumors about sorcery. The village committees had to caution the people: generous financial aid would keep rolling in so long as all the "friends of the Indians" remained confident. Witchcraft rumors upset white people. That was a fact they had to live with.

SEXUAL RIVALS

EL FEO HAD NEVER had sex with such a delicious woman as Angelita. It was because she was so powerful that she excited him so much. He had got aroused just listening to her reasons for secrecy about Engels and Marx. El Feo had pulled Angelita on top of himself on their bedrolls in the bushes where they retreated for "classified activities."

"Ah! Talking about your sexual rivals, Engels and Marx, has excited you," Angelita said. El Feo was only able to nod before he buried his face between Angelita's heavy brown breasts. He imagined the warmth of the darkest, deepest forest in an early-summer rain; he imagined he was burying himself deeper and deeper into the core of the earth until he lost himself in eternity where wide rivers ran to a gentle ocean that included all beings, even Engels and Marx. El Feo felt how greedy this wild woman Angelita was, her eyes closed tight, lost in the imaginary embraces of fierce Marx, or the gentle caresses of the lesser presence

Engels. Luckily El Feo had never been jealous. That had been one of the worst aspects of the Cuban, who thought women were private property once they had been his sex partners.

Bartolomeo was a complete failure in El Feo's view because communal living meant share and share alike. Bartolomeo had never lost his taste for bourgeois women. Bartolomeo was responsible for the handbills of Menardo's corpse and the Marxist slogan. Bartolomeo had printed the handbills because Menardo had fucked Alegría while Bartolomeo was fucking her. Bartolomeo had had her first, not her "husband." Bartolomeo was always thinking with his dick, and Cuban aid or no Cuban aid, the people's army had enough trouble without dick brains such as Bartolomeo. El Feo knew better than to press his luck with such a woman as Angelita; he wanted to, but dared not ask what exactly she imagined Engels and Marx were doing.

Politics didn't add up. In the end only the Earth remained, and they'd all return to her as dust. El Feo left books and politics to Angelita, who was strong enough to stomach the poison about taxes, authorities, and the existence of states. El Feo himself did not worry. History was unstoppable. The days, years, and centuries were spirit beings who traveled the universe, returning endlessly. The Spirits of the Night and the Spirits of the Day would take care of the people.

The United States allowed huge stores of grain and cheese to rot; El Feo had watched on television: the waste, great hills of discarded lumber and wire, and his heart had beat faster because he had realized someday the United States would spend all its money and sell off and strip everything they could take from the land. Finally, the United States would be poor and broke, and all the water would be gone; then the people would see European descendants scurrying back across the ocean back to the lands of their forefathers.

El Feo focused all his energy into one desire: to retake the land. El Feo's work was to remind Angelita and the others not to lose sight of their task. There had been too many masks and disguises already, too many times government police had posed as rebel guerrillas to slaughter poor villagers in the mountains, while rebel guerrillas dressed as government police to rob motorists.

El Feo had seen enough of television and its effect on people to know the citizens could never trust what they were seeing or hearing from television, newspapers, or radio. Because the politicians now were trained actors, and on television, actors dressed as undercover police in beards, dirty hair, and beggar's clothes. Ordinary citizens would never again be certain who was who or what was what; no matter whether they were peasants or workers, video images and sounds were not to be trusted. Not even Angelita or El Feo himself could be trusted speaking from a television screen because electronic images were easily tampered with.

El Feo had devised a simple and clear test to reveal whether so-called "leaders of the people" were true or only impostors sent by the vampires and werewolves of greed. The test was easy: true leaders of the people made return of the land the first priority. No excuses, no postponements, not even for one day, must be tolerated by the people. Even before the burial of the dead, who did not mind waiting because they had died fighting for the return of the lands. Before bridges, roads, electricity, or phone lines were restored, the land must be returned to the people whose ancestors had lived on the land for twenty thousand years continuously. Big talk and promises of free gasoline, free gener-ators, free chain saws and motorcycles—all of this was the wool the false leaders pulled over the eyes of unwary citizens. First the land. Without the land there was no need for chain saws or motorcycles; without the land, there was no place to set the generator or TV.

El Feo understood he had been chosen for one task: to remind the people never to lose sight of their precious land. He had listened to Angelita describe early betrayals of Marx, and the revolutions in France and later in Russia. True leaders of the revolution would deed back thousands of millions of acres of land. Even city people might identify the true leaders because true leaders would immediately seize all vacant apartments and houses to provide shelter for all the homeless.

El Feo warned the people to beware of the talkers and the foot-draggers; land first, talk and ideology later. Those were the rules. Leaders caught stalling or lying would be shot. The rules were simple. To any whiners or grumblers in his teenage army, El Feo said, "Shut up! Quit sniveling! We've been sent to take back the land. You can get 'rich' afterwards, if you have to."

ON TRIAL FOR CRIMES
AGAINST TRIBAL HISTORIES

BARTOLOMEO HAD BEEN incredulous. He refused to believe he was about to be tried before the people's committee assembled in the plaza sipping orange soda he had provided for them. He, Bartolomeo, had been generous enough to obtain the arms and other supplies they had requested; he, Bartolomeo, had many times argued on their behalf when Cuban officials had wanted to cut off aid to these mountain villages. Bartolomeo had looked intently at Angelita as if to remind her of those long sweaty afternoons in bed together; Angelita smiled and shook her head. It was time to get on with the people's case against Bartolomeo. "Unbelievable!" Bartolomeo said. "You Indians are serious!"

All the people present in the village plaza would constitute the people's committee; the verdict would be reached by a count of hands. Angelita would interpret the people's discussion for Bartolomeo in Spanish.

Bartolomeo's first offense concerned the picture of the dead capitalist on pamphlets that falsely discredited and endangered the people's army for the sake of cheap Marxist propaganda. The second charge against Bartolomeo was for crimes against the people's history.

"What *history*?" Bartolomeo had fired back in a sneering tone. "Jungle monkeys and savages have no history!" Bartolomeo had gone on to make scornful remarks about "dumb and gullible squaws" who had confused themselves reading too many books with ideas that were over their heads—like water too deep. "How deep?" Angelita asked, and imagined Bartolomeo on the morning they would lead him to the new pine two-by-fours nailed into a gallows; not as deep as Bartolomeo was going to dive that morning from the new pine lumber.

Bartolomeo had been clever enough to attempt to mobilize village jealousies and gossip aimed at Angelita and her wild ideas and the Devil's books she read. Here Angelita pointed out Bartolomeo's attempt to use that worn European ploy: set one faction of Indians against another. But Bartolomeo had not known when to stop his attacks on Angelita. He had demanded to take the stand to testify on his own behalf. Angelita knew it was better if Bartolomeo did talk, otherwise people might begin to feel sorry for him standing mute as they might before a village council or before the soldiers or police. On the stand, Bartolomeo had harangued everyone—all of them—unit leaders, village council members, even idle spectators. It had been as if he, Bartolomeo, were not on trial but *they* were.

Bartolomeo had continued sarcastically about their "primitive animalistic tribalism," which was "the whore of nationalism and the dupe of capitalism." Nationalism such as theirs, he said, "had to be cut out and burned like a tumor." Even while Bartolomeo had been speaking, the people who had crowded under the long tin drying shed where the trial was being held had whispered and joked with one another. The people had thought it amusing and typical of a white man to make a fool of himself in court. The people themselves had had hundreds of years of the white men's courts, and they knew the one on trial was not supposed to argue and talk back the way the Cuban had.

But Bartolomeo had wanted to argue. He seemed to relish his role as defense attorney for himself. Bartolomeo seemed unable to comprehend who was on trial. What right did they, ignorant Indians, have to put educated Cuban citizens on trial? "*You* set foot in *our* sovereign jurisdiction. That is where we get the 'right,' Comrade Bartolomeo," Angelita had answered. If he kept talking that way, everyone would raise a hand and vote the death penalty. But Comrade Bartolomeo had not finished. His handsome face was pinched with intensity. This was not an official, authorized court. This was not fair. Angelita nodded. At least Bartolomeo had understood one thing: the trial wasn't really a personal matter or about personal dislike of Bartolomeo. The Committee for Justice and Land Redistribution had no time for mere personal matters. This was a trial of all Europeans. More than five hundred years of white men in Indian jurisdiction were on trial with Bartolomeo.

Angelita might have translated Bartolomeo's ridicule and scorn differently for the people's committee, who didn't understand much Spanish. She might have tipped off Bartolomeo to say nothing—certainly not to argue. Angelita might have got Bartolomeo a commuted sentence if she had wished. But that afternoon in the plaza, Angelita had watched Bartolomeo, so handsome, so presumptuous, so ignorant, and she knew he finally had to go. Oh, well, who was Bartolomeo anyway? What did he matter? Who would remember him?

Angelita announced to the Committee and the people assembled in the village plaza she would read a list that was only a small sample of the great mass of Native American history that Bartolomeo and the other white men, so-called Marxists, had tried to omit and destroy. The list would be in Spanish to prove Bartolomeo had no excuse for his ignorance. Native uprisings and rebellions in the Americas had been exhaustively reported by the Church clergy, and colonial flunkies who had sent frantic dispatches to the Spanish throne from the New World pleading for more weapons and soldiers. Indigenous American uprisings had been far more extensive than any Europeans wanted to admit, not even the Marxists, who were jealous of African and Native American slave workers who had risen up successfully against colonial masters without the leadership of a white man.

"Here, listen to this," Angelita said. "Here's what the Europeans don't want us to know or remember," and Angelita had begun reading the dates, names, and places rapidly in Spanish for Bartolomeo to hear, since he was the perpetrator of crimes against history. "Each day since the arrival of the Europeans, somewhere in the vastness of the Americas the sun rises on Native American resistance and revolution. Listen to the history that Europeans, even Marxists, hope we Native Americans will forget! These are only a few of the *big* uprisings and revolutions. These don't include all the rebellions, all the mysterious fires, all the lost horses and other acts of resistance. She began to read:

1510—Cuba—Hateuy leads the first Native American revolt against European slave hunters.

1521—Colombia—Colonial slave hunters outrage coastal Indians, who destroy Dominican convent at Chiribichi, killing two priests.

1526—U.S.A.—Pee Dee River, South Carolina; Indian and Negro slaves rise up.

1536—Peru—Incas rise up against Pizarro and lay siege to Cuzco and set it afire. Rebellion spreads down Rimac Valley where Incas lay siege to Lima.

1538—U.S.A.—Zuni Pueblo Indians kill the Moor, Esteban, sent by Spanish to scout the Grand Chichimecas for cities of gold.

1540—U.S.A.—Zuni Pueblo Indians fight Coronado to prevent starving Spanish expedition from entering village.

1540—U.S.A.—Hopi Pueblo Indians fight and repel de Tovar and his men.

1540—Mexico—Alvarado argues that two kings of the Cakchiquel Quiche must hang, otherwise they will incite revolt.

1540–41—Mexico—Great Mixton War led by Tenamaztle and others against de Guzmán.

1541—Mexico—*July:* Alvarado dies in freak accident impaled on his own spear. *August:* Colonial capital of Guatemala is flooded by volcanic crater lake; Alvarado's wife drowns.

1542—Mexico—Indian rebellion at Mixton is put down, and all the rebels are branded and sold into slavery. In Jalisco, 4,650 women and children are branded on grounds of rebellion.

1545—Mexico—Two hundred thousand Indians die of flu around Mexico City and Chiapas.

1590–94—Mexico—Nacabeba leads rebellion of Indians at Deboropa; Catholic priest, Father Tapia, is killed.

1598—U.S.A.—Acoma Pueblo people fight Onate's troops and kill assistant commander Zaldivan.

1600—Mexico—Revolt by mountain tribes, Chicoratos and Cavametos. Churches are burned. Revolt by Toroacas Indians on San Ignacio Island.

1610—Mexico—Two Mayas declare themselves "pope" and "bishop" in revolt against the Europeans' exclusive control of the sacred.

1616—Mexico—Great Tepehuan Rebellion at San Pablo, northwest of Durango, led by "Cobameai" on the feast of the Virgin; three hundred Europeans die.

1617—Mexico—Yaqui warriors defeat Spaniards; Captain Hurtado and men narrowly escape death.

1622—U.S.A.—Indian uprising at James River, 347 Europeans dead.

1624—Mexico—Rebellion at the royal mines of San Andres led by Nebomes.

1633—Mexico—Pimas revolt at Nuri, east of the Yaqui River.

1648—Mexico—Tarahumara Rebellion at Fariagic, southwest of Parral. Priest is hanged from an arm of a cross in front of the church. Tarahumaras say church bells attract the plague.

1680—U.S.A.—Great Pueblo Indian Revolt. Pueblo tribes join

Apache and Navajo tribes to drive Europeans south across the Rio Grande at El Paso. Three hundred ten Europeans dead.

1690—Mexico—Quaualatas of the Tarahumaras leads the Tepehuan Revolt in northwestern Mexico. Four hundred Spaniards killed, including four priests. Quaualatas promised any Indian who died fighting would be resurrected.

1712—Mexico—Tzeltal Maya revolt in Chiapas, take control of the Church and sacraments.

1720—Paraguay—Successful Indian revolt.

1760—Jamaica—The Great Jamaican Rebellion led by Koromantin, a Gold Coast Negro, oracle who promises magical preparations to ward off bullets.

1761—Mexico—Caste war and revolt led by Jacinto Canek and Mayas who sought to purge themselves of all things European. Canek is a half-breed educated by the priests.

1762—U.S.A.—Pontiac, of the Algonquin Confederation, warns all tribes to rid the continent of white people.

1766—Mexico—Lower Pimas rebel and in 1768 are joined in the revolt by the Seri Indians from the shore of the Sea of Cortés.

1778—U.S.A.—Taos, New Mexico, hosts annual "trade fairs" where Indians are bought and sold by whites.

1781—Mexico—Yumas kill Franciscan father Garcia near the Gila River junction with the Colorado River.

1781—Peru—Half-breed who calls himself Condorcanqui proclaims himself the long-lost Tupac Amaru, the Child of the Sun. Spaniards execute him.

1791—Haiti—The first successful slave rebellion in the New World. In 1801, slaves and the first "black Indians" hold off Napoleon's brother-in-law and twenty-five thousand French troops.

1805—Simón Bolívar visits European courts and salons. He refuses to kiss the Pope's slipper, and the Pope says, "Let the young Indian do as he pleases." Bolívar has not one drop of Indian blood, but Europeans believe any babies conceived in the Americas undergo changes in skin, hair, and eyes; in other words, colonials are believed to be slightly tainted.

1807—U.S.A.—"The Meteor" or "the Shooting Star," Tecumtha, notifies the governor of Ohio that all former treaties are invalid: "These lands are ours. No one has a right to remove us, because we are the first owners."

1812—U.S.A.—Red Eagle leads the Creek tribe to resist the Europeans. "Red Sticks" reject all things European.

1819—Florida—Spanish territory is "annexed" by the U.S.A. to wipe out nests of hostile Indians and runaway slaves who use Florida as a base camp for guerrilla raids on plantations across the border.

1825—Mexico—The Yaqui whose Spanish name is Bandera leads a rebellion in which the Yaquis declare themselves a sovereign nation not liable for taxes to Mexico; a Catholic priest is killed at Torim.

1910—Mexico—Eight hundred Mayo Indians rise up and take over three thousand federal troops at garrison at Navajoa.

1911—Mexico—Zapata leads the Indians, who demand "land and liberty."

1915—Mexico—Although promised land after the revolution, the Mayo Indians get none. So Bachomo leads a guerrilla band in the Fuerte River valley.

1923—Peru—Mariatequi founds Sendero Luminoso.

1945—Bolivia—Indians form National Federation of Peasants to restore Indians' rights.

Angelita skipped from the dates to the tables of facts and read the figures for the Native American holocaust:

1500—72 million people lived in North, Central, and South America.

1600—10 million people live in North, Central, and South America.

1500—25 million people live in Mexico.

1600—1 million people live in Mexico.

The village people murmured over the figures; the people were not in the habit of looking at the "bigger picture," as Angelita liked to call it. Of course the white man had never wanted Native Americans to contemplate confederacies between the tribes of the Americas; that would mean the end of European domination.

Angelita had to take a break. Rattling off all the names and dates had left her mouth dry. But the people in the crowd had begun clapping and cheering when she paused; the names and dates had touched off a great deal of excitement among the people, who immediately added dozens of other uprisings and rebellions that had occurred in that region alone. Angelita stepped away from the microphones to watch the people. Voices buzzed with enthusiasm and she realized that for a moment the crowd had forgotten the Cuban on trial as people began to recall stories of the old days, not just stories of armed rebellions and uprisings, but stories of colonials sunk into deepest depravity—Europeans who went mad while their Indian slaves looked on.

El Feo pointed at the sun. Time to get on with the trial; they didn't have all week; help could always arrive for Bartolomeo in the minivan of radical Catholic Church people or a surprise visit from Bartolomeo's superiors in Mexico City might interrupt.

Angelita returned to the microphone, and applause and shouts for "land" and "justice" and more "land" rang out, mostly from the young soldiers of the people's defense units. But others in the crowd had also cheered, and drunks made jokes and called out, "Beer! Television!" Angelita detected a change; she felt strange energy in the air—something generated by the people themselves in their anticipation and excitement. It was as if the recitation of rebellions and rebel leaders had radiated energy to the people gathered in the plaza.

"All this is only a short list. A beginning. But Comrade Bartolomeo here has no use for indigenous history. Comrade Bartolomeo denies the holocaust of indigenous Americans! Seventy-two million people in 1500 reduced to ten million people by 1600! Comrade Bartolomeo is guilty! Guilty of crimes against history!"

The people cheered and clapped, but Angelita could see they were tiring; small children had begun whining, and the old men who weren't asleep coughed, spat, and raised their straw hats to scratch.

The crowd had shifted toward the small speaker's platform with two PA speakers nailed at each corner. Behind them, the new gallows was leaning slightly in the direction of the wind. The workmen had not wanted to bother with much bracing since the scaffold would only be used once.

People were not sure about killing an outsider such as the Cuban, crime against history or no crime against history. First there were the questions concerning the white man's spirit or ghost, and where it would go after they hanged him.

El Feo shook his head slowly. The gallows should never have been built. It looked oddly like an elevated outdoor privy without its walls, with only a simple hole in the boards for the shit to drop through. El

Feo sighed. Someone would have to think of something better to do with traitors like Bartolomeo. Once the people got their land back the killing would be stopped.

The execution took place as the sun was getting low in the west. Bartolomeo wet his pants and had to be carried and dragged up the gallows steps to the noose.

"Next time *don't lie* about our history!" shouted an old woman standing near the gallows as Bartolomeo fell through the hole and dangled.

"So, sadly, they have been forced to terminate their relationship with dear comrade Bartolomeo," as a wisecracker at the graveyard had put it.

Angelita, El Feo, and the others with their volunteer units scattered in all directions from the village. Because this time, the people had *really* done it and there was no turning back. Sure, there was going to be a lot of shooting all right. Angelita was realistic about that, because after all, this was war, the war to retake the Americas and to free all the people still enslaved. You did not fight a war for such a big change without the loss of blood.

Angelita felt inspired. She talked to the people again. Change was on the horizon all over the world. The dispossessed people of the earth would rise up and take back lands that had been their birthright, and these lands would never again be held as private property, but as lands belonging to the people forever to protect. The old people had said over and over again, "Remember, tell your children so they will remember; never forget the identities of the days or the years because they shall *all* return to bring bitterness and regret to those who do not recognize the dangerous days or the murderous epochs."

If the Cubans or government authorities started asking questions, all they had to say was Comrade Bartolomeo had tried to involve them in the cocaine smuggling business.

Angelita told the people not to worry. Both governments wanted Bartolomeo dead anyway. He had outlived his usefulness.

BOOK TWO

RIVERS

MR. FISH, THE CANNIBAL

EVEN AS A CHILD, Beaufrey had realized he was different from the other children. He had always loved himself, only himself. He could remember lying in a crib sucking on his own hand, perfectly content, even blissful, when he was all alone. He disliked noise and disruptions in his perfect, drowsy pleasure and daydreams. He felt indifferent toward his mother and father, and the kindest nannies. Beaufrey understood their acts signified care and love from them, but he felt only indifference toward them. They did not matter, therefore their feelings, love, or concern did not matter either.

His selfishness gave him great satisfaction. He never altered his behavior for others; others did not fully exist—they were only ideas that flitted across his consciousness then disappeared. For as long as he could remember, Beaufrey had existed more completely than any other human being he had ever met. That was why the most bloody spectacles of torture did not upset him; because he could not be seriously touched by the contortions and screams of imperfectly drawn cartoon victims. Beaufrey knew only he could truly feel or truly suffer. The others had nervous systems like earthworms, and the torture that gave so much pleasure to audiences scarcely raised Beaufrey's blood pressure. The cries and the cringing always seemed excessive and self-indulgent; sometimes even manipulative and false. The photograph or diagram of a tortured human body had more impact for Beaufrey than film or video of the victim moaning in handcuffs and leg irons.

Beaufrey had taught himself to read by the age of three. By the time he had turned eight his parents were taking him for psychiatry twice a week because his indifference had frightened them. Dr. VM had been a stupid hack, a parasite associated with wealthy families stricken with depression, mania, or psychosis. Beaufrey had talked circles around the psychiatrist. Beaufrey at age eight had set up the shrink. Beaufrey had insisted he wanted to talk about the books he had read. Yes, Dr. VM could not disagree with this. The child was quite precocious. Which books were his favorites? Those about crimes, and those with pictures.

Crimes? Ah, the picture books. Picture storybooks?

"No," Beaufrey said rudely, "not storybook pictures! Crime pictures! Ones that show dead faces. And blood."

"And the books you read? Which one is your favorite? I don't mean picture books now."

Beaufrey had loathed the psychiatrist's air of condescension. "Stories about crimes. Famous crimes," Beaufrey had said in a bored tone of voice, watching Dr. VM scribble rapidly on a stenographer's tablet. Beaufrey's favorite book had been about the Long Island cannibal, Albert Fish.

Dr. VM had wanted to know what in particular he found interesting about the cannibal. The Fish family had been blue bloods directly off the *Mayflower*. The Fish family had been politically prominent. Dr. VM did not look up from his notes. "And?" the old quack tried to push him. "And nothing!" Beaufrey said, excited by the frown on the old doctor's face. "Mother says there are no aristocrats in America."

Albert Fish had been a cannibal and a child molester. He peeled carrots and potatoes to cook with roasts of leg or arm. Mr. Fish had been quite particular about the age and size because they affect flavor and tenderness. Mr. Fish had explained his recipes to police after they had arrested him. Dr. VM had scribbled notes furiously and leaned forward in his chair. Why did Mr. Fish kill the children? So he could eat them. Why did Mr. Fish eat the children? Because he was hungry for the taste of human flesh. Psychiatry's questions were useless and stupid.

The English called it blue blood; on the endless plains of Colombia, they called it *sangre limpia* or *sangre pura*. Albert Fish had belonged to a wealthy family. His craving for the flavor of roasted human meat had got the best of Mr. Fish, and the police had captured him carrying a human arm roast in his shopping bag.

As a child, Beaufrey's intuition and imagination had been strangely acute. He had felt Albert Fish and he were kindred spirits because they shared not only social rank, but complete indifference about the life or death of other human beings. As Beaufrey had read European history in college, he had realized there had always been a connection between human cannibals and the aristocracy. Members of European aristocracy were simply more inclined to hunger and crave human flesh and blood because centuries of *le droit du seigneur* had corrupted them absolutely. Beaufrey was bored by anything less than the absolute; of course "blue bloods" such as himself were different. Bluebeard in his castle hung "his" wives from meat hooks in the tower; the "wives" had been the brides of serfs raped by the master on the evening of their wedding night.

In the beginning, European aristocracy had risen above the common soil; the royalty had been superior beings who had survived the test of combat's fire and steel. But two world wars had consumed Europe's best blood; after the First World War, true aristocracy had virtually been annihilated. Beaufrey's mother had talked about nothing else while she had searched in vain for a young woman of a lineage as august as theirs.

So much for blue blood. Those with *sangre pura* were entirely different beings, on a far higher plane, inconceivable to commoners. They might crave roasted human flesh. What of it? There was nothing in the world that money could not buy. Beaufrey was especially interested in things, places, or beings that were not for sale; he got a thrill out of what was unavailable or forbidden.

The words *unavailable* and *forbidden* did not apply to aristocrats. Laws in England and the United States traced their origins to the "courts" of feudal lords who had listened to complaints and testimony and then passed judgment on the serfs.

SANGRE PURA

THE *FINCA* BELONGS to Serlo; he is the only genuine blue blood. Beaufrey likes to make this point to David; that Serlo is a blue blood, but all David's got is bloody hands. The change of locations is deliberate. There had been hundreds of telephone calls for David after the show had sold out; "Too much publicity, Davey," Beaufrey had told him. But then there had been the mess with the bitch over the child. David still believed the bitch was hiding the baby somewhere with her prostitute friends, maybe in Tucson, and had made up the kidnapping story. The grassy plains of Colombia were the ideal location to weather political and legal storms.

David had loved his baby son. Beaufrey enjoyed watching David's dumb pain over the disappearance of the child. Fathers who gushed over sons made Beaufrey want to smash in their faces. He despised public sentimentality over infants and small children. In private, these same infants had their heads smashed or vaginas ripped; after all, they were the private property of their fathers. The poor might be excused for their sentimentality since their offspring were all that would ever be theirs, however briefly the infant survived. Breeding was for animals; Beaufrey himself had been a byproduct of his mother's last menopausal fling in Paris. She had never wanted children because of the nuisance and the damage they did to the figure. But bless her, his mother had feared abortion more than she had feared a baby at forty-six.

Beaufrey had underestimated David's need to see himself reproduced, to see his own flesh live on; it was a common hang-up Beaufrey had seen in gay men, especially the men who called themselves "straight" because they wanted to see their face reproduced on a tiny, shitting, screaming baby. Humans were like monkeys delighted with the little mirror images, until they realized any likeness was only illusion. Children, in fact, grew into total strangers. Beaufrey and his parents had loathed one another.

Beaufrey had taken David's girlfriend, Seese, to the abortionist once before, but that had been when she and David had first been lovers, before Seese and Beaufrey had begun to hate one another.

At first David had not spent much time at the apartment Beaufrey had rented for Seese and the baby. They could not live in the penthouse with a baby screaming day and night. But later, David had begun to bring the baby up to the penthouse where he spent entire afternoons photographing the infant posed on white rabbit fur. Beaufrey had been strangely intrigued by David's obsession with the infant's supposed resemblance to himself. David had shot dozens of rolls of color film of the baby sleeping, close-up studies of the baby's face.

The change in David's attitude had been obvious. David wanted the child. He did not want that cunt to have that essence of himself, his child. Seese was nothing but an addict and a drunk; at her best, she was a whore. As David talked, he got more excited. He had a plan. David wanted to take the child and leave the United States. David had overheard Beaufrey and Luis talk about the ranch or *finca* in Colombia. Colombia seemed far enough away from the U.S. courts.

David was almost delectable when he was serious and his nostrils had a slight flare. Beaufrey had to smile. Here was one of life's little mysteries: aristocratic bloodlines seemed genetically incompatible with physical beauty. Beaufrey would be the first to admit the rich were ugly; only great fortunes had made it possible for ugly blue bloods to continue reproducing themselves. Beaufrey knew that David, Eric, and all the other "rough trade" only stayed as long as there was dope and money. Street punks looked blank if they heard the term *blue blood;* occasionally one might confuse the word with *blue ball* or scrotal congestion. Still, life's mystery was that the loveliest, most tender pieces of beauty were "rough trade"—the boys of the street dripping their pearls in the soot.

The idea of the game was to permit gorgeous young men such as David to misunderstand their importance in the world. The objective was to fool the young men before they could fool Beaufrey. Artists were the most fascinating to Beaufrey because they were often shattered and easily manipulated emotionally. Artists were quite exciting to destroy. Because they participated so freely. Eric had made his suicide a sort of visual event or installation, which Eric had somehow known would be irresistible to a visual artist such as David.

Beaufrey loved the theater. Players such as Eric or David and the cunt were a dime a dozen; Beaufrey was the director and author; he was the producer. One act followed another; Eric had performed the last act of his life farce perfectly; uncanny how Eric's blood and flesh had become a medium consumed by a single performance.

David had been triumphant after he had snatched Monte from his playpen. Beaufrey had made all the arrangements, including the purchase of passports and papers for the infant. They had left the same afternoon for Cartagena by chartered jet. They could count on Seese to stay drunk and coked up for hours before she got desperate enough to contact the police.

The first week in Cartagena it had seemed possible to endure David's child's remaining with them. The child seldom cried for its mother and slept long intervals in the afternoon when Beaufrey preferred sex. But at the beginning of the second week, the child had begun crying and rocking its crib against a wall while they were having sex. Beaufrey had been furious about the interruption, but pretended he did not mind

David's fussing with the child. Beaufrey had cut more lines of cocaine on the mirror and filled both glasses with champagne. David must have no suspicion. Later Beaufrey discussed the schedule: they could not fly out to the *finca* until the end of the week.

The baby seemed to sense David's rising frustration and had cried for hours despite the best efforts of the night nurse, a chubby, young Colombian woman with three children of her own at home. Beaufrey had rented another suite for himself and Serlo on another floor because the baby's crying had annoyed him so much. David had pretended he did not mind being left behind in the hotel suite with a crying baby and its nurse; but David had always been jealous of Serlo. Only a few nights before, David had demanded Beaufrey tell him everything he and Serlo did in bed together.

Beaufrey marveled at the odd chemistry. David pretended he was not jealous. But he had started fucking the chubby night nurse, who taught him to mix paregoric in the baby's formula. Before the end of the week, David had begun leaving the baby with the nurse in the suite to join Beaufrey and Serlo upstairs in the penthouse for drinks and dinner followed by cocaine and videos of police torture, autopsies, or other new acquisitions. Beaufrey claimed he wanted David to see what others had done with "still-life studies" such as Eric, but Beaufrey had enjoyed watching the expressions on David's face as the torture had progressed conveniently into the "autopsy" of the victim.

David had enjoyed watching torture and killing videos before; most men did. Beaufrey divided the world into those who admitted the truth and those who lied. But that night David denied the videos gave him pleasure. David had been sullen throughout cocktails and the lovely dinner Beaufrey had ordered in their suite. That night, David had leapt up from his chair the instant he saw the surgery paraphernalia appear on the video screen. David had left the hotel without stopping to check with the nurse about the baby. Beaufrey had to smile to himself. David's reaction was too powerful to overlook; David was afraid to feel how much he enjoyed the scalpel sinking through skin and flesh.

Beaufrey always relied on intuition to know when a situation or a sucker was ripe. Beaufrey had been intrigued by the process of deterioration in Eric; now in David, he was beginning to detect a similar pattern. Separate David from G. and the gallery with all the ass lickers, adulation and hoopla, and David would diminish a little more each day until there was nothing. No David. He would no longer exist except when he stared into the face of a baby. But soon David had not even looked at his baby.

David's reaction had been typical of U.S. citizens too long insulated from foreigners and strange climates. At first, David had been exhilarated by the novelty. Cartagena had soon drained David, and he had lost a certain edge as the days passed and the hotel switchboard seemed unable to connect him with his gallery more than twice a week. Finally David had become depressed and weepy over imagined infidelities between Beaufrey and Serlo.

David was ripe. Beaufrey could feel his excitement rising as the final moves of the game were being made and it was clear his prey could not escape. Beaufrey had purposely waited three weeks in Cartagena to make the kidnapping seem more plausible. Seese would need time for everything to sink in; that Monte had been taken, that David was responsible, that her only hope was to hire someone to find them. Seese had old connections in Tucson who could track Beaufrey; that had been another reason Beaufrey was ready to make his new headquarters on the remote Colombian plains. Or at least these were the stories Beaufrey had already fed to David, who wasn't completely stupid. The plan required enough time so retaliation by Seese was possible.

The flight to the *finca* had been scheduled for early the next morning. David had gone out with Serlo to buy darkroom equipment and supplies he would need at the ranch. Beaufrey had arranged for the four gunmen to enter David's hotel suite and to leave the nurse unharmed, locked in a closet. The nurse had identified the gunmen as foreigners, Mexicans she thought. Beaufrey had specified Mexicans to further implicate the connections Seese had in Tucson.

The shock of seeing police, hotel staff, even journalists, crowded around his door had left David pale and withdrawn. Beaufrey had shown David to the red leather armchair and asked Serlo to bring them some brandy. Beaufrey did all the talking because his friend did not speak Spanish fluently. As soon as the police and other authorities had grasped the possibility the child's mother from the U.S. had taken the baby, the excitement immediately subsided. Oh! Oh! That was a different matter! Very soon the hall outside the suite had been cleared of all but a few police inspectors who were required to complete reports.

Beaufrey had coaxed David to drink the brandy and to snort some cocaine to settle his nerves. Beaufrey wanted David to know he was prepared to charter a return flight to the United States. Nothing was more important to Beaufrey than for David to find his infant son.

David had snorted a line of cocaine and settled back on the sofa with his eyes closed, pinching his nostrils shut with one hand. Beaufrey especially enjoyed watching David when David was angry or upset. David's pouting mouth aroused Beaufrey. He had the urge to cross the room and lick the traces of cocaine powder from David's nostrils. Dull or ordinary people were so much more interesting when you and they were drunk and high on coke, just as the most ordinary street boys became special after their nipples sported diamond or gold studs. Nothing stimulated the cerebral cortex like cocaine unless it was coffee. "The deadly 'C' plants from South America," he said, giggling. Beaufrey was drunk. He was high. He must not giggle again because David's baby had been stolen only hours earlier. He snorted more coke. A great tingling rush came over Beaufrey's entire body all at once. Bliss! Bliss! Nothing matters but bliss! Beaufrey and David stayed in the hotel suite for two days while Serlo took all telephone calls from local authorities and police, who wished to contact the United States to locate the missing child's mother. But after numerous assurances from Serlo that the infant's mother had kidnapped it, police authorities marked the case file "inactive."

Beaufrey persuaded David to fly with him and Serlo to the *finca*. David seemed to have forgotten he had kidnapped Monte in the first place, and that the police in San Diego might be looking for David. Or they might not be looking for him, since Monte was David's own son and the child's mother was an addict and a whore.

At the *finca*, David had regained much of his former vigor. He wasn't going to let Seese keep the child. The child was his. Beaufrey had nodded and pretended to agree with everything David said. The first few days at the ranch had been a replay of the last days in the hotel in Cartagena, where Serlo had been relegated to the role of receptionist while Beaufrey and David had lain naked in the king-size bed snorting gram after gram of cocaine watching torture videos or soccer games on big-screen satellite TV.

ALTERNATIVE EARTH UNITS

SERLO HAD REMAINED perfectly calm. Only he, of all the others, had the rare gift of perfect calm. Serlo was there to keep watch; in all directions, farther than the eye could see, the infinite blue sky enclosed the plain. Serlo was *sangre pura;* years before they had all the mestizos and Indians relocated to work on their ranching operations in Argentina. The *finca* was to become a stronghold for those of *sangre pura* as unrest and revolutions continued to sweep through.

Serlo preferred that Beaufrey be dominant; danger was exciting. Their most engaging conversations together had concerned the importance of lineage. The United States had vulgarized wealth by allowing the lowest levels of humanity to worm their way into political power in a so-called democracy. Beaufrey and Serlo both agreed lineage was all that mattered. Those of highest lineage had never lost their great wealth; lesser lines of nobility had found themselves with lineages but no money.

Serlo had dedicated himself to a cause. Really it wasn't as quixotic as all that; other great leaders and thinkers had shared Serlo's concern. He believed the human race would die out without a proper genetic balance. All along the *droit du seigneur* had been aimed at constant infusion of superior aristocratic blood into the peasant stock, just as Serlo had heard his uncles laugh about the rubber plantations years before where they had raped six or seven young Indian women, not because they had been lustful men, they were not, but because they believed it was their God-given duty to "upgrade" mestizo and Indian bloodstock.

Serlo was the first to concede that a great deal of weak genetic material in the human population was Caucasian, the results of improper mixing of bloodlines. For example, the matings of Polish and Irish resulted in hybrid individuals worse than either of the parents. Serlo had studied at the private institutes for eugenics research, which even he had felt were questionable because researchers had refused to consider the factor of the mother. Serlo had studied a large body of psychological and psychiatric writings that clearly demonstrated that even the most perfect genetic specimen could be ruined, absolutely destroyed, by the defects of the child's mother. Serlo believed the problems that Freud had identified need not occur if a child's "parents" were both male. The nature of the female was to engulf what was outside her body, to never let the umbilical cord be severed; gradually the mother became a vampire.

Serlo did not mind Beaufrey's cheap street boys, or the gringos, not even Eric; how could Serlo have possibly felt anything at all about them? Jealousy was out of the question. Serlo had *sangre pura;* "blue blood" deserved "blue blood." In the end there could be nothing better. The *finca* would become his research center. An institute also. They would be able to conduct research in complete seclusion. While Beaufrey was not interested in the scholarly details, still he understood simple political realities. Riches meant little if the cities were burning and anarchy reigned.

At the *finca* they would have everything; the underground vaults and storage units had been built to accommodate the bales of U.S. dollars, deutsche marks, and other currency put in storage by certain of Beaufrey's clients. Other underground units contained giant, sealed tanks of water and barrels of wine. Other units contained immense stores of dehydrated foods. But Serlo had not stopped here; he had made a generous research grant to a young scientist from Geneva, who had traveled to Colombia and lived on the *finca* for a year as he designed and supervised the construction of an underground chamber or "Alternative Earth" unit. Once sealed, the Alternative Earth unit contained the plants, animals, and water necessary to continue independently as long as electricity was generated by the new "peanut-size" atomic reactors.

But Serlo's interest in Alternative Earth module research extended far beyond mere survival or self-defense from anarchy with underground caches of supplies and weapons. In the end, the earth would be uninhabitable. The Alternative Earth modules would be loaded with the last of the earth's uncontaminated soil, water, and oxygen and would be launched by immense rockets into high orbits around the earth where sunlight would sustain plants to supply oxygen, as well as food. Alternative Earth modules would orbit together in colonies, and the select few would continue as they always had, gliding in luxury and ease across polished decks of steel and glass islands where they looked down on earth as they had once gazed down at Rome or Mexico City from luxury penthouses, still sipping cocktails.

The colonies in earth's orbit would periodically be recharged with water and oxygen from earth, but the Alternative Earth modules had been designed to be self-sufficient, closed systems, capable of remaining cut off from earth for years if necessary while the upheaval and violence threatened those of superior lineage.

DAVID'S INFANT SON

SERLO HAD ALMOST persuaded Beaufrey to forget the one-man theater experiments with Eric in San Diego when David had appeared on the scene with the woman not far behind. Serlo had never cared for beauty or virginity since neither were as lasting as one's lineage, which not even death could diminish. Serlo never failed to take new visitors, such as David, down the long hall to see the portraits. Those along the north wall had been his mother's lineage; these along the south wall were his father's lineage, which was perhaps somewhat less distinguished.

Serlo had been interested in Beaufrey's preoccupation with David's girlfriend and David's child. Serlo knew Beaufrey wanted Seese dead. He was curious to know what Beaufrey would do with the infant. If Beaufrey did not have the infant killed, Serlo wanted it raised by two men in what would be his institute's first important experiment. The child was of common blood, but one did not waste aristocratic blood unnecessarily. Serlo did not bother with questions; whatever Beaufrey had done with the infant would undoubtedly be recorded on videotape or with photographs anyway.

Serlo had been watching David's attentions toward him; odd how David had ignored Serlo until he saw the landing strip and the ranch buildings of the *finca*. David was street trash; street boys were the same the world over, whether they were from the U.S. or from downtown Bogotá. Serlo liked a good dog; a good dog wagged its tail when it sniffed fresh meat. Serlo was amused at U.S. street boys who called themselves "musicians" or "painters," but not "prostitutes." David had misunderstood his status entirely after the success of his one-man show. Of course Beaufrey used to play along to set them up. Beaufrey loved to see their faces fall and their eyes brim with tears, these street boys who had thought they were his "equals." Suddenly one day Beaufrey would put them in their place.

SECRET AGENDA

DAVID HATED SEESE so much he had failed to recognize how unlikely it would have been for Seese to stay off vodka and cocaine long enough to arrange to have them tracked to Cartagena. All David understood was his baby son, Monte, had been taken by kidnappers hired by that cunt Seese. David had even returned to San Diego once from the *finca* because the whore had insisted she did not have the baby. Beaufrey had stayed up all night with David, snorting cocaine and arguing about having the woman killed. If Seese were dead, they might find who was hiding the baby for her. But David had feared they might never find his baby with Seese dead.

Serlo hoped to wean Beaufrey gradually from street boys and psychodramas because they would spend most of the year living on the remote *finca*. Serlo had calculated David's departure for later in the year. Although Beaufrey would deny it, Serlo knows Beaufrey is obsessed with David. Beaufrey confided he had felt strangely excited that he had stolen David's son but David had no inkling, no suspicion. How Beaufrey relished the deceit. Beaufrey does not want to lose his plaything; otherwise, why bother to fabricate the kidnapping at the hotel, why let the child's mother live any longer?

At the *finca*, Serlo and Beaufrey allowed nothing to interfere with horseback riding. Serlo and Beaufrey each had competed at the international level for equestrian teams—Serlo riding for Colombia and Beaufrey for Argentina. At first David had gone to his new darkroom, equipped with computerized color enlargers and color-processing systems, while Serlo and Beaufrey rode the practice course on their dressage horses. But after a few weeks, David could not bear to listen to the dinnertime conversations about their horseback rides together. Serlo secretly savored David's feeling of isolation and purposely had launched dinner-table conversations about the Polish royal cavalries and the origins of dressage in the military use of horses.

Serlo had talked coyly about the "incomparable exhilaration" one experienced as one's slightest touch commanded instant response from the powerful volatile animal quivering under one's own body. David was determined not to be left out. Darkroom work bored him. Taking the photographs was more exciting. He wanted to ride horseback too, he had announced. The big Dutch dressage horses were too ugly and clumsy for David's taste. In the pasture with the polo ponies David had noticed a small chestnut mare with four white feet; *that* was the horse he wanted. Serlo had watched David struggle to mount the small, nervous mare; no reasonable man would ever have chosen the crazy-eyed mare.

David did not ride gracefully, but he did not fall off either. David had chosen the worst horse on the *finca*. The undersized Thoroughbred mare had been too high-strung to use for polo. The open space and unfenced distances of plains to all horizons affected the mare strangely, and the grooms speculated the mare had been born and reared in box stalls then ridden indoors inside equestrian arenas until the mare had been sold to the *finca*. Once out of the box stalls and away from the confines of paddocks and fences and buildings, the mare had become increasingly excited. The grooms called the affliction "rapture of the plain" or "rapture of the wide-open spaces"; local people reported similar strange afflictions in dogs brought from the city accustomed only to enclosures. Unkenneled for the first time on the vast plain, the dogs bolted away, to run and run past exhaustion to death.

David had been able to hold the mare in check at a walk inside the exercise paddocks; but when he had allowed the horse more rein, she had taken both bits in her teeth and head high, she had bolted. Serlo thought David would fall, but the mare had not bucked, and David had clung to the mare as she raced around the paddock. Serlo had to check his horse sharply as it pulled at the bit to follow the mare. Beaufrey's mount was well seasoned, and Beaufrey's confidence soothed the horse. But Serlo was riding a less-finished horse, a recent purchase. Serlo had been buying different breeding stock so the *finca* would be self-sufficient, with different horses for different purposes. Serlo believed the day would come when the world was overrun with swarms of brown and yellow human larvae called natives. Serlo carefully planned and prepared for the days of chaos about to arrive. But Beaufrey himself was not so sure. Beaufrey had never voiced his doubts to Serlo, of course. Serlo was extremely sensitive about his global theories. He was a charter member of a secret multinational organization with a "secret agenda" for the entire world.

There was little use in bringing a genetically superior man into a world crowded and polluted by the degenerate masses. The history of the secret agenda had begun with the German Third Reich, but it had not ended with Hitler's death. The group's secret agenda had been right on schedule actually because European Jewry had been destroyed. Jewish holocaust survivors were too few and too haunted to reproduce themselves effectively in Europe any longer. For all practical purposes Jews were extinct in Poland. But the most persuasive evidence of the Third Reich's success could be seen in Israel, where Palestinians kept in prison camps were tortured and killed by descendants of Jewish holocaust survivors. The Jews might have escaped the Third Reich, but now they had been possessed by the urge to inflict suffering and death. Hitler had triumphed.

If the Israelis wished to incite the Moslems in order to justify a war to wipe them off the face of the earth, then all the better for the hidden agenda. Yellows, browns, and blacks, let them slaughter one another. The agenda was concerned with survival, not justice. The old man had taught Serlo years before that to kill a man was unjust in the first place, so why bother about rules of "fair play"? A bullet in the ear or a bomb under the front car seat was not fair, but it was final.

BIOLOGICAL WARFARE

THE OLD MAN did not attempt to hide the nature of his relationship with Serlo. His parents were divorced and neither had wanted him. The old man did not consider massaging the boy's arms and legs at night homosexuality. Homosexuality involved others, other men who attempted to penetrate or who wanted to be penetrated. Serlo had learned sexual penetration was silly, unnecessary, and rotten with disease.

One night when Serlo was thirteen, the old man coughed three times then lost control of his bladder and died. Serlo had not allowed another human being to touch him in a sexual way since his grandfather's death. Serlo had battled constantly to protect his cleanliness and health. Beaufrey had first sought Serlo in Paris because rumors claimed Serlo was the last and oldest boy virgin on the Continent. Serlo had been ahead of his time with his fetishes of purity and cleanliness; there were insinuations his sex organ touched only sterile, prewarmed stainless steel cylinders used for the artificial insemination of cattle. Tantalizing gossip had circulated throughout the long Mediterranean coast about Serlo, the pale eyes and milky skin, the pride of European nobility reared on the remote plains of Colombia.

Ordinarily Beaufrey had not sought out "celebrities" of sexual kinks, but he found the stories about Serlo irresistible.

Serlo's grandfather had been a science enthusiast. The old man had ordered artificial insemination implemented for the cattle herds on all his vast *fincas*. The old man had practiced only masturbation into steel cylinders where his semen was frozen for future use. His grandfather had influenced him, Serlo admitted. The old man had dreamed that someday nobility and monarchy would be restored in Europe. The old man had left behind his seed of noble blood so the masses of Europe might someday be upgraded through the use of artificial insemination. The old man had looked far into the future and had seen that reproduction needn't involve the repulsive touch and stink of sex with a woman.

Beaufrey and Serlo had argued over tactics; the group that Serlo met with had wanted to focus upon "positive" action—research laboratories and sperm banks where a superior human being would be developed. The group had obtained reports from research scientists working to develop an artificial uterus because women were often not reliable or responsible enough to give the "superfetuses" their best chance at developing into superbabies. Yes, Serlo admitted, he was saving all his sperm in a freezer for use in future generations. Nothing was impossible, Europe was full of living monarchs; Serlo had loved to rattle off the list—all of them his distant cousins: Michael in Romania, Otto in Austria, Niko in Montenegro, Simeon in Bulgaria, and of course dear Constantine in Greece. Serlo was anxious to get his institute under way and to obtain sperm contributions from European males of noble birth lest rare and distinguished lineages disappear without issue.

Although they required time, biological and chemical agents were far superior to bullets and bombs because they worked silently and anonymously. No one could prove a thing. The AIDS virus, HIV, had not been detected for years, and by then the targeted groups had been thoroughly infected. Beaufrey had claimed the U.S. CIA developed HIV, but Serlo knew that was a lie. Years of research into rare cancers, rare viruses, and *hepatitis* had been required; followed by radical experiments in cloning bacteria and viruses. Researchers in Johannesburg had experimented with monkey viruses. The great biological bomb that had exploded was the result of international collaboration. It had been determined the first biological bomb should be detonated in Africa where researchers hoped malnutrition would enhance the virus's power. Hepatitis B had been the model they had followed to plot the spread of the immune-deficiency virus. In Africa they had simply contaminated whole blood and blood plasma supplies to be sent to remote hospitals where patients were primarily women who had just given birth. Thus husbands and subsequent newborns were infected. They had modeled their immune-deficiency virus on hepatitis B because the targeted groups had already proven their susceptibility to hepatitis B.

Serlo had learned a great deal about virology and molecular biology from attending the group's meetings. Serlo was able to appreciate the beauty of HIV in a way that Beaufrey could not understand. Hepatitis B was a disease of the poor, the nonwhite, the addicted, and the homosexual, but hepatitis B was curable. HIV had no cure. Members of the research team bragged that they had created the first "designer virus" specifically for targeted groups. The filthy would die. The clean would live. "Think of the greatest army on earth!" one of the researchers had exclaimed. "Imagine an army of billions and billions of deadly troops! What do we have? Yes, gentlemen! We have the virus army! Deadly and silent!" Of course Serlo and his associates had always been acutely aware secrecy was the group's cornerstone, but at their core lay the conviction that an endangered species fought for survival with no holds barred. HIV was the perfect weapon for those who found themselves vastly outnumbered in a final battle for survival.

Beaufrey was always bragging about the work of his friends in the U.S. CIA. Beaufrey claimed the abundance of cocaine in the United States had been planned by U.S. strategists who were concerned that heroin users in ghettos would not spread the HIV infection fast enough. Beaufrey always had to have the last word. Serlo had heard the stories about the U.S. CIA, but he doubted very much the U.S. CIA had been so well coordinated. It had only been a lucky coincidence that cheap, abundant cocaine had appeared when HIV did. Running cocaine against heroin had been a long shot, but the U.S. CIA had had little choice. The CIA's Company had lost billions of dollars in opium revenue after Saigon fell. The cocaine had been part of a deliberate plan to finance CIA operations in Mexico and Central America with the proceeds from cocaine sales in the United States. Without cocaine, the millions of young black and Hispanic men and women confined to ghettos in U.S. cities would riot. Without a cheap, abundant supply of cocaine, it would be "Burn, baby, burn!" all over again as it had been in New York, Washington, Los Angeles, Detroit, and Miami. Secretly, Beaufrey did not believe the rioting natives of the earth would have enough energy or ambition to overrun it. Uprisings and revolts always petered out after the revolutionists and their followers started watching television and had a little more to eat.

To call England or the United States a "democracy" was a big joke because in neither country did the citizens bother any longer to vote. What did it matter? Both governments had secret agendas and employed "private contractors" such as Beaufrey, while their stupid citizens muddled along in terror of new taxes. Monarchy had many advantages over corrupt elected officials; in noble family lineages, accountability extended even to the monarch. No lineage dare allow even their monarch to abuse his divine office, otherwise they might all be ruined by popular unrest, even civil war. The masses, the common folk, desperately wanted a monarch; one had only to look at the United States, where presidents and their families were embraced by the citizens as quasi-royalty. The lowly gray masses of England had paid and paid billions over the years to retain their beloved royal family. There was a strict biological order to the natural world; in this natural order, only *sangre pura* sufficed to command instinctive obedience from the masses.

BABY PICTURES

IN ORDER TO CONTROL the mare it was necessary to pull her head sharply to one side, pulling her into a tight circle that gradually slowed the mare to a walk again. David found the speed and danger exhilarating. He refused to try another horse and was bored at the slow pace Beaufrey and Serlo kept on their huge Dutch geldings. Serlo and Beaufrey sometimes performed dressage exercises as they rode along to illustrate obscure refinements. Absolute obedience, and absolute control. David could not resist making tasteless remarks about man and horses "becoming one" and other stupid sexual innuendos. The mare sensed

David's impatience with the slow pace, and she had begun to prance nervously and toss her head, rattling the bits against her teeth. The clatter of the steel against her teeth set Serlo's nerves on edge.

Beaufrey could see Serlo was offended by everything David did or said. David was a darling in that regard. David was entirely predictable. Beaufrey had even guessed which horse David would choose. Beaufrey enjoyed riding between Serlo and David to feel the tension as it grew and grew until the little mare was prancing and even the Dutch gelding Beaufrey rode became restless and steadily more agitated by the antics of David's mare. But before long David got tired of fighting to rein in the mare; and abruptly, without a word, David had let the reins go slack. The mare half-reared and took off with David like a rocket, leaving Serlo and Beaufrey behind in a cloud of dust.

Serlo thought it was really quite funny. He liked to look at David and smile because David would misread everything, blinded by egotism. David was expecting Serlo to make a big play for his body soon. They were sitting on a long dark leather couch in the *sala,* which opened into a center ballroom with a thirty-foot ceiling. With David, perhaps Serlo could teach Beaufrey a lesson about the common street trade. David's photographs were not art, they were disgusting pornography no different from Beaufrey's loathsome videotapes. Maybe all gringos were as dull witted as David. Sometimes Serlo wondered. The Texas boy Eric, he had been the same. Toys, little trifles, those boys had been punks. David never even suspected Beaufrey had arranged the kidnapping. Serlo had not asked Beaufrey about the child. He had perfected indifference to Beaufrey's weird fixations. Serlo was not curious about the fate of insignificant beings; he had not felt the thrill Beaufrey felt watching Eric, David, and Seese waltz one another closer to suicide.

The rooms were full of a rich, diffuse light from the tall windows. Long porches shaded the rooms from the bright burning sun. Beyond the yellow-blossoming trees, the plains flattened away in every direction until the light blue of the sky folded over them. There were no other tall trees in sight on the *llano,* only shrubs. Bees and large black flies browsed in the trees' blossoms. Huge black flies clung to the window screens and did not move even when the wind caused the screen to flex in and out. Serlo spoke softly.

"Down here, the hottest months are July and August. You look out these windows, and the heat is so thick it quivers—" David had a lens brush and was making delicate sweeps across the face of the telephoto lens. David did not respond. Serlo was forced to finish: "Like quicksand." David smiled because he had forced those last words from Serlo.

"Quicksand?" David wondered. David did not think of heat as quicksand, but he knew there were people who were like quicksand. David was not as sure about Beaufrey now; he took trips alone to Bogotá and refused to allow David to accompany him. David had intended to fly to San Diego, to stay there until he located where Seese had hidden Monte. But Beaufrey's unexpected trips to Bogotá had worried David. David did not believe Beaufrey's story that Serlo was asexual, and he did not believe Beaufrey was flying to Bogotá to sell videos either. Beaufrey's eye had strayed from Eric to David; David was determined not to let anyone or anything come between himself and Beaufrey. All of his life David had imagined an older man like Beaufrey—rich, aristocratic, and ruthless; someone who would be his patron, so that David would be invited to shows all across Europe.

Eric had accused David of being heartless like Beaufrey. At the time, David had said nothing, but he had been pleased with the comparison. Eric had cried too often, and the dampness on his cheeks and the downturned corners of his mouth had nearly driven David insane with the compulsion to smash the crybaby's face to bloody pulp. The dampness and moisture of Seese after the baby was born had also disgusted David. The morning David had left Seese, the last morning they had been together, David had pulled the sheets off the bed, screaming at Seese—not even words, only sounds—screaming his rage, rage over the stickiness of the bed sheets from the humidity, rage at the odor and pale-yellow stains of milk that leaked at night from her nipples while she nursed the infant in bed with her.

Even after David had taken Monte away to Cartagena, David had felt revulsion when the baby had spit up on the edge of the blanket as he held him. The nannies had been instructed to dress the baby freshly before they brought him to his father. At first David had taken many rolls of film of the baby for comparison with David's own baby pictures, which his mother had mounted in the blue leather baby books she had kept for him. David still got tears in his eyes when he thought about his mother dying. If his mother had been alive, she would have been delighted to see how much the baby looked like him. David had spent a great deal of time alone with his mother because his sister and brother had already been in school when David was born. His father had been an accountant who used to leave for his office then vanished on a three-day drunk.

David had been careful to keep all his mother's family albums; she had taught him to look at photographs of all the family branches and to identify certain family characteristics in the eyes, cheekbones, or postures. David remembered his father as a silent, angry man whose thinning gray hair stood on end when he was drunk. David had been happiest as a child on the nights when the old man did not come home. The photographs in the albums had been their favorite pastime to share— far from phone calls from police who had found his father passed out in his car. After David's sister and brother graduated and left home, the albums of photographs had been the best and most real part of his mother's life, except for David. David was her very soul, she said; without him she would simply have died. She had her gin and tonic in the morning after David went to school.

LAWSUITS

DAVID HAD WANTED Serlo to notice him; David enjoyed the charged atmosphere of sexual tension that had developed between the three of them. Beaufrey claimed Serlo was asexual; who could blame Serlo when Beaufrey refused to uncover his body? Beaufrey always had sex in silk pajamas or the clothes he was wearing. Beaufrey did not allow himself to be seen *or* embraced *or* touched. He ignored his partners. "On rainy days we wear our raincoats" had been Beaufrey's standard line about condoms. He had such potent sensitivity he was able to wear one over another for added safety. Beaufrey said he knew too much about secret biological research and the use of sexual transmission. HIV had only been the beginning.

David had been prepared to return to San Diego to make things happen, to have the bitch beaten until she revealed where Monte was hidden, when G. had called; new lawsuits over the photographs of Eric's suicide had been filed against G., the gallery, and of course David. Fortunately David and the negatives and the color transparencies were not in the United States. G. reminded David he had warned him about the risk of a lawsuit involved with the Eric photography series; but at the time, David had been confident Eric's family wanted no further publicity or embarrassment. The lawsuit, filed by Eric's parents, asked millions of dollars in punitive damages. Of course G. could no longer sell David's prints in the United States, but G. had already made arrangements with a gallery in Munich.

G. kept telling David not to worry, not to worry, the publicity was worth millions and millions. G. was handling everything. David need not worry. But David had been angry about the attorney's fees. G. was charging David's account thousands per month for attorneys. Prints of Eric's suicide were selling briskly, but David's share had been consumed by payments to lawyers. David was furious. He had waited years and years for this success to come; Eric's family and their lawsuits had ruined everything. G. said not to worry, but that was because G. knew there was little chance of losing David to a rival gallery after controversy and lawsuits. Of course the "Eric series" would still be sold abroad and to private collectors, but naturally lawsuits cast shadows over anticipated profits. G. was optimistic about David's next show; how was the new series progressing? "Great," David had lied. There was no new series. Why should there be? David had just created a brilliant series. The Eric series was his masterpiece, and the show had been a huge success until the shitbag lawyer's bills came in the mail. David blamed G. for mishandling the entire situation. He did not trust G. or G.'s bookkeeper either; just like that $100,000 was gone. Now G. had condescended to lend David $5,000, but he wanted more prints from the Eric series sent air express before G. would wire the cash.

David slammed down the telephone receiver. He felt tears in his eyes. G. had mismanaged the show and sale of his best new work. Hysteria and prejudice had turned the art critics against David. None of them understood how important the Eric series was; none of them realized David's work was about to redefine the terms *portrait* and *still life*. G. had been too anxious to sell sets of the Eric series before further lawsuits were filed by Eric's family. G.'s attorneys were his old school chums as well, and they had backed down in the face of a team of top-rate lawyers the Texans had hired. Suddenly it was as if all the work David had done to create the Eric series had been destroyed, because all the sets of limited-edition prints had been sold and less than $10,000 remained after the lawyers had been paid. G. talked vaguely about a gallery abroad where the effects of the U.S. lawsuits would not interfere. After that, what was the point of work?

Serlo rode horseback early in the morning when Beaufrey was away. He had not invited David to ride with him, but David did not care; he invited himself. He spoke no Spanish and the hired help spoke no English.

Serlo had been as deliberate and dull as a nun riding horseback. Poor horsemanship appalled Serlo, so he said little to David while they were riding. David did not care how he looked in the saddle; all he cared about was hanging on at a dead run because he felt transformed into the pure sensation of the horse pounding across the earth devouring space and distance.

David already knew Serlo found him attractive; Beaufrey had confided Serlo was aroused by watching men ride horses. The horseman was potent and virile. David knew how much the danger aroused Beaufrey. Serlo undoubtedly had similar attractions; otherwise, Serlo would not have ridden a horse at all. Horses were dangerously strong. David had met Serlo-types before: pale, aristocratic, and passionless.

With Beaufrey gone most of the week, David had become bored with satellite TV. He had begun grooming and feeding the chestnut mare himself. The mare learned to whinny when David came to the stables. The ranch hands made jokes among themselves about the stable boy. David didn't care. *Sangre pura* was bullshit. David was from the United States, and he knew only money mattered.

Serlo did not vary his route on the rides. Beside the dressage and jumping courses, there was an indoor course for bad weather. Serlo preferred to ride only the roads and paths because the *llano* grass often concealed hazards, treacherous rodent holes and narrow, deep gullies. Here the *llanos* were not as flat. There were gently rolling hills covered with grass and shrubs, and far far in the distance mountains stood so blue and so tall they were lost in clouds and sky. No sensation ever equaled the absolute thrill David had felt on the back of a racehorse. David had raced motorcycles and cars, but they were not alive; they did not risk shattered bones.

All had seemed so near, almost within David's grasp, until the injunctions and lawsuits. He knew his Eric series was sheer genius. The Eric series should have launched his career. But it had all turned out wrong, as wrong as the pathologist's report when his mother had first got sick. Some things were never meant to be, such as his own birth after his father was too old and too drunk. In the beginning David had expected Beaufrey to defend his Eric series, to hire additional lawyers to help G.'s lawyer bring out the big guns, because Beaufrey loved art, especially David's art, and of course, because Beaufrey loved David, or at least he loved David the artist. But Beaufrey had been strangely complacent about the attacks on David's work; Beaufrey's response was that

G. and the gallery should handle the matter entirely. "Survival of the fittest, dear David," had been Beaufrey's only comment.

GAMES

AFTER THE NIGHT rain, a blue mist rose above the rolling green *llanos* from dawn until noon. A hundred miles in the distance, the high mountains were still hidden in clouds, and it had been easy for David to imagine he was Adam in the Garden. For as far as he could see to the south and the west, there were no jet vapor trails, no engine sounds, no glitter of metal or glass, no dogs barking, no human voice; only the insects whirring and the calls of birds. There were no sounds of cattle or horses and none in sight; he might have been the last man on earth. No wonder Serlo had all those bizarre ideas; Serlo had been too long on the *llano*.

Except for ancestral portraits hung along the halls, the only art in the ranch house had been nineteenth-century landscapes of the Spanish countryside with winding roads and neatly kept olive groves behind ancient stone walls. The landscape paintings were some of the most stupid David had ever seen. He found conventional landscapes completely boring. All that mattered in the landscape was the human form, the human face, which was our original "landscape" as infants. So-called still lifes and landscapes were only analogues for the artist's perceptions and emotions. Eric's body had become a new landscape, and his colors had been scattered all over the bedspread, ceiling, walls, and floor.

The midday heat after the night rain had left David exhausted, but the air-conditioning in his room was in poor repair and he had been unable to sleep. Beaufrey was still in Bogotá on business. Serlo spoke with Beaufrey almost daily. Serlo had no answer when David asked what business had suddenly required so much of Beaufrey's attention. Serlo promised to have the ranch foreman fix the air-conditioning unit in his room and suggested David might sleep more comfortably on the screened porch. The heat had produced a strange fatigue during the day; David lay on his bed but could not sleep. Although he knew it was quite impossible, fantasies about Beaufrey's suddenly taking charge still flashed through David's head. He imagined Beaufrey's handsome, cruel face as he announced his lawyers in Bogotá had taken care of everything for David. David daydreamed that Beaufrey had arranged secret meetings with European gallery owners to plan a stunning international debut for David and the Eric series. All it took was money. Beaufrey had the money.

David had known men like Beaufrey before. They betrayed no feelings; their eyes were expressionless. They claimed to have no attachments. They gave no gifts or money, but paid all travel, hotels, meals, whiskey, and cocaine. Beaufrey had even let David keep Seese, the way he had let Eric stay on too. Beaufrey had only been curious, not generous. Beaufrey was attracted to artists because he was easily bored.

Throughout dinner Serlo watched David eat and chatter about riding racehorses. To Serlo, English sounded like parrot chatter anyway, and he had paid little attention. What he was interested in were David's presumptions and delusions. David had been trying to interest Serlo in a race horse; Serlo did not bother to explain to David the vulgarity of competition, especially horse racing. David's ignorance was of course part of his attraction for Beaufrey. Serlo had to admit he was interested too. Serlo had never seen such arrogance coupled with such ignorance, but Beaufrey had assured him all men in the United States were like David. Beaufrey had deliberately left Serlo alone at the *finca* with David. "The next move is yours," was all Beaufrey had said.

Beaufrey's games. Serlo was tired of games; he had the institute to work for now. For years, Beaufrey had tried to seduce Serlo with luscious young men procured all over the world. Serlo had enjoyed them—pretty blonds hung like donkeys and willing to do anything, anything Serlo might want. He had enjoyed their confusion and shame when he'd revealed he wanted nothing to do with them or any filth.

David, of course was unique, a special case; Beaufrey's game had abruptly turned to obsession, and Serlo wanted to end the game. David was only incidental now; Beaufrey was obsessed with David's child. The instant the child had been conceived, Beaufrey despised it, even more than he had hated the first fetus Seese had aborted. Serlo had been shocked at Beaufrey's behavior. Serlo had known even then, the time had come. Those of *sangre pura* must stop playing games and take action before the world was lost.

BAD NEWS

THE SORREL MARE'S presence was soothing, and David hoped to meet Serlo in the stable area. At the dinner table the night before, Serlo had smiled at David and had asked if David would be joining him for a ride in the morning. David had not felt so much energy or excitement since Beaufrey left; the prospect of fucking Serlo was the source of his new enthusiasm. He would fuck Serlo and see what *that* did for Beaufrey. David would show Beaufrey.

All his childhood, David had wanted a pony or horse to ride far away from the houses and schools and people. Now the sorrel mare was David's childhood dream come true. David knew he could always remain on the *finca* even if Beaufrey no longer wanted him, because of Serlo. Serlo wanted David; David felt certain. There was no mistake when a man as remote as Serlo began to smile over the dinner rolls and inquired about morning horseback rides.

The little mare had gone lame after the ride, and David had been racked with guilt. The swelling of the mare's knee and foreleg had reminded David of his mother's cancer. Both Beaufrey and Serlo had warned David before about speed on the mare.

Serlo had said nothing as the grooms had mixed medicinal plasters to bandage around the mare's knee. David had not meant to let the mare run until she injured herself, but the sensation of speed over the endless rolling plain had been irresistible. Distances fell away, and the earth was a blur; the little mare had wanted to race beyond all barriers and restraints, and David had not wanted to stop; he had wanted the horse to run the plain forever.

David had remained in the box stall with the lame mare after Serlo and the grooms had left. He had brushed her, then wiped her with a damp chamois, repeating her name softly over and over: "Roja, Roja, Roja." David felt great sadness rise from his chest into his throat. It was no use. Nothing mattered. Everything he had tried, everything he had done, had turned out wrong.

The injury to the little mare had abruptly ended the horseback riding and Serlo's smiles across the dinner table. David had spent most of his days in the box stall stroking or grooming the horse. Serlo had made it quite clear he thought David was a vulgarian and a fool for riding so recklessly. The mare whinnied when David entered the stable; hers had been the only greeting David had got. Serlo had only stared at him silently when David spoke. The ranch hands and grooms suddenly were mute.

David had lost interest in photography; he hated the tedium of the darkroom and the odor of chemicals. David had given them his best work and they had watched as the exhibit had been ruined. G. was crazy if he thought David was going to complete a new series or make any more Eric prints either. David was finished with the art racket; galleries were as sleazy as casinos. There was no big money in art unless you were a dealer or a dead artist.

David massaged the mare's knee and took her on daily walks to rebuild muscle tone and strength in the foreleg. The mare had quickly recovered, and David was triumphant, leading the horse past the grooms and stable hands. David hardly cared whether Serlo had noticed that David no longer ate at the long dining table with him. He preferred to take meals alone in his room because Serlo had made unforgivable remarks to David when the horse had been injured. Serlo had called him "mongrel," "misfit," and "pervert." Serlo jerked off to fill his private sperm bank yet called himself heterosexual; David had never known such a *queer* before.

David had made a special effort to keep the little mare on short rein and at a walk to prevent reinjury. He wanted the mare sound when Beaufrey returned. David had practiced with the mare on the dressage course, and she seemed to relax and work on a looser rein. Alone, David had ridden farther and farther from the ranch house, deeper into the grassy, gently rolling *llanos*. All the emptiness, all the space, the green of the land and the purity of the blue sky, were lovely but also unearthly. He could understand how Serlo might dream of space colonies orbiting earth, because across the endless plains, the ranch buildings had appeared to be tiny satellites in the vast space of the plains.

So ten days had become ten weeks in Bogotá for Beaufrey. He had returned one Monday afternoon and offered no explanations and made no comments about his business in Bogotá. Beaufrey had asked David no questions, and he didn't expect any questions from David. David had lost his temper. Beaufrey didn't have to ask any questions because Serlo watched and reported everything David did anyway. David knew

Beaufrey and Serlo had no secrets; he knew Beaufrey had described every detail of every sex act with David to Serlo—wasn't that part of their game? David knew all about the mind-fuck games. Beaufrey had left David for ten weeks in the middle of nowhere, ten weeks in which the only English David had heard had been over the telephone or off satellite TV.

Beaufrey had burst out laughing when David had complained about hearing English only on TV. Poor thing! Foreign languages in foreign countries! Beaufrey's laughter had infuriated David. Serlo had smiled faintly. David was sick of their secrets. He demanded to know everything. Beaufrey seemed amused by David's outburst. He had been unpacking the new handguns and carbines he had brought back for the *finca*'s arsenal. Serlo called it "the gun collection." David had seen the underground arsenal once; all the walls had been lined solidly with rifles and carbines; dozens of glass cases had been filled with revolvers, automatics, derringers—every kind of handgun.

Some things it was better not to know. Beaufrey looked at Serlo. Didn't Serlo agree? Look at these 9mm pistols. David might enjoy the Glock. With the unrest and guerilla activity so widespread, no Caucasian should be without a handgun on his person.

"Don't change the subject," David said. He picked up the gun, and Beaufrey handed him the empty clip. In another minute Beaufrey would bring out the cocaine as he usually did after they had quarreled. Beaufrey's eyes were expressionless; his lips did not move. Serlo kept wiping the barrel of a .45 automatic; he didn't look up. "I want to know all of it—everything." Beaufrey and Serlo exchanged brief glances. "Everything?" Beaufrey repeated, smiling cruelly. "You want to know *everything?*" The long dining table was covered with packing debris, shipping boxes, and fifteen or twenty revolvers and automatic pistols. The giant grandfather clock ticked loudly down the hall.

"It was all bad news, I'm afraid." Beaufrey's eyes had been gleaming again, and David felt hopeful they would still be lovers. He did not understand Beaufrey: What bad news? "It all required more time than I had anticipated," Beaufrey continued, watching David's face closely.

"The galleries in Europe . . . ?" David felt his heart leap.

The room was quiet again, except for the hall clock, and the sound of Serlo slitting open the cardboard packing around the guns. "I said 'bad news,' nothing about art." Both Beaufrey and Serlo watched David closely. David's mouth hung open stupidly as he began to understand. "The baby," David said in a flat voice, "you mean the baby." Beaufrey nodded; he was wiping shipping grease off the cylinder of a brand-new Colt .357 magnum.

"I really am sorry, David, but with that woman, what could you do?" Beaufrey had never spoken to David so sincerely. David experienced a flood of feelings, a great expansion in his chest from his beating heart. "With a creature like that you expect the offspring to be lost. Isn't that true, Serlo? You see that here all the time with horses and cattle, don't you?" Serlo had been cataloging the serial numbers of the new handguns in a huge old ledger bound in brass and leather. Everything that had ever been purchased for the *finca* was described in the ledger. Serlo nodded yes to Beaufrey's comparison of the woman with a cow, but did not lift his head. He was sick of David's stupid, pouting mouth and Beaufrey's reptilian gaze each time the lovers' eyes locked on one another. Serlo had watched Beaufrey before. Beaufrey became aroused watching the young men break down. When the young men bored Beaufrey, they angered him; and quite unintentionally Beaufrey was compelled to break them down. Serlo wondered what the American would do or say if he was told the truth about the child. David would shit his pants. Or maybe David would be so stupid that even if he was told the truth, he would not believe it. Serlo decided to tell the gringo, "Some are only fit as organ donors. That is the only useful function left for common rabble." Of course David did not understand Spanish or Serlo's meaning, except to know it was derogatory.

Beaufrey had looked at Serlo sharply, but Serlo had been refilling the fountain pen and pretended not to see. Serlo didn't care if David found out; the David game was about played out. Serlo was sick of Beaufrey's pretending to console David. Beaufrey brought out more cocaine and offered it first to David before he passed it to Serlo.

RAPTURE OF THE PLAIN

DAVID HAD BEEN pleased at how sharp Beaufrey's glance at Serlo had been. The excitement of having so much of Beaufrey's attention and concern had made even the painful loss of the infant recede naturally into the distance. With Beaufrey in love with him, even *that* loss seemed bearable. David had been surprised at Beaufrey's sudden change of heart just when David had feared everything might be over between them. He did not want to upset Beaufrey any further. He did not press Beaufrey for details. Beaufrey said only the child had died in Tucson of natural causes. Whores such as Seese produced defective offspring; nature's way was best; only the fittest survived. David felt strangely relieved now that Beaufrey had confirmed the worst. There was nothing more David could do for the dead child. If he ever saw Seese again, David vowed to kill her.

Beaufrey's games ended when he wanted them to, and not until then. Serlo refused to be suckered into a shouting match by Beaufrey. They fucked while Serlo rode horseback alone. They rode horseback for hours together while Serlo supervised the ground-breaking for the institute facilities. Serlo had spoken to Beaufrey once, even twice, each day by phone while Beaufrey had been in Bogotá; now they slept under the same roof but did not speak to one another, sometimes for days. Beaufrey was soft, Beaufrey was a slave to urges and desires of the flesh. Beaufrey confided that the secret had greatly increased his sexual desire for David. Beaufrey really got hot because David had never even suspected what had happened to the infant: something terrible. Nothing got Beaufrey hotter than pumping away at an unsuspecting asshole such as David; ignorant of everything.

Time was getting short; unrest was spreading across the Americas; Serlo and Beaufrey had both lost ancestors to the guillotine. Epidemics, accompanied by famine, had triggered unrest. Mass migrations to the North, to the U.S. border, by starving Indians had already begun in Mexico. Serlo and the others with the "hidden agenda" had only a few more years to prepare before the world was lost to chaos. Brown people would inherit the earth like the cockroaches unless Serlo and the others were successful at the institute. Dedicated to the preservation of the purity of noble blood, the facilities would provide genetically superior semen.

Serlo blamed the United States for the crisis in the hemisphere because the U.S. CIA had encouraged government authorities, the worst criminals, to smuggle cocaine for them. Very soon the others had learned the fabulous profits that could be made, and the U.S. CIA had fierce competition in the cocaine trade from mestizos and Indians. Serlo had seen the black men and the brown men with semiautomatic carbines they had bought with the profits of the trade. Serlo had seen a message in the eyes of these people: guns make us equal, white motherfucker.

Enemies of the United States had actually tried to cut off the supply of heroin to the United States near the end of the Vietnam War. During the summer of the disruption of heroin supplies, dozens of U.S. cities had burned night after night. Without cocaine and heroin, the U.S. faced a nightmare as young black and brown people took to the streets to light up white neighborhoods, not crack pipes. Secret U.S. policy was to protect the supply of cocaine. Without cocaine, the U.S. would face riots, looting, even civil war. The downfall of the United States had been those civil rights laws passed after the Korean War.

Serlo seldom joined them horseback riding since Beaufrey had returned from Bogotá. David spotted Serlo approaching rapidly on his black hunter-jumper across a grassy, dry lake-bed; he had not seen Serlo ride a horse so fast before. Beaufrey had reined in his horse when he saw Serlo. David was intrigued because Beaufrey acted genuinely surprised, as if he had not expected to see Serlo. Beaufrey had always denied Serlo was jealous, but David knew better.

The sorrel mare tossed her head and opened her mouth wide to escape the bit. Beaufrey was critical of David's lack of control of the mare. Whenever Beaufrey felt out of sorts, he liked to criticize David's "seat," and the atrocious position of the reins in his hands. This bitching at David was meant to cheer up Serlo. David dug his heels into the mare's ribs and pulled her around sharply as she leaped into a gallop in a tight, clockwise circle around them. Beaufrey was worried about David's control; well, let him watch this! Serlo saw David's horse break away from Beaufrey's mount, but instead of riding in the direction Beaufrey had gone, Serlo had turned his horse to follow David.

David had turned hard in the saddle to try to see Beaufrey's reaction, but the little mare seemed to accelerate even as David struggled to rein her into a circle. Then he could see Beaufrey was galloping after Serlo. David felt a big smile on his face. How romantic and dramatic! The thrill of the chase across the grass and through the scrubby trees across dry lakes had overcome David. He could feel the little Thoroughbred did not want to stop; the farther she ran, the faster she ran. The speed whipped tears in his eyes as he fought to pull the mare's head around; he would let her run in a big circle until she was exhausted. To otherwise stop or control the horse was hopeless. Serlo had kept shouting at David, but the excitement of a chase was too keen to halt. David glanced over his shoulder and saw Beaufrey's horse stumble and nearly go down. Neither Beaufrey nor Serlo dared race as fast as David had over the grassy plain.

The sorrel mare had gradually slowed as she tired; David pulled her to a stop. Sweat dripped from her neck and legs. David had dismounted and was walking the horse when Serlo rode up. David heard Serlo's words, but had difficulty making any sense of what Serlo said. David had stopped to allow the mare to rub her sweaty head and ears against David's shoulder. He looked up at Serlo on the lathered hunter-jumper. What was Serlo's news that simply could not wait?

But Serlo had said nothing; instead he had handed David an eight-by-ten manila envelope. To see was to believe. David stared at proof sheets of 35mm color negative strips; most of the proof images had been almost too small to see without a magnifying lens, but a cold chill and then sweat had made the hairs on David's neck stand up. Beaufrey rode up while David was still holding the proof sheets in both hands helplessly. Beaufrey did not answer when David asked him if what Serlo had said was true. David kept his eyes on Beaufrey's eyes as he deliberately trampled the proof sheets under his boots, then remounted the mare.

David refused to let Serlo or Beaufrey, but especially Serlo, play any more mind-fuck games with him. Serlo had tried all along to drive David away from Beaufrey. David did not doubt that Beaufrey had videotapes and enlarged color photographs of autopsies and organ harvests of Caucasian infants. David simply refused to believe the tiny cadaver in the images was that of his infant son, Monte. That simply was not possible because the cadaver had been considerably larger than his baby.

Beaufrey hated surprises such as the one Serlo had just sprung. Beaufrey had been furious, but he pretended the photographs were only Serlo's sick joke. Of course the photographs were off the black market; it had been a bad joke. Beaufrey's lips gradually drew back in a sly smile; he winked at David and shrugged his shoulders. Serlo was Serlo. Only the greatest passions drove men to deeds such as these. Serlo had only pretended cool detachment. Serlo was a man of great passion. But David would not be outdone. The sorrel mare's coat was still damp from the previous run, and she trembled with anticipation; David held the reins tight and the horse stepped backward nervously. David had not ridden so far onto the *llano* before; off in the distance, a great open plain dropped away from the scrubby trees and ran forever to the horizon. A light breeze swept across the *llano*.

David wanted to reassure Beaufrey that he did not believe the lies Serlo had told. Serlo must have lost his mind completely to accuse Beaufrey of something so gruesome. David blamed the stupid institute for Serlo's delusions and accusations. Nazi-thinking caused mental illness. David did not care if Serlo heard what he said to Beaufrey. David had never trusted Serlo. Beaufrey should be careful. Serlo considered himself heterosexual; he might turn against his friends and lovers any day. Beaufrey should remember Hitler's solution for homosexuals.

David guided the little mare into a slow canter, keeping the mare's head tucked under the arch of her neck. For weeks David had ridden the mare to practice control. He had practiced to please Beaufrey, but also to prove to himself he could control the mare. Sports and games were always about control; control was everything. One person wanted to control the other. Dope or sex, it was all about control, and the slave, the one who served and obeyed. Seese had taught David that; she had asked David to fuck her while he was shooting her up. He had hated her for wanting that, and he had wanted to hurt her, to miss the vein. But his cock had got hard and curved up to his belly just as he got the needle in the vein; warm and white he fed it to her in steady streams and spurts.

The sorrel mare heard the hoofbeats of Serlo's and Beaufrey's horses behind and raced faster over the plain until the scrubby trees and yellowing grass were blurred from the mare's speed. His arms ached from fighting the mare. He hated the fever of the mare's need to run. He hated Beaufrey's gibe that the rider must "husband" his horse. As the ranch hands said, the mare suffered from the rapture of the *llano,* the rapture of space and endless horizons.

David had tried. What more could a man do? He rejected that responsibility bullshit. If the horse wanted to run, let it run. The little Thoroughbred had fought to break loose for miles, and David was beginning to tire. If the horse wanted to run, let it run. Serlo and Beaufrey were far behind. The mare would slow as she began to tire.

David felt a great sense of relief and freedom as he let the reins go slack. He crouched low over the neck and clutched mane and reins in both hands. For an instant the little Thoroughbred hesitated, then she bolted forward, hooves scarcely touching the earth, her sinew and muscle cracking as she raced over the plain toward the horizon's pale blue. "You want to run? Then run! Run goddamn you! Run!" David had screamed, but the speed of the mare swept the words from his mouth almost before he could make their sounds. Let Beaufrey try to forget this! Truly he had the sensation he was flying. The faster the horse ran, the smoother the ride. He wanted Beaufrey to see how fast the little sorrel could run so Beaufrey would agree to sponsor the horse next season in Caracas. None were as surefooted as this mare! None had her guts, her heart! She leaped the grass clumps, brush, and gullies of the *llanos* like a deer; she never missed a beat across rocky terrain. The mare's balance and surefootedness were phenomenal. David had left Beaufrey and Serlo miles behind on their thick, slow dressage horses.

When the ranch hands came, one of the grooms examined the tracks and the position of the fallen horse. The sorrel mare had run until her heart stopped in midstride and she had dropped like a rock. David had not been thrown free, but had become entangled with the falling horse so that Beaufrey and Serlo had had to drag the dead horse by the tail and bridle reins to roll it over to free David's battered corpse. Serlo watched Beaufrey's face for signs of regret, but Beaufrey was grinning. He had sent a ranch hand to bring his camera. They rode a short distance to some scrubby trees to escape the flies that swarmed over David's corpse and the horse carcass. The late-afternoon light gave the entire *llano* a violet-blue-green color. A refreshing breeze stirred while they waited for the camera.

David was worth more dead than he had been worth alive. The Eric series would appreciate in value, and even pictures of David's corpse would bring good prices. Beaufrey knew Serlo disapproved of selling these photographs; but here was what gave free-world trade the edge over all other systems: no sentimentality. Every ounce of value, everything worth anything, was stripped away for sale, regardless; no mercy. Serlo and his associates feared the rabble were about to seize control of the world, but Beaufrey knew the masses in the United States and England were too stupid to turn on their masters; all slaves dreamed of becoming masters more cruel than their own masters. Serlo and the others had to realize the best policy was to allow the rabble their parliaments, congresses, and assemblies; because the masses were soothed and reassured by these simulations of "democracy." Meanwhile, governments followed secret agendas unhindered by citizens.

Serlo and the others were alarmists. Socialism would never be a threat because it was too soft on the weak and unproductive. Capitalism stayed ahead because it was ruthless, Beaufrey said after he had finished the roll of film. They left the ranch hands to bury David. Carrion birds were welcome to the horse.

PART FIVE

THE
FIFTH WORLD

BOOK ONE

THE FOES

FROM THE ANCIENT ALMANAC

LECHA COULD READ the old notebooks and scraps of newspaper clippings for hours and forget all about the pain. The first time Lecha opened the notebooks, she had recognized here was the real thing. Despite all of Yoeme's lying and boasting, the "almanac" was truly a great legacy. Yoeme and others believed the almanac had living power within it, a power that would bring all the tribal people of the Americas together to retake the land.

For hundreds of years, guardians of the almanac notebooks had made clumsy attempts to repair torn pages. Some sections had been splashed with wine, others with water or blood. Only fragments of the original pages remained, carefully placed between blank pages; those of ancient paper had yellowed, but the red and black painted glyphs had still been clear. The outline of the giant plumed serpent could be made out in pale blue on the largest fragment. The pages of ancient paper had been found between the pages of horse-gut parchment carried by the fugitive Indian slaves who had fled north to escape European slavery.

Lecha speculated that some keepers of the old almanac had been illiterate, but had not bothered to hire someone to read the pages for them. If they had any curiosity about the writing, then their fear, which was greater, had prevailed. What they had feared were the spirits described in the writing and the glyphs on the pages. There was evidence that substantial portions of the original manuscript had been lost or condensed into odd narratives which operated like codes.

The great deal of what had accumulated with the almanac fragments had been debris gathered here and there by aged keepers of the almanac after they had gone crazy. A few of the keepers had fallen victim to delusions of various sorts. Here and there were scribbles and scratches. Lecha found pages where old Yoeme had scribbled arguments in margins with the remarks and vulgar humor Lecha and Zeta had enjoyed so many times with their grandmother.

Whole sections had been stolen from other books and from the proliferation of "farmer's almanacs" published by patent-drug companies and medicine shows that gave away the almanacs as advertisements. Not even the parchment pages or fragments of ancient paper could be trusted; they might have been clever forgeries, recopied, drawn, and colored painstakingly.

Europeans called it coincidence, but the almanacs had prophesied the appearance of Cortés to the day. All Native American tribes had similar prophecies about the appearance, conflict with, and eventual disappearance of things European. The almanacs had warned the people hundreds of years before the Europeans arrived. The people living in large towns were told to scatter, to disperse to make the murderous work of the invaders more difficult. Without the almanacs, the people would not be able to recognize the days and months yet to come, days and months that would see the people retake the land.

Yoeme alleged the Aztecs ignored the prophecies and warnings about the approach of the Europeans because Montezuma and his allies had been sorcerers who had called or even invented the European invaders with their sorcery. Those who worshiped destruction and blood secretly knew one another. Hundreds of years earlier, the people who hated sorcery and bloodshed had fled north to escape the cataclysm prophecied when the "blood worshipers" of Europe met the "blood worshipers" of the Americas. Montezuma and Cortés had been meant for one another. Yoeme always said sorcery had been the undoing of people here, and everywhere in the world.

Fragments from the Ancient Notebooks

The Month was created first, before the World. Then the Month began to walk himself, and his grandmothers and aunt and his sister-in-law said, "What do we say when we see a man in the road?" There were no humans yet so they discussed what they would say as they walked along. They found footprints when they arrived in the East. "Who passed by here? Look at these footprints. Measure them with your foot." The Mother Creator said this to the Month, who measured the footprint.

The footprint belonged to Lord God. That was the beginning for Month because he had to measure the whole World by walking it off day by day. Month made sure his feet were even before he began the count. Month spoke Day's name when Day had no name. So the Month was created, then the Day, as it was called, was created, and the rain's stairway to Earth— the rocks and the trees—all creatures of the sea and land were created.

Death Dog traveled to the land of the dead where the God of death gave him the bone the human race was created with.

Scorpion uses his tail as a noose to lasso deer. Scorpion is a good hunter. He has a net bag in which he carries his fire-driller and fire-sticks.

The sign of the human hand = 2. The hand that holds the hilt of the dagger is plunged into the lower body of the deer.

Those cursed with the anguish, and the despairers, all were born during the five "nameless" days.
On the five nameless days, people stay in bed and fast and confess sins.

Black Zip whistles a warning. He is the deer god.
In the year Ten Sky, the principal ruler is Venus.

Big Star is a drunkard, a deformed dog with the head of a jaguar and the hind end of a dog with a purple dick. He staggers like Rabbit, who also is a drunkard. Nasty, arrogant liar! Troublemaker and experimenter in mutual hate and torture!

Venus. Color: red. Direction: east. Herald of the dawn and measurer of night.
Envious Ribald;

Sin in his face and in his talk; he had no virtue in him.
He is without understanding.

He had no virtue in him. Mighty carnivorous teeth and a
body withered like a rabbit.

Deities return. Better get to know them.

Venus of the Celestial Dragon with eight heads; each head
hurls shafts of affliction down on mankind. Europeans call
Venus "Lucifer, the Bright One," who fell from grace long ago.
Venus resides in darkness until he rises as Morning Star. Dog-
face partially blackened, a fish in his headdress, he swims up
from the dark underworld.

Error in translation of the Chumayel manuscript: 11 AHU
was the year of the return of fair Quetzalcoatl. But the mention
of the artificial white circle in the sky could only have meant
the return of Death Dog and his eight brothers: plague, earthquake, drought, famine, incest, insanity, war, and betrayal.

Xolotol, the Death Dog, is playing his drum. He wears
bird and snake earrings, which is a rebus for Quetzalcoatl.
Xolotol, ribs and skull with a knife in the teeth.

Jade water = rain.

Dead souls travel branches and roots of the ceiba trees to
reach the land of the dead. The outline of the tree's roots and
branches has the appearance of the outline of the lizard, Imix,
earth monster, crocodile. The land of the dead is a land of
flowers and abundant food.

Ik is three. Ik is wind on the edge of the rain storm; deity
of the rain carries pollen; Lord of the night of the hollow drum,
God of caves and conch shells. Earthquake is a scale off the
back of earth monster Crocodile.

Kan is four. Kan is the lizard from whose belly sprang all
the seeds for grain and fruit.

Chichan is five. Chichan is a giant snake half human and half feathered. The four chichans are the rain deities who live in the four directions.

Cimi is six and is called death, owl's day. Lord of the underworld and Lord of death. Nonetheless day six, day of the skull, is a good-luck day.

Manik, the deer, is number seven.

Eight is the day called the Dog. Bloody pus pours from the ears of the dog. Persons born on the day of the dog will be habitual fornicators and will be obsessed by dirty thoughts.

[Numbers nine and ten are illegible.]

Eleven is the day of the monkey, whose head appears like the sun high in the trees. Jealous elder brothers sent the youngest brothers climbing high trees after monkeys so they'd fall to their deaths. The Big Dipper is the monkey constellation where the youngest brothers remain in the sky.

[Manuscript incomplete.]

Eb is the blackish mildew caused by too much rain or mist or dews and damps that ruin crops. A good day for obtaining advice concerning misfortunes. A good day for prayers for prosperity. The souls of the dead return as little gnats and bees. The souls of women who died in childbirth descend every fifty-two days to harm mankind, especially small children and babies.

Obsidian butterfly.

Seventeen is the number of Earthquake.

Nineteen is the day of flint knife.

[Manuscript illegible.]

> the deer die: drought
> maize in bud: women of sexual maturity
> sprouting maize: marriage

Rain god sits on coiled snake enclosing a pool of water; the number nine is attached. Nine means fresh, uncontaminated water.

The snake god with the green symbol on the forehead means "first time," "new growth," "fresh."

Dog = rainless storms. The dog carries a lighted torch: drought, great heat, heaped-up death.

Fine paper of bark cloth finished with lime sizing; a single, continuous piece of paper twenty-two feet long, folded like a Chinese screen, to be read from left to right. Ink of black and red; blue background, green, dark and light yellow. Short glyphic passages give the "luck" of the day planets and stars, ceremonial and sacrificial anniversaries, and prophecy.

A day began at sunset. "Reality" was variously defined or described.

Narrative as analogue for the actual experience, which no longer exists; a mosaic of memory and imagination.

An experience termed *past* may actually return if the influences have the same balances or proportions as before. Details may vary, but the essence does not change. The day would have the same feeling, the same character, as that day has been described having had *before*. The image of a memory exists in the present moment.

1. Bring the sun. Bear it on the palm of your hand. Bring the green jaguar seated over the sun to drink the sun's blood. A lance is planted in the center of the sun's heart. [The sun is a fried egg; the lance in its center is a green chili pepper.]

2. Bring me the brains of the sky so I may see how large they are. [The thick gray clouds of smoke from the copal incense suggest the gray mass of the brain.]

3. Son, go bring me the girl with the watery teeth. Her hair is twisted into a tuft; she is a very beautiful maiden. Fragrant shall be her odor when I remove her skirt and other garments. It will give me great pleasure to see her. Fragrant is her odor and her hair is twisted in a tuft. [A green ear of corn]

The unrestrained, upstart epoch is the offspring of the harlot, and a son of evil. The face of the Katun is covered with mud, trampled into the ground as he is dragged along.

The face of the Lord of the Katunsi is covered; he is dead. There is mourning for water, there is mourning for bread.

Bloody vomit of yellow fever.

Four piles of skulls: Spaniards, mestizos, Indian slaves, Africans.

The rope shall descend.

The poison of the serpent shall descend.

Pestilence and four piles of skulls; living men lie useless.

A dry wind blows. Locust years.

Bread is unattainable.

The sun shall be eclipsed.

Eleven Ahau is the Katun when the aliens arrived.

A beginning of vexation, a beginning of robbery with violence. This was the origin of service to the Spaniards and priests, of service to the local chiefs, of service to the teachers, of service to the public prosecutor by the boys, the youth of the town, while the poor people were harassed. There were the very poor people who did not escape when the oppressors appeared, when the anti-Christ had come to earth, the kinkajous of the towns, the coyotes of the towns, the blood-sucking insects of the town, those who drained the poverty of the working people. But it shall come to pass that tears will fill the eyes of God. Justice shall descend from God to every part of the world, straight from God, justice shall smash the greedy hagglers of the world.

Twenty-year drought: the hooves of the deer crack in the heat; the ocean burned so high the face of the sun was devoured; the face of the sun darkened with blood, then disappeared.

A time of dissolution.
Priests were called from distant towns.
Acolytes were seen carrying baskets full of small mummified creatures—lizards, toads, wrens, desert mice. Four years had seen grasshoppers devour bean and corn seedlings. Torrential rains that came too late had caved in roofs of empty granaries and storerooms.
Priests sprinkle corn pollen and meal and bits of coral and turquoise on the stone snake's forehead. They whisper to the stone snake leaning close so no one may see their lips.
Inside the cloudy opal, four years of grasshoppers devour bean and corn seedlings. Torrential rains arrived too late and caved in roofs of empty granaries and storerooms. Any children still alive were sent away with great sorrow.

Quetzalcoatl gathered the bones of the dead, sprinkled them with his own blood, and recreated humanity.

Marsha-true'ee, the Giant Plumed Serpent, messenger spirit of the underworld, came to live in the beautiful lake that was near Kha-waik. But there was jealousy and envy. They came one night and broke open the lake so all the water was lost. The giant snake went away after that. He has never been seen since. That was a great misfortune for the Kha-waik-meh.

1560

The year of the plague—intense cold and fever—bleeding from nose and coughing, twisted necks and large sores erupt. Plague ravages the countryside for more than three years. Smallpox too had followed in the wake of the plague. Deaths number in the thousands.

May 18, 1562—sickness and death still rampant at the end of the sixty-third year after the Katun was completed.

May 1566—between one and two in the afternoon an earthquake caused great destruction. Severe earthquakes lasted *nine* days.

1590

In the sixty-seventh year after the alien invasion, on January 3, 1590, the epidemic began: cough, chills, and fever from which people died.

In the sixty-eighth year after the alien invasion, the face of the moon was covered with darkness soon after the sunset. It was really a great darkness and the moon could not be seen. The surface of the earth could not be seen at all.

1594

Today, September 23, a land dispute between the Xevacal Tuanli is decided according to law.

1595

The mayor was struck by lightning. Ten days later lightning struck the church and main altar. In December, the great bell of Tzolola was begun. A thousand *to-stones* were collected from community funds in order to pay for the bell.

1597

Thus, September 3, three days before the feast of the Nativity of Mary, there was an eclipse of the sun and the day became as dark as the night.

1600

Nine Ymox, Saturday, June 16, Mary, grandmother of the sun and all creatures.

1617–24

Smallpox.

1621

Five Ah, the plague began to spread. Great was the stench of the dead. People fled to the fields. The dogs and vultures devoured the bodies. Your grandparents died, *we all became orphans.* We were children and we were alone; none of our parents had been spared. The younger brothers were oppressed and baby boys were flayed alive. His face was that of the war *capitán,* of the son of God.

This shall be the end of its prophecy: there is a great war. A parching whirlwind storm. Katun 1 Ahau. There is a sudden end of planting. Lawsuits descend, taxes and tribute descend.

One day a story will arrive in your town. There will always be disagreement over direction—whether the story came from the southwest or the southeast. The story may arrive with a stranger, a traveler thrown out of his home country months ago. Or the story may be brought by an old friend, perhaps the parrot trader. But after you hear the story, you and the others prepare by the new moon to rise up against the slave masters.

THE GREAT INFLUENZA
OF 1918

OLD YOEME HERSELF had added a number of pages to the almanac; Lecha easily recognized the handwriting:

Late in the summer, the pigs chew green corncobs, and I wait for execution in the Alamos Jail. I have been convicted of sedition and high treason against the federal government. They hate me because I am an Indian woman who kicked dirt in the faces of the police and army.

They stand outside my cell and gloat over my death. Soon I "must" die because I had "already lived too long," I have blemished their "honor." Me, "the short, square-shouldered woman with deadly aim," that's my title.

In twos and threes they come to stare at me. They relish the words they repeat again and again—their daydreams of my hanging and dismemberment.

My execution is delayed by their needs for pageantry. Elected officials from other jurisdictions arrive. I am on display, an example to all who dare defy authority. Postponement is due to the governor's busy schedule. They don't miss a day outside my cell.

The police chief carries a paper with days crossed off in charcoal. "Count them," he tells me in low tones. He is outraged because an Indian can read and write, while he, a white man, can not. I laugh and call him "barbarian" in my language.

"You will die! That is certain!" All the others of my kind have already been sent to hell, he says. My death is certain. I am not afraid to die. I am sorry to leave the people I love when the struggle is only beginning. I pray to God for justice. For myself and all our people I pray for the success of the revolution.

The day before my execution the news reaches town. At first the officials refuse to believe the reports of so many sick and dead. Influenza travels with the moist, warm winds off the coast. Influenza infects the governor and all the others. The police chief burns to death from fever. The jailer leaves a bucket of water and a bowl of parched corn.

"The authorities want to keep you alive," he says, "until they recover enough to hang you." The jailer has bloodshot eyes. He says entire households have the dead lying next to the living, who are too ill to drag corpses outside.

I laugh out loud but the jailer reacts slowly.

"Someone will come to hang you," he reassures me, but when I ask who, the jailer shakes his head. He is tired this morning or he would kill me himself. The town is silent. Church bells no longer ring the Angelus, and I listen with all my strength for the footsteps of my executioners.

I could hear the big buzzards and smell what they ate with such relish. I was still locked up. Human scavengers followed, and I heard the sounds of looting. I did not think anyone would come. But then they came to loot the jail's guns and ammunition. The scavengers were afraid to open my cell because they saw my legs and wrists were shackled. But I told them the Blessed Virgin of the Indians had just worked me a miracle; I had been saved by the hand of God and they must set me free.

OLD YOEME'S ADVICE

THAT OLD WOMAN! Years after her death, Lecha still could not top her. The story of Yoeme's deliverance had been carefully inserted among the pages of the old almanac manuscript. Why had Yoeme called the story "Day of Deliverance"? What good was the story of one woman's unlikely escape from the hangman? Had old Yoeme known or cared that 20 to 40 million perished around the world while she had been saved? Probably not. Lecha could hear the old woman's voice even now.

"You may as well die fighting the white man," Yoeme had told them when they were girls. "Because the rain clouds will disappear first; and with them the plants and the animals. When the spirits are angry or hurt, they turn their backs on all of us."

Of course the white man did not want to believe that. The white man always had to be saved; the white man always got the last available water and food. The white man hated to hear anything about spirits because spirits were already dead and could not be tortured and butchered or shot, the only way the white man knew how to deal with the world. Spirits were immune to the white man's threats and to his bribes of money and food. The white man only knew one way to control himself or others and that was with brute force.

Against the spirits, the white man was impotent. "You girls will see someday. Look what happened to your grandfather. Those mine shafts into the earth turned against him, and his bones broke to mush."

How fitting that Yoeme had required the single worst natural disaster in world history to save her. Nothing could change Yoeme's view of her "deliverance." She had had "a vision" that told her the influenza had saved many others as well as revolutionists such as herself sentenced to die.

Yoeme had made margin notes after the pages describing her deliverance. Yoeme had believed power resides within certain stories; this power ensures the story to be retold, and with each retelling a slight but permanent shift took place. Yoeme's story of her deliverance changed forever the odds against all captives; each time a revolutionist escaped death in one century, two revolutionists escaped certain death in the following century even if they had never heard such an escape story. Where such miraculous escape stories are greatly prized and rapidly circulated, miraculous escapes from death gradually increase.

It had been with Yoeme that Lecha had first seen rain clouds in the fat of sheep intestines. As children in Potam, Lecha and Zeta and their cousins had played with the lamb and pretended he was one of their make-believe herd. They stirred mud in tin cans and served it to him on plates of cottonwood leaves. He followed them when they ran. His long, woolly tail wagged while he nursed the black rubber nipple on a pop bottle. Later in the summer his tail was thick with fat and wool; burrs had tangled in his tail wool. Then one Saturday afternoon in August, old Yoeme had brought out her sharpening stone and long, curved butcher knife. She had also brought out the enamel dishpan. Uncle Ringo tied the big lamb's legs together with rope, but the lamb did not struggle and lay on its side calmly as old Yoeme held a small tin pail under the lamb's throat. Uncle Ringo pulled the lamb's head back by the muzzle slit its throat. As its blood pulsed into the pail, the lamb made a weak struggle against the rope on its legs.

In the opened belly of a deer, the old woman told them, was where she herself had first seen distant skies revealed in membranes of blue and purple, translucent as clouds before a snowstorm. The strands of pure white clouds were pearls of belly fat strung on thick loops of tallow the old woman saved for soap making. She told the girls there were ways the clouds might be summoned with the belly fat of deer or sheep. In the winter, steam off the body cavity summoned up snow mists and fogs around the dry mountain peaks. Old Yoeme had turned the lamb's stomach inside out, and the bright green grass spilled out for the old dog to eat.

Old Yoeme's gift to Lecha had been peculiar: Lecha's gift finds only the dead, never the living. For a long time Lecha had blamed herself; she thought she had only to focus herself more intensely and quickly. By the time Lecha had returned to Potam, Yoeme had been so old and shrunken she had to lie in a child's hospital crib. Lecha had barely been able to suppress a reflex to gag; she hated the smell of all of them crowded in the old house—cousins and in-laws in every room. It had been that day, long ago, when Lecha had begun to realize she could never be buried anywhere near the graves of other family members. Old Yoeme had seemed well cared for, although they left her alone most of the day. The old woman had recognized Lecha immediately. They had given Yoeme the room off the kitchen, and although Yoeme was as alert and cunning as she had ever been, she had got so old and shrunken up she could no longer walk. Even her bones seemed to have withered up, so all that remained were her small dark eyes still glittering with mischief.

Yoeme had claimed she had lived as long as she had because she was curious. Yoeme laughed loudly and had opened her lips and licked her tongue across yellow pegs of teeth. She still had a taste for life, what could she do for her dear grandchild?

"What if the only ones you find are dead?" Lecha had asked.

"Well, yes," Yoeme had answered. "That is common enough. What do you want to know?" Yoeme had laughed as if Lecha's question were a joke.

FAMILY CEMETERY

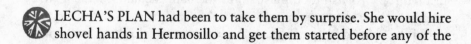 LECHA'S PLAN had been to take them by surprise. She would hire shovel hands in Hermosillo and get them started before any of the

rest of the family found out what was happening. Word had come from Potam that the big house had caved in; the adobe walls had melted like fresh dung after days of torrential rain. As soon as the message had arrived, Lecha had visualized the cemetery as she had seen it as a child: the ocean below the hill was as bright blue as the sky filled with white clouds blossoming in the spring wind. Hollyhocks that had been cut before dawn were tied to weathered crosses, but hours of the breeze and the sun had left the flowers drooping like the heads of captives tied to the stake. Around Yoeme's unoccupied grave, the shifting dunes were held back by round, smooth ocean rocks the size of fists. In Lecha's memory, there were no traces of the other graves of uncles and aunts, not even her mother's. The blue of the sky swelled into the blue of the Sea of Cortés.

The idea had come to her suddenly, and Lecha had to laugh out loud. She who had spent nearly all of her so-called "professional life" watching coroner's assistants open shallow graves would now watch as shovel hands dug up a few more.

Who would calculate how fast a family graveyard might fill up? The crowding had been the fault, of course, of their cousins' breeding like flies. Lecha had endured them for more than sixty years, but she damn sure didn't have to lie there for eternity with them. The big house at Potam had been sinking into the hill with each rainstorm. The seaward walls were going fastest, but the summer storms drove rain hard out of the southeast. White stucco had buckled and fallen long ago. The adobe bricks exposed had lost their edges and angles. With luck the house would cave in after two rainy, gray weeks in January. Then Uncle Ringo, Cucha, Popa's husband, and any children remaining could be buried in the ruins of the house. The adobe walls would mound into soft pink clay terraces, and from the center, spidery branches of the lively old bougainvillea would scatter scarlet petals over fallen roof beams. As the years passed, after late-summer cloudbursts, a village child might find a curious shard of china or a shell button, or the tiny bone of a fingertip. Some year a man returning from a wood-hauling trip might see something reflect the late-autumn sun. He would find not the engraved silver bowl he had imagined, but the top of Uncle Ringo's skull.

Popa would be one of the first they would dig up. Lecha herself would scatter Popa's bones in the mounds of broken glass, rusted tin cans and rotting dog carcasses at the town dump. Popa had insisted old Yoeme leave the big house to live in Popa's shack. Popa had wanted the big house of course, and once old Yoeme had been moved into Popa's shack, Popa moved herself and family into the big house. A deaf woman from the hills was hired to live in Popa's shack with old Yoeme. Popa tore out the interior walls of the big house, remodeling, she said, but Lecha knew the old whore had been looking for the almanac notebooks. The walls were redone with pink wallpaper that matched the color of rouge the undertaker used on babies' cheeks. Lecha knew Popa had not found the notebooks because Yoeme had given Lecha the notebooks long before she died. When Popa had confronted Lecha in a great fury, the morning after the funeral, Lecha had only laughed at her and stepped into the taxi waiting outside the big house. Popa's feebleminded children had followed her like quail chicks as she ran after the taxi screaming, "Thief!"

The family graveyard in Potam had been nearly empty when they were children. Although Lecha had not gone back, not even when Popa was killed, she got reports. Popa's sister, Cucha, had served her family kidney stew gone bad in the summer heat, and three of the youngest had died, while Cucha lingered paralyzed in a hammock on the long porch that ran the length of the big house. Popa herself had been killed in a train wreck, returning before Christmas from a shopping spree in Nogales on the bullet train. That had left Uncle Ringo in charge of Cucha, her three older children (her husband had gone to find work in California and never returned), and Popa's epileptic husband and four idiot children. Uncle Ringo had not managed the big house and its inhabitants very well. Popa's children, though quite large, still stole matches or begged them from American tourists driving past to stare at the two-story adobe mansion on the highest hill in Potam. Uncle Ringo, an albino with watery, pale eyes and poor vision, had failed to notice the four huddled over a small pyre they'd constructed from dry weeds and bits of palm fronds. When the pinheaded boy named Dennis came running, his shirt and hair were on fire. The others with halos of smoke and flame had begun running down the road toward town, afraid of the beatings Uncle Ringo had given them for playing with fire before. The family graveyard had filled up quickly.

Uncle Ringo told everyone he'd done his best, but Uncle Federico had insisted on adopting Cucha's remaining three—all lovely little girls, the oldest being thirteen. Lecha had laughed when her spy from Potam told her about Uncle Federico's adoption of the girls. Once Uncle Federico had taken Lecha and Zeta to the train station in Hermosillo. Both Lecha and Zeta already knew what Uncle Federico liked to do when he found them alone in the hall on the third floor of the big house or caught one of them in the pantry off the downstairs kitchen. His forefingers were as thick and ugly as the Cuban cigars he smoked. Once Lecha had seen a large dog turd in the courtyard that she mistook for a cigar her uncle had lost. He could slide the finger under the elastic of the panty leg with the same smooth motion he used to lift the little girls up into his arms. It happened so quickly he used the next motion to slip it out and smooth down the skirts of their little dresses. As they got older, he took each girl for a ride in his two-ton livestock-hauling truck and bought her a Chinese parasol out of red and gold paper, then explained that it was a delicate matter. "I studied at the seminary for the priesthood, as you know. Thus it is I who is chosen by your mother to look after you young girls. Sister Josefa has had you girls study the catechism, hasn't she? You know the importance of your purity, your virginity, then. Yes? Well, my little dove, I am only watching out for it, a simple checkup. I am a doctor you know, I understand the human body."

The forty-mile ride to the train station in Guaymas had not been simple.

The girls were fourteen. They had talked to other girls, inquiring awkwardly about the other girls' uncles. When none of the other girls volunteered any information, not even a blush or warning about secret and delicate subjects, the girls began to get the picture. They stopped for orange soda pop at San Isidro, a small town that served as a supply center for the cattle ranches and remote villages. Uncle Federico had inquired after Father Lopez from the woman behind the counter at the little store. Oh, yes, Father Lopez was there. He had a new house, one of those modern house trailers, parked next to the church. Lecha looked at Zeta and Zeta looked at Lecha. They shook their heads. They were both aware of how Uncle Federico was staring at their breasts. There was nothing in the store. The wooden shelves from floor to ceiling along the walls were empty except for a deep layer of gray dust. The soda-pop vending machine had rattled and hummed constantly but left the soda lukewarm. There were dusty harnesses hanging from nails in the wall, but the leather was brittle and cracked. No one there had the money to own horses anyway, the girls knew. Their poorest Indian relatives lived in San Isidro. Their father had sent them each a ten-dollar bill for the trip to Tucson. Zeta tried on the sunglasses, the only other merchandise in the little store. They were a man's sunglasses, and the layer of dust on the lenses made them look like blind insect eyes. The girls laughed at each other in the glasses. They waited outside on the shady side of the store building until Uncle Federico came huffing and panting across the plaza from the direction of the church. "Surprise!" he said. "Father Lopez can hear both your confessions. You go over right now and I'll wait for you in his beautiful house trailer. Come to me right away—just as soon as you've finished."

The confessional box was low and hot and smelled of mutton fat. Lecha went first because she had nothing to confess except that she was angry their father had sent for them instead of letting them live with old Yoeme. The priest had a soft, whispery voice. He asked questions. Was she sad her mother had died? Yes, she was, but her mother had taken a great deal of time to explain that they would meet up again. Only if you get to heaven, my child. She didn't say that, Lecha told the priest, but probably she forgot. "Five Hail Marys and go right away to the trailer. Your dear uncle is waiting for you."

Lecha had brushed against a whitewashed wall coming out of the church. She rubbed the black cotton of her skirt against itself to remove the chalky smudge. She walked to the shiny new house trailer slowly. Everything seemed so strange now that their mother was gone. The father who sent for them had not seen them for years. Yet when her mother died, he had sent for them.

Before Lecha could knock on the yellow and white metal door of the house trailer, Uncle Federico opened it wide. "Ah, my dear! All cleansed of sin. Yes. Come inside." All the floors in the trailer were covered with bright yellow linoleum. Lecha thought of bugs that had splattered across the windshield as they had neared the town.

"Lie down in here for a little nap," Uncle Federico said. "Take off your dress. Don't wrinkle it!" He closed the door and left her in a room so small that she could spread her arms and almost touch the walls on either side. She had just lain down when he came in. He felt Lecha's forehead, then took out the stethoscope he always carried in the pocket of his sport coat. His breath smelled like sour wine and onions. He felt her stomach through her slip. He rubbed her stomach round and round and told her to close her eyes.

"Appendicitis is very common nowadays. Because children eat too many sweets. Now let me feel. Ah, there! Is that where it is? Yes, my dear, now keep your eyes closed and relax. Don't peek, I am just going to insert my finger in here and probe around." He was leaning on the bed and she could feel him tiptoe, and the narrow bed creaked under his weight. Lecha had started to open her eyes, but this time Uncle Federico had ordered them shut in a frightening tone. Still Lecha knew how to cheat at hide-and-seek; through slitted lids she say he held something in his hand. One of his thick, dark cigars. Strange that he would want a cigar during an examination.

ADIÓS, WHITE MAN!

SEESE DROVE the big Lincoln sixty-five and seventy all the way from Nogales to Hermosillo. Lecha was giving her directions and coaching her on driving in Mexico.

"Step on it! Don't ever hesitate! They'll move out of the way!" Sterling had learned to get out to piss when they stopped for gas because Lecha demanded they drive straight through. They still had to stop to hire shovel hands.

"My information comes from here," Lecha said as they pulled up to a small whitewashed house with strings of blue morning glories trailing up the front walls. The sun was dropping low, and Seese looked tired. When she glanced at him in the rearview mirror, Sterling thought Seese looked sad. The sun was on the southwest horizon, and the crickets were noisy; a light breeze fluttered the blue morning glories. Lecha had hired teenage boys, around fifteen or sixteen; all three wore clean, mended blue jeans and white T-shirts. They were too shy to speak to Lecha, who rattled on at them in Spanish. She was apparently explaining what she wanted them to do. They answered her with nods of the head. They seemed afraid to brush against Sterling and gave him plenty of room on the back seat. They were a strange group—these teenage boys, Sterling, Seese, and Lecha.

The family graveyard was on a sandy ridge above a salt flat on the southeast side of the bay. The last twilight was fading. Seese had been driving for hours. She was still seeing white lines on pavement although they were winding down a hill on a sandy wagon road. A breeze came across the salt flat and salt crystals glittered in the last light. The sea beyond was thick, blue, and motionless. The family cemetery was surrounded by a low, crumbling wall of ocean cobblestones. Wire fencing, now rusting and sagging, enclosed the entire west and north sides where the wall had fallen and stone was scattered over the ground. The recent graves were still mounded high. The white wood crosses that marked them were entwined with red and yellow plastic roses and plastic wreathes of green ferns and pink carnations. Graves in the older sections were marked with flat wedges of dark basalt from the low volcanic peaks, *cerros,* they'd passed driving from San Isidro. Some of the black stones had been patterned with crude white crosses gradually weathering away. Around the stone markers the plastic roses and carnations had been planted into the white dune sand as if they had always grown there.

Lecha leaned over the wrought-iron fence and pointed at the graves of Federico, Popa, Cucha, and the others. She had turned to Seese and Sterling and glanced at the three boys. She made a disgusted sound against her teeth with her tongue and shook her head. The three boys leaned on the pick and shovels and watched the strange woman tour the graveyard.

Sterling leaned on the pick and stared off toward the west. He was sorry they had come so late. It would have been nice to see the ocean water of the California Gulf. He had seen the ocean many times from Long Beach where he liked to vacation and visit the amusement park. His favorite ride had been the giant roller coaster. He liked the part of the ride over the ocean in the early evening when the mist and fog rose up and left his jacket and hair soaking. Looking at the smooth, dark-blue surface loosened the big knot of loss in his chest. There were other places he could retire to besides Laguna.

Seese watched Lecha walking from grave to grave. Seese shivered although the air was warm. She had suddenly wanted to get away. Anywhere but Tucson or the Southwest. But Lecha had warned her certain matters take time. They would have to work on the almanac. Seese wandered to the far end of the graveyard where the stone wall was most intact. The graves were closer together here and the stones and crosses were smaller. She stopped at a white stone marker with two baby angels lifting a lamb.

"I didn't know it would be this easy!" Lecha said triumphantly as the three boys lifted out the first coffin. The pale beach sand on the ridge made easy digging. Lecha had been too excited to notice Seese had turned pale and had stumbled away in the dark.

In the distance, Sterling could hear the town dogs barking. He was nervous. He figured he'd probably get fired, but after all this it would be just as well. These people in Tucson were too strange for him. He'd try to find his cousin in Phoenix. High wages weren't everything. Sterling was worried about what the Mexican police did to people who disturbed graves. He held the flashlight while Lecha directed the boys. The coffin was old and the wood was half-rotted. The boys carried it easily. They seemed unconcerned at what they were doing. Sterling had seen the roll of bills Lecha carried in her big black pouch. Maybe she would buy off the police too if they showed up. Sterling was beginning to think that what had happened back on the reservation with the Hollywood movie crew was hardly an incident as compared to the crimes committed in places like Tucson.

Lecha threw open the trunk lid. She did not seem very sick, though Sterling could see her black pouch and suitcase were full of pill bottles and syringes. Of course, Sterling reasoned, Lecha could be relying on that mysterious strength he'd read about in the *Police Gazette*—the strength that crazy people and killer maniacs possessed as they fought off platoons of police with tear gas and live bullets. Lecha gave orders in Spanish. The oldest boy caught the edge of the coffin lid with the toe of his cowboy boot and popped it loose. "Dump it in here," she said in English, and pointed at the deep trunk of the Lincoln. Sterling was holding the flashlight for them, but he turned his head away, as the boys did, to avoid the fine dust that spumed up. "Well, well, Uncle Federico, here is all that remains of you and your thick, hairy fingers!"

Next came Popa. "We'll see how you like *your* new home, Auntie." Lecha directed the boys to enlarge one hole and dump in all the remains of the coffins. When an end of a coffin protruded, she had grabbed the pick from Sterling's hands and smashed it into kindling. "That's what we brought tools for," she said, giving it back to Sterling. He could tell how badly his hands were shaking by watching the beam of light on the beach sand pouring from the boys' shovels over the remains of the coffins. At the town dump they scattered the bones and remains. Lecha had paid the teenage boys very generously to keep this night confidential. People would accuse her as they had accused old Yoeme of sorcery.

Lecha had got all the news about the war in the South from the teenage gravediggers. The young men had been excited about the rumors and television reports about two brothers from a small mountain village near the Guatemalan border. Spirits talked to one of the twins and told him what the poor people must do, what the poor Indians must do. Spirits talked to him and scolded the people for being lazy and weak, for selling out to the Europeans. The spirits spoke through two big macaws. The macaws had flown out of the jungle to perch on the shoulder of one of the brothers.

Before they left Hermosillo for Tucson, Lecha had directed Seese to the street with the newsstand where she bought all the Mexico City newspapers. Before the blue and yellow spirit macaws had alighted on the brother's shoulder, theirs had been just another pitiful group of rural squatters hounded to death by the Mexican army and police.

The big excitement each day was the thousands of Indians and mestizos as well as hundreds of whites who gathered to learn what spiritual messages had been received. The spirit macaws promised spiritual strength and satisfaction to all who marched north. North was the direction of Death, but they must not be afraid. The number of the landless and the homeless and those who joined them had grown steadily, but now the authorities were dealing with a religious cult that seemed not to fear death much because they already talked to spirits of the dead anyway.

Nearly as remarkable as the spirit macaws was the Indian woman leading an all-tribal army that traveled with the spirit macaws to protect the twin brothers who served the macaws and the other faithful followers. The woman had lived with the other twin brother. The woman had been trained by a Cuban Marxist unit, but other reports circulated that other Cubans, only posing as Marxists, had trained La Escapía or the Meat Hook as she called herself.

The all-tribal people's army had sent a shocking video to local government television stations. La Escapía's big Indian face had filled the whole video screen. Her big Indian teeth flashed in the close-up. She said she chose the name La Escapía for battle because she thought it was hilarious. Hilarious how terrified the whites were of Indian wars. To further terrorize army and police officers, La Escapía promised if she captured high-ranking officers in battle, she would feed them the steel of her namesake and cook their testicles for lunch. The enlisted men had nothing to fear, she promised. They were welcome to quit the government forces and join the people's army at any time.

Newspapers reported that the latest messages from the macaw spirits had warned that soon unrest would spread like wildfire across Mexico and U.S. military forces would invade. To save money, La Escapía has videotaped another message for later broadcast, after the U.S. invasion of Mexico. She wants to terrify the young U.S. troops; on the screen flash color photographs of the severed heads of the U.S. ambassador to Mexico and his aide floating faceup in a canal at Xochimilco Garden.

"Adiós, white man," La Escapía's voice accompanies the video images of severed heads floating among flowering water lilies. La Escapía wants U.S. troops to understand they are fighting an Indian war. Commander La Escapía's brown, smiling face fills the TV screen. The people of the all-tribal army understood that U.S. troops had no choice but to follow orders; still, Commander La Escapía invited U.S. military personnel to become conscientious objectors to this Indian war, and she promised deserters safe conduct to Oslo or Stockholm.

The interior of the white Lincoln had been uncomfortably warm despite the air conditioner, which was on full fan. But Lecha had felt a chill spread over her body as she read about the videotape of floating heads and the offer to relocate U.S. military deserters in Europe. Suddenly Lecha felt awake and refreshed; her body felt cooler. As soon as she got back to Tucson, Lecha would learn more about the two brothers, the spirit macaws, and the woman commander of the pan-American tribal army. Money, money, money. All armies needed money. Lecha wondered what Zeta had done with all the cash she and Ferro had made smuggling; Lecha wondered what Calabazas had done with his money or if those two Brito sisters had pissed his money away pampering Catholic priests.

GREAT LORD IGUANA

SEESE HAD NOT FELT well since the trip to Mexico. The evening at the graveyard had been difficult; and then reentry at the border had been a nightmare because U.S. border agents had refused to believe Lecha and Sterling were American citizens. A jeepload of GIs slouched in the shade outside Border Patrol headquarters. Border Patrol agents had looked at Seese closely and asked her to repeat her name twice before they slammed down the trunk lid and allowed her to take the Lincoln through. She waited in the car, and finally Lecha and Sterling had come out a sliding glass door. Sterling clutched the back of Lecha's wheelchair grimly. "They almost forced me to live in Mexico," Sterling said in a shaky voice. "They didn't want to believe my driver's license or voter's registration card because they'd expired. But I told them to look at the picture—look, that's me, see. It is still my face and my name even if the license has expired."

Lecha laughed. "Well, I guess this is war," she said. "I've been hearing rumors all about it. U.S. army tanks lined up in rows all along the border. Jeeploads of GIs to patrol all roads and highways along the border."

Lecha had talked to the gravediggers and to the gas station attendant in Hermosillo. Seese didn't have to understand Spanish or Yaqui to realize they had given Lecha serious news. The summer before, angry crowds had set fire to the courthouse in Hermosillo after the outgoing mayor and his council had refused to turn over the courthouse to the newly elected mayor, who was a grandson of a former Nazi who had fled to Mexico. Lecha pointed out that the Indians had nothing to do with elections. Whatever happened among the political candidates and parties did not matter to the millions and millions who were starving.

The confrontation with the Border Patrol had invigorated Lecha. She had sat up talking bright-eyed in the front seat with Seese, while Sterling napped in the backseat. Lecha said the white man had always been trying to "control" the border when no such thing existed to control except in the white man's mind. The white man in North America had always dreaded a great Indian army moving up from the South. The gringos had also feared that one day there would be a spontaneous mass migration—millions of Indians coming out of the South.

Even with Lecha talking and laughing and the car windows open, Seese had to fight off sleep. She hoped Sterling could drive if she couldn't. The excitement of travel and the hours at the graveyard had taken a toll.

Lecha was ready to take on the old notebooks and Yoeme's bundles of notes and clippings. She wanted Seese to plan to work at the word processor full-time. Lecha said she was full of ideas; the news of the spirit macaws had inspired her. It had been years since she had felt so many thoughts swarming.

Back in Tucson, Lecha had begun to make notes and sift through the piles of paper and old notebooks. Seese had been surprised when Lecha had skipped the late-afternoon and midnight shots of Demerol; Lecha no longer took Percodan at noon because she wanted to stay alert to decipher the old notebooks. Old Yoeme had had her own peculiar ways to spell Spanish, and she had made up spellings for Yaqui words.

The trip to Mexico had had the opposite effect on Seese. The morning after their return Seese awoke exhausted, although she had slept ten hours. Later in the day at the word processor she had dozed off. She had been working on a strange passage in Lecha's transcriptions of the notebooks, which had an almost narcotic effect on her.

Transcriptions From the Old Notebooks

The old priest's hair is matted with dried blood.
The hair forms a long, stiff cape. The beads of
dry blood crust rattle softly as the old priest leans over the boy-
sacrifice
a lovely young prince. The young sacrifices eat their last meal
together.

Barbarians may sacrifice prisoners of war or slaves;
but the truth is, the spirits only listen when
the bloodshed is royal from the rich.

Lord Iguana carries all the seeds of the World in his tail.

In the dark around the altar
the sound of their soft breathing sends aches of desire down
the old priest's legs.

The lizard's head is full of fruit and flowers.
Each day has its own name and spirit.
Days form like buds.
The dawn is their flower.
The old priest wanted the boy so they did not take the boy
with the others.

The stone lizard shines with blood.
By morning, the lizard has lost
the iridescence of fresh blood.
Clots darken to brown then black.

A dark skin forms on the blood,
the rind of a fragrant fruit
which he inhales deeply.

At night he whispers to the sleeping child
there are other gods they must serve now.
The flesh starves, the flesh craves until
flesh devours itself.

The long afternoon
raindrops tick against the roof.
One dancer stumbles and ruins the luck of the new year.

The room is narrow.
Light the color of granite sways
behind a paper shade.
The lamp had been hung in the window
still shaking dust
golden swarms of luminous ants.

The sun is in the North corner of Time
and no longer moves. This is a dream of another day
or this day.
He cannot remember if they have come
or if they are still approaching.

The old woman sits alone and thinks.

The liquid in the basin is the color of garnets.
The heat bruises the datura, the blossom closes.
The cotton sheet laps up his fever like a village dog.
The edge of the curtain floats, then soars in the wind.

Is it yesterday now? Fragrant odor of flowers
jewel-colored the size of a boy's thumbnail.
All afternoon the wings of heat
shiver with voices
their moisture like yellow fruit
overripe now
decay trickles over the stone floor.

They talk to the open sky above the altar.
The most casual prayers:
the seeds were cut loose,
dripped down, scattering.
The moon is a woman tonight.
Throat to groin down the center.
He only struggled a little.

All that week Seese had taken naps and gone to bed early; but during the day she was aware of the weight of her body and felt as if she were drowning in air and light. Seese thought "bacteria" and "amoeba"; she thought about the flu. She thought about the suitcase pushed to the back of her closet, and the cocaine she had not wanted for months.

Seese blamed the old notebooks for the dream. She had awakened from the dream in tears, and hours later the effect of the dream had not subsided. Seese had sat at the keyboard and let the tears stream down her face. Instead of Lecha's transcriptions, Seese had typed a description of the dream:

In the photographs you are smiling
taller than I have ever seen you
older than you were when I lost you.
The colors of the lawn and house behind are indistinct
milked to faded greens and browns.
I know I will never hold you again.

It had been as if Seese had not felt the enormity of Monte's loss until the dream. She shoved the chair back from the keyboard. She lay facedown on the unmade bed. The pain in her chest took her breath away and she hoped she would die. All her life she had done everything wrong—she had ruined or lost any love she had ever had. Seese wept until her eyes and throat were dry. She had no one left, nothing to live for with Monte gone. Lecha must have known from the beginning; Seese was furious. Why hadn't Lecha told her? Lecha could find the dead. Why didn't she find Monte?

All at once she was sliding the suitcase out from the back of the closet. She put the newspaper-wrapped bundle on the bed. She had remembered to stash a quart of vodka just in case she ever started snorting cocaine again. She poured a glass of vodka and took large burning gulps to steady herself. She had not wanted to start with cocaine again, but now it hardly mattered if Lecha found out or Zeta kicked her out. Monte was dead, and Seese wanted to die too. Seese scooped a vial full of cocaine from the kilo. She had snorted line after line as if she were starving. She needed to get to town, to find Root or maybe even Tiny, to see if she could sell the kilo.

C O C A I N E   G L U T

ROOT WAS NOT surprised to see the blonde on his doorstep again. The first time she had come looking for Lecha, but this time she was looking for him. She was holding an overnight bag. Root looked around for a vehicle. "I took a taxi," Seese said, and Root motioned her inside the trailer. "I want to ask you not to tell Lecha I came here." Root looked at the blonde's face intently. He had always thought she might come back, and he sensed they would have sex that afternoon. Seese had been sipping vodka from a purse flask; she was nervous and talking too fast. Root was not surprised when she opened the train case and unwrapped a kilo of cocaine. Root shook his head slowly.

"Everybody has some," Root said, putting a pinch under his tongue, "but this is pretty good. Ether, not acetone." Root went to the refrigerator for a beer and turned off the TV.

"Can you sell it for me?" Seese had switched from vodka to beer; she got out the little mirror and vial and cut lines for Root and herself. If Root wasn't interested, there was always Tiny; but she wouldn't go to Tiny until she was desperate.

Root snorted a line in each nostril, then closed his eyes and let his head fall back on the couch. He got a big smile on his face. "The market here is flooded. You won't get more than ten or twelve."

"For a kilo?" Seese was not sure she had understood Root. Root lit a marijuana cigarette and passed it to Seese. She inhaled but started coughing—she coughed until tears filled her eyes.

"Strong?"

Seese nodded and wiped her eyes; she felt like crying. All he had said was ten or twelve. That was better than nothing. That was better than snorting or shooting coke until she was dead, wasn't it?

Seese had cut more lines of cocaine, but after they finished the marijuana, Root locked the trailer doors and led her to the bedroom by the hand. He didn't remove her clothes right away but embraced her on the unmade bed.

She was so skinny and white compared to Lecha. Root could feel her sharp bones while he fucked her. He went on and on with her because the cocaine and marijuana had that effect. Root tried not to get gouged by her pubic bone or pelvis. Lecha had spoiled sex for him with skinny women. Lecha made fun of men who secretly desired young boys instead of real women. Lecha said the white men kept their women small and weak so the women could not fight back when the men beat them or pushed them around.

Seese was seldom aroused by her lovers the first time. She had whispered the information to Root after he had pumped for half an hour; going on and on was no problem for him, he told her, a beneficial effect of brain damage, the tireless erection. Seese had kept her eyes closed so she did not have to see the peeling panel on the ceiling of the trailer's tiny bedroom. If she let Root keep humping, he might come, and if he came, he might help her.

Root didn't know what it was—the combination of drugs or the strange woman—but he didn't want to stop. He wanted to keep fucking her as if each thrust might take away the sadness.

Afterward they had smoked more marijuana, but Seese dropped the vial of cocaine in the train case and closed the lid. Root mixed a pitcher of frozen orange juice. Root stirred the orange juice with a wooden spoon and stared at the train case. "All the kilos in town right now are packed in blue Samsonite," Root said casually, but Seese sensed some question, some suspicion.

Seese laughed. "They gave me this overnight bag. I would never buy this color of blue."

"Someone did," Root said, turning down the switch on the evaporative cooler. "They probably got a good deal on a thousand *powder blue* suitcases."

Seese felt happy and high. Somehow sex had made the cocaine-craving disappear.

"I don't know about buyers," Root said. "Tucson is snowed under, snowbound."

Seese started to argue, "Two years ago—"

"Two years ago the world was a different place," Root said. His abrupt interruption hurt her feelings, but Seese blamed herself for expecting help from a man she hardly knew. Root probably had no respect for secretaries who screwed their employer's boyfriends either. She must be crazy again; coming to Root had been a dumb mistake.

"I don't know what I was thinking," Seese said. "I didn't want to get started with coke again. I need the money to find my little boy."

"Don't you work for Lecha anymore?"

"I do, but Lecha has cancer."

"You believe that?"

Seese looked closely at Root. He was difficult to figure out. She shrugged her shoulders and got a hairbrush out of her purse. She would take a taxi to the Stage Coach and have a talk with Cherie. The two of them could go back into the business together. They could turn one kilo into two kilos with baby laxative just like old times. Seese watched out the window for the taxi; if Root wanted to talk, let him. She wasn't saying anything he could carry back to Lecha and use against her. "I may be able to get rid of that for you—I just can't make any promises on the prices."

Seese saw the taxi turn into the trailer court entrance; she picked up the light-blue train case and shook her head at Root. "That's all right, don't bother," Seese said. "I have other people interested." Root stood in the door and Seese sensed how much he wanted to embrace her, but she was finished with him.

Let her find out for herself about the changes in Tucson. Root remembered downtown when it had been alive, before the malls had killed downtown. No one had thought the big malls would die out either. But then the U.S. economy had begun to falter. Prominent corporations had been avoiding or abandoning Arizona steadily over the years because corporate employees balked at living in Arizona. The quality of life was substandard. Root thought it was really funny. Guam and Puerto Rico spent more on schools and mental health programs than Arizona did. No new industry or business would ever come to Arizona again; all the tax breaks and cozy deals, all the cheap land Arizona offered to attract corporations—all was for naught. Analysts said Mexico's civil war would be nasty and spill across to the United States. Tucson's fate was closely tied to the fate of Mexico. Tucson's malls had depended on wealthy Mexicans; but the rich Sonorans had fled the angry mobs of peasants and relocated to Argentina or Spain. Rumors about violence across the border had begun to scare off wealthy patrons at Tucson's spas and health resorts.

Root had to laugh. Merchants who sold arms and munitions did a "booming" business. Tucson had always depended on some sort of war to keep cash flowing. Root's own great-grandfather had got rich off the Apache wars. Calabazas had told Root all about it. Root's parents never discussed the family's social prominence or the family wealth. After Calabazas had described the bootlegging to the Apaches and the army, the whores and the skimming off army supply contracts, Root understood why his parents and Tucson's "social elite" had so little interest in local history.

As far as Root was concerned, he was dead to his family, he had died on the day of his accident. The only family Root had was Calabazas and maybe Mosca. He could never be sure about Mosca or Lecha either; they both loved him but they were both crazy too. Root did not know if he loved them or if he had ever loved anyone. Had he ever loved his mother? He hardly even thought about his father.

Sometimes Root even amazed himself. He should never have fucked Lecha's assistant or nurse or whatever she was. As soon as the urge and the hunger had been hammered away, the floating ecstasy had given way to doubt. The town was full of strangers carrying suitcases packed with cocaine or U.S. dollars to trade for dynamite. Lecha had psychic powers, but she still made mistakes where her personal life was concerned; hiring the blonde might have been a mistake. Root turned on the TV, but he could not get rid of the sad feeling. No wonder Mosca only "used" prostitutes. That was money well spent because there were no regrets.

Root had started hating television while he was in the hospital. But after he got out, he had begun to hate radio too; most of all, he had hated the new state lottery, and all the stupid ads for the suckers. Local radio stations had to give away cash all day long to be assured of listeners. No one did anything for anyone anymore except for cold cash. The deliverymen and receptionists, telephone operators and line repairmen, grocery checkers and department store clerks—the stupid suckers listened hour after hour while radio deejays pimped them with trash promotional merchandise.

In the hospital, prize money and prize merchandise had been all the nurses or nurse's aides and therapists ever talked about. At home they paid baby-sitters to watch television in case the lucky phone call came at their house. They had all been making payments on new carpet or new living room furniture. The whole question came down to what it was a person stayed alive for.

Root once sat in a neighborhood coke dealer's kitchen one day and watched. Around three P.M. the first of the "clients" had got off work and stopped by for a "boost" to get them home. For a small extra charge clients were allowed to shoot up in the bathroom. They had all been white, and the dealer was sympathetic. The clients had spouses, families, and jobs to think about. Root watched the steady parade. Legal secretaries, mechanics, postal workers, receptionists, dental hygienists, and others Root could not guess—they might have been real estate agents or high school teachers. But all had the same expression of anticipation and relief on their faces. All day they had thought about only one thing. They had shut out the tedium and humiliation of their jobs—they had endured because they knew there was a full syringe waiting. This was what they lived for; this was why they went to work.

Root understood. Anyone who could see and reason clearly and logically would have found a painless way out—handgun, any caliber, its barrel nuzzled by the ear that would never hear the blast. Everyone had made his or her choice—a personal strategy for survival. New carpets, new dinette sets, new automobiles; something to live for, reasons to go to the jobs they hated. The coke dealer was an addict himself; he complained about the fall in cocaine prices. He said less cash was circulating around town; regular customers had been laid off or had had their work hours cut back.

COMMUNIST PRIESTS
AND NUNS

MOSCA HAD LEARNED not to bother with those smart, nervous women even when they were dark and beautiful like the two sisters. In a way, Calabazas had wasted his life with those two Brito sisters.

First, Sarita, his "lawful wedded wife," had been in bed with a dead monsignor—that was a good one! Fucked him into a heart attack. Second, Liria, Calabazas's "true love," had gone behind his back and with Sarita had joined a Catholic radical group to help smuggle refugees from Mexico and Guatemala to the United States. Mosca had overheard most of the argument when Calabazas had found out. Mosca thought most of the neighbors had at least heard the loud voices, which had quickly dropped to angry whispers. Mosca had been the one who had found out. Mosca had told Calabazas. See how fast word got around? What was that bitch Liria trying to do? What if they came investigating Liria and her communist nuns and priests.

Mosca had heard all the arguments before—both sides. Those who said you helped when you fed them, and those who said people needed "saving." Mosca liked to brag that he only voted what his stomach told him. Calabazas had reminded Liria that all the farmers were relatives or clanspeople of his in Mexico. Theirs was a family business; all the marijuana had been from family farms, carefully packed inside truck-loads of pumpkins.

Liria had pointed out that she was not telling him to stop his business. The Indians had been left the poorest land; it was true. In the hills only marijuana would grow; pumpkins and gourds only grew down in the small valleys. Liria had remained calm. Each person chose the work they would do. Her work was to give sanctuary to people fleeing bullets and torture. Liria did not see how her work or Sarita's work with the refugees would interfere with his work.

Then Mosca had heard Calabazas make an inspired argument about the dangers of smuggling political refugees versus smuggling gourds full of cocaine. People were too large and too noisy to smuggle easily. Liria's church group was too open to infiltration by government agents.

Calabazas had been walking on shaky ground; suddenly Liria had become furious with Calabazas.

"Just listen to yourself, old man! What chicken shit you men are!" Liria had stormed out, and later she had thrown two suitcases in the trunk of her Toyota and drove away. Mosca knew that Calabazas was in the dark about a lot of the subversive work the Catholic Church was doing. Mosca had never trusted nuns, priests, any of them. Mosca had brought up the subject gently because he knew Calabazas had spent years madly in love with that woman Liria.

Mosca had been able to detect wizards or sorcerers, and assassins and spies, but only as he was driving past them. Mosca's explanation had been that sorcerers, like antelope or coyotes, did not seem to fear detection from moving vehicles.

Mosca would be minding his own business, driving down Drachman at Miracle Mile, when suddenly he would see a dark wizard disguised as a clean-cut, young Hispanic college student. Mosca did not care if Root, Calabazas, or that bitch Liria laughed at him and called him, "Loco, loco, loco!" Mosca had made careful observations. The weirdos all hit the streets at the same time—they all lurched out of their cheap apartments and trailers to walk along Ft. Lowell Road laughing and talking to themselves. How had they all known it was time to step outside? Weirdos were on the same brain wavelengths as lizards and

migrating birds and possessed the mysterious ability to converge simultaneously on the same location. Sometimes witches and wizards even
hit the streets together. Mosca had never figured out why those who
hated and feared one another so much would all want to stroll together
on the same streets. Yet Mosca had often seen the sorcerers, witches of
both sexes, *curanderos*—whatever you wanted to call them—they all
circulated together no different from the whores, male and female, who
also walked South Sixth Avenue.

Speeding past a witch on the street, Mosca sometimes had a split
second to see a light—sometimes a flash, sometimes a glow—around
the face or the feet. Compared to the old-time stories about sorcerers,
his power, Mosca had to admit, was limited.

Mosca opened another beer and scooped four big snorts from the
plastic bag of coke shoved in the pocket of his western shirt. Mosca
didn't care about the teasing and the jokes. Calabazas, Root, or Liria—
the rest of them—could laugh until they choked. The alcohol and the
dope, were only the doorways; alcohol didn't do the talking. All the
notions, the suspicions, the schemes, the reveries, the theories, and the
hunches belonged to him. They were locked up inside compartments of
flesh and bone deep in Mosca's body. Mosca could feel what he knew:
the surge of a great flood, the muddy, churning water of what, he couldn't
yet say. Mosca's eyes were shining. Tribal people in South America had
navigated the most treacherous rivers and had traveled icy mountain
paths with the aid of Mama Coca.

SOULS OF THE DEAD

MOSCA HEARS and remembers so many voices and so many
places he forgets where they all came from. Two or three beers,
and three or four good snorts, and if everything else is level and smooth,
then all the doors and gates of memory swing open. Every time Mosca
had ever been arrested, there had been an intervening circumstance—a
witch, a devil, a spirit thing. Mosca went on talking about zombies,
open graves, and ghost armies traveling in green fireballs because they

were and had always been a part of Mosca's life. Root had asked Mosca how old he was when he had first seen one of the weird things.

"Oh, man, I was just a little baby! They had me sleeping in a banana box. It must have been cold, because they had me and the box up on a table or something in a kitchen." Mosca claimed he could remember everything, even being born. Though he had only been an infant, had sensed something was watching him from the ceiling. The first of thousands of things Mosca would "see."

Mosca had watched the steam rise off the Santa Cruz on mornings when cold mountain air settled over Tucson. He understood how the steam was the moisture of the river rising, so that you had a river running into the sky, in all directions of the winds—but also that these were the souls of the dead rising out of the purgatory where they'd been imprisoned hundreds and thousands of years waiting to be released so they could return to help their beloved descendants.

In the Sonoran desert foothills the winds were supernatural. *Los aires,* the air currents—tricky breezes, little updrafts, and ferocious jaws of downdrafts—that crushed small aircraft into the mountains. A sorcerer of some prowess could ensorcell a minor wind or strong breeze off a prominent mountain cliff. A sorcerer might grow rich and powerful if he could manage to secure just the right wind at just the strategic place. Naturally every sorcerer dreamed and bragged and schemed after the great winds—seldom seen except in sudden gusts that engulfed armies in desert sand or scuttled war fleets against coastal rocks.

One afternoon, the sky is overcast-gray, and damp heat is pushed ahead of big thunderclouds. Mosca is moody and strange. Root finds Mosca standing outside Calabazas's house facing west. Thousands of waxy cottonwood leaves click together in the damp wind. Mosca does not acknowledge Root for a while, and then Mosca just starts talking about the souls of the dead. You can hear them, Mosca says, on rainy afternoons, summer or winter, because the dead souls are out on cloudy days to bring rain. "Dead souls are always near us," Mosca continues, "watching over us." The talk about spirits begins to excite Mosca. His dark eyes gleam as he gathers momentum. He says white people got the idea of guardian angels from the spirits who help us. Except the poor souls could not really "guard," but they always accompanied you wherever you went. They came from the place of complete peace in which silence was the answer, and silence was truth.

"Dead souls stay near us, but they don't break the silence," Mosca said. Because talk was not necessary so long as you remembered everything you knew about your ancestors. Because ancestor spirits had the answers, but you had to be able to interpret messages sent in the language of spirits.

Souls of the newly dead hover like gray and brown moths at the window screens and by doors of places they'd once lived. Newly dead, they have not yet learned the ways of the dead, so the dead souls cried piteously outside their houses. Europeans did not listen to the souls of their dead. That was the root of all trouble for Europeans. They never seemed to hear the cries of their dead swarming outside windows and doors of courthouses and office buildings whining for money they had not been able to take along with them. Mosca did not agree with what the communist priests and communist Indians from Mexico had said, but Mosca did agree the dead souls of Europeans cried out.

"We are outnumbered here!" was their message, endlessly, in the "séances" the Barefoot Hopi had conducted for them in prison. The Europeans not only did not feed the souls of their dead for four days afterward, family members took all things precious to the dead and scattered them. Thus Europeans were haunted by the dead in their dream life and were driven mad by the incessant cries of unquiet ancestors' souls. No wonder they were such restless travellers; no wonder they wanted to go to Mars and Saturn.

Souls of the dead sometimes appeared as butterflies before a spring rain in the desert. Which dead souls brought blizzards and hailstorms and torrential rains that collapsed roofs and washed away garden seedlings? Calabazas wants to know. Mosca is more confident than Root has ever seen him. Mosca does not erupt in fury as he once had if anyone dared question one of his beloved theories. Dead souls that brought too much rain or too much of anything were suspected of working for sorcerers.

High plateaus and rugged mountain passes were hazardous. They were places to be avoided because where clouds were found, so were the souls of the dead. Wise travelers avoided mountain or high-land travel except in dry, cloudless weather because lightning, hailstorms, and sudden blizzards had trapped and frozen countless travelers before them. Mosca had heard the stories.

In a high mountain pass, stranded travelers huddled around a fire in darkness and blizzard. Then, on the edge of the light of the fire, through lacy veils of snow, the travelers made out a silhouette the shape of a horse. Bewildered, they staggered from their fire toward the white horse emerging from the blowing snow.

"Here!" Mosca said. "Here is the miracle of it: the Christ Child! The Holy Infant as a tiny baby, sitting astride a white horse!" When the infant smiled at them, the travelers saw the infant had a full set of teeth.

" '*Tengo los dientes,*' the Holy Infant said, and then rode away on the white horse into the snowy night." Mosca smiled when he finished his story.

Liria had been listening from the kitchen. She shook her head. "That wasn't the Christ Child! That was the Devil!" Liria started laughing. Mosca's mouth tightened into a pout. Who asked her to butt in? Mosca demanded to know. Couldn't anyone talk without someone listening in? What did she know anyway about the Infant Jesus? If He was God, He could have anything He wanted, including death on the cross and a white horse to ride as a baby.

Mosca hates Liria most at moments like that. Hates her laughing, hates her fucking her sister's husband, hates her sister who fucks priests, hates the stiff-prick priests and their scandal of holy orders. Liria knows nothing. The Devil never rides white horses. Jesus had traveled the length and width of the continents called the Americas years before the Romans had directed the Jews to nail Him up on the cross. Jesus had been seen by the wandering tribes that walked the Great Plains. Jesus had been seen in Mexico. Liria and her sister were ruined by their mother, who had raised them to be white women. The Jesus they prayed to had blue eyes and blond hair.

Mosca had not always believed all the notions of the old tribal people, but he had seen for himself over the years the old people had told the truth.

Mosca's body had been so full of natural electricity, he had never been able to wear a wristwatch of any kind because his body's electricity interfered with the tiny watch mechanisms. Flocks of birds migrated thousands of miles and lizards communicated with one another using the same sort of electromagnetism. The circulation of the blood around and around a living body created electric current; moving electric currents in living bodies created a sort of magnetism. Performers and TV people were addicted to the jolts of electricity they got during performances in large stadiums with thousands and thousands of human bodies massed together to focus energy on a small stage. The barefoot Hopi had explained all this to Mosca while they'd shared a cell.

Mosca blamed his bad luck with women on what he called "too much electricity." Women became uneasy around Mosca because he aroused so much sexual desire in them whenever he was near. Unfortunately most women did not follow their instincts, but blamed Mosca for everything.

A few women had got so upset on first dates with Mosca they had even hallucinated what they heard Mosca say. Once Mosca had asked a date if she could see a clock; the woman had misunderstood and thought he said, "Can you suck my cock?" The woman had nearly jumped from the moving vehicle until Mosca's denials had convinced her.

Mosca believed in the power of sunspots. Sunspots sent great waves of electromagnetism to collide with radio waves throughout the galaxy. Mosca had learned not to date women except in the "dark" of the moon. Otherwise, embarrassments and misunderstandings were certain to occur; even prostitutes had wild fantasies about someone loving and marrying them. Mosca would never get married; they'd have to shoot him first. Mosca had to remain absolutely free. He knew he had a higher calling than ordinary men.

Mosca could not make out what his special calling would be, but he could feel the revelation would arrive soon, a messenger was approaching. He wasn't afraid to die. He knew the electricity that formed the soul merely escaped the body, and nothing was destroyed or lost. The dead remembered everything; the dead still loved us and watched over us. Mosca would never be lost to the people in their struggle; he would be with them, he would float around as spirit energy, giving jolts to the police, the military and the clergy.

A few nights later, Mosca had slept the wrong way on his neck. Next morning, to work the stiffness from his neck, Mosca was stretching his arms up over his head when suddenly he heard a strange sound. Then Mosca realized the sound was the cry of a spirit voice that had settled in his neck, near the base of his right shoulder. Before Mosca had left his house, he knew he would have to get advice from someone who knew about these voices because when he had tried to lift the coffeepot full of fresh water, there had been shooting pains and complete weakness in his right shoulder joint and forearm. He had been able to lift the coffeepot only with the greatest willpower and effort while a constellation of shooting pains shot like electrical charges up his arm and neck to the base of his brain.

Mosca went to consult an old woman who could talk to spirit voices. The old woman wanted fifty dollars to talk to the spirit in Mosca's shoulder because the first statement the voice had made had been about suffering and perhaps despair. Talk to dangerous voices cost more. Mosca had always been leery of "medicine people" he did not know; most of the good medicine people had already passed on. The only ones left called themselves healers, but they were mostly blackmailers and sorcerers. When Mosca told the old woman she charged too much, the old sorceress had begun to move her eyes up and down his body, slowly, like hot hands. She had lifted her skirts flirtatiously and said if she were not short of cash, she would have done it for free. He was in some danger, and she would hate to see him get hurt. The old woman had been a setback for Mosca; she had probably laid spells on him with lice larvae in his hair. The lice shampoo had turned his hair orange. Mornings came when Mosca had awakened with a great sadness he could not identify. Mosca felt a burden, not his alone—ancient losses, perhaps to war and famine long ago.

ONE WHO "READS" BODY FAT

MOSCA HAD ABRUPTLY stopped snorting cocaine when the voice in his right shoulder had begun to speak. He had begun to smoke far more marijuana to "calm his nerves"; he ate a great deal of candy and ice cream, and suddenly Mosca could pinch little spare tires of fat from his belly.

Mosca had contacted his friend Floyd, in prison for life, to get the name of a reliable reader of body fat. Fat readers were virtually unknown outside the remote mountains of Chihuahua and Sonora. For too many years during the Spanish and Mexican occupations there had been no fat to read, only skin and bones of Indian corpses. Rumors and stories claimed that the remaining readers of fat had been enslaved or retained, often for life, simply to read the fat of the idle rich who were addicted to astrologists, faith healers, and mountain Indians who could "see" lucky numbers in the dimples and puckers of a client's body fat.

Mosca had never seen a woman quite as fat or quite as majestic in his life. Immediately Mosca's heart had begun to beat faster, and he could feel the fat reader was about to change his life. The fat reader had examined his hands first, and then she had touched his cheeks, forehead, and chin. "You used to be skinny most of your life. Until now," she had commented, as if to herself. "Take down your pants," she said, and Mosca felt his face flush. When he hesitated, the fat reader had laughed; readers of fat, she said, preferred to read the belly, buttocks, or thighs of men and women both. Belly fat on a man means one thing; belly fat on a woman, however, means something quite different. Fat that has always been carried by a person tells a different tale than fat that appears suddenly. Fat that had been with a person all his life related to the past; fat that had appeared suddenly was related to events in the future.

The best readers of fat could tell a client a great deal more than winning lottery numbers. Fat readers were able to enhance and increase sexual pleasure by "talking to the fat" and massaging messages into the body. Belly fat increased the width and depth of the orgasm, pulsing showers of ecstasy reverberating in every cell; body fat was the great generator of sensual pleasure. Fat had its own timetable: first, relentless, consuming lust.

The fat reader had glanced at the television set in the corner of her consultation room, tuned without sound to the Telemundo station. She was still amazed, she said, at today's people and their fear of body fat. The human body grew to the size necessary for its survival. Mosca was delighted the fat reader had interpreted the television news the same way she interpreted television commercials. The starvation of others had caused the killers to diet obsessively because they feared detection; they feared the starving would see how fat the rich had grown off their suffering. The rich dieted frantically lest one day they be killed for their fat by the starving people.

The fat reader had poked and prodded Mosca's little folds of skin and fat with her eyes closed. From time to time she would make a deep sigh, as if she were sad or tired. "You might go one direction or you might go the other," she said. "You tend to be thin, so you are at risk." Thin ones tended to be not well attached to life. Without capacity for pleasure, thin ones preferred the sensation of denial and pain. Injury and illness could easily carry off a thin woman or man. Skinny ones burned up in fires and blew away in big winds. "One more thing," the fat reader had said as Mosca was leaving. "The voice in your shoulder says, Fatten up! There's a great storm brewing in the South. In the big flood that's coming, only the fat will float."

Mosca had not told anyone about his visit to the fat reader. Liria and even Calabazas would make fun of him the way they had when Mosca told them his ideas about death. The old people used to request that their remains be left out in the hills for the scavengers to eat. That way they started "living" again within a matter of hours, surging through the blood veins of a big coyote as she raced across the desert to suckle her pups. Calabazas had wisecracked about becoming coyote shit. Mosca had only nodded; he didn't mind being coyote shit because the rain carried the shit to the desert roots and seeds, and all kinds of beings and life. Fed back to the earth, Mosca believed he would bound and leap in the legs of the mule deer and soar in the wings of the hawk.

What had depressed Mosca was the way Calabazas, Root, and Liria had been so quick to laugh and make jokes whenever Mosca tried to discuss the ideas and theories that filled Mosca's head more and more each day, like gifts from God. Mosca did not know what was wrong with Calabazas and Root; they both should have known better—Calabazas because he had been reared by old-time people, and Root because he had almost died in that scooter wreck. Mosca did not expect anything worthwhile from Liria because she wanted to be a white woman.

Liria stood up to excuse herself. Conversations about turning to shit after death did not interest her. Liria's air of superiority had infuriated Mosca.

"You think the mortuary does any good?" he shouted. "Morticians take a last fuck on top of you while the machine replaces your blood with embalming fluid!" Liria had been laughing by then, and she shook her head as if she could not care less what Mosca was saying.

"Embalming fluid turns your bones to jelly," Mosca said, but Liria had slammed the door, laughing wildly; then she had abruptly opened the door a crack to taunt Mosca. "And what was *your* plan for the bones, eh, Mosca?" Liria had taunted.

"I'd jump your bones!" Mosca said, startled by the answer he had given. Liria had snapped the door shut and laughed down the hall. Mosca's face was hot, and he glanced quickly out the corner of his eye to see if Calabazas was pissed off. But the old man had been laughing. So had Root. To them, Mosca knew he was a joke; for a long time he had not minded their laughter, but lately his feeling had been changing.

TUCSON, CITY OF THIEVES

HIMSELF, Mosca preferred to call Tucson "City of Thieves" because there were fourth- and fifth-generation thieves living there. Tucson was a place where betrayals ticked off with each second, most of them little stabs in the back, and then, once a day, a murder or two. Mosca could feel sorry for the old and the weak or ill who had to live in a place such as Tucson where the police were as predatory as the mob and the gangs. There was no honor among the generations of thieves in Tucson. Mosca himself had never felt even the slightest sensation of loyalty. He understands loyalty exists for some, and therefore Mosca recognizes loyalty as a variable, though Mosca sees loyalty is more easily bought and sold than most commodities.

Mosca did not have any embarrassment about killing the Santa Fe poet. He hadn't been disloyal to Calabazas or the others. The police were always killing innocent bystanders with stray bullets. FBI agents in Phoenix had accidently shot their own female agent. Mosca wondered what the true story had been in that case. Mosca did not claim to be anything more than who and what he was, and guys in his line of work often had to fire guns around innocent people. Mosca had never sworn or promised to serve or uphold anything for anyone. If Mosca had ever sworn himself to any cause, the cause would have been land and justice for native people. The Santa Fe poet had been an intruder. It was one thing for a crazy guy such as Mosca to shoot someone, but it was a whole worse matter when the *locos* were the police with .45 automatics.

Mosca believed his mother's illness during his childhood had been the cause of his mistrust of people who were close to him. Mosca believed he had been affected by nursing his mother's milk laced with the strange natural chemicals of her poor schizophrenic brain. Mosca had listened to radio show experts discuss human milk; weak mother's milk had left Mosca shorter than he should have been. Mosca did not thank his mother. No one had asked him if he wanted to be born short, skinny, dark, and dirt-poor in southern Arizona. Mosca's mother had betrayed

Mosca when she had conceived him in the swirling rainbows of her deranged blood.

Mosca had always enjoyed imaginary plots, fantasies in which he was a traitor. Mosca loved to imagine the expressions on all their faces— Calabazas and Root, the bitches Sarita and Liria, when they learned of their betrayal by Mosca. Mosca reveled in the pain they would feel at the moment his treachery was revealed to them. The betrayal of Jesus was Mosca's favorite Bible story. Mosca and the other street kids had gone to Mass on Palm Sunday to rip palm fronds out of the hands of rich Catholics outside the Tucson cathedral. Mosca had laughed wildly as he seized palms the priest had blessed for old, rich women because the rich were suffering a little, suffering to remind them of Jesus' suffering. The betrayal of Jesus had not stopped with the crucifixion; Paul and Peter had corrupted Jesus' creed of forgiveness and brotherly love. Mosca had seen all the gold and silver and silk and satin on Catholic Church altars. Mosca had seen the big Cadillacs, new every year, parked in the drive of the monsignor's residence.

Mosca did not expect women to be loyal because men threatened them and their babies and slammed them against walls. Mosca did not blame women, but he was careful around women. Treachery was everywhere throughout history. The prophet Muhammad had preached tolerance and love, as Jesus had; but when Muhammad had passed to heaven, the Moslems, like the Christians, forgot the teachings of their God.

Christians and Moslems had lost contact with their Gods whenever they had slaughtered their own brothers in so-called holy wars. Only God had the right to kill everything because he had created everything. Accidents, plagues, and famines would carry away the unbelievers; it was not necessary to make war, to take God's will into puny human hands.

Mosca thought someday the Moslems might take over the world. They might simply settle for Western Europe because European Christians would be dangerous and troublesome captives who would require the Moslems' undivided attention; or perhaps the Moslems would simply wait a few hundred years until fertility and birth rates among Moslem immigrants in Western Europe gradually overtook them, overwhelmed the Christians. What would Moslem Germans or German Moslems resemble? Mosca imagined the bellowing cattle sounds of German opera side by side with the nasal caterwauling of Arab music. Would there be a Moslem Reich? The Europeans should never have left their homelands in the first place.

KILO OF COCAINE

SEESE TOOK A CAB to a cheap hotel on Miracle Mile, and while the driver waited, she hid the kilo under the foot of the bed. She kept telling herself over and over that Root hadn't rejected her, he had only refused to buy the cocaine. Wholesale prices were low, Seese could believe that. If something happened to Lecha or her job with Lecha, Seese would need cash. If she was able to endure the old routines, Seese knew she could easily sell the cocaine to the pimps on Miracle Mile. The easy way out was to sell the kilo for what she could get from Tiny because Tiny had everything worked out with the undercover cops— Tiny always had things worked out with the law.

The Stage Coach was quiet on weeknights. The married men stopped by on their way home from work, but after seven there were only bikers playing pool and the diehards watching the dancer under the black lights. Seese did not recognize the girl on stage—a skinny, boyish blonde in black panties and bra. Three bikers nursed bottles of beer and watched the topless dancer in silence. In the corner Seese saw the same jukebox she had danced to in the old days, when she had worked for Tiny. An "out of order" sign was taped to the front. Nothing had changed; Tiny was still as stingy as he had been when Seese had danced at the Stage Coach. The jukebox used to stay broken for weeks. There had been days when Tiny told the dancers to turn on the radio because no one cared about the music except the girls; the afternoon crowd only wanted titties, ass, and crotch.

Seese didn't see the bartender, but saw the storeroom door was open. She knocked on the door to Tiny's office. Tiny always kept a .38 on the desk beside the phone. Seese had seen the pistol many times while she had worked for Tiny. If there was a knock at the door, Tiny always slipped his hand over the .38. Tiny didn't care whose voice it was outside the door; Seese knew he didn't move his hand from the gun until he could see the visitor in the doorway. Tiny was a fat man, but Seese had watched him, and he was faster than he looked. Seese and Cherie and some of the other dancers used to joke about Tiny's shooting someone in the tit if she forgot to knock. Tiny did not lock the door, but Seese knew he liked privacy to snort coke at his desk and sip whiskey all evening long.

Seese had to repeat her name three times before Tiny said, "Come in." Tiny seemed surprised to see her. He was sitting at his desk with bookkeeping ledgers and computer printouts stacked around him. Cherie said Tiny had another bar, on the east side, not a dump like the Stage Coach, but a cocktail lounge that booked *Playboy* playmates of the year. Off- duty Tucson police and sheriff's deputies drank at Tiny's other bar. Tiny had been in the Marines and so had most of the deputies and cops. Cherie said Tiny had a rule; he never talked about the other bar, and he never wanted to see any of the Stage Coach dancers near the east-side place.

Tiny had gotten even fatter, but still wore a Marine Corps haircut. Seese was reminded of the color illustrations in children's books of Humpty-Dumpty. Seese had never felt comfortable with Tiny, and not just because he had been in love with her once. There had been something else too—only a feeling really; Seese thought it might be Tiny's connection with the military and her father. Seese glanced down; the .38 was on the desk by the telephone. Tiny stood up from his chair behind the desk and took both her hands in his; suddenly he seemed very happy to see her. He buzzed the bartender for a bottle of whiskey and brought out a brown vial and a little spoon from a desk drawer. Seese shook her head and set her vial of cocaine on the edge of the desk.

"See what you think of this," she said. Tiny looked at her closely. Seese knew he was trying to figure how she had managed to turn her luck around in Tucson. Tiny could see the glitter of pure crystals that had not been "cut"; Tiny held the vial, then set it back on his desk without opening it. There was a voice and a knock. Seese watched Tiny's hand settle on the snub-nosed .38. Suddenly Seese wished she had taken the taxi back to the ranch. The bartender brought two glasses and whiskey. Seese needed the whiskey; otherwise she was going to have to reach for the vial of cocaine. Seese had forgotten the negative charge in the air when Tiny knew he could only look but not touch. She should have taken the train case home and pushed it to the back of the closet until she thought of someone else besides Tiny or Root who might buy the kilo.

Tiny wasn't interested in buying cocaine, he was interested in her. After all that time the fat pig was still after her. No money—nothing— was worth the clammy, bulging belly or thick black hair that grew out of the crack of his ass. Seese reached for her purse on the floor by her feet. Returning to the Stage Coach was always a mistake. Seese wondered if she would ever learn. She hardly knew Cherie anymore; there wasn't much they could safely discuss in front of Cherie's boyfriends or husbands. A few years had made a lot of difference. Cherie's eldest was in sixth grade. Tucson was seedier and more run-down. The pavement on big streets such as Oracle and Broadway had cracked and left potholes. Stores and restaurants where Seese had once shopped with Cherie were gone. Even the shopping malls were partially vacant; real estate FOR SALE signs were everywhere. "Money's been tight in Arizona ever since the feds took over all the banks," Tiny said, as if he had read her thoughts. The apology in his tone was unmistakable. "I'll see what I can do," Tiny said, his eyes on hers. "How much do you want for it?" Seese took a big swallow and finished the whiskey. "A kilo for twenty thousand," she said. "It's never been cut." Seese knew she should have started at thirty because Tiny would take the price down five thousand right away. All the bluffing and bullshit in drug deals bored Seese. "Ten max," Tiny said. Seese stood up to leave. Her hand was on the doorknob. "All right, twelve. But not tonight." Seese nodded and walked out the door before Tiny could get out from behind the desk. Tiny followed her past the bar to the pay phone.

"Use the phone in my office," Tiny said.

"Oh, thanks, I'm just calling a cab. I need to use the ladies' room." Seese knew if she went back to his office, Tiny would try to kiss and fondle her. Tiny knew he had lost his opportunity and had a disappointed expression on his face. Seese smiled and winked at him as she went into the ladies' toilet. She had outmaneuvered Tiny tonight, but she would have to be careful next time. When she came out of the rest room, Tiny was gone, and the cab honked outside. Seese got the train case with the kilo from the motel room, and the cab took her back to the ranch. No wonder Beaufrey had been so generous with Seese. The wholesale price of cocaine had probably started to slide back then. A kilo was cheaper than hiring a gunman, and nothing had to be explained because Seese was an addict. Beaufrey had really counted on Seese to OD.

Seese gave the cabdriver a big tip for driving her over the dirt road to the ranch house. Some cabdrivers were afraid to drive inside the gate because of the snarling guard dogs behind the chain-link fence on each side of the driveway. Seese shoved the train case to the back of the closet and lay down on the bed to smoke a joint. She regretted she had asked Root to help her sell the kilo. Root probably thought she had fucked him for the favor. A man with a limp and slurred speech was not likely to have many girlfriends or get much sex unless he went to whores. Seese thought she might like another evening with Root. He seemed different from other men; he seemed more gentle. But now Root would not trust her. She had ruined her chances with him because of the cocaine. Going to Tiny at the Stage Coach had been a mistake too. Seese didn't know Tiny anymore; she didn't even know Cherie.

All night Seese had nightmares about losing the train case, or about how the kilo had spilled open all over the floor of Tiny's office, but then the cocaine had congealed like white pus or sperm. Lecha might help her get rid of the cocaine, but Seese did not want to ask. Lecha had been working past midnight every night, poring over the old notebooks. Lecha said there would be old acquaintances at an upcoming convention who might have questions about Yoeme's old notebooks.

Seese telephoned Tiny's office at noon the next day. Her hands were perspiring as she waited for Tiny to answer. She wanted to get rid of the kilo as soon as possible; every week the wholesale price of a kilo fell lower. The whole U.S. economy had gone soft. She had nothing else to sell; no other way to hire a detective to find Monte.

BAREFOOT HOPI

ROOT HAD STILL felt sad the next day when Mosca drove up with a hail of gravel. Root could see Mosca was flying high. Mosca said he had not slept two nights running because the Barefoot Hopi had come to town. They had been chewing peyote and talking for more than forty-eight hours. "I couldn't stand it, man," Mosca told Root. "I got so excited I had to tell someone. "I went by Calabazas's, but no one was home. So I came here!" Mosca had left the big Blazer idling in the driveway; he wanted Root to come with him right away.

Root was still in his bathrobe. Mosca had been complaining lately about how boring the work was. Smuggling was just another dumb job. Mosca had his truck paid for, but now he complained that he had everything he wanted. Mosca couldn't think of what else to buy except more semiauto rifles. Calabazas had teased Mosca for buying so many firearms; Calabazas and the other Indian smugglers had not armed themselves in the old days; but all of that had been changing. The old-timers who used remote trails still did not arm themselves, but suddenly there were more players, complete strangers. The new players were Salvadorians and Guatemalans.

Root pulled on a dirty T-shirt and some jeans he found on the floor. Mosca had started to tell his story while Root was tying his shoes, but refused to tell the good stuff until they were safely in Mosca's truck. Root shook his head. Mosca thought the authorities might have bugged Root's trailer, but when Root asked him about "bugs" in his truck, Mosca had been indignant. Root left his trailer for hours at a time, while Mosca seldom left his truck unattended. At night Mosca parked the truck outside his bedroom window. No one in the neighborhood dared come near Mosca's adobe shack because they feared Mosca. Root had learned to fasten his seat belt and save his breath; no one could win an argument with Mosca, especially not an argument about Mosca's power or invincibility. Root watched cars and pedestrians scatter in front of them as Mosca casually ignored red lights at intersections. For Mosca this was it. The message had arrived. The Barefoot Hopi was the messenger.

The Hopi had no permanent location but kept moving—one week in Ontario, the next in Guatemala, then to New Mexico to lead demonstrators protesting police brutality in Albuquerque. Because the Hopi traveled around so much there had been other rumors too, rumors the Hopi was a spy or special agent. The Hopi traveled the world to raise political and financial support for the return of the land to indigenous Americans. After five hundred years of colonialism, and the terrible bloodbath in South Africa, the African tribal people had retaken Africa. Now the Hopi had received not only encouragement but financial aid from African nations sympathetic to the Hopi's cause.

Mosca drove to the big arroyo where the homeless people had made small camps and shelters under mesquite trees. In the beginning, the homeless had mostly been white men who wintered in Tucson then fled the heat; but now the big arroyo sheltered families, and the women and children did not leave when the heat came. Two men wearing green berets watched Root and Mosca from the homeless Vietnam veterans' camp, which had expanded since the last time they'd seen it.

Mosca seemed slightly embarrassed about the Hopi's accommodations. Mosca was anxious for Root to understand the Barefoot Hopi traveled like this because of the police and FBI. "He travels like this *on purpose*," Mosca said in a confidential tone. "The government's been tracking him since he got out of prison. They don't know what he's up to, but he worries them. See, the Hopi talks to the Mexicans and Africans; he even talks to the whites. People will listen to the Hopi. Even bikers and Ku Klux Klan, because what the Hopi talks about is the day all the walls fall down. Ask him if he means earthquakes or riots and the Hopi smiles and says, 'Both.' "

But the Hopi was not under the mesquite tree; a neat circle of river cobbles held ashes that were still warm. A pair of green shower sandals and a small canvas pack were in the crook of the tree. Mosca said the sandals were the Hopi's so he must have gone for a walk along the river to feel messages from the earth through his bare feet. The Hopi wouldn't mind; they'd wait. The Barefoot Hopi's entire philosophy was to wait; a day would come as had not been seen in five thousand years. On this day, a conjunction would occur; everywhere at once, spontaneously, the prisoners, the slaves, and the dispossessed would rise up. The urge to rise up would come to them through their dreams. All at once, all over the world, police and soldiers would be outnumbered.

The Barefoot Hopi was not more than five feet five inches tall, but he must have weighed almost three hundred pounds. Root did not think the Hopi looked fat; more like the Hopi was built like a brown boulder. The Hopi's full-moon face was always wider with a big grin; his teeth large and perfect. Root did not think the Hopi looked old enough to have spent ten years in federal prison or five years out already. The Hopi shook Root's hand warmly and smiled. "So we both know this *loco coyote*," the Hopi said, looking at Mosca. Root nodded his head. "I told him you're all right," Mosca said, touching Root's arm. "I told him you're my brother."

The Hopi had been a celebrity in prison. The media had followed his crime closely; the cameras had loved the bare feet and the traditional Hopi buckskin moccasins the Hopi carried in his woven-cotton shoulder bag. The cameras had loved the Hopi's mouthful of perfect, pearly teeth, and his wonderful laugh. He was not sad or angry at all for going to prison. The Barefoot Hopi had confided to Mosca and a few others that he had no regrets about shooting down the helicopter. The helicopter had been hired by rich tourists from Beverly Hills to hover over the Snake Dance at old Oraibi.

Nothing had equalled the exhilaration and joy everyone at the Snake Dance had shared the day the Hopi had shot the helicopter out of the sky. The Hopi had used the carbine he had "liberated" when he had been shipped home from Vietnam. The Barefoot Hopi regretted the injuries to the pilot and passengers, but he did not regret prison. In prison he had discovered the work he must do for the rest of his life; he must work tirelessly until all prisoners went free, and all the walls came down. The Hopi knew he might work to make preparations the rest of his life, yet never see the day when prisons and jails all over the U.S. were hit with riots and strikes simultaneously. But that didn't discourage the Hopi. One human lifetime wasn't much; it was over in a flash. Conjunctions and convergences of global proportions might require six or seven hundred years to develop.

They sat under the mesquite tree in the shade. The Barefoot Hopi took a plastic bottle from a crook in the tree and offered Root water. Mosca fished a fat marijuana cigarette from his shirt pocket, and the Hopi struck a match. For a long time they sat in the shade and shared the cigarette in silence. The cicadas in the mesquites were already buzzing. Drought and heat were international news on TV, but in Tucson and the surrounding Sonoran desert, the rainfall had been normal. The cicadas had almost drowned out the whine of semi trucks on Interstate 10 across the big arroyo.

"You going to that conference they're having here next week?" the Hopi asked. He had stretched out on the ground with a mesquite trunk for a headrest; his eyes were closed. "I'm too old to sit up two nights running with old man Peyote."

"What conference?" Mosca wanted to know. Mosca sat up and took off his dark glasses; he glanced at Root to see how Root liked the Hopi so far. Root nodded. "Indigenous healers. Native healers," the Hopi said, "from all over the world." He was sitting up now, massaging his feet with both hands. He put the palms of both hands flat on the sand in front of him and closed his eyes. "Earthquakes," the Hopi said. The tribal people had tried to warn the Europeans about the earth's outrage if humans continued to blast open their mother. But now all the warnings were too late. The Hopi could feel the earth grinding and groaning from Alaska to the South Pole. For days at a time, the ground had not been still in northern California; dozens of volcanos had erupted along the Aleutian chain, land of ten thousand smokes. Underground nuclear test explosions in Nevada had destabilized critical faults along California's coastal plain. A gigantic earthquake centered in a populous U.S. city might be just the occasion for their national prison uprising.

The Hopi explained that he and his followers were biding their time; they had to watch the rest of the world for signals; they were in close contact with their sisters and brothers on the streets and in the hills on reservations. They were waiting for the right moment—for certain conjunctions between the spirit forces of wind, fire, water, and mountain with the spirit forces of the people, the living and the dead. Otherwise, the prisoners and the people in the streets and hills were certain to be crushed. The U.S. government would not hesitate to fire-bomb the jails and prisons or hundreds of city blocks. If anyone needed proof of this, the Hopi only had to point to the Attica prison riot years ago and to the blocks of rowhouses fire-bombed by the Philadelphia police.

But the time was drawing closer; the right moment might come after Mexico had been engulfed by unrest and violence. U.S. troops would be sent to Mexico to protect factories owned by U.S. corporations. At the same time, human waves of refugees would pour across the U.S. border from the south. The U.S. government might have enough fire-power to crush the coordinated prison-jail uprisings; the government might have enough fire-power to halt the people in the streets and in the hills. But the Barefoot Hopi did not think the U.S. government would be strong enough to fight its own people at home while millions of refugees stormed the border. The Hopi had paused to take a drink of water from a plastic bottle. "Oh yeah," the Hopi said, "while all this is happening, California, Nevada, Utah, Colorado—all the southwestern states will run out of drinking water."

Just then a black man and a white man, both wearing green berets, approached them from the 'Nam veterans' camp. The Barefoot Hopi rolled to his feet gracefully for such a big man. He excused himself and went to shake hands with the black man. The black man introduced his companion, and the Barefoot Hopi grinned and shook his hand. Root heard the Hopi tell the black man he'd meet them later.

Root watched the Hopi curl his toes into the sand and wondered what signs or messages the Hopi was getting. Mosca and Root stood up too and shook hands with the Barefoot Hopi. "You should come to this healers' convention," the Hopi said, "I'll make a speech there. You might be interested." Mosca swore absolutely he would be there; Root had nodded too, although Root thought the Hopi was crazy; no one got prison inmates to cooperate. If they could have helped one another and organized to work together, they would not have been locked up in prison in the first place, that's what Root thought.

Mosca kept talking as they were driving to Calabazas's house. The Hopi had begun writing letters while he was in prison and kept writing letters once he got out. The Hopi had written thousands of letters to prisoners all over the United States, Guam, and Puerto Rico. The Hopi had sent cigarettes and food boxes to hundreds and hundreds of men;

otherwise the Hopi would have been rich because he had found a deep freeze full of hundred-dollar bills buried in the desert. In a dream, a giant snake had showed him where to dig, or that was the Hopi's story. There had also been rumors the Hopi had befriended an armed robber or an investment banker dying of AIDS in the prison hospital. The disclosure of the hidden cash had been made on the death bed.

Mosca had not actually seen one of the Hopi's letters, but he knew the Hopi wrote to the prisoners about their dreams. The Hopi worked only in the realm of dreams; the Hopi's letters made no mention of strikes or uprisings; instead the letters had consisted of the Hopi's stories about the Corn Mother, Old Spider Woman, and the big snake. The black convicts and the Hopi talked about African spirits. Even redneck bikers ate up the Hopi's stories, but that was because the Hopi had already infiltrated their dreams with the help of the spirit world.

CLOSE CALL

ROOT HAD NOTICED Mosca kept glancing into the rearview mirror, so Root looked over his shoulder and saw a Border Patrol car on their tail. Mosca had pretended to ignore the Border Patrol car and kept talking, but Root saw Mosca was tense. Root watched Mosca's hand on the .357 magnum between them on the seat. Root had not prayed so much as he had focused all his mental energy at Mosca's brain with a message. Don't reach for the gun, they'll go away; or they'll run names and they'll let us go; please, Mosca, please, Root had concentrated. Don't get mad, Mosca, don't blow their heads off while I'm with you. The last time the Border Patrol had stopped Mosca, he had sworn he would never again give any *migra* pig ID or answer any questions except with his .357. By some miracle the Border Patrol unit had turned off the street without stopping them. Root wiped sweat from his forehead.

Mosca glanced in the rearview mirror as he spoke. His dark eyes glistened with feeling. "Well, you are right. I almost killed me some pigs then." Mosca watched Root's face for a reaction. "Only one thing stopped me—"

"You didn't want me to go to the gas chamber with you," Root joked.

Mosca shook his head. "Because pigs are low on my list." Then Mosca slammed his fist into the padded dash. Root thought he heard bones crack. Mosca crushed the accelerator to the floor. The big four-wheel-drive truck leaped forward, and Root thanked the god or spirit who had given Mosca empty lanes ahead. When Mosca was upset, his truck became a lethal weapon. Big tears rolled down Mosca's face. "I wanted to blast the pig's face off! I wanted to smash his teeth down his throat so much! Fucking *gringo* pigs! Where's my green card? I'm a fucking U.S. citizen! I don't fucking need no kind of card! My people lived here in palaces while Englishmen still lived in caves!"

Root was relieved when he saw the side street to Calabazas's place; Mosca turned off Oracle so fast he drove over the curb and the tires squealed. Root felt the seat belt harness tighten around him; this wouldn't be the first vehicle Mosca had rolled over. Root didn't blame Mosca for his fury; there were Border Patrol agents all over Tucson stopping anyone who looked dark complected or "foreign." Root himself had been stopped at Pima College where the agents waited outside classrooms where students learned English as a second language.

"Yeah, it's really fucked," Root said, "and all the white people in Tucson love it because it makes them feel safer." Root had listened to his family for years. They had Mexican relatives, it was true, through Root's grandfather. But Root's mother and the others had been careful not to socialize with the Mexican cousins and kinfolk. Root's father liked to joke the Irish weren't choosy. But his father had lied; his father had not wanted a son who limped or sounded like a retard when he tried to talk. Root had learned a lot about his family and about white people when he was eighteen. They were afraid when they looked at him. They didn't want to be reminded of what had happened to him. They would have been happier if they had buried him. What was Caucasian was perfect, and Root's skull and brain were no longer perfect. His mother was not surprised. Root listened to her tell her friends who had come to visit him in the hospital; one of her five was bound to be a "wild one." His mother never said "crazy Mexican," but they all knew what she meant.

"But that's okay," Mosca said through clenched teeth as he turned onto the gravel of Calabazas's driveway. "We'll take care of the pigs when the big day comes!" Mosca slowed the truck and looked intently at Root. Root shook his head. The Hopi must be crazy. White inmates hated black inmates and Hispanic inmates, and vice versa. Snitches were everywhere. Even if rioting started, what was the purpose? Mosca had been driving down Calabazas's driveway and braked sharply. "The purpose? What's the purpose?" Mosca started laughing, then stamped the accelerator so hard the big four-wheel-drive fishtailed and splashed gravel all the way to the big cottonwood tree in the yard. "Making big trouble is the purpose," Mosca said. "Those fucking pigs won't know which way to run!"

A SERIES OF POPES
HAD BEEN DEVILS

ROOT SAW CARS he did not recognize parked next to Calabazas's pickup; Mosca shrugged his shoulders. "Church people," he said. Mosca did not care, but the strange cars made Root nervous. Liria and Sarita knew better than to hide refugees there, but sometimes they held meetings at the house.

Calabazas had been sitting outside under the cottonwood tree in the remains of an old recliner chair, drinking a beer. There was a beat-up Styrofoam ice chest next to the chair. The sun had already dropped behind the trees along the river. Calabazas grinned at them. His hair was white at the temples and his mustache was silver. As they dragged lawn chairs to the tree, Calabazas popped open two more cans of beer. Calabazas looked a little drunk.

"You still trying to figure out the meaning of life, old man?" Mosca said.

"That's right," Calabazas said, "I thought I better get started on it while I'm still alive." A cool wind rose from the river and stirred the cottonwood leaves. The three men drank silently and watched the sunset blaze red-orange across the sky. Actually Calabazas had been thinking about time.

In the darkness Mosca could make out figures, but the voices were whispers. Cars started and turned down the driveway. The meeting was over. Mosca was already drunk. Mosca said he didn't trust *anything* connected with the Catholic Church, and he didn't trust *anyone* connected with the Catholic Church either. Mosca was always ready to bicker with Liria or Sarita over the Church. Mosca had been restless for weeks. He wanted action, he wasn't happy with the things he had bought. The new clothes, new truck, and better whores had been exciting to dream about, but once he had them, he had realized how worthless they were. The clothes and the truck had changed nothing. The whores had worked like vacuum cleaners sucking him off, and for the money, Mosca understood why men invested in plastic inflatable women or Japanese battery-operated vaginas.

What did the Church want? Was it different from what the generals wanted, or from what the rich wanted from the poor and the Indians? All the Church had ever done was snatch food from the mouths of the hungry in the name of Jesus Christ. The nuns and priests who called themselves the Liberation Church were puppets used by the Church to give poor people the illusion the Church was on their side. Anytime they wanted, the Church could have stopped their clergy from smuggling political refugees out of the South. But over the centuries the Church had learned to keep potential troublemakers, priests and nuns and "penitents" such as Sarita and Liria, safely occupied.

The Church demanded the Indians pray only to Jesus. The Church didn't want the people to listen to the spirits of ancestors or animals or rocks. The Church wanted Indians to feel and think like whites. Mosca wasn't fooled; it was like the routine the pigs had: bad cop, good cop. The Church played the good cop. Smuggling out a few political refugees gave the Church good publicity.

Mosca had got himself worked up. From the Catholic Church he had leaped to the Italians and the Mafia; the pope was part of the Mafia. Mosca knew his catechism. Mosca had been swatted with a flyswatter by the nuns if he did not repeat his catechism. The pope could stop Church sacraments to anyone for any reason; yet the pope had not stopped the sacraments to the army officers who hunted down and shot Yaqui women and children. The Church had two faces it wore in Mexico; both were mask faces. The truth was the Devil had taken over the Catholic Church sometime after Saint Peter died. After the takeover, the

Devil had declared himself pope; a series of devils had been pope, and often the popes had had numerous wives and illegitimate children. The popes had been poisoners and sexual inverts because the devils lived in them and in their priests and nuns, whom Martin Luther had finally caught at their devil Masses and lewd celebrations. The Devil, the Church, and the Mafia were a world conspiracy as Mosca saw it.

Root had been baptized a Catholic, but had refused to have a priest visit him in the hospital. Root had stopped believing a couple of years before the accident. He didn't care what Mosca said about the Mafia and the Church; but he had been surprised when Mosca started talking about Max and Sonny Blue. Root had not heard Mosca talk about the Italians for a while; the Tucson families had had the pie split up before the Italians ever got to Tucson. The Mafia had been warned by the other white men; leave the border to the Indians unless you have wings. The Indians were allied with the desert inferno; all others died there. Mafia nephews and son-in-laws bought "legitimate" small businesses—sausage shops in shopping malls, or pinball and vending-machine concessions or private garbage collection. Max Blue's wife kept buying real estate.

Mosca had always enjoyed imaginary plots in which he surprised everyone and betrayed them all. Mosca loved to imagine the expression on Calabazas's face when he discovered his wife had fucked to death a Church monsignor. Even with the old monsignor dead, Calabazas had lost his wife to the Church. Having the other sister was no consolation that Mosca could see; both women were under the control of priests. Sarita had taken up the refugee work only because the priests had threatened her with eternal hell for killing the old monsignor with sex. Churches had always made clever use of the money and manpower of sinners. Penitent sinners would do anything the Church told them to do.

THE HOPI HAS ANSWERS
FOR EVERYTHING

ROOT WANTED to get Mosca off the subject of the Church so he could find out more about the Barefoot Hopi. Root asked Calabazas if he had ever met the Hopi. Mosca had, of course, answered before Calabazas himself could speak; no, only Mosca knew the Hopi, but soon people all over the world would hear about the Hopi. The Hopi was the organizer. The Hopi had dedicated his life to one day of mutual cooperation among all incarcerated persons in North America and in Mexico. Mosca was high and drunk. After his release, the Barefoot Hopi had traveled to prisons all over the United States where he had petitioned federal courts to obtain special permission as a clergyman to perform religious rites for imprisoned Native Americans.

In prison they'd all learned to respect the Hopi because he had continued to practice his religious beliefs. The Hopi claimed his religion included everyone; everyone was born belonging to the earth. Some Hopis and other Indians had called the Barefoot Hopi a witch because he talked about the dead as if their spirits still hovered among the living. Those who objected to talk about the spirits of the dead were either Christians or staunchly traditional Navajos and Apaches uncomfortable with the subject of dead souls.

Mosca had attended all of the Hopi's Sunday services while he was in prison, and he had watched how the Hopi's strategy worked. At first there had only been Indians and Mexicans; that week the Barefoot Hopi had talked about desecration. Earth was their mother, but her land and water could never be desecrated; blasted open and polluted by man, but never desecrated. Man only desecrated himself in such acts; puny humans could not affect the integrity of Earth. Earth always was and would ever be sacred. Mother Earth might be ravaged by the Destroyers, but she still loved the people. Mosca had listened to the Hopi talk for over an hour.

As the months passed, more guys showed up, and they had permission to meet for two hours. Then a few blacks had come, blacks who believed they had Native American ancestry. After the black Indians, then other blacks had showed up; these guys had been quiet and never spoke; last came the white guys—some who *were* mixed bloods, and others who felt like Indians in their hearts—whatever that meant. The Hopi's religion made no distinctions. A few had showed up because they had heard wild rumors. The Hopi was always aware some might be spies.

Mosca took a big hit off the joint and passed it to Calabazas; he puffed out his cheeks and chest and held his breath until he started coughing. "You should hear the Hopi tell it," Mosca said. "He's in town for some kind of healers' convention. You should go." Calabazas and Root had both nodded, and the three sat listening to the sirens and what sounded like gunshots in the distance. A police helicopter flew over the neighborhood flashing searchlights over roofs and backyards. Mosca's attention shifted briefly to the police helicopter. "The Hopi has an answer for everything," Mosca went on dreamily. "We know what the Hopi's answer to a helicopter is. Boom!" Mosca pointed his finger at the sky.

"You they'll put in the gas chamber," Calabazas said. "The Hopi had an excuse; he was protecting his religion."

"They might shoot me, but they won't put me in no gas chamber," Mosca said. "There won't be any more prisons or gas chambers left by then anyway."

Calabazas and Root had learned not to argue with Mosca. Root could tell Calabazas was as skeptical as he was about any plans to organize a national uprising of prison riots and jailbreaks all over the United States. It wasn't likely all the prisons and jails would participate, and everything in the Hopi's plan depended upon simultaneous riots so that police and other law enforcement would be overwhelmed. Calabazas had asked what the Barefoot Hopi planned to do about the National Guard and the U.S. army. Even if state police and law enforcement were overwhelmed, there were still the military and of course, citizen volunteers. The air force would drop bombs on jails and prisons to stop the uprisings. Root had expected an angry outburst from Mosca when Calabazas asked about the air force; instead, Mosca had remained calm.

"Well, you're thinking just like the white man thinks, aren't you?" Mosca said. "Listen to the Hopi. Army, Air Force, or Marines—the Hopi doesn't worry about them. When the time comes, they'll all be busy too. Anyway, bombs and guns are the least important weapons. The power lies in the presence of the spirits and their effect on our enemies' morale." The Barefoot Hopi was not the only one in contact with the spirits. Mosca reminded Calabazas and Root about the spirit voice in his own right shoulder. So far the spirit voice had not said much. A spirit didn't actually need a voice to communicate; the spirit put the idea into your head out of the blue. When the spirit had filled the people, then all at once the people would know what they must do. The Hopi didn't mean any Christian Holy Spirit either.

The Hopi refused even to argue whether it was one spirit with many dimensions or many spirits with singular dimensions. That was white man talk. Instead the Hopi had talked about Buffalo Man, who had seduced Yellow Woman in the old stories. Buffalo Man's spirit had moved from a human body to a buffalo bull's body effortlessly.

BOOK TWO

THE WARRIORS

GETTING OLD

IT HAD BEEN a long time since Calabazas had got so drunk by himself; Mosca and Root had left hours before. Calabazas liked the way the sound of the crickets and his own breathing were in harmony. The whole world had gone crazy after Truman dropped the atomic bombs; the few old-time people still living then had said the earth would never be the same. Human beings could expect to be forsaken by the rain clouds, and all the animals and plants would disappear. All over the world Europeans had laughed at indigenous people for worshiping the rain clouds, the mountains, and the trees. But now Calabazas had lived long enough to see the white people stop laughing as all the trees were cut and all the animals killed, and all the water dirtied or used up. White people were scared because they didn't know where to go or what to use up and pollute next.

It was after three but neither Liria nor Sarita had come home. The U.S. government did not want the people Liria and Sarita and their Church comrades were smuggling across the border. Zeta and Lecha would say right there was the best reason to do it—because the U.S. didn't want any more brown Indians or white Spanish-speakers on the streets of Los Angeles or El Paso. Still Calabazas tended to agree with Mosca that the motives of the Church might not be as simple and pure as the fervent nuns and priests imagined.

Calabazas took full responsibility for how things had turned out with Sarita and Liria. At one time Calabazas had spent a great deal of time with Zeta on his mind. The two beautiful sisters hadn't been enough trouble; Calabazas had not been able to resist Zeta, who called herself an enemy of the United States government. Zeta swore each shipment of contraband was a victory against the United States government.

Calabazas liked to watch sunrise the way the old people had when he was a child. He thought it was funny the way the human mind only copied itself over and over, yet everything found itself radically changed. He watched the sky but he did not see what they had seen. Perhaps the earth was spinning faster than before; rumors like this had circulated among tribal people since the First World War. Calabazas had heard the arguments the traditional believers had had among themselves— each accusing the other of being tainted by Mormonism or Methodism or the Catholic Church. But he had also heard them discuss the increased spin of the earth; others disagreed and had asserted it was instead the universe running downhill from a great peak and the increased speed was only temporary, before it reached the plain to slow gradually and regain a measure of stability.

Calabazas himself had no proof about the speed of the earth or about time. He did not think time was absolute or universal; rather each location, each place, was a living organism with time running inside it like blood, time that was unique to that place alone.

Calabazas no longer recognized himself in the stories Mosca or the others told about Calabazas's adventures thirty years before. The man in the stories sounded familiar, and Calabazas could recall what had happened, but the man he had once been was gone. Liria and Sarita had recently accused him of getting soft inside like white-bread dough; maybe they were right. Most of his life Calabazas had traveled back and forth across the border in a beat-up old truck or leading a string of pack burros on his little spotted mule. Calabazas had not been careful with money. If he had worked alone, and for himself, he might have been rich, though who knows? But Calabazas had worked with the people who had loved and cared for him as a child; he had worked with his relatives and his clanspeople in the Sonoran mountain villages. He had routinely made advances and gave out loans for no interest. He split profits fifty-fifty with village farmers, but he paid all the expenses himself as his pledge to them. He had not been a good businessman. He had not bought land and new houses; he had not bought gold or guns as Zeta had. He had given Sarita and Liria all the money they had ever asked for.

Calabazas could also feel his own time running inside himself, pounded out by his heart. The bones and meat hauled the soul around for fifty or sixty years then let go. He had seen a great many changes in the United States and in Mexico during his lifetime, and they had all been ominous. Calabazas had asked the elders, but native people around Tucson could not remember when they had seen so many white people—women and children—living in cars and in camps under the trees.

Now even crackpots such as Mosca's pal the Hopi were planning and plotting. All the past summer, Calabazas had watched the riots and the looting in a dozen U.S. cities. Calabazas had noticed an important difference: this time the rioters did not loot or set fires in black neighborhoods. They had set fire to Hollywood instead, and hundreds and hundreds of both black and white youths had blocked fire fighters and fought police on Sunset Boulevard. The rioters had chanted, "Burn, Hollywood, burn!"

Calabazas remembered the riots and looting in the sixties vividly. The U.S. president and Congress had done nothing for the poor until the poor had taken their anger to the streets. The people had high hopes for the war on poverty, but soon U.S. strategy makers had seen a better way to stop the riots in U.S. cities. If those young black and brown men rioting wanted to fight, then the U.S. had *just the place* for them in Southeast Asia. Those who had managed to survive Vietnam had been returned to their neighborhoods by the United States government addicted and maimed to ensure they wouldn't take to the streets and fight anymore.

Calabazas had given up on politics. Politics got you murdered in short order. Calabazas didn't trust any government; Calabazas didn't trust the Catholic Church either. Mosca had a good point: what business did the Church have removing political dissidents and activists? How were the people of those areas ever to rise up without their own leaders? The Church removed dissidents thousands of miles to the United States to keep them from causing any more trouble.

Maybe there was something wrong with him, maybe time had worn something down inside Calabazas, as Liria had accused, and the flame had burned out. He was not ignorant. He had listened to the old ones bitterly recount the stories of the great war for their land; the people had never got tired of recounting Yoeme's narrow escape from the hangman's noose during the flu epidemic. Yoeme had been a big troublemaker among the Yaquis even before the revolution. The Mexican government had kept a bounty on her scalp; only Zapata might have pardoned her for her fierce war against the government, and the whites had murdered him.

Calabazas had been lucky with his life; he had been born during the lull in the great war and had bought himself a safe perch. But now the war was spreading, and in a few years there would be no safe perch for anyone. Yoeme's great war for the land was still being fought; only now it wasn't just the Yaquis or even the Tohano O'Dom who were fighting. The war was the same war it had always been; the people were still fighting for their land. The war would go on until the people took back the land.

Calabazas reached into the ice chest for another beer but found only melting ice and water. He went inside to get another six-pack from the refrigerator and rolled himself a fat joint to smoke outside. He had not stayed up all night for years, not since he had worked across the border. But tonight he was wide-awake. He could not stop thinking about Mexico. Rumors and conflicting reports came from village couriers, and from Salvadorian and Guatemalan refugees. Mexico was chaos. The Mexican economy had collapsed, and fleeing government officials had stripped the National Treasury for their getaway. The army and police had not been paid for weeks. Battles had broken out between the Federal police and the local police. The citizens were fighting both the army and the federal police. Fighting between the Citizens' army and the Mexican army had cut off the Federal District from deliveries and food supplies. Electrical power lines and water-main lines to the center of the city had been dynamited. Thousands in Mexico City were starving each day, but Mexico's president had refused the people emergency food. The Mexican air force had opened fire on thousands of squatters rioting for food at the entrance to the city's main dump. Hundreds of squatters, women and children, had died as army bulldozers had leveled miles and miles of shanties and burned lean-tos. Within hours of the big fire at the city dump, hundreds of thousands of rats had swarmed through Mexico City, where starving people in the streets had caught the rats and roasted them. There were rumors of bubonic plague and of cholera.

The army and police had seized food and livestock so the Yaquis and other people once more headed for the high mountains where they had fled during the last revolution. In their mountain strongholds the people had already begun the vigil; the people were praying the white men would kill off one another completely. All the people had to do was be patient and wait. Five hundred years, or five lifetimes, were nothing to people who had already lived in the Americas for twenty or thirty thousand years. The prophecies said gradually all traces of Europeans in

America would disappear and, at last, the people would retake the land.

The old-time people had warned that Mother Earth would punish those who defiled and despoiled her. Fierce, hot winds would drive away the rain clouds; irrigation wells would go dry; all the plants and animals would disappear. Only a few humans would survive. Calabazas knew the story by heart, but he was not sure if he believed it anymore.

DEAD BRITISH POET
AT YAQUI EASTER DANCE

THE SPIRIT VOICE in Mosca's right shoulder groaned and creaked odd messages. Mosca had not been the same since he had discovered the spirit voice in his right shoulder. Root did not ridicule Mosca because he had heard Mosca's shoulder make creaking or popping sounds even when Mosca had not moved. Root didn't think the spirit voice could be any crazier than Mosca was himself; the spirit voice might even be an improvement. The spirit voice had told Mosca to get Sonny Blue and his brother and cousin. So Mosca had spent the day at the racetrack, consulting his paid informants in the shade of the grandstand.

Sonny Blue and Bingo had brought two strippers from the Stage Coach to watch Angelo's filly race. They had made a high-profile arrival in a red Testarossa followed by a Lincoln. Mosca's spies had taken in everything. Sonny Blue and Bingo had been laughing, bragging to the strippers about "being met" at the airstrip near Yuma. The people behind Sonny and Bingo were so big that a special code had been radioed to the Border Patrol and state police advising them to ask no further questions and to let them go. The authorities had not even opened the back of Greenlee's truck or touched a single suitcase. "They think they own this town," Mosca told Root with a big grin. "Those Italian boys are crazy." Mosca's spies had got a great deal of information, and he had plans in his mind already. Root had nothing to worry about; Mosca wanted to work on this alone.

Mosca refused to admit he had done anything wrong. The confusion and crowds of tourists milling with Yaqui men and old Yaqui women on lawn chairs had been exactly what Mosca had counted on for his strike. A great tactician took advantage of the unexpected; Mosca's spies knew Sonny Blue's big buyers from New York had been warned about doing business in Tucson. The New Yorkers had demanded a crowded public place for the meeting. Oddly enough, the New Yorkers had specified the Yaqui Easter Dance as the meeting place because they wanted to see real Indians.

The British poet had been much taller than the other spectators at the Yaqui Easter deer dance, and Mosca's bullets had gone high and missed just about everyone. The bullets had missed children, and anyone seated or kneeling. Mosca said it was the white man's own fault the bullet had got him between the eyes; the poet had been too tall, and he had been impolite to stand in front of all the other spectators when really, he should have stood far at the back where he belonged. The bullet wouldn't have found him back there.

What a sight! Here was the British poet lying dead in the dirt under the big ramada of freshly cut cottonwood boughs, and the poet's three ugly girlfriends all were hysterical and crying. The cops pointed guns at the sobbing women as if they had shot the poet, and not the gunman, who witnesses said was small, thin, and wore a Yaqui pharisee mask, a cowboy shirt, blue jeans, and beat-up cowboy boots. The stupidity of Tucson's police was amazing. They had immediately suspected the victim—the dead tourist—because he had carried a British passport and lived at a Santa Fe address. Tucson police generally worked on the assumption that victims somehow deserved what they had got; the police task was to determine exactly how the poet had earned a bullet between the eyes. The easy and most reliable assumption for Tucson police had been that the Santa Fe quartet were smuggling cocaine to the rich artists.

The dead poet had immediately been forgotten because the Tucson police now had the three sobbing women. The report of a short, dark Indian male seen leaving the area with a handgun, did not interest the police as long as they had three attractive women to interrogate. By the time the dead man's three female companions had been cleared of all suspicion, the trail of the gunman was cold. Mosca's excuse for his bad aim with the pistol had been the mask; the bullet had whizzed over the short wop's head into the poet standing a few feet behind him. Sonny Blue had known instantly the bullet was intended for him, and Sonny had panicked and both had pulled out pistols. Bingo was already running and pushing and stumbling through the crowd. The New Yorkers had tried to follow.

The crowd watching the all-night deer dance had not been alarmed at the sound of shots because all evening Yaqui children had been lighting firecrackers. If Bingo and Sonny had not panicked, if they and their New Yorker pals had remained calm, the Tucson police might never have noticed them in the crowd. Mosca's years of experience with police had shown him cops were like sharks or stupid fish that respond only to sudden movement.

After he had fired the shot, Mosca had casually tucked the 9mm in his pants under his T-shirt, then coolly moved through the crowd to the attaché case Sonny Blue had dropped. Mosca picked up the case and walked in leisurely mannner until he reached the darkness in the church parking lot, where he removed the mask and tossed it in the back of a parked pickup truck. He didn't mean any disrespect to the mask or to the deer spirit, but this was war. The 9mm had a date with old man Santa Cruz River, but Mosca had stayed around in the parking lot to watch the police have fun with Sonny Blue and Bingo.

The New Yorkers had been lucky enough to be arrested in the deer dance ramada surrounded with hundreds of witnesses. But Sonny Blue and Bingo had been caught in the dark parking lot. Mosca had watched the undercover cops take turns kicking Sonny Blue and Bingo between the legs and in the belly and face. Mosca had heard the cracks and thuds, Bingo's groans, and Sonny's muffled profanity.

Mosca thought it was funny. The cops had got their wires crossed. Max Blue had paid off the police chief, and in return the police had mashed Sonny's balls and had knocked out two of Bingo's front teeth. Mosca had waved the attaché case above his head with both hands. "Finders keepers!" he said; he was triumphant. The attaché case was full of New York money.

Calabazas has told Mosca before that he had not expected Mosca to last six weeks, let alone six years in the smuggling business. Mosca always laughs and shakes his head, fully in agreement. He is sincere too. Because Mosca may refuse to admit he has done anything stupid, but Mosca is as surprised as Calabazas about his own survival. As far as Root has been able to figure, Mosca counts survival as the absolute proof. And here he is again, Root thinks. Everything done wrong, the worst possible sequence of events—but Mosca gets away with everything: the money, even the shooting. Because Sonny Blue had stepped right in the trap, panicked after the shooting.

Although things might have gone better, Mosca had been hurt that Calabazas had called him "loco" when almost everything had gone exactly as planned; and now Mosca would begin phase two, which was "drop a dime," dial 911 and leave the names of Bingo and Sonny Blue. When Calabazas saw the results, he would understand that the shooting at Yaqui Easter marked the beginning of the end for Max, Sonny, and Bingo. Blow away your Blues! Mosca was counting on maximum trouble and misunderstanding between the Tucson police and old man Blue and his ass-wipe sons. Whatever the "arrangements" were between Max Blue and the Tucson PD, shooting tourists from Santa Fe hadn't been one of them.

Mosca had been so delighted he had even done a little victory dance before he got in his truck. None of it would have been possible if Sonny Blue had not frozen with panic. Everyone had seen the "Italian stallions" with their pistols pulled after the tall tourist fell dead. Calabazas was getting old and soft; his mind was coming unstrung almost like a white man's. In time, Calabazas would see the genius of Mosca's plan.

TUCSON POLICE BRUTALITY

SONNY COULD FEEL his chest tighten and his heart pound when he remembered them swarming over him with .45 automatics shoved hard against both ears and the top of his head. They had smiled as they'd kicked him in the balls, then in the back; and then they had kicked him in the stomach and in the balls again. Sonny had been on the ground puking when a pig in uniform walked up and kicked him in the side of the head. The cops were talking about the briefcases and who had grabbed what; a suspect had been seen fleeing with a briefcase.

Sonny had let the waves of nausea and pounding pain in his ear and head drive his anger harder and deeper; he wouldn't just get mad, he would get even. If it took the rest of his life, he was going to fight his own little war with the pigs; and his father would never have to know about it. Fuck the million-dollar payoffs to the Tucson pigs. Fuck all the money! What difference did money make if pigs were all over your ass every time you stepped out the door? What good was anything if the pigs beat you up whenever they felt like it?

Sonny had taken the worst beating because too many curious people had gathered before the undercover cops could start beating Bingo. People standing nearby had helped pull the undercover cops off Bingo, but there had been no one to pull the pigs off Sonny. Sonny had been trapped on the far side of the car in the darkness.

Max had promised that the undercover officers and cops in uniform who had kicked Sonny would get what was coming to them. Max had asked Sonny to trust him, to leave the matter in his hands. Angelo and Bingo had both tried to calm Sonny, and to remind him everything was okay, and there had been no arrests except for the New Yorkers caught with the cocaine. But Angelo saw the reassurances had only made Sonny Blue more furious, so Angelo and Bingo kept quiet. They would have to leave Sonny alone for a while, and they would meet the shipments for Mr. B. as scheduled. Angelo and Bingo had even talked to Max Blue alone, to ask if Max could send Sonny on a Caribbean vacation for a while. Because all Sonny had wanted to talk about had been ideal assassination weapons and schemes for getting the undercover cops or the pigs in uniform. Sonny had bought detailed information as well as the names and home addresses of undercover police from the county attorney's office computer. Angelo noticed Max got pale when he learned that Sonny had already got the cops' work schedules. The three of them were silent for a moment, then Max had excused himself. Sonny Blue refused the offer of a Caribbean vacation.

Angelo had noticed a change in Bingo since the cops had jumped them; Bingo seemed happier and more confident about himself. Bingo told Angelo he had always been scared of pain—terrified of being slugged and kicked. But now that Bingo had been hit and kicked by the pigs, he was no longer afraid. He had imagined the pain and the humiliation to be far worse than they had actually been. Of course the big Yaqui Indian women had dragged the undercover pigs off him; the cops had been disgraced by the three-hundred-pound women.

Max Blue was angry at the Tucson police over the missing briefcase full of cash, not because they had kicked the shit out of Sonny Blue. Sonny had needed the beating; Bingo too. Max had been surprised at how angry Sonny Blue was; Max didn't want Sonny to do something stupid. The Tucson police had their days numbered anyway. Once a U.S. border crisis alert began, Tucson and the entire Mexican border area would be placed under the jurisdiction of the military police or Federal marshalls. Large amounts of cash made the pigs piss their pants. "National security" flights and shipments had been hijacked and stolen by local police in Miami and Baton Rouge. That had been Mr. B.'s reason for hiring Max Blue and for the relocation of his operations in Tucson.

When the senator and Max played golf alone, Max received his "national security briefing." The senator served on the select committee on National Security. The senator had invaluable sources to leaks at the highest levels. The senator had already been deeded ten acres of prime commercial property in future downtown Venice, Arizona.

The senator claimed the CIA had bought members of the Mexican aristocracy fifty years ago, and it was only a matter of time before the Mexican president and his cabinet would request U.S. military aid and intervention to prevent the antigovernment forces from taking Mexico City. How could the senator be certain of the events to come in Mexico? Their mutual friend, Mr. B. Mr. B. had been working for more than ten years against the communists in Mexico and Guatemala.

AMBITIONS

MAX PLAYED ALONE on the back eighteen holes after the judge and the police chief had gone. With each stroke he was driving away the stink of the judge and the police chief. He loved to watch the arc of the ball and the way wind currents held the ball aloft perfectly suspended as if time no longer existed. Max enjoyed the collision of the fairways and greens with the desert boulders, cactus, and shrubs. Desert mesquite and paloverde trees along the edges of the fairway grew tall from the golf course water. Some players were disturbed by the desert setting, and before they left the clubhouse, they would ask Max about rattlesnakes and coyotes. Max had never walked into the desert from the fairway. The desert meant danger and death, but he did not mind that they were close by. The whole thrill of the game was to follow the little ball on its hazardous journey from hole to hole safely. Max feared nothing as long as the sky was open, high overhead and no low, gray clouds of overcast closed overhead like a coffin lid.

Max had laughed at what Tucsonians called "rainstorms"; compared to New Jersey's gray, suffocating overcast with rain for days on end, even Tucson's violent summer thunderstorms were trifles. The sun was almost always shining or partially visible in some part of the valley even as torrential rains fell at other locations. Even downpours did not last long; Max would wait five minutes wrapped in a rain parka, then go right on playing. Max did not stop even when the wind gusted violently and rain mixed with sand stung his face; he kept his head down and swung with all his weight behind the golf club. Storms were invigorating. When the lightning sirens were sounded, the other golfers scurried to the clubhouse for shelter; but Max loved the desert storms. Nothing compared with the first smell of rain in the dry desert air.

Max had briefed Sonny, Bingo, and Angelo. The job was simply to count the suitcases as they were unloaded from the plane. No screwups; that had been Mr. B.'s peeve with others he had worked with in the past—real lowlifes, military and former enlisted men from Florida to Louisiana. Max doesn't tell the boys that for an operation such as Mr. B.'s, Tucson is a minor-league pit stop. Max let Sonny, Bingo, and Angelo eat it up when Mr. B. said, "Arizona is a welcome change"; B. was a liar. B. had owned the airfield west of Tucson all through the Vietnam War. Max had been introduced to B. by the senator. The government later had got cold feet, but Max had been paid a fabulous sum anyway. The deal had been to supply professional assassins for certain "targets" in a half dozen U.S. cities.

Max knew how Sonny and Bingo felt about the vending machine business—rancid sandwiches and video games jammed with metal slugs. Those jobs had been good experience when they first got out of school, but now Sonny especially was impatient to make money. If everything went smoothly, then Max planned to let the boys run the operation. Max looked at Sonny and Bingo and felt uneasy about the offspring, who did not resemble him or Leah. Not that he thinks Leah cheated. Sonny and Bingo are his sons, but Max saw the family resemblances; they had favored the weaker side of the family. Max remembers his older brother, Bill. Bill is written all over that kid Angelo. Max has never known what to make of the family—his family, and the business. Max feels nothing anymore for "family"—not even his own sons. Leah used to argue with Max that his feelings for people would return, that the doctors had already warned her that Max might experience temporary personality changes including anger, depression, or some memory loss. When Max looks at Leah, he tries to recall memories with feelings for Leah but there is nothing.

Max felt an obligation to offer Angelo something better than watchdogging crooked racetrack managers. Family could be trusted. If Sonny did not want to work with his cousin Angelo, Max wanted to know then, not later. The first few times Max wanted Sonny to take Bingo and Angelo to see how things were done. Mr. B. had assured Max that all arrangements had been made. All Sonny and the boys had to do was to meet the plane and watch the transfer of the shipment to the truck while the plane was reloaded with Mr. B.'s cargo for next-day departure back south.

Sonny was excited. This contract work for Mr. B. would be a piece of cake. Mr. B.'s southbound cargo was secure in Leah Blue's warehouses. There were no cash transactions. The pilots worked for Mr. B. For the occasion, Sonny had rented a new Ferrari for twenty-four hours. The stupid Tucson police could not imagine anyone would dare drive to a million-dollar cocaine delivery in a bright red Testarossa. Sonny had rented a big Lincoln town car for Bingo. From now on they would call themselves "commercial land sales executives." The landing strip was eighty miles from Tucson in the desert west of Casa Grande. Arrival time had been scheduled for five P.M. when Border Patrol and radar surveillance personnel changed shifts. Sonny had insisted Angelo ride with Bingo in the Lincoln, then gave them a half-hour head start.

Bingo had been sipping gin and tonics since lunch; he had a double in a plastic glass with a lime wedge but no ice. Bingo claimed the cocaine helped clear the gin from his head, but Angelo decided to drive anyway. The Lincoln's clock had a digital readout for elapsed travel time; Bingo seemed gloomy, so Angelo had made a bet with him about how long before the Ferrari screamed past them in a blazing red streak. Angelo and Bingo had never had much to say to each other because Sonny had done all the talking for both of them. Angelo glanced into the rearview mirror watching for the Ferrari—a red speck on the horizon. The Lincoln handled like a huge motorized sofa compared to Angelo's Porsche. Angelo might have won if he were driving his Porsche, but Sonny always had to have the advantage.

Bingo stared straight ahead at the highway with the gin and tonic between his legs. Angelo remembered how easy it had been to stay pleasantly drunk, removed from noise and confusion, detached from the pain of the loss. Who or what had Bingo lost? "You see him yet?" "No. He can't open it up until he gets clear of traffic." Angelo glanced into the rearview mirror; on a hill back in the distance he thought he saw a red speck. Bingo, his face flushed from gin, turned awkwardly to look for the Ferrari's approach. Sonny was closing on them in the left lane. For a moment the red streak seemed to rise straight up from the earth to materialize into a Ferrari grill, the windshield filled with a maniac's grinning face. "Bastard!" Bingo said as the Ferrari flashed past them and disappeared again into the horizon line. "Sometimes I really hate the fucker," Bingo said, squeezing a wedge of lime into his gin and tonic. "But I can't complain. Sonny Boy does all the work. He makes all the decisions. He even tells me which women I'm allowed to fuck."

Angelo set the cruise control at seventy-five. He did not want to talk about Sonny. And Angelo was not sure he could trust Bingo. Too many drunks repeated everything they heard to get free drinks or because they were desperate for attention. Angelo could not stop thinking about Marilyn with Tim. Tim was in trouble if a creep like Mr. B. was looking for him. Mr. B. had lied. Tim had never been a pilot. Mr. B. might want to locate Tim, but Angelo would bet rehiring wasn't what Mr. B. had planned. Tim might already be dead meat, and Marilyn might come back.

SUITCASES FOR MR. B.

BINGO FINISHED the gin and tonic and dropped the clear plastic glass on the floor mat. He grimaced drunkenly at Angelo to acknowledge his sloppiness, then shrugged his shoulders to make clear he didn't care about that or anything. Bingo kept talking about when they were kids in New Jersey. Angelo hoped Bingo would quit talking and sleep until they got to the landing strip. Driving on the empty highway under a wide blue sky always reminded Angelo of Marilyn and New Mexico. Bingo slammed his fist into the palm of his hand. "Sonny came down there to my own place, my own house, and he threw her things into garbage bags. She was crying and calling out to me to help her." Bingo started coughing and rolled down the window; he had leaned so far out the window to puke, Angelo feared he might fall.

Finally Bingo had passed out, and Angelo could think about Marilyn in peace. Marilyn loved the wide-open spaces; that was all New Mexico had going for it anyway, she used to say. She had showed Angelo how people drive in the Southwest. On straight, empty stretches of highway Marilyn loved to give a whoop and holler, "Pedal to the metal!" as the

Porsche had surged ahead. In the West, people were wild, she said. Mostly Angelo remembered the good times; there hadn't really been a bad time until she left. Marilyn had read Angelo a poem once. She had taken classes at the university in Albuquerque, and the poem had been assigned in a class. The only line of the poem Angelo remembered was, "You will never know the last time we make love." She might have been trying to let him know her feelings, but instead of talking, Angelo had wanted to make love.

Angelo had tried to push inside Marilyn, but she was too tight, closed to him. He could not look at her face because he knew he would cry, although he did not understand the reason. With his eyes closed, Angelo had seen thick, black shapes twist and turn continually, changing and transforming themselves. Sweat ran from his armpits down his sides. Marilyn had been soaked and their bodies made smacking, sucking sounds together. He did not want to hurt her. He had rolled off her and hit the damp sheet facedown. Marilyn had not seen Angelo cry before. Her eyes filled with tears. She told Angelo how beautiful his body was, his thighs so muscular and full from riding horses, his cock thick and dark, long enough to enter her from behind. No woman had ever loved him the way Marilyn had. She played with the lock of hair at the nape of his neck, making a loose curl around her finger.

Sonny Blue had followed orders step by step, marking off each item as he worked down the list, but Mr. Big's people had screwed up big time. The pilot had flown the correct north-south corridor, but border surveillance radar personnel had apparently not been briefed. Angelo, Bingo, and Sonny had been standing on the dirt landing strip watching Mr. B.'s pilot and copilot move the suitcases from the plane to a delivery van when a Border Patrol pursuit plane appeared overhead. Mr. B. had guaranteed no problems, even if the worst happened and some hot-dog Border Patrol unit happened to intercept a delivery. Once a pursuit plane had been dispatched to chase suspicious aircraft, it could not be called back without arousing suspicion. Certain procedures would be taken if such interceptions did occur; after one phone call, law enforcement officers would be instructed to take down names of suspects for "further investigation," but no one would be taken into custody. Mr. B. had acknowledged this was a lame cover story, but it had worked again and again in southern Arizona where the citizens were suspicious but stupid.

The pilot and copilot took off just as the pursuit plane had touched down. Bingo and Angelo had started to run for the car, but Sonny Blue motioned for them to stay put. The truck driver ignored the pursuit

plane and continued to slide the big blue suitcases into the van. Two
men in dark blue coveralls and sunglasses sat inside the van, with shotguns across their laps.

Bingo had been pale and sweating as if he might puke, so Sonny
nudged him and whispered they had nothing to worry about. After the
first phone call, other phone calls would be made. Sonny felt cold sweat
on his hands and on the back of his neck. The seven hundred pounds
of cocaine in the suitcases were what was most important. Mr. B. had
had trouble in the past with suitcases that had been lost or had disappeared. In the event of trouble, instructions were to lock the suitcases
in the van, or in the Lincoln should the van be lost. Sonny had been
warned to watch local law enforcement officers closely; hundreds of
kilos of cocaine disappeared each year before they ever reached police
headquarters.

The Border Patrol pursuit plane taxied past them and Sonny could
see the copilot talk on the plane's radio, to call in ground units while
they took off again after the plane. Sonny made a call from the Ferrari
to the number Max had given him for emergencies. At the sound of the
beep Sonny punched in the message: *"Call off the dogs."*

Greenlee had got his start by selling old furniture and junk out on
East Twenty-second Street. He went to government auctions of surplus
and used military property and had bid on anything, provided it was
dirt cheap. Then Greenlee had got lucky. He had bid two thousand
dollars for a scrap metal lot that included spare aircraft parts; sixteen
months later U.S. troops had been dispatched to Southeast Asia and the
U.S. air force had paid Greenlee five hundred thousand dollars for the
badly needed spare parts.

Greenlee walked briskly down the landing strip, glancing in the
direction of the highway for signs of headlights from Border Patrol
ground units. He wanted to know if Sonny had dialed the emergency
number. Sonny could not make out Greenlee's mood except he did not
seem particularly concerned, not even when a dozen sets of headlights
could be seen bobbing and weaving at high rates of speed down the dirt
road to the landing strip.

THE THURSDAY CLUB

JUDGE ARNE was annoyed that his clerk had scheduled lawyers on a Friday morning. After Thursday-night blowouts at the club, he did not like to come to his office until noon. He especially did not want to see the attorney on the county prosecutor's staff who was a regular at the club, and who, the night before, had made a spectacle of himself with—of all things—a broomstick. As a life member of the Thursday Club, Judge Arne could hardly be absent from their weekly meetings this year because they were celebrating their hundred-year jubilee; one hundred years of fellowship and mutual support between the judiciary and law enforcement officers of southern Arizona. Judge Arne was one of the few remaining members who knew club history from the beginning.

The U.S. or "gringo" takeover of Mexican territory, later called Arizona and New Mexico Territory, with the Guadalupe Hidalgo Treaty, had been bitterly resented by the people throughout the Southwest. Circuit-riding judges and prosecutors from El Paso were forced to take rooms in the homes of local law officers, who, like the judges and the prosecutors, were non-Catholics, and white men. A year or two later the bachelors among the deputy marshals had rented a large house together on Main Street. When the circuit-riding judges and other prominent bachelors visited Tucson, the accomodations and a membership at the Thursday Club became a coveted social prize. The bachelor son of a prominent Tucson family had become police chief, and from that time on, relations between the police and the local bar had been unusually cordial; more than once, Tucson had gained national attention as an example of harmony and understanding between law enforcement and the local business community. A great deal had been made of the prohibition of women on the premises of the Thursday Club because Main Street had been notorious for its bordellos.

"Brotherly *camaraderie* and socializing between law enforcement officers, judges, and lawyers, a phenomenon unheard of east of the Mississippi, is a weekly ritual at the exclusive Thursday Club," an issue of the *Tucson Territorial* had reported. Young deputy marshals with blond mustaches as sparse as their experience sat on the long mansion porch at night and smoked Cuban cigars with assistant U.S. attorneys and federal magistrates. During those early years, they had been out-numbered in Tucson. The gringos had to stick together or they'd be overrun.

Within a few years the Thursday Club had boasted a membership with every socially prominent Tucson family represented. The word on the street was the Thursday Club hired pretty Mexican boys to chop wood bare chested all winter while club members watched them from the sun-room as they sat in chaise lounges, sipping cocktails or sucking on small oranges. The clubhouse had boasted the first evaporative cool-ing system in Tucson. All summer, young brown boys carried water buckets to the roof to saturate cotton wadding in wooden frames. Jeal-ousy over the cool-air system in the rooms at the top of the Thursday House had resulted in rumors about the source of the heat on the top floor. The rumors alleged it was the young Mexican boys frolicking with certain club members who had heated things up on the top floor.

Club members ignored or casually dismissed rumors, citing com-radeship, man to man, as the most precious commodity on the treach-erous frontier. They had found themselves in the last corner of the United States, the desolate, troubled Southwest territories. There was only one direction to go after Tucson; that was *down* to Mexico, and they'd all rather have died first. "Hang together or hang one by one," was the gringo motto.

After World War One, club membership had become exclusive and hush-hush. The Thursday Club's name had been changed to the Owls Club. Security had been cited, but it was evident the club's members wished to lay to rest rumors—the stories that had circulated in the bars and brothels for years—tales of "the closet club," "the old fags sleeping society," and "sucky-fucky." The old guard at the club had been ada-mant about discretion and total privacy. The sudden sale of the club's mansion during the eighties real estate boom had been very carefully calculated. They made immense profits off the sale, while at the same time they had left behind the so-called "scene of the crime"—the attic rooms in the mansion where Tucson police were rumored to have posed nude for the pinup calendar called Cop Cakes.

The club had already been in decline before the Cop Cakes pinup calendar scandal. Membership had fallen over the years as the club had become more exclusive. The young deputies and law clerks who had in past years always created such delight and excitement were no longer eligible for membersip; a mistake which Judge Arne believed had been fatal to the club. But Tucson's so-called social elite were deeply concerned about "good breeding." Tucson's "gentry" seldom talked about anything else at their parties. It often required all of the judge's abundant good breeding (himself a blue blood from a Mississippi timber dynasty) to suffer the hilarious pretensions of Tucson's "aristocracy," spawned by the whiskey bootleggers and whoremasters who had fattened off the five thousand U.S. troops who had chased Geronimo and fifty Apaches for ten years. Ah, Tucson high society! With their pedestrian little fortunes skimmed off government supply contracts for army rations of weevil-infested cornmeal and wagonloads of spoiled meat.

THE YOUNG POLICE CHIEF

JUDGE ARNE preferred the company of honest working men to the pretensions of Tucson's social elite. The judge did not consider himself homosexual; he was an epicurean who delighted in the delicacies of both sexes. In classical times it had not been necessary to talk about contact between men. Contact was action, and action was behavior. Behavior was not identity. A gentleman had a myriad of choices open to him at appropriate places and times. The judge had always been certain of his sexual identity: he was a man with a cock tip big as a fist, and balls that hung like a bull's. His was merely a cocks man's taste for strange fruits.

The judge had taken care to make friends with the young police chief. The judge had always been strongly attracted to "black Irish," as the Tucson police chief identified himself. The deep blue eyes, the black curly hair, and traces of five-o'clock shadow on Irish cops were almost irresistible. The young police chief had grown up in Phoenix. He still made jokes about living in Tucson. He had never visited the Thursday Club, and he was married with three children. Still, the judge had learned from years at the club that cops were the ones who would surprise you because they had more personality quirks and twists to them than attorneys, who lacked imagination beyond panty-hose worn with a butthole cut into the panty. The judge had learned that cops were uniform freaks, and when they got drunk at the Thursday Club, their favorite attire had been nurse uniforms. Cop tastes ran to cock rings and color photographs of animal castrations.

Around the young police chief, Judge Arne always felt very heterosexual, he wasn't sure why. He found it exciting to ride through downtown in the police chief's cruiser. The judge wanted to see what might develop with the police chief. The judge had always preferred watching over touching or performing with others. Under certain circumstances, the female genitalia greatly aroused the judge. He had studied human embryology in college. Each male prostate had almost been a uterus, while the clitoris was merely a penis shrunk by estrogen. In one textbook there had been a page that showed freak female sex organs erect and as large as a young boy's penis; female organs that size dripped pearly juice when they climaxed. Some places in the world, the juice sold for hundreds of dollars, like rhino horn ground to powder to get old men aroused.

Then at a border law enforcement convention in El Paso the judge and police chief had taken a taxi together. They had been drinking margaritas, and the police chief asked the taxi driver to take them to a whorehouse across the border. The judge had felt radiant as the driver took them down dusty lanes and narrow alleys; it had been as if the police chief had been able to read the judge's mind. Nothing brought men closer than fighting side by side; then later, there was nothing like fucking women together.

The run-down mansion was a block from a Juarez police annex; not surprisingly, many of the regular customers were police. The madam was a Mexican American in her late forties who drove across the border every night to her country club home in northwest El Paso. As she led them up the stairs, she complained loudly about business. Her hot breath stank of brandy and cigarettes. She had guessed they were from the law enforcement convention over in El Paso. She wasn't surprised to see Americans because few Mexicans could afford her girls. Anyone could see Mexico was plunging into deep trouble when a thousand pesos didn't buy ten tortillas. The Mexican police inspectors and detectives had got rich off the drug trade, but she did not approve of her girls servicing men who had been police interrogators because they had developed "sadistic perversions." As the madam said this, she had looked sharply at both the judge and the police chief. "I don't want my employees to get hurt."

These upstairs girls were reserved for special customers, the madam said, opening the door. One rule the judge had was never to look at a woman's face; women's faces did not attract him. The judge imagined the police chief ramming it in from behind dog-style while the whore braced herself with both hands against the steel bedstead. The judge felt his cock twitch and his balls shift against his inner thighs as he imagined the police chief's cock, swollen, stiff, and blood-red, its nob oozing sperm. That got the judge ready. When he thrust his cock into her, the whore had gasped and pressed her hands against her belly, moaning that he was too deep and too large for her. She tried to move out from under him, but he seized her nipples and pulled her back under him, thrusting even harder and faster. He slid a hand down to her cunt, engorged and swollen so tight; the pressure had popped out her little pink jalapeño, wet and erect as he seized it. His fingers were locked tight so she could not protect her little pepper, and he would pull and squeeze until he milked her dry, until her little jalapeño was flat and white with a trace of dried blood on its tip. The judge could not remember when he had enjoyed a visit to a whorehouse so much; of course all the pleasure had been due to the police chief's companionship.

Judge Arne had not seen the police chief since the El Paso lawmen's convention. The judge had no interest in the cocktail and dinner parties in Tucson. He preferred to work with his dogs or play a little golf. The judge and the senator played golf with Max Blue on Thursday afternoons when the judge was free and the senator was in town. This week though, the police chief would join them. There had been trouble between Tucson police and Sonny Blue over a shooting. A few days later, the judge had got a call from the senator's office about Sonny Blue and a mix-up with Customs and DEA over one of the "special planeloads." Sonny Blue was batting zero.

After the U.S. military had been accused of smuggling drugs from Southeast Asia and Central America in military aircraft, Mr. B. and others had turned to the private sector, to independent contractors such as Max Blue and his wife, Leah. The arrangement had been for Customs and the DEA to look the other way; "authorized" aircraft were allowed to cross border radar without identifying themselves or destination. The judge had learned about the national security plan some years before. He had been approached by special Treasury agents on behalf of a convicted cocaine smuggler the judge had been about to sentence to thirty years in prison.

The judge had startled the special Treasury agents with his cooperation; they told him many judges at the federal level were reluctant to cooperate even after the national security issues had been explained.

The judge luxuriated in the praise of the special agents. They were relieved to be dealing with a man of his intelligence and sophistication. They confided that other federal judges had demanded numerous delicate telephone calls from senators and even higher before they had agreed to cooperate. Occasionally, the special agents even had to withdraw their requests from judges who refused to acknowledge the urgency of the secret strategy and agenda for national security.

The judge was sophisticated enough to understand the strategy for national security: cocaine smuggling was a lesser evil than communism. Cocaine smuggling could be tolerated for the greater good, which was the destruction of communism in Central and South America. The fight against communism was costly. A planeload of cocaine bought a planeload of dynamite, ammunition, and guns for anticommunist fighters and elite death squads in the jungles and cities of El Salvador, Guatemala and Nicaragua. Communism was a far greater threat to the United States than drug addiction was. Addicts did not stir up the people or start riots the way communists did. Addicts didn't live long, and what time they had was devoted to scoring to get high or stealing money to score with.

In recent years the judge had received more and more requests from various agencies involved with issues of national security. The judge, like all dedicated conservatives, understood the greatest dangers to a nation lay within, among its own people who had become degenerate and had betrayed their Christian nation. The judge had not been fooled by the communists; he knew their secret agenda to rule the world had not been altered. All civilized nations had secret agendas known only to a select circle of government figures. Fortunes and national fates could not be left in the hands of the ignorant masses. The judge was proud to do his part against the spread of communism in the Americas.

Max Blue wanted to meet for a golf game pronto because Tucson police had roughed up Sonny Blue and Bingo pretty badly the other night and a large amount of cash had been "lost." The judge had seen police out of control before in Tucson. One of the reasons the city council had hired the new police chief was because he had grown up in Phoenix and had no relatives in Tucson. Tucson's last police scandal had involved police officers fencing stolen goods for family and friends involved in car-stereo thefts.

Police were useful to the secret agenda, but only as long as they were kept under control. Control and order were all that mattered; even the senator and Max Blue had agreed on that. That was why they played golf every Thursday; to keep all lines of communication open; to minimize accidents or mistakes such as the ones Sonny Blue had made the week before. Mistakes led to disorder; accidents led to loss of control. The judge planned to ask the police chief to have lunch with him soon so he could give the chief a little "fatherly" advice. The judge would particularly have to caution the police chief about the gradual deterioration that had taken place with law enforcement in Pima County. From two or three cops stealing car stereos for extra cash, the ring of car-stereo thieves had grown until the police had been working with the largest retail car-stereo sellers in the state. The judge recalled the burglary ring might never have been detected except that the cops had devoted more and more time to stealing and fencing car CD players, and less and less time to their actual patrols and paperwork. Finally, other officers had got fed up with the extra work and someone had ratted to the local press. What had been lacking was control; the former police chief had been a lazy bastard who only wanted to collect his piece of action.

Max Blue had asked the judge to call the senator too, but the judge had persuaded Max to cool off a little, that he was upset and trying to make federal cases out of a little misunderstanding and an unfortunate mix-up. There was no need for the senator to be there when he and the police chief were coming. The matter was trivial. No one had really been hurt except a tourist, and Sonny Blue had not fired the fatal shot.

Somewhere the judge had read about a South American country, maybe Brazil or Argentina, where the police force had started by using torture to interrogate political prisoners but had soon become so addicted to torture they no longer wanted to leave work at the end of their shifts; they'd take short naps, eat, and come back for more torture. The judge blamed lax supervision; there were valuable lessons to be learned from Argentina about the necessity for control over the police.

GOLF GAME

AS THE JUDGE pulled his car into the clubhouse lot, he checked the horizon for thunderclouds. Sudden, violent storms occurred in late afternoon all summer and ruined golf games. Max Blue reputedly ignored precautions even when the lightning strikes were close. Official policy on all municipal and resort golf courses was mandatory closure at the approach of thunderclouds, but Max was exempt from that policy. The back eighteen holes were his private course.

The old man had used thunder and lightning to terrorize Arne when he was a child. The old man said balls of lightning would bounce out of the chimney, then come bouncing up the stairs into Arne's bed. Lightning melted zippers that burned off your balls and cock. The old man had teased him mercilessly when Arne had visited at the old man's ratty mansion. Electricity in Tucson had not been reliable before the Second World War. Lights in the mansion blinked on and off and fuses blew out. The old man preferred candles and had left boxes of matches everywhere. "Little boys who play with matches pee their beds! Little boys who dance on tables at night make the lights go out!" The judge could still hear the old man's voice. He blamed the old man for the nervousness he still felt about lightning.

The skies to the west were hazy blue, which might signal extra pollution drifting down Interstate 10 from Phoenix, or it might be the first traces of rain clouds drifting off the Sea of Cortés. But the judge didn't worry about those clouds; he worried when he saw purple, big-headed clouds that billowed into anvil shapes thousands of feet high. The judge had read all about bolts from the blue; they were true occurrences, not old wives' tales.

The police chief had not arrived yet, but the judge knew Max would already be out on the course. He took some practice drives and did some practice putting while he waited. The putting greens were parched and hard as brick. The judge did not care much about golf. Billiards was a refinement, down to the perfection of green felt instead of weeds and turf, without the worry of lightning or heatstroke. In Tucson, billiards had another advantage over golf: the green felt did not require millions of gallons of water every year. The judge had not known or cared how much water a golf course used in a year until the water rights dispute had come into his court. Water for golf courses was top priority because tourism was all the industry Arizona had left. Tucson had steadily lost population after the U.S. economy had faltered, and Arizona's banks had all failed. The blue-chip companies such as IBM or Motorola had become more and more fearful of the political developments and upheavals in Mexico and had relocated in Denver.

Judge Arne was the last of his line, and he was glad of it. Let Tucson slide back to its rightful place in history, which was as a dusty, flyblown village of bootleggers, whores, and soldiers. Mexicans and Indians the judge didn't count because they had lived in Tucson so much longer and were, in any case, much different than white people. Mexicans and Indians grew connected to a place; they would not leave Tucson even after all of Arizona's groundwater was polluted or pumped dry. He had seen the evidence, the exhibits by hydrologists, in the water rights lawsuit. Arne didn't care; he would probably not live to see it: Tucson and Phoenix abandoned by the hundreds of thousands after all the groundwater had been consumed.

The judge had been practicing with his woods on the driving range when the police chief joined him to take warm-up swings. The police chief wore baby-blue shorts and a baby-blue polo shirt, then had the bad taste to top it off with a navy-blue baseball cap with SWAT in white letters across the crown. The judge chuckled as he shook the chief's hand; the cop just couldn't leave his SWAT cap home. The police chief was more nervous about the meeting than he wanted to admit.

The judge had not witnessed Max Blue betray emotion before, not even in golf games after other players made idiotic drives or talked nonsense. The judge could hardly blame Max Blue for being upset. Sonny Blue was supposed to get Tucson police protection, not Tucson police beating.

The police chief had squinted off in the distance at the Rincon Mountains while the judge talked to Max Blue. Max had been too upset to play golf. Instead, they had gone in two golf carts, followed by Max Blue's cartload of bodyguards. They parked the golf carts under a tall mesquite tree in the rough beyond the twelfth hole. Max had been upset that the judge had not invited the senator also. The incident on the landing field near Yuma was the senator's responsibility. Someone had been doing a sloppy job of alerting the Border Patrol radar units to let their planes and pilots through.

The judge had gently reminded Max that with only two telephone calls, the entire mix-up at the landing field had been resolved. No one knew better than the senator how important safe landings were. The senator's reelection campaign fund depended on those shipments; other party candidates had been financed as well with the proceeds from the shipments. Max had the goods on the senator. The judge knew that. Max had saved the senator's ass with a bundle of dynamite under the car seat of a certain Los Angeles investigative reporter who had alleged the senator's involvement in a San Diego real estate fraud.

The judge watched the police chief: the more angry Max Blue got, the more nervous the cop got. The police chief began with an apology, but Max had cut him off. Max held a seven iron in his hand and made gestures that worried the judge. What was the use of spending a million dollars on the Tucson police if all they did was kick your boys in the balls and steal their cash?

The police chief tried to explain that the undercover officers worked by rules of their own, and it was unfortunate that Sonny Blue and Bingo had chosen the Yaqui village for the drop. The judge listened to their voices—Max Blue's voice was quivering with fury while the police chief's voice was even and conciliatory. Arne was bored with their bickering. He hoped Max would get off the police and get back to the lawsuit over water for Leah Blue's Venice development. Arne had good news. His clerk had located a number of possible legal theories and strategies to legitimize sending the water rights lawsuit back to state court where Leah Blue had already won against Indian tribes and environmentalists.

Max Blue had promised the judge a house next to the golf course Leah was planning for her Venice dream-city. Players could reach the back eighteen holes in quaint gondolas or in golf carts.

Arne, of course, would never consider leaving the home place. Mother had planned for everything. She had even removed the old tennis courts to make way for the dog runs and kennels. She had recognized immediately that Arne had no interest in coarse outdoor sports; basset hound breeding was a perfect hobby. She seemed not to have acknowledged warnings from nannies and later from teachers that her son showed "unnatural" curiosity and interest in the sexual habits of dogs. In high school, Arne had openly proclaimed to horrified classmates his preference for watching dogs fuck over watching a Chaplin comedy. Arne had always hated the mute little tramp and did not think Chaplin funny or poignant at all.

Arne had begun to regret they were not playing golf after all. Hitting the practice balls had awakened the urge to whack the little balls to kingdom come. Acting as liaison between the police and Max Blue was just one of the duties Judge Arne performed; there was also an entirely different realm of border crossings and dealings with certain local businessmen who secretly worked for the U.S. government.

Max had refused to let go of the police beating once he had started ranting and raving about the undercover cops. Here was where Arne's role as liaison got tedious. The police chief said payment did not buy protection for transactions occurring in "no-man's-land"—the term Tucson police had given to those parts of town where they feared to go even in force. The Yaqui village fit the police chief's definition of no-man's-land, at least no-*white*-man's-land; only undercover police dare enter no-man's-land. "Then why were your men there?" Max Blue had asked. The police chief seemed to shrink inside his baby-blue golf shirt and shorts; the judge noticed how thin the chief's thighs were. What a disappointment at the crotch! The cop was hung like a canary! The judge enjoyed watching other men argue and struggle as if the world itself depended on them, and all the while the judge already knew who would win and who would lose.

The undercover cops could have the cocaine, but Max demanded the return of the cash. The police chief shook his head. In the confusion of the shooting, the bag full of cash had been lost. Sonny was at fault for choosing a Yaqui village for his rendezvous with the New York buyers.

Now the police chief and Max were sitting in Max's golf cart hunched over a notebook comparing calculations and figures. The judge saw Max's face had relaxed, and he knew the little tempest had passed. But off to the southeast and southwest the judge could see big puffy, white clouds hugging the shoulders of the high blue mountains. There was no sign of lightning yet; the clouds were still silver-white. He had learned to keep an eye on the clouds when he was a boy riding his horse alone on the old man's ranch. Gradually over the next few hours, the clouds would swell and darken purplish blue until thick bolts of lightning and their thunder shook the ground. The old man had taught Arne that sunshine and blue sky over his head were no protection. If there was a big thunderstorm across the valley, distance was no guarantee, the old man used to cackle. Because lightning might travel diagonally for twenty or twenty-five miles, before the bolt struck the ground.

The judge took no chances with lightning. He would keep an eye on the cloud mass above the mountain peaks. He had certain rules regarding lightning that he had followed since he was a boy riding his horse. At the first clustering of purplish, big-bellied clouds, Arne used to spur his horse home. The judge did not care if Max and the young police chief were discussing the matter of the "national security" shipments; at the first rumble of thunder, the judge was going to excuse himself and take cover in the clubhouse.

After Max Blue and the chief had concluded their business, Max had called over his walkie-talkie, and a golf cart approached slowly. Arne saw a waiter had ridden down from the clubhouse with a picnic basket and ice chest. They ate sitting in the golf carts parked under a grove of mesquite trees near the back boundary fence of the golf course.

Arne had heard rumors that Max Blue had armed guards who secured the desert area outside the golf course fence; and if a small aircraft circled from time to time, it was part of Max Blue's security against assassination attempts from the air. Max did not worry about reprisals from the victims' families; he worried about former clients and his own associates. Max had made "arrangements" to solve "problems" for a great many interest groups including the "family," foreign governments, even the U.S. CIA. Max had the goods on everyone, and that was dangerous.

The judge ate his club sandwich and potato salad. Max Blue always served the same lunch. If Max wanted to make a deal, plenty of champagne and beer would be served; if Max was chewing a new asshole for someone, such as the police chief, then there would only be ice water or ice tea. They ate without small talk. Cicadas droned in the trees, and there were the sounds of chewing and potato chips; for an instant there had been no city sounds, no jets or cars, no dogs barking or voices. The judge watched as the clouds began to darken over the mountains; he heard the first rumble of thunder. Max Blue had heard the thunder too and he grinned at Arne. Max and the judge had a private joke about Arne's dislike of lightning and thunder.

The judge started to speak, but Max had cut in, "I know, I know—your grandfather showed you corpses of sheepherders split in half by lightning!"

"And stone walls four feet thick reduced to shattered rock by a single lightning bolt," Arne himself had continued.

"You'd never know what hit you," the police chief said. "It beats the gas chamber."

"How do you know?" Max Blue said, looking sharply at the police chief. Max always forgot how dull-witted police were until he spent a few hours with a cop.

BELOVED BASSET HOUNDS

ARNE COULD HEAR the thunder from the storm over the Rincon Mountains quite distinctly now. He was tired of sitting in a golf cart in the heat. The misunderstanding had been resolved, and Arne had given Max the good news: Leah Blue could begin to pump water from her deep wells at her Venice, Arizona, development whenever she wanted. The judge wanted to go home. They left Max preparing to tee off on the fourteenth hole. The police chief drove the golf cart as fast as it would go.

Arne much preferred the company of his bassets to the company of humans. His grandfather had felt the same; more than once the old man had declared that his dog's mouth was cleaner than a human's mouth. Arne only wanted to go home and recover from the heat and the sun. But the young police chief wanted to talk about the "national security" shipments. Others in the department had been complaining they got no cut off the "national security" shipments. Suddenly the judge had not been able to restrain himself. Something about the little-boy cowlick on the police chief's head infuriated him; stupidity passing for innocence. "Greed is so ugly in the police," the judge said, "and really, it is quite useless to talk about law and order if you can't control greedy 'pigs.' " Arne was delighted with the police chief's shocked expression at his use of the term *pigs* in the conversation. Arne had continued, "The French call the police *vaches*—'cows.' All I can picture are the milk cows on the old man's ranch with bright green shit smeared all over their asses." The judge wanted to make a point clear to the young cop: they had hired him out of Phoenix to work for them.

Arne waited for some response, but the police chief had been too stunned by the attack. "Get too greedy and see what happens," the judge said. "I've been on the federal bench for twenty-five years. There's only so much pie to go around. Get out of line too often and the feds will call secret grand juries and flush you down the crapper like they did your predecessor." The young police chief nodded soberly. The judge put a hand on the chief's arm. "No hard feelings, Sean," Judge Arne said, "I only tell you this for your own good. Clean house the first chance you get." The young police chief nodded solemnly; the judge saw big circles of sweat under both the cop's arms. "The men call what they take 'combat pay' and 'fringe benefits,' " the police chief said hopefully, but the judge had turned away abruptly, leaving the police chief in midsentence. Arne was in no mood to argue about police salaries or Arizona's brain-dead economy. Arizona had been sliding toward the financial abyss for years. One disaster had followed another. Arizona's tax revenues had plunged. Hughes, Motorola, IBM—the list ran on and on; like rats off a sinking ship they had relocated to Denver or Las Vegas.

The judge did not bother to look back or wave to the police chief. The senator had let the cat out of the bag the other night at the Thursday Club. The senator had been too drunk to stand up or focus his eyes, but he had delivered one of his spontaneous sermons, this time in front of the big urinal in the downstairs bathroom. "Things are looking up! Things are looking up," the senator said, all the while letting his limp cock droop in his hand and piss on his own shoes. The judge had stayed close by to be sure the senator did not let too many cats out of the bag. The senator had just finished briefings about top-secret U.S. border policy. Yes, Arizona's economy would certainly look up if suddenly, overnight, Tucson became command headquarters for all U.S. military forces assembled along the Mexican border.

Judge Arne eased the Mercedes onto the dirt road to the home place. He was thinking about Max Blue's wife, Leah, the real estate tycoon. She had spent millions drilling the deepest water wells in North America. The water from her deep wells had been salty, but all the better for her "canals of Venice." Leah Blue was a gambler. Even the most expensive spas and resorts for the rich in Tucson had lost money, but that did not discourage Leah about her dream city in the desert. Leah Blue was lucky. Thanks to the judge's directed verdict, she had all the water she wanted without interference from environmentalists or Indian tribes. If U.S. troops were sent into Mexico to restore order at the request of the Mexican president, then Tucson and all the border states would be booming again, and Leah Blue would be rich beyond imagination. Beside her, Max Blue would be a minor league player even with his assassination franchise.

It was always a relief to come home to his basset hounds after a day in the courtroom. The judge had the maid and cook leave each night by six because he wanted to enjoy his privacy. The judge rather liked how fierce the badger hunters were with their huge basset heads, and thick dirt-digging claws; and yet bassets were nearly helpless without human assistance during mating. Bassets and basset-breeding weren't for everyone; how many people wanted to guide a wet, pink, banana-size basset-hound prick into a bitch in heat? The judge certainly didn't mind, but he knew he was not like others. Basset-breeding had required the utmost dedication for hundreds of years, by European nobles who had selectively bred the dogs for badger hunting.

The judge poured himself a martini from the chilled shaker the cook always prepared and refrigerated before she went home. He went outside to sit on the patio where he could watch the kennel runs and his bassets, all barking their greetings to him. He closed his eyes, took a sip, and settled back on his chaise lounge. The martini warmed his veins and he began to relax. It was always a mistake to work with the dogs if he was tense or had had a difficult day. More and more he enjoyed being alone with only his dogs for companionship. During his sexually active years he had always preferred prostitutes of either sex. He did not think gender really mattered; sex after all was only a bodily function, a kind of expulsion of the sex fluids into some receptacle or another. Now at the Thursday Club, Arne found he was far more excited by watching the antics of the other club members or the sex videos on the club's big-screen TV. Even the two or three words one had to speak to a whore were too many words to waste on such creatures. Sex had always been filthy and deadly even before the outbreak of AIDS.

How much better the old man's methods had been—how casually the old man had unbuttoned the fly of his trousers, then slipped his hard dick into the milk cow's heifer tied and hobbled in the barn. Arne had watched his grandfather speechlessly. The heifer did not seem to mind. The old man's dick was long and rather thin like a bull's pizzle anyway. Afterward the old man had talked about the Greeks and their gods and the offspring of the gods who were part man and part horse or part man and part bull. Even as a young boy, Arne had not been confused. He knew there could be no such thing as minotaurs or centaurs. But even then, Arne had understood the old man's urge to fantasize that he was no longer a man, but a bull.

The bassets were pure and noble. They waited their turns with him one by one; it was their ritual, their excited barking in anticipation; then, after martinis, he had sex with the four bitches. His basset stud was a good sport. The bitches were receptive to the dog only twice a year, but they had been trained to accept their master from behind anytime. The stud dog smelled what went on in the bedroom off the patio; by the time it was his turn, the basset stud had performed gloriously on Arne, who lay belly down on Mother's carved mahogany bed. Nothing was as deliriously potent as the orgasms that seized Arne when he fucked his basset hounds.

TUCSON'S SEX MALL

LEAH BLUE was already late for her meeting with Trigg, but she stopped her Mercedes anyway to look at the site of her dream city. Grayish gravel and yellowish creosote bushes were all that were there now, but since Judge Arne had thrown out the last motions for an injunction, Blue Water Development Corporation could begin construction on the hundreds of miles of canals that would crisscross the entire development. She imagined how stunned, then proud, her father and her brothers would be when they saw all the maps and blueprints. The water wasn't just decoration either; the sight of foundations and canals everywhere was reassuring to newcomers in the desert. Surveys showed both residential and commercial buyers responded most strongly to property with flowing water; in the absence of a bubbling stream, fountains or canals greatly enhanced chances for quick sales. Leah closed her eyes and could see it all—sapphire water in canals weaving between brilliant white walls of palazzos and villas bordered with lawns that ran into fairways and greens. No vulgar wire fencing or asphalt parking lots in Venice, Arizona.

Leah had been afraid Trigg might be angry because she was late. But as she drove into the Arizona Inn parking lot, she saw Trigg had been late too. He had just started down the sidewalk in his wheelchair. Leah called and waved for him to wait. Trigg seemed surprised she was late. When she leaned down to kiss him, he pinched both her breasts. "See if *that* arouses you," he said. The last few times they had met at the hotel for sex, Trigg had kept asking Leah what excited her. He claimed he wanted to find out what women really preferred sexually, but Trigg was a liar. He got aroused when she told him what excited her, and for Trigg that had been all that mattered.

Leah sat in the bed with the sheet pulled around her, watching Trigg lift himself from the chair to the toilet. He took great pride in his bladder and bowels, which emptied when he massaged and pressed his abdomen. These partial functions were evidence *not* everything had been severed; and Trigg talked constantly about his hope, his belief, that someday there would be transplants, a cure, for spinal cord injuries. Trigg talked the whole time she sat on top of him, his cock inside her hard and dead as a dildo. She ignored Trigg as she always did when they had sex, and she visualized a brutal French dwarf in a medieval castle who forced her to ride his huge, hairy rod instead. Trigg said he had to watch her excitement before he could come; but lately Leah had begun to wonder if Trigg really got that much out of sex, or if his "mental" orgasms were imaginary, his denial that paralysis had made him a eunuch.

Lately Leah had noticed their afternoons for sex at the Arizona Inn had dwindled from hours of nonstop sucking and bouncing with cocktails and a light lunch afterward, to fifteen minutes in which Leah bounced on top while Trigg used his tongue only to talk about the outcome of "their" bid on the bankrupt Tucson shopping mall and a partially completed resort hotel. Finally Leah told Trigg to be quiet or she'd never come; if she got sweaty, filthy, and rubbed raw while his chattering distracted her and she didn't come, that would be the last time she bothered with Trigg.

She looked down at his face for a reaction as she spoke. His eyes opened wide and blue, and for an instant Leah was seized with the urge to slide herself up over his chest so his neck was between her thighs to strangle him or break his neck.

Instead, she slid up his chest and thrust himself at his mouth and leaned into his tongue, his most lively member. She whispered to Trigg, "Don't waste your tongue talking." They could talk about money later. Trigg had been trying to persuade Leah to sink more of her money into his sex mall scheme. Trigg's bankers in Phoenix had all been sent to prison for making sweetheart loans. Trigg had depended on his banker friends in Phoenix for the "financial packages" Trigg had used to buy blocks of downtown Tucson, and to finance the plasma donor centers.

Leah was getting bored with Trigg, although she still got a sexual kick out of his helplessness; however, his financial helplessness was boring. Trigg talked about the past—how he had flown to Phoenix for a million-dollar unsecured loan and his banker friends had made the loan to him that same afternoon. Finally Leah had lost patience. She told Trigg what "used to be" was gone. Screw the loans Trigg had got before. They were talking now. Trigg had tried to discourage Leah about building her dream city of white marble palazzos and canals in the desert. He said it wasn't just because he wanted her to invest in his project; American and foreign manufacturers and businesspeople had still not forgot Arizona's last paralyzing water crisis. But Leah Blue had thought about water before she had thought about anything else for her Venice plan.

Arizona's worst water problems had accidentally been solved after the closure of the copper mines and the rapid loss of jobs and the drop in population in Tucson and Phoenix. Leah had the research and statistics; Arizona's last water crisis had been blown out of proportion by the world news media. The drama of millions of middle-class, white Arizonans waking up one morning to find no water in their faucets had obscured the facts. Arizona would not have run out of water that infamous summer if federal water-management officials had not allowed too much of the Colorado River to escape to Mexico.

Leah Blue had got her idea from reading about oil-field bankruptcies and court-ordered auction sales in Oklahoma and Texas. She had read with fascination about the deep wells and the gigantic drilling rigs that were required, rigs costing millions of dollars. Leah remembered how Trigg and the others had made fun of her flying to Houston to bid on a deep-well rig; she had got it for a flat five hundred thousand dollars— a savings of almost a million dollars. Max had even caught wind of Leah's purchases from the senator, who had heard about it from Judge Arne. Max had only mentioned the gossip in passing; he never interfered with Leah or how she spent the money. Trigg had bet Leah Blue's rigs would hit salt water at two thousand feet; she could drill to China or to hell, but salt water was all she would get. Leah had not worried. If the canals and lakes of Venice, Arizona, ran with salt water that lent authenticity; salt water could be used to flush toilets. For drinking water, Leah would provide bottled glacier water from the Colorado Rockies. Trigg had anticipated that Arizona's Indian tribes and the environmentalists would go to federal court to stop Leah's deep-water well from ever pumping. Opponents argued that the salt water threatened to ruin the last of Arizona's potable water. What Trigg had not anticipated was the quick denial of the injunction against Leah's deep well by Judge Arne. Leah's attorneys had argued that the deep wells were Arizona's last hope for precious water. Leah Blue was a visionary, her attorneys said, because her deep wells would pump water even during drought years when the Colorado River had dried up. A little salt in the water was still preferable to no water at all.

Trigg sat in a white terry-cloth robe eating French toast and arguing with his mouth full of bacon. The water supplied by the deep wells might be enough now, but Leah had no guarantee in ten years or even five. Trigg was still trying to "sell" her more stock in his sex mall. Arizona's financial collapse had begun to spook little guys such as Trigg as they watched their banker friends fall. When two-bit hustlers got scared, they started to think small. Leah had always thought big, but Trigg saw no reason for Venice when thousands of residential properties in Tucson were still empty, unrented and unsold, or inhabited by squatters. Leah shook her head. Trigg knew nothing about real estate. Residential property priced over a million was still reliable. Leah's homes in Venice would be priced beginning at two million. Leah did not mention that Mr. B. had already inquired about forty units for himself and business associates.

Trigg was not interested in hearing about the security features that the canals and lakes would provide; he wanted to know who were these people and why would they bother to come to, much less buy property in, a state such as Arizona, the first state ever forced into federal receivership by her creditors. As both the U.S. economy and the civil war in Mexico got worse, Arizona's population would continue to drop. Why build a new city from scratch when you could buy Tucson already built for ten cents on the dollar? "That's all I want to know," Trigg said, lifting each leg into his trousers before he lay back on the bed to pull the trousers over the dead weight of his thighs and hips. Trigg wanted Leah to invest in the Tucson that was already there. They had to get Tucson back on "her" feet; they had to counter the ugly rumors. Had Leah looked at the faces on downtown Tucson streets lately? They were all Mexican and Indian; the only whites downtown were police, lawyers, and the clerks and workers in the county and city courts.

Leah had put the cart before the horse, Trigg told her. The city of Tucson was standing there all around them; commercial property was 85 percent vacant with residential properties running at a 47 percent vacancy rate. The Federal government owned all the vacant property by default. Here was a golden opportunity. Tucson was desperate. Attorneys for the City of Tucson had unsuccessfully sued to stop a network broadcast that called Tucson a "ghost town" or "ghost city." People didn't want to see empty storefronts and empty houses; empty buildings scared people off. Even the Hollywood rich came less often to Tucson's fat farms because limousine rides from the Tucson airport to the spas passed through acres of open desert shrubs dotted with the tents and the shelters of the homeless.

Leah looked at her Venice blueprints, then at Trigg. Even if he lied about feeling orgasms in his brain, Leah admired the man's energy. Trigg never gave up, but he wasn't very bright either. Her dream city had been calculated with Arizona's financial collapse and Mexico's civil war in mind. Venice, Arizona, would rise out of the dull desert gravel, its blazing purity of white marble set between canals the color of lapis, and lakes of turquoise. The "others" had to live someplace; let it be Tucson. Leah didn't care how cheap real estate was, all she saw were dingy, decaying storefronts and defunct shopping malls in Tucson. Tucson had been run-down too long; forget Tucson and start over.

Leah pulled on her panty hose and combed her hair. She watched Trigg in the mirror as he pulled himself into his wheelchair. Leah didn't bother to argue. She had noticed the pattern in Trigg all along. Trigg was always ready to steal what was there and make the best of it as fast as he could. Maybe that had been the effect of his accident, Leah wasn't sure; but she knew it was important to Trigg to brag about sex with her and the imaginary threat Max posed. Max got reports that Trigg liked to say he might be in a wheelchair, but he still had more balls than the others did because he fucked Max Blue's wife. Trigg didn't know that Max had spies. Trigg didn't know Leah told Max everything. Sex was unimportant to Max—something Trigg would never understand because Trigg was obsessed with standing up; more than anything Trigg himself wanted to be erect.

"What are we doing arguing?" Trigg had said, suddenly widening his blue eyes at Leah. He pointed at a large blank area on one map: "Venice, Arizona, City of the Future," he said to show Leah he had been persuaded to accept her plans; now Trigg wanted Leah to support what he called his "comprehensive plan." Trigg's plan took a hard look at Arizona's economy. Even in the best years, Arizona's economy had never been famous. Arizona mined some copper and grew some cotton, but mostly Arizona had been the place Americans went when they went on vacation or got sick. Politics across the border had become so explosive that the wealthy vacationers and rich fitness addicts might be difficult to lure back to Tucson. But patients confronting fatal illnesses would be willing to take the risk Mexico might blow up while they were in Tucson. The terminal patients would not notice that Tucson's parks and arroyos were full of homeless people. Tucson was already a heart-lung transplant capital. Trigg's comprehensive plan would make Tucson an international center for human-organ transplant surgery and research.

The beauty of Trigg's plan was it took advantage of existing facilities and personnel already located in Tucson. Trigg kept development costs down that way. He wanted Leah Blue to realize that starting from scratch cost too much. All he had to do was to redesign the defunct Tucson resort hotels he had bought in bankruptcy sales and voilà! They would have luxury hospital accommodations to lure billionaires for organ transplants and other delicate operations. They would offer luxury out-patient treatment centers where new transplant patients might reside permanently in a luxury condominium only minutes away from the transplant center emergency room.

Trigg was convinced his plan took everything into consideration. Since the international market for organ transplants might at first be unpredictable, Trigg had been careful not to scrap his faithful standbys, the plasma donor centers, or his private hospitals for substance abusers and disturbed children and teens. Trigg dreamed of making Tucson and southern Arizona the health and beauty capital. The Arizona water crisis a few years previous plus recent border violence had frightened visitors away. Trigg would lure them back with his grand resort hotel in the mountain foothills where a luxury hospital and outpatient accommo-dations for cosmetic surgery would be featured. The beauty of this business was even when the fat came off or was sucked out, yards and yards of sagging wattles and crepey skin remained to be snipped off or tucked.

Trigg's proposal even took into account the possibility of war in Mexico; even if the trouble in Mexico scared off wealthy transplant and tummy-tuck patients, Trigg wasn't worried. If Mexico blew up, the beds of Trigg's hospitals would be filled with wounded U.S. soldiers paid for by Uncle Sam. And of course, if civil war broke out in Mexico, there would be no shortages of donor organs in Tucson. Trigg wanted to draw transplant patients from all over the world to one location. The secret was how to obtain the enormous supply of biomaterials and organs which was necessary, and the civil war in Mexico was already solving that. Even if there were no war, still Trigg had come up with a brilliant solution. Trigg had a gold mine. Hoboes or wetbacks could be "har-vested" at the plasma centers where a doctor had already examined the "candidate" to be sure he was healthy. A lot of those people on the street were full of worms and sick but didn't look it.

Leah Blue felt the hairs on her neck rise on end. She rerolled the blueprints slowly while she chose what she would say. At the core of Trigg's plan was a research center for nerve-tissue transplants for spinal cord injuries. Tucson had barely been able to keep the heart-lung transplant center after the university hospital had gone bankrupt, much less support an even more experimental transplant research program. Trigg's capacity for self-delusion was inexhaustible. "All your millionaire transplant surgeons and their wives will have to live in Venice," Leah said. "I can't imagine they will tolerate living in Tucson." Trigg had a puzzled expression. He didn't get it. "I mean the surgeons and their families won't want to live in Tucson once you get the 'sex mall' going," Leah said.

Trigg reminded Leah that he and his business partners preferred to call it the Pleasure Mall. Trigg was touchy about the use of the right terms. The defunct Tucson shopping mall had been a blight on Tucson's face; gangs of homeless had broken in and squatters had been living in the Penney and Sears stores. The mall would be completely renovated; first class all the way. Nothing would be cheap or dirty about the Pleasure Mall, Trigg argued. The finest food and liquors would also be available as well as luxury hideaways with hot tubs and pools for nude swimming. All the shops would be tasteful or at least educational. Theirs would be the first shopping mall of its kind in the world. Lingerie shops would be next door to video rentals and adult bookstores. The Pleasure Mall would feature a gallery of erotic art. Sex toy stores would offer live demonstrations to promote safe sex. If all that wasn't educational enough, Trigg had been negotiating with a promoter in London to lease a rare collection of specimens in jars and under glass consisting of the scrotums and penises of all species, including a number of human specimens. Trigg also hoped to lease a nineteenth-century wax museum devoted to unnatural sex positions and unnatural sex partners. This was only the beginning, Trigg said. The best was yet to come. Not even the Japanese had devoted an entire shopping mall only to sex.

Leah glanced at her wristwatch. She smiled and shook her head. Trigg could argue all he wanted, but no one who could afford better was going to live in a town with a sex mall. The ugliness of Tucson would only make the white marble palazzos and canals of cobalt-blue water more irresistible. Leah was getting tired of Trigg and his obsession with his paralysis. She lied and said she was late for an appointment and left him with his Pleasure Mall blueprints spread open on the bed. Trigg's dream of nerve transplants for spinal injury patients was pathetic.

BOOK THREE

THE STRUGGLE

LUXURY CRUISE

THE EASY PART had been emptying the vaults, packing the car, and driving to the airport in Oaxaca. Once Menardo was dead, the others had immediately shunned her; even the maids and cook had left after Tacho had disappeared. They had fled back to their barrios or villages until the official investigation had been completed or abandoned. No one had expected the new widow suddenly to disappear before the funeral, not even the police chief and the general, who had been suspicious of Alegría from the start. Alegría had made her moves while all the attention was focused on dead Menardo.

Alegría felt her heart beat more slowly as the jet taxied down the runway. She had cleared everything from the vaults—Menardo's "savings" in uncut emeralds, pearls, and gold nuggets from Peru. The most important contents of the vaults had been the half dozen bank safe-deposit-box keys and the worn address book with the locations of the banks in San Diego and Tucson. Within a few hours after Menardo's death, Alegría had made all the necessary arrangements. The travel agent in Culiacán had been the brother-in-law of the doctor's wife Alegría knew from the country club canasta tables. The travel agency "specialized" in group tours to the United States.

Alegría had been instructed by the doctor's wife to request the "deluxe luxury tour"; the doctor's wife had been born in San Salvador, and a number of her cousins and their friends had taken the deluxe luxury tour to the United States. Sure it was expensive—$2,000 U.S.—but from start to finish you traveled in complete luxury and safety. You could carry with you as much as you wished because special arrangements had been made with the authorities. There were no stops for inspections. At the border itself there would be a short walk—nothing more than a mile or two—and then waiting on the U.S. side would be air-conditioned motor homes stocked with ice-cold beer. A large truck followed with excess baggage and crates containing art objects or antiques. After refreshing showers in the motor homes and a change of clothing, members of the tour would be allowed to examine their luggage and crates traveling by truck, to assure group members their precious belongings had made the border crossing intact. A champagne brunch would be served during the drive to the train depot in Yuma. The doctor's wife had giggled; certain art and antiquities dealers took the "tour" regularly for "business" reasons. Others went because they had heard about the "love bus" and the wild parties that went on all night while the tour bus cruised north.

The luxury bus tours operated out of a travel agency located in a run-down mansion in the old residential district of Culiacán. The wide doors of the old mansion's dining room and ballroom had been rolled back to accommodate the bus tour passengers and their belongings. Alegría's companions appeared to be an assortment of Mexicans and Central Americans—all light skinned and well dressed—who kept their hands on their briefcases and other carry-on luggage at all times; the wealthy Salvadorians were all young married couples. The women were dressed much like Alegría, in linen suits and lizard-skin pumps; the men wore stylish golf shirts or seersucker trousers and blazers.

The travel agent introduced himself as Mario. "Welcome to the luxury bus cruise." They would be getting under way within a few hours. Boxes, trunks, and suitcases were stacked in a great mound in the center of the hardwood floor of the mansion's ballroom. Alegría watched Mario's eyes dart from tour members to the pile of luggage and back, over and over, as if he were sizing up each of them and their belongings. Mario had then met privately with each tour member in the mansion's library. When Alegría went into Mario's office, he asked for her payment, then counted the cash twice before slipping the money into a briefcase between his feet. Alegría felt relieved that Mario's attention was on the money, and not on questions about the weight or the contents of her luggage. That's what $2,000 U.S. bought: no questions and no need for passports or visas because the buses took "special routes" through the mountains at night to reach the border.

Mario had been looking at lists on the desk when he asked if Alegría had any questions. She could sense immediately he did not expect questions or maybe he didn't want any questions. Alegría had been curious. What shoes should she wear? She had been told there was a distance to walk. "The walk? A short walk!" Mario had answered, nodding rapidly as his eyes darted to her feet, then to the briefcase between his own feet. "You walk from one bus to another," Mario said as he walked Alegría to the door. "Relax! Enjoy! There's nothing to worry about," Mario said as he motioned for a young Costa Rican couple to enter the office.

There was no music, but maids brought out glasses of champagne and little crackers covered with anchovies, green olives, peppers, and cheese. Some of the Salvadorian women, friends since grade school, had taken suitcases to dressing rooms upstairs where they had changed into party dresses, chattering gaily about the interior decoration of their new homes in the U.S. They would have their babies there. This tour made it all so easy and convenient. They could bring jewels, antiques, and art without duties, or taxes. Alegría had gone to boarding school with young women who had enjoyed similar privileges of wealth and white skin. Alegría was just like them; they were all on the run, taking as much family wealth as possible as they fled north to the United States. They wanted only to burp babies wearing satin baptismal gowns and to enjoy the wealth that rightfully was theirs, without fear of bloodshed. Alegría could see only one difference between herself and the others: they thought they had a right to their wealth, and she knew that she did not have any right to wealth—no one did—but she had taken as much as she could. Alegría had learned to take and take; because those who didn't ended up dead.

More champagne had been served while Mario announced a slight delay with their luxury cruiser bus. Two hours later when the bus had finally arrived, all the tour members, including Alegría, had been drunk on the cheap champagne. Mario had disappeared upstairs, and soon disco music began to pound from intercom speakers in the ballroom. The young Salvadorian couples were in a party mood, and the young husbands had got drunk enough to change to their tuxedos for the luxury bus cruise. Why not celebrate? They had almost reached the United States; they were almost to begin exciting new lives. They were proud they were not like others; they did not have to run and scramble or arrive as the peons did with backs wet from sweat or river water. The young Salvadorians were proud of their wealth and the privileges wealth had bought them.

The luxury cruiser had two levels; the sight-seeing level had a cocktail bar, with a disco music setup that the bartender could control with the touch of a finger. New orange carpet covered the bus interior; the bus seats had been freshly upholstered in orange velvet. The men's and women's rest-rooms were no larger than closets, but each had tiny lavatories with lighted mirrors, new yellow vinyl wallpaper, and yellow vinyl floor tile to match. Two "bus hostesses" in maid uniforms had been drinking with the bartender. The bus swayed and lurched and the hostesses staggered and giggled in the aisles as they gave out blankets and pillows and took orders for cocktails with crackers and cheese or beer served with popcorn or peanuts.

Alegría could feel the approach of a headache from the champagne. She sat with the reading light out and her seat back fully reclined. The throb of the disco music overhead played against the roar of the big diesel engine as the bus raced through the darkness. Alegría closed her eyes and listened to the voices around her. When wealthy Mexicans got drunk, they had to brag to each other about all the money they had stashed in U.S. banks. On and on they went, speeding north through the night; the driver was "making time" in the light traffic and the bright moonlight. Money was all that the Tuxtla country club couples had ever talked about, and Menardo had been no different from the others. They had talked about the good years, when money had flowed from the foreign bankers: money, money, everywhere; millions and millions in U.S. dollars! Enough they could afford to live anywhere. The billions and billions owed to foreign bankers the people of Mexico never even saw.

Bartolomeo had confronted Alegría about that. Wasn't it so? Hadn't Menardo and the governor stolen millions from the hydroelectric project that was never completed? Alegría had laughed and nodded her head. Of course the accusations were true. Of course the money had been stolen, but the common people had never expected to see any benefits for themselves. Alegría had never been afraid to argue with the Marxists or others because she believed each was born to a fate. The poor had been born to suffer; suffering was their fate. Alegría could not change her fate, which had been always to enjoy wealth and luxury effortlessly. She had studied philosophy at two universities and had got no further than to call it "fate." Bartolomeo had called it "accident."

The celebrating Salvadorians had finally passed out or fallen asleep in their party clothes, the young marrieds with their arms thrown around one another. A few women had kept overnight bags with them, but all other luggage had been transported separately by truck, so they could not change clothes. Alegría watched the silver light of the moon reflect off the dry coastal mountains in the distance. The Salvadorians had been the only talkers; the others and the Mexicans like herself traveled alone and each had remained aloof. They all had secrets they carried in their luggage, or perhaps secrets pursued them—Alegría could not guess. She had heard the wives at the country club talk about cousins and sisters married in Honduras and Costa Rica now frantic to escape the spreading civil wars. The paperwork took months; even priority and privileged lists at the embassies were eight to ten weeks behind. Hundreds of travel agents offered U.S. tours like Mario's. As the doctor's wife at the country club had said, the question wasn't the expense but the quality and the guarantee of no embarrassments; no scrambling or running, no swimming across rivers, no wet backs.

Back in Tuxtla the authorities would begin to search for Alegría after she failed to appear at the church for Menardo's funeral. The police chief and the general would issue bulletins to locate her for "questioning." The federal police would find the Mercedes parked at the airport in Oaxaca. They would lose her trail in Culiacán, and neither the police chief nor the general wanted to trouble himself further except to issue alerts to customs officials on all flights departing to foreign cities. They were happy to be rid of her; whatever funny business had gone on between Menardo and the Americans or Menardo's wife and the communists, the police chief and the general both wanted to keep it confidential. The increased unrest in countries to the south had only added to the burden of providing protection and security in Tuxtla. The general wanted no scandal at a time when Universal Insurance and Security was about to make him even more rich than before.

Sometime in the night Alegría had felt the bus turn off the pavement to a gravel road. At dawn the bus stopped, and Alegría saw four men standing by a pickup truck. One of them was Mario, who appeared to be angry and shouting at the others. Alegría washed up in the ladies' closet-size toilet; as she combed her hair, she imagined how good a shower would feel. She heard someone vomit in the other bus toilet and decided fresh air and a walk might help.

Mario the travel agent was all smiles as Alegría stepped down from the bus steps; he snapped his fingers at one of the men near the pickup, and instantly Alegría had a paper cup full of hot coffee. She could feel cool breezes stir as the sun climbed over the horizon; Alegría shivered. She was not accustomed to the dryness of the air or the chill of the desert night. Jungle was either moist or moister; either warm or warmer. The jungle was lush, its vegetation seemed to promise all-around protection and plenty; the desert was all distance and exposure and emptiness—dry, gray foothills ascended flat, blue mountain ranges that ended in jagged peaks.

Mario's deluxe luxury tours. Mario handed out paper cups filled from quart tins of orange and pineapple juice. The bus hostesses served coffee boiled over the campfire by the truck. The Salvadorians were sick with hangovers and asked for medicine. Mario had produced a large bottle of aspirin, but apologized for his helpers, who had remembered cups, sugar, orange juice, coffee, pineapple juice—everything but the breakfast pastries. That was all right because they had plenty of coffee and juice for everyone.

A SHORT WALK

ALEGRÍA LOOKED around to see if she could locate any indication of the international border. The foothills were scattered with dark volcanic rocks the size of fists, yet the underlying ground was curiously hard and white, volcanic ash packed hard as concrete. The Salvadorian women pretended to be afraid to step from the bus to the hard gray desert in their high heels and party dresses, but they had already seen how easily Alegría had walked in the desert in her high heels.

Mario instructed everyone to remove their purses and other carry-on items from the tour bus, which was due back in the city. While his assistants refilled cups with juice or coffee, the travel agent explained that the sumptuous new motor homes bought expressly for this tour had had minor difficulty negotiating a steep ravine down the road. Fortunately this would be no problem at all because they would simply walk a short distance where they would find the motor homes and drivers waiting for them on the U.S. side of the border. The group would be reunited with their luggage and other belongings, and the motor homes would then depart, but in five different directions, with one bound for San Diego, another for Los Angeles, and the others to Phoenix, Tucson, and El Paso.

After the tour bus had disappeared, the only sound had been the men arguing behind the pickup truck. Mario acknowledged the men with a smile and wave of his hand; Indian guides—no one knew the desert better. Nowadays they didn't want to work; they only wanted money. The travel agent glanced at the sun still low in the eastern sky but already heating the dry air. Time to get under way; otherwise they would keep the drivers in the motor homes waiting with the engines and air conditioners running needlessly. He nodded to the guides, then slid behind the wheel of the pickup and started the engine for the trip back to Culiacán.

Good-bye, Mexico! Alegría was not sorry to walk across that invisible line because, bless her, poor Mother Mexico had been gang-raped by the world. Alegría knew she had been destined for the luxuries and refinements of life, and she was not sorry to leave behind the sadness and the mess. Mexico would only become more violent. Alegría was sad for Mexico, but she had watched Bartolomeo and the Marxists struggle to teach the people and it was hopeless; there was nothing to be done. The masses were naturally lazy everywhere, and they often starved; that was nature. Her destiny had always been different; she had tempted fate by associating with university radicals. Bartolomeo had been Alegría's peculiar weakness, but even he had not been able to stop her. She had stepped across the threshold to her new life in the United States. She could not think anymore about Mexico. She was almost within reach of Sonny Blue. Sonny had been all she had allowed herself to think or dream about on the tour bus. She had put aside all damaging thoughts or fears. The police chief and the others had bigger fish located closer, if they wanted someone to fry.

The foothills were broken by wide, sandy washes and gray basalt boulders as big as motor homes; around every curve and over each rise Alegría had visualized five shiny new motor homes waiting for them. If not over the first or second foothill, then behind those boulders up ahead a little farther. At any moment Alegría expected the blinding reflections of the sun flashing wildly off the windshields and mirrors of the motor homes. Walking agreed with Alegría. She imagined how she would design the gardens for the new home she would build in Tucson.

The volcanic ash packed firmly under the heels of Alegría's shoes.

Concrete or pavement were not always necessary; she wanted her rock garden to appear to be a natural desert landscape. Perhaps she might have a knack for landscape architecture too. Alegría stopped to look around. The sun was still climbing and the dry desert air was pleasantly warm. The tour had broken into four groups: the Indian guides walked a distance ahead, then the men; Alegría followed with the other women; and last came the five Salvadorian couples, who were complaining loudly and calling at the guides to stop. Tempers were short. Where were the motor homes? How much farther must they walk? The Salvadorian husbands shouted angrily and began to fling pebbles at the guides, who ignored them and kept walking.

Alegría had observed that treacherous chauffeur Tacho long enough to know when Indians were going to make trouble, and her heart had beat faster when she saw the three guides disappear over a hill. Behind the hill must be the motor homes and drivers. As she neared the summit, a sudden gust of wind had chilled the sweat on her neck and scalp. A moment later as she stood on the hilltop, she realized what had happened. There were no motor homes and drivers waiting for them; there never had been; the Indian guides had been instructed to abandon them.

The guides had carried away all the drinking water in their big backpacks. The four Mexicans still clutched their briefcases, but they were not much farther ahead of her now. She wondered why, in this heat, they did not remove their sport coats to make covers for their heads against the intense sun. Alegría stopped to look at the others behind her; they had all drunk too much of Mario's free liquor the night before. The Salvadorians appeared to have the worst hangovers; the young husbands in their tuxedos were far behind, almost as far back as their wives, who still wore last night's party dresses and high heel shoes. Alegría had wished she had a camera then for a snapshot; otherwise no one she told would ever believe this had happened.

Alegría had snapped the high heels off her shoes after the second hill. She had been mistaken about the sun in the North. To hear those fools along the equator talk, no sun was more fierce than theirs; but they had never seen skies seared white above the parched earth. This northern sun smoldered fiercely for hours above a red horizon before it disappeared only briefly.

Alegría argued with the voice of panic inside her head. Over the next hill they would find the motor homes and drivers waiting with the guides in the shade. The voice of panic was understandable in view of the strain Alegría had been under since Menardo had been killed. This tour company had been highly recommended; traveler safety had been one of Mario's big selling points. Alegría adjusted the pink nylon underslip she was wearing on her head to prevent sunstroke. The Salvadorian husbands were carrying their wives piggyback now. The men had covered their heads with their jackets, and then the women had copied Alegría and wore underskirts on their heads. Just over the next hill and they'd be home-free; ice-cold beer and ice-cold water waited. They would take cool showers and rest in the air-conditioning of the motor homes.

Alegría soon overtook the four Mexicans. They had sunburnt their faces before they had removed their jackets to cover their heads. They were standing on the big gray hill Alegría had nicknamed the Elephant's Ass. Alegría used silly, funny words to keep her mind off the heat and to keep herself moving. Elephant's Ass was a good name all right because that had been exactly where they were: a place where only shit could rain down. From the grayish clay hilltop they were able to look out over a vast barren plain that wobbled like a mirage in the waves of heat rising. Up the Elephant's Ass and into the Blast Furnace. There were no more hills to hide the air-conditioned motor homes and drivers or the three Indian guides; there were only miles and miles of pale, arid plains broken by odd black volcanic formations and scattered with volcanic rocks.

Alegría looked at the faces of the four Mexicans. They had begun to realize they had been abandoned. One of the four kept muttering, "This has never happened before"; he was one of Mario's satisfied customers. He had made the journey twice before and nothing like this had ever happened. "This is *not* right!" the Mexican said forcefully; even the route they had taken this time was unfamiliar. "Why tamper with success!" the Mexican had repeated until one of the others told him to shut up. The other three men had grim expressions on their faces; Alegría saw they believed Mario had abandoned them deliberately. All along Mario had been setting them up for this big one. Mario had safely delivered them and their "goods" across the U.S. border a number of times to gain their trust. But Mario would not get away with it. "Too many of our families know," the man said, wiping his face across the sleeve of his white shirt. "He won't get away with this!"

Alegría thought it must be the heat; she burst out laughing at the four Mexicans and their threats of what they were going to do to Mario when they caught him. She told them if they didn't get out of the sun, they were all going to die. They had to find shade and rest until the sun went down; then they had to find water. She knew the highway should lie parallel with them and to the west. After dark, they'd walk in the sandy wash because the night air was cooler in the wash, walking was easier. The four men stared at Alegría in a daze; they were not accustomed to Mexican women making decisions without men. They nodded and moved slowly down the hillside to the dry wash to find shade. Alegría looked back at the others. The Salvadorians were moving again, but in slow motion; the husbands no longer carried their wives. They had broken the high heels off the women's shoes too late, and the women's feet had become too blistered and swollen for shoes. Alegría saw six of them huddled together under a shade canopy they'd created by hanging sport coats and petticoats on the branches of tall yucca plants. If they stayed under the makeshift shade by the yucca plant, they might survive; but the best bet was the dry wash where the temperatures were a few degrees cooler, and the steep clay banks of the arroyo provided good shade. Below her, Alegría saw two Salvadorian men about to pass the others huddled under the shade by the yucca. Alegría considered for an instant returning to tell the Salvadorians and the others about the dry wash on the other side of the hill. But the voice of panic whispered she must conserve her own strength or she'd die in the desert too, with the rest of them. They were silly, ridiculous people anyway, those bourgeois Salvadorians and Mexicans; they wouldn't listen to a woman either.

Alegría sank into the cool shade of the steep north bank of the arroyo. She tried not to think about water; the coolness of the shade refreshed almost like a sip of cold water. The shade and coolness in the arroyo must have revived the four Mexicans because when Alegría awoke later, the men were gone and Alegría found four sets of fresh footprints following the arroyo west. Men always had to be first; let them go. Before any of the others straggled into the arroyo, Alegría had made certain she could not be seen, then had reached inside her blouse and under her skirt to make sure her money belt was securely fastened. Mario and his thugs could have her trunks and suitcases full of "art" Menardo's first wife had collected, but the emeralds and the safe-deposit keys in the money belt were a different matter; anyone who wanted the belt would have to kill Alegría first.

Sobs and swear words woke Alegría. The Salvadorian couples had managed to reach the arroyo while Alegría had dozed. The sun was low and motionless in the sky and reminded Alegría of a blowtorch she had once seen at a construction site; the torch had been on one side of a steel panel burning a hole through. She had only been a first-year architecture student then, and the professors and male students had made lewd comments as they watched the torch cut the steel. They had forgot a woman was present; Alegría had got used to vulgarity in architecture school. Alegría did not move or speak. She watched the Salvadorian husbands half-carry and half-drag their wives on their backs and shoulders.

The four Mexicans were in better condition. They did not stop. They were walking in the shade of the north bank of the arroyo. Alegría could not see them, but she heard their voices in the distance; the men sounded strangely exhilarated as they talked. The shade in the arroyo would be enough; no need to wait. They would start walking now and be that much closer to the highway and water. Alegría watched the last Salvadorian couple disappear as they rounded a curve in the arroyo. She estimated the temperature was still above 110° F, but the humidity was also less than 8 percent. The real danger was dehydration, not the heat.

Alegría woke again after sundown. She had dreamed of nothing; the perfect, dark blank of nothingness. She had feared the torment of dreams about drinking water, or ice cubes in iced teas, and cold beer in chests full of ice. She had started walking; she could feel thirst take over the voice inside her head. Thirst was chanting its name over and over. Alegría put a pebble in her mouth because she had read in a novel once that a pebble might help. But the novel had not showed what happened after a while; novelists used poetic license that architects never got to use. After a while, the pebble in her mouth had not helped because all the saliva the pebble had stimulated had been used up. Alegría had read about death from thirst in Bartolomeo's nasty little counterinsurgency training manual captured from the U.S. CIA. He had asked her to read everything because he loved her and he wanted her to know the risks. Thirst had seldom been used as a torture method by the CIA, the manual asserted, because the tongue swelled out of the mouth as thirst intensified, and the "subject" could not talk if he wanted to.

Alegría knew she had only hours to find water or reach help at the highway after she saw the Salvadorian women. The two had died in each other's arms, sitting upright against the arroyo bank. The contents of both their purses had been emptied out on the sand. At first Alegría had thought the husbands or maybe even Mario's treacherous guides had sneaked back to empty the purses. Then she had realized the two women had been delirious from thirst and had dumped the contents from their purses in a last desperate search for something to drink. One woman had drunk her French perfume; the empty bottle was in her lap.

Their expensive party dresses had held up under the ordeal very well; the fuchsia ruffles and pink crepe pleats had somehow remained clean and untorn, and only a little wrinkled. Alegría thought how odd death was to leave the party dresses without a tear or even a stain. She did not look at the faces, not for fear she might see black, swollen tongues or buzzard-eaten eye sockets, but because she had not noticed the women's faces while they were alive and certainly did not want to bother with these Salvadorian cows now that they were dead.

The white arroyo sand reflected the light of the three-quarter moon so Alegría could see plainly a hundred yards away. She squatted in the sand and cupped her hand to catch her own urine. She drank it all. She didn't see what difference it made when it was her own; men routinely required lovers or wives to swallow their sperm. The urine brought the saliva back, and Alegría hardly bothered to notice the identity of the corpses she passed. She wasn't curious or interested in those who had died. They hadn't meant anything to her alive, and now they meant even less. She alone was going to live; she herself would survive. Alegría felt euphoric each time she passed another corpse. Guatemalans and Hondurans seemed to die in twos and threes; the Mexicans dropped like flies, one by one alone. She had lost count, but she knew the "secret system": each corpse she passed advanced Alegría closer to safety. The more the others died, the more likely it was that Alegría would be saved; that was only simple mathematics.

Alegría had walked steadily all night. After dawn she passed the corpse of one of the four Mexicans; his briefcase was gone; before he had died, he had torn off all his clothes. Alegría did not stop again until the rotting smell was left behind. Before the sun got high, Alegría searched for shade where she could sleep until darkness. The arroyo was much wider now and there were desert trees growing along both banks. In the shade, under the desert trees, Alegría sat down with her back against a tree trunk. At her feet, half-buried in the sand, were empty cans and brittle, cracked plastic bottles that had once contained water. Alegría held a plastic bottle up to the sky in both hands; when she had first seen the bottle partially buried in the sand, she had thought it might still contain some water. But then she had noticed the gaping hole in the lower half of the bottle, filled with fine white sand. Alegría tried to sleep, but she was too thirsty. She had been weeping when suddenly Alegría had had no more tears. Her eyes felt burned and swollen. Now when she urinated, she had difficulty passing more than a few drops, which burned her cracked lips and tongue.

Alegría refused to die. She didn't care how weak and sick she was, she would sit there under that tree, and she *would not* die. She could feel the money belt with the pouch of emeralds against her ribs. Menardo used to spend hours examining and admiring them when he brought them out of the vault. Their intensity of color and the almost supernatural light that shone out of the emeralds, together with their flawlessness, made the emeralds worth millions. Only the Japanese had better emeralds, Menardo said. Now she had the emeralds. As long as she had the emeralds, Alegría refused to die. She was too thirsty to sleep, but she could think about the emeralds; they were hers now and they would keep her alive. In their endless depths of green, Alegría saw lagoons and pools of pure water surrounded by thick jungle leaves; the bluish-green light was a tropical rain-mist spread across the sky. She was determined not to die. Sonny Blue was in Tucson. So were hundreds of thousands in gold and in cash, even a town house. All that was hers now. She was going to live to enjoy it no matter how thick or dry her tongue got.

Alegría had not truly slept, but she had dreamed and hallucinated. From the shade under the tree Alegría had watched as the large basalt boulders and big rocks had slowly moved down the wash as if they were beasts grazing on the sand; next Alegría had heard the sound of a car engine, the Mercedes engine, and before she could move, she saw Menardo's car driven by Tacho, moving slowly through the arroyos as if Tacho were following or tracking her. Alegría saw Tacho's face clearly, but he did not see her; he seemed to be gazing out of the car window at the sandy ground where Alegría saw rounded stones transformed into human skulls the farther the car drove up the wash. Then the car disappeared, and Alegría could smell the dampness of rain in the air, although the sun burned in an empty blue sky. Alegría could smell roast turkey and saw that where the stones had been human skulls, there were now roast turkeys on silver platters that reflected the sun. Alegría heard voices from the direction the ghost Mercedes had taken; she could feel the blood in her veins begin to thicken, to dry up gradually in her veins. Her eyes no longer opened because the eyelids had swollen, then shriveled shut.

Alegría had always known life meant nothing, so dying was nothing at all either. She did not wish for her mother or father. There was no love between them. Her father would turn the story of her death into after-dinner conversation; her mother would say nothing, as if Alegría had never been born. Alegría rested her hands on her belly to feel the bulge of the pouch of emeralds inside her money belt. If her eyes dried up forever, she would replace them with two big emeralds. A natural blonde as she was would look even more stunning with green eyes.

Alegría woke with water pouring off the top of her head, down her face and chest; she rubbed at her eyes with her hands. She heard a woman's voice in Spanish call out, "This one's still alive." Someone knelt beside her with a canteen and helped Alegría rinse her mouth and tongue with water to moisten her throat so she would not choke when she drank. Alegría tried but could not focus her eyes. She could hear men's and women's voices in English and Spanish now. They gathered around her. Alegría could make out their shoes and their legs. Something was very familiar about the identical black shoes the women wore. Alegría thought it had to be another hallucination because she was surrounded by a half dozen Catholic nuns, and two Catholic priests. The nuns wore modern short veils, white blouses, and dark skirts; they were clearly *gringas* chattering excitedly in English. The dark woman who spoke Spanish returned with a woman who appeared to be her sister. They had both looked closely at Alegría, then shook their heads. She wasn't one of theirs. They had expected none by that description: blond hair. It must be the *coyotes* now were crossing a higher class of people as the civil wars in the South worsened.

In the back of the van Alegría had managed to whisper in Spanish to one of them, "Please, no police or hospital." Liria and Sarita had nodded in unison. Nothing to worry about, they told her in soothing tones. Relax. Sleep. Everything was going to be all right. Alegría tucked her knees up to her belly and felt the pouch in the money belt against her ribs. She closed her eyes and whispered to her emeralds, "Oh my little beauties! I love you, I love you; I owe you my life."

ENEMY LIGHTNING

ZETA HAD NOT HEARD from Awa Gee in days. He had not returned messages left at a computer answering machine. All his other phone lines had been busy, including a private line Zeta had been paying for, a line that supposedly was always open to her. Awa Gee was obsessed with telephone lines, and in a closet he proudly showed Zeta his "official" telephone-lineman coveralls complete with a fake Asian name embroidered on one pocket. New identities were one of Awa Gee's many specialities. Zeta did not ask, but she assumed Awa Gee tapped into other phone lines for special jobs.

Zeta went to find Awa Gee. He had recently located what he called his "dream house" in a block of seedy, crumbling bungalows on Glenn Street off Stone Avenue. Two large arroyos cut through the neighborhood where vacant lots and yards had been retaken by the desert plants, the creosote bush and paloverde, which had always grown in the gravel floodplains of the desert washes. Before Awa Gee had located the dream house, he had moved frequently. He was wary of being caught by the telephone company and seemed always to be listening for unfamiliar sounds. Night and day he expected federal agents to knock at his door. But worse than federal agents, Awa Gee feared and hated lightning. Awa Gee had ridden all around Tucson on his old Vespa scooter, looking for "safe pwace, safe pwace." Awa Gee's enemies were lightning, power outages, and any and all interruptions of telephone lines. The neighborhood Awa Gee had chosen was flat and had few living trees taller than mailboxes—all excellent recommendations against lightning strikes. Awa Gee used to close his eyes and pretend to shiver at the mention of lightning. A pellet-shaped aluminum trailer was parked next to the little house he had rented. He had bought the trailer; it was necessary to house all the small computers he had wired together for the hundred-digit project.

Whenever Awa Gee talked about lightning's threat to his precious computers and programs, Zeta was able to detect a bitterness that Awa Gee kept concealed with his wide grins and apparent cheerfulness. They had been standing in the semi-darkness that Awa Gee preferred for work at his terminals. Awa Gee said U.S. military and foreign governments had taken steps to secure their computer centers much too late. Only rank amateurs and blunderers had ever been detected or identified for computer-network break-ins. The biggest heists, the best penetrations, would not be detected for years; millions and millions of dollars per hour had evaporated out electronic circuits. Awa Gee said international banking and finance were all part of a great flowing river where immense quantities might disappear before the river level fell noticeably. Theoretically, somewhere, someday, the figures would catch up with themselves and somebody would come up short; but in fact, unless all the lights went out, the electronic river would never stop flowing, and the two-nanosecond lead that the deposits had would forever keep them ahead of the debits.

Awa Gee had a great deal of money in offshore bank accounts. He need never lift a finger again if that was his pleasure. Awa Gee collected "the numbers." His prospective clients were asked to supply entry codes. Ninety-nine percent of his clients had been former employees motivated by revenge. His collection of numbers had saved Awa Gee the innumerable hours of computer time required for random "safecracking" as he called it. Of course he had always kept meticulous records of every entry and entry attempt he had ever made. To assure that he would not duplicate sets of numbers in his search for new networks to penetrate. Awa Gee screened prospective clients according to whether he had any interest in the particular network that was to be entered. Naturally Awa Gee could have demanded top dollar for his expertise, but he had been careful not to get greedy. Awa Gee called the global networks "a big-tit cow" he was going to milk and milk; but always before he had stopped short. Up until then. But now Awa Gee saw the day approaching when he must strip "the cow" of everything, milk her, then bleed her dry. On that day he would set loose a host of allied computer viruses and time bombs that would combine and interlock to alter financial records and data in systems around the world.

Zeta had never asked any questions, but sometimes the strange little yellowish man talked nonstop when she came to make inquiries about the work he was doing for her. Awa Gee had recommended Zeta demand all payment in gold. Gold, always gold, because anything else was only paper or a few electronic impulses encoded on bank systems vulnerable to tampering.

Awa Gee had carefully taped blackout cloth all over the windows of the little house. The only light had been from a huge fish tank and from a mute color TV in the center of the room near the zebra-hide sofa. Awa Gee had dumped pillows and bedding to the floor to make space on the sofa for Zeta to sit. Awa Gee perched himself on his work stool; his eyes, strangely magnified by his glasses, shifted from her eyes to the terminal screens and blinking red, yellow, and green lights that filled the room from floor to ceiling. Awa Gee did not show Zeta what was inside the trailer, but they had stepped over two bundles of heavy cable that seemed to connect the little house to the trailer. The cable had been carefully wrapped in plastic garbage bags and taped securely.

Awa Gee had been working night and day for weeks on an international project. "All goodwill—no pay! By invitation only!" he told Zeta proudly. All the other participants had had billions of dollars of research facilities behind them. Awa Gee had been the only "little guy" to reach the last level for entry to the project. Split the atom? They had done that easily with sheer force. But to split a one-hundred-digit number into two primes! That had not been accomplished until last week, Awa Gee said, smiling.

Awa Gee had acted as if he had not seen another human being for weeks; the little man could not seem to stop talking. Zeta told Awa Gee he must feel very pleased with himself, but the little Asian shook his head and the bitterness had returned. No, he could feel no pleasure, not while there was injustice. Injustice allowed others with inferior brains, intellectual imbeciles, to receive all the millions in research grants, while he, Awa Gee, had to settle for what he could make from the junk he found in the dumpster behind the university's computer-science center.

Awa Gee's last outburst seemed to tire him, and he sat down muttering to himself in Korean. Zeta settled back on the zebra-skin couch to watch the huge lion-fish. Awa Gee reached into a Styrofoam ice chest on the floor by his feet for a cold can of beer. He offered it first to Zeta, who shook her head.

They sat in the dim light, and Awa Gee drank the beer while they watched the lion-fish beg for food. Awa Gee seemed to revive after the beer and was ready to talk some more. During the special prime-number project he had barely had time to call orders to the liquor store. He had paid cabdrivers to deliver cases of beer because his constant attention to the project had been indispensable. He had gone days without sleep. A brooding expression spread over Awa Gee's face. "The others, they had all they needed—not like Awa Gee!" Awa Gee had been forced to string together an odd assemblage of old computers considered obsolete by others. Strands of computers had been Awa Gee's secret of course, and his "strands" could match the best the universities might have, though not the government. Of course, the government researchers themselves had third-rate brains; without human intelligence computer power hardly mattered. Awa Gee's face tensed when he talked about the "government." The advantage the government and the universities had was *no lightning*. They could all afford the latest protective devices for their precious equipment. But not Awa Gee. One bolt of lightning, one great electrical surge, and the genius of all his endless months of circuitry intermeshing and wires would be vaporized. Zeta picked up a book with huge slashes and forks of lightning blazing across the book's dustcover.

"Lightning," Awa Gee said. "I am learning all I can about my—my worst enemy!" Zeta flipped through pages of lightning photographs; lightning leaped out of volcanic eruptions, lightning coiled inside tornado funnels, and zigzagged across the mushroom cloud of an atomic blast.

Awa Gee was sorry the special project had taken him away from his best customers, but the prime-number project had been absolutely essential. The governments of many nations had not wanted the hundred-digit prime-number project to continue because project results might jeopardize national security by facilitating hackers who broke through elaborate secret entry codes. Citing national security, the U.S. government had seized all Awa Gee's project notes in Customs and had prohibited further work with codes by Awa Gee. "But they can never find me," he had told Zeta proudly, "because to them, I am connected by way of Seattle and San Francisco. To them, I am a certain Professor Kew on sabbatical leave from Stanford University."

One of Awa Gee's specialities had been the creation of new identities complete with passports, driver's licenses, social security numbers—everything obtainable through computer records. Awa Gee had created a great many identities for himself while he had lived on the West Coast, where Asian births and deaths were plentiful. "The dead are my friends," Awa Gee had confided to Zeta. "I go to find birth dates on the gravestones or in the newspaper, then I write to the state capital for a new birth certificate." Awa Gee had already created three new identities for Zeta, complete with U.S. passports. Awa Gee charged extra for Canadian or Mexican identities because it required him to travel.

SOLAR WAR MACHINE

AWA GEE FINISHED his beer and with a big smile brought out another. Zeta could see he was just getting warmed up. She thought about making up excuses to get out of there, but Awa Gee was easily insulted. Alcohol brought round red splotches to Awa Gee's cheeks. He went to the corner where two speakers sat on the floor. "Hear this," he said. Ocean waves crashed rhythmically and endlessly on the sound track. Zeta saw the petals of the lion-fish's gills undulate in rhythm with the ocean sound.

Awa Gee sat at a keyboard where his left hand worked a terminal while the right hand dialed phone numbers. Awa Gee's fingers moved over keys with amazing speed. Awa Gee did not need the company of other human beings. He was most relaxed, most "at home," with his own thoughts and the numbers. Numbers were alive for Awa Gee; some numbers "sang," while others flashed complex patterns of iridescent colors as if they were exotic blossoms or jungle birds. Numbers were his companions, his roommates, and his allies. One morning the "big cheeses" would wake up to discover how the numbers had suddenly all added up to zero for them. The power of the numers would reside with the poor and the dispossessed.

For Awa Gee it had become increasingly clear that the people were up against the giants. But the giants had been ruthless for too long; the giants had become deluded about their power. Because the giants were endlessly vulnerable, from their air traffic control systems to their interstate power-transmission lines. Turn out the lights and see what they'd do; turn out the lights on one of their state executions. Awa Gee had already infiltrated emergency switching programs. No interstate backup transfers, no emergency at all would register even after miles of high-voltage transmission line were gone. They'd never catch him. They'd blame the ecofreaks.

Awa Gee had no interest in personal power. Awa Gee had no delusions about building empires; Awa Gee did not plan to create or build anything at all. Awa Gee was interested in the purity of destruction. Awa Gee was interested in the perfection of complete disorder and disintegration. At first Awa Gee had experimented with disorder by unwinding spools of rope to snarl and tangle deliberately into mounds of thick knots; then he studied the patterns of the snarls and tangles as he worked to remove them. Empire builders were killers because to build they needed materials. Awa Gee wanted to build nothing; Awa Gee wanted nothing at all to happen except for the lights to go out; because then he would top them all with his "necklace" of wonder machines so efficient they operated off batteries and sunlight. Earth that was bare and empty, earth that had been seized and torn open, would be allowed to heal and to rest in the darkness after the lights were turned out. The giants of the world would fight of course, but their retaliation would serve Awa Gee at every turn. The greater their retaliation, the greater the destruction.

The University of Arizona was a giant that must die soon. The university had fired Awa Gee and sent him to hell at a photo-finishing lab. Awa Gee had written the computer programs for polishing the giant mirrors and lenses the university had developed for the government's secret space-laser project. Awa Gee had planned to stay with the university for a few years longer to perfect his solar war machine, but one of the old white professors had caught Awa Gee polishing the war machine's special components after hours, in the university's optics plant. That had been the end of Awa Gee's top-security clearance, but the end had also been the beginning for Awa Gee.

Although the lens of the solar war machine weighed at least forty pounds, Awa Gee had mounted the machine on the back of his bicycle, to show it was indeed a weapon for the poor masses, who had little or nothing in the way of transportation. The simplicity of the solar lens was also an important feature. A one-day demonstration and briefing was all it would take. No prototype could be expected to be perfect. The solar war machine had to be unpacked and assembled on a tripod that fit onto the bicycle frame. Awa Gee had many modifications to make, but the single most important element had been the glass lens he had salvaged from the university optics department.

Awa Gee watched Zeta relax with her eyes closed. He watched the rhythmic flutter of the gills of the lion-fish and regretted he could not tell Zeta about the success of the machine's first test. But Awa Gee had made himself a few simple rules, and he intended to live by them. Complete secrecy had been the first rule. Awa Gee had loaded the machine and his video camera on his bicycle and pedaled down Stone Avenue to the corner of Speedway. Awa Gee had been planning and preparing for some time for the test target: a motel coffee shop where city cops drank coffee and ate lunch. Two or three Tucson police cars were usually parked outside.

Awa Gee had recorded all the tests of his weapon in order to make improvements.

First Awa Gee had set up the video camera on its tripod. The camera took attention away from the war machine on its short, stout tripod. The video camera was an old model, and its bulk was just what Awa Gee liked in case of gusty winds. Awa Gee set the video camera on auto and zoomed in first on a police motorcycle, then a squad car.

Awa Gee had kept his breathing slow and deep like the lion-fish sleeping in his tank. He had taken a leisurely look at the sky. No clouds for a hundred miles. Perfect weather for the solar war machine. Awa Gee squinted up at the sun and began to adjust the legs of the war machine's tripod. The glass face of the lens remained hooded in black velvet. Awa Gee had sewed the cover himself. The lens had been a prototype—one of a kind—and Awa Gee wanted no scratches or dust to mar the surface of the powerful lens.

Awa Gee had not worried about passing motorists or people on the sidewalk in Tucson. Because people in Arizona were generally ignorant and assumed that all Asians with video cameras were wealthy tourists. Awa Gee knew he was practically invisible to almost everyone driving by or sitting inside the coffee shop. He removed the velvet hood from the solar war machine and adjusted the angle of the tilt of the war machine's lens until a tiny point of blinding white light light was focused on the windshield of the police car. Awa Gee had watched through the telephoto lens of the video camera and counted the seconds. Suddenly the point of blinding white light had been surrounded by a flash of red as the interior of the car burst into flames. Awa Gee had walked casually to the war machine and turned the lens away from the sun. He had kept the video camera recording as he carefully repacked the war machine on the back of his bicycle. The police eating lunch in the coffee shop did not emerge until a fire engine pulled up to the flaming patrol car. Awa Gee watched the motorcycle cops scramble to move their machines and wished he could have aimed for their gas tanks while he was at it. But that might have caused suspicion, and Awa Gee was no fool.

English words that he had once studied and memorized to impress a lovely English teacher suddenly came to mind: *Euphoria. Euphoric.* Awa Gee had never felt anything so powerful sweep over his entire being. The fire had made roaring, popping sounds loud enough to be heard over the sirens' noise and the shouts of firemen spraying water over the cop car. Awa Gee had visited the fat brown whores walking Sixth Avenue, but he had never confused trivial amusement with profound pleasure. He was the mighty author of the comedy scene that had played in the motel coffee shop parking lot. He was the sole author of the comedy's opening lines: a series of small pops and explosions. The best part had been that the police and firemen had no idea what had happened. Awa Gee had zoomed the camera onto the faces of the cops just as the car's gas tank had exploded. The brown whores were delicious, yet one visit didn't last Awa Gee long; but the thrill of the burning police car did not diminish.

TURN OUT THE LIGHTS!

AWA GEE HAD FALLEN a little in love with Zeta. Zeta had always made it quite clear to Awa Gee that she was not interested in anything physical. Awa Gee felt both of them would remain quite safe this way. Awa Gee would act out his love for her through his work with the computer entry codes he cracked for her. There were always the ladies on South Sixth Avenue for sex. He loved Zeta because she understood what he could do with computers and numbers, and she had trusted him enough to pay for any experiments he wanted.

Awa Gee had tinkered with the solar war machine in his spare time. War machines were his hobby. The war machines he was most interested in were the machines that did not require electricity or high technology. After hours and hours each day with computers, Awa Gee's mind had been refreshed by the contemplation of wind machines and catapults. The giant had many vulnerabilities, but the greatest was the giant's massive dependency on electrical power. The giant had made a great tactical error with electricity in the United States; all high-voltage transmission lines were unguarded in remote locations. The first strikes must be made against electrical power sources.

Awa Gee knows he is not the only one who hates the giant. He knows there are others like himself all over North America; small groups but with unusual members who would bring down the giants. It is not necessary to know more than this, Awa Gee tells himself; there are others of us and we will know when the time is at hand. No leaders or chains of command would be necessary. War machines and other weapons would appear spontaneously in the streets.

Zeta was always amazed at Awa Gee's freewheeling discourses. His black, slanty eyes twinkled. He loved to go on and on about the computers he had "broken and entered." "Arpanet, Internet, Milnet," Awa Gee intoned. "Mean anything to you?" Zeta shook her head. "Well, don't worry, my friend," Awa Gee told her, "these names are just a sample of the connections I have !" Awa Gee was drunk. His face was flushed from the alcohol. Awa Gee bragged about his employment record: it read like a nightmare—beginning with the best university computer-science departments, but with a fast decline after the Stanford job. His last job had been at a photo-finishing lab where he had presided over simple button-pushing amid deadly chemical fumes.

Awa Gee loved to brag about himself. Zeta had to smile and shake her head as he rattled on about the secret German computer hackers' club that called itself Kaos. Awa Gee had been in regular communication with club members until he had broken inside their data storage systems. Awa Gee called this "ransacking"; he said he could confess to Zeta because she was a friend. All his life Awa Gee had not been able to resist snooping and peeking—of course he would never do such a thing to Zeta! Zeta had only nodded; she didn't want to bet on it. Awa Gee's first task had been to reroute phone calls to Max Blue's home and to the pay phone at the golf course locker room. Awa Gee's system had automatically put the calls through a special relay modum that recorded the caller's number and entire conversations for later playback.

As Zeta had suspected, the actual calls had been nothing. The calls had been taken by secretaries, who were merely told the day and time for golf at the Desert Golf Course in northwest Tucson. But mostly the information Awa Gee had gathered for Zeta had merely confirmed what Zeta had already suspected: the federal judge, the senator, and the police chief all got calls from Max Blue. Something had changed; Ferro had got reports from their people in Mexico.

Awa Gee had worked for months with equations in which he had altered slightly the value of one factor consistently throughout the entire computation. Over time, the error would multiply itself, and the enemy would be far off course before he realized anything was wrong. Now Awa Gee was working to create little "leaks" in their shipment pipeline. Zeta could then make use of the "leaks and spills" as she wished. Awa Gee's small, deep-set eyes glittered. He needed just a few more numbers, a clue from the wastepaper basket—old printouts or a floppy disk—then Zeta would see results! Zeta visualized the layout of Greenlee's desk and computer terminal in the basement vault. She knew how to get a disk from Greenlee.

If Zeta wanted to throw a monkey wrench into the computer networks of business associates, competitors, or enemies, then Awa Gee swore to see it was done! Zeta stood up to leave. She could not be sure how much of Awa Gee's enthusiasm was due to the beer and how much was lust. The longer he had talked, the closer Awa Gee had inched toward her on the zebra-striped sofa. "You are a beautiful woman,"

Awa Gee said, still sitting but staring up at Zeta's breasts. "Never mix business with pleasure, Mr. Gee," Zeta answered. "Business *is* my pleasure!" Awa Gee said, jumping up to walk Zeta to the door. They had not yet discussed his plans to divert electronic cash transactions before they infected the rival systems with the virus. But Awa Gee had saved that discussion for another day. Soon Zeta would have results; whatever network of traders Zeta wanted to sabotage, Awa Gee felt confident he could bring them down with his software.

Awa Gee's dream was to create the equivalent of a hydrogen bomb, a computer program that would destroy all existing computer networks. He dreamed of a series of secret "raids" into networks across the earth in which he would use computers to destroy other computers. Awa Gee realized computer time-bombs alone were not enough. Awa Gee had to watch and work and wait until other conditions were optimum. One person alone could do little, but Awa Gee knew if the timing was just right, then only a few warriors like himself could change forever the contours of the world. When the time came, the people would sense it; they would feel it in their blood without recognizing what they were about to begin. They would seize whatever was at hand and they would bring down the giants.

Awa Gee had to admire the arrogance of the U.S. government. They had not been able to imagine that emergency reserves or alternate power systems might be needed. Always the assumption was "everything would be all right"; no matter what had happened, Americans believed it could be rebuilt or repaired in a matter of hours or at most days. But Awa Gee had intercepted messages between individuals who traded maps and diagrams of interstate power-transmission lines. The maps and diagrams had not been in code, but the accompanying messages had been, and Awa Gee had been intrigued. He had easily deciphered the code.

At first Awa Gee had thought the messages might be one of those government decoys; but after he had monitored the messages for a few weeks, Awa Gee had detected no traps. The maps located the high-voltage transmission lines; diagrams showed the concrete and steel towers that supported the huge high-voltage cables. The coded messages with the maps and diagrams outlined procedures for placing explosives to topple the high-voltage towers. Awa Gee had been elated! He had jumped up and down for joy. He had turned to the lion-fish in its tank and shouted, "Aiiii!" He had been right all along. Out there in the wide world there were indeed others, others like himself who were making preparations, secretly working until suddenly all the others realized the time had come.

They would know the time had come by certain signs. The signals would be in the air—they would feel it! No organizations, no leaders and no laws were necessary; that was why success would be certain.

Awa Gee was content to leave the dynamite and crashing steel towers to the mysterious group that used code names such as Earth Avenger and Eco-Coyote. He monitored their communications daily. They became his favorites. Someone called Eco-Grizzly had sent out long-winded, angry ravings in code, and Awa Gee had worked on the "memos" as if they were great puzzle games. Eco-Grizzly and the others practiced what they called "deep ecology," and from what Awa Gee could tell, "Back to the Pleistocene" was their motto. Eco-Grizzly and the others genuinely wanted to return to cave living with the bears as their European forefathers had once lived. To Awa Gee, such a longing for the distant past was a symptom of what had become of the Europeans who had left their home continent to settle in strange lands. Awa Gee estimated it took two or three thousand years before migrant humans were once again comfortable on a continent. But Eco-Grizzly and the others were truly aliens because Awa Gee could always return to Korea, but they could not get back to the Pleistocene. Not unless something cataclysmic happened, and if something cataclysmic occurred, they would still not find the pristine planet their Pleistocene ancestors had enjoyed.

Awa Gee had spent hours each day and many nights scanning thousands of transmissions. All his life he had seldom needed more than two hours of sleep, and this had enabled Awa Gee to accomplish a great deal with his studies and experiments in computer cryptology. No one could scan as fast as Awa Gee. But Awa Gee could only scan for a few hours before he needed a break to rest his eyes. Then he would get on his bicycle or if he felt tired, the little motor scooter, and he would take a ride at midnight or two A.M. to refresh his brain and stretch his legs. As he rode around Tucson, Awa Gee always marveled at the wastefulness. Everywhere on the northwest side of Tucson, Awa Gee saw acres of new buildings in so-called industrial parks. But the offices and warehouses had stood empty and unrented since completion. It was about time someone pulled the plug on the waste! The eco-terrorists were right about that. Awa Gee was not alone. There were others dreaming just like him.

Change was coming! Awa Gee could fee it! Chills ran down his arms and back; he shivered, then laughed out loud. He was the only one on the street. He was the only one who knew about all the others. As he pedaled and coasted, his thoughts had soared away. All over the planet there were other small, secret groups; what they believed or what they grieved over was not important. All that mattered was these people burned with the blue flame of bitterness and outrage. They would not have to wait much longer. Awa Gee had intercepted a long memorandum from Eco-Kamikaze. In what appeared to be a farewell memorandum, Eco-Kamikaze had announced that "he was going out on a limb": Machine-gun station wagons driven by pregnant mothers of five; build a wall across the U.S.'s southern border to keep out all the "little brown people." Then Eco-Kamikaze had got down to the substance of his memorandum: don't linger with an expensive, painful post industrial malignancy in your brain or liver; and don't just swallow that handful of capsules or connect a hose to the auto exhaust; "contact us first!"

Balls to the wall, U.S.A.! Awa Gee was gleeful. The eco-terrorists were recruiting the terminal and dying, the suicides and the eco-true believers who were fed up, who saw the approach of the end of nature and who wanted to do some good on their way out. The eco-terrorists were making final plans: kamikaze hang-gliders and kamikaze balloonists to bomb the White House; trained dogs with payloads of TNT strapped to their bellies; eco-kamikazes in wheelchairs wearing vests of plastic explosives outside the U.S. Supreme Court building. Awa Gee could hardly believe what he was reading. Political assassination was of limited interest to Awa Gee, although he thought the U.S. Supreme Court was a very good place to begin. Human bombs had been sent to great hydroelectric dams and electrical generation plants across the United States. The human bombs would leap at the most strategic points of the dam's structure. All the interstate power transmission lines had been scheduled to go down simultaneously after the dams had been destroyed.

Zeta had left Awa Gee hunched over a computer terminal muttering to himself. Zeta agreed with Awa Gee; they must secretly try to aid Eco-Grizzly and the others in their efforts to hit interstate power lines, dams, and power plants all at once. Awa Gee had developed a computer virus to disable the emergency reroute systems in computers of regional power stations so the U.S. blackout would be complete. But before Awa Gee could investigate any further the "cocaine for guns" transactions, he needed more numbers. Awa Gee didn't try to weasel money from Zeta, only more numbers. Now Zeta would have to decide what to do before she visited Greenlee. She had thought about driving past Calabazas's place to talk to him, but she drove back to the ranch instead; there were too many people coming and going at Calabazas's place. Anyway, the decision didn't really involve anyone but Zeta.

FERRO IN LOVE

FERRO HAD SPENT as much time as possible away from the ranch house since Lecha had returned. The bitch thought she could appear out of the blue in a taxi one day and pick up where she had left off. Ferro had never felt he had a mother; Zeta had always made it clear she was a stand-in for Lecha. He was not sure how he felt about either of them. Ferro had rented a town house on Ina Road after Lecha had returned. Paulie was left back at the ranch to sleep in Ferro's room. Ferro drove to the ranch each morning. He could not sleep under the same roof with Lecha. Her sudden appearances and disappearances throughout his childhood had triggered nightmares and bed-wetting.

Ferro had told Paulie nothing about Jamey's moving into the town house with him, but Paulie had sensed a rival almost at once. Ferro hated the puffy, bloodshot eyes staring at him mournfully.

Ferro had thought Jamey was too beautiful even to consider him. Ferro was thick around the belly and face while Jamey was lean and blond and perfectly proportioned.

Jamey said himself he was no Einstein. The university was only a place he and friends of his had heard about for good parties. But even when Jamey did not bother to go to his classes, Ferro had not been able to get over the awful feeling Jamey would find a new lover on campus, someone who was as blond, slender, and blue eyed as Jamey. Ferro could not stop making comparisons between Jamey and a runt like Paulie. Paulie was rough trade; Paulie was a sucker. Whatever white powder or substance was put before him, Paulie had lapped it up. Paulie had a grimy face and the close-set eyes of a rodent. Paulie had wandered up like a stray dog that got fed and had stayed. Ferro had never wanted Paulie. Paulie had only been there to work for the old woman, Zeta.

Later Ferro recalled conversations with Jamey; and Ferro hated himself for not guessing Jamey's secret then. Ferro blamed distractions for his lapse: Lecha's unexpected return, the unrest and the U.S. troops

along the border; Jamey himself had been a distraction. The mere sound
of Jamey's name had caused Ferro's heart to beat faster and sent chills
down his neck. Ferro had never been so in love before. He had been
consumed with pleasure as long as Jamey had remained close by; but if
Jamey was away, Ferro's pleasure had suddenly given way to the most
terrible sensations of doubt and fear that somehow Jamey and Jamey's
love for him were about to be lost.

Ferro savored each moment and all the pleasure he got with Jamey.
Jamey and Ferro. Ferro and Jamey. Ferro wanted to stop Jamey's nights
on the town without him. Ferro had offered to match whatever "Perry"
paid Jamey for the drops and pickups, but Jamey had lightheartedly
refused. Ferro was reacting to the stress and the pressure, Jamey said.
There were important details Ferro could not work out when his mind
was always whispering, "Jamey, Jamey." It seemed funny how Jamey
had eclipsed all the rest of it—the return of Lecha, the trouble with Max
Blue, even the rumors of war in Mexico. Ferro was relieved he was about
to retire. He did not want to take any chances of losing Jamey; all the
nights Ferro had to spend with Paulie moving shipments might jeopardize
their love. The reappearance of worthless Lecha was another sign it was
time for him to retire with Jamey and enjoy life far from the dirt landing
strips and desert jeep trails. Ferro wanted to escape the stink of women
in the ranch house. Zeta had always said half was his. Half of all the
gold and the guns Zeta had hidden in abandoned mine shafts on the
ranch property. He would finance Jamey's calendars, and later they
might branch out and publish a men's magazine. As magazine publishers,
they would travel the world together. Ferro was glad to take his share
before Zeta gave away all of it to the Mexican rebel Indians or worse,
to the new religious cult founded by the twin brothers who took their
orders from two blue macaws.

UNDERCOVER
SPECIAL ASSIGNMENT

JAMEY LOVED the purple, pink, and violet of the sky over the Catalina Mountains after sundown. He loved feeling the warm desert breeze against his face when he drove the Corvette with the top down. He knew wind-whipped hair got split ends that looked tacky on long hair. Appearance was nine-tenths of undercover work or any other police work for that matter. The undercover assignment had been a disappointment because Jamey had loved how he looked in his police uniform. But the new police chief had chosen Jamey right out of police academy to begin a special undercover assignment, to be part of an internal security unit for the police chief. The others in the narcotics undercover unit had no idea Jamey was there to watch them as well as to work with them.

Jamey loved the mock orange blossoms' perfume in the air, and he loved his role of "boy toy" for a shakedown at the Stage Coach later in the evening. Jamey liked to sing along with the radio and talk to himself. Working undercover two years had changed Jamey's idea about wearing a uniform and being a cop. All the uniform cops ever talked about was their dicks and how much they hated homosexuals. Jamey had felt so lonely he wanted to quit the department, but then Ferro had come into his life.

Jamey had never responded so strongly to a man before, and Ferro had wanted to keep fucking all night. Jamey had not been taken to an expensive resort suite before; he had been accustomed to the hurried brutal thrusts and abrupt embraces in the dark with balding fraternity alumni brothers. Ferro had been different from the start for both of them. Jamey had not felt so captivated in years; Ferro's blazing dark eyes made Jamey weak with desire.

The police academy had not really been Jamey's idea; he had followed two fraternity brothers to the police academy after graduation. His two buddies had dropped out the first week, but Jamey had stayed because it seemed easier to stay. He liked being with the rest of the guys, and he didn't mind having someone else make the decisions. That was what Jamey had enjoyed most about Ferro; Ferro took command and told Jamey what they would do. Jamey got chills whenever Ferro gave him instructions. Jamey had got chills too whenever the police chief called him into his office alone to brief Jamey on his special assignment. Upon graduation Jamey had left the academy immediately on special assignment to narcotics and vice. The police chief said they liked his "blond, blue-eyed good looks" so necessary for undercover work at university fraternity and sorority parties.

Jamey was proud of his versatility; he could look preppy and clean-cut or grow out his hair like this and walk on the wild side. Jamey enjoyed watching his own reflection in the plate glass as he eased the Corvette up Oracle. Tonight he wore tight black leather pants and a black leather shirt with silver studs open to his navel. His blond hair had grown so long it had reached his shoulders. He looked perfect. He loved his life undercover, dressing up and pretending to be someone he was not.

Jamey had told Ferro about his passion for uniforms, and he had told Ferro about his fraternity brothers who had wanted to be cops. Jamey remembered vividly how Ferro had spat at the mention of cops. Right then Jamey had known that silence was better, silence had always been better than trouble. Jamey had intended to explain to Ferro that police work was only a job; but Ferro had not wanted to talk so Jamey had let the subject drop. Jamey had learned as a rookie not to be surprised when he saw the undercover officers and cops in uniform fill their pockets with the cash and the drugs they had confiscated for evidence. Jamey had learned the rules. He let the others know he was easy. When they offered him a share or cut, Jamey took it. Jamey had played the dumb fraternity jock who did anything the others told him to do.

The chief had asked Jamey to watch for any suspicious behavior he might notice among his fellow undercover officers. The chief had spent an uncomfortable interval staring directly into Jamey's eyes after he said that. It was crazy, but when Jamey was under intense pressure such as that, he sometimes imagined straight men were coming on to him. At first, it had seemed to Jamey, the police chief had done him a favor by assigning him directly from the academy to narcotics under-cover work; others waited years walking a beat or writing traffic tickets. Undercover narcotics was the big cookie jar. But very soon Jamey had sensed jealous undercurrents within the department, and suspicion focused on him. Jamey didn't know why the police chief had singled him out from the other recruits, but others in the department thought they knew. Jamey was one of the new chief's pets, and a spy sent to report on the others in the narcotics unit. Jamey found his picture from the Cop Cakes calendar taped to the door of his department locker. Jamey had felt all their eyes on him, but Jamey had been cool; he had laughed it off. He knew the sergeant and the others behind desks had the best jobs of all; they got thousands in cash just for passing on classified police information, or for zealously "cleaning out" files or for evidence in the department vault that had mysteriously disappeared.

Jamey drove past the Stage Coach to check out the vehicles in the parking lot to see if the others were there yet. He drove under the freeway overpass to the bridge on the Santa Cruz River. The water in the river came from the city sewage treatment plant; still the cattails and other greenery along the banks looked succulent. Jamey parked the Corvette and walked down the riverbank. He was always a little nervous before a shakedown, and this one at the Stage Coach was important. According to Perry, the guy Tiny who managed the Stage Coach owed them because his dancers didn't keep their pussies covered. Anyway, Perry said all they had to do was wait until they saw the blonde go into Tiny's office. Tiny had called them about the blonde with the kilo of "top grade"; Tiny was setting up the blonde so they would get a kilo worth five times what he owed them.

Jamey was supposed to pull his .38 to make the shakedown look convincing. Jamey let the others handle the details; he was content to follow orders. Still, he could feel his stomach tense and his bowels heat up as he parked the Corvette next to a row of Harleys in the parking lot. It all seemed simple enough. They would wait until backup units had surrounded the bar parking lot. They wanted to give Tiny and the blonde enough time to cut up some lines to sample before they rushed the office door. Perry would give the signal, and uniformed officers would kick in the back door to the office a moment before Jamey came through the front door.

SHOOT-OUT AT
THE STAGE COACH

SEESE REMEMBERED a horror movie she had once seen in which blood had flowed out elevator doors in waves and had flooded a hotel lobby. The police had forced Seese to sit in the chair with her feet in the pool of Tiny's blood. The blood had soaked through the soles of her shoes and through her stockings, but the police refused to move her. She sat handcuffed in the chair until six o'clock the following morning while internal affairs investigators came and went. Seese had closed her eyes but kept remembering the movie with the blood flowing from the elevator doors, oceans of blood. Tiny had been a huge man, over three hundred pounds. How many pints in a quart? How many quarts in a gallon? Seese could not stop her thoughts from spinning; her brain was a slot machine rolling up words and images from everywhere. Her father's blood in the South China Sea. The undercover pig had deserved what he got. Maybe Tiny had deserved it. Or maybe the police had got sick of Tiny. Now they were rid of him and they had got his bar and assets too. Seese couldn't stop thinking. She had been drinking vodka tonics with Cherie before she took the train case into Tiny's office.

Seese had watched the police all night. They regularly had different interrogators ask her the same questions again and again. Did she remember *who* came through *what* door first? Who was shot first? Who shot the undercover officer? Who shot Tiny? No questions about the kilo of cocaine in the train case. The train case had been removed by the first undercover-unit officer into the room after the firing had ceased. She had hit the floor after she had seen Tiny reach for his gun. She had been splattered with the undercover cop's blood after Tiny had fired and had dropped the cop in his tracks as he came through the door. She had been facedown on the floor when the other cops in uniform had opened fire on Tiny, so she had only heard him hit the floor.

Seese began to notice the odor of the blood almost at once. The police had turned off the air conditioner in the office, and the big pool of Tiny's blood was beginning to spoil. They had removed the dead undercover cop almost at once, but they had left Tiny on his back near Seese's feet. Somehow the police had assumed Tiny was her lover, and the sight of his body was intended to shake some information loose from Seese. Where had the kilo come from? They had already assumed the cocaine did not belong to her because bitches might haul coke for their men, but it wasn't theirs.

Seese could think of no reason why she was still alive. Why hadn't the police shot her? They had shot fat Tiny full of big holes. The explosive force of the bullets had blown out his fat like pillow stuffing. Human fat was bright white. She had dived to the floor to save herself; but for what? Every chance she might have had to find Monte and all her hope were gone now.

Seese had lapsed into dreamlike states while she was awake; she saw David's face on Tiny's body, which seemed to be bloating from the heat. This was cop fun; to display their trophy; this must be a big one. The police chief himself and the sheriff stood away from the blood at the back of the office and had listened as the detectives questioned Seese about the sequence of events.

Maybe David was dead and Monte was dead. Maybe she would soon be dead. The handcuffs and her arms bent back around the chair had caused her upper body to go numb. The police refused to let her use the toilet. Seese slipped into a trancelike calm, as if she had just polished off a pint of whiskey and a half a gram of coke. A strange form of exhaustion had agitated her thoughts while her body gradually became numb. *Yes* or *no; wet* or *dry*. Seese had not thought about the precise meanings of words since she quit school. Seese wet her pants and smiled as she saw how this had excited the police; they had left her handcuffed to the chair because this was what they had wanted. She had not overheard them discuss freeing her until three or four in the morning.

Finally Seese had passed out from exhaustion; she woke up when a sheriff's deputy decided to unlock the handcuffs because her hands and arms had swollen. The police were rolling Tiny's old-fashioned box safe out the door; behind them were the ambulance crews with body bags. Seese saw then that the dead narc had only been taken outside and left facedown on the floor by a pool table. His long blond hair was soaked with blood, but no one had bothered even to throw a bar towel over him. She had assumed when they took the dead pig out of the office, they were taking him to his glorious reward; to lie in state at a local funeral home, then the police honor guard and twenty-one-gun salute at the graveyard.

Seese tried to figure it out. She wasn't sure she trusted her own senses, but something seemed odd. The behavior of the others was not what she had anticipated; sheriff's deputies and police whispered and walked past the corpse without looking down or stopping. When the police chief and the sheriff had arrived at the scene, they had studied the close-ups the police photographers had taken hours earlier, before the corpse of the cop had been moved from the office. Then Seese knew. The dead cop had been set up by his own people. Cops took care of their own kind if they stepped out of line. They had kept asking her if she was sure the undercover man had come in the door first because the department had certain guidelines and procedures to prevent confusion during police raids. Uniformed officers broke through doors first; undercover followed. Otherwise, suspects pulled guns the way Tiny had. Was she *certain* the undercover cop had come through the office door first? Yes, she was *certain*. Had he yelled "Police"? No, he had not yelled "Police." Could she be mistaken? Wasn't she snorting cocaine with the deceased that night, wasn't she drunk as well? Was it possible she had not heard the officers come through the back door first? Maybe she had only imagined the undercover cop coming first. Then Seese knew. Seese got the picture.

Seese said nothing. She let them ask the questions over and over. Could she be mistaken? After all, she had old arrest records for misdemeanor prostitution in Tucson. Hadn't the uniformed officers shouted "Police!" as they broke down the back door? Didn't the undercover man shout "Police!" too as he came through the front door? Seese understood what they wanted her to remember; if her memory improved, they would be happy to see her leave town, and even the state, and she wouldn't ever be asked to return to testify. In fact, they would recommend Seese leave Arizona and never return again, if she knew what was good for her. For all Seese knew, the police had shot their own man; Tiny had only fired once, and he might have missed. The police had sprayed Tiny's office with bullets; stray bullets had torn big chunks out of the phone book on Tiny's desk, and bullets had shattered the fake maple paneling like the plastic or fiberglass it really was. Police bullets had pierced the cheap plasterboard walls of Tiny's office. Yes, her memory had improved; it was clear now, the uniform cops had come through the door first. Then Seese had remembered Cherie and the other dancers and the customers who had been in the Stage Coach when the shooting started. She had not heard if there had been other injuries.

The police chief himself had talked to her alone in the backseat of his unmarked car. Seese had seventy-two hours to gas up and get out of town. If she was caught in Tucson after seventy-two hours, they had a list of charges they would slap her with; for starters, they had accomplice to felony murder. Seese did not know why she felt giddy at a moment such as that; she felt like laughing because the police chief did not want to get too close to her because she stank of her own urine and Tiny's blood. She had watched how his eyes had examined her breasts and thighs; she wanted to laugh out loud. Luckily she had been a mess because the police chief looked as if he might like to fuck her.

She did not want the police to follow her so she did not call a taxi. Instead Seese had left on foot from the Stage Coach. She hurried across the frontage road. She was nothing to the police really; she wasn't even a problem. Probably the police chief and sheriff were already riding together in the helicopter back downtown to prepare statements for the press. They were already erasing her. No woman had been in the office with Tiny, contrary to early reports. Seese imagined that by next week and the funeral, they would already have forgot the real reason the narc had got blown to kingdom come. By the time the big state funeral for the narc rolled around, they would only remember that the dead man had been a cop and one of their own, whatever else he might have been. All they would remember was the fat fucker at the titty bar had killed a good man.

Seese waited in the scrubby greasewood bushes that grew on the plain of old river gravel the city had bought for a park that was never built. She heard loud police radios in cars that raced over the bridge, and she wondered if the police were trying to follow her. She felt strangely relaxed and calm, certain she was safe, crouched in the sand, hidden by the greasewood as if she were a desert animal. The police would expect to find her hitchhiking down Interstate 10. Seese was shivering and could not stop. She did not feel either cold or afraid: it was as if the shivering of her muscles had been separate from her, from her real self. She stretched out on the ground under the greasewood; she was nauseous with exhaustion but still her eyes would not close. Her eyes were wide open and she knew she could not force her hands to cover her eyes. She saw the sandy ground close up with the tiny yellow greasewood leaves scattered over it; she saw, only inches from her eyes, the gnarled, twisted trunk of the greasewood.

When Seese and Cherie had worked for Tiny, the police used to find dead whores dumped in the greasewood flats near the bridge. Naturally whore killers didn't take the trouble to haul the bodies very far; Seese had hidden deep in the greasewood thickets where people could hardly get through. Seese lay on her side and stared at the river gravel; the ground resembled a map with villages and cities marked with pebbles of varying size as one might expect to see, if one could fly over a map instead of the earth.

How cool it felt to lie on the ground with the greasewood for shade; in a few hours the sun would be high enough to penetrate the thin shade. Seese knew she'd have to move, but by then, the police would be gone. Seese wished she had her picture of Monte with her then because something had happened. Probably it was exhaustion, but she was having difficulty remembering Monte's face. Her memories of his face as a newborn had blurred together with her memories of Monte on the day he had disappeared. Even the strange dream Seese had had of Monte as a much older child had become part of her memory, and she cried because she could no longer remember how Monte looked.

Seese took deep breaths to help her relax and remember. She rolled over on her back and saw the bright blue sky through the spindly branches and twigs. A mother always remembers; a mother never forgets. Tears filled her eyes. She had to remember. She had to remember because she had to find Monte. Nothing else mattered. In the distance, she heard police radios and car doors slamming. She knew she should be alert for footsteps, but it had been as if her veins were flooded with morphine, and she felt powerless to move. Dying was like that, easy and natural as breathing out and in. If the police found her, she would never know; a bullet in back of the head and she would simply not wake up. That was fine with her; she didn't want to be awake anymore. In her dreams she could be with Monte and with Eric again. In her dreams she could forget she had lost everything; she wanted to sleep forever.

When Seese woke, her face and body had been sticky with sweat, and tiny black ants had been crawling over her feet and hands. She jumped up and brushed off the ants. She rubbed the skin on her legs and feet through torn panty hose. The dried blood had worn off her shoes and left only a dark stain. Seese imagined Tiny's corpse as a pig's carcass with a man's head; she could feel an invisible film of rancid oil on her ankles and feet, wherever Tiny's greasy blood had touched her skin. She could hear the rush-hour traffic on Interstate 10 and on Silverbell Road. The cops who had been searching for her would have finished their shift. It was almost nine A.M. Seese tried to wash up a little in the river so she could use the pay phone at the I-10 truck stop without attracting attention. The water felt so cool Seese had been tempted to drink some; she had expected the water to stink like shit, the way the air smelled near the sewage treatment plant. But all she had been able to smell had been the terrible odor of Tiny's blood as she tried to wash off her shoes and feet in the shallow water.

SCATTERED IN ALL DIRECTIONS

STERLING WOULD NEVER forget the morning Seese had not returned from town, and Ferro had learned his friend was dead. Lecha had rolled herself out to the kitchen in the wheelchair to get her medication. She had asked Sterling if he knew where Seese might have gone, then she had gone back to her bedroom. Sterling had been bundling up the garbage in the kitchen while Zeta sat at the table with Ferro and Paulie watching the morning news on TV. Ferro had been drinking from his cup of coffee when suddenly he had let the cup drop from his hands. Coffee had splashed the wall, and broken pieces of the cup scattered across the tile floor. Zeta and Paulie had both looked at Ferro, but Sterling saw Ferro's eyes were fixed on the TV screen, and the close-up photograph of a handsome young man with blue eyes and blond hair. The video report that had followed showed the interior of a dingy bar and two corpses in body bags leaving the bar one after the other. Ferro had bellowed like a wounded animal—"No! No!" Sterling heard Lecha's telephone ring, and then Lecha had called his name. "Sterling! Sterling! Quick!"

Sterling had wanted to alert Lecha to the developments in the kitchen, that someone Ferro knew had been killed, but Lecha had been in a hurry. She gave Sterling the keys to the old Lincoln and slipped a pistol from under a pillow into her purse. Then she got out of bed in her red silk robe and stepped into the wheelchair. She had seemed healthy enough to walk, and she wasn't crippled. She rolled herself around in a wheelchair; for sympathy and to fool the cops, she said, but still, Sterling had felt something was odd.

In the kitchen Paulie was on his hands and knees wiping up the spilled coffee; Sterling saw the paper towel had spots of blood where Paulie had cut himself on shards of the broken cup. Zeta had her arms around Ferro, who stood rigidly, resisting her comfort, shivering as if he were about to explode. Sterling saw wet streaks down Ferro's pale, fat cheeks. Lecha had looked at Ferro and Zeta, and at Paulie; Lecha had seen Ferro was upset, but Sterling knew her mind was on the phone call, and they had to hurry. Lecha had not told him, but Sterling thought he knew: it was Seese who had just called. Lecha didn't want Zeta to find out Seese was in trouble. Zeta had focused all her attention on Ferro as she tried to console him, and she did not look up even when Lecha and Sterling came into the room. Paulie had kept his head down, but Sterling saw the tears in his eyes.

Zeta could not stop the stampeding horses that had scattered in all directions—that had been her nightmare after the police shootings. Now Ferro had gone off with Paulie. Paulie wanted to park a junker car loaded with dynamite next to the Prince Road police substation. Zeta had seen the expression in Paulie's eyes; Paulie wanted more than anything to prove his love to Ferro now that the rival was dead. Paulie's devotion had only made Ferro's grief more fierce and Zeta was afraid Ferro might want to follow his boyfriend to the grave. Zeta's grief had surprised her, and she felt a terrible pain in her chest as if her grief had crowded her heart against her ribs.

She and Calabazas had been fools. Their lives were nearly over and what had they done? What good had all their talk of war against the United States government done? What good had all their lawbreaking done? The United States government intended to keep all the stolen land. What had happened to the earth? The Destroyers were killing the earth. What had happened to their sons? She loved Ferro; she didn't want him to die.

The time had arrived more quickly than any of the people had ever dreamed, and yet, all the forces had begun to converge. Lecha had learned a strange story from the gardener, Sterling.

A giant stone serpent had appeared overnight near a well-traveled road in New Mexico. According to the gardener, religious people from many places had brought offerings to the giant snake, but none had understood the meaning of the snake's reappearance; no one had got the message. But when Lecha had told Zeta, they had both got tears in their eyes because old Yoeme had warned them about the cruel years that were to come once the great serpent had returned. Zeta was grateful for the years she had had to prepare a little. Now she had to begin the important work.

Packing a great sidearm put a rare glow in Zeta's eyes. She had walked the dingy street along the railroad tracks and felt light on her feet because the .44 magnum was in her purse. Greenlee had phoned to say he was ready to do business. Zeta told Greenlee she'd sell him the .44 Blackhawk he wanted. Her hands weren't as steady anymore, and she wanted to buy a pistol that was less demanding.

Greenlee had never realized how much Zeta hated him. The more tense and stony faced she had been, the more animated and friendly Greenlee had become. Zeta had allowed the misunderstanding to continue for years because he had sold her guns without any questions. But now, messages from the South had indicated Greenlee was a key man.

Greenlee had waved off the six security men pointing Uzis when he saw it was only Zeta with the .44 Blackhawk in its holster. She was one of their "best customers," Greenlee had exclaimed as he pretended to scold the security guards for not recognizing Zeta. Zeta had always let Greenlee think she was swallowing the flattery with the lies. Today she smiled and winked at him. She wanted to be left alone with him in the huge basement vault; she wanted plenty of time, no hurry. She let Greenlee show her special laser scopes to fit handguns and examined an automatic rifle he had taken from the rack on the wall.

He had a hilarious new Indian joke for her too, Greenlee said as he answered the red phone next to the computer terminal. Zeta could barely stomach Greenlee's jokes; she knew the jokes were his way, his little test, for dealing with Mexicans or Indians and blacks. His theory had been that anybody who got huffy or hot while he told his nigger and beaner jokes would eventually try to cut his throat. "Cheaters win, and winners cheat," Greenlee liked to say. So he got them first. Greenlee thought his jokes and "tests" were foolproof.

Today Greenlee seemed enormously pleased with himself; Zeta knew business was good; Awa Gee had just intercepted computer data that revealed big transactions between Greenlee and Mr. B. Greenlee's small, pale-blue eyes were bloodshot. He had always watched Zeta's eyes as he told the jokes, and she had never flinched. Greenlee really liked this one, he said, "because it's about that TV broad—you know, what's her name? Bah-bah Wah-wah! So anyway the bitch is talking—interviewing this Indian chief."

Zeta smiled; she still had to marvel at the hatred white men harbored for all women, even their own.

"Oh, by the way," Greenlee added, "the joke's title is 'Never Trust an Indian.' "

Zeta had burst out laughing.

"I knew you'd really like that!" Greenlee said.

Zeta was still chuckling and had nodded her head. Zeta really was going to enjoy this one.

"So Bah-bah Wah-wah asks the chief why he has so many feathers, and he tells her, 'Me fuck them all—big, small, fat, tall—me fuck them all!' " Greenlee tried to imitate a falsetto scream. " 'Oh, you ought to be hung!' " he lisped, then Greenlee had bellowed, " 'You damn right me hung! Big like a buffalo, long like a snake!' "

Zeta had laughed out loud because everything essential to the world the white man saw was there in one dirty joke; she had laughed again because Freud had accused *women* of penis envy.

Greenlee had mistaken her laughter as a compliment and preened the hair at the edge of his shirt collar. "So Barbara Walters cries out, 'You don't have to be so hostile!' The chief says, 'Hoss style, dog style, wolf style, any style, me fuck them all!' " Here Greenlee had doubled over with laughter until his pale eyes watered.

Zeta smiled and had nodded to encourage Greenlee to laugh harder.

"So she cries out, 'Oh, dear!' The chief says, 'No deer—me fuck no deer. Asshole too high! Fuckers run too fast! No fuck deer!' " Greenlee had not laughed so hard before. Zeta could feel a chill at the base of her spine. Greenlee was almost hysterical, and Zeta could not resist laughing at the bright pink color of his face. How perfect his face was for this one moment! Ah, his laughter! How it echoed up and down air-conditioned aisles of the basement vault. "No fuck deer!" Greenlee kept repeating the punch line over and over.

"Bombproof, bulletproof, fireproof, but not foolproof!" Greenlee had loved to brag about his office in the basement vault. Because only a fool would dare attack this vault. Zeta had let the revolver rest comfortably on her lap after she had removed it from the holster. She had used both hands with the barrel at a perfect forty-five-degree angle the pistol butt braced against her stomach. "No, not foolproof," Zeta said as Greenlee's grin went flat on his face when he saw the pistol was cocked. "Soundproof though," Zeta said as she squeezed the trigger. Soundproof but not foolproof because only a fool fired a .44 magnum without earplugs. Zeta took her time. Greenlee's security unit would not return for hours unless Greenlee called them. The vault was off-limits. With her ears ringing, deaf as dirt, Zeta had gathered the disks and readouts Awa Gee needed to complete his work.

PART SIX

ONE WORLD, MANY TRIBES

BOOK ONE

PROPHECY

THE INTERNATIONAL HOLISTIC
HEALERS CONVENTION

ANGELITA LOOKED AROUND the ballroom of the Tucson resort carefully. She was alert for familiar faces from the Freedom School in Mexico City. If the Israelis or Chinese had sent spies to the International Holistic Healers Convention that meant they were on to the plan. She saw none of the familiar faces, but that did not mean there were no spies. She had left Wacah and El Feo in the mountains with the people. Hundreds of people kept coming to listen to Wacah talk about the ancient prophecies and explain the future. German and Dutch tourists had witnessed Wacah's sessions with the people, and soon a German television crew had trekked up the muddy paths with their equipment to record the odd new mystical movement among Indians in Mexico, who were growing their hair long and painting their faces again in imitation of the twin brothers, who served the macaw spirits, and who promised the people the ancient prophecies were about to be fulfilled.

The video cameras had recorded a slow but steady trickle of people, mostly Indian women and their children, trudging along muddy, steep paths and rutted, muddy roads. The people came from all directions, and many claimed they had been summoned in dreams. Wacah had proclaimed all human beings were welcome to live in harmony together. People from tribes farther south, peasants without land, *mestizos*, the homeless from the cities and even a busload of Europeans, had come to hear the spirit macaws speak through Wacah. The faithful waited quietly by their sleep shelters and belongings. After the German television report, the cash had started flowing in from "Indian lovers" in Belgium and

Germany. They had received a large amount of cash from a Swiss collector of pre-Columbian pottery in Basel. A people's army as big as theirs would not need weapons. Their sheer numbers were weapons enough. A people's army needed food. Wacah said the people would eat as long as they were with him. All they had to do was walk north with him.

After the cable news report there had been trouble. Authorities heard rumors that the native religion and prophecies were a cover, and the true business of Wacah and his brother was to stir up the Indians, who were always grumbling about stolen land. The Mexican federal police had sent truckloads of armed agents to search the mountains for secret caves suspected to contain caches of weapons the Indians had allegedly received from the Cubans. But even the four-wheel-drive trucks the police drove could not cross the landslides which the mountains had shaken down in previous weeks. Straggling in to the villages on foot, the police had found nothing; all the able-bodied had followed the twins. Those too sick or weak to travel said the mountain spirits were shaking the earth and would not stop until the white man's cities were destroyed.

The cable television news crew had still been at Wacah's camp when the federal police arrived; the calm of the people and the frenzy of the police had been televised all over the world. But the police had soon realized they were greatly outnumbered and they had withdrawn. Wacah's invitation to address the world convention of holistic healers had arrived within days of the federal police raid. But the spirit macaws would not permit Wacah or El Feo to leave. They had to walk with the people. Wacah and El Feo must not ride in automobiles or helicopters. The spirits required that the people walk. Wacah and El Feo had sent Angelita to the healers convention to make apologies for them, and to invite all those gathered to join them. All were welcome. It was only necessary to walk with the people and let go of all the greed and the selfishness in one's heart. One must be able to let go of a great many comforts and all things European; but the reward would be peace and harmony with all living things. All they had to do was return to Mother Earth. No more blasting, digging, or burning.

Wacah's message to the holistic healers assembly was to be prepared for the changes, welcome the arrival of the people, and send any money they could. All money went for food; the people were protected by the spirits and needed no weapons. The changes might require another hundred years, until the Europeans had been outnumbered and the people retook the land peacefully. All that might be okay for Wacah and El Feo, but Angelita had plans of her own. What Wacah and El Feo didn't know, wouldn't hurt them. Angelita was in charge of "advance planning." From villagers in Sonora, Angelita had heard about certain people and families living in Tucson who might wish to help.

Wacah, El Feo, and the people with them believed the spirit voices; if the people kept walking, if the people carried no weapons, then the old prophecies would come to pass, and all the dispossessed and the homeless would have land; the tribes of the Americas would retake the continents from pole to pole. They did not fear U.S. soldiers or bullets when they reached the border to the north because they did not believe the U.S. government would bomb its own border just to stop unarmed religious pilgrims. But Angelita wasn't so sure. The U.S. Treasury might be nearly empty, and the United States might be caught in civil unrest and strikes—but the white men would spend their last dime to stop the people from the South. The U.S. government might have no money for the starving, but there was always government money for weapons and death. The Mexican Treasury had been bankrupt for months, but still the federal police got paid. The U.S. was no different. The people themselves might be finished with wars, but their generals and business tycoons were not.

El Feo and Wacah had to obey the spirit macaws. What they might personally think did not matter. Wacah believed the spirits would protect them, but personally El Feo had agreed with Angelita La Escapía, his comrade-in-arms: the U.S. government might not wait for the twin brothers and the people to reach the border. The unarmed people would most likely be shot down before they even reached the border, but still they must have faith that even the federal police and the soldiers would be caught up by the spirits and swept along by the thousands. How long could the soldiers and police keep pulling the triggers? They might fall by the hundreds but still the people would keep walking; not running or screaming or fighting, but always walking. Their faith lay in the spirits of the earth and the mountains that casually destroyed entire cities. Their faith lay in the spirits outraged by the Europeans who had burned alive the sacred macaws and parrots of Tenochtitlán; for these crimes and all the killing and destruction, now the Europeans would suffocate in their burning cities without rain or water any longer.

El Feo told Angelita she must do what she felt was best. What was coming could not be stopped; the people might join or not; the tribal people of North America could come to the aid of the twins and their followers or they could choose not to help. It made no difference because what was coming was relentless and inevitable; it might require five or ten years of great violence and conflict. It might require a hundred years of spirit voices and simple population growth, but the result would be the same: tribal people would retake the Americas; tribal people would retake ancestral land all over the world. This was what earth's spirits wanted: her indigenous children who loved her and did not harm her.

The followers of the spirit macaws believed they must not shed blood or the destruction would continue to accompany them. But Wacah did say the pilgrims would be protected by natural forces set lose, forces raised by the spirits. Among these forces there would be human beings, warriors to defend the religious pilgrims. These warriors were already waiting far to the north. Wacah believed that one night the people would all dream the same dream, a dream sent by the spirits of the continent. The dream could not be sent until the people were ready to awaken with new hearts.

Angelita did not see how any spiritual change could take place overnight, especially not in the United States where the people of whatever color had become desperate in the collapse of the economy. Angelita did not believe in leaving the people or the twin brothers defenseless, even if the spirit macaw had said the end of the Europeans in the Americas was inevitable.

Angelita did not care if El Feo teased her or called her by her war name La Escapía, all the time. She wasn't taking any chances. She had come to the healers convention in Tucson to make contacts with certain people, the people with the weapons she needed to protect the followers of the spirit macaws from air attacks. Those amazing shoulder-mounted missiles worked as simply as holiday skyrockets. Angelita had fired one herself and it hadn't been much different from holding a Roman candle. The missiles were purely defensive measures, of course, against government helicopters and Wacah and El Feo need never know. Angelita heard from spirits too—only her spirits were furious and they told her to defend the people from attack.

WILSON WEASEL TAIL,
POET LAWYER

NO COP TROUBLES, no shootings, nothing was going to keep Lecha away from the International Holistic Healers Convention in Tucson that week. Newspaper ads for the convention had headlined native healers from all the continents, including medicine men from Siberia and Africa, and an Eskimo woman who might be her old acquaintance Rose. Lecha also did not want to miss the spectacle of Wilson Weasel Tail, who was on the convention program.

Lecha had met Wilson Weasel Tail on a cable-television talk show originating in Atlanta years before. Weasel Tail had gone out of control on the talk show; from the pockets of his powder-blue polyester suit, Wilson had taken a handful of index cards covered with the illegible scribbles of his "statement" in poem form. Studio technicians behind glass doors and behind the cameras had scurried and gestured frantically as blue, yellow, and red lights blinked. One of the Indians on the guest panel had seized the microphone! The talk show hostess had opened and shut her pink mouth like a beached fish, but no words came out. No one and nothing stopped Weasel Tail. His mission had come to him by virtue of where he had been born. Weasel Tail was Lakota, raised on a small, poor ranch forty miles from the Wounded Knee massacre site. Weasel Tail had dropped out of his third year at UCLA Law School to devote himself to poetry. The people didn't need more lawyers, the lawyers were the disease not the cure. The law served the rich. The people needed poetry; poetry would set the people free; poetry would speak to the dreams and to the spirits, and the people would understand what they must do.

Lecha had never forgot the success of Weasel Tail's rampage that afternoon on cable television. As soon as the producers realized they had another harmless nut case reading off greasy note cards, they had signaled security to stand by. The talk show hostess and studio audience were given reassuring messages on studio monitors and teleprompters.

Privately the assistant producers had probably congratulated themselves
for their shrewd choice of a militant Sioux Indian lawyer-poet for the
guest panel. A crazed Indian who commandeered the talk show was
exactly the true-life drama the home viewers endlessly craved.

Weasel Tail had introduced his poetry by explaining he had abandoned law school because the deck was stacked, and the dice were
loaded, in the white man's law. The law crushed and cheated the poor
whatever color they were. "All that is left is the power of poetry," Weasel
Tail had intoned, clearing his throat nervously.

> Only a bastard government
> Occupies stolen land!
>
> Hey, you barbarian invaders!
> How much longer?
> You think colonialism lasts forever?
> *Res ipsa loquitur!*
> Cloud on title
> Unmerchantable title
> Doubtful title
> Defective title
> Unquiet title
> Unclear title
> Adverse title
> Adverse possession
> Wrongful possession
> Unlawful possession!

Cable television was an enormous beast consuming twenty-four
hours a day; but even live television had to be choreographed. An assistant producer guided two huge blond women in security uniforms
through the tangle of cables in the direction of Weasel Tail. Weasel Tail
saw they were women cops with their revolvers drawn, so he could not
resist blurting out, "There will be no happiness to pursue; there will be
no peace or justice until you settle up the debt, the money owed for the
stolen land, and for all the stolen lives the U.S. empire rests on!" A
whole squad of cops had swarmed over the television studio but the
studio audience had refused to be evacuated from their $50 seats and
miss the drama and any violence. Still, Weasel Tail knew he would have
to hurry if he was going to read the full text of his indictment against
the United States of America and all other colonials.

We say, "Adios, white man," to
Five hundred years of
Criminals and pretenders
Illicit and unlawful governments,
Res accedent lumina rebus,
One thing throws light on another.

Worchester v. *Georgia!*
Ex parte Crow Dog!
Winters v. *United States!*
Williams v. *Lee!*
Lonewolf v. *Hitchcock!*
Pyramid Lake Paiute Tribe v. *Morton!*
Village of Kake, Alaska v. *Egan!*
Gila River Apache Tribe v. *Arizona!*

breach of close
breach of conscience
breach of contract
breach of convenant
breach of decency
breach of duty
breach of faith
breach of fiduciary responsibility
breach of promise
breach of peace
breach of trust
breach of trust with fraudulent intent!

Breach of the Treaty of the Sacred Black Hills!
Breach of the Treaty of the Sacred Blue Lake!
Breach of the Treaty of Guadalupe Hidalgo!

Res judicata!
We are at war.

"You of the *turpis causa!* Unlawful, unelected regimes! We the
indigenous people of the world demand justice!" Just as Wilson Weasel
Tail was saying "justice" four large male cops had lifted him off the
studio floor, two on each side, and had carried him away. Wilson Weasel
Tail had disappeared after his arrest on cable television, and now, years

later in Tucson, he had reappeared, but this time not as a lawyer-poet. This time Wilson Weasel Tail had billed himself as "a Lakota healer and visionary." Lecha wanted to hear what Weasel Tail had to say this time; as far as Lecha knew, Weasel Tail had no training of any kind in healing, Lakota or otherwise. Weasel Tail had sworn to take back stolen tribal land; he was a political animal, not a healer. Lecha wondered what new angle, what new scheme, Wilson Weasel Tail had up his sleeve. She wondered what someone from the Northern Plains was doing so close to the Mexican border.

Lecha wandered through a maze of dingy, carpeted hotel corridors that were lined with long Formica-top tables where hundreds of "the new age of spiritualism" converts displayed their services and wares for sale. Lecha had always tried to avoid "spiritualists" in the past; old Yoeme had taught them ninety-five percent of spiritual practitioners were frauds. Lecha was looking for Zeta or the little Asian who worked for her. Zeta claimed Awa Gee had intercepted coded fax messages from radical eco-terrorists who were planning to appear at the convention. Lecha had not asked what interest Zeta or Awa Gee had in the eco-terrorists or why the eco-terrorists wanted to address a world convention of natural healers.

MEDICINE MAKERS— CURES OF ALL KINDS

LECHA COULD ONLY shake her head in wonder. She had never seen German root doctors or Celtic leech handlers before. But most of the new-age spiritualists were whites from the United States, many who claimed to have been trained by 110-year-old Huichol Indians. Lecha searched the schedule of conference events for familiar names. Scheduled in the main ballroom that morning had been the following lectures:

. . .

Tilly Shay, colonic irrigation therapist, editor of the *Clean Colon Newsletter,* discusses the link between chronic constipation in the Anglo-Saxon male and the propensity for violence

The cosmic Oneness of Red Antler and White Dove (adopted members of the Abanaki Tribe). "Feel the nothingness of being through the emanating light of the sacred crystal"

George Armstrong—Intuitive Training and Meditation Power Sites
Jill Purcee—Tibetan Chanting
Frank Calfer—Universal Experiential Shamanism
Lee Locke—Women's Spirituality
Himalayan Bells—A Rare Concert at 2 P.M., Poolside, Donations
Soundscape, Rainbow Moods, Cosmic Connection, and the
     New Age: Where Next for Healing? 8 P.M., Tennis Courts

It would have been difficult to overlook Wilson Weasel Tail's portion of the program schedule because it filled half the page. Lecha had to laugh; Weasel Tail really knew how to get people's attention:

Stop time!
Have no fear of aging, illness, or death!
Secrets of ancient Native American healing
Hopi, Lakota, Yaqui, others
Kill or cripple enemies without detection
Summon up armies of warriors' ghosts!

Lecha glanced at a clock: there was half an hour before Weasel Tail spoke. Lecha had felt her heart beat faster when she read the last line in Weasel Tail's program about summoning armies of ghosts. Who had spiritual possession of the Americas? Not the Christians. Lecha remembered their mother had forbidden old Yoeme to slander Christianity in their presence, but of course that had not stopped Yoeme from telling Lecha and Zeta anything she wanted when their mother wasn't around. According to old Yoeme, the Catholic Church had been finished, a dead thing, even before the Spanish ships had arrived in the Americas. Yoeme had delighted in describing tortures and executions performed in the name of Jesus during the Inquisition. In a crude catechism book Yoeme had even showed them pictures, wood-block prints of churchmen burning "heretics" and breaking Jews on the wheel. Yoeme said the mask had slipped at that time, and all over Europe, ordinary people had understood in their hearts the "Mother Church" was a cannibal monster. Since the Europeans had no other gods or beliefs left, they had to continue the Church rituals and worship; but they knew the truth.

Yoeme said even idiots can understand a church that tortures and kills is a church that can no longer heal; thus the Europeans had arrived in the New World in precarious spiritual health. Christianity might work on other continents and with other human beings; Yoeme did not dispute those possibilities. But from the beginning in the Americas, the outsiders had sensed their Christianity was somehow inadequate in the face of the immensely powerful and splendid spirit beings who inhabited the vastness of the Americas. The Europeans had not been able to sleep soundly on the American continents, not even with a full military guard. They had suffered from nightmares and frequently claimed to see devils and ghosts. Cortés's men had feared the medicine and the procedures they had brought with them from Europe might lack power on New World soil; almost immediately, the wounded Europeans had begun to dress their wounds in the fat of slain Indians.

Lecha had not appreciated Yoeme's diagnosis of Christianity until she had worked a while as a psychic. Lecha had seen people who claimed to be devout believers with rosary beads in their hands, yet they were terrified. Affluent, educated white people, upstanding Church members, sought out Lecha in secret. They all had come to her with a deep sense that something had been lost. They all had given the loss different names: the stock market crash, lost lottery tickets, worthless junk bonds or lost loved ones; but Lecha knew the loss was their connection with the earth. They all feared illness and physical change; since life led to death, consciousness terrified them, and they had sought to control death by becoming killers themselves.

Once the earth had been blasted open and brutally exploited, it was only logical the earth's offspring, all the earth's beings, would similarly be destroyed. The international convention had been called by natural and indigenous healers to discuss the earth's crisis. As the prophecies had warned, the earth's weather was in chaos; the rain clouds had disappeared while terrible winds and freezing had followed burning, dry summers. Old Yoeme had always said the earth would go on, the earth would outlast anything man did to it, including the atomic bomb. Yoeme used to laugh at the numbers, the thousands of years before the earth would be purified, but eventually even the radiation from a nuclear war would fade out. The earth would have its ups and downs; but humans had been raping and killing their own nestlings at such a rate Yoeme said humans might not survive. The humans would not be a great loss to the earth. The energy or "electricity" of a being's spirit was not extinguished by death; it was set free from the flesh. Dust to dust or as a meal for pack rats, the energy of the spirit was never lost. Out of the dust grew the plants; the plants were consumed and became muscle and bone; and all the time, the energy had only been changing form, nothing had been lost or destroyed.

Lecha had to laugh to herself. The earth must truly be in crisis for both Zeta and Calabazas to be attending this convention. Calabazas must be getting old because he had been listening to his loco lieutenant, Mosca, who had wild stories about a barefooted Hopi with radical schemes, and new reports about the spirit macaws carried by the twin brothers on a sacred journey north accompanied by thousands of the faithful.

The hotel conference rooms and lobby areas were swarming with people of all ages and origins. Lecha could sense their urgency and desperation as they milled around ushers who collected ten dollars at the entrance of the ballroom where Wilson Weasel Tail was scheduled to speak. Lecha saw a hotel conference room full of women chanting over and over, "I am goddess, I am goddess." In the next room freshly cut evergreen trees were tenderly arranged in a circle by white men wearing robes; it looked as if tree worship was making a comeback in northern Europe. In the corridors there were white-haired old hippies selling cheap crystals and little plastic bags of homegrown chamomile. There were white men from California in expensive new buckskins, beads, and feathers who had called themselves "Thunder-roll" and "Buffalo Horn." African medicine men seven feet tall stood next to half-pint Incas and Mayas selling dry stalks of weeds wrapped in strips of dirty rag. Lecha watched for a while; she had watched the hands. The hands had gripped the cash feverishly as they waited for their turn; old Yoeme used to brag that she could make white people believe in anything and do anything she told them because the whites were so desperate. Money was changing hands rapidly; fifties and hundreds seemed to drop effortlessly from the white hands into the brown and the black hands. Some bought only the herbs or teas, but others had bought private consultations which cost hundreds of dollars.

Lecha had not been able to get close enough to the Incas or the Mayas to hear what they were saying. Two interpreters appeared to be attempting to translate for the crowd, but they had momentarily been involved in disagreement over the translation of a word. Lecha could not help noticing a short, wide Maya woman who seemed to be studying the crowd; suddenly the Maya woman had turned and looked Lecha right in the eye. Yoeme used to warn them about traveling medicine people, because witches and sorcerers often found it necessary to go to distant towns where their identities were not known. Lecha turned and saw a woman holding a walrus tusk, surrounded by spellbound listeners. Lecha's heart beat faster and she felt a big smile on her face; she would have recognized that Eskimo anywhere!

Rose had talked to Lecha as if the crowd of spectators had not been there. The more Rose seemed to ignore the people, the more quiet and intense the crowd had become as they sought to hear each word between the two short, dark women. Rose had begun talking about the years since Lecha had abandoned the dogsled racer for warmer country and faster men.

Rose had learned to talk to her beloved little sisters and brothers who were ghosts in blue flames running along the river. Of course Rose did not speak to them the way she was talking to Lecha now. The blue flames burned with a loud blowtorch sound that would have made words impossible to understand even if her sweet ones could have talked. But no sounds came from their throats; when they opened their mouths, Rose saw the words written in flames—not even complete words, but Rose could understand everything they had to say.

Lecha had felt the crowd press closer, but at that instant, Rose stood up and caused the spectators to step back quickly and respectfully. Rose pointed at a big suitcase near Lecha's feet. Rose lifted the lid; inside, all Lecha saw were white river pebbles and small gray river stones. Rose nodded at the rocks and then at the well-dressed young white people lining up obediently to buy whatever the Yupik Eskimo medicine woman had to sell. "Some of us are getting together later in my room," Rose said, "after Weasel Tail and the Hopi speak. Room twelve twelve."

THE RETURN
OF THE BUFFALO

WILSON WEASEL TAIL strode up to the podium and whipped out two sheets of paper. Weasel Tail had abandoned his polyester leisure suits for army camouflage fatigues; he wore his hair in long braids carefully wrapped in red satin ribbon. Weasel Tail's voice boomed throughout the main ballroom. Today he wanted to begin his lecture by reading two fragments of famous Native American documents. "First, I read to you from Pontiac's manuscript:

" 'You cry the white man has stolen everything, killed all your animals and food. But where were you when the people first discussed the Europeans? Tell the truth. You forgot everything you were ever told. You forgot the stories with warnings. You took what was easy to swallow, what you never had to chew. You were like a baby suddenly helpless in the white man's hands because the white man feeds your greed until it swells up your belly and chest to your head. You steal from your neighbors. You can't be trusted!' "

Weasel Tail had paused dramatically and gazed at the audience before he continued:

"Treachery has turned back upon itself. Brother has betrayed brother. Step back from envy, from sorcery and poisoning. Reclaim these continents which belong to us."

Weasel Tail paused, took a deep breath, and read the Paiute prophet Wovoka's letter to President Grant:

You are hated
You are not wanted here
Go away,
Go back where you came from.
You white people are cursed!

The audience in the main ballroom had become completely still, as if in shock from Weasel Tail's presentation. But Weasel Tail seemed not to notice and had immediately launched into his lecture.

"Today I wish to address the question as to whether the spirits of the ancestors in some way failed our people when the prophets called them to the Ghost Dance," Weasel Tail began.

"Moody and other anthropologists alleged the Ghost Dance disappeared because the people became disillusioned when the ghost shirts did not stop bullets and the Europeans did not vanish overnight. But it was the Europeans, not the Native Americans, who had expected results overnight; the anthropologists, who feverishly sought magic objects to postpone their own deaths, had misunderstood the power of the ghost shirts. Bullets of lead belong to the everyday world; ghost shirts belong to the realm of spirits and dreams. The ghost shirts gave the dancers spiritual protection while the white men dreamed of shirts that repelled bullets because they feared death."

Moody and the others had never understood the Ghost Dance was to reunite living people with the spirits of beloved ancestors lost in the five-hundred-year war. The longer Wilson Weasel Tail talked, the more animated and energized he became; Lecha could see he was about to launch into a poem:

We dance to remember,
we dance to remember all our beloved ones,
to remember how each passed
to the spirit world.
We dance because the dead love us,
they continue to speak to us,
they tell our hearts what must be done to survive.
We dance and we do not forget all the others
        before us,
the little children and the old women who fought
        and who died
resisting the invaders and destroyers of Mother
        Earth!
Spirits! Ancestors!
we have been counting the days, watching the
        signs.
You are with us every minute,
you whisper to us in our dreams,
you whisper in our waking moments.
You are more powerful than memory!

Weasel Tail paused to take a sip of water. Lecha was impressed with the silence Weasel Tail had created in the main ballroom. "Naturopaths," holistic healers, herbalists, the guys with the orgone boxes and pyramids—all of them had locked up their cashboxes and closed their booths to listen to Weasel Tail talk. "The spirits are outraged! They demand justice! The spirits are furious! To all those humans too weak or too lazy to fight to protect Mother Earth, the spirits say, 'Too bad you did not die fighting the destroyers of the earth because now *we* will kill you for being so weak, for wringing your hands and whimpering while the invaders committed outrages against the forests and the mountains.' The spirits will harangue you, they will taunt you until you are forced to silence the voices with whiskey day after day. The spirits allow you no rest. The spirits say die fighting the invaders or die drunk."

The enraged spirits haunted the dreams of society matrons in the suburbs of Houston and Chicago. The spirits had directed mothers from country club neighborhoods to pack the children in the car and drive off hundred-foot cliffs or into flooding rivers, leaving no note for the husbands. A message to the psychiatrist says only, "It is no use any longer." They see no reason for their children or them to continue. The spirits whisper in the brains of loners, the crazed young white men with automatic rifles who slaughter crowds in shopping malls or school yards as casually as hunters shoot buffalo. All day the miner labors in tunnels underground, hacking out ore with a sharp steel hand-pick; he returns home to his wife and family each night. Then suddenly the miner slaughters his wife and children. The "authorities" call it "mental strain" because he has used his miner's hand-pick to chop deep into the mother lode to reach their hearts and their brains.

Weasel Tail cleared his throat, then went on, "How many dead souls are we talking about? Computer projections place the populations of the Americas at more than seventy million when the Europeans arrived; one hundred years later, only ten million people had survived. Sixty million dead souls howl for justice in the Americas! They howl to retake the land as the black Africans have retaken their land!

"You think there is no hope for indigenous tribal people here to prevail against the violence and greed of the destroyers? But you forget the inestimable power of the earth and all the forces of the universe. You forget the colliding meteors. You forget the earth's outrage and the trembling that will not stop. Overnight the wealth of nations will be reclaimed by the Earth. The trembling does not stop and the rain clouds no longer gather; the sun burns the earth until the plants and animals disappear and die.

"The truth is the Ghost Dance did not end with the murder of Big Foot and one hundred and forty-four Ghost Dance worshipers at Wounded Knee. The Ghost Dance has never ended, it has continued, and the people have never stopped dancing; they may call it by other names, but when they dance, their hearts are reunited with the spirits of beloved ancestors and the loved ones recently lost in the struggle. Throughout the Americas, from Chile to Canada, the people have never stopped dancing; as the living dance, they are joined again with all our ancestors before them, who cry out, who demand justice, and who call the people to take back the Americas!"

Weasel Tail threw back his shoulders and puffed out his chest; he was going to read poetry:

The spirit army is approaching,
The spirit army is approaching,
The whole world is moving onward,
The whole world is moving onward.
See! Everybody is standing watching.
See! Everybody is standing watching.

The whole world is coming,
A nation is coming, a nation is coming,
The Eagle has brought the message to the tribe.
The father says so, the father says so.

Over the whole earth they are coming.
The buffalo are coming, the buffalo are coming,
The Crow has brought the message to the tribe,
The father says so, the father says so.

I'yche'! ana'nisa'na'—Uhi'yeye'heye'!
I'yche'! ana'nisa'na'—Uhi'yeye'heye'!
I'yehe'! ha'dawu'hana'—Eye'ae'yuhe'yu!
I'yehe'! ha'dawu'hana'—Eye'ae'yuhe'yu!
Ni'athu'-a-u'a'haka'nith'ii—Ahe'yuhe'yu!

[Translation]
I'yehe'! my children—Uhi'yeye'heye'!
I'yehe'! my children—Uhi'yeye'heye'!
I'yehe'! we have rendered them
desolate—Eye'ae'yuhe'yu!
I'yehe'! we have rendered them
desolate—Eye'ae'yuhe'yu!
The whites are crazy—Ahe'yuhe'yu!

Again, when Weasel Tail had finished, the ballroom was hushed; then the audience had given Weasel Tail a standing ovation.

"Have the spirits let us down? Listen to the prophecies! Next to thirty thousand years, five hundred years look like nothing. The buffalo are returning. They roam off federal land in Montana and Wyoming. Fences can't hold them. Irrigation water for the Great Plains is disappearing, and so are the farmers, and their plows. Farmers' children retreat to the cities. Year by year the range of the buffalo grows a mile or two larger."

Weasel Tail had them eating out of his hand; he let his voice trail off dramatically to a stage whisper that had resonated throughout the ballroom speaker system. The audience leapt to its feet with a great ovation. Lecha had to hand it to Wilson Weasel Tail; he'd learned a thing or two. Still, Weasel Tail was a lawyer at heart; Lecha noted that he had made the invaders an offer that couldn't be refused. Weasel Tail had said to the U.S. government, "Give back what you have stolen or else as a people you will continue your self-destruction."

GREEN VENGEANCE— ECO-WARRIORS

THERE WERE FORTY-FIVE minutes of recess before the Barefoot Hopi made the keynote speech. Lecha had searched until she located Zeta, sitting with her computer expert, Awa Gee. Awa Gee had intercepted a coded fax message that the eco-warriors planned to make a surprise appearance at the healers convention. Zeta looked exhausted and nervous. Neither of them had had much sleep since the shooting. Ferro had not known his lover was an undercover cop. But then Lecha had not known Seese had kept a kilo of cocaine in her closet either. Secrets and coincidences involving cocaine didn't surprise Lecha anymore; how odd that Zeta seemed so upset. Lecha whispered in Zeta's ear, "What's the matter?" Zeta had looked around, then leaned close and whispered, "I killed Greenlee yesterday." Lecha nodded. So the time had come.

Ferro was the problem now; Ferro had loaded a junker car with six hundred pounds of dynamite to park outside the Prince Road police substation. Zeta had tried to persuade Ferro to hold off retaliation at least until the preparations she and Awa Gee had been making through the computer networks had been completed. They only needed time for Awa Gee to run Greenlee's access numbers, but Ferro had refused to listen. Still Ferro couldn't make a bomb that size overnight. Awa Gee's guess had been it would take a week for a competent bomb maker to load the car properly and wire it correctly to the detonation device.

Just when Zeta was beginning to think the holistic medicine convention was a bust, a great commotion had developed near the steps to the ballroom stage and podium at the far end. Zeta and Lecha had both stood up, but they were too short; Awa Gee leaped up on his chair where he could see over all the heads. "There!" Awa Gee said. He excitedly patted Zeta on the shoulder. "I told you they'd come!"

The two eco-warriors wore ski masks and identical camouflage jumpsuits; they did not appear to be armed and Zeta saw no bodyguards around the podium. The eco-warriors had motioned for the audience to take its seats, and there on the stage with the eco-warriors Zeta saw the Barefoot Hopi impeccably dressed in a three-piece suit and tie and wearing Hopi moccasins instead of boots or shoes. The Hopi stood close to the eco-warriors, who were listening intently to the Hopi. The rumors about the alliance between the Hopi's organization and the Green Vengeance group apparently were true. Zeta was in agreement with the tactic. Green Vengeance eco-warriors would make useful allies at least at the start. Green Vengeance had a great deal of wealth behind their eco-warrior campaigns.

A convention organizer had announced the Hopi was going to introduce a special unscheduled appearance of Green Vengeance, who came with an urgent message. The noise in the main ballroom and in the corridors outside had hushed as the Hopi approached the microphone; a buzz of whispers began as the Hopi had pressed a button on the podium, and a giant video screen lowered to the center of the stage.

"Friends, you have all heard state and federal authorities blame 'structural failure' for the collapse of Glen Canyon Dam. Now you are about to see videotape footage never before made public by our allies in the struggle, Green Vengeance, eco-warriors in the defense of the earth!"

The ballroom's overhead lights had dimmed, and a jerky sequence, videotaped from a moving vehicle, filled the giant screen. The sound track and any voices on the videotape had been deliberately removed. The brilliant burnt reds and oranges of the sandstone formations and the dark green juniper bushes flashing past appeared to be Utah or northern Arizona. Next came interiors of motel rooms with figures in ski masks and camouflage clothing standing by motel beds stacked with assault rifles and clips of ammunition. The camera had avoided the masked faces and focused instead on the hands carefully arranging black boxes in nests of foam rubber; the foam-rubber bundles were packed carefully inside nylon backpacks. A close-up of a black box before its lid was closed showed a nine-volt battery and wires. On the worn gold motel bedspread, the hands had strung the six backpacks together with bright blue wire. Awa Gee leaned over and whispered in Zeta's ear, "I can't wait to see this!"

Next, the screen had been filled with highway signs and U.S. park service signs; in the background was the huge concrete mass that had trapped the Colorado River and had created Lake Powell.

GLEN CANYON DAM; the sign had filled the entire screen. Next the concrete bulwark of the dam came into focus; tiny figures dangled off ropes down the side of the dam. At first none of the park service employees or bystanders and tourists appear to notice. Then the camera had zoomed in for close-ups of each of the six eco-warriors, each with a backpack loaded with explosives in the motel room. Zeta had been thinking the six resembled spiders on a vast concrete wall when suddenly the giant video screen itself appeared to crack and shatter in slow motion, and the six spiderlike figures had disappeared in a white flash of smoke and dust. The entire top half of the dam structure had folded over, collapsing behind a giant wall of reddish water. Zeta heard gasps from the audience.

"A massive structural failure due to fault asymmetries and earth tremors," the eco-warrior said in mocking tones amid the excited voices and cheers. Zeta looked around; the audience was on its feet. "Your government lies to you because it fears you. They don't want you to know that six eco-warriors gave their lives to free the mighty Colorado!" The audience cheered. The eco-warrior handed the microphone to his partner. Zeta glanced at Awa Gee, who sat motionless, spellbound by what he was seeing and hearing.

The eco-warrior who spoke next was a woman. She spoke calmly about the choice of when and how one was going to die. She continued calmly, relating the states of awareness she had passed through; for a time, she said, she had not wanted to resort to the destruction of property or the loss of human lives, but after their beloved leader had been murdered by FBI agents, her eyes had been opened. This was war. The new enemies, she said, were the space station and biosphere tycoons who were rapidly depleting rare species of plants, birds, and animals so the richest people on earth could bail out of the pollution and revolutions and retreat to orbiting paradise islands of glass and steel. What few species and what little pure water and pure air still remained on earth would be harvested for these space colonies. Lazily orbiting in the glass and steel cocoons of these elaborate "biospheres," the rich need not fear the rabble while they enjoyed their "natural settings" complete with freshwater pools and jungles filled with rare parrots and orchids. The artificial biospheres were nothing more than orbiting penthouses for the rich. Three thousand eight hundred species of flora and fauna are required for each artificial biosphere to attain self-sufficiency. Eco-warriors had infiltrated the artificial biosphere projects at all levels; plans had already been made for the final abandonment of earth. At the end, the last of the clean water and the uncontaminated soil, the last healthy animals and plants, would be removed from earth to the orbiting biospheres to "protect" them from the pollution on earth.

The eco-warrior paused to clear her throat. People in the audience raised their hands frantically to ask questions, but she ignored them. "All orbiting telescopes and space stations will be turned back on the earth to monitor the human masses for as long as they survive. The orbiting biospheres will require fresh air and fresh water supplies from time to time; giant flexible tubes will drop down from the sky to suck water and air from the earth. If the people on earth attempt to destroy or sabotage the giant feeding tubes, lasers from satellites and space stations will destroy the rebels and rioters." The eco-warrior paused, then shouted, "This is war! We are not afraid to die to save the earth!"

"Hard act to follow," Lecha had whispered to Zeta as the eco-warriors left the stage.

Zeta had read the messages Awa Gee had intercepted from the eco-warriors. The eco-warriors had lost their beloved leader to a car bomb. They were determined to give him glory. They were determined to turn out the lights on the United States one night. They were determined to destroy all interstate high-voltage transmission lines, power generating plants, and hydroelectric dams across the United States simultaneously. Their scheme did not seem quite so improbable now that Zeta had seen the videotape. The six kamikaze eco-warriors disappearing into the collapsing wall of Glen Canyon Dam was a stunning sight, Zeta agreed. No wonder the U.S. government and Arizona state authorities had blamed the destruction of Glen Canyon Dam on "structural failure." Naturally the authorities had feared copycat bombings of hydroelectric dams.

Awa Gee knew from the intercepted messages the government had begun sweeping arrests of all persons affiliated with environmental action groups; even people with the Audubon Society and the U.S. Forest Service employees had been accused of being "secret eco-warriors." Awa Gee was always reminded of South Korea when he heard about mass arrests by police. The United States had been different when Awa Gee had first arrived from Seoul by way of Sonora. Awa Gee remembered that back then the world economy had still been riding on the big wave; to Americans, Awa Gee had looked Japanese. Back then, all the Americans had been able to talk about were Japanese cars this and Japanese cars that. Love-hate between Japan and the United States, two countries Awa Gee had despised for their racism and imperialism. Zeta had thought Awa Gee could not hope to get much help from the eco-warriors now that the government had begun to round up all of them for "protective custody." But Awa Gee thought about the situation differently; the police had only caught the law-abiding eco-warriors with families and jobs. Awa Gee didn't think people with jobs and families were worth much as subversives anyway.

Awa Gee had high hopes for these Green Vengeance eco-warriors. Green Vengeance was hard-core; one of the eco-warriors who had died blowing up Glen Canyon Dam had been a gay rights activist ill with AIDS. No wonder government authorities had denied all reports of sabotage or loss of human life at Glen Canyon Dam's collapse. Awa Gee had intercepted the gay eco-warrior's last message to his family, colleagues, and friends. Awa Gee had kept the computer readout of the eco-warrior's message although he knew it was risky to keep such evidence.

Dear lovers, brothers, mothers, and sisters!
Go out in glory!
Go out with dignity!
Go out while you're still feeling good and *looking*
    good!
Avenge gay genocide by the U.S. government!
Die to save the earth.
Mold long underwear out of plastic explosives and stroll past
the U.S. Supreme Court building while the justices are hearing
arguments. Bolt in the exit door and flick the switch! Turn out
the lights on the High Court of the police state!

Awa Gee believed very soon these last remaining eco-warriors
would push forward with their plot to turn off the lights. From messages
he had intercepted he had concluded that a good many eco-warriors
had gone underground at the time their leader was assassinated. Awa
Gee decided he would help the eco-warriors turn out the lights, although
they might never even know Awa Gee's contribution.

The regional power suppliers had emergency generating plants and
used sophisticated computer systems to deal with brownouts, storms,
or other electric power failures by automatically rerouting power reserve
supplies to black-out areas and by switching on emergency power-gen-
erating systems. But Awa Gee had already developed a protovirus to
subvert all emergency switching programs in the computers of regional
power-relay stations. Awa Gee's virus would activate only during extreme voltage fluctuations such as might occur after the coordinated
sabotage of key hydroelectric dams and interstate high-voltage lines
across the United States. To destroy every last generator and high-voltage
line would be doing the people a favor; alternating electrical current
caused brain cancer and genetic mutations. Solar batteries were the wave
of the future. The plan was a long shot; Awa Gee was counting on the
"cost cutting" of the giant power companies to curtail or cancel auxiliary
emergency systems. But if the plan worked, if the lights went out all
over all at once, then the United States would never be the same again.

DESTINY'S PATH

MOSCA HAD INSISTED it was safe for him to drive Calabazas and Root to the holistic healers convention to hear the Barefoot Hopi. Mosca announced he wasn't hiding or leaving town; he had some other tricks yet to play; Mosca was just getting started. The Tucson police believed Mosca had fled to Mexico; the Tucson police had ruffled some feathers and they did not want to think about the little Mexican Indian. Mosca enjoyed the stupidity of the Tucson police. To them he was a nothing, a coincidence, a sneak thief accidentally in the right place at the right time to snatch the briefcase.

Mosca could feel his life and his fate shifting inside him; the voice in his shoulder gave good advice and strategy. Mosca wasn't the least worried. Something was happening, and the earth would never be the same again. So far, thanks to his genius, Mosca had the white men in Tucson fighting one another—all part of the Hopi's strategy, all part of the coordinated effort. Mosca couldn't stop himself; on the drive to the convention he had to brag to Calabazas and Root: the Barefoot Hopi had given Mosca a sneak preview of his keynote speech. One strategy the Hopi had emphasized had been the "international coordinated effort." The Hopi had traveled to Africa and Asia; he had been around the world to meet with indigenous tribal people. The strategy was to ensure when the time came, the United States would get no aid from foreign allies to crush the uprisings in the United States. The Hopi believed the Europeans would be too concerned about their own civil unrest and the mass human migrations north from Africa, to care what happened inside the U.S.

In his lectures the Barefoot Hopi had emphasized the similarity between the tribal people of Africa and the tribal people of the Americas. Many in his audiences had been shocked that the Hopi dare refer, even indirectly, to the South African holocaust in which thousands of whites and Africans had died after white South Africa had refused to give back the land. The Hopi said black Africans talked about the price they had paid in blood to take back the land; the spirits had been furious and had demanded blood in retribution for the sacrileges the people had allowed against the spirits. Their lands had been reconsecrated to Ogoun and Damballah with European as well as African blood. The Hopi had got promises from a dozen African nations; if the natives of the Americas rose up, the African nations would not remain neutral. The Hopi's plan depended upon the help of "foreign allies" in the Persian Gulf region also.

As they pulled into the hotel parking lot, Mosca had announced he was quitting Calabazas to work with the Hopi. Calabazas had looked relieved. Root knew Calabazas hated to fire anyone; Calabazas had hired Mosca in the first place because no one else in Tucson wanted the risk. Root thought Calabazas looked tired and older since Mosca had shot the British poet. There had also been the matter of Sarita and Liria with their secret meetings and mysterious two-day treks into the desert, and the vanloads of smuggled Guatemalan refugees driven by nuns and priests. All that worry might make even a young man old before his time, but Calabazas was no colt.

As they walked from the hotel parking lot, Mosca had asked Root to come with him and the Hopi. "Go where? Do what?" Root did not believe any of that spiritual horseshit. Mosca looked a little hurt at Root's snippy reply. "Look, man, we use handicapped people in our army. You're good enough for us—aren't we good enough for you?" Mosca turned to Calabazas and ignored Root. I talked to the Hopi. The way we used to move dope—now we move supplies to the people across the border." Calabazas laughed and shook his head. "Your Barefoot Hopi is crazy. The government will stop him." Mosca began nodding his head excitedly. "But don't you see? They can't stop the Hopi because he *is* crazy. But a crazy man can get things done. Especially a crazy man like the Hopi."

Calabazas had never seen anything like the natural healing convention; hundreds of people had filled the ballroom, and all or nearly all of them were young and white. Calabazas had been surprised at the prices these so-called native healers demanded and received from white people who looked too intelligent to believe in nonsense. But of course what could be expected of people who thought they could buy a cure in a tablet? Calabazas looked over the booths in the area; he saw slow brown hands receive cash from anxious white hands. "You know, all this time we were in the wrong business," Calabazas had finally said, nodding in the direction of a display of rock crystals and wind chimes for a hundred dollars. Root had nodded. He was beginning to see what the Hopi had in mind; holistic medicine was a worldwide phenomenon that had generated billions of dollars. The Hopi planned to make thousands of white "converts" to aid and protect the twin brothers and their followers.

Angelita had never seen anything like it, not even at the May Day rallies they had celebrated at the Freedom School in Mexico City. She was relieved she did not actually have to address the convention but only had to say a few words, to relay the greetings from the twin brothers and their followers bound on destiny's path north. Angelita felt the undercurrent of excitement in the audience. Were the twins right? Was the time ripe? But then came the Barefoot Hopi.

The audience settled into its seats as the Barefoot Hopi approached the podium. He was looking closely at the audience, but the expression on the Hopi's face was serene. "The brave liberators of the Colorado River left a farewell message," the Barefoot Hopi said. "Here's what they wrote: 'Rejoice! Mountains and valleys! The mighty river runs free once more! Rejoice! We are no longer solitary beings alone and cut off. Now we are one with the earth, our mother; we are at one with the river. Now we have returned to our source, the energy of the universe. Rejoice!' "

When the Hopi had finished reading, there was silence in the ballroom. The Hopi continued, "We know death awaits all living beings as part of a single continuing process. The brave eco-warriors focused all the energy of their beings to set free the river, and so they merged instantly in the explosion of water and concrete and sandstone. They are no longer solitary human souls; they are part of a single configuration of energy. Their spirits are close with us now as we all gather here. They love us and watch over us with our beloved ancestors."

Lecha looked around at the audience; the Hopi's performance had been flawless. Mosca was right; the Hopi seemed to know exactly what the audience had wanted to hear. Lecha was fascinated with the Barefoot Hopi; he was as tall as he was round. He weighed over three hundred pounds easily, but his flesh was solid, and he moved with the energy and odd grace of a bear. Lecha guessed his age to be somewhere around forty; her information had come from Calabazas, who had heard it from Mosca. The Hopi had spent more than a year with various tribal groups all across Africa. Mosca claimed the Hopi had been meeting with African leaders to get them to send money when the people began the final struggle to retake ancestral lands in the Americas.

The Hopi had paused to look the audience in the eyes, row by row.

He cleared his throat and began, "The eco-warriors have been accused of terrorism in the cause of saving Mother Earth. So I want to talk a little about terrorism first. Poisoning our water with radioactive wastes, poisoning our air with military weapons' wastes—*those* are acts of terrorism! Acts of terrorism committed by governments against their citizens all over the world. Capital punishment is terrorism practiced by the government against its citizens. United States of America, what has happened to you? What have you done to the Bill of Rights? All along we Native Americans tried to warn the rest of you; if the U.S. government kills us and robs us, what makes the rest of you think the U.S. government won't rob and kill you too? Look around you. Police roadblocks. Police searches without warrants. Politicians and their banker pals empty the U.S. Treasury while police lock up the homeless and poor who beg for food. The U.S. government dares to outlaw the Native American Church religion. Butt out of our religion!" the Hopi's voice boomed out. "You spiritual bankrupts! You breeders of child molesters, rapists, and mass murderers! We are increasing quietly despite your bullets and germ warfare. You destroyers can't figure out why you haven't wiped us out in five hundred years of blasting, burning, and slaughter. You destroyers can't figure out what is going wrong for you. You don't know how much the spirits of these continents despise you, how the earth hates you; now your cities burn from the sun, and millions abandon cities in the Southwest for lack of water. This is nothing! This is only the beginning!"

The people in the audience rose to their feet simultaneously. Lecha felt the hair on her neck stand up; the people had been mesmerized by the Hopi's voice. Affluent young whites, fearful of a poisoned planet, men and women both, had fallen in love with the strong, resonant voice which promised that all human beings belonged to the earth forever. He promised a force was gathering that would counter the destruction of earth. Lecha could tell the Hopi knew when he had a winner; she imagined the Hopi had been able to raise a great deal of money in Europe and in Asia, because even in a dirt-water town that hated brown people as Tucson did, the Barefoot Hopi already had people fumbling for their checkbooks, and he was only getting warmed up.

"All the riches ripped from the heart of the earth will be reclaimed by the oceans and mountains. Earthquakes and volcanic eruptions of enormous magnitude will devastate the accumulated wealth of the Pacific Rim. Entire coastal peninsulas will disappear under the sea; hundreds of thousands will die. The west coast of the Americas will be swept clean from Alaska to Chile in tidal waves and landslides. Drought and wildfire will rage across Europe to Asia. Only Africa will be spared because the anger of the spirits has already been appeased by the rivers of blood in the great war that freed South Africa."

Zeta had turned to Lecha to nod her approval of the Hopi; then Awa Gee tapped Zeta's shoulder and began whispering excitedly in Zeta's ear. Lecha could see that Mosca had jumped up from his chair he was so excited. Even Calabazas had sat up in his chair, wide-awake. Lecha could see the Hopi gather himself for his finale; he spread his short legs and held the podium with both hands.

"Now on the eve of the final destruction of mankind, now when all seems hopeless and the greed of the destroyers unstoppable, now in our time of greatest peril, the twin brothers who have always helped our people, the twin brothers are on their way!"

Lecha heard gasps all around her; the room began to buzz with excitement. The Hopi continued in an even voice, "In Africa and in the Americas too, the giant snakes, Damballah and Quetzalcoatl, have returned to the people. I have seen the snakes with my own eyes; they speak to the people of Africa, and they speak to the people of the Americas; they speak through dreams. The snakes say this: From out of the south the people are coming, like a great river flowing restless with the spirits of the dead who have been reborn again and again all over Africa and the Americas, reborn each generation more fierce and more numerous. Millions will move instinctively; unarmed and unguarded, they begin walking steadily north, following the twin brothers."

The Hopi paused and motioned at the big Maya Indian woman Lecha had noticed earlier. "We are privileged to have with us today Angelita La Escapía, with a message from the twin brothers."

As soon as the big Mayan woman reached the podium and looked out at the audience, Lecha had seen she was no ordinary envoy; in fact, Lecha saw the woman was at least as powerful as the twin brothers she claimed to serve. The Maya woman spoke calmly and clearly in Spanish, but the conference had provided no interpreter. Lecha wondered how many in the audience understood her. The message was quite simple. There was nothing to fear or to worry about. People should go about their daily routines. Because already the great shift of human populations on the continents was under way, and there was nothing human beings could do to stop it. Conflicts and collisions were inevitable, but it was best to start from scratch anyway. Nothing European in the Americas had worked very well anyway except destruction. All the people needed to remember was the twin brothers and the people from the south were coming to stop the destroyers. Converts were always welcome; Mother Earth embraced the souls of all who loved her. No fences or walls, would stop them; guns and bombs would not stop them. They had no fear of death; they were comfortable with their ancestors' spirits. They would come by the millions.

MEETING IN ROOM 1212

LECHA DIDN'T CARE if she was the last one to Room 1212. She had to telephone to see how things were at the ranch. After the Barefoot Hopi's speech, Zeta had told Lecha about Greenlee and his last joke; Lecha had felt her entire body tingle; even her scalp had prickled. Everyone had gone crazy: Mosca at Yaqui Easter, Seese at the Stage Coach, and now Zeta killing the gun dealer. Lecha spoke with Sterling and told him to tell Seese to start packing. The craziest one had been Ferro since the death of his lover. Ferro blamed the police, but he had also blamed Lecha for bringing Seese. Ferro refused to hear the truth: Jamey had been living on borrowed time, like any crooked undercover cop. No matter how many times Lecha or even Zeta had tried to talk to Ferro, to reason with him, he had exploded into a rage, screaming like a wild animal, not a human. Ferro had declared war on the Tucson police, and Zeta said no one would stop Ferro unless they killed him. Worse yet, Zeta had not been able to prevent Ferro from recruiting Awa Gee. Awa Gee refused to listen to Zeta after he learned Ferro wanted him to build car bombs. Awa Gee was even crazier than Ferro was, Zeta said. Awa Gee had babbled that the Tucson police were only a warm-up, only the beginning.

Year by year, Zeta had watched Tucson change. The years the snowfalls had fallen short in the Colorado Rocky Mountains had left the Southwest without water. Hundreds of fancy foothills houses in Tucson stood vacant. Block after block of small businesses in Tucson had closed or gone bankrupt. Affluent young professionals had been transferred out of Arizona or recalled to the safety of Phoenix, one hundred miles farther from the Mexican border.

The air force base in Tucson had been reopened, and military personnel were pouring into Tucson but without families. It was clear what the high command felt about the security of the U.S. border. Zeta remembered the Vietnam War and the names of the Vietnamese cities as they had fallen and the U.S.-backed forces had been forced back until at last they had been driven out of Saigon.

Already in Tucson and southern Arizona military and government vehicles patrolled the streets, ostensibly to seize illegal immigrants; but now they stopped everyone with brown skin and demanded identification. Any white people in Tucson who were not riding in health-spa limousines with bodyguards were also routinely stopped and questioned by Tucson police, who "advised" the homeless to leave town.

There were rumors the U.S. wasn't worried about the civil war in Mexico because the U.S. had CIA all the way to the top. Rumor had it that the Arizona governor had requested military aid not against Mexicans, but to control the thousands of homeless and destitute Americans fleeing northern winters. It did Zeta's heart good to see the white men so nervous. She had to laugh when Mosca told her about the squads of homeless veterans and the homeless families occupying vacant condominiums in the foothills.

When Lecha knocked on the door of Room 1212, she could hear a voice speaking English with a British accent. When Rose had opened the door, Lecha saw a blue-black African in bright yellow and red robes addressing the others seated around the room. Mosca had been sitting next to a black man in army fatigues wearing a green beret; Lecha saw by Mosca's maniacal grin the African and the black man were probably Mosca's guests. Zeta and Calabazas were on the sofa with the Maya woman sitting between them. Wilson Weasel Tail and the Hopi were sitting on the floor with their backs against the bed. Weasel Tail was tying knots in the shag carpet, but the Hopi was taking notes while the African talked. Rose had motioned for Lecha to sit down on the bed.

All night long in Room 1212 they had discussed a network of tribal coalitions dedicated to the retaking of ancestral lands by indigenous people. Europeans were welcome to convert, or they might choose to return to the lands of their forebears to be close to Europe's old ghosts. The sun was just rising over the mountains as the meeting in Room 1212 ended. Only Calabazas looked tired, and that had been because he was skeptical. When the Hopi talked about a national or even multinational prison uprising coordinated with the activities of say the eco-warriors dynamiting power plants and high-voltage lines, Calabazas had shook his head. Calabazas feared the jail and prison uprising riots were likely to deteriorate into race riots with the whites and Hispanics and others against the blacks. The Hopi had listened to Calabazas's doubts respectfully; the Hopi smiled and shrugged his shoulders. Of course it would not be an easy task because the prisons were designed to keep inmates at war with each other. The Hopi knew he had his work cut out for him, but the Hopi also had a growing number of disciples inside and outside jails and prisons all over the United States. At that point, Clinton spoke up; Clinton said he was skeptical too, but so far he had seen homeless white men and homeless black men work together for a common cause—survival—just as black men and white men had fought side by side in Vietnam.

Calabazas had been stubborn. They were crazy, he said; they had seen too many Hollywood movies. The minute there were prison riots and unrest in the cities the battle lines would fall along skin color. No, the Hopi had explained patiently, if anything happened, it would be more like the haves, whatever colors they were, killing the have-nots. Anyway, the African Americans would not be the focus of attention; the hundreds of thousands of Native Americans making their way north with the twin brothers would be. Calabazas had been skeptical of the Mexican Indian woman and her account of the spirit messages the twins claimed they got from the big blue macaws the people carried with them. But the Hopi said he believed it was necessary for the hundreds of thousands of Indians to appear from the South to prevent whites from turning on blacks in the United States. Almost immediately whites would look to blacks and Hispanics as buffers or shields, and mediators between themselves and the great migration of Native Americans. Calabazas was skeptical that the millions of U.S. citizens who called themselves Christians would even tolerate, much less support, a Native American religious movement to reclaim the Americas from the destroyers. Still, the heat waves and droughts had already driven thousands north to cooler temperatures. All the big shade trees in Tucson had died as the water table plunged precipitously.

Until the twin brothers and the people had reached the border, the Hopi advised they should all make preparations and then simply wait. As Wilson Weasel Tail's Ghost Dance song had stated, white people seemed to be having nervous breakdowns and psychotic episodes in record numbers. The Hopi said perhaps the whites could sense the changes that were approaching. What they had done to others was coming back on them; the tables had turned; now the colonizers were being colonized.

Calabazas said he didn't believe in miracle conversions of Christians or Jews or Moslems back to tribal religions, and the Hopi winked and said, "But you do believe in mass hysteria? The collective need to see drops of real blood on Church statues during Lent? You know something about mass hypnosis and subliminal messages." The Hopi smiled. "Anyway, no one says it will happen right away tomorrow. No one says anything like that. Native American people have been on these continents thirty thousand years, and the Europeans have been here for five hundred."

The Hopi had talked about peaceful and gradual changes as if he believed voting would become the solution as soon as millions more Indians became U.S. citizens. Lecha watched the expression on Angelita's face as the Hopi had outlined the possibilities for peaceful changes. Each time the Hopi said "nonviolent free elections," Angelita had grimaced. Lecha could see Angelita suspected the truth: there would be no elections; great struggles were about to sweep all through the Americas as far north as Alaska and Canada. Angelita La Escapía was one tough she-dog; Lecha could see that in the Mayan's barrel figure and steely, dark eyes. Angelita only pretended to agree with the twin brothers and their followers, unarmed and humble as they walked northward to fulfill an ancient prophecy. Lecha had seen the twin brothers on satellite TV. They looked to be hardly more than twenty-two or twenty-three years old, and easy to manipulate by the likes of Angelita. Lecha wasn't fooled; it was that big Mayan woman who was behind the twin brothers. Lecha had watched Angelita whisper to Zeta, and Zeta had made a lengthy reply. Later when Lecha asked her, Zeta admitted Angelita had asked about buying a few army surplus Stinger missiles. Lecha thought Angelita was right. The Hopi and the twin brothers might sincerely believe their recovery of the Americas could take place without bloodshed, but Lecha had her doubts especially since the hideous slaughter that had occurred in South Africa. These American continents were already soaked with Native American and African blood; violence begat violence, but if the destroyers were not stopped, the human race was finished.

Calabazas took the words of the Hopi to heart. He believed the change was in motion and was a process that had never stopped; it would all continue with or without him. Calabazas could sit back and do nothing if he wanted to and still the changes were inevitable. All the same, Calabazas felt uneasy. He had trusted the men who had been in Room 1212, but he wasn't sure about the women, especially not the Eskimo or the Maya woman. Those two looked like troublemakers; they looked like *killers* if a man didn't cooperate. The Eskimo woman said "quality, rather than quantity," and she had been talking about the Indigenous People's Army of the North. They might be few, but they were fierce and well armed. The Army of the North would sweep down behind the U.S. forces along the Mexican border. Before Weasel Tail knew it, his Lakota armies had been absorbed into the Army of the North. Weasel Tail was a smart man because he didn't object. No objections or resistance would stop the Maya woman or the other one, the Eskimo. Fire. All the Eskimo woman had talked about was fire. Forests and tundra burning. The earth burning. La Escapía—why, just her name—she was no better. She had talked about the fire macaw who brings destruction.

Wilson Weasel Tail and the Hopi could talk all they wanted about peaceful revolutions, but Calabazas had seen the Maya La Escapía talking to Zeta, and he knew what that meant. For years Zeta had been buying and stockpiling weapons in the old mine shafts. Calabazas was content to retire from smuggling, politics—everything; he had put in his time and had earned a rest in the shade with his little mule and burros. Calabazas would sit back and let the others make the decisions and give the orders, the way he always had, since he was a child with the old-time people in the Yaqui mountain strongholds. They had told him what must be done and he had done it. Since he was an old man now, maybe the women would give him something easy to do, something that wasn't too strenuous or too dangerous—maybe answering the phone or mailing letters.

RISE UP!

THE TUCSON POLICE had used SWAT teams to raid the homeless camps. They had used armored vehicles to smash down the cardboard and tin lean-tos and tents pitched under mesquite trees. The SWAT team had hit the camp with the women and children too, and the screaming children had been taken from their mothers to "protective custody" in State foster homes. But at the war veterans' camp, the SWAT team had stopped as if by hypnosis. They had seemed paralyzed by the sight of the homeless war veterans standing at attention in their raggedy army-surplus uniforms without any weapons. Clinton would never forget that moment. Rambo-Roy had addressed the men: "You didn't fight and almost die for the United States to end up like this. You didn't crawl on your belly through bullets, blood, and poison snakes in foreign countries just to starve and sleep in a ditch when you got back home!"

Other homeless men and women had witnessed the face-off between the SWAT team and the veterans; in their faces Clinton thought he had detected a flicker of recognition. Clinton had listened to the Barefoot Hopi, and he had talked day and night with the African. Both had preached patience, the patience of the old tribal people who had been humble enough not to expect change in one human lifetime, or even five lifetimes. Maybe not tomorrow or next week, but someday Clinton knew, the other homeless people would remember the defiance of the homeless vets; the dumpy, pale women and their skinny, pale men would remember the absolute surge of pride and power the veterans' defiance had given them. Like little seeds, the feelings would grow, and the police violence that had rained down on the people would only nurture the growing bitterness.

Clinton had been headed out anyway when the police came looking for him and Rambo-Roy. Naturally the Tucson police had got the details confused and had arrested the first white man and black man they had located wearing camouflage clothing. Clinton had not been sure if it was right for him and Rambo-Roy to let two other "brothers" take the rap for Trigg's murder. The police claimed they had genetic evidence from the crime scene that linked the two men in police custody to the killing. Clinton and Rambo-Roy both knew any genetic evidence found at the crime scene belonged to them, not the men in police custody. So actually the Tucson police had found no evidence at the scene, but after they had arrested the two men, the police detectives had taken hair and skin-cell samples from the men to put in the evidence bags with other material collected at the murder scene. Rambo said once the police had planted your hair or skin cells at the scene of the crime, you were finished. There was nothing that could be done. So even if Clinton had turned himself in, it wouldn't be *his* hair or *his* skin cells in that police evidence bag. Rambo-Roy said the brothers were doing their part by taking the rap for them. Clinton had to get back to the big cities. He had to try to reach the black war vets before they got misled by fanatics or extremists screaming "Black only! Africa only!" because Clinton had realized the truth: millions of black Indians were scattered throughout the Americas. Africans in the Americas had always been "home" because "home" is where the ancestor spirits are. From the gentle giants, Damballah and Quetzalcoatl, to the Maize Mother, and the Twin Brothers and Old Woman Spider, Africa and the Americas had been possessed.

Clinton was heading for Haiti after he visited some of his black Indian cousins in New York City. Black Indians living in Manhattan had long been supplying aid and arms to the Mohawk nations at war with Canada and the United States. The African had been discreet about the modest financial aid certain African nations had sent to the Mohawks. The African had called the aid a "symbolic gesture" of the solidarity between the African tribal people and the Native American tribal people. Now that black Africans had finally recovered their ancestral land the spirits would not allow the Africans to turn their backs on the tribes of the Americas as they fought to take back their land.

Clinton wasn't going to waste time with the whiners and complainers who had made wine or dope their religion, or the Jesus junkies, who had made religion their drug. Talking to Weasel Tail and the Barefoot Hopi had given Clinton so many more ideas than he and Rambo-Roy had ever got by themselves. Rambo-Roy and he had been right about the homeless and their plan to organize the homeless poor around an army of homeless war vets. On the Indian reservations the surviving war vets were at the core of the preparations. As Weasel Tail and the Hopi said, they might kill and cripple thousands, or even millions, of us, but those who did survive would indeed become a power to be reckoned with. All around them, all their lives they had witnessed their people's suffering and genocide; it only took a few, the merest handful of such people, to lay the groundwork for the changes.

Ignorance of the people's history had been the white man's best weapon. Clinton had continued to fill his notebook with fragments of the history the people had been deprived of for so long. The Hopi had given Clinton a book that the Hopi said might shine some more light on black Indians. Clinton had written in bold letters at the top of the notebook page *Thank you, Herbert Aptheker*!

1526   Pee Dee River, South Carolina: Negro slaves rise up, flee
        to live with the Indians.

1663 Gloucester County, Virginia: Indians aid black and white slaves.

1687 Westmoreland County, Virginia: Negro slaves rebel.

1688 Maryland: "Sam," slave belonging to R. Metcalfe, leads uprising.

1690 Newbury, Massachusetts: Mysterious white man from New Jersey leads Indian and black slaves to French Canada.

1691 Middlesex County, Virginia: "Mingo" leads other black slaves on rampage.

1702 New York, South Carolina: Mild unrest among slaves.

1708 Newton, Long Island: Indian and black slaves rebel and kill seven whites.

1709 Counties of Surry, James City, and Isle of Wight in Virginia suffer rebellions of Indian and black slaves.

1711 South Carolina: Great terror among whites as "Sebastian" leads other black slaves in uprising.

1712 New York City: Indian and Negro slaves kill nine white men during uprising.

1713 South Carolina: Slave rebellion plot blamed on slave preacher recently arrived from Martinique.

1720 South Carolina: Slave uprising coincides with drought, economic depression, and Indian troubles.

1722 Rappahannock River, Virginia: Slave unrest and conspiracies.

1723 Gloucester and Middlesex, Virginia: Slaves plot to flee to Florida and freedom promised by Spanish officials. Boston, Massachusetts, and New Haven, Connecticut: slaves set fire to numerous buildings.

1727 Louisiana: Captured Indian slave reveals secret outlaw village of "Natanapalle" where runaway black and Indian slaves live.

1729 Virginia: Black slaves flee to Blue Ridge Mountains with guns and agricultural implements.

1730 Louisiana: French arm adult black slaves to fight Chonachee Indians, but blacks conspire with Indians against the white men.
Virginia, South Carolina, Louisiana: Unrest and rebellion blamed on rumor among black slaves that the king had freed all baptized slaves.

1733 Unrest among black slaves increases everywhere after the Spanish government announces all slaves of the British who reach Florida will be free.

1738 Charles Town, Virginia: Conditions approach guerrilla warfare as black slaves try to reach Florida, which they call "the promised land."

1739 Stono, South Carolina: Uprising of black slaves blamed on Spain's war with England.

1740 New York City: Slaves poison their masters' water.

1741 New Jersey: Arson blamed on black slaves.

1747 New York City: Uprising among black slaves.

1751 South Carolina: Law enacted against slaves poisoning masters.

1755 Virginia, Maryland: the French and Indian War causes slave unrest.

1765 South Carolina: "Maroons" hiding in mountains grow more troublesome.

1767 Alexandria, Virginia: Rebellious black slaves.

1771 Georgia: British agent blamed for stirring up black slaves.

1772 Perth Amboy, New Jersey: In the center of the slave trade, a rebel conspiracy is uncovered.

1774 Boston: Black slaves rise up and seek aid of British and Irish.
St. Andrew's Parish, Georgia: Slaves rise up.

1775 North Carolina: Black slaves plot to rise up and join British forces.

1776 Bucks County, Pennsylvania: Black slaves rise up to aid British.

1778 Albany, New York: "Tom" arrested again for stirring up minds of Negro slaves against their masters.

1782 Spanish Louisiana: Rebellious "maroons" and Negroes led by one "St. Malo" make trouble for whites.

1786 Savannah River, Georgia: Negro slaves calling themselves "soldiers of the King of England" carry on guerrilla warfare from a stockaded village in Bell Isle swamp.

1791 Santo Domingo (Haiti): Successful black slave uprising. News does not reach U.S. slaves for a year or two.

1791 Western Virginia: Indians defeat General St. Clair and unrest stirs among black slaves while militia is gone fighting Indians.

1793 North Carolina: Cherokee Indians fight whites and black slaves threaten to rise up.

1793 Richmond, Virginia: Black slaves discuss successful rebellion in Santo Domingo.
Charleston, South Carolina: Mysterious fires sweep the city, and black slave unrest is blamed on revolt in Santo Domingo.

1796 Massive sell-off of black slaves by white masters such as Thomas Jefferson and George Washington due to economic hard times.

1797 Charleston, South Carolina: Three black slaves executed for "plots" and arson.

1800 Denmark Vesey buys his freedom.
Nat Turner is born. John Brown is born.

1800 Henrico County, Virginia: "Gabriel," slave of T. Prosser, leads a conspiracy.

1804 New Orleans: Slaves are restless and cruelly punished during war between France and Spain.

1804 Philadelphia: Whites attack blacks, but blacks rally together shouting, "Show them Santo Domingo!"

1810 Virginia: Slaves rise up and kill four whites.

1811 St. John and St. Charles Parish, Louisiana: Charles Deslondes, a free mulatto from Santo Domingo, leads a rebellion of black slaves.

1812 War with England stirs up slave unrest.

1813 Washington, D.C.: When British are near, black slaves rebel.

1815 Maryland, Virginia, South Carolina, Louisiana: Widespread unrest among black slaves.

1819 Florida, a Spanish territory, is "annexed" by the U.S. to wipe out nests of hostile Indians and runaway slaves who use Florida as a base camp for guerrilla raids on plantations across the border.

1819 Severe droughts and starvation in Virginia and South Carolina lead to numerous slave revolts.

1822 Charleston, South Carolina: Denmark Vesey's plan for a Great Revolt is betrayed. Vesey was counting on aid from blacks in Haiti and in Africa. Of 131 black slaves arrested, 38 were hanged.

1826 Louisville: Seventy-seven slaves being transported by five white men rise up, kill the slave traders, and escape.

1828   Richmond, Virginia: Nat Turner hears the voice of God
       tell him he must lead his people to rise up when the signs
       come from God.

1829   Virginia: Free-born Negro Christian Tompkins writes
       pamphlet foretelling the coming of a mulatto savior who
       is huge, bearded, and invincible and comes from Grenada
       to destroy slavery in the U.S.

1829   Slaves bound for sale in New Orleans from Norfolk rebel
       and only after great struggle are controlled.

1829   Rains in Louisiana damage crops and cause famine and
       slave revolts.

1830   David Walker, a free man, publishes his "Appeal," which
       Nat Turner may have read.

1831   The signs from God come and Nat Turner leads a slave
       rebellion in Southampton County during which fifty-
       seven whites are killed. Hundreds of black slaves are
       killed without trials across the U.S. as whites panic and
       give way to hysteria.

1835   Texas: Black slaves escape and join Mexican forces
       against Texans.

1846   Pensacola, Florida: Martial law declared after slave re-
       bellion plans revealed.

1861   Arkansas: Slaves rise up and kill enslavers on July 4.

1862   Richmond, Virginia: Slave named Bob Richardson ex-
       ecuted for plotting uprising.

1862   Yazoo City, Mississippi: Slaves rise up and burn court-
       house and homes of fourteen whites.

Clinton knew racism had made people afraid to talk about their Native
American ancestors. But the black Indians would know in their hearts
who they were when they heard Clinton talk about the spirits. The people
had to be reminded that the spirits were all around, and the tribal people
torn from Mother Africa had not been deserted by the spirits. Rather
the people had deserted the spirits; overwhelmed by their losses, the
people had no longer prayed or believed because they blamed the spirits
for their slavery on alien soil.

Clinton was heading for the remote mountains in Haiti. He didn't
care if everyone was dead and all traces were gone. He wouldn't be
surprised. The white man and white-man imitators had tried to destroy
all traces of the mighty spiritual forces that had united in Haiti's moun-

tains five hundred years ago. Clinton just wanted to set his feet on the soil where the spirits of three continents had been manifested, where the first black Indians had been born and their descendants had triumphed against the French fleet.

Clinton suspected many African Americans secretly grieved for the spirits they believed had been lost or left behind in Africa centuries before. That would be his main work, to explain to the people that many of the African spirits also inhabit the Americas too. Clinton reclined his seat after take-off from Tucson International Airport. He didn't bother to look down or say adiós because he knew he'd be back. Nothing could be black only or brown only or white only anymore. The ancient prophecies had foretold a time when the destruction by man had left the earth desolate, and the human race was itself endangered. This was the last chance the people had against the Destroyers, and they would never prevail if they did not work together as a common force.

Clinton had promised the Barefoot Hopi he would spread the word among the brothers and sisters in the cities. He would tell them to prepare; a day was coming when each human being, man, woman, and child, could do something, and each contribution no matter how small would generate great momentum because they would be acting together. The Barefoot Hopi's plan called for a nationwide jail and prison uprising to be triggered by the execution of a prisoner or the outbreak of riots in the cities. The people had to make their moves while the police and military were busy trying to put down the prison riots. Once the people had hit the streets, the authorities would call military and police units back into the cities to protect the government from the people. The secret was for the people to park themselves smack in the middle of the rich man's backyard, so any firebombing the city police did would burn out the rich man for a change. At this stage the people would suffer immense casualties; the government would firebomb the crowds of angry citizens as they marched from the ghettos down Madison Avenue, State Street, and Sunset Boulevard.

Clinton had talked with brown people, mostly women, because so many men were sick or dead. Talk about casualties and all you got was laughter, jokes, and more laughter. Two hundred or three hundred dead from police bullets or firebombs? That was funny! Hundreds more of the people died every year from starvation and its complications, which were slow and painful. They weren't afraid to die. Clinton had heard it said again and again, mainly by the women. Black women, Hispanic women, white women, homeless with starving children; they all said they'd rather fight. They'd rather burn down the city, take a police bullet, and die quick, because that way they died fighting, they died warriors, not slaves.

Roy was going to lie low until cooler weather came, maybe contact camps of eco-warriors in the mountains of Montana or go to the homeless veterans' camps Clinton had visited in the winter. Roy had a scheme for a big November Veterans Day celebration. All over the country, Roy hoped to persuade homeless veterans to contact local authorities for permission to build authentic firebase camps to show the public. The scheme called for the model firebase camps to be built just outside military bases where Veterans Day activities were held.

Everything would be exactly as it had been in Vietnam; they would bury and sandbag mortar and missile launchers and dig underground bunkers for protection from counterattacks. The catch was that when Veterans Day festivities were over, a few of the homeless vets would continue to occupy the model firebases. Roy was realistic. Not every city in the U.S. was sentimental and guilty about homeless war veterans, but Roy figured most cities would not bother to evict the homeless veterans from their model firebases once Veterans Day had passed. The ploy was a long shot. They had no mortar shells or little missiles, and there was no guarantee they'd be able to get any, but the Hopi had some promising leads. Still, firebases manned by a few vets and the young would-be's could draw fire from the police and military and buy time for the prison uprising and the rioters in the cities. The Barefoot Hopi's plan depended upon coordination and timing. Ideally, just as the Florida State electric chair was about to be used, the eco-warriors would conduct their "simultaneous hit" on significant interstate power-transmission lines and power generators. The Hopi had dreamed that when the warden threw the switch, the lights would go out and the condemned man would be unharmed, then prison and jail inmates would begin their riots. Emergency generators had fuel for at most seventy-two hours.

The night the lights went out and didn't come back on, the tables would turn. The poorest, those living on the street or in the arroyo, they would laugh at the others because the homeless and poor lived everyday without electricity or running water. Turn out the lights and the police had no computers, no files, no names, no spy cameras, and police radios went dead. As Wilson Weasel Tail had pointed out, the Lakota, Cheyenne, Crow, Hidatsa, as well as the Navajo and Apache—none of their people depended much on electricity. The same for the Eskimos. But they all had weapons and they all were ready to fight. Because if they didn't fight, they would be destroyed and Mother Earth with them.

Poor Engels and Marx! Angelita La Escapía had to smile at the two old white men who had waited and waited, year after year, for the successful revolution until their time ran out. They had been close, but they hadn't quite got it. They had been on the right track with their readings on Native American communal economies and cultures. For Europeans, they had been far ahead of their time; they had been close, but they still hadn't got it quite right. They had not understood that the earth was mother to all beings, and they had not understood anything about the spirit beings. But at least Engels and Marx had understood the earth belongs to no one. No human, individuals or corporations, no cartel of nations, could "own" the earth; it was the earth who possessed the humans and it was the earth who disposed of them.

Now it was up to the poorest tribal people and survivors of European genocide to show the remaining humans how all could share and live together on earth, ravished as she was. Angelita La Escapía was confident. All hell was going to break loose. The best was yet to come.

SMOOTH SAILING

LEAH BLUE SAW only smooth sailing once Judge Arne had dismissed the last of the injunctions and lawsuits to stop her from pumping her deep-water wells. Leah's lawyers had argued that since the U.S. banking collapse and the crash of Arizona land prices, Arizona had been losing population. Of course the political turmoil in Mexico and the thousands of refugees massed along the border had not helped. Leah's lawyers maintained that Arizona's loss of population as well as the shutdown of the copper industry had suddenly changed the entire outlook for water resources in Arizona. Water was plentiful, expert witnesses had testified for Leah Blue. Of course the environmentalists and the Indians had brought in their own experts, who had testified that Leah Blue's deep wells would destroy shallow wells throughout the valley. Leah Blue had got a kick out of watching Judge Arne pretend to weigh both arguments.

As for the trouble between the Tucson police and Sonny and Bingo, Leah felt confident the senator could clear up any misunderstandings. Everything was coming up roses. Preliminary estimates showed that construction costs had plummeted because so many skilled workers were unemployed. Leah had paid next to nothing for the land because it had been worthless without water. Every morning Leah drove to the wellheads. She was pleased to see the security service had assigned four armed guards in the day as well as at night. Terrorist ecologists had made threats to dynamite the deep wells, and to fill them in with concrete.

Leah had a way with the construction foremen and crews that was friendly but distant, and she liked things that way. She liked to step on the concrete pedestal at the deep wellhead, to gaze out over the brownish desert shrubs and grayish desert gravel and visualize the sleek, low villas of pale marble with red bougainvilleas and even water lilies for the floating gardens in the canals. She could not understand why the Indians or the environmentalists had bothered to sue even if her deep wells *did* harm other wells or natural springs, which her deep wells *did not;* what possible good was this desert anyway? Full of poisonous snakes, sharp rocks, and cactus! Leah knew she was not alone in this feeling of repulsion; most people who saw the cactus and rocky hills for the first time agreed the desert was ugly. In her dream city, the water lilies and cattails, the giant cypress trees and palms, would soothe their eyes, and people could forget they were in a desert.

Leah had been driving back from her deep wells when the call came over her car phone. It was Max, and the instant she heard his voice she knew someone was dead. Not Sonny! Sonny had been talking about getting even with the cops. Leah had worried about the boys. Max had never spent more than five minutes with either of them, even when they were babies.

No, Sonny, Bingo, and Angelo were all right as far as Max knew. It was Trigg. Trigg had been found with his skull smashed, neatly arranged in an organ-freezer compartment in the basement of the Bio-Materials headquarters. Leah had started to protest; she had just seen him late yesterday afternoon, but Max cut her off. That was yesterday. Today Trigg was dead. The police chief still had a hair up his butt over the deal with Sonny and Bingo; now the police had another excuse to come sniffing around. The police claimed they had to check out all leads, including the theory of the jealous husband. Max already had his lawyers mobilized.

"I thought the senator had all that cleared up," Leah said. "Isn't he supposed to set the police straight?" Leah talked to Max, but another part of her mind had been racing at the same time. Trigg had been her lover, but Leah didn't feel anything—she wasn't even surprised he was dead. Trigg had always been in a lawsuit or a dispute with someone. Leah wondered if something was wrong with her because she wasn't sad and she didn't cry, even after Max hung up. She drove to her office for business as usual. If the police wanted to talk to her, she would cooperate because that young police chief was really quite sexy. Maybe the transplant doctors had got him. Trigg used to say not even the lowest street addicts were as greedy as surgeons. His "silent partners" at the medical school had made millions with their heart and lung transplant racket, but routinely they had accused Trigg of skimming profits. For some reason, the thought of Trigg's empty wheelchair brought tears to Leah's eyes. Poor stupid Trigg. He had always believed he would walk again before he died.

Trigg had told Leah the trouble had started when the surgical team had transplanted the wrong lungs and heart in a patient who had later died. Trigg said his partners had come begging and pleading first; then they had gotten nasty. They had wanted to shift liability for the error to Bio-Materials, Inc.; after the court judgment, they would declare bankruptcy and form a new corporation. Trigg had refused. The police were looking for motives; here were some motives. With Trigg out of the way, the surgeons could fix the blame any way they wanted; they could testify the lungs and heart had arrived from Bio-Materials incorrectly labeled. Of course Leah had understood later when she learned the police detectives had not questioned the "silent partners." After all, except for fat farms and tennis resorts, Tucson's only booming business these days was human organ transplants. Tucson police had wisely concluded Trigg had been killed by two homeless men, a black and a white man who had both worked for Trigg as night watchmen.

Leah had thought she might cry for Eddie Trigg later; the loss might suddenly hit her later, in a week or two, but it never did. She didn't cry for Eddie and she didn't cry for Max either. How odd it had been. Suddenly they were both gone, one right after the other. Luckily Max had been struck by lightning on the golf course; otherwise, the stupid Tucson police would probably have made her a suspect in both deaths. She had to fight an impulse to laugh. The lightning had melted the putter in Max Blue's hand on the sixteenth hole. Max's bodyguard had cried when he told Leah Max had refused to leave the course to take shelter because he had almost finished the game. Leah had pretended to dab her eyes as she listened, but she felt relief, not loss.

Leah asked the boys and Angelo to give her some time alone; she asked Angelo to make the funeral arrangements and to notify the family. She felt restless indoors. She sat by the pool and watched the sun disappear behind the mountains. The violent thunderclouds and lightning had dispersed, leaving swirls and strands and fluffy masses of clouds to catch the colors of the sunset—silvers and golds becoming chrome-yellow, fire-orange, fire-red, fire-purple. Max had been right about one thing; the Arizona sky was spectacular. The Arizona sky would make her a billionaire.

A D I Ó S , T U C S O N !

STERLING HAD NEVER been the same after the time he had spent in Tucson. Loud noises such as firecrackers or gunshots or thunder sent him straight up in the air, ready to run again the way he had that afternoon the gunmen had come to the ranch. After the gunshots, Lecha's old white Lincoln had come careening down the hill. Seese had flung open a car door so Sterling could throw in his shopping bags and suitcases. The car had still been moving as Sterling jumped in the backseat. Lecha had gunned the big engine, and they had left a big rooster's tail of dust behind them as the Lincoln plowed down the driveway. Sterling was certain they would crash the security gate, but then he saw the gate was already open, and ahead there was something dark lying in the middle of the long driveway.

Lecha never hesitated. The big Lincoln had surged over the dead dog. Sterling had gasped and tried to look back through the car window to see which dog they had run over. Then Lecha had pointed out the other dogs. They were lying scattered near the outer security gate; their swollen tongues hung from their mouths. Lecha had slowed to look at the dead dogs. They had been shot with little silver darts. Sterling had been impressed that Lecha could remain so calm with gunfire behind her and the dead guard dogs in front of her. Seese had hidden herself crouched down in the front seat; Sterling could hear Seese crying. Lecha had not looked back. She drove eighty miles an hour all the way to the New Mexico border.

Sterling had so many questions. How had the gunmen got past the alarm devices and the TV cameras? Maybe Paulie had forgot to activate the system as he left for town. Paulie had become more and more upset. The last week, after Ferro's friend had been killed, Paulie had drowned all but one of the pups nursing the red Doberman bitch.

Lecha talked as she drove and didn't seem to care if anyone was listening. Seese had fallen asleep slumped low in the front seat. Sterling had been too upset at the time to follow everything Lecha had said during the trip, but later much of it had come back to him. Lecha had said it was a good time to get out of Tucson for many reasons. She had had a dream about war. She had dreamed hundreds of big green helicopters, U.S. gunships flying in low from the south over the saguaro cactus forests outside Tucson. The cargo doors of the helicopter gunships had been wide open; and inside, Lecha had seen dozens of wounded soldiers in U.S. army uniforms. Lecha said she knew the helicopters were evacuating wounded U.S. troops from Mexico. Very soon the U.S. would send troops and tanks across the border to help the white men who ran the Mexican government keep all those Indians under control. The U.S. had always feared Mexico might fail to control her Indians. Sterling didn't know what to think about such a dream. He thought it sounded more like a nightmare. When the shooting started, women and children, the old and the sick, the innocent and the weak, would die first. For all the trouble Sterling had had with the Tribal Council, he still respected the Tribal Council and the people; because they had all met and discussed Sterling's offenses, and they had at least let Sterling speak before they had voted to banish him.

Lecha had stopped for gasoline in Willcox. Sterling was glad to get to the men's room. He had been careful not to drink any of the coffee in the thermos Lecha had brought along because of his aging bladder. Seese seemed exhausted; she had hardly stirred in her sleep even when the car door slammed. Out of Willcox heading for the New Mexico state line, Lecha had talked about the gunmen. Ferro had got the drop on two of the gunmen right away. Zeta had shot the third gunman through the back of the head as he had tried to flee across the patio. The gunmen were coyote food now. Lecha was taking Seese and leaving Arizona for a while as a precaution. They would return when the heat was off—Lecha had laughed at her pun. Would the heat be off for

Sterling with his own people? Lecha had invited Sterling to come along. She and Seese were headed for South Dakota to the secret headquarters where Wilson Weasel Tail and the others were making preparations. Lecha wanted Sterling to join up because they could use him. Weasel Tail had plans to ally his Plains army with Mohawk forces.

Sterling had thanked Lecha for her kind offer. He told her he thought his grandnephews might let him live in the stone shack at the family sheep camp. The next time the Navajo sheepherder quit to celebrate the Navajo Tribal Fair, Sterling thought he could probably have the job. Sterling didn't care to return to Aunt Marie's house in Laguna village. It wasn't the banishment order from the Tribal Council that stopped him. Sterling knew if a person stayed away for a year or so, the way he had, usually no one mentioned the banishment, unless of course there was trouble again. To return and see Aunt Marie's empty armchair by the window would have caused Sterling too much sadness, and Sterling was not sure he could endure much more sadness.

He knew he could never again live as he had before. Aunt Marie and the other old folks used to scold Sterling when he came home from Indian boarding school to visit because he wasn't interested in what they had to say and he wasn't interested in what went on in the kivas. Sterling had only been interested in his magazines and listening to the radio as he did at boarding school. Sterling had never been disrespectful of the old folks' beliefs, he just had not cared either way about religion. This indifference had been used against Sterling during the banishment proceedings of the Tribal Council. Before, it seemed Sterling had not known enough and had not caught on fast enough, and that had got him in deep trouble with the Tribal Council over the movie crew. But now, after Tucson with all the violence and death, after everything Lecha had revealed, Sterling felt as if he knew too much, and he would never be able to enjoy his life again.

On the long drive, Sterling had awakened and for an instant forgot where he was and what had happened. But the instant he saw Seese huddled in the front passenger seat, Sterling had remembered. Somehow Seese had been crushed by whatever had happened the night of the shoot-out at the bar. All Sterling knew was two others in the room with Seese had been killed by the police. Since that morning, all Sterling had said to her was "Can I bring you anything?" and "I hope you're feeling better" because even the most simple words seemed to break Seese down, and tears had welled up in her eyes whenever she tried to speak.

Lecha had stopped in Albuquerque for gas before they headed west.

Albuquerque still looked normal, as if nothing were happening because Albuquerque was five hours by car from the border—a distance safe enough that those fleeing Tucson and El Paso had relocated there. Albuquerque appeared to be booming. Sterling looked out the window at people walking to their cars from the shopping malls and from the K marts. The faces he saw were placid. The shoppers didn't seem to have a clue about what was happening. Maybe they had noticed a few more U.S. government cars on the street, or increased military-helicopter flyovers, but that was all. On the West Side, Sterling could tell the people didn't know either, because the faces had been excited, happy, even joking. They didn't know, and Sterling knew even if someone told them, they would not believe it. Sterling had not believed the old prophecy either, but he had seen what was happening in Tucson with his own eyes.

Lecha had claimed certain human beings sensed danger and began reacting without being conscious of what they were preparing for. They had no idea others like themselves existed as they worked alone with feverish plots and crazed schemes. But all that mattered was, they were making preparations. When the time came, all these scattered crazies and their plans would complement and serve one another in the chaos to come. The people would be smarter this time. They had learned from Watts and from police bombs in Philadelphia; the people would head for the fancy high-rent districts so when police firebombed the protest marchers, the Ferraris and the fur coats would go up in smoke too.

What would these people in Albuquerque do when they heard about the twin brothers and their followers? How would the Native Americans and Mexican Americans in New Mexico react when the U.S. military opened fire on the twin brothers and thousands of their followers, mostly women and children? How many of these Chicanos and these Indians had ever heard the old stories? Did they know the ancient prophecies? It all seemed quite impossible, and yet one only had to look as far as Africa to see that after more than five hundred years of suffering slavery and bloodshed, the African people had taken back the continent from European invaders. Sterling shuddered when he remembered the terrible price the tribal people of South Africa had had to pay while the nations of the world had stood back and watched.

Lecha warned that unrest among the people would grow due to natural disasters. Earthquakes and tidal waves would wipe out entire cities and great chunks of U.S. wealth. The Japanese were due to be pounded by angry earth spirits, and the world would watch in shock as billions of dollars and thousands of lives were suddenly washed away. Still there would be no rain, and high temperatures would trigger famines that sent refugees north faster and faster. The old almanac said "civil strife, civil crisis, civil war." Allies of the United States would decline to intervene or send military aid. England and France would cite the distances and the costs and point out that no "armed force" threatened the U.S. border, only thousands of defenseless and hungry refugees from the war-torn South. Lecha's reading of the old book had Canada alone proclaiming herself a U.S. ally in this last big Indian war. The Germans would follow the lead of the Japanese, who wanted to watch and to wait until the dust settled. Of course all of the northern European nations would find themselves in similar predicaments with massive onslaughts of refugees from the South. Lecha had even dreamed the streets of downtown Amsterdam were full of Indians from all the tribes of the Americas. She had seen only Indians crowding the streets of Amsterdam and no Dutch; many of the Indians had looked pale, as if they had been born there.

When Sterling caught a glimpse of the distant blue peaks of Mt. Taylor, his throat tightened and tears ran down his cheeks. Woman Veiled in Rain Clouds was what the old people had called the mountain. Sterling was home. Sterling asked Lecha to drop him off near Mesita Village where Interstate 40 cut through the red sandstone. Seese had been crying too hard to say good-bye; she had clung to Sterling. "It's all right," he heard himself say over and over, "don't worry," but the roar of the vehicles that sped past had obliterated his words. The emergency lane of Interstate 40 was no place for long good-byes. Lecha had pulled an envelope from her purse. "You might need some money," she said. They shook hands. Seese had hugged Sterling one last time, tears streaming down her face, and then Sterling had slammed the car door, and the old white Lincoln had roared off.

HOME

STERLING HIKED over the little sand hills across the little valley to the sandstone cliffs where the family sheep camp was. The windmill was pumping lazily in the afternoon breeze, and Sterling washed his face and hands and drank. The taste of the water told him he was home. "Home." Even thinking the word made his eyes fill with tears. What was "home"? The little stone shack seemed to be deserted although Sterling had found an empty Vienna sausage can on the little woodburning stove. On the shelf there were two coffee cans; inside he had found dry pinto beans and some sugar.

Sterling didn't think what he was experiencing was depression; it felt more like shock. For three days Sterling lay stunned; he could barely swallow water. On the fourth day Sterling awoke and no longer felt exhausted, but he had felt different. He didn't have the heart to look at his magazines anymore. He didn't even glance in the direction of his shopping bags. The magazines referred to a world Sterling had left forever, a world that was gone, that safe old world that had never really existed except on the pages of *Reader's Digest* in articles on reducing blood cholesterol, corny jokes, and patriotic anecdotes.

Sterling cooked beans in the tin coffeepot and went for a walk in the field of sunflowers below the windmill. He had never spent so much time before alone with the earth; he sat below the red sandstone cliffs and watched the high, thin clouds. Far in the distance, he could hear jet airplanes, Interstate 40, and the trains. But Sterling found it was easy to forget that world in the distance; that world no longer was true. He purposely kept his mind focused on the things he could see or touch; he avoided thinking about the day before or even the hour before, and he did not think about tomorrow. He watched the tiny black ants busily gather food for the ant pile. Aunt Marie and the old people had believed the ants were messengers to the spirits, the way snakes were. The old people used to give the ants food and pollen and tiny beads as gifts. That way the ants carried human prayers directly underground. Sterling had spooned out a few cooked beans on the ant hill, but he couldn't think of a prayer to say, or even a message to send to the spirits of the earth. But the ants didn't worry about prayers or messages; they swarmed excitedly over the beans. Sterling watched them work for a long time; sometimes the ant workers had almost been crushed under beans they were carrying. The ants worked steadily, and by sundown they had taken all the beans underground. Sterling did not understand why, but the success of the ants had lifted his spirits. He wished he had listened more closely to Aunt Marie and her sisters, for he might have understood better the connection between human beings and ants.

The next day Sterling got up before dawn and took a bath in the shallow creek Laguna people call "the river." Sterling gasped as the cold river clay squeezed between his toes and the cold water reached his ankles. He washed his hair with soapweed root left behind by some sheepherder too poor or too stingy to buy real shampoo. The day after that, Sterling had walked for two or three hours along the river enjoying the smell of the willows. When he stopped to rest, he realized he had walked north almost as far as the mine road. The open-pit uranium mine had been closed for years. Sterling walked away from the shoulder of the road in the weeds although there were no signs of any traffic, or other human beings for miles.

Sterling knew what was at the mine, but he wasn't afraid. Without realizing what he was doing, Sterling had been walking in the exact direction of the mine road where the shrine of the giant snake was. Sterling knew the visit to the giant snake was what he must do, before anything else, even before he went to buy food.

Sterling felt stronger as he walked along. The wild purple asters were blooming, and Sterling could smell Indian tea and bee flowers; in the distance, he heard the field larks call. As long as Sterling did not face the mine, he could look out across the grassy valley at the sandstone mesas and imagine the land a thousand years ago, when the rain clouds had been plentiful and the grass and wildflowers had been belly high on the buffalo that had occasionally wandered off the South Plains. Lecha had talked about the Lakota prophecy while they were driving from Tucson. Lecha said that as a matter of fact, the buffalo were returning to the Great Plains, just as the Lakota and other Plains medicine people had prophesied. The buffalo herds had gradually outgrown and shifted their range from national parks and wildlife preserves. Little by little the buffalo had begun to roam farther as the economic decline of the Great Plains had devastated farmers and ranchers and the small towns that had once served them. Sterling had to smile when he thought of herds of buffalo grazing among the wild asters and fields of sunflowers below the mesas. He did not care if he did not live to see the buffalo return; probably the herds would need another five hundred years to complete their comeback. What mattered was that after all the ground-water had been sucked out of the Ogalala Aquifer, then the white people and their cities of Tulsa, Denver, Wichita, and Des Moines would gradually disappear and the Great Plains would again host great herds of buffalo and those human beings who knew how to survive on the annual rainfall.

Sterling still had two miles to walk, but already the mountains of grayish-white tailings loomed ahead. He had not understood before why the old people had cried when the U.S. government had opened the mine. Sterling was reminded of the stub left after amputation when he looked at the shattered, scarred sandstone that remained; the mine had devoured entire mesas. "Leave our Mother Earth alone," the old folks had tried to warn, "otherwise terrible things will happen to us all." Before the end of the war, the old folks had seen the first atomic explosion—the flash brighter than any sun—followed weeks later by the bombs that had burned up a half a million Japanese. "What goes around, comes around." Now he was approaching the shrine of the giant snake.

Sterling tried to remember more of the stories the old people used to tell; he wished he had listened more closely because he vaguely recalled a connection the giant snake had with Mexico. Tucson was too close to Mexico. Tucson *was* Mexico, only no one in the United States had realized it yet. Ferro had called the exploding car bomb outside Tucson police headquarters his "announcement" that Tucson wasn't United States territory anymore. Sterling had been terrified of Ferro from the start because Aunt Marie and the old people used to talk about how fierce the Mexican tribes were—how quickly and casually they had killed.

Long time ago, long before the Europeans, the ancestors had lived far to the south in a land of more rain, where crops grew easily. But then something terrible had happened, and the people had to leave the abundance and flee far to the north, to harsh desert land. Hundreds of years before the Europeans had appeared, sorcerers called Gunadeeyahs or Destroyers had taken over in the South. The people who refused to join the Gunadeeyahs had fled; the issue had been the sorcerers' appetite for blood, and their sexual arousal from killing. Aunt Marie and the others had been reluctant to talk about sorcery in the presence of young children, and Sterling had not paid much attention to what his playmates had told him about the Gunadeeyahs. Still Sterling knew the Destroyers robbed graves for human flesh and bones to make their fatal "powders." Aunt Marie had cautioned Sterling and the other children always to be careful around Mexicans and Mexican Indians because when the first Europeans had reached Mexico City they had found the sorcerers in power. Montezuma had been the biggest sorcerer of all. Each of Montezuma's advisors had been sorcerers too, descendants of the very sorcerers who had caused the old-time people to flee to Pueblo country in Arizona and New Mexico, thousands of years before. Somehow the offerings and food for the spirits had become too bloody, and yet many people had wanted to continue the sacrifices. They had been excited by the sacrifice victim's feeble struggle; they had lapped up the first rich spurts of hot blood. The Gunadeeyah clan had been born.

Sterling wished for a drink of water. No wonder the blood sacrifices and the blood-spilling had stopped when the people reached this high desert plateau; every drop of moisture, every drop of blood, each tear, had been made precious by this arid land. The people who had fled north to escape the bloodshed made rules once they were settled. On the rare occasions when the sacred messengers had to be dispatched to the spirit world, the eagles and macaws had been gently suffocated by the priests; not one drop of blood had been spilled. Permission had to be asked and prayers had to be made to the game animals before the hunters brought them home. The people were cautioned about disturbing the bodies of the dead. Those who touched the dead were easily seduced by the Gunadeeyahs, who craved more death and more dead bodies to open and consume.

Now the old story came back to Sterling as he walked along. The appearance of Europeans had been no accident; the Gunadeeyahs had called for their white brethren to join them. Sure enough the Spaniards had arrived in Mexico fresh from the Church Inquisition with appetites whetted for disembowelment and blood. No wonder Cortés and Montezuma had hit it off together when they met; both had been members of the same secret clan.

Sterling made his way up a sandy hill and then slid down the crumbling clay bank of a small arroyo. He tore a cuff on his pants crawling through the barbed-wire fence that marked the mine boundaries. Ahead all he could see were mounds of tailings thirty feet high, uranium waste blowing in the breeze, carried by the rain to springs and rivers. Here was the new work of the Destroyers; here was destruction and poison. Here was where life ended. What had been so remarkable about the return of the giant snake had been how close the giant snake was to the mountains of tailings. Two mine employees from Laguna had discovered the giant stone snake on a routine check for erosion of the tailings. Sterling had heard Aunt Marie and the others talking excitedly about a giant stone snake. At first Sterling had thought a fossil snake had been found, but then he had realized the stone snake was only an odd outcropping of sandstone. Sterling remembered his skepticism about the giant snake. He had not believed the mine employees who swore there had never been anything at the foot of the tailings before—nothing but sand and a few weeds. Sterling had thought that probably the strange sandstone formation had been lying there for hundreds of years and no one had noticed it; or if they had, the people had lost track of the rock formation after the mining began. But Aunt Marie and the others had pointed out the sheep camps nearby and the road that passed within a hundred yards of the giant stone snake. Rabbit hunters familiar with the area had come to agree with the miners, sheepherders, and the others. No way had they overlooked a sandstone snake thirty feet long! Overnight, the giant stone snake had appeared there. The old folks said Maahastryu had returned. Sterling had forgotten all about the stone snake after that. He had heard Aunt Marie talk about the stone snake from time to time with her nieces; but back then, talk about religion or spirits had meant nothing to Sterling, drinking beer with his section-gang buddies. Back then Sterling used to say he only believed in beer and big women bouncing in water beds. For Sterling, the stone snake had been a sort of joke, and he had forgot all about the snake until the Hollywood film crew had tried to film it and all hell had broken loose.

Sterling was not sure how much farther he had to walk; he had been to the snake shrine only a few times, and the last time, Sterling had been in the backseat of a tribal police car as they had raced to stop the movie people from filming the stone snake. Suddenly there it was. The stone snake's head was raised dramatically and its jaws were open wide. Sterling felt his heart pound and the palms of his hands sweat. The ground near the snake's head was littered with bits of turquoise, coral, and mother-of-pearl; there were streaks of cornmeal and pollen on the snake's forehead and nose where those who came to pray had fed the spirit being.

Sterling had no idea what to do; he had no idea why he had walked all that distance to the stone snake. He sat down near the snake to rest. He had to think. What had happened to him? What had happened to his life? Education, English, a job on the railroad, then a pension; Sterling had always worked hard on self-improvement. He had never paid much attention to the old-time ways because he had always thought the old beliefs were dying out. But Tucson had changed Sterling. In Africa the giant snakes talked to the people again, and the buffalo ran free again on the Great Plains. Sterling felt haunted—he would never forget the child Seese had lost. Marching through his brain day and night were Lecha's "armies" of Lakotas and Mohawks; Sterling saw them over and over in dreams; ghost armies of Lakota warriors, ghost armies of the Americas leading armies of living warriors, armies of indigenous people to retake the land. Sterling tried to forget the blood and the gunshots. He tried to forget everything Lecha had told him because she and the others at the meeting in Tucson were crazy. "Rambo of the Homeless," "Poor People's Army," the Barefoot Hopi and Wilson Weasel Tail—the world was not like that. Tucson had only been a bad dream.

When the giant stone snake had first reappeared, Aunt Marie and the old folks had argued over the significance of the return of the snake. Religious people from all the pueblos and even the distant tribes had come to see the giant stone snake. The snake was so near the tailings it appeared as if it might be fleeing the mountains of wastes. This had led to rumors that the snake's message said the mine and all those who had made the mine had won. Rumors claimed the snake's head pointed to the next mesa the mine would devour, and Sterling had believed the mine had won. But the following year uranium prices had plunged, and the mine had closed before it could devour the basalt mesa the stone snake had pointed at.

Sterling sat for a long time near the stone snake. The breeze off the junipers cooled his face and neck. He closed his eyes. The snake didn't care if people were believers or not; the work of the spirits and prophecies went on regardless. Spirit beings might appear anywhere, even near open-pit mines. The snake didn't care about the uranium tailings; humans had desecrated only themselves with the mine, not the earth. Burned and radioactive, with all humans dead, the earth would still be sacred. Man was too insignificant to desecrate her.

Sterling didn't show himself in Laguna for a long time, and then only to buy food. He had held his breath, but the Tribal Council had ignored him. His grandnephews and grandnieces let him stay at the sheep camp, but they didn't trust him with sheep right away. There was gossip and speculation about what had happened to Sterling in Tucson. Sterling didn't look like his old self anymore. He had lost weight and quit drinking beer. The postmaster reported Sterling had let go all his magazine subscriptions. Sterling didn't care about the rumors and gossip because Sterling knew why the giant snake had returned now; he knew what the snake's message was to the people. The snake was looking south, in the direction from which the twin brothers and the people would come.

▲
NORTH
TO ALASKA

Rose and the burning children
the dogsled racer

The wild herds of
buffalo return.

ALMANAC OF THE DEAD
FIVE HUNDRED YEAR MAP

Through the decipherment of ancient tribal
texts of the Americas the Almanac of the Dead
foretells the future of all the Americas. The
future is encoded in arcane symbols and old
narratives.

Wilson Weasel Tail
the Barefoot Hopi

● Winslow

Trigg
Leah Blue
Max Blue
Sonny Blue
Bingo

Marilyn
John Dillinger
Geronimo
Clinton
Mosca
Calabazas
Liria
Sarita

Zeta
Lecha
Ferro
Jamey
Paulie
Awa Gee

The Senator
The Judge
The Police Chief
Mr. "B"
Greenlee

Angelo
Rambo
Clinton
Peaches
The Army of the Homeless

● Phoenix

San Diego

Seese
David
baby Monte
Eric

Beaufrey
Serlo
Mr. J's gallery

● Yuma

Seese seeks help

M E X

PACIFIC OCEAN

● Potam

Mario's Luxury Bus Tours

● Cuílican

Yoeme
Zeta
Lecha
Guzman
Amalia
Uncle Federico
Uncle Ringo

Aunt Cucha
Aunt Popa

cocaine to finance arms

military arms, aircraft to private

PROPHECY

When Europeans arrived, the Maya, Azteca,
Inca cultures had already built great cities and
vast networks of roads. Ancient prophecies
foretold the arrival of Europeans in the Amer-
icas. The ancient prophecies also foretell the
disappearance of all things European.

Menardo
Iliana
Alegría
Bartolomeo

Tacho-Wacah
Angelita
El Feo
La Escapía

● Tuxtla Gutiérrez